*It's a sultry summer in the city
and three of the toughest, sexiest men
have gone undercover to take on the most
dangerous mysteries, the darkest secrets
and the hottest women...*

DESI
& D

in the

heat of the
night

**Steamy, sensual novels from
three bestselling authors:**

LORI FOSTER

GINA WILKINS

VICKI LEWIS THOMPSON

heat *of the* night

LORI FOSTER

GINA WILKINS

VICKI LEWIS THOMPSON

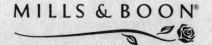

MILLS & BOON®

First published in Great Britain 2002.
Harlequin Mills & Boon Limited,
Eton House, 18-24 Paradise Road, Richmond, Surrey TW9 1SR

HEAT OF THE NIGHT © Harlequin Enterprises II B.V., 2002

The publisher acknowledges the copyright holders of the individual works as follows:

CAUGHT IN THE ACT © Lori Foster 2001
YESTERDAY'S SCANDAL © Gina Wilkins 2000
COMPROMISING POSITIONS © Vicki Lewis Thompson 2001

ISBN 0 263 83622 3

49-0602

Printed and bound in Spain
by Litografia Rosés S.A., Barcelona

CAUGHT IN THE ACT

LORI FOSTER

LORI FOSTER

Mills & Boon published Lori Foster's first Sensual Romance™ in 1996, and since then her rise to stardom has been nothing less than astronomical. Just six years and some twenty plus books later, she is a bona fide bestselling author. Not bad for a wife and mother and 'housewife extraordinaire' whose first novel was written longhand and never saw the light of day! Still, Lori's priorities haven't changed: family first, writing second. She lives in Ohio, USA with her high-school sweetheart husband and three strapping sons, who inspire her to create exceptional heroes.

Caught in the Act *is linked to two stories coming soon in* Sensual Romance™ – *both by Lori Foster.*
Treat Her Right *is available in October 2002, and* **Mr November** *is on the shelves in November 2002. Don't miss them!*

Dedication:

I want to give a very special thanks to
Officer LaDon Laney,
who exemplifies the types of heroes I enjoy writing about. While helping me with my research, Officer Laney spoke of his family, his community, his co-workers and his job with admirable love and respect. His help was invaluable to me.

And to Kathy McCutter for medical assistance, and Lynda Sue Cooper for answering 'cop' questions.

You're all wonderful!

CHAPTER ONE

RAIN DRUBBED THE WINDOW sluggishly, but Mick Dawson could still see out, still see all the different people milling around with colorful umbrellas and hats. He was so intent on watching for her he listened to the conversation with only half an ear. But then, half an ear was the most required when his friends got started on that particular topic.

"See that gorgeous blonde?" Josh Marshall said, deliberately baiting as usual. "The one who just came in? She's wearing a push-up bra."

"Is that right?" Zack Grange kept his tone dry. "How can you tell?"

"I know women." Josh's reply held an overdose of world-weary cynicism. "And I especially know women's breasts." He added, "At your age, I'd think you would, too."

"Yeah, and at your age," Zack retorted, "I'd have thought you'd outgrown your adolescent obsessions."

The three of them sat in the corner booth at Marco's, a casual Italian restaurant they'd first discovered five years ago. It was central to where they each worked, in the downtown area.

They came often, more so every year, it seemed, until now they met almost daily for lunch and often for dinner, too. None of them was married. Josh remained a confirmed bachelor, Zack was now a widower and Mick…well, Mick hadn't met the right woman. His criteria were strict, but to his mind, marriage was forever. He'd seen the worst quite often, marriages made in hell and sustained with sarcasm and cheating and drink. He'd also witnessed that elusive best, unions overflowing with love and trust and support. No way would he settle for less than what he knew could and should be.

Because of their different jobs—each of them stressful—and their lack of romantic ties, meeting at Marco's was about as close to a domestic routine as the three men ever saw.

The restaurant served as a place for celebration—a promotion, a new house, whatever came up that seemed celebration worthy. They also commiserated with each other there, as when Zack's young wife had died and he'd wanted to retreat from life, not seeing anyone, not doing anything except coddling his little girl. Or after Mick had gotten shot in the leg and missed several weeks of work, making him edgy.

Mick's life was all darkness and threats and caution. Ugly. Except here at Marco's, and with the people he trusted—his two friends, his family.

No one else. At least, not yet.

No woman had ever snagged his attention long enough to build a trust, certainly never for anything serious. Until now.

Now he was intrigued.

"Mick, tell this fool that breasts don't lift to the sun like a flower." Josh laughed at his own jest. "If they're damn near touching her chin, she's wearing a push-up bra."

Mick glanced at Zack and grinned. "Josh is an idiot where women are concerned—including his insane fascination with breasts, which, I agree, he should have outgrown years ago."

Josh shook his head in a pitying way. "Men do not outgrow their fascination with breasts. You two are just weird."

"A real woman," Mick told him, "would chew you up and spit you out."

"A real woman?" Zack asked, feigning confusion. "You mean someone with an IQ higher than ten? Why would Josh date anyone smarter than he is?"

Josh said, "Ha-ha. You're just jealous." He grinned and added, "Besides, the ladies have better things to do with their mouths when they're around me. Chewing is definitely out."

All three men laughed. "So," Josh said, "if you two abnormal specimens aren't turned on by a woman's breasts—which should be soft and natural, not shoved heavenward—then what does do it for you?"

Mick groaned. "Didn't we have this discussion back in high school?"

"Yeah, but it's still interesting."

"Bellies," Zack blurted.

Josh raised a brow. "Excuse me?"

For the moment, Mick felt content to just listen.

"I love a woman's belly." Zack leaned back, smiling to himself. "Not all muscled up the way some women want to do these days. Just a nice soft smooth woman's belly.'' He nodded, confirming his own conclusions. ''Very sexy.''

Josh considered that, then nodded, too. ''Okay, I'll give you that one. Bellies are hot. But not belly button rings.''

''No,'' Zack agreed. ''A good belly doesn't need decoration.''

''What about you, Mick?'' Josh prodded. ''Long legs? Great ass? What?''

Mick took another bite of his BLT, almost by rote, not because he was hungry. He considered his reaction when he'd seen *her* for the first time. What had he noticed? What had caught his eye and kept him so interested, to the point he almost felt obsessed?

He glanced out the dim window again. It was a miserable, dank July day, breezy, with fat purple clouds hanging low in the sky.

She should be coming along any minute now.

He'd first noticed her at his old neighborhood. He'd been there to rent out the upstairs apartment of the building he still owned, the same building he'd once lived in as a child. There were a lot of…*unpleasant* memories for him there, along with a few special ones. He kept the building as a reminder to himself that his life had changed, *he* had changed, but he was still a product of his upbringing.

Evidently, she rented from the building next door, because she had come down the walkway to the street and headed toward the post office, letters in her hand. It worried Mick, because no one traipsed around unprotected in that area. To call it rough would be a gross understatement.

But there she'd been, strolling along without a care. He hadn't hesitated to follow her, making certain she remained safe, enjoying the back view of her as she strutted along, her stride long and sure and almost cocky.

The sun was blistering hot that day, shining down on her blue-black, shoulder-length hair, hair so silky it appeared fluid when she moved. Soft, light blue eyes looked beyond everything and everyone, including Mick, as if a great distraction held her. He'd been nearly spellbound by her tall, willowy body with its incredibly long, slim legs and broad, fragile shoulders. Strangely enough, even when she came back out of the post office and went past him, again oblivious to her surroundings, he hadn't noticed her breasts. All his attention had been on her face, with its strong jaw, straight nose, pale eyes.

Mick wondered for an instant what Josh would think of his oversight.

Because he wanted to meet her, wanted to get to know her and have sex with her until he passed out from sheer exhaustion, he wasn't about to discuss her with Josh or Zack. So he merely shrugged. "It's a combination of things, and it's different with every woman."

Before either Josh or Zack could respond to that obscure reply, Mick saw her. Blindly, he laid his sandwich aside and twisted in the booth to better see out the window. Regardless of the drizzling rain, the gray sky, he'd expected her. A little rain wouldn't chase her inside. No, not this lady. She jogged every day around the same time, the same place. Or at least she had for two weeks now. It felt like fate, seeing her first in an area where he owned property, and then here again, where he routinely visited.

Zack, being a reasonable sort, hadn't complained much when Mick had made him move so he'd have the window seat. Josh, though, was unreasonable, always. Outrageous bordering on obnoxious. He'd demanded, all with laughter and taunting grins, for Mick to admit who he was watching for. Mick had refused, but now it didn't matter.

The second he shifted his attention, going on alert, Josh noticed.

"Aha! There you go, Zack. I think we'll get to see this mystery lady any second now."

Mick told him, rather succinctly, what he could do with his speculations. But that didn't deter Josh; if anything, it made him more curious.

Both Josh and Zack twisted around, and they, too, watched through the window. The streets were crowded during the lunch hour. Open umbrellas jumped with the breeze as people milled up and down the sidewalk.

And there she was, weaving in and out of human traffic as she jogged, her head uncovered, her clothes better suited to a bright spring day than drizzling rain. Funny thing was, she went right past them, inky-black ponytail bouncing, rainwater dripping off her nose and darkening her sweatshirt, and still Josh and Zack looked, searching the crowds.

They hadn't realized she was the one.

Mick's body knew that she was. Just seeing her now, bedraggled and wet and distracted, he wanted her. His muscles felt tight, his blood hot, his flesh prickly. Damn, if just watching her jog did this to him, how would it feel to kiss her, touch her, to slide deep inside her and hear her moan out a climax?

He felt the stirrings of an erection and muttered a curse. Insanity, he decided, but it couldn't be helped.

To hide his reaction, he grinned and leaned into the corner of the booth. Now that she'd gone by, he could face Zack and Josh and still keep an eye on her for about half a mile on the long, straight street. He glanced, and saw there was almost no jiggle to her firm little butt in the skintight biker shorts. His large hands would cover that bottom completely, and he'd hold her still, keep her steady for his thrusts....

Josh interrupted his very interesting imagery. "So? What are we looking for?"

"Nothing now." Mick deliberately sipped his coffee, knowing he had to get control of himself. And he had to get her; maybe after he'd made love to her for no less than ten days, he'd be able to get her out of his system.

A comical look on his face, Josh stretched past Zack, nearly knocking his plate off the table, and pressed his nose to the window. He looked and looked and finally said, "Damn it, there's nothing, no one, out there worth staring at!"

Mick and Zack shared a look. Zack shrugged. "If you're only looking for breasts, that could be. Maybe Mick was looking for something else."

Josh frowned at Zack. "No way. You know he's straight. We've both seen him with women."

Mick spewed his coffee. Zack burst out laughing,

and several women in the restaurant looked their way. They kept looking, smiling, flirting, and Mick shook his head. "You're drawing attention to yourself again, Josh."

"Me? I'm not the one laughing like an idiot."

"You don't need to laugh," Zack told him, "to be an idiot." Then slowly, as if speaking to a half-wit, he said, "I meant Mick was maybe looking at a woman who wasn't top-heavy. Just because it's your ultimate definition of what makes a woman, that doesn't mean the rest of us agree."

Josh studied Mick. "That right?"

"That you have strange ideas about women?" He took another sip of coffee and shrugged. "Yeah."

"I meant," Josh said, exasperated, "is she… lacking in the upper works?"

"As far as I can tell," Mick told him, a little annoyed and not sure why, "she's not lacking anywhere."

That only perplexed Josh more.

Mick again peeked out the window, and to his surprise, he saw her turn at the corner, cross the street and start back toward him. There was no more jiggle from her front than there'd been from her back. When she was just opposite the restaurant, she slowed and finally stopped. She rested her hands on her knees while she breathed deeply, heedless of the light rain and his avid attention.

When she straightened again, she stretched her arms high. Her shirt rose, showing a very sweet belly that Zack no doubt would have adored. Captivated, Mick continued to stare at her while a slow heat stirred deep inside him. She walked into the jewelry store located directly across from the restaurant, and Mick made up his mind.

Pushing aside his plate, he stood. So many times over the past few weeks he'd considered following her, initiating a conversation, introducing himself. He didn't want to rush her, but he'd dreamed about her twice, so he knew his fascination wasn't about to go away. Now seemed like as good a time as any to make his move. "I'll be back."

Josh and Zack stared at him, blank faced. Mick was aware of a thread of urgency vibrating through his blood. It had been like that from the second he first saw her, and every moment after when he watched her. He couldn't put his finger on it, couldn't tell anyone outright what it was about her that appealed to him, what pushed him over the edge. He only knew he wanted her. *Bad.*

As he dodged cars and puddles in the roadway, and muddy, slick spots along the curb, he wondered—for about the hundredth time—if she'd been in the area awhile, or if she'd only recently moved in when he first saw her. He'd been buried in work for the past two months, putting in seventeen-hour days, so it was possible she'd been close by for longer than two weeks.

He could get another assignment any day, so he had to take advantage of the opportunity now.

He hoped like hell she was single. Since first seeing her, he'd studied her closely. There weren't any rings on her fingers, but then he knew women who didn't wear them, especially while jogging. Not once in the two weeks of his awareness had he seen her with anyone, definitely not a man, but that, too, could be a fluke.

Mick turned up the collar on his windbreaker and darted across the sidewalk, trying to keep as dry as possible. He didn't have to look behind him to know both Josh and Zack would be craning their necks, their noses pressed to the window, spying on him. It was totally unlike him to chase a woman.

It was totally unlike him to be interested enough to bother chasing.

Thunder boomed, echoing over the street and rattling windows just as he stepped through the jewelry store's ornate front door. Air-conditioning hit him, chilling his damp skin. He brushed his hair back from his forehead and looked around. Glass cases were everywhere, some large, some smaller to showcase a certain piece, and there, in the far corner, she stood. Dressed in her running wear she looked very out of place, conspicuous and unique in the upscale, glitzy store. She also looked sexy as the original sin with her skin dewy from the drizzle and sweat, her cheeks flushed from exertion, her hair as much out of the ponytail as in, wet and sleek.

Damn, he thought, annoyed with himself. She wasn't that pretty, was in fact kind of plain. She wore no makeup, but her lashes and brows were as dark as her hair. Her nails were short, clean. She had a nice body, strong and sleek, fine boned, but not overly curved, not typically sexy.

Not the type of body to make him sweat at the sight of her.

She didn't give out signals or flirt or even pay much attention to men, not that he'd noticed.

His eyes widened. God, maybe she didn't even like men. That'd be a kicker, one he wouldn't, couldn't accept. Not when the mere sight of her turned him on. He didn't just want her; he felt as if he had to have her, just as he had to sleep or eat. It was the damnedest feeling, and he wasn't happy with it or himself.

She didn't appear interested in any particular item as she moseyed from case to case, peering inside, then shaking her head and moving on. For the moment, Mick was content to watch her. He slipped his hands into his jeans pockets, then quickly pulled them out again when he realized that negligent pose might expose the weapon in the waistband holster at his back. Being off duty, he didn't need the gun, but he always carried it.

In this day and age, his cover wouldn't have been believable without it. Drug dealers, prostitutes, gamblers…they all expected you to be armed, and if you weren't, you were considered an idiot, or worse.

Usually, even when conditions didn't call for a weapon, he managed to smuggle in the Smith & Wesson 9 mm in an ankle holster. There were times, though, when he had to go without, leaving him feeling naked, and those were the times when he got most tense, when the adrenaline rush was all but blinding. He always wanted a woman afterward, a way to release all that pent-up energy.

He wanted a woman now.

He wanted her.

Moving closer, watching her, he was amazed that she didn't feel his attention, so acute that it had him half-hard again with expectation. It had always been his experience that blatant staring was felt like a stroke of ice. But then, she was a civilian, and he'd already noted the first day he saw her how heedless she could be of her surroundings. It amazed him sometimes that people could survive with so little caution.

The door chimed behind Mick and more people entered. Two men, dressed much like Mick in jeans and T-shirts, wearing sneakers, one in a ball cap. They appeared to be in their mid-thirties, clean, middle-class. As a cop, Mick automatically took in everyone and everything. He'd already noted the two salesladies, the older couple looking at cocktail rings for an anniversary. He picked up on actions and quiet dialogue and expressions.

Caution was as basic to him as breathing. And because he wasn't a civilian, wasn't oblivious, he immediately detected the sudden charge in the air despite the nonthreatening scene and apparently ordinary people. It had come in like the wind with the men, and Mick didn't like it worth a damn. He had a keen sixth sense, and he trusted it more than he trusted appearances.

The woman looked up, around, made brief eye contact with the two men who'd entered, then again with Mick. Their gazes locked and held for an instant, an instant that made his gut clench with awareness. She gave him a small smile, a simple, friendly smile that nonetheless heightened his tension, before she turned away again.

Senses on alert, Mick followed her, not too close, in no way obvious, but keeping her within reach. Because the shop was small and crowded with displays, the air thick and humid from the rain outside, he could detect her scent. It was earthy and rich, warm woman, damp skin and clean female sweat. His heart punched hard, a little fast; his sex thickened. He'd been too long without a woman, too long without any sexual relief. Sometimes being a contrary bastard was a real pain.

Her wet running shoes squeaked on the ceramic tile floor as she browsed, appearing to study the shop, not just the wares but the structure, the setup. Mick frowned as he watched her, further intrigued and a little distracted. Out of the corner of his eye he saw one of the men reach into his jacket pocket, and a silent alarm screamed inside Mick's head.

He jerked around, but not quickly enough.

"Everyone stay still and calm." The guy waved a SIG Sauer .45 around the room with menacing intent. "No one panic or do anything stupid," he said with a sneer, "and I won't have to kill anyone."

Damn, damn, damn. Mick took a quick, inconspicuous glance around. The elderly woman, clinging to her husband, looked ready to faint, while the salespeople stood motionless, frozen in horror. His movements so slight that no one paid him any mind, Mick edged closer to the woman he'd followed. She stared at the gunman, her blue eyes darker now with fascination, but he saw no real fear.

"We'll do our business," the guy in the ball cap said, "and then leave and no one will be hurt."

Mick didn't buy it for a second; the words sounded far too rehearsed, far from sincere. And there was an anticipatory expression on the man's face.

Things never worked out the easy way—not life, not love, sure as hell not an armed robbery.

The second man hitched his gun at the saleswoman. "You, come open the register and make it quick."

She balked, more out of surprise than rebellion. Mick had a similar sensation. They were surrounded by diamonds and gold of unbelievable value, yet this idiot wanted what little cash might be in the register? The robber had to realize that most sales would be handled with credit cards or checks; his demand didn't make sense.

Mick's hands twitched. He wanted to grab his gun; he wanted to be in control. Right now, control meant keeping everyone alive. It meant keeping *her* alive.

Without warning, the man who'd issued the order shouted, "*Now,* goddamn it!" and everyone jumped, the saleslady screeching and stumbling over her own feet as she rushed to obey.

A predictable panic reaction, Mick thought, to the threat of sudden violence, not something a robber intent on keeping things calm would have instigated. Mick's suspicions rose.

The older woman quietly wept, one saleslady turned white, the other shook so badly she had a hard time working the register. Before she could get it open, distant sirens broke the quiet, making both men curse hotly. Mick tensed, waiting for another outburst, for them to turn and run, for them to retaliate by shooting the saleslady. He'd learned early on that criminals did the most absurd and unaccountable things, often causing death without reason. He prepared himself for any reaction.

But what they did took him totally by surprise.

They didn't yell, didn't run. They focused their blame on the young woman next to Mick.

"Bitch," the guy in the ball cap snarled. "You set off an alarm."

Startled, she blinked, looked around, backed up two paces. "No," she breathed. It was the first time Mick had heard her voice, which quaked with fear, bewilderment. "I don't even know where—"

The man took aim at her and, without thinking, Mick blocked his path. Both gunmen froze at his audacity. He felt the woman's small hands against his back, clutching at his jacket. He felt her face press into his shoulder, was aware of her accelerated breathing, her trembling. She was deathly afraid, and anger surged in his blood.

His voice as low and calm as he could make it, Mick said, "She's a customer. She doesn't know where the alarm is."

He was ignored.

"Everybody get down!" As the guy in the ball cap yelled his order, a car screeched up in front of the shop, motor idling. The customers all dropped to the floor, panicked, including the woman at Mick's back. He felt her jerky movements, could hear her panting in terror.

Mick moved more slowly, his mind churning as he

tried to buy himself some time. If he could get his gun… His elbow touched the woman's wrist, he was so close to her. She, like the others, had stretched out flat, covering her head with her arms, shaking. Mick kept himself balanced on his elbows, ready to move, watching without appearing to watch.

The sudden shattering of glass—again and again as each case was destroyed—caused the older woman to wail, the saleslady to whimper. The woman next to Mick never made a sound. He wanted to look at her, to somehow reassure her, but he didn't dare take his attention off those weapons. The two men grabbed a few large items of jewelry, but it was as if they destroyed the store just for the sake of destruction.

It was by far the most pathetic, disorganized and unproductive robbery Mick had ever witnessed—and that made him more suspicious than anything else might have. By rights, they should have known where the most valuable items would be, and should have concentrated their sticky fingers there. Instead, they seemed to take whatever was at hand without thought to its worth. No one robbed a jewelry store without casing it first, without knowing what would be found inside and where.

The two men finally headed for the door. The tension tightened, grew painful, static crowding the air until it seemed impossible to breathe—and the bastard in the ball cap turned to fire.

Mick moved so fast, he barely had the thought of moving before he was over her, his arms covering her head, his muscular body completely blanketing her delicate one. Though she was tall for a woman, about five-nine, she was small boned and felt fragile to his six-three frame. He was plenty big enough, and more than determined enough, to be her protection.

She gasped at the feel of him on top of her and immediately stiffened, forcing her head up, twisting. "No! What are you doing?"

He jammed her head back down, then cursed when her cheek hit the hard tile floor. Knowing what she likely thought and wishing he could spare her, Mick said into her ear, "Be still."

She wiggled more furiously, trying to free herself, confused and frightened, unsure of his intent. "He's going to—" Mick began to explain, and then it was unnecessary.

The crack sounded loud and startling; the sudden pain in his right shoulder was a lick of pure fire. For only a moment, his arms tightened around her and he ground his teeth together. "Oh God," she whispered, trying to turn toward him.

Mick grunted, but didn't move. No, he wasn't about to move. For whatever reason, they wanted her dead, but they'd have to get through him first.

He felt the blood spreading on his back, sticky and warm; he was aware of the woman squirming beneath him, gasping, crying. But it wasn't until he heard the door open that he rolled and drew his gun at the same time. He blocked the awful pain, any distractions, and got off a clean shot through the glass door, clipping the man who'd tried to shoot her. The hollow-point bullet hit him high in the left thigh before he could get into the car. The leg crumpled beneath him and he went down in an awkward heap, howling in pain, grabbing for the open car door in desperation.

The car lurched away, spewing gravel and squealing tires, tossing the man back. The side of his head cracked solidly against the curb. He lay there unconscious, sprawled out like a wounded starfish.

Surging to his feet, Mick ran out the door. He spotted the car, drew careful aim and fired again. The back window exploded, but the car didn't slow. It careened around the corner on two wheels and disappeared.

Already the streets had filled with onlookers, people too damn stupid to stay inside and away from gunfire. Mick's arm rapidly went hot, cold and then numb; his fingers throbbed. His hand shook as he tried to hang on to his gun, to steady himself.

Josh and Zack appeared, having witnessed the tail end of the robbery from the restaurant. Josh, smooth as silk, slipped the gun from Mick's hand and dropped it into his trouser pocket. They'd arrived just seconds before the police cars. More people from all over the street converged, whispering, curious. Josh caught Mick's upper arm and supported him. "Jesus, man. You're shot."

Zack came to his other side and yelled, "Someone call the paramedics. He needs an ambulance." That made Mick laugh, since Zack was an EMT. Zack shook his head wryly and pulled out his radio, putting in the call himself.

"Here, sit down," he said, and led Mick to the rain-wet curb.

"I don't want to sit in a damn puddle," Mick

grumbled. "I'm fine." Fine enough that he wanted to find the woman. He looked around, and when he didn't immediately see her, terror started to take hold. He located the elderly couple leaning against the brick building. The old woman clung to her husband and cried, while he peered around in dismay and impotent anger. Mick saw the two salespeople, huddled together, dry eyed but white as snow, apparently in shock. Cops swarmed everywhere, separating the witnesses so they couldn't share stories. Two police cars took off to give chase, while another radioed in the call. An officer headed Mick's way.

Where the hell is she?

When the cop reached him, frowning, his hand resting on his holster, Mick said quietly, "I'm Mick Dawson, Vice." He started to reach inside his jacket for his badge, but his arm wouldn't cooperate and he cursed.

Josh said, "I'll get it." He retrieved the badge and flipped it toward the officer, who nodded and yelled for someone to get a blanket.

Frustrated, Mick could do no more than stand there, getting weaker by the second, while Zack gave instructions into his radio and Josh more or less held him upright.

Zack told the officer, "The ambulance is on its way. I'm an EMT. I'll see to him until it gets here."

The officer, frowning in worry, handed Zack the blanket and then set off to clear the street.

Mick started to pull free, desperate to find the woman and make certain she was okay, but just then she stepped around the elderly couple. Her face, her beautiful face, was creased with worry, with disbelief. From a slight distance, they stared at each other, and there was no distraction in her gaze now, no oblivion. The horror of what had just happened darkened her eyes to midnight.

A bruise discolored her cheekbone from when he'd pushed her head down. His stomach cramped with that realization. She trembled all over, and Mick shook off Zack to go to her, needing to hold her, to apologize, though he didn't even know her name, had no idea who she was or why the robbers had wanted to kill her.

Zack, who'd been looking at the wound in his shoulder, drew him back. "Damn it, Mick, you're ready to drop."

Mick started to deny that, but then his legs gave out, and if it hadn't been for Josh and Zack supporting him, he'd have been sitting in the middle of the sidewalk instead of on the curb with a folded blanket beneath him. His vision swam, closed in.

"You're losing a lot of blood," Zack said in his calm, professional voice, but Mick heard the concern, the anger, as his friend began first aid.

"Don't let her get away." Mick meant to say it loud and clear, an order that couldn't be ignored. But the words emerged as a faint whisper, and that infuriated him. He'd finally met her—sort of—and he sounded weak, looked weak.

At the moment, he was weak. Too weak.

But she'd felt so good beneath him for that brief, charged moment, adding to his adrenaline rush, further arousing him though they'd been in the middle of a very dangerous situation. It was so absurd, but even as he'd braced for that bullet, he'd been aware of her under him, her ass cuddling his groin, her head fitting neatly under his chin.

He forced his head up and said again, trying for more than a whisper this time, "Don't let her get away."

He knew Josh heard him because he leaned closer. "Who?"

"In…the running clothes. Black hair." That was the very best description he could muster under the circumstances.

Josh looked up, eyes narrowed as he scanned the crowd and then settled on someone. He said, "You've got it, buddy. Now you just rest. I'll take care of it." He got to his feet and stalked forward purposefully, saying in a tone that brooked no argument, "Miss? I need to see you, please."

And Mick blacked out.

CHAPTER TWO

"WHERE IS SHE?" The sound of his own voice, foggy and dark and thin, appalled him. Mick tried to clear his throat, but it was impossible.

"Shh," he heard Zack say. "Take it easy."

Mick struggled to open his eyes, then wished he hadn't. What the hell had they done to him? His shoulder didn't hurt, at least not at the moment, but he felt as if his brain might explode, and every muscle he possessed was sluggish, refusing to cooperate with his brain's commands.

More cautiously this time, he cracked his eyes open and found Zack on guard at his bedside. Where was Josh? Where was *she?*

"The woman?" he asked again, and he sounded like a dying frog.

Zack lifted a glass of water with a straw to Mick's mouth. He wanted to tell Zack to jam the straw in his ear, but he couldn't. He gave in to his thirst and took several quick sips. He started to move his arm, and fire burned down his side. *Now* his shoulder hurt. He ground his teeth, hissing for breath.

"The anesthesia is wearing off," Zack explained. "You'll be groggy a little longer, but overall you're fine. They left the bullet in—that's two for you now, right? Taking it out would only have caused more damage. You lost too much blood already.''

Mick was still registering what Zack had said when his friend leaned forward and growled, not two inches from his nose, ''You scared the hell out of me! Don't you know if you get shot you should stay down? Swinging your arm around that way just encouraged it to bleed more.''

Mick grunted, as much from the pounding in his head as in reply. ''Where the hell is she?''

Exasperated, Zack sighed. He didn't need to ask *She who?* ''Josh has been keeping a close eye on her, since right before you passed out and bashed your damn head on the ground. Yeah, that's why your head feels like it's splitting. I'm surprised you don't have a concussion, as hard as you hit. If you didn't have to be so damn macho, if you'd just tell someone when you were ready to faint—''

''I did *not* faint.'' Mick's voice, his words, were gaining strength, and he grumbled, ''I passed out from blood loss.''

''Yeah, well, they look about the same when you drop right in the middle of a crowd.''

It hurt, but Mick narrowed his eyes and said, ''Zack? Come closer.''

Zack, filled with new concern, leaned down close.

''Where the hell is she!''

Zack jerked back and grimaced. ''All right, all right, you don't have to bust my eardrum. You said, all ominous cloak and dagger, 'Don't let her get away.' Neither Josh nor I knew if that meant she should be arrested, or if she was the lady you'd been watching for.''

Mick jerked—and the sudden movement squeezed the breath right out of his lungs. Damn, he'd forgotten how badly a bullet hurt. Through clenched teeth, he snarled, ''You didn't…?''

''Turn her over to the cops? Nope. They questioned her, of course, but Josh followed them to the station and then picked her up afterward. She's fine, just shook up and babbling about you being a hero—no surprise there, I suppose. She claims you took that bullet for her, and she wants to see you, overflowing with gratitude and all that, but, of course, since we didn't know what the hell was going on…''

''I'm going to kill you.''

Zack grinned. ''We collected her for you, but she's none too happy right now. Josh is more or less, er, detaining her. No, don't look like that. You know he wouldn't hurt her. But he's taxing himself; it's been over four hours, after all.''

Four hours! Mick wanted to groan again, thinking of her waiting that long, Josh coercing her into hanging around….

''No,'' Zack said, correctly reading his mind, ''she didn't want to leave, she wanted to see you. And she's not happy when she doesn't get what she wants. She's actually—'' Zack coughed. ''She's a very determined lady.''

Zack looked at Mick's IV and added, ''Evidently, she wants you.''

That was a revelation, one he could easily live

with. His head pounded, but Mick held back all wimpy sounds of distress and said, "Get her for me."

"Don't be an idiot! You're hardly in any shape to start getting acquainted." Zack stood, towering over the bed. "I assumed once you came to, you'd explain what the hell's going on, we could then explain it to her, and then we'd let the lady go home so you could get some rest."

"Do *not* let her leave here alone." Mick had awakened with a feeling of panic, again seeing that gun aimed at her—just her, no one else, and for no apparent reason. Until he figured things out, he wanted her watched. He wanted her protected.

It pissed him off royally that he had to ask others to do that for him.

"Mick, we can't just refuse to let her leave."

Giving Zack a sour look, Mick said, *"Get her."*

"Damn, you're insistent when you're injured."

"And I've heard more 'damns' from you in the last five minutes than I have since your daughter was born."

Zack shrugged. "Well, Dani isn't here to listen and emulate. Besides, it's not every day I see a friend shot."

"You say I need to recoup, Zack?"

"That's right."

"So how is it going to help my recuperation when I get out of this bed and kick your sorry ass?"

Zack hesitated before giving in with a laugh. "I can't fight you now, because you're already down and I feel sorry for you. If I let you get up and attempt to hit me, you'd probably start bleeding all over the place again and rip your stitches, and I'd have to let you win.'' He held up both hands. ''Stay put. I'll find out how soon you'll be moved to your room and when Delilah can join you.''

Pain ripped through his shoulder as Mick did a double take. ''Delilah?''

Zack stared. ''Don't tell me you didn't even know her name.''

''So?'' Learning her name hadn't been his top priority. Touching her had, and he'd accomplished that while also protecting her. A nice start, except for the fact that someone wanted her dead, and had shot him trying to accomplish the deed. But he'd figure that one out eventually. In the meantime, he had no intention of letting anyone hurt her.

''So you took a bullet for a complete stranger?''

Very quietly, Mick asked, ''Wouldn't you have done the same?''

And because Zack already had once, long ago, he turned and walked out.

The second Zack pushed aside the curtain and left, a nurse stepped in, ready to check Mick's vitals and reassure him. She lingered, and Mick couldn't help but smile at her, despite his discomfort and his current frazzled frame of mind. She was about five years older than he, putting her in her early thirties. She was attractive even in sensible white shoes and a smock. She smoothed his hair, her fingers gentle, while she explained that he'd be there overnight, but would likely leave in the morning, and that they'd put him in his own room very soon.

Still being polite, Mick was careful not to encourage her. He wanted to meet Delilah, wanted to talk to her, hear her voice when she wasn't frightened, see her smile again. She was the only woman he wanted at the moment, and he was relieved when the orderly showed up and announced it was time to take Mick to his room.

Any minute now he'd meet her, really meet her. And he promised himself that not long after that he'd kiss her...and more. He didn't know how he'd manage that, all things considered, but he would. He had to taste her, had to stake a claim in the best way known to man.

He discounted his wound. It wouldn't slow him down; he wouldn't let it slow him down.

He needed her.

"I'M CAPABLE OF WALKING on my own."

Josh, the man "escorting" her to Mick's room, gave a disgruntled sigh and removed his hand from her arm. He'd been pushy and demanding, a total stranger insisting she follow his orders. She'd done so, once she realized he was a friend of the man who'd protected her.

But she didn't like him, and she definitely didn't like the distrustful way he loomed over her. He pretended gentlemanly qualities, but she knew he held on to her so she couldn't get away. She'd already told him a dozen times that she had no intention of leaving.

Not that Josh paid any mind to what she had to say.

He had "slick" written all over him, from the way he held himself to the way he noticed every single female in the vicinity. She understood his type. Josh was one of those men who felt superior to women, but covered that nasty sentiment with charisma and a

glib tongue. No doubt, given his good looks and outrageous confidence, women regularly encouraged
him.

Del just wanted to get by him so she could meet
the other man, the one who'd risked his life for her.

Josh slanted her one of his insulting, speculative
looks. "I hope you don't go in there and give him
any grief."

When she didn't answer him, he added, "He did
save your sorry, ungrateful little butt, after all."

She could hardly ignore that! Del whirled and stuck
a finger into his hard chest. "I know. I was *there*,"
she snapped. Her control, her poise and any claim to
ladylike behavior were long gone. Today had been
the most bizarre and eventful day of her life. "You're
the one who doesn't seem to understand that I need
to see him, that I should have been there with him all
along, to thank him—"

He glared at her, rubbed at his chest and walked
away. Del had to hurry to catch up to him. A few
seconds later they turned a corner, and Josh pushed a
door open. "Here we go," he said. And then under
his breath, but not much under, she heard him mutter,
"Thank God."

Through the open doorway, Del could see the occupied hospital bed, and she drew up short. Heavy
emotion dropped on her, making her feel sluggish in
the brain—which was a first. Her breath caught. Her
stomach flipped. Her heart fluttered.

He lay almost flat, his long, tall body stretching
from one end of the narrow bed to the other. She
remembered his height when he'd covered her, protecting her and all but dwarfing her despite her own

height. She remembered the power of him, too, the vibrating tension and leashed strength.

His beautiful, dark brown hair now looked disheveled, spikey from the earlier rain and his injuries and… Her bottom lip quivered with her loss of composure.

He was the most beautiful man she'd ever seen, though she hadn't really seen him until he threw himself on top of her and saved her life. At first she'd thought he was with the robbers, and she'd known so much fear she'd actually tasted it.

Instead, he'd taken a bullet meant for her.

Her heart stuttered to a near stop. What kind of man did that? He didn't know her, owed her nothing. She'd barely noticed him in the store before that.

But when he'd chased the bad guys just like a disreputable Dirty Harry clone, she'd looked him over and hadn't been able to stop looking. He'd been all hard, flexing muscle, animal grace and speed.

Now he was flat on his back in a hospital bed. She sighed brokenly, choking on her emotions.

He turned his head at the sound she made, and those deep brown, all-consuming eyes warmed. A slight, heart-stopping smile curved one side of his mouth, and he looked sexy and compelling. In a deep, dark voice hoarse with pain, he whispered, ''Hi.''

Just like that her heart melted and sank into her toes. There was so much inflection, so much feeling, in that one simple hello. Vaguely, she heard Josh saying, ''Delilah, meet Mick Dawson. Mick, Miss Delilah Piper.''

Del paid no attention to Josh, her every thought and sense focused on the large dark man in the bed. In the bed because of *her*. No one had ever done anything even remotely like that for her. Her life in the past few years had been, by choice, a solitary one. Even before then, though, her relationships had been superficial and short-lived—nothing to inspire such protective instincts.

The reality of what he'd done, what he'd risked for her, threw Del off balance emotionally, just as the sight of him stirred her physically.

Without another thought, she moved straight to the bed. Mick looked at her, still smiling, but now with his eyes a bit wider, more alert, a little surprised. She sat near his hip and stroked his face. She *needed* to touch him, to feel the warmth of his skin, the lean hardness of his jaw.... Unable to help herself, she kissed him.

Against his lips, she said with heartfelt sincerity, "Thank you."

He started to say something, but she kissed him again. It felt...magically right; she could have gone on kissing him forever. His mouth was firm, dry. Five o'clock shadow covered his jaw, rasping against her fingertips, thrilling her with the masculinity of it. Heat, scented by his body, lifted off him in waves, encompassing her and soothing her. He tasted good, felt good, smelled good.

A little breathless, bewildered by it all, Del said, "I'm so sorry. It should be me in that bed."

"No!" His good arm came up, his hand, incredibly large and rough, clasped her shoulder, and he levered her away. For a man in a sickbed, he had surprising strength and was far too quick.

And he looked angry. And protective.

Excitement skittered down her spine, while tenderness welled in her chest.

The door opened again and Zack, the man who was a little nicer than Josh, started in. He jerked to a halt when he saw them both on the bed, nose-to-nose. Startled, Zack began to backpeddle, only to change his mind once more when he spotted Josh standing in the corner, smirking.

"Uh, Mick?" Zack sounded ridiculously cheerful and vastly amused. "I see you're feeling…better."

Josh chuckled. "I imagine he feels just fine right about now, since she's in here."

Slowly, not wanting to upset Mick, Del stood and cast a quick glare at both men. In her fascination with Mick, she'd all but forgotten them and how they'd bulldozed her, refusing her every request, evading her questions.

"I'd have been with you sooner, but they wouldn't let me," she said to Mick, feeling piqued all over again. "I didn't know what was going on or why—"

"Only family could see him before he got to his room," Zack said, some of his cheerfulness dwindling.

Del had heard the same lame explanation at least ten times, yet Zack had pretty much stayed with Mick, except for when he'd taken a turn guarding her so Josh could look in on him. They were friends, not family, or so they'd told her, so their excuses held no weight. They'd insisted she come to the hospital, insisted she wait around, and then they'd refused to let her do anything useful—like see Mick and thank Mick and…

She brushed her stringy bangs out of her face, still annoyed, still frustrated. "You could have taken my suggestion and told them I was his wife. Then they'd have let me in."

Josh choked; Zack raised one eyebrow and looked at Mick. Mick grinned, then reached out for her hand with his good arm, which meant stretching across the bed. When she took his hand, he said, "I'm sorry you were worried." And in a quieter tone, "Are you all right?"

Dismissing the other two men, she again sat on the bed. She wanted to kiss him some more, but his friends were standing there, not only ogling them, but bristling like overprotective bulldogs. Besides, after her run through the rain, and the burglary, she probably wasn't all that appealing.

"I'm fine."

Mick touched her bruised cheek with gentle fingertips. His eyes were nearly black with concern. "Damn, I'm sorry about that."

His tone made her heart beat faster, made her skin flush and her insides warm. They'd only just met, but she felt as if she'd known him forever.

Catching his wrist, she turned his hand and kissed his palm. Again he looked surprised, and if she didn't miss her guess, aroused. His eyes were hot, his cheekbones slashed with color. He stared at her mouth.

Was it possible he felt the same incredible chemistry?

Del had to clear her throat to say, "You saved me. I'm sorry I freaked. I thought…well, at first I thought you were with them and you intended to…"

"I know." He continued to stare at her mouth, which made her belly quiver, her nerves jump. "I'm sorry I scared you."

The irony didn't escape her. Here he was, in bed, wounded, and he kept apologizing to her. She'd never met a man like him. "You kept me alive," she stressed, which discounted any side effects, such as a small bruise, as unimportant. "I'm the one who's sorry. Well, not sorry that I'm alive, but sorry that you got hurt in the process."

"It's just a flesh wound."

Zack coughed and Josh snorted.

She looked at his two friends, then peered at Mick suspiciously. Was it worse than she thought? But the nurse had told her he'd be okay.

Her ire resurfaced and she said to Mick, "I wanted to come in and see you, but they wouldn't let me. Waiting was awful. When we found out how long it would be, I planned to go home and shower and change, and try to make myself presentable, so when you came to I wouldn't be such a sight, but he—" she directed a stiff finger at Josh "—wouldn't be at all reasonable about any of it."

"Don't blame Josh," Mick said, smiling just a bit. "I asked him to keep you around."

"You did?"

"I was afraid you'd disappear and I wouldn't get to see you again."

His words were so sweet, she forgot about her sweat and ruined clothes and stringy hair. "I wouldn't have done that, I swear! I would have come right back."

Again she leaned down and kissed him, but this time he was ready for her and actually kissed her back. His tongue stroked past her lips for just a heartbeat, then retreated. Her breath caught and she sighed. *Oh wow.*

With a numb mind and tingling lips, she heard him rumble in a low voice, "I want to see you, Delilah."

She lowered her voice to a mere whisper. "I want

to see you, too. I just wish I'd had time to clean up. I'm all sweaty and I have mud on my feet and my clothes are limp and wrinkled. I smell like a wet dog.''

His hot gaze moved from her eyes to her mouth and back again, his expression devouring. "You smell like a woman.''

She almost slid right off the side of the bed. Much more of that and she'd be sweating again, that or she'd self-combust.

He was just so darn sexy! The dark beard shadow covering the lower part of his face made him look dangerous. After witnessing him in action that afternoon, she knew he *was* dangerous. His brows were thick, his lashes sinfully long, his high-bridged nose narrow and straight, his mouth delicious. And those dark eyes... This man had singled her out and risked his life to save her. It was beyond comprehension.

It was the most exciting thing that had ever happened to her.

Only a thin hospital gown and a sheet concealed his entire gorgeous, hard body from her. She looked him over, saw the width of his chest, the length of his legs. His feet tented the sheet, and as her attention slid back up his body, she noticed something else was beginning to tent, as well.

She returned her gaze to his, saw the burning intensity there, and froze. He wasn't embarrassed and made no attempt to conceal his growing erection.

Using his left hand, Mick lifted her fingers and caressed them gently. His eyes were direct, unapologetic, and when she glanced at the other two men, it was to see them looking out the window, at the ceiling, anywhere but at the bed.

She was unimpressed with their show of discretion after everything they'd already put her through. It didn't matter that they'd directed their attention elsewhere; they were still in the room, their presence noticeable. They'd more or less forced her to stay, at Mick's request, but it was obvious they still didn't want her alone with him.

If they'd really been polite, if they'd trusted her at all, they'd have left the room. But no, they weren't ready to budge an inch. She supposed they didn't know her well enough to trust her and, after all, he'd just been shot, but still…

Mick looked vital and strong and all-male, and his effect on her was beyond description. She'd long since decided men weren't worth the effort, but oh, she hadn't met this man yet.

"Are you sure you're going to be okay?" She gripped his hand hard, trying to accustom herself to the unfamiliar feelings of tenderness and worry and explosive desire. It had been forever since she'd felt so much awareness for a man. Well, actually, she'd never felt it—not like this. Which was the main reason she seldom dated anymore. Men didn't appreciate her emotional distance.

She felt far from emotionally distant now. "The nurse said you'd be fine, but…"

"Yeah." His voice was rich with promise. "I should be out of here soon."

"Tomorrow," Zack said, still keeping his eyes averted, "as long as you agree to take it easy. They'll send you home with antibiotics and painkillers, but knowing you—"

A noise in the hall alerted them to more visitors. Mick released his hold on Del and bunched the blan-

kets over his lap to hide his partial erection just seconds before a man and woman pushed through the
door. They entered in a rush, heading straight for
Mick.

Not being much of a people person, Del faded
aside, inching into the corner opposite Zack and Josh.
Mick frowned in displeasure at her retreat, and Josh
said, "No worries. I've got it covered." When he
moved to stand between Del and the door, Del realized he meant that he'd continue to keep her around.

As if she'd leave now!

Del's attention snagged on the pretty blond woman
now hovering over the bed, kissing the top of Mick's
head, his high cheekbone, his chin. "Thank God
you're all right!"

The woman's lips were all over Mick, and Del
didn't like it at all. But she knew she had no right to
complain.

"I made Dane drive like a demon to get us here."

"Angel," Mick protested, all the while grinning
widely so that Del knew he didn't really mind her
attention at all, "you didn't need to rush. I'm fine."

Del wondered if Angel was her name or an en-
dearment.

The woman pressed her cheek to Mick's. "But you
were shot!"

Zack laughed. "I told you on the phone he'd be
all right."

"I had to see for myself."

Josh crossed his arms over his chest and smiled. It
was apparent to Del that they all knew each other,
that these were more of Mick's friends. These people
Josh trusted; she could see that.

Feeling like an outsider, or worse, an interloper, Del frowned.

"According to the doctor," Josh said, addressing Angel, "he'll need some baby-sitting."

Zack nodded. "Luckily the bullet hit at a tangential entry. It was expended enough that the force didn't carry it into the chest cavity, which could have injured his lung, or in a through-and-through injury that could have caused more damage to his arm."

"Yeah," Mick mumbled, tongue in cheek, "I'm real lucky."

Del's heart ached for him. This was the most she'd heard, and it hadn't been revealed for her benefit. Rather, the information was for the new arrivals, especially the woman with the lips.

The female who was trusted.

It all sounded so horrendous, worse than Del had imagined. If the shooter had stepped just a little bit closer, if his aim had been a little higher... She closed her eyes, fighting back a wave of renewed fear and impossible guilt. Mick could so easily have been killed.

Her eyes snapped opened when she heard Angel say, "You'll come home with me, of course."

Del had no real rights to jealousy or possessiveness, but she felt them just the same. Who was this beautiful woman who felt free to kiss and touch Mick?

And then the thought intruded: was he married?

Del's stomach knotted. She tried to see Mick's hand, but couldn't with both people crowded near his bed.

The man with Angel said, "The kids would love a chance to fetch and carry for you. They adore you, you know that."

With incredible relief, Del realized that if they had kids, they must be a couple. Which meant Mick was safe from any romantic entanglement with Angel.

Del was just beginning to relax again, feeling on safer ground, when yet another couple pushed through the door. This woman was lovely, too, but the man with her held her close to his side, leaving no doubt that they were together. He was large and dark and so intense he looked like Satan himself. Del stared, but no one else seemed alarmed.

Mick even rolled his eyes. "Angel, did you drag Alec and Celia down here, too?"

Angel touched his face. "They were visiting when we got the news. Of course they insisted on coming."

The room was all but bursting with large men. Josh and Zack were big enough, but their physical presence was nothing compared to Dane's and Alec's, both of whom were in their prime and exuding power.

And Mick, even flat on his back and wounded, was a masculine presence impossible to ignore. He had an edge of iron control, of leadership, that couldn't be quelled by an injury. All in all, the men made an impressive group. Del expected the walls to start dripping testosterone any moment.

She watched them all, memorizing names and studying faces as they shared familiar greetings. The women were all-smiles, and even Dane looked somewhat jovial. Alec, however, looked capable of any number of nefarious deeds.

Just as Del thought it, she saw his piercing gaze sweep over Mick from head to toe, and he grinned a surprisingly beautiful grin, making his black eyes glitter and causing Del to do an awed double take.

"I knew you wouldn't go much longer," Alec

drawled, and even his deep voice sounded scary to Del, "without getting yourself shot again. It's a nasty habit."

"I'll try real hard to keep that in mind," Mick said.

"Zack tells me you got shot on purpose this time." Alec crossed his massive arms. "At least I try to avoid it when possible, and when Celia isn't around."

Celia, slim and elegant, leaned over Mick's bed and kissed his forehead. To Del's way of thinking, there was far too much kissing going on, and far too many visitors. At this rate, she'd never get him alone.

But that concern was secondary to another. Judging by what Alec had said, this wasn't the first time Mick had been shot. Del looked at Josh and Zack, to judge their reactions to that news. Their expressions were impassive, leading her to believe they already knew Mick had been shot before this.

"Don't let Alec tease you, sweetie," Celia said. "He's glad I got him shot. Otherwise we'd never have ended up together."

Alec looked very dubious at her statement, whereas Del was completely floored. What in the world did these men do that they took turns catching bullets?

Celia continued, saying, "If you stay with Angel, then we can visit you."

Del knew that any second now Mick would agree to Angel's offer, and then she'd lose her chance. She took a deep breath, unglued her feet and tongue, and declared, "I'm taking him home with me."

The room fell silent, and as one, all eyes shifted her way. The women and two men stared, as if seeing her for the first time.

Mick smiled.

Under so much scrutiny, Del squirmed. Thanks to

the rain and her long jog and the events at the jewelry store, she looked like something out of a circus sideshow. But determination filled her. She wasn't a coward and she wouldn't start acting like one now.

Moving out of the corner, she edged in around Angel, who kept kissing Mick's forehead. Del got as close to him as she could, then stated again, "I'll take care of him." She made her voice strong, resolute.

Angel blinked, looked at the other people, then back at Del. "You will?"

"Yes. After all," Del explained, "it's my fault he's hurt."

Everyone's gaze shifted from her to Mick. Expressions varied from male amusement, astonishment and fascination, to female speculation.

Del wanted to wince, to close her ears so she wouldn't have to hear what Mick might reply to her appalling assumption. They were strangers in every sense of the word, but he'd claimed to want to see her again. What better opportunity would there be than for her to take him home? She'd never played nurse to anyone before, but how hard could it be?

She stood by his bed, refusing to budge, blocking Angel and her lips, in particular, and waited in agony.

Expectation hung in the air, along with a good dose of confusion.

Mick grinned, managed a one-shoulder shrug and addressed all six people at once. "There you go. Looks like it's all taken care of."

"WHAT DO YOU KNOW ABOUT her?"

Josh looked down at Angel and shrugged. They stood in the hallway outside Mick's door, which was as far as Angel would go. "Not a damn thing," he said, "except that Mick is in a bad way."

Angel pressed a hand to her chest, looking as if she'd taken the bullet herself. "The wound?"

Josh knew how close she was to Mick—practically a surrogate mom even though only nine years separated them. Mick's real mother, from what he understood, had been plagued by too many personal weaknesses. She'd died long ago, and Angel and Dane's family had become Mick's. "I'm sorry, I meant that he's been acting...infatuated."

Relieved, Angel bent a chastising look on him. "Mick is a grown man, a very levelheaded man. He doesn't get infatuated."

Josh knew that, which only made it more baffling. Beautiful women flirted with Mick and he hardly noticed. But this one... Josh shook his head. "Call it what you want, but today he chased her down, took a bullet for her without even knowing her name. And according to Zack, the first thing he asked about, even before he got his eyes open, was Delilah."

A slow smile spread over Angel's face. "This is wonderful!"

"Did you hear me?" Beyond respecting her a great deal, Josh knew Angel was one of the chew-'em-up-and-spit-'em-out women Mick had mentioned during their lunch, so he carefully measured his words. "Today, just a few minutes ago, is the first time he officially met her. Before that, he just watched her jog every day." Josh thought about Mick's preoccupation with Delilah and added, "She's not even all that eye-catching."

Angel smacked him on the shoulder. Not hard, but it still stung.

He refused to rub it.

"Looks are nothing, and you should know it by now. Besides, I think she's cute."

Dane, carrying two colas, strolled up behind her. He handed one to his wife and asked, "Who's cute?"

"Mick's woman."

Grinning, Dane said, "That little dynamo in there telling him she won't leave now that he's awake, not even to go home and get a change of clothes? And if she does leave, she absolutely will not take a bodyguard with her?" Dane laughed as he sipped his drink. "Both Alec and I offered, at Mick's insistence. Alec even promised her we wouldn't leave him alone, that one of us would be sure to stay with him until she returned. But she's not convinced. If anything, that seemed to have the opposite effect on her."

"I wonder why."

"Because she likes being difficult," Josh pointed out, disgruntled.

Dane grinned. "Actually, I believe she's jealous of Angel."

Angel frowned. "Of me? But Mick and I are like…"

"You don't have to convince me," Dane told her. "But then I know you both well. She doesn't."

"Why would she need a bodyguard?" Angel asked, changing the subject. Dane spent a few minutes explaining about the bizarre aspects of the robbery, and Mick's concerns.

"For whatever reason, I don't think Mick has told her that he's a cop," Dane said. "He tried telling her she could be in danger, but she's blowing the whole thing off as nothing more than a fluke, or a coincidence. I get the feeling he'll have his hands full with that one.''

Josh glared toward the closed door. ''After spending several hours with her today, I can tell you that she's about the most contrary woman I've ever met. All she did was bitch at me.''

Dane raised both brows. ''Let me guess, you tried treating her as you do most women, flirting, teasing—''

''Condescending,'' Angel added.

''I was charming!''

''—and,'' Dane continued, ''she was too smart to fall for it.''

''She wants to do things her own way,'' Josh grumbled, still amazed that she'd taken exception to his manner, ''and damn the consequences. She's far too…independent and stubborn for my tastes.''

Barely stifling a chuckle, Dane clapped him on the shoulder. ''It's good for you, teach you a little humility around the ladies.''

Josh wasn't interested in learning humility, thank you very much. He and the ladies got along just fine. Delilah Piper—well, she was just an aberration, a woman who couldn't be swayed with sound male logic, smiles or compliments. In fact, she'd been rude enough to scoff at his compliments, as if she'd known they were false, which, of course, she hadn't because he was damn good at flattery when he chose to be.

Josh felt renewed pique; no woman had ever scoffed at him before. ''Do you want me to go drag her out of there?''

Dane's expression filled with anticipation. ''Oh yeah, I'd love to see you try.''

True, Josh thought. Knowing her—and, after

spending hours closed up with her in the waiting room, he did indeed feel that he knew her—she'd probably kick him someplace dirty. His groin ached just thinking about it. She'd threatened to do him in once today already, when he wouldn't agree to label her Mick's wife, just so she could sneak in and see him sooner. Obstinate woman.

And besides, brute force wasn't something he'd ever used on a female. He'd only been mouthing off because he'd used up his other tricks on her without success. "I'll see if I can dredge up some diplomacy," he told Angel and Dane, and sauntered into the room with all the enthusiasm of a man headed to the gallows.

One look at Delilah and he was again filled with confusion. What was it about her that had Mick going gaga? The woman was...*lanky*. That's the only word he could think of that described her. Her arms and legs were long, her body slim, her breasts small. She appeared delicate when he knew she was anything but.

He had, however, noticed that she had a very nice tush, not that it made up for the rest of it.

And now she watched him, on alert, as if he had no right to be in the room seeing one of his best friends. His gaze met Alec's and Alec shrugged. Celia stared wide-eyed.

None of them were used to Mick being thwarted. Most times, he told people what needed to be done and they did it. Mick had an air about him that demanded obedience. Women especially went out of their way to make him happy. Not that Mick took advantage of his appeal to women. Just the opposite, he seemed unaware of how they gravitated to him and he was the most discriminating male Josh had ever known. Beautiful women came on to him, but more often than not, Mick showed no interest at all.

Until now.

According to Angel, Mick had been that way since he was sixteen. Always a take-charge guy, always irresistible, but at the moment he looked ready to pull his hair out.

With flagging patience, Mick said, "I want you to be comfortable, Delilah. Go home and take the shower you mentioned earlier. Change your clothes if you want, get something to eat."

"I'm not hungry and I'm used to the clothes now." Her every word exuded stubbornness, though an edge of desperation could be heard, too.

Alec and Celia stood at the foot of the bed. Celia shook her head and Alec narrowed his eyes in contemplation.

Mick looked tired and frustrated and pained as he said, "I don't need you to baby-sit me, Delilah."

Josh decided enough was enough. Mick wasn't in top fighting form or the conversation never would have gone on for so long. He hated seeing his friend this way, wounded and weak.

Josh had handled plenty of women in his day. This one was no different—at least not in the most important ways.

"Of course you need a damn baby-sitter." Josh leaned against the wall, ready to take on Delilah and win. "Good God, Mick, you were dumb enough to get shot in the first place, then dumb enough to pass out. I can understand why she doesn't trust you now to do as the doctors and nurses tell you. You'd probably yank out your IV, wouldn't you? Or get up and parade around the room until you keeled over again. If she doesn't stay right here like a good little mother hen to make sure you behave yourself, you might even—''

Predictably enough, Miss Delilah exploded. She went stiff as a spike, sputtered, then practically shouted, ''Don't you talk to him like that, Josh!''

Celia jumped a good foot at Del's explosive outburst. Alec coughed to cover a laugh. Zack, always laid-back and calm, watched the drama unfold with interest. But then Zack knew Josh and likely suspected his motives.

''Well,'' Josh reasoned, extravagant for the sake of their audience, ''why would you refuse to go home and change out of your rumpled clothes unless you didn't trust him to act intelligently?''

Delilah fried him with a look before bending down to Mick. She said very sweetly, ''I'll be right back.''

When she stalked around the bed, both Celia and Alec scurried to get out of her way. Josh didn't know if it was the scent of mud and sweat that motivated them, or the intent look on her face.

As she passed Josh, she snagged his shirtfront and dragged him out after her. Biting back a victorious laugh, Josh looked over his shoulder in time to see Mick chuckling. Josh sent him a salute.

Once in the hallway, Delilah rounded on him. She opened her mouth to speak, but he beat her to it. ''You need to shower. I can see sweat stains under your arms, and I can smell you.''

Her face flaming with color, she kept her gaze glued on Josh, then turned her head the tiniest bit and sniffed. She wrinkled her nose and frowned.

Josh almost laughed. Truth was, Delilah smelled

kinda nice, like shampoo and lotion and woman, not that he'd ever tell her that. Calmly now, because he didn't want to offend her, he said, "Mick needs you here. I know that. Hell, you're all he's talked about since he came to."

"Really?" She looked skeptical, and hopeful.

"Yep." Seeing her uncertainty, Josh softened. Most of her aggression had been on Mick's behalf, so he couldn't really hold it against her. "He'll be uneasy if he thinks he's imposing. You don't know him like I do. He's not used to relying on anyone. Do you really want to start a relationship that way?"

She stared down at her muddy sneakers and mumbled, "No."

Such a small voice for Delilah! And he noticed she didn't deny the relationship part. Good. At least that meant she was as interested as Mick. Josh would hate to think his friend was the only one smitten.

"He also doesn't want you to be alone. He doesn't worry about women often, so you could show a little gratitude and go easy on him."

Seconds ticked by before she finally admitted, "I didn't—don't—know those men." She looked at him, her eyes troubled. "And I don't want a total stranger waiting around on me while I shower and change. I don't like to impose on others, either."

Josh wanted to curse, to end this awful day by heading home and phoning a reasonable woman, a doting woman who'd give him the comfort of her body and her feminine concern. He did not want to spend more time with this particular woman, who treated him as an asexual nuisance.

But he knew what he needed to do. He drew in a breath and made the ultimate sacrifice. "All right.

Then let me take you home. You can do what needs to be done, then I'll bring you back. You can stay until visiting hours are over. I know he'd appreciate that.''

As if he hadn't made the grand offer, she said, ''Maybe Zack could drive me home?''

If it wasn't for Mick... Josh drew a deep breath and reached for control. ''Zack can't. He has a four-year-old daughter and he needs to get home to her.''

''Oh.'' Delilah eyed him, apparently liking his plan as little as he did. ''I suppose Dane or Alec would be okay....''

He should have said fine, should have let Mick deal with her. Instead, he heard himself say, ''Dane and Alec just drove two hours to get here, and I'm sure they'd like to spend their time visiting Mick, not chauffeuring your stubborn butt around town.''

Stiffening, she said, ''I could take a bus....''

''And Mick would still worry. Someone shot at you today, lady.'' From what Josh understood, someone had singled her out as a victim. It didn't make sense, and he understood Mick's concern. ''You witnessed a burglary and it doesn't matter that you told the police you didn't recognize anyone, that you have no idea what's going on, it's still strange.''

She didn't relent, and he said, his patience at an end, ''Hell, I promise not to speak to you, all right? I won't even look at you if it'll make you happy.''

Using both hands, she covered her face. Her normally proud, straight shoulders hunched and she turned partially away.

Thinking she was about to cry, Josh froze. Damn, but he couldn't deal with weeping women. There was nothing he hated more, nothing that made him feel more helpless. His stomach tightened, cramped. Delilah acted tough and talked tough, but she was still female, delicately built, and she'd been through an ordeal.

But she didn't so much as sniffle. "I don't mean to be nasty," she said from behind her fingers. Her voice was miserable but strong, and devoid of tears. "It's just…" She hesitated for a long minute, then dropped her hands and sighed. "I feel so responsible."

Josh's hostility and impatience melted away. She'd been involved in a robbery, shot at, stuck in the hospital all day in wet, grubby clothes with total strangers. If he'd known her longer, he'd have offered her a hug. But he'd just met her—and so had Mick. Josh was still worried. It wasn't like Mick to fall so hard so fast. He'd never even seen Mick trip. On rare occasions, Mick dated, and then moved on.

Josh couldn't think of a single female, other than family, who Mick would have invited to stay at the hospital with him. Not only would he have found it an intrusion, he was far too private to want anyone around him when he wasn't up to full speed.

In his line of work, Mick naturally had to be careful, and that caution had carried over into other aspects of his life. Or perhaps it had always been there, left over from a less-than-wonderful childhood. But whatever the reason, Josh could tell that for this woman, Mick was throwing caution to the wind.

Settling for a friendly arm around her shoulders, Josh steered her back toward the hospital room. "The last thing Mick would want is for you to feel bad. About anything. As to responsibility, it sure as hell isn't *your* fault those idiots showed up and started shooting. Okay?''

"Thanks." She nodded, and even managed a small smile for him. Josh was struck by that smile, and for the first time, he had an inkling of what Mick felt.

They walked through the door, and she seemed to forget all about Josh the second her gaze landed on Mick. Nonplussed, he watched her hurry back to Mick's bedside. "Josh is going to drive me home, but I'll be right back."

Mick's surprise at the quick turnaround was plain to see as he looked from Josh to Delilah and back again. Josh winked. Oh yeah, he'd have fun ribbing them later with this one. He'd gotten her to do what the rest of them couldn't. He hadn't lost his touch, after all.

"Don't worry, Mick," Josh said, feeling in good humor for the first time since the shooting, "I'll keep a real close eye on her."

That earned him a frown from both Delilah and Mick. Delilah apparently didn't think she needed to be watched, and Mick obviously didn't want any male looking at her too closely. Jealousy, Josh decided, and was glad he'd never suffered such a miserable emotion.

"You really don't have to rush," Mick told Delilah after dragging his attention away from Josh. But it was plain to Josh that Mick wanted her back where he could be the one keeping an eye on her, protecting her, not any other man, not even a friend he trusted. He was also in pain and doing his best to hide it. Damn stubborn fool.

Delilah glanced around the room. "Will your visitors stay all night?"

"No," Mick said, making the decision before any-one else could answer.

Alec coughed again. Celia rushed to assure her. "We'll be at a nearby hotel for the night, but we'll stay here until you get back. How's that?"

As if it was up to her, Delilah nodded. "That'd be perfect. Thank you." Then she bent to kiss Mick again. "I'm going to give my cell phone number to the nurse, just in case." She turned to Josh. "Are you ready?"

"I'll be right there."

She looked suspicious at his delay, but didn't ques-tion him on it. She turned and moseyed out.

The door had barely closed before Angel and Dane came back in. Angel propped her hands on her hips and said, "Now that she's not within hearing dis-tance, tell me the truth. Does your shoulder hurt?"

With a crooked grin, Mick admitted, "Hell, yes." Then he turned to Zack. "If you could see about some pain medicine…?"

"The doctor ordered it for when you woke up, but you were too bullheaded to take it."

"It would've made me sleepy."

Josh shook his head. "And God forbid he miss a single second of Delilah Piper's visit."

Zack, always something of a peacemaker as well as an EMT, laughed. "I'll go get your nurse and she can take care of you."

Josh walked over to the bed, where both Dane and Alec now hovered. Josh knew they were dying for some answers. Together the two men ran a private investigations firm, and they could sniff out trouble without even trying.

"The other men got away. The police are still looking, but they haven't turned up anyone."

Mick's curse was especially foul. "What about the one I shot? Did they find out anything from him?"

"The idiot had ID on him. He's Rudy Glasgow, and he's still unconscious." Josh knew that despite Mick's injuries, he'd want to know it all. Still, he hesitated before saying, "It doesn't look good."

Mick dropped back onto the pillow with an aggrieved sigh. "I know my shot to his leg didn't put him under. Was it the head wound from when he fell?"

"Yeah. You two mirror each other—both shot, both with conked heads. Only his was worse. He rattled something in his skull and the docs don't know when he'll come to, which means they don't know when he'll be able to answer questions, if ever. You were lucky that you landed more on Zack than the concrete when you fell."

Not amused, Mick cursed again.

"I also turned your gun over to the officer first on the scene. He insisted, of course, and with you passed out cold…" Josh shrugged.

"That's standard procedure," Mick assured him, not worried. "I'll be issued a new one."

Josh nodded. "I notified your sergeant and he's getting in touch with Internal Affairs."

"Which means I'll have to see the damn psychiatrist, too." He groaned.

"Just procedure?" Josh asked, though he already knew any shooting required a follow-up visit with the shrink, just to keep the officers healthy in mind and body.

"Yeah." Mick looked weary beyond belief. "When she leaves here tonight—"

Dane held up a hand. "We won't let anything happen to her. I promise."

And Josh assumed that meant one or both of them would be tailing her the rest of the night, even after she finished her hospital visit. Delilah wouldn't like it if she knew. But then, Dane and Alec were damn good, so she wouldn't find out unless they wanted her to know.

Alec looked thoughtful, and with his intense, dark features, the look was almost menacing. It had taken Josh some time to get used to him. "So you think the robbery was a sham? Just an excuse to shoot her?"

"They aimed for her head," Mick rumbled in disgust, describing how he'd covered her, and the shooter's angle. He gave details he hadn't given when Delilah was in the room. "They didn't threaten anyone else. Hell, they didn't even look at anyone else."

"But why her?" Dane asked.

"I haven't got a clue. Far as I can figure, she was just a customer, like the other two in the shop."

Though Mick said it, he didn't look quite convinced. Josh didn't like any of it, especially since his friend seemed determined to be in the middle of it all. "I'd better get out there or she'll leave without me."

"She doesn't have a car here, does she?" Mick asked, concerned over the possibility.

"No, but believe me, that wouldn't stop her. Prepare yourself, Mick, because she's about the most obstinate, bullheaded woman I've ever run across." He squeezed Mick's left shoulder. "Take it easy while we're gone."

"You won't let her out of your sight?"

"Just when she showers." He grinned at Mick's warning growl. It amused the hell out of him how possessive his friend had gotten, and how quickly. "Quit worrying. I'll bring her back safe and sound."

CHAPTER THREE

MICK WATCHED JOSH GO, and though he trusted Josh implicitly, he cursed the injury that kept him confined to bed. "She could have been killed today."

Angel sat beside him on the narrow mattress. "Is that why you agreed to go home with her? So you can protect her?"

He nodded, but he saw that both Alec and Dane knew his reasons were more varied than that. And more territorial, more sexual. Protecting wasn't the only activity he had in mind. He'd never burned for a woman before, but now he felt like an inferno ready to combust.

Why the hell would someone want her dead?

Mick remembered the way she'd been looking the place over, the way she'd initially smiled at the men—a smile he'd considered merely polite, stranger to stranger.

Zack came back in, the nurse trailing him. She gave Mick a dose of morphine through his IV, and seconds later the discomfort receded and lethargy settled in.

Mick relished the relief from the searing pain, even while he fought to stay awake and sharp enough to think.

"Relax," Dane ordered him.

"I have to figure out what's going on." A vague sense of impending doom, of limited time plagued him.

Dane shook his head. "No. You're in no shape to start snooping around. Let it go for now. The bastard who shot you isn't going anywhere, and he won't stay out forever. When he comes to, you can question him. Or better yet, let someone else do it."

"No." Even with the morphine clouding his mind, Mick knew he wasn't about to pass up the opportunity to get some answers. "I need to call my sergeant, to tell him I want to stay advised. And I need to talk to the head nurse. I need to—"

Angel pressed her fingers over his mouth. "You need to sleep. I have a feeling when Delilah gets back, you'll be determined to stay awake and alert."

Alec cocked a brow while cuddling Celia to his side. "He wouldn't want to miss a minute of that, as Josh said."

Mick relaxed, thinking of Delilah's emotional strength, her boldness, how she'd kissed him, her taste, her heat. They were right—he didn't want to miss that. In the next instant, he fell asleep.

MICK WOKE TO THE SOUND of quiet tapping. The room was dim, with only one light glowing in the corner. The curtains were all closed, but he could tell it was night. He'd probably slept another four hours or so, and it enraged him. There was a lot to consider, a lot to do, not the least of which would be getting to know Delilah.

The tapping continued, light and quick. He bit back

a groan as he turned his head on the soft pillow and zeroed in on the source. There, sprawled in the room's only chair, a laptop resting across her thighs, was Delilah.

God, she was lovely.

A nurse had evidently brought her a pillow and blanket in an effort to help make her comfortable. The padded lounge chair could have served as a bed in a pinch. Delilah had the back reclined, the pillow behind her shoulders, the blanket thrown over the arm of the chair.

Her rich dark hair, freshly washed, swung loose and silky around her shoulders. The light from the laptop cast a soft blue halo around her. Her eyes looked mysterious, purposeful, as she typed away. Mick watched her, aware of the acceleration in his pulse, the expanding sexual tension.

She'd changed into a pair of baggy jeans and a miniscule, snowy-white, cropped T-shirt. Her sandals were off, tucked beneath the chair, her bare feet propped on the edge of the counter in front of the window. Two flowering plants now sat there, no doubt from Angel and Celia.

Delilah's slim legs seemed to go on forever, and Mick, still only half-awake, pictured them around his hips, hugging him tight while he rode her, long and slow and so damn deep. He visually followed the trail of those incredibly long legs, and when he came to her hips he imagined them lifted by his hands, her legs sprawled wide while he tasted her, licked her and made her scream out a climax.

A groan broke free from him and Delilah jumped, nearly dumping her laptop. "Mick!"

Heat throbbed just below his skin. He was so aroused he hurt, but he'd done nothing more than look at her and give his imagination free rein. What would it be like to actually have her?

He swallowed and said with a drawling, raw deliberation, "I don't suppose you'd like to give me another kiss?"

Slowly, her gaze glued to his, she set the laptop on the floor and stood. "I didn't mean to be so brazen earlier. I just…it amazed me that anyone would do what you did."

"So you kissed me?"

Arching one dark brow, she half laughed. "I wanted to devour you, actually."

The shadows in the room did interesting things to her body. "Do you always say exactly what you think?"

She shrugged. "I guess so. I know I shouldn't, but I'm out of practice when it comes to this sort of thing."

"You can say whatever you want to me, okay?"

She nodded. "You saved my life, and you got hurt in the bargain. I saw you and I just…wanted to kiss you."

That didn't sound right to Mick. "So it was about gratitude?"

"Yes…no. I'm not sure." She made a helpless gesture, then shifted her feet and tucked her silky hair behind her ear. "The thing is, touching you seems…right."

He understood that. Touching her seemed right, too. Hell, devouring her seemed right. He'd have gladly gotten started right that minute, but she stood there, waiting, uncertain, very different now that they were alone. She wasn't as defensive, and there was no reason for her to be protective.

No woman had ever been protective of him. Except Angel, but that was back when he'd been a boy. With Delilah it felt different.

"Everyone else has left?"

"Yes. Angel and Celia gave me the number of the hotel where they're staying so you could call if you needed them. The man, Alec, said you had his cell number if you wanted to make sure he was on duty. Whatever that means."

Mick nodded, understanding perfectly. Alec would wait and watch for Delilah to leave. He'd protect her until Mick could take over. There wasn't a more capable or harder man than Alec Sharpe. Knowing he'd keep his eye on Delilah gave Mick a new measure of relief.

When he didn't speak, she gestured at the flowers and said, "The women bought these in the gift shop."

"That's just like them."

She fidgeted. "They're…friends of yours?"

"More like family. As close as family can be without all the baggage."

"Oh." A mix of emotions crossed her features—confusion and relief. "Josh and Zack said they'd be in touch in the morning."

"I figured as much." She stood there before him, barefoot and fidgety, and Mick used the opportunity to look at her. The loose jeans hung low on her slim hips, showing a strip of pale belly between the waist-band and the hem of her shirt. He saw the barest hint of her navel, enough to fire his blood, to make his mouth go dry.

He glanced at her breasts and found himself smil-ing. She was indeed small, but still so damn sexy he ached all the way down to his toes. As he stared, her nipples tightened, pushing him over the edge.

He needed her closer. Because she looked uncer-tain, he asked, "You didn't like kissing me?"

"I did!" she blurted, then bit her bottom lip. She twined her fingers together and shifted her bare feet again. "I just didn't want you to think that, you know, just because you were nice enough to save me that you had to…"

"Had to what?" Inside, he grinned, knowing what she thought, but in the mood to tease her.

"You know. Be sexual with me." His gaze shot to her face and she rushed to add, "I wasn't sure if you felt the same way I did. I mean, you're incredible. Gorgeous and sexy and hard and…what woman wouldn't want you? But I'm just me. I didn't know if you wanted to—"

Just that quickly, his humor fled. "I want to."

"You do?"

He was hard, and there wasn't a damn thing he could do about it. "Come here, Delilah."

As if reassured, she strode to the bed and sat beside him, this time to his left. "You want me to kiss you again?"

Unwilling to rush her or scare her off, he didn't

move. He wanted her to be as free as she'd first been, taking what she wanted from him, when she wanted it. Was there a better male fantasy than having a bold woman who knew her own mind and went after what she needed?

Holding himself still, Mick said softly, "I'd love for you to kiss me again."

"You don't need anything first?" She searched his face, looking him over, he assumed, for signs of discomfort. "A drink? More pain medicine?"

I need you. "No."

Tentatively, she laid a hand on his chest. "You're so warm," she whispered, her fingers lightly caressing, edging under the loose neckline of the hospital gown. "I watched you sleep for a while and it made me nuts." She glanced at him, meeting his gaze. "You even look good when you sleep. I had to get out my laptop to keep busy, just so I wouldn't end up touching you. I didn't want to wake you."

Mick had no response to that, other than a rush of heat. The thought of her watching him and wanting him fed his awareness of her, making it more acute.

She touched his throat, then slid her slender fingers over his uninjured shoulder. "I think," she whispered, watching the progress of her hand, "that you're about the sexiest man I've ever seen."

If they'd been anywhere other than a hospital room, he'd have pulled her under him. He shifted, felt the pain deep in his shoulder and cursed.

She quickly pulled away, then poured him a drink of water and lifted the straw to his mouth. "Shh. This will help."

Getting her under him would help, but he didn't say so. He drank deeply, hoping the icy water would cool his urgency, return a measure of his control. It was insane to want a woman this way.

After setting the paper cup aside, Delilah again rested her hand on his chest. Her gaze locked with his. "Your heart is racing."

"I'm horny," he explained, because anything more eloquent was beyond him while she continued to touch him.

Her light blue eyes twinkled and her lush lips curled into a satisfied feminine smile. "No sex for you, at least not until you're healed."

That "not until" stipulation—which pretty much guaranteed he'd eventually have her—about stopped his heart. Without another word she leaned down and touched her mouth to his. She was gone before Mick could respond.

Her blue eyes were warmer, softer, and he rumbled, "Again."

She looked at his mouth, bent, stroked his bottom lip with her hot little tongue. "Do you like that?" she breathed.

He groaned.

Still so close he tasted her breath, she asked, "You're not married or anything, are you?"

"No."

"At first, I was afraid Angel or Celia—"

"No." Using his left hand, he touched her hair. Warmth, softness. "I love your hair." He tangled his fingers in the silky mass and brought her mouth back flush with his.

"Thank you," she murmured, and obligingly gave him the longer kiss he wanted.

Dull pain pushed at Mick, but he blocked it from his mind. It was nothing compared to the feel of her. "Open your mouth."

She did, then accepted the slow, deliberate thrust of his tongue. He stroked deep, taking her mouth, exploring all the textures and heat, and the taste that was uniquely Delilah.

They both groaned.

Delilah pulled back. She touched his jaw and asked, "Did I hurt you?"

He had to stop this or he'd lose it completely. "Of course not."

"I'm not married or anything, either."

Mick, still on the verge of a meltdown, managed to lift a brow at that candid disclosure, and she shrugged. "I just thought you should know," she said, her words coming in soft, uneven pants, "being as we're...well, doing this."

"This?" She stayed close and the scent of her, lighter now and touched with lotion and powder, filled him. He wanted to wrap himself in it, wanted to hold her close to his body until their scents mingled.

"The whole sex thing." She drew a breath, but kept her gaze steady, unwavering. "I assume that's where we're headed. I mean, I'll have you all to myself in my apartment and I want you. I assume you want me, too."

He could hardly believe what she'd just said. No woman had ever come right out and so boldly stated her intentions to have an affair with him. Women sometimes chased him, but they were subtle, never so up front with their motives. They teased, flirted, advanced and retreated.

They didn't advance and advance.

"What is it you do?" she asked, unconcerned with his bemused astonishment—maybe even unaware that she'd astonished him. "I've never known anyone who carried a gun and shot people."

He should have been prepared for that, because he knew she'd ask. But he was still stuck on that affair statement, attempting to get his head back together—a near impossible feat because all he could think about now was starting that damn affair. The sooner the better.

"Mick?"

He wanted to tell her the truth, but he knew nothing about her except that she evidently had an enemy, someone who wanted her dead, someone who would have succeeded if that bullet hadn't been sidetracked by his shoulder. He also knew she was eccentric, a woman heedless of her surroundings, honest to a fault, brazen and stubborn one minute, shy and uncertain the next. And he knew she wanted him, not as much as he wanted her, but enough.

His innate caution warned him against going too fast. Thinking of Dane and Alec, he lied. "I'm a private investigator."

Her eyes widened with unrestrained excitement. "Seriously?"

She looked so comically surprised, he grinned. "Yeah." Starting things off with a lie wasn't the best course of action, but he had few choices until he found out what was going on. If all went as planned, he'd be able to tell her the truth soon enough. She'd understand his reasoning and forgive his deception. He'd see to it.

"Wow." She settled on the side of his bed, her hip against his, her hand still resting on his chest. "I could use you for research."

Mick did a double take, momentarily getting his mind off the idea of pulling her down on the narrow bed beside him. "Research for what?"

She shrugged in the direction of the laptop. "I'm a writer. I'm always looking for easy ways to research. From the horse's mouth is always the easiest."

A writer? Now, somehow that fit. The creative types were always a bit different, as far as he knew. "What do you write?"

"Mysteries." She waggled her eyebrows. "Fun stuff. Whodunits with a few laughs and some racy romance thrown in."

It was Mick's turn to say, "Wow." Then he added, "Have you ever been published?"

"Well, yeah." She seemed to consider that a stupid question.

She'd said it so casually, as if it were nothing. He'd never met a novelist before, and now he planned to sleep with one. "How many books have you done?"

"I've had four published so far, with two more in the works." She nodded toward her laptop. "I'm working under a deadline right now."

"How old are you?" Mick didn't think she looked

old enough to have one book published, much less four. He'd always pictured writers as more seasoned, scholarly types.

His question made her grin. "Twenty-five, almost twenty-six. I sold my first book when I was twenty-three."

Mick eyed her anew. A mystery writer. He had to shake his head at the novelty of it. And here he'd claimed to be a PI. A match made in heaven. "I'll be damned," he said, still dealing with his amazement. "Maybe I could read one sometime?"

"Sure. I'll show them to you when we get to my apartment. By the way, I drove myself here so I could take us both home tomorrow. Your friend Josh was pretty ticked off about it. He was going to tattle, and you should have seen his face when we found you asleep. He looked so frustrated, I thought his head would explode. Of course, for that one, it might be an improvement."

Mick closed his eyes. Some maniac had tried to kill her, and here she'd been on the road alone again, vulnerable. He could just imagine Josh's frustration. "Delilah."

"Del."

"Excuse me?" He opened his eyes again and stared at her. Hard.

"If we're going to be friends, you may as well call me what everyone else does."

"And everyone else calls you...*Del?*" It sounded like a man's name to Mick.

She shrugged. "It's what I've always gone by. Only my father called me Delilah, usually if he was angry, and he died a few years ago. Now I only use my full name when I write.''

Mick wondered how her father had died, if she had any other family left.

He shook off his distraction. He'd have time to ask her about her family later. Keeping his tone stern, he said, ''Josh was right to be angry. Someone tried to shoot you today. You shouldn't be alone, not until I—'' He pulled back on that, quickly saying instead, ''Until the police can figure out what's going on.''

She flapped her hand at him, waving away his concerns, then let it settle on his abdomen. He nearly shot off the bed. Every muscle in his body clenched and his cock throbbed. He'd never been in such a bad way before.

If she moved her fingers just a few inches lower, she could make him feel so much better. He closed his eyes against the image of her soft hand holding him, stroking him. Too fast, he was moving way too fast.

''I don't think,'' she murmured, watching her hand on his body, ''that they were really shooting at me. Why would they?'' She looked up at him, her hand thankfully still. ''I mean, they aimed at me, but I think it was just a random thought. They were criminals and they got thwarted because the police showed up, and they were mad, so they wanted to shoot someone.''

Nearly choking on an odd combination of explosive desire, frustration and protectiveness, Mick asked, ''And you think they chose you, a woman who didn't have a thing to do with anything, a woman just visiting the store? They didn't look rattled or frenzied. They looked like they meant to shoot you—you specifically—before they took off.''

Her fingers spread wide and her brow furrowed. ''I don't know. I didn't notice anything like that.''

Her baby finger was a quarter inch from the head of his penis. His body strained, fighting against his control. He *needed* to lift his hips, to thrust into her hand.

''You,'' he rasped, ''are the person they accused of setting off an alarm, when you hadn't moved and weren't anywhere near anything that could have triggered an alarm.''

That made him think of something else, and he forced himself to concentrate on things other than her touch. ''How did the cops know? Did anyone tell you?''

She stared blankly at his bandaged shoulder, deep in thought. ''The officer who questioned me said someone on the street noticed the guns when he was walking by, and he used his cell phone to call them.''

''Honey, listen to me.'' Mick put his left hand on her bare waist, between the bottom of her shirt and the top of her jeans. Her skin was smooth and warm, her muscles taut. ''Did you recognize either of them? Was there anything at all familiar about them?''

''No, of course not.'' She looked at her hand on his abdomen, then at his erection. He read her thoughts as if she'd spoken them aloud. Instinctively, he tightened, which brought forth a moan of pain from both physical discomfort and sharp anticipation.

''You're in a bad way,'' she said in a hushed,

husky tone filled with understanding and her own measure of need.

He wanted to howl. He wanted to ask her to go ahead and stroke him, hard and fast, that she use her mouth…

"Delilah…"

"Del," she whispered, and started to glide her hand lower.

Using his left hand, Mick caught her wrist. His hold was tight, too tight, but he felt stretched so taut he was ready to snap. "I'm in worse than a bad way," he rasped. "I'm on the very edge, and if you touch me I won't be able to control myself."

She tilted her head, staring at him as if she didn't quite grasp his meaning.

"I'll come," he said bluntly, then watched for her reaction.

She stayed still, but probably only because he held her slender wrist in an iron grip, refusing to let her move.

"This is difficult for me," he explained, watching her, needing her to understand. He felt more tension than he had at fifteen, when he'd seen his first fully naked female, there for the taking. He'd lost control then; he was ready to lose control now. He ground his teeth and insisted, "I'm not usually like this."

Her eyes, warm and heavy-lidded, looked him over. "You're hurt, in bed. This is a strange situation."

"It has nothing to do with any of that and everything to do with you. I want you bad, and have since the first time I saw you."

He could tell that admission pleased her. "To-day?" she asked,

Gently, he lifted her hand away from his body so he could carry on a coherent conversation. He brought her hand to his chest and kept it there. "I saw you two weeks ago, near a building I own. You were heading to the post office."

Her frown reappeared. "I never noticed you," she said. Then, chagrined, she added, "I was probably plotting, and I don't pay much attention then. My mind tends to wander."

He thought about how she'd been examining the jewelry store, studying it, prowling from one corner to the other. "Plotting…what?"

"My book, of course."

She said it as if it should have been obvious to him.

"So," she asked, "you saw me a few weeks ago?"

"And many times since then. I eat at Marco's a lot, and you—"

"Jog by there a lot." Her smile was very sweet. "Whenever I have a deadline, I need to get outside at least once a day to clear my head so I can really think and plot. So I jog. But I've never noticed you before."

"I've watched you almost every day. Today when I saw you actually stop and go into the jewelry store, I decided it was time to introduce myself."

Her countenance darkened. "Instead you saved my life."

They stared at each other. The air was charged, until a nurse started backing in, dragging a cart with her.

Delilah moved so fast, Mick was stunned. She snagged the pillow from her chair and dropped it over his lap. To the nurse she said, "Time to check him again?"

The nurse looked over her shoulder and smiled. "I'll only be a minute." Then she turned to Mick. "For an injured man, you're about the healthiest thing I've ever seen."

Mick was in no mood for small talk. "Is that right?" he asked, while watching Delilah.

"Yep. Great lungs, great reflexes. The epitome of health. I wish everyone would take such good care of their bodies."

Delilah made a choking sound at that observation. "I'll, uh, just get out of your way." She tapped a few buttons on her laptop, closed it and set it on the window ledge. She picked up a large tote from the floor and swung the strap over her shoulder, saying to Mick, "I'm going to run down to the coffee shop and grab a bite to eat. Do you want anything? You slept through dinner."

The nurse said, "We can still get him a tray."

Delilah leaned close and whispered, "It was nasty-looking stuff. I'd pass if I was you."

The nurse heard and grinned. "The coffee shop has pretty good sandwiches and chips and desserts. You're not on a restricted diet, so if something sounds good…"

Delilah started out. "I'll surprise you."

"Delilah—"

"Del," she said, then added, "Don't worry. I'll be right back. We'll pretend we're having a picnic."

And before he could warn her to be cautious, she was gone. Mick sank back against the pillows, the ache in his shoulder receding to no more than a dull, annoying throb. The nurse offered him more pain medication, but he passed. He needed all his wits about him to deal with Delilah Piper. Otherwise, he thought, grinning shamelessly, she'd probably take sexual advantage of him in his weakened physical shape.

He could hardly wait.

The nurse finished her poking and prodding, changed his bandage, and then, at his request, handed him the phone.

He called Josh. A woman answered—no surprise there—and Mick heard her grumbling, heard the squeaking of bedsprings, before Josh came on the line.

"You're either feeling much better or much worse if you're making a call."

"Much better," Mick told him, and he knew it was only a partial lie. "Can you bring me a change of clothes tomorrow? The nurse said I should be ready to get out of here by eleven."

"Sure thing, but it'll have to be early. I'm on duty starting at eight."

As a fireman, Josh worked varying hours, usually four days on, four days off. On his off days—today being one—he spent a lot of time with women.

Zack, an EMT stationed right next door to the fire department, was just the opposite. He spent all his spare time with his daughter and only rarely made time for women, and then only when his hormones refused to let him put it off any longer.

"If it's inconvenient, I can ask Zack."

"It's no problem. I'd planned to check up on you anyway, just to make sure your little woman hadn't done you in."

"You don't like her?" Mick asked, not really caring, but curious all the same. Personally, he found everything about Delilah unique and enticing, even her damned stubbornness, which had earlier about driven him nuts.

"She's…different."

True enough, Mick thought.

"And she took exception to me right off the bat."

Mick grinned. That was probably a first for Josh.

"She's not like other women, and she'll take some getting used to. But it appears she's as nuts about you as you are about her, and I suppose that's all that really matters." There was a muffled sound as someone snatched the receiver away from Josh and he apparently wrestled it back. Mick heard him growl, "Just hang on. I'll only be a minute."

Chuckling, Mick said, "I won't keep you."

"S'no problem. She'll wait. So, what's it to be? Jeans? And I guess some type of button shirt?"

"That'd be easiest. I'm sure you can find your way around my house."

A feminine whisper, insistent and imploring, sounded in the background. Mick grinned again. "G'night, Josh."

"Hey, before you go, you should know that Alec

is hanging around, waiting to take care of things for you.''

Mick appreciated the subtle way Josh explained that with his lady friend listening. ''Thanks. I'll ring him next.''

He disconnected his call with Josh and punched in Alec's number. He imagined Delilah would return any minute, and he wanted to make sure things were set first.

''Sharpe.''

''It's me, Alec. Where are you?''

''Hanging out in the parking lot.''

''Damn, I hate to do that to you.''

He could hear the smile in Alec's tone when he said, ''Celia's with me. It's no problem.''

That made Mick smile, too. He could just imagine the two of them necking like teenagers. Alec was still a bad ass of the first order, but with Celia, he was a pussycat. ''Why don't you head out and I'll call you when she decides to leave?''

The door opened and Delilah came through, her arms laden with paper bags and disposable cups of steaming liquid. Mick eyed her cautiously, not sure how much she'd heard.

She set everything down and turned to him with a smile. ''Is that Josh?''

''No, it's, uh, Alec.'' He could hear Alec laughing in his ear. He knew they all appreciated the unique effect Delilah had on him.

''Alec?'' That surprised her, he could tell, but not for long. ''Well, tell him to go home and go to bed.

I'm not leaving tonight, so I don't need a body-guard.''

Mick scowled. "Delilah…"

"Del." She sat on the side of the bed and took the phone from his hand, then said into the receiver, "I'm going to stay the night. But thanks for thinking of me, anyway."

And then she hung up.

CHAPTER FOUR

AT TEN O'CLOCK, the doctor gave Mick the okay to leave, together with a long list of instructions. Del listened intently and felt confident that she could take care of everything that needed to be done.

Angel and Celia, along with their husbands, had come and gone already. They'd been there since early morning, but because Delilah now realized that they were in fact Mick's family, she enjoyed the attention they lavished on him. He treated both women with an avuncular ease, not with the heated awareness he'd shown her.

Unfortunately, Josh had shown up, too, at the crack of dawn. She'd been asleep when he'd arrived, and was forced to awaken to his scowling face. He'd seemed suspicious of her overnight stay, as if he thought she might have molested Mick in his sleep. Stupid man.

Though Josh was uncommonly handsome, and could be witty when he chose to be, she wasn't at all certain she liked him. Whenever he looked at her, his demeanor plainly said he found her lacking. He distrusted her interest in Mick, and showed confusion at Mick's interest in her.

Nevertheless, she did appreciate his friendship with

Mick. Willingly, he'd brought Mick clothes to wear home, then insisted she leave the room while he helped Mick dress. She would have stubbornly refused—*she* wanted to help him dress!—except Mick had wanted her to leave, too.

Delilah had already washed her face and brushed her hair and teeth while his family visited. They'd shown up just as Josh was leaving, and she couldn't help but feel a twinge of poignant sadness, seeing how loved he was. He had a good family, loyal friends, and she envied him that.

Hoping to make a better impression on them today than she had yesterday, she'd applied a little makeup and exchanged her slept-in T-shirt for a dark-rose tank top. Though the hospital was cool, out the window she could already see heat rising off the blacktop in the parking lot.

Now that they were alone again, Mick paced around the room, waiting for an orderly to bring a wheelchair. To Del's discerning eye, he looked ruggedly handsome with his morning whiskers and tired eyes. He also looked a little shaky. She wanted to coddle him, but she'd already figured out that he wasn't a man used to relying on others.

"Does your family live close?"

He glanced up at her, clearly distracted. With his arm in a sling and his eyes narrowed, he looked like a wounded pirate. "A coupla hours away. They'll be back over the weekend, I'm sure." His dark gaze sharpened. "Will that be a problem?"

"To have them visit? Of course not. For as long

as you stay with me, I want you to be completely comfortable. It'll be your home, too.''

He looked undecided, as if there was more he wanted to say, then he just shook his head. ''We need to come to a few understandings.''

''Oh?'' Seeing Mick flat on his back in bed was one thing. Him standing straight and tall—all six feet three inches of him, moving around the room with flexing muscle and barely leashed impatience—was another. He was an intimidating sight. An arousing sight.

''I want a few promises from you.'' He stalked toward her, as if ready to pounce, and she felt her heart tripping.

She was a tall woman, meeting many men eye-to-eye. Not so with Mick. He looked down at her, his dark eyes drawing her in, and without thought Del went on tiptoe and touched her mouth to his.

He froze for a beat, then slanted his head to better fit their mouths together, and caught her with his good arm at the same time. He carefully gathered her close, his large hand sliding up her back to her nape and holding her immobile.

Del was acutely aware of his arm in the sling between their bodies. Her breast brushed against the stiff cotton restraint and she shuddered, trying to keep space between them so she wouldn't inadvertently hurt him.

''Relax,'' he whispered, and then his hand left her neck to coast down her spine, down and down until he was squeezing her bottom, cuddling, drawing her up and in until her pelvis nudged his groin. He made a rough sound of pleasure.

Del pulled her mouth away and rested her forehead on his chest. "This is incredible," she groaned.

"I know." He kissed her temple and asked, "How many bedrooms do you have?"

Her nerve endings jumped with excitement. "I have two, but I was thinking we'd—"

The orderly pushed into the room with the wheelchair and gave them a cheery greeting.

Del felt heat flood her face, more so when Mick gave her a scorching look of understanding. He started to pick up the small bag of items he had to take home, but Del rushed to beat him to it.

"You just sit," she said, trying to regain some composure, "and I'll get this." Mick kept her so flustered, she could barely think, and she almost left her laptop behind. Without preamble, the orderly plopped nearly everything into Mick's lap and started out the door. Del hustled after them.

"It's stupid to ride in a wheelchair when I'm perfectly capable of walking."

"And smooching," the orderly said in agreement, even more cheerful now that he knew what he'd interrupted. "But it's hospital policy."

Mick stayed silent until they got into the car and were on their way. He seemed inordinately alert, watching everything and everyone, and he soon had Del on edge.

"Do all PIs act like you?"

Mick didn't bother to glance her way when he said, "Yeah."

"Are you going to do this the whole time you're with me?"

Again, he said, "Yeah." But then he turned to face her. "You were shot at, Delilah. I wish I could blow it off as bad luck on your part—being in the wrong place at the wrong time—but I can't. Not yet. Not until the police have a chance to talk to the guy I shot, and that can't happen until he comes to."

She bit her lip. "Do you think he'll die?"

"I doubt it." He turned to look back out the window, hiding his expression from her, but she heard the contempt in his tone when he added, "But don't feel bad if he does."

"I wouldn't. I mean, I don't. He could have killed someone."

"That's about it."

Given his surly tone, she decided a change of topic was in order. They stopped at a light and she looked Mick over. His hair was thick and shiny and a little too long. The whiskers on his face, combined with the tiredness of his eyes, made her heart swell. Today he wore the softest, most well-worn jeans she'd ever seen on a man. They hugged his thick thighs and his heavy groin and his lean hips and tight buttocks.

Her pulse leaped at the thought of that gorgeous body beneath the clothes. Tonight, she'd get to see all of him. She'd make sure of it. She was so wrapped up in those thoughts, she almost missed the light turning green.

She eased the car forward, while her thoughts stayed attuned to Mick.

The shirt Josh had brought him was snowy-white

cotton, buttoned down the front, and looked just as soft as the jeans. The thick bandage on his shoulder could be seen beneath, as could the heavy muscles of his chest, his biceps. "The doctor says you can shower," she told him with a croak in her voice. "But he doesn't want you to soak."

"Right now, a shower will feel like heaven."

"Will you need anything in particular? I could run by your place after I drop you off and pick you up anything you need."

"Josh grabbed me a change of socks and boxers. Angel's taking care of the rest later today. For now, whatever soap and shampoo you have will work." He glanced at her, smiling just a bit. "Do you use scented stuff?"

"No."

His eyes went almost black. "Good. I love the way you smell. I'm glad it's you and not from a bottle."

Del tightened her hands on the wheel. Boy, much more of that and she wouldn't make it home. Luckily, he stayed silent for the rest of the ride, and Del didn't bother trying to draw him out again. Her heart couldn't take his idea of casual conversation.

She pulled up to the garage in front of her building. She had to pay extra to park her car there, but she knew if she left it on the street, it'd likely get stripped. She said as much to Mick as she turned off the ignition.

"Yeah, I know. I told you I own that building next door, right?"

Del rushed around to his door to help him—and got a disgruntled frown for her efforts. He was suddenly in an oddly defensive mood, and she didn't understand him.

"You told me. I wasn't sure if you meant the building to the left or the right."

He grunted. The building to the left was a shambles. His building was nicely maintained. "Alec used to rent from me, before he married Celia. The agency where he works is located between here and where he lives now."

Del cocked a brow. "If he doesn't live *here* now, why did he follow us?"

Mick jerked around. Wary, he asked, "What are you talking about?"

She rolled her eyes. "Your friend is pretty hard to miss, looking like Satan and all. I saw him a few cars behind us. I suppose this is more of your protection?"

Tilting his head back, Mick stared at the heavens. "Something like that." When he looked at her, she could almost feel his resolve. "I don't have a gun right now. The cops confiscated it as evidence."

Del gasped. "They're not going to accuse you of anything, are they?"

"No, it's routine to take any weapon used in a shooting. I'll get another one before the day is out, but until then, I wanted someone armed to keep an eye on things."

Fascinating. He spoke about guns with the same disregard that she gave to groceries. "This is all really extreme, you know."

"It's all really necessary, as far as I'm concerned." Then he added, "Trust me, honey. This is what I do, and I'm not willing to take any chances with you."

That sounded nice, as if he might be starting to like her. But maybe, Del thought, all private detectives were as cautious as Mick. She had no comparisons to go by; she'd never known a PI before.

Shrugging, she decided not to fight what she couldn't change, and hefted out her laptop. She put the leather strap of the carrying case over her shoulder along with her tote, and then reached inside for his bag.

Mick caught her shoulder with his left hand. "Something we need to clear up."

Del peeked up at him. He looked too serious, almost grim. Getting to know this man, with all the twists and turns of his personality, would be exhilarating. "Yes?"

He relieved her of his bag, then her laptop, holding both casually in his left hand as if they weighed no more than a feather pillow. "I'm not an invalid."

Her temper sparked. "No, of course not. But you are wounded and you're not supposed to strain yourself."

Without warning, he leaned down and gave her a loud, smacking kiss. His expression was amused and chagrined and determined. "It doesn't strain me, I promise."

"But you can only use the one arm."

Slow and wicked, his grin spread. "I can do a lot," he whispered in a rough drawl, "with one arm."

Her stomach curled at the way he said that and what she knew he inferred. She cleared her throat. "I see."

"Good. Now lead the way."

She didn't want to. She wanted to insist that he let her help him. He'd done enough already, more than enough. Too much. The man had a bullet in him, thanks to her.

She turned and marched toward the front stairs. The entry door was old and heavy, and she hurried to open it, anxious to get Mick settled inside.

Together they climbed the steep stairs to the upper landing, where she used her key on both of the locks for her apartment door, one of them a dead bolt. Being a runner, she made the climb with ease, breathing as normally as ever when she reached the top. She half expected Mick, with his injuries and his load, to huff at least a bit, but he didn't.

He did, however, keep a vigilant watch. "I'm relieved to see the landlord keeps the place secure. Not all the buildings in this area are safe."

Del looked at him over her shoulder as she reached inside and flipped a wall switch. She didn't tell him that she'd had the dead bolt installed recently. The front door opened directly into her living room, and one switch turned on both end-table lamps. She said only, "I'm not an idiot. I wouldn't endanger myself."

She tossed her tote onto the oversize leather sofa to her right and reached for her laptop. Mick, who'd been looking around, taking in her modest apartment, held it out of reach, lifting it over his head as if he didn't have a bullet in his other arm, as if the pain wasn't plain on his face. His strength amazed her.

"Where do you want it?"

Sighing, Del pointed to her desk in the corner, where a half wall separated her kitchen area from the rest of the room. Her desk was the only modern, truly functional piece of furniture she had. A computer occupied the center of the tiered piece, with a fax machine, a printer and a copier close at hand. There were file folders and papers stacked everywhere, notes, magazines, interviews she hadn't yet put into the file cabinet behind the desk. Reference books littered the floor.

Mick lifted a brow and boldly glanced at her papers as he set the laptop down.

His curiosity would have to be appeased another time, Del decided. She took his arm and steered him toward the narrow hallway on the opposite side of the room. "The bathroom is this way. You can shower while I change the sheets. Are you hungry?"

He'd never admit it, she knew, but he looked ready to drop, pain tightening his mouth and darkening his eyes. Twice she'd seen him rub at his temples when he didn't know she was looking. The doctor had told her that he was as likely to have headaches from his fall as pain from his wound. Del had a hunch the two were combining against him.

"After you finish," she said gently, but with as much authority as she could summon, "you'll need to take your medicine."

Mick stopped in the bathroom doorway and caught her chin with his hand. His gaze burned, touching on her mouth, her throat, her breasts. "After I finish," he said, his fingertips tenderly caressing her skin, "I intend to see about you."

Her knees almost went weak. "Me?" It was a dumb question; she knew exactly what he meant.

Nodding slowly, he said, "All that teasing you've been doing, all that talk about starting an affair, and your bold touching. I'm beyond ready."

She really did need to learn a little discretion, she thought, now wishing she hadn't told him all her intentions. But she was used to going after what she wanted, and he'd been irresistible, a man unlike any she'd ever known. Everything about him turned her on, from the protectiveness she'd never received before, to his strength and intensity, to his rough velvet voice and drool-worthy bod. The man was sexy emotionally and physically, and she wanted him.

She caught his wrist and kissed his palm. "Mick, you need to rest. There'll be plenty of time for..."

He carried her hand to the thick erection testing the worn material of his jeans. Her heart dropped to her stomach, then shot into her throat.

"You think," he whispered roughly, his eyes closing at the feel of her hand on him, "that I can rest with that? The answer is no."

Her palm tingled and of their own accord her fingers began to curl around him. He lifted her hand away, leaned down and kissed her. "I just need fifteen minutes to shower and shave."

Carrying his bag into the room with him, he turned and closed the door, leaving Del standing there with her lips parted and her eyes glazed and her muscles quivering. She sucked in a breath and let her head drop forward to the door, bracing herself there until she stopped trembling.

His effect on her was startling, almost too much to

bear. She'd given up on men as too much trouble, with not enough payoff. But with a mere look, Mick could make her hot, and when he touched her, or she touched him, the need was overwhelming.

She heard the shower start and realized she hadn't reminded him to be careful. She leaned close and said loudly, "Don't soak your shoulder! The doctor said that was a no-no."

Just as loudly, he retorted, "I was there, Delilah, remember?" And then she heard the rustling of the shower curtain and knew he was naked, knew he was wet....

She turned and hurried away.

When he'd answered her, he'd sounded distinctly irritable. Well, hell. Heaven knew, he was likely to be doubly so when he found out she had no intention of making love with him today. It would be too much for him, and there was a good chance he'd injure his shoulder anew.

No, she couldn't let him do that.

She also couldn't let him go unsatisfied. She closed her eyes, feeling wicked and sinful and anxious. There was only one thing to do. Granted, *she* was likely to end up the frustrated one, but that was a small price to pay to a man who'd played her hero, a man who'd saved her life. And she had no doubt he'd make it up to her later. She may not have known him long, but she knew that much about him already. The man wanted her—more than any man ever had.

It was a heady feeling. She liked it.

She especially liked him.

MICK FOUND HER in the kitchen, staring into her refrigerator as if pondering what to fix. A glass of iced tea sat on the counter.

He shook his head, not yet announcing himself. Foolish woman. How could she possibly think he'd want food when she stood there looking more than edible? Oh yeah, he wanted to eat her up. And he would, slowly and with great relish. "Delilah."

She whirled around, first appearing guilty, then abashed when she saw his naked chest. He'd done no more than pull on snug cotton boxers; he had no need of the sling right now, though he kept his right arm slightly elevated to relieve his shoulder of pressure. The bandages there were made to withstand showers and would dry soon.

Any clothes he would have put on would just be coming off again, so he hadn't bothered with them, either. By look and deed she'd made her willingness, her own desire, clear. It didn't matter that he hardly knew her, not when everything about her felt so right.

He braced his feet apart and let her look her fill.

Her eyes widened and then traveled the length of him. Twice. She touched her throat. "If I looked as good as you, I'd have skipped the boxers."

Though he appreciated the sentiment, Mick was too far gone with lust to manage a grin. "Want me to take them off?"

She shook her head and said, "Yes. But not yet. If you were naked now, I'd forget you're hurt and do something I'd regret."

"Like what?" She continued to stand there, her gaze returning again and again to his straining hard-on, which the snug cotton boxers did nothing to hide.

"Like throwing you down on the floor and having my way with you."

He did grin this time. "The bed is right around the corner. Why don't we go there now?"

Just that easily, he saw her resolve form, harden. He may have only known her a day, but he already knew that look.

"You need to take your medicine. Good as you look, I can see that you hurt."

The pain in his shoulder and head were nothing, certainly not enough to make him want to wait another day to have her. "I'll take a pill after I've sated myself with you."

Her gaze locked on his. "Oh boy, you don't pull any punches, do you?"

"From what I remember last night in the hospital, neither do you." And to encourage her, he added, "But I like it when you speak your mind."

She nodded. "Okay, yes, I want you to sate yourself with me. I want to sate myself with you, too." Her expression was one of worry, regret. "But I figure that'd probably take me hours, maybe even days, so we should maybe put it off until you're not likely to die on me."

Damn, her brazen words mixed with the sweetness of her expression and the obvious worry she felt for him was an aphrodisiac that fired his blood. She was a mix of contradictions, always unique, sometimes pushy and too stubborn. Mick took two long steps toward her, ignored the continual throbbing in his shoulder and head, and gathered her close.

He wasn't prepared for her stiffened arms, which

carefully pushed him back again. Shakily, she said, "We have to make a deal."

The need stalled, replaced by innate suspicion. What possible deal could she need to make at this moment? Thoughts flew through his head as he remembered numerous deals offered to him by prostitutes, drug dealers, gamblers, people from his youth and the people he now came into contact with every day of his life.

He also thought about the robbery, about her uncommon interest in the jewelry store, her interest in him, her willingness to bring a near stranger into her home and have sex with him.

By nature, he was overly cautious. From his upbringing, and then working undercover, he'd become suspicious of almost everyone and everything.

Because of his background, he often doubted the sincerity of women in general.

Dropping his hands so he wouldn't accidentally hurt her with his anger, Mick growled, "What kind of deal?"

She blinked, confused by his temper. Carefully, her words no more than a whisper of sound, she explained, "I can't stand seeing you in pain. I want you to take your medicine first, then we'll go to bed."

Mick made sure no reaction showed on his face, but once again she'd managed to take him off guard. Her deal was for him, not for her. "The medicine makes me too groggy."

"Not for fifteen minutes or more. I've watched you after you take it. It doesn't kick in right away, and you only go to sleep when you let yourself."

Still not touching her, he said, "What I have in mind will take more than fifteen minutes."

She inhaled sharply at his words, then touched him, her hand opening on his chest, her fingers splayed, sifting through his body hair. The reflexive clench of his muscles brought a sharp ache to his temples, his shoulder.

"You're welcome to stay here until you're completely recovered," she said, still stroking him with what seemed like acute awe, probably attempting to soothe him, when in fact each glide of her delicate fingers over his muscles wound him that much tighter. "There'll be plenty of time for both of us to indulge ourselves."

He didn't answer right away, trying to figure her out in the middle of an intense arousal that kept rational thought just out of reach.

"Please," she added, both hands now sliding up to his shoulders. One edged the bandage that came over his shoulder from the back. "I won't be able to enjoy myself for fear of hurting you."

He didn't want that. He fully intended for her to experience more than mere enjoyment. He wanted her ripe with pleasure, numb with it. He wanted to give her the kind of explosive release she'd have only with him.

Yet, she was right. In his present condition, it wasn't likely to happen. With her insistence, she was probably helping him to save face.

Mick brought her close and said against her hair, "I'm sorry. I'm not used to wanting a woman quite this much." He wasn't used to wanting to *trust* a woman, either. But he wanted to trust Delilah. He wanted to involve himself with every aspect of her life. He needed to tie her to him in some way.

Nodding, she said, "I know the feeling. You blow my socks off."

He tilted her back so he could see her face. Her honesty humbled him, and pleased him.

"We haven't discussed it," he said, thinking now was as good a time as any, "but I want you to know the nurse was right, I come with a clean bill of health—in all ways. Not only have I always been discriminating, but I'm very cautious, too."

That brought a beautiful smile to her face. "Same here. I can't claim to have been a recluse, but I haven't met many men that I wanted to get involved with. Not like this, not enough to let them interrupt my life. And men take exception to that. They don't like to be neatly compartmentalized."

"Is that right?"

She nodded. "You may not have noticed, but I get really wrapped up in my work, and most of the time I'm not even aware of men around me. At least, not for long."

Mick grinned. "I noticed. At first I wondered if maybe you were a lesbian."

Her mouth opened, then closed. She frowned at him, her pale blue eyes burning bright. "I'm not."

His grin widened. "I noticed that, too."

Still scowling, she said, "Not that there's anything wrong with—"

"Of course not. But I have to tell you how glad I am that you're interested in men."

"I'm interested in *you*."

He appreciated her clarification. "Which means I'm one lucky bastard."

She snorted. "If you were so lucky, you wouldn't have gotten shot." She turned and grabbed up the pills. "Take these."

He downed them in one gulp, washing the bitter taste away with sweetened tea.

"Are you hungry? You really didn't eat that much yesterday, and you hardly touched your breakfast."

He'd been too caught up in his thoughts, in mentally organizing all the things that had to be done that day, to concern himself with breakfast. And the truth was, he felt hollow down to his toes. He could probably eat two meals, but not yet. "No. I just want you. And now that I've swallowed the damn pills, time's wasting."

Her eyes warmed, the vivid blue darkening. She took his hand and turned to lead him down the hall. Without looking at him, she said, "Let me see if I can help you to sleep soundly for a few hours."

It took a great deal of resolve not to turn her against the wall and enter her right there, standing up, without the benefit of a soft mattress. At twenty-six, he'd known lust, but he'd never known anything like this, an all-encompassing need to devour a particular woman.

Her bedroom was small, holding a bed that would barely accommodate his size. The beige spread was tossed half off the bottom of the mattress, pooling on the floor and showing matching beige sheets. Across from it sat a triple dresser with a mirror, the top cluttered with papers and candles and receipts.

A wooden rocker sat in front of one window. The other window held an air conditioner, softly humming on low, keeping the room pleasantly cool. Over the bed a ceiling fan slowly whirled, barely stirring the air but making the room comfortable.

The building didn't have central air, of course. None of the buildings on her street did. Some of them didn't have heat, either. Thankfully, Delilah's apartment building was kept up, just as Mick kept up his building next door. And she wasn't on the first floor, so she could open her windows without fear of intruders.

Her bedroom wasn't what you'd call neat, not with laundry piled on the chair and shoes tossed haphazardly over her closet floor, but it was orderly. He had the distinct impression Delilah could walk into this room and find anything she needed without effort.

She went straight to the bed and propped up the pillows. ''Sit here.''

Bemused, Mick allowed her to take control. She always seemed less reserved when she was the aggressor, as if taking control gave her more confidence. He wanted her without inhibitions, so he gladly let her lead.

He settled himself, easing his injured shoulder back against the headboard. Delilah stood in front of him and unsnapped her jeans. The sound of her zipper sliding down nearly stopped his heart. Transfixed, he watched her disrobing in front of him. There was no false modesty, no timidity, but no real brazenness, either. She revealed her body with a no-nonsense acceptance that touched his heart; she wouldn't flaunt, but neither would she cower. Mick tightened his fists in the bottom sheet and held himself still.

He'd been half-afraid he was rushing her, moving too fast. But judging by her willingness now, she was finally as ready as him.

But then, he'd been ready from the first moment he saw her.

CHAPTER FIVE

DELILAH'S JEANS DROPPED, and she smiled at him as she stepped away from them, using one foot to nudge them aside. "I'm not as perfect as you," she stated, again with that simple acceptance of her own perceptions, "but somehow I have a feeling that won't bother you."

Oh, he was plenty bothered, on the point of going insane. Her comments weren't geared toward gaining compliments, but he could only give her the truth. "You're the sexiest woman I've ever seen."

Her mouth twitched and then she laughed. "Yeah, right. With small boobs and a straight waist and gangly limbs?"

He wanted to correct her, to point out everything he found enticing, yet when she caught the hem of her tank top and tugged it over her head, he went mute. His heart struck his rib cage, his breath caught.

The bra she wore had no shoulder straps, and the cups only half covered her. When she flipped her hair back, he could have sworn he saw the edge of a mauve nipple.

He swallowed hard. "This is insane. Come here."

"In a minute. Don't you want me naked?" she teased.

"God, yes." He shifted his legs. He was uncomfortable, drawn tight, ready to come from just the sight of her. "I want to touch you, too." *And taste you and bury myself deep.*

Reaching behind her back, she unhooked her bra and let it drop. Her breasts were round and firm, with small, tightly puckered nipples now darkened with desire.

She left her miniscule panties on and walked toward him, her gait long and sure and purposeful. Without reserve, she climbed into the bed and straddled his lap. Mick groaned as her rounded bottom nestled on his thighs and her breasts came even with his face. He reached for her.

"Shh," she said, catching his right arm and holding it still. "Let me. You just sit back and relax."

Blood rushed through his head. He gritted his teeth and nodded. He didn't tell her that relaxing was out of the question.

"Tell me what you want." As she spoke, she looked at him and touched him, and his vision narrowed to only her.

"I want to taste you."

Her eyes smoldered, encouraging him even as her hands attempted to ease him. It was a wasted effort. Each soft stroke of her hands—over his chest, his uninjured shoulder, his waist, his throat—inflamed him.

He saw the pulse fluttering in her throat when she asked huskily, "Where?"

"Everywhere, but for now, I want your nipples."

Her thighs tightened around his, giving her away.

She wasn't nearly as detached or in control as she pretended. He didn't quite understand her forceful determination, but he knew at least part of it was inspired by reciprocal lust.

She drew a shaky breath and slowly, so slowly the anticipation damn near killed him, she leaned forward.

Mick struggled to stay calm. He couldn't stop himself from bending his knees, forcing her farther forward, couldn't stop the flexing of his cock against her tantalizing ass. But he made certain to gently kiss the rounded softness of her breasts, to nuzzle against her until she moaned. He teased her, licking close to her nipple but not quite letting his tongue touch it.

She twisted, attempting to hurry him, but Mick held himself in check. She needed to catch up to him—if that was possible.

With a rough, impatient sound, she finally murmured, "Mick, please…"

He placed a wet, soft kiss directly over her nipple, briefly drawing her into the heat of his mouth with a gentle suction, and then releasing her. It wasn't easy, considering he wanted to feast on her.

She moved against him, one small jerk on his thighs before she stopped herself. Panting, she said, "I like that."

"I thought you would." He did it again, then again and again until she gasped for breath, until her hands settled in his hair and her nipples were tight wet peaks. Likely with more force than she realized, she brought his mouth to her breast, saying without words that she now needed more.

And he suckled her, strong and deep and long.

The combined sensations rocked him: the taste and feel of her on his tongue as his mouth tugged at her, the heat of her sex pressing insistently against his abdomen, her scent and softness and her unique determination.

The physical bombardment on his senses was enough, leaving him confused and wild with need. But the emotional storm also overwhelmed him. He wanted to consume her savagely, brand her as his own, hear her cries and feel the bite of her nails. And he wanted to hold her gently to his heart, to let her feel protected and know that he'd take care of her. Basic, elemental instincts rolled through him in a way he'd never felt before.

As he continued to tongue and suck, her back arched and she released a ragged moan. Then she moved against his thighs, a riding motion that rubbed the damp silk of her panties along the length of his shaft.

He replaced his mouth with his fingers and said harshly, "Kiss me, Delilah."

She did, stealing his breath as her tongue licked in to tease his. As wild and out of control as he felt, she was more so.

"Let's get these panties off you," he murmured, knowing he couldn't last much longer.

She pulled away, trembling, gasping for breath. Her head dropped forward. After a moment, she dipped down and kissed his throat, her mouth open and hot and wet. Mick wanted to protest, but he loved the feel of her mouth on him.

The pills had muddled his mind some and it took more effort than he could dredge up to stop her as she sank lower, biting at his chest, hotly licking his own nipples, tasting and teasing him.

His arm hurt like a son of a bitch and his head continued to throb dully, but raging lust and crushing need overrode it all. Using his good arm, he tangled his fingers in her silky hair, letting it slide over his chest and then his abdomen as she moved lower and lower down the length of his body.

When her tongue dipped into his navel, he nearly shouted with the pleasure of it. "God, Delilah," he managed to rasp, "baby, you have to stop."

She ignored him. Her hand crept up his tensed thigh, higher and higher until she cuddled his testicles for a brief, heart-stopping moment before grasping his erection and slowly stroking.

He stiffened, all sensation, hot and thick, rushing into his groin. Her mouth, still gentle but hungry, kissed him through the cotton boxers, and the pleasure-pain was so excruciating it blocked everything else.

He cursed, feeling himself sinking, out of control. He had to stop her, but he didn't want to. He wanted her to—

As if she'd read his mind, she eased the boxers down.

"No," Mick protested with a long groan, knowing he sounded less than convincing. The damn pills had melted away his determination, made him forget all his plans. He could only focus on Delilah, on what she did, how she touched him.

"I've been thinking about this all day," she breathed.

He opened his eyes, needing to watch. The look on her face mirrored his own emotions of fire, need, possession. She watched her hand driving him to distraction, her grip firm, her thumb curling over the end of his erection with each long stroke, pushing him closer and closer....

Mick felt a surge of release and desperately fought it off, but she saw the drop of fluid at the head of his penis and leaned forward.

He shuddered, cursed, held his breath—then shouted in reaction when her mouth closed over him, not tentatively, as he'd expected, but sliding wetly down the length of him, taking all of him in, sucking.

Maybe if he hadn't taken the damn pills, maybe if it had been any woman other than her, he could have controlled himself.

But from the moment he'd seen her he'd wanted her, and he couldn't hold back, couldn't stop himself from coming. His fingers knotted in her hair and he held her head to him, not that it was necessary because she didn't pull away. She drew him deeper and made a low sound of pleasure that he felt in his soul. He tightened, surged, and experienced the strongest release of his entire life. He growled with the force of it, his body taut, arching, his mind going blank.

His only realization in that turbulent moment of rioting sensation was that no other man would ever touch her; she was his, and he intended to keep her.

MICK DIDN'T SLEEP LONG this time, probably no more than an hour, but he awoke half-frozen. The air conditioner, on the highest setting, hummed loudly, and the ceiling fan whirled overhead. He felt his hair blowing, felt his skin prickle with goose bumps.

He'd passed out just as she'd left him, half propped against the headboard, his legs now limp, his shoulder cushioned by a soft pillow. At least she'd pulled the spread up to his waist, he thought, a bit disgruntled.

He felt like an idiot as he looked around and realized the room was empty. He cursed. Then cursed again when he pushed the spread away and became racked with chills. It was like sleeping on the wing of an airplane, for crying out loud!

He swung his legs to the floor, stood—and nearly fell. Weakness had invaded every muscle. The pain pills had no effect on his aches, not after that mind-grinding orgasm, where every muscle in his body, clear down to the soles of his feet, had knotted in pulsating pleasure. She'd wrung him out—no doubt that had been her intent.

He grunted, unable to believe what she'd done, and unwilling to accept that after she'd done it, he'd had the gall to fall asleep.

If the room hadn't felt like a meat locker, he'd probably have been hot with embarrassment.

He glanced down at his boxers, still around his thighs, and shook his head. It was too much, far too much.

He straightened his underwear, whipped the spread off the bed and around his shoulders to ward off the cold, then went to the window to turn the unit down. The air conditioner sputtered and died with a sigh.

Forcing himself forward on shaky limbs, Mick left the bedroom. The apartment was quiet, other than the rattling of pans in the kitchen area. On his way down the hall, he decided to take the offense. Delilah knew he'd wanted to make love to her, but she'd taken the choice away from him. *How* she'd taken it away had been beyond incredible, but still, she needed to know that he wouldn't be so easily manipulated. Not ever again.

He was appalled that he'd proved so easy this time. But then, maybe that's why she'd given him the pills, to weaken his resolve. He'd be sure to ask her that.

When he reached the arched kitchen doorway, she had her back to him, stirring a pan of something on the stove. Whatever she was cooking smelled good, as did the coffee in the coffeemaker. She'd pulled her tank top back on, but not her jeans, and the sight of her bottom in the silky panties did a lot to obliterate his other concerns.

Before he got distracted, he asked, "Did you talk me into the pain pills so you could keep us from having sex?"

She yelped, dropped her stirring spoon and jerked around to face him. Their gazes locked.

The sight of her face made his mind go blank, his heart trip. *She'd been crying.*

"Delilah?" he asked around a sudden lump of emotion. Damn, that bothered him. He didn't get lumps of emotion. In his job, he saw the worst life had to offer and he handled it dispassionately, with a distance that could be applauded. Always, from the time he'd been a young boy, he'd kept his emotions in check.

But God, she looked like hell with her eyes swollen and wet, her cheeks blotchy, her nose red. Seeing her made his heart thump.

She bit her bottom lip and turned to the stove again. He heard her sniff. "Yes."

Mick shook his head. He wanted to hold her, to comfort her. Yet she'd turned her back on him. "Yes what?"

"Yes, I gave you the pills so you wouldn't complain when I...eased you. It was the only thing I could think of. I didn't want you to strain yourself, and the doctor said it was too soon for you to have sex."

Talking with Delilah was like wading through syrup. He kept getting stuck, but damn, it was sweet. He cleared his throat, forcing the emotion away so he could think and react clearly. He slowly approached her and stood at her back, close enough to breathe in her sexy scent and see the enormous pot of spaghetti sauce she stirred. "You spoke with the doctor about us having sex?" Her initiative amazed him—and aroused him.

"Yes. Right after I bought the condoms."

Mick paused. *Bought the condoms?* Before he could ask, she said, "I snuck them into the bedroom, in the nightstand drawer, just in case you didn't go to sleep after you came."

She spoke as bluntly as any man, but then, she'd done that from the first, speaking her mind with candor. Unlike other women he knew, she didn't measure her words. She was so female she made him crazy, yet she didn't always act female. Damn if that didn't arouse him, too.

Hell, everything she did aroused him. Just moments before he'd thought himself fully satisfied, but now...

"The hospital sells rubbers?"

She glanced at him over her shoulder, and he watched one fat tear track down her cheek. "Yeah, of course they do. It's a hospital, and they understand about unnecessary risks."

She'd managed to distract him, after all.

Mick shook his head and wrapped one arm around her waist. Resting his chin on top of her head, he asked, "Why are you crying, sweetheart? Did I hurt you?"

"Of course not." She leaned into him, then pushed back with a frown. "You're shivering." Twisting, she put her hand to his forehead in a maternal gesture of concern. "Are you sick?"

"Just cold." He turned her back around and laced his hands over her middle. Her bottom pressed into his groin. "The room was like ice."

She nodded. "I figured you'd like it cold. Most men get warmer than women, right?"

He had no idea, but he doubted any man would relish the igloo accommodations she'd provided him. She'd obviously had some sexual experience, and she was comfortable with her body, with her sexuality. But she was far from knowledgeable about the opposite sex. Mick shook his head at the added contradictions. "Why are you crying?"

She shrugged and leaned back against him. "I'm

just a little sad. I'm sorry you have to see me like this. I'm a terrible crier. Very ugly. The news just took me by surprise."

"What news?" He rubbed his chin against her hair, spread his hand over her belly. He loved the feel of her, her softness, her sleekness. She was so feminine, but not in a frail way.

"A guy I know died. I just read it in the paper."

Mick stiffened, caught between conflicting reactions. He wanted to comfort her from any upset, and he wanted to jealously demand information about the guy who'd made her cry. He must have been important to her to bring on the tears.

It shouldn't have mattered. They'd only just officially met, and hadn't officially consummated their relationship yet. But it did matter. A lot.

"Who was he?" Mick asked, keeping her pressed into him by his hand on her belly.

After a long, shuddering sigh, she put the spoon down and turned into his arms. Her face nuzzled into his chest and she whispered, "Just a guy who helped me with research." He felt her wet cheek on his pec muscle and groaned.

"I'm sorta known for my research methods, you know," she continued. "They've become part of my publicity." She leaned back to stare up at him earnestly, and in case he hadn't understood, she clarified. "For my books, I mean."

"How is research a publicity stunt?"

She lifted one shoulder. "People are amazed by the strangest things. But whenever I write about something in a book, I try to experience it first so that I get it right. When I can't experience it, I try to talk to someone who has.''

''So what type of research did this guy help you with?'' Mick hoped like hell it wasn't a love scene. He could handle anything but that.

Turning away, she reached for a napkin and mopped her eyes. Mick heard another loud sniff. ''He was a small-time criminal. I had a scene in my book where a guy stole a car. I couldn't really steal a car—'' she glanced at him and added ''—not without getting arrested, I'm sure.''

''Better not to try it,'' he agreed, smiling.

''That's what I figured. So I hired this guy, and he took me through all the ins and outs of car theft. For a criminal he was a really nice guy.''

Mick glanced at the coffeepot. ''Mind if I have a cup?''

''Oh, of course.'' But she didn't let him get it himself. ''Sit down and I'll pour it for you.''

Since his knees were still shaking, Mick sat. More than most things, he hated being weak, and for now there was nothing he could do about it. He pulled out a chair at the black, wrought-iron parlor table and gratefully dropped into it.

''Cream or sugar?''

''Black, please.''

She set the steaming mug in front of him. His first sip made his body hair stand on end, and he nearly spat it back out. His throat raw, he rasped, ''Damn, that's strong.''

Delilah didn't take his comment as a complaint. She smiled, looking adorable in her skimpy top and panties, her nose bright red. "I figured you being a man and all, you'd want it strong."

It was a wonder new hair hadn't sprouted on his body. He coughed, and because he didn't want to hurt her feelings, he said, "I think I'll take the cream and sugar, after all."

She happily got them for him, then went back to the stove to check her sauce. To Mick, it looked like there was enough to feed an army. Hopefully, she didn't expect him to eat it all—because he was a man.

Making sure she didn't notice all the sugar he dumped into his coffee, he asked, "So where did a nice woman like you meet a car thief?"

"In prison."

The mouthful of coffee—still too bitter to enjoy—got spewed across the table. He continued to choke as Delilah grabbed up a dish towel and patted his back.

"Mick! Are you all right?"

He wheezed, trying to regain his breath enough to speak. With his eyes squeezed shut, he finally demanded, "What the hell were you doing in prison?"

Tilting her head, she smiled. Given her swollen eyes and the tear tracks on her cheeks, it didn't have the usual effect on his libido. "More research." She chuckled. "You didn't think I meant I'd been serving time, did you?"

Actually, he had, but he wasn't dumb enough to say so. Relief warred with confusion. "Of course not. But can you explain all this research for me?"

She pulled out her own chair at the table. "Okay, but don't let me forget the spaghetti sauce. Your friends are coming over for dinner and I want to impress them.''

"Josh and Zack?''

She snorted. ''I meant your other friends, the ones you said were like family.''

"Dane and Angel are staying for dinner?'' He didn't like putting her out, especially since she was so upset.

"I invited them. Angel called and said she had your things, and wanted to know when it'd be a good time to drop them off. I know she's still worried about you, and she doesn't exactly trust me, so I thought this would be a way to make her feel better.''

Cautiously, Mick asked, ''What makes you think Angel doesn't trust you?''

Del made a face. ''I'm not dumb.''

Mick let that go. He'd have to talk to Angel first to see what had been said. He knew Angel would never insult Delilah, but she was protective. ''Why do you want to impress them?''

"They're like your family. I like you, so of course I want them to like me.''

Mick almost told her it didn't matter what anyone else thought, that he intended to make her a part of his life. But he'd never gotten so deeply involved with a woman, and to do so now, at Mach speed, was just plain foolish. He liked her, all her quirks and unique qualities. He liked her different way of viewing things and her outspokenness mixed with occasional glimpses of uncertainty. And God knew, the sexual chemistry between them was explosive.

But most of her background was still a mystery to

him. So he forced himself to be cautious, to go slow. He tucked a tendril of her silky hair behind her ear and asked, "Are you sure you're up to a dinner party?"

"Why wouldn't I be? You're the one who got shot."

"*You* were the target. And you've been crying."

She waved that away, ignoring his first comment and only responding to his second. "I'm overly emotional about the people I care for. There aren't that many. Being a writer keeps me isolated, so I don't get into the social swing of things often. Neddie became a friend as well as a teacher. We had a lot of fun hot-wiring my car."

This time Mick just stared. She gave an impatient sigh and went on. "It's true. We were alike in a lot of ways, reacting to our place in society. Neddie became a misguided criminal, just trying to fit in. I became a writer."

"It's hardly the same thing."

"Of course not. I just meant that we understood each other. Neddie was wrong, and he knew that. But he always said he never hurt anyone who didn't deserve to be hurt. Anything he did, he did among other criminals, including stealing cars. And from what he told me, I believe him."

"Criminals always have excuses, Delilah."

"Well, he was a nice criminal, okay? And very patient. We took my car to a deserted lot and practiced on it for hours. Once I got the hang of it, Neddie timed me."

Mick's left hand, resting on the tabletop, curled

into a fist. "You went to a deserted lot with a convict?"

"Can you imagine how the cops might have reacted if they'd seen me hot-wiring a car around here?"

She needed a keeper. *She needed him.* He drew a calming breath, something he found himself doing often around her. "Back up and tell me what you were doing in prison."

"I had a character in a book who had spent a good portion of his life in prison. I couldn't very well write that without knowing what the inside of a prison was really like."

"Ever heard of research books?" he asked dryly.

She laughed. Though he knew her humor was aimed at him, he was glad to see her mood lightening. "I use research books when I have to. But I think it's always better to get firsthand, in-person information whenever I can."

"You said that's part of your promotion?"

"Yep. It didn't start out that way. But then this one reporter got wind of it when my last book hit the *New York Times* bestseller list. She interviewed me and asked me all kinds of questions about my research, and since then the media is real accommodating. They always make a fuss about my way of researching."

His head throbbed. "Media?"

"Yeah. Silly, huh?"

His tongue felt on fire as he sputtered, "You're a celebrity."

Delilah wrinkled her nose and with a note of dismissal said, "To some people, I guess."

"You do this often?"

She shrugged. "Often enough. I was on a talk show once, and not too long ago I got featured on the news."

"The news?"

"About my newest book, and my research for it. It was fun."

In that moment, a thousand questions went through his mind. What the hell was a celebrity doing living in this neighborhood? How much money could she possibly make and what other types of research had she done?

Could any of that have to do with the incident at the jewelry store?

Before he could start on his interrogation, and that's what it would have been because he fully intended to get a lot of answers, she said, "We better get a move on. Everyone will be showing up in about half an hour. I still need to shower and change and make the bed and boil the spaghetti and fix a salad—"

Mick caught her hand as she rose. He tugged her between his legs. "I can help."

This time her laughter had the desired effect. He got hard as a stone. "Mick," she said playfully, and cupped his neck in both hands. "I think I can handle a shower on my own."

Damn, that brought an irresistible image to his mind. Delilah naked and wet, water streaming down her body, over her belly and between her thighs....

He released her hand and curled his arm around her waist, keeping her close when she tried to impatiently edge away. "I meant," he said, his voice now hoarse, "that I can handle spaghetti or a salad."

"No," she said in that unrelenting tone he already recognized. Delilah was used to making all the decisions, and used to holding her ground.

He'd have to work on that flaw.

She leaned down and quickly kissed him. "Not one-armed, you can't, and the doc specifically said you shouldn't use your right arm."

Mick was ready to explain a few things to her, but she added, her voice sweet and cajoling, "Please, Mick. Just let me take care of you, okay?"

He opened his hand on the small of her back, then slipped it down her spine to her bottom. He filled his palm with one firm cheek. "All right," he agreed. "But on one condition."

Her eyes narrowed. "What?"

"Tonight, after everyone is gone…" He let his fingers drift lower, pressing in to touch the heat of her, pleased with her gasp and small moan. "Tonight you'll let me show you exactly what I *can* do with one good arm."

Breathless, she said, "Sex is—"

"I know, not on the agenda." His fingers caressed her. "But I can return your favor of today."

Her lips parted, her eyes glittered and her cheeks looked warm. Several heartbeats went by, then she whispered, "Yes, okay."

Mick felt like a conquering warrior now that she'd given in to him at least a little. He grinned and smacked her butt. "I'm glad you can see reason. Now go get your shower. I'll pull on my jeans and park myself in front of the TV.''

"And you won't lift a finger?''

He stood, kissed her forehead and replied, "Not until tonight.''

With a comical look on her face, she turned the sauce down to warm and left the room. Mick flexed his aching shoulder, winced and decided to make a fresh pot of coffee while Delilah was otherwise occupied. He could only imagine Dane's expression if he took a gulp of that thick, bitter brew. It would probably prove amusing, but then Mick would have to drink it, too, which would negate all the fun.

So far, her coffee, her air-conditioning and her lack of discretion in dangerous situations were the only things he had trouble with. Those things aside, Delilah Piper was one hell of a woman. With each passing minute, he fell a little harder.

CHAPTER SIX

IT TURNED OUT TO BE a hectic evening, and Delilah was glad to see it winding down. Not only had Dane and Angel come to dinner, but Alec and Celia had called, and she'd invited them along. She figured she might as well get the family gathering over with. She was used to people not understanding her, to assumptions that her preoccupation with her stories was sheer daydreaming, motivated by lack of intelligence or attention.

She wasn't used to caring, to going out of her way to be accepted, and she'd felt on edge. Added to that was her urge to write. She had a deadline looming, and her mind kept wandering to her story.

Then Zack had dropped in with his four-year-old daughter, Dani. She was about the cutest thing Delilah had ever seen, and strangely enough, writing took second place to other thoughts. Dani had blue eyes like her father's, but her hair was blond and curly, and she had dimples when she smiled.

It took only a moment for Del to see that the little girl adored Mick. With her father's admonition to be careful of Mick's injury, she'd rushed to him, climbed into his lap and kissed his cheek as if he were a favorite uncle. Then she'd given him three more kisses to "make him all better." Mick had claimed to feel much improved on the spot, which prompted Dani into giggles.

Something about seeing Mick with a little girl in his arms made Del's heart swell. It was an incongruous sight, Mick so strong and darkly handsome, holding such a delicate, fair child. But it also looked very right, as if Mick were made to be a father.

Del frowned at that. Their relationship, started only a day before, hardly warranted thoughts of parenthood. She shook off the strange aberration and concentrated on being a perfect host.

She wasn't used to entertaining and she definitely wasn't used to so much company. But she didn't resent the intrusion on her writing time. In fact, it was all really nice.

During dinner, Josh phoned, and minutes later another man called for Mick, though he didn't introduce himself and Mick didn't tell her who it was. During his whispered conversation, she saw Alec and Dane share a look.

Her small apartment felt like Grand Central Station. Celia kept watching her closely, as if she was waiting for something, though Delilah had no idea what. Both she and Angel were cautiously nice.

Other than Mick, Del hadn't entertained a man in ages. And she'd never entertained a man's family before now. She had no idea if she was doing things right.

Mick caught her alone in the kitchen getting ready to make more coffee. He wore the sling again, but he still managed to drag her close for a kiss.

"Dinner was great."

He sounded sincere, and she smiled against his mouth. "Thank you." It had been a guessing game, trying to figure out how much sauce and spaghetti to make. After she'd done her best calculation, she'd doubled it for good measure. And that was a good thing, because the men had eaten far more than she'd ever anticipated. "Everyone is so nice. I like them."

"Even Zack?"

"His daughter is wonderful."

Mick laughed at that careful evasion. "You still holding a grudge?"

That sounded infantile, so she shook her head. "No, of course not. I understand why they were so protective of you."

"They were protective of *you*, Delilah."

She didn't agree, but saw no point in arguing. "I suppose for Zack to have such a sweet daughter, he must be a good father."

"He is that." Mick stroked her hair, then added, "Zack likes you. He told me so."

Staring at his chest, Del asked, "What about the others?"

He tipped up her chin. "Angel is cautious because I don't normally get involved with women."

Del wasn't at all certain she understood that. "You're not a virgin."

He choked on a laugh. "No."

"Then what do you mean—"

"I mean I'm real choosy. I already told you that, right?"

"The same is true for me, but maybe for different reasons. I've never had much time for men."

"You're making time for me."

There was no denying that. But Mick was... different. Well worth any effort.

"And," he added, still explaining Angel's reserve, "we've been moving pretty fast."

Delilah chewed over that obvious bit of information. "She's afraid I'll hurt you."

His eyes warmed, and his hand on her cheek was so gentle. "She's afraid you could, and that's a first." He kissed her again. Then once more. "Damn, I have to quit that or they'll wonder what we're doing in here."

She didn't want him to quit. "We're just kissing."

"I want to do a lot more."

So did she. "Tonight, I wouldn't mind—"

His hold tightened. "Tonight," he growled, "it's your turn."

Her heart tripped. She was still aroused from the afternoon. She'd been aroused since the second she saw Mick in that hospital bed.

Knowing he wanted to touch her and...do things to her made her whole body feel tight and too hot and somehow empty. Sighing shakily, she said, "All right."

"An agreeable woman," he teased, and took her mouth with a kiss that curled her toes and made her breasts tingle.

A knock sounded on the wall behind them. Mick lifted his head and turned.

Del groaned, then went on tiptoe to peek over his

shoulder. Celia stood there smiling. Alec stood next to her, looking amused.

"I—I was just about to make more coffee," Del stammered.

"Why don't you let Alec do that?" Mick suggested, putting his good arm around her shoulder.

That idea didn't sit right. "But he's a guest."

Alec raised a brow and gave Mick a curious glance. "I don't mind. Coffee is my specialty. Besides, I think my wife is dying to ask you something."

Celia elbowed him, then stepped closer. She looked anxious, her hands clasped together, and she kept glancing from Del to Mick and back again. Finally she blurted, "Are you *the* Delilah Piper? I mean, I saw some books on your shelves and I know it seems crazy, but..."

Mick looked at Del with surprise, and Celia stood there holding her breath. "That's me," Del said.

Mick frowned. "You've heard of her, Celia?"

"Are you kidding? She's fabulous! One of my favorite authors."

That got Del's attention. "Thank you. You've read me?"

Celia rushed closer. "Each and every one. Ohmigosh, that last one had me on the edge of my seat. When the car went off the bridge into that river..." She shivered, as if remembering the scene.

"I did that, you know," Del told her. When Celia stared wide-eyed, Del nodded. "It's true. Of course, I took some lessons first, so I wouldn't drown myself, but then we found this old bridge that no one uses anymore, and the instructor and I took the car right off the side.''

Beside her, Mick growled, ''What the hell are you talking about?''

And in an awed whisper, Celia said, ''Angel didn't believe me that it was you. I mean, that you're the author who really did all those things.''

''The coffee will be done in a minute,'' Alec said, interrupting another angry outburst from Mick. ''Why don't we go back in the living room and Celia can grill you like I know she's dying to?''

Del loved talking about her work, and she allowed herself to be tugged into the room. Mick held her hand tight, and as soon as her backside found a couch cushion, he demanded, ''What the hell do you mean, you drove your car off a bridge?''

Angel gasped. ''Then it's true? It's really you?''

Mick didn't give her a chance to answer. ''Delilah, what's going on? What are they talking about?''

''You don't know?'' Alec asked, then shared a look with Dane. To Del, all those shared looks felt like a conspiracy. Regardless of her attempts, she was still an outsider in their group.

''Know what?'' Mick's gaze narrowed on Del, dark and almost…predatory. A hush fell, everyone watching with expectation.

Del turned in her seat to face Mick, unsure of his sudden change in mood. He sounded angry for some reason, and he looked more than a little disturbed.

Maybe he needed another pain pill, though he kept refusing them. ''I explained how I do my research, and about the interviews, Mick.''

"You said you visited a prison, not that you drove your car into a river."

She took exception to his tone, especially in front of their guests. She wanted the visit to go well, not be ruined by an argument.

Attempting to sound reasonable in the face of his growing ire, she explained, "I knew what I was doing. I took diving lessons and a class that teaches you how to keep from panicking. I learned all kinds of neat things. You see, under murky river water you sometimes get disoriented because it's so dark." She shivered. "Really nasty, if you want the truth. But if you let out just a little of your breath, the bubbles will rise and show you the way to the surface."

Mick groaned.

"Also, if you stay calm, your heartbeat is slower and you use less oxygen, so you can hold your breath longer. I wasn't very good at that part of it, though. I couldn't hold my breath long at all. Still, it was pretty exciting to—"

"Drive your car," Mick rasped in an ominous voice, "deliberately off a bridge?"

Del frowned. Unlike Angel and Celia, Mick didn't seem at all impressed with her career. Not that she expected or needed him to be impressed. In fact, it was kind of refreshing that he didn't seem in awe.

She was used to a variety of reactions, most of them gushing, some fascinated, even disbelieving. But not angry. That was a reaction she'd never encountered. "It was kind of neat."

"Neat?"

That one word held a wealth of scorn and incredulity. Del lost her temper, too. "I may have done a lot of…eccentric things, but it's my life and I can damn well—"

"What other eccentric things?" he demanded. "What else have you done?"

She heard Dane mutter something, and Alec chuckle in return. Those two seemed to find everything amusing, and this time Del had the distinct impression they were laughing at her, or rather her predicament.

Indignant, she gave them each a look of censure, not that it had any visible effect; Dane winked at her, and Alec continued to smile. *Men,* she thought, and decided to ignore their misplaced humor.

Though her heart hurt and embarrassment threatened, Del stood and walked to her bookcase. She pulled out her first book and addressed the women, while deliberately disregarding the men—Mick especially. "For this story I learned skydiving."

"I've always wanted to try that," Dane admitted.

Despite her resolve to ignore him, Del glanced his way. "I learned how to do it without a chute. Another jumper passed me one in midair."

Mick closed his eyes and groaned. He definitely sounded in pain this time.

"For heaven's sake," Del said, thoroughly exasperated. "I *had* a chute! I just pretended I didn't. And there were plenty of other people jumping with me, trained for that sort of thing. Rescue jumpers were there in case something went wrong. Besides, we practiced a lot first in simulated jumps before I actually did it."

Angel piped up and said, "I remember the villain in that book had to steal a chute off another man. That man almost died, but being the male protagonist, he didn't."

"I never kill the male leads." She looked at Mick. "That would ruin the romance aspect of the books."

He groaned again.

Celia, like a true adventurer at heart, asked, "Did you take a chute off someone else?"

Alec immediately hauled her to his side and wrapped his brawny arm around her shoulders. "Don't even think it," he warned, and he looked deadly serious, his expression fierce. Celia just smiled.

"I didn't want to go that far," Del said, a little distracted. It fascinated her the way Celia and Alec interacted. He looked so savage, so menacing, yet Celia wasn't the least threatened by him. Just the opposite; Celia cuddled closer. "I learned how to put a chute on in the air."

Mick bolted to his feet. He looked ready for a full-fledged rage. The only other time she'd seen him like that was the day of the robbery, when he'd rolled to his feet after being shot, and raced out the door. That day his eyes had been nearly black with rage—as they were now. His jaw had been clenched tight, too—as it was now.

She wasn't quite sure what to make of him.

Lifting her chin, Del pulled another book off the shelf. "In this one, I learned how to navigate through an underwater cave."

"That was the creepiest scene," Celia whispered.

"There were sharks and poisonous snakes. It gave me nightmares." Then she added, "It was also my favorite book."

Del went to her desk, pulled out a pen and signed both books. She handed one to Celia and one to Angel. "Here, a gift."

Celia clutched the book to her chest. For a long moment she was speechless, then she blurted, "Thank you!"

Angel looked amazed. "You don't have to do this."

Del shrugged. "I get some copies for my own use." She hoped to change the subject so Mick would quit scowling. It didn't work.

Attempting a relationship was hard work. Now she remembered why she'd never much bothered. Of course, that was before Mick, with guys who were easy to dismiss.

She couldn't dismiss Mick.

Angel scooted to the edge of her seat. "Where do you get your ideas?"

She'd been waiting for that question; without fail, it always got asked. She smiled, then for almost half an hour answered questions and explained about her work and laughed and had fun. Mick didn't appreciate hearing about her research techniques, but the women, especially Celia, hung on her every word.

When Del admitted that she had a looming deadline and intended to put in a few hours of writing that night, Alec pushed to his feet. "We need to be heading home. It's getting late and Celia—" he gave his wife a cautious look "—is getting ideas."

Dane also stood, saying in an aside to Del, "Alec is a worrier."

Del looked at the big dark Alec, towering protectively over his petite blond wife. He looked like a marauder, not a worrier. "If you say so."

Angel leaned against Dane and sighed. "We'll let you get to your work."

Del blushed. "I didn't mean to run everyone off."

"Not at all. Dinner was wonderful and the company was even better. But the kids will be getting antsy at their grandmother's."

"You have children?"

"We have two," Angel told her. "Grayson, who's twelve, and Kara just turned ten."

"Our Tucker is nine now," Celia said, "and looks just like his daddy."

Alec's frown lifted into a smile of pride. "The kids would love to meet you, Delilah."

Mick forestalled Del's reply by saying, "I'll tell you all about them tonight."

Del seemed to be the only person who heard his lingering undertone of annoyance.

Angel bent a fond look on Mick. "He does love talking about the kids, so prepare yourself."

"That's because they worship him," Dane added. "It's almost nauseating how they fawn all over him. Especially Kara. The boys aren't quite as bad as she is. But as you probably noticed with Zack's daughter, females love Mick."

Angel elbowed Dane hard, which made him grin and kiss her mouth. Del had already noticed what an affectionate bunch they were, always touching and teasing and kissing.

Mick obviously loved these people, and they loved him, but now, rather than making her feel excluded, the sight of them all together touched her heart and made her yearn for things she'd never considered before. They were wonderful people.

At the moment, though, Mick was busy throwing them all out.

Del watched as Mick herded everyone toward the door. She had the distinct feeling he wanted privacy so he could yell at her. Not that she'd let him. No one had yelled at her since she was a little girl, and she wasn't about to let Mick start now.

Celia surprised her by giving her a hug and telling her she'd cherish the book. Del felt a little silly. It was only a book, but she enjoyed Celia's enthusiasm.

Angel followed suit and hugged Del, too, whispering in her ear, "It's so nice to see Mick confused by a woman." She leaned back and grinned. "Thank you for taking such good care of him."

"My pleasure."

Angel's mouth quirked. "I can see that it is."

Mick stood at the door until everyone had gone. Del didn't wait around for him to start complaining or questioning her. She gathered up the coffee cups and carried them to the kitchen.

He stepped up close behind her. "Delilah."

She could feel the tension emanating off him in waves. It made her tense, too. "Call me Del."

Her hands shook. She refused to turn and face him,

choosing instead to rinse out the cups and put them in the dishwasher.

He ignored her order. ''Why,'' he asked in a barely audible growl, ''do you do all this crazy stuff?''

''You mean like bringing strange men home to my place? I was just wondering the same thing.''

She'd meant to distract him from his grievances, but her ploy didn't work.

''Hell, yes, that's part of it. Don't you have any sense of self-preservation at all?''

She tightened her hands on the edge of the counter. ''I learn what I need to know and I don't take unnecessary risks.''

He stepped closer, crowding her against the sink. His anger was there, pulsing between them. But there was something else, something more. Her skin prickled with awareness as she felt his erection nestle against her bottom. Her breath caught.

''Tell me why you do it, babe.''

She swallowed hard. ''The media claims I do it because I like writing about heroes, about guys who can win against all odds, solve twisted mysteries and get the bad guy every time. They psychoanalyze that I'm setting myself up as a heroine.''

''Are you?''

''No.'' It was difficult to think with him so close, and so aroused. ''My parents say I've always been too creative and too frenetic. I'm not content to sit idle.''

His hot breath touched the side of her throat as he spoke. ''I can see that.'' He nuzzled her, making the fine hairs on her nape tingle, her breasts swell.

''You've got more energy than any woman I've ever met. And you don't think about things, you just act.''

''You're…you're complaining?'' His words sounded disgruntled, but his touch was so gentle, so exciting.

His good arm came around her waist and squeezed her. ''The things you've claimed to do are insane, Delilah.''

''Look who's talking! A man who deliberately takes a bullet in the back.'' She forced enough room between them so that she could turn and face him. Her hand trembled from a mix of anger and excitement as she reached up and touched his jaw. ''What if that bullet had hit something vital? A lung or your heart or your spine? You could have been killed.''

''I'm trained to react.''

She snorted at that bit of idiocy. ''They don't train you to get shot, do they? I thought PIs did sleuthing, not gunplay.''

He looked away from her gaze and focused instead on her mouth. ''We do what we have to do.''

''And that includes nearly getting killed for a stranger? At least I take every precaution when I do my research.''

His eyes, when they met hers again, were so dark, so intense that Del felt consumed by him. ''I couldn't bear the thought of that bullet hurting your soft skin,'' he whispered. He leaned lower and kissed her, tiny biting kisses from her throat to her ear, to where her neck met her shoulder.

Del shivered, then forced herself back in control.

"I can't change who I am, Mick. This is what I do, what I enjoy doing."

He pressed his face into her throat and simply held her. It was a tender, possessive embrace and made her heart rap hard.

"Not since before Angel married Dane have I felt the need to protect someone."

She slipped her fingers through his silky hair, over his neck and the hard joint of his shoulder. "I don't need you to protect me," she assured him softly. Then, touching the bulky bandage on his back, she added, "I don't even want you to try to protect me. Especially not when you get hurt in the bargain."

His head lifted and he stared at her hard. "*Tough.* We've forged a bond, you and I, whether you like it or not." He tangled his hand in her hair and tipped her head back. "You *did* take me in, not just into your home but into your bed. If you didn't mean it, you shouldn't have started it."

"Mean it?" She found it hard to breathe with him watching her so intently, as if he could see her soul. "What…what does that mean?"

"It means you're mine now."

He continued to study her, probably waiting for her to refute his claim, but Del had no intention of doing so. No one had ever wanted to protect her. No one had ever wanted to claim her.

She swallowed. "I was going to clean the kitchen—"

"Leave it," Mick ordered.

"—but I'd rather go to bed with you."

His jaw hardened and his pupils flared. He caught

the back of her head and drew her up for his kiss. He tasted so good, and she leaned into him until she heard him groan.

"Mick..." Very gently, she pushed him back. "You should take your medicine."

"Not this time, sweetheart."

"Your shoulder—"

"Will be fine. I promise." He took her hand and started toward the bedroom.

Del admitted to herself that she wanted to let him have his way. Never in her life had she felt so hungry for a man. Never had a man been so hungry for her.

The bedroom door closed behind them and Mick leaned against it. "In the morning," he said, "we're going to talk. Without distractions."

Del had no problem with that plan. "You'll tell me more about the kids and how you and Angel met and about your background?"

There was only a slight hesitation before he nodded. "All right."

"I'm curious about you, Mick."

His gaze moved over her, hot and anxious. "We haven't had much time for talking, but we'll catch up. For now..."

"For now, I want what you want."

He pushed away from the door, his smile slow and lazy. Hot.

"As long as you don't hurt yourself," she qualified.

Mick again caught the back of her neck and lifted her to her tiptoes. Against her mouth he said, "You can help me out by taking your clothes off."

She smiled. "And yours, too?"

"God, yes."

MICK KNEW HE SHOULD HAVE put off the lovemaking in favor of getting a few things straightened out, but he seemed to have little control around her. That in itself was a worry. He was used to an icy indifference in most situations, an iron discipline that never wavered.

Especially where women were concerned.

Too many things didn't add up, and now that he understood the lengths she went to for research—his blood nearly froze every time he thought of it—new questions were beginning to surface about the robbery. He couldn't let lust make him lose sight of the possibilities.

She kicked out of her sandals while unbuttoning her blouse, and his discipline shattered. She didn't undress slowly to tease him. Rather she tore her clothes off as if she felt the same burning urgency as he.

Mick braced his feet apart to keep himself steady while she stripped bare. Her frenzy fired his own.

Tomorrow they would talk. But tonight, he'd make her his in every way.

CHAPTER SEVEN

IN NO TIME, Delilah stood before him wearing only a lacy bra and skimpy panties. He was so hard he hurt. He could feel the hot pulse of blood through his veins, the heavy, rhythmic beating of his heart.

Slowly, savoring the moment, Mick walked to her. With just his fingertips he touched one taut nipple straining against her bra. "Don't move," he whispered, and bent to take her in his mouth.

Her moan was raw and real and satisfying. Mick took his time, suckling her, teasing with the tip of his tongue, the edge of his teeth. He felt the heat rising from her slim body, her restless movements, her heavy hot breath.

"Mick, please." Against his instructions, she tangled her fingers in his hair and tugged. He straightened and began working his own buttons loose.

He held her gaze as he asked, "Are you wet for me right now, Delilah?"

Her pupils dilated, she shook her head. "I don't know."

"Check for me."

Her lips parted. "But…"

"Put your fingers between your legs," he urged, "and tell me what you feel."

Her pulse thrummed wildly in her throat. She swallowed hard, her gaze locked with his, and when her hand moved between her thighs, Mick had to bite back a groan. He locked his knees against the wash of raging lust.

"I...I'm swollen. And hot."

Triumph exploded through him. "And?"

Trembling, she whispered, "And wet."

He cursed low. The damn shirt pulled at his shoulder as he tried to wrest it off. Delilah stepped up to him, her entire body quivering. "Let me."

With gentle hands she eased the shirt from him, then went to her knees to work on his jeans. *Not this time,* he told himself, seeing her on her knees, knowing how ready she was for him.

He let her get his jeans unsnapped and unzipped, then he stepped away. "Stand up, Delilah."

"But—"

"It's your turn tonight, remember?"

Staring at his erection, she licked her lips with blatant insinuation and said, "I know."

Mick laughed, a harsh, hoarse sound. She looked as if she wanted to make a feast of him, and that nearly cost him his control. "You are such a tease." Then, with more command in his tone, he said, "I want you to finish stripping, then sit in the chair."

Startled, she cautiously stood and looked over her shoulder. The chair was piled with clothes, positioned in front of the window. Her bewildered gaze met his. "The chair?"

"That's right." He looked at her breasts, straining

against the lace. "Take off your bra. I want to see your nipples."

She glanced again at that straight-backed, hard-seated chair. A shiver ran through her before she reached behind herself to unhook her bra. The position thrust her breasts out more. Mick hardened his resolve, doing his best to remain unaffected by the luscious sight of her. Looking at him, Delilah dropped the bra. Her breasts rose and fell with her accelerated breathing.

"Now the panties," he said, feeling sweat dampen his back and shoulders. His hands shook with the need to touch her, but instead he went to the chair and removed the clothes, dropping them onto the floor. He turned to face Delilah—and she was breath-takingly naked.

As if she was overwhelmed, her head hung slightly forward, her hair shielding her expression. Her long legs were pressed together, her knees locked. Her hands flexed, opening and closing in small, nervous movements.

Mick was caught between wanting to stand there and look at her forever, and needing to be inside her now, this very instant.

Her nipples had flushed a dark rose, puckered tight. The black curls between her thighs looked silky, shielding her secrets.

"Don't be shy with me, Delilah."

Her head lifted, their gazes clashed. "I want to throw you down on the carpet. I want to strip your jeans off you and taste you again." She licked her lips, panting. "I don't understand it, but I'm not shy with you at all. I just want you. A lot."

Mick held out his hand. "Then come here. Let me help you."

She strode to him, her small breasts jiggling, her silky dark hair swaying. He caught her and held her away, but tipped up her chin so that she looked at him. "I want you to sit in that chair and let me pleasure you."

She blinked hard and a slightly worried frown pulled at her brow. "Couldn't we just—"

"No." Mick moved her to the chair and urged her onto the hard seat. He smiled at the way she sat so straight and proper, her spine erect, her knees together and her hands in her lap. But not for long.

Going down on one knee, he sat back on his haunches. "Open your legs as wide as you can, Delilah."

Her shoulders stiffened and color rushed into her face. "What are you going to do?" she asked, both breathless and excited.

"I'm going to kiss you." He glanced at her face, then back to her sex. "Here." Pressing his fingers between her thighs, he cupped her in his warm palm and felt her spontaneous jerk. Though she was tense, her breathing suspended, he could feel her, soft and wet, just as she'd said.

Shifting slightly, he stroked her, his fingertips opening her more, touching her distended clitoris. "Relax for me," he murmured.

Instinctively, she curled forward before catching herself and, with some effort, leaned back in the chair.

She took several deep breaths, and her thighs went limp, yielding to him as he pressed her legs wide. "Scoot to the edge of the seat."

Her head tipped back and her eyes closed. He saw her throat move as she swallowed audibly. "Mick, I feel...exposed."

"You are exposed," he whispered, watching as she slid forward in a delectable sprawl. "I wish I had two good arms right now so I could touch you everywhere."

Her eyes snapped open. "You're not hurting, are you?"

"Shh. I'm fine." He moved between her thighs and leaned forward to kiss her mouth, taking his time, enjoying her while he breathed in the spicy scent of her arousal. She curled her fingers around his upper arms and held on, making no move to push him away.

He could feel her impatience and drove her as far as he could, wanting her to remember this night forever. When she couldn't stop squirming beneath him, he cuddled her breast in his left hand. He wanted to hold both breasts, but his right arm and shoulder felt numb with pain.

He teased her nipple, stroking with his thumb and carefully tugging until her back arched. "Give me your other breast."

Her eyes slowly opened. "What?"

"I want you in my mouth."

Understanding dawned and her look turned equally hot and gentle. She cupped her breast and raised it high. At the same time her other hand went to the back of his head and brought him forward.

At the sight of her offering herself so sweetly, Mick growled. He kissed her softly at first, plucking with his lips, lapping with his tongue. She moaned, pressing herself into him, and he suckled greedily, unable to get enough of her taste, her incredible scent. Delilah moaned and writhed and managed to raise herself enough to rub against the fly of his jeans.

Mick cursed the injury that kept him from taking her in all the ways he wanted.

''Mick!'' She cried out, straining against him.

It was too much. He moved back and opened her legs even more. Her pink flesh glistened, wet and ready, and he leaned forward to taste her deeply, his left hand curving around her bottom and holding her still.

Delilah raised her hands and covered her own breasts, crying, moving with his mouth. He loved the taste of her, so hot and sweet. He pressed his tongue into her, slow and deep, then stabbed with quick motions, swirled and licked and teased, and when he knew she was near, when he felt the tremors going through her slender thighs, her belly, he caught her clitoris and drew on her gently.

Her contractions were so strong she nearly escaped him. Fingers biting deep into her soft ass, he held her close and did his best to block the pain of his injury, enhanced by her thrashing.

With one long, last, shuddering moan, she stilled. Her breathing remained ragged, loud, and she seemed boneless in the narrow chair, her long limbs sprawled for him, around him. Her hands dropped to her sides.

Shaken, Mick put his good arm behind her and

rested his face on her belly. Though he stayed perfectly still, which eased his physical aches, his mind still reeled and his emotions rioted.

Damn, he thought. This level of connection was more than he'd expected, more than he'd even known existed.

It scared him spitless, because he wasn't a hundred percent sure he could trust in it, in her. He just knew he wanted her now, and he couldn't bear the thought of any other man with her like this.

His arm tightened and he forced himself to say lightly, "You okay, sweetheart?"

"Maybe."

He raised up to smile at her. "The taste of you is enough to make me insane."

Her eyes remained closed, but she smiled. She took several deep breaths to calm her racing heart and said, "Know what I'm thinking?"

He lightly kissed her belly button, then nuzzled the soft skin of her stomach. "Vague, soft, happy thoughts, I hope."

"I'm thinking I want you inside me."

Mick clenched his jaw. He wanted to be inside her, but he didn't see how he could. Much as he hated to admit it, he wasn't invincible. His arm hurt like a son of a bitch, more so with every breath.

Her position in the chair had taken a lot of the physical stress off his arm and shoulder, but her soft moans had caused his muscles to tighten, to flex, and now his pain felt very real.

Delilah sat up. She cupped his face in her hands and said, "Did I tell you I took riding lessons?"

His shoulder screamed a warning, but his erection was more than willing to listen. "On a wild stallion, no doubt?"

Her smile was still softened by her climax. "No. As a little girl, my parents gave me riding lessons. C'mon." She pushed at him gently until he moved back and gave her room to stand. She reached a hand down to him, and with a laugh, Mick came to his feet.

"First," she said, "a pain pill for you. And no arguing. I promise to make it worth your while."

Mick pulled her up short. "You don't have to do this, sweetheart."

"But I want to." Her expression clearly showed her confusion. "I'm not doing you a favor by making love to you. What you just did…it was so wonderful. I had no idea."

Mick wanted to know which part had surprised her, but he kept quiet.

"The only thing is that now I feel empty." She flattened her hands on his chest and stared up at him. "I meant it when I said I want you inside me."

Holding her gaze, he slid his hand down her belly. "My fingers would probably do," he said, and matching actions to words, he pressed two fingers deep inside her.

"Oh, God." Still sensitive from her climax, she dropped her head forward and curled her hands, clutching at him. They both breathed hard. "That's…that's wonderful," she whispered, delighting him with her honesty, her openness.

Her hand moved down his body and curled around his hard-on.

Mick had to fight to keep from coming the second she touched him. He felt primed to the max, and her hand was so soft and feminine. ''Delilah,'' he warned, closing both hands around her shoulders.

''This,'' she whispered in a sultry voice that coasted over him like rough velvet, ''will feel even better.''

He had to laugh, though it sounded more like an agonized groan.

She released him, patted his butt and said, ''Now quit trying to distract me.'' Taking his hand again, she led him toward the kitchen, where she kept the pain pills. ''I have the feeling you like to control everyone and everything, but I've been on my own too long for that nonsense.''

She wasn't looking at him, so it felt safe to smile. She was the most endearing woman he'd ever met.

Her insight was also uncanny. It was true he liked to have control, but more than that was the fact he wanted to take care of her, protect her. He'd never even come close to feeling that with any woman other than Angel, and then it had been a clear-cut feeling. They'd both been going through bad times and had quickly learned to trust each other, to help each other. They were friends and there'd been no confusing possessiveness or lust or this irrational need to make her a part of him, to somehow meld her body and soul with his own.

He loved Angel, just as he loved Dane and their children, and by extension Alec and Celia and Tucker.

He'd protect any one of them with his life, but that instinct had never been put to the test. Dane and Alec were more than capable of taking care of their own, so Mick's sense of protectiveness was blunted by their presence.

Not so with Delilah. There was nothing and no one to soften the raw edge of volatile emotions consuming him.

He knew it was too much, too strong and overwhelming. It put him at risk, a risk he'd never faced before because he'd never met a woman who hit him so hard on a gut level.

He had absolutely no idea how to deal with her.

She stopped beside the kitchen counter, unmindful of her nudity, although Mick relished the sight of her under the bright fluorescent lights. While she filled a glass with water, he looked her over. Her shiny dark hair was mussed, half hanging over her brow, framing those incredible, bright blue eyes. Her lips were still slightly reddened from her climax, her cheeks still flushed.

Her nipples still tight.

He sucked in a breath and accepted the pill she handed him, tossing it back and washing it down with the entire glass of cold water. Delilah stepped behind him and peered at his shoulder.

"I think we should change the bandage."

He didn't want her taking care of him, and turned to face her. "It's fine."

She propped her hands on her slim hips and frowned up at him. He'd never had a naked woman remonstrate him before. It put a new slant on things.

"I'm changing your bandage, Mick." When he started to speak, she interrupted, saying, "It's early yet and I have a feeling you won't be falling asleep despite the pain pill."

"God, I hope not." He still smarted over the fact that he'd fallen asleep on her earlier.

"Then that means, being as you're so determined and you refuse to listen to common sense or a doctor's orders, we'll be making love for some time yet. You need to be comfortable and relaxed so that you don't hurt yourself."

He gave her a lazy smile, eyeing the glossy dark curls over her mound and the long length of her legs, now braced apart as if for battle. "Relaxed, huh? You think your lovemaking is so boring I'll be able to just sit back and yawn?"

Her eyes got heavy, her smile wicked. "I think you need to let me handle things. It'll be a novel experience for you. I'll be gentle…but thorough. I promise."

He must be getting used to her, Mick thought, because her boldness didn't shock him at all, it just fired his lust. He shook his head, but heard himself say, "All right."

Her soft smile broke into a triumphant grin and she turned, giving him a view of her saucy behind as she marched away. Crooking one finger, she called back to him, "Come along, now. I'll see to everything."

He was in so deep he could barely breathe, and strangely enough, he didn't give a damn. Everything would work out, he'd see to it.

Later.

DEL COULDN'T REMEMBER ever having so much fun. Mick was astounding, giving over to her and trusting her. At least as far as his body was concerned. His thoughts were still a secret, but she understood that. Her life wasn't one she openly discussed, either. Not that it had been bad, only that it had been different, and not many people understood her or her choices.

At the moment, she had Mick stretched out on his back, a pillow cushioning his head, his shoulder freshly bandaged. Together they had showered, touching and teasing anew, then taking turns drying each other. While she'd brushed her teeth, he'd commented on her body, complimenting her in the most outrageous ways.

She returned the favor, savoring the sight of him naked at her sink, his razor and aftershave there as if they'd always been a part of her home, as if they, as well as he, belonged with her.

He had an incredible physique, tall and strong and wholly masculine. While he brushed his teeth with amazing dexterity, considering he used his left hand, she watched the play of muscles in his shoulders and biceps. Still damp from the shower, his dark hair clung in curls to his nape and temples. Her blood raced at the beauty of him.

There wasn't a single flaw to his body—except for that obscene bullet wound.

Her heart nearly broke at the sight of it, and without thinking, she'd moved to kiss him above and below his stitches, where dark bruises marred his olive skin.

His groan, one of mingled awareness and physical pleasure, encouraged her. He'd braced his hands on the sink and allowed her to do as she pleased—and she pleased quite a bit.

After that, she'd spent a good fifteen minutes just touching him, caressing his aching muscles and hopefully massaging away some of the pain and stiffness from the injury.

Even with his head dropped forward and his body totally relaxed, Mick still looked so powerful, so strong and capable. It made her stomach jumpy to know he wanted *her,* desired *her.*

Had nearly died for her.

He grew impatient with the subtle touches and teased, ''Is it your plan to taunt me all night? Because I'm a hair away from taking control again.''

She laughed at him, then squealed as he hurried her to the bed. She had to regain the upper hand so he didn't do more damage to his injury, and it took her several minutes to convince him that she needed to wrap his shoulder again.

He'd finally given in, but only because she let him touch her anywhere he wanted while she saw to that chore. It was apparent that, even though she lacked his physical beauty, Mick felt the same fascination for her body that she felt for his.

Now he reclined in her bed, his eyes dark and hot, watching her as she leaned over to the nightstand and withdrew a condom.

''I hate to sound unsophisticated,'' she said, ''but I've never put a rubber on a guy before. Tell me if I do it wrong.''

He didn't reply, merely watched her as she tore the small package open and reached for him. She felt the subtle clenching of his muscles, the heat rising off him in waves. She glanced at his jaw and found it locked hard.

"Like this, right?" she asked, knowing she was pushing him, and enjoying it.

"Good enough," he growled, and his abdomen tensed as she slid the condom over the head of his penis and then midway down its length.

Del surveyed her handiwork. "Not bad," she announced, trying to drag out the anticipation as long as she could. It wasn't easy; already her hands were shaking and a weakness seemed to have invaded her bones. Mick was thick and hot and silky in her hand.

"I've always been really careful," she whispered, trying to regain lost control, "about protection. Not that I'd mind having children someday, but not until I meet the right man."

His body taut and expectant, Mick rasped, "I want kids someday, too."

Del soothed him, stroking his right arm, his chest and shoulders. She met his smoldering gaze and asked, "With the right woman?"

"Yes."

Sliding her leg over his hips, she positioned herself. "Well, this woman is going to make you crazy with pleasure tonight."

His back arched. "I'll get my turn," he told her.

She laughed. "Not until the doctor says you're able." Slowly, so slowly every nerve ending sparked, she lowered herself. He'd barely penetrated at all, just the thick head of his penis inside her, her inner muscles gripping and quivering around him, when she stopped with a gasp. "It's…it's been so long for me," she muttered, trying to explain, her words broken and breathless and fast. Already she felt stretched, uncomfortably tight, yet tantalized. "I'm…I'm not at all sure."

Mick strained beneath her, sweat dampening his forehead, his chest. Delilah knew she couldn't wait any longer or he'd hurt himself. Swallowing back her own discomfort and uncertainty, she braced her hands on his chest, drew a deep breath and pressed down until he was fully, completely inside her.

An explosive curse broke from Mick. She whimpered in response. For long moments, neither of them moved except for a slight trembling of rigid muscles and a spontaneous flexing of sexes as they each struggled to adjust.

Forcing her head up, Delilah looked at Mick through a sweltering haze of sensations. "Are you…all right?"

"No." His left hand lifted, spread wide over her hip. "I need you to move, baby."

Del licked her lips. "It's just that you're…bigger than I thought."

Without his permission, his hips rose, pressing into her, deepening his penetration. "I can't do this," he groaned.

And Delilah's heart tumbled over.

"Mick." Leaning down, she kissed his mouth, his throat, licked at his salty skin. Very gently, subtly, she rocked her hips. His fingers contracted on her flesh, biting hard as he urged her to continue.

She slid up, her wetness making it easy and

smooth, then all the way down again, harder and faster with each turn. Suddenly, despite his injury, Mick gripped her hips in both hands and pumped into her, holding her tight to him, not letting her retreat. He looked feral and explosive and so sexy she felt her own climax begin.

This was what she'd wanted, him filling her, his body a part of hers, wild and real with no reserve between them. She tipped her head back and cried out her pleasure, then heard Mick's answering moan of completion.

A few seconds later his fingers went lax and she lowered herself to nestle against him. He grunted, and she mumbled, "Did I hurt you?"

It took him a little while to answer, but she didn't mind. She felt the bellowing of his chest beneath her ear, felt his sex still deep within her. "Mick?"

Using his left hand, he smoothed her bottom. "I'm feeling no pain. Even my brain is numb."

She didn't want to, but she raised herself to her elbows. "Will it hurt you if I sleep here with you?"

His dark eyes opened. "It'd kill me," he said huskily, "if you didn't."

Tears clung to her lashes. She hurried to blink them away and sat up more. After a deep, calming breath that helped to chase away the excess emotion, she said, "I'm ready for bed. You?"

The way he looked at her told her she hadn't fooled him one bit. He knew she was mired in sentiment, that making love with him had thrown her for a loop. She'd had sex in the past, but this wasn't sex. This was... She wasn't sure what to call it. Sex had been easy to give up, but she couldn't imagine giving up Mick.

More tears clouded her vision, but he didn't seem to mind. In fact, he looked…satisfied.

Del snorted at herself as she swiped at her eyes. He'd come, so of course he was satisfied. "I'll just get rid of the condom and turn on the air conditioner and—"

Mick moved out of her reach. "I can take care of myself, thank you, and I'll set the air conditioner. I'd like to wake up without hypothermia."

"I set it too cold?" She watched him climb from the bed, and was gratified to see he shook just a bit, too.

He stood in front of her and touched her chin. There was a silly smile on his face, in contrast to the male triumph in his dark gaze. "Yeah. You set it too cold," he agreed. "I'm a man, not a polar bear."

Then he went down the hall to the bathroom. Del stood there, bemused, until she heard the water turn off and the toilet flush.

She rushed to straighten the bedclothes and reposition Mick's pillow. She'd sleep on his left side, to keep from injuring his shoulder, she decided.

He walked into her room, as comfortable with his nudity as she was. After setting the air conditioner a tiny bit higher, he got into bed as if sleeping with her were nothing. She wasn't sure if she liked that or not, considering it seemed like a very big something to her. But then he turned off the light and settled back, and when she crawled in next to him, he put his arm around her, drawing her close. The darkness added a new level of intimacy, filling her with contentment.

Her mind peaceful, her body sated, she kissed his chest and asked, "Will you tell me if you get uncomfortable during the night?"

"No." She pushed up to frown at him, but he only laughed and pressed her face back to his chest. "Shh. Go to sleep, Delilah. You've worn me out and I need to recoup so I can get even tomorrow morning."

Feeling smug, she said, "You'll have to wait to even the score. I have to go out in the morning."

His arm tightened. "Where to?"

"Neddie's funeral is tomorrow."

"Neddie?"

Because she'd already told Mick all about him, she sighed. "Neddie Moran, the man who helped me with my research."

A volatile silence followed her statement, then seemed to detonate. Mick turned, pinning her beneath him in one hard, fast movement, his expression furious. "Neddie *Moran* is the criminal who taught you how to steal cars?"

Watching him warily, she said, "Yeah, so?" He'd sounded ready to fall asleep one moment, then outraged the next. "Mick, you're going to hurt your arm."

For some reason, he looked astounded that she would even mention his arm. He jerked around and flipped the light back on. "Forget the morning. We've got to do some talking right now."

"We do?" Del scooted up in the bed and pulled the sheet over her breasts.

''Damn right we do. Do you know how Neddie Moran died?''

''He drowned.''

''He didn't just drown. Someone else drowned him.'' Mick drew a breath. ''Sweetheart, he was murdered.''

CHAPTER EIGHT

MICK AWOKE TO AN EMPTY bed. Again.

This time, in light of everything he now knew, fear hit him before anything else. He glanced at the bedside clock. Three-thirty. They'd finished their talk almost four hours ago. Where the hell was she in the middle of the night?

He was out of the bed and heading for the door on silent feet before he'd even given himself time to think about it. The reality of her association with known criminals had his skin prickling with unease, his every sense on alert.

She saw no connection between Neddie's recent death and her own very near escape from death.

Mick, however, was positive that the two events were in some way related. She'd associated with Moran, formed a strange friendship even, and now the man was dead. It had been tricky, telling her what he knew of Moran's death without telling her how he knew, or giving away confidential information. The death was still under investigation, but thanks to reporters, it was public knowledge that Neddie had been drowned in the river, so Mick had no problem sharing those details.

Not that they'd swayed her. The most he'd been

able to get out of her was a promise that she'd let him escort her to the funeral. Mick planned to avoid even that, using a deception to keep her away, while he had men checking into any possible associations between Neddie and the robbers at the jewelry store. He didn't like himself for it, but he felt it necessary to protect her.

Hours of talking to her had proved that reason and logic wouldn't work. Not with Delilah Piper, and definitely not when she felt an obligation to a friend.

Mick went only a few steps down the hallway before he saw the dim blue light of her computer shining in the otherwise dark apartment. He heard the light tapping of her fingers on the keyboard, and peered around the hallway corner.

Sitting there in front of her computer, her glossy hair mussed, a T-shirt her only clothing, Delilah looked totally absorbed in her writing. Mick leaned against the wall and watched her, aware of a strange twisting in his heart.

Never had he allowed himself to consider hearth and home and a family of his own. He'd become so discriminating with women, so particular, that he'd doubted any woman would have ever appealed to him on that level.

But standing in a dark hallway looking at Delilah, he felt a contentment unlike anything he'd ever known. She was a woman of constant change and contradictions. She made him hot with her careless, comfortable air, and she kept his emotions turbulent with her daring and her stubbornness. And now that he'd laughed and argued and made love with her, he couldn't imagine not having her in his life.

Insane, he insisted to himself. But his pulse continued to riot and his lungs constricted, and only a small part of that reaction was due to lust. Hell, he shouldn't even have felt lust. It hadn't been that long since she'd wrung him out.

But he looked down at himself and, sure enough, he was already semihard. What could you do with a woman who affected you so strongly, except keep her close and make sure she didn't have the chance to affect any other man the same way?

Delilah paused, bit her lip, stared at nothing in particular and then smiled and began typing again. Mick shook his head. She amazed him, amused him, and she turned his libido red-hot.

Not wanting to startle her, he said softly, "Am I interrupting?"

She glanced up, then held one finger in the air, indicating she needed him to wait.

He should have been annoyed. They'd finished making love for the first time and she'd sneaked away to write, and now had the gall to make him wait. He smiled. No woman had ever treated him as she did, and damned if he didn't like it. Probably because her reactions, her responses, were all so real. Delilah didn't have a deceptive bone in her body. She said what she thought, did as she pleased, and that meant she could be trusted—the most appealing factor of all.

Mick sidled closer and stood behind her. He moved her heavy hair off her nape and used his thumbs to stroke her.

Delilah froze, then twisted to face him. "Um…I can't write with you there."

"Why not?"

She frowned, then turned off her monitor. Shadows closed in around them. "It makes me jittery for anyone to look over my shoulder. I don't want you to read anything out of context and think it's lame."

"I wasn't reading," he explained, still holding her neck easily between his hands. "I was considering the possibility of dragging you back to bed."

Delilah faced the computer again, her hands in her lap, her head bent forward. Finally she said, "I'm running behind, Mick. I need to finish up this scene, okay?"

"It's almost morning."

"I know. But the scene is there now, in my head." She twisted again, this time in a rush. "I'm sorry. I know this probably seems odd to you. But writers write…whenever. And I do have a deadline that is quickly closing in." She shrugged. "I've never had anyone live with me, so I've never had to not write when I wanted to. Know what I mean?"

Mick grinned. She meant that she didn't want him to interfere with her writing, but was trying to be tactful. He said only, "How long do you think you'll be?"

Again she shrugged. "I don't know. As long as the words are coming, I want to keep at it. Once this scene's done, I'll have some free time before I need to start the next one."

A thought occurred to Mick: if she stayed up all night writing, perhaps she'd forget about the damn funeral, and he wouldn't have to deceive her. "Okay, sweetheart. You take your time, okay?"

"You don't mind?"

"Of course not. There'll be times when I'll be gone all night working." Even in the dim shadows, he saw her scowl and had to fight from laughing out loud. "I'm sure you'll be understanding, too, won't you?" he teased.

Very grudgingly, she muttered, "I guess."

"Then I'll see you in the morning."

She continued to stare up at him. "Since you're here anyway, will you give me a good-night kiss?"

"My pleasure." Mick made it a kiss to singe her eyebrows—and felt himself burned instead. In that moment, he wondered if he'd ever get enough, if a lifetime of tasting and touching her would ever satisfy him.

He had his doubts.

"Wow," she said when he lifted his mouth. "You think I can work a kiss like that in with a murder scene?"

Mick stared at her blankly and she waved her hand toward the computer. "That's where I'm at in the book. All your talk about Neddie and connections and conspiracies gave me an idea for the murder scene. Do you think my hero would stop in the middle of trying to chase down the escaping madman to kiss the heroine?"

Mick shook his head. "If the heroine was you, I'm sure of it."

He saw the white flash of her teeth, then heard her chuckle. "You're outrageous. Now go on before I totally lose my train of thought and end up with them making love in the middle of the street instead of doing the responsible thing.''

Thinking of the ''responsible thing,'' Mick pushed any remnants of guilt from his mind. He'd do whatever was necessary to protect her. ''Take as long as you need,'' he said. ''Good night.''

As soon as he turned away, he heard the tapping on her keyboard resume. Madmen and making love and responsibility. Somehow they were all tied together with Delilah, and probably with her research pal, Neddie Moran, and the shooter, Rudy Glasgow, and the robbery.

All Mick had to do was find out how.

His mind filled with possibilities, both intimate and protective, so it was no wonder he slept fitfully. He had just awakened again when he felt Delilah slipping into bed beside him. He glanced at the clock and saw that it was only an hour or so until dawn.

Turning toward her, he slid his good arm beneath her head and murmured sleepily, ''Did you finish your scene?''

''Yes.'' She snuggled down, fitting herself to him as if they'd been doing this for most of their lives. That's how it was with Delilah, natural and comfortable and *right*. Her hand settled on his chest, her fingers twining in his body hair, caressing. ''I'm sorry I woke you.''

''You didn't.'' Mick pressed his mouth to her crown, drawing in the sweet scent of shampoo and Delilah. ''I've been thinking.''

''You should have been sleeping.''

"I'll sleep with you." He felt her smile against his chest. "What were you doing in the jewelry store, honey?"

Startled, she looked up at him, then with a shrug, nuzzled into his side again. "I was researching."

Their voices were both low, mere whispers over the hum of the air conditioner and the lazily twirling ceiling fan.

"What kind of research?"

Her fingertips sought and found his nipple, toying with him, making him stiffen even while half-asleep. "In this book," she whispered, "the hero has to break into a jewelry store and steal something that the madman is after, before he can get it. So I was trying to see how I'd break into that store if I was a madman."

Mick chuckled. "Neddie couldn't tell you how to do that, huh?"

"He told me a lot of things, gave me a lot of ideas, but not details on a robbery." She pressed her face against Mick in a show of emotion. "I'd contacted him about it, and even left a message, but he hadn't returned my call. I realize now that he probably couldn't."

Shit. If she'd left a message on a machine, then that could be the link that had led them to her. Mick squeezed her closer. No way in hell would he let anyone hurt her. "What exactly did you say on the message?"

"Mick." She rose up on one elbow to look at him. "I do like talking to you in the middle of the night like this, but—"

"Actually, it's morning," he said softly, pushing a curl away from her face.

"That's my point. I really would like to get some sleep."

He chuckled. "No sparing my tender sensibilities, huh?" That made her frown with concern, and he added quickly, "I'm just teasing."

"Are you sure? Because I guess I could stay awake and talk more about this if you really wanted to."

"Actually," he murmured against her mouth, "I was thinking about sports."

She again pushed away, peering at him through the dark with interest. "Are you an athlete?"

Snorting, he said, "Hell, no."

"You don't like sports?"

"I have no idea. I just never played any."

"But all little boys play baseball and football and—"

"I didn't."

She seemed to have forgotten all about sleeping, and her frown was back. "Well, why not?"

He didn't want to talk about his childhood, about his mother's shortcomings. Not now. Preferably not ever. "I was thinking about a sport you taught me."

Despite his best effort, there was an edge to his tone, a deliberately forceful change of subject that she picked up on. She might often be obtuse to her surroundings, but Mick found she was very attuned to him. It unsettled him, and turned him on.

She cupped his jaw in a gesture so tender, his heart ached. "What," she asked, lightly touching the corner of his mouth, "have I taught you?"

"Riding." He rasped the word, forcing it past an emotional lump in his throat, desperate to change his ache to a physical one, one that she could easily appease.

In the next instant, Delilah kissed him—everywhere. The emotional and the physical commingled, a variety of needs that stirred him on every plane.

After she rolled the condom onto him, she mounted him with a smile and leaned down to kiss his mouth. She slid her body onto his with a snug, wet fit, and whispered wickedly, "Giddyap."

DELILAH GROANED as she managed to get one eye open. Her entire body ached in places she hadn't known she had. And her butt was cold.

She forced her head up and saw that Mick had kicked the covers to the bottom of the bed. Her front, curled into his side, was warm enough. But her behind faced the air conditioner and was numb with cold.

When she looked Mick over, gloriously naked, she quickly heated. Until she noticed the alarm clock.

"Noon!"

Beside her, Mick groaned and he, too, opened one eye. "What is it?"

"I overslept!"

"Don't worry about it," he mumbled, and tried to draw her close again.

"But Neddie's funeral! I'll never make it now." She couldn't be sure, but Mick looked very satisfied over the situation. Del frowned. "Did you keep me awake all night on purpose?"

Both eyes opened and he stared at her breasts. "Yeah."

"Mick!"

"I'm not into making love with comatose women, so of course I had to keep you awake."

"Oh." She subsided, but only a little. "That wasn't what I meant."

"All I did," he informed her, reaching out to smooth his hand over her hip, then her belly, "was mention riding." He glanced up, his dark eyes unwavering. "You're the one who did the rest."

Because he was right, and because his hand felt too good on her body even now, she flushed. "I feel terrible," she admitted.

Mick cupped his fingers between her legs, fondling, seeking. His voice morning-rough, he crooned, "I think you feel very nice."

She frowned at him and said, "I'm sore, so forget it."

His smile made him look like a pirate. A dark sexy pirate, set on pillaging. "I'll be understanding," he promised, "and run you a nice hot bath. I'll even get the coffee." Then he added deliberately, "But forgetting about it is impossible."

"Mick." She said his name on a sigh.

His tone, his look, turned serious. "You're about all I can think of these days."

She melted. And she wasn't that sore, she decided. But he'd taken her words to heart and slid out of the bed. He stretched, careful of his wounded shoulder, and she sighed yet again at the sight of him. *Much more of this,* she thought, shaking her head, *and I'll begin sounding like a wounded coyote.*

"Since it's already too late to make the funeral, would you like to come with me today?" He looked expectant—and just a bit too watchful.

"Where are you going?" she asked.

"I need to set up something with a therapist for my shoulder."

"I thought the doctor said to give it two weeks first."

Mick shook his head. "I can't wait that long." He flexed his right arm, winced, and added, "I don't like being less than a hundred percent."

He started out of the room and she scurried after him. He detoured into the bathroom, so she had to pull back. Damn, he shouldn't be pushing himself. But how could she stop him? He far outweighed her and had double the stubbornness she possessed.

She waited in the hallway until she heard the bath-water start. She called through the door, "Mick?"

The door opened and he snagged her, pulling her inside. He looped his left arm around her waist, kissed her pursed mouth and said, "You soak while I get coffee. I'll shower when you're done."

"You're supposed to be resting!" she said, trying for a stern expression.

"Making coffee won't tax my meager strength, I promise." He kissed her nose and swatted her on the behind left-handed. "Now, soak."

"Take your medicine!" she yelled to his back.

She was submerged in the hot water, letting it ease her aches and pains, when Mick came in carrying two mugs of steaming coffee. To her disappointment, he'd pulled on jeans, and she frowned at him. "No fair me being naked and you being dressed."

He handed her a cup of coffee. "It's the only way I can guarantee we'll make it out of here today." He grinned and added, "Otherwise I'm likely to join you in the tub. You're a helluva temptation."

She ignored his outrageous compliment and sipped—and moaned with pure, unadulterated pleasure. "Oh, that's good."

"Just what I wanted to hear. I'll take over all the coffee duties."

"You could just show me how to do it."

"I'm not quite that trusting."

Wondering just how trusting he might be, she splashed him. "So you're saying you don't like my coffee, either?"

"I had a hairless chest before drinking it."

Del tried to feign insult, but she ended up laughing instead. "Okay, so I made it stronger for you. I thought all men wanted their coffee strong and black."

He nodded. "So you know a lot of men with iron stomachs, impervious to the cold, fearless and reckless and invincible?"

"No, but that's how I write them," she teased.

Sounding far too serious, he asked, "Is that the kind of man you were looking for?"

Del considered getting serious, too. She considered telling him he was exactly what she'd been looking for, even though she hadn't realized it until she met him. Instead, she shook her head. "I know the difference between reality and fiction, but I don't have much experience with men's preferences. And for the record, I wasn't looking. I didn't really think there was room in my life for a man, not since I've kinda thrown myself into my writing.''

Mick put the toilet lid down and sat. "You really enjoy writing, don't you?''

Her need to write wasn't always a pleasant one. "I suppose it's a love-hate relationship. I feel the craving to write almost all the time. Sometimes it's inconvenient. People think I'm dumb because I plot a lot. They consider it daydreaming, and write me off as being too fanciful. But I doubt I'd feel like me if I wasn't writing.''

She hesitated, then tilted her head to look at him. "I hope you can understand. There'll be a lot of times when I'm trying to listen, but my mind will go off track. And I get up a lot at night to write. It seems like as soon as I try to sleep, my brain starts churning and I just can't shut down.''

"I'll persevere.''

"It doesn't mean I'm not aware of you. It doesn't mean you're not important.''

"I understand.''

His acceptance was just a tad too quick, making her suspicious. "Do you? Not many guys I've dated have.''

He gave her a measuring look, then asked, "Have you dated many?''

"Sure. In my younger days, when I was curious about things.''

"Things?''

She grinned. "Sexual things, though the sex was never enough to keep me…engaged for long. I outgrew my curiosity and my fascination with men. These days, writing is more interesting, and more important than any guy—especially when I have a deadline, which I almost always do." She thought about that, and added softly, "Of course, those guys weren't as important as you."

Mick looked down at his coffee cup for a long moment. "Because I protected you?"

"Partly," she agreed. "No one has ever tried to protect me before. You blew me away, putting yourself in line for a bullet."

"What about your folks? Surely they're protective."

"I guess." She idly soaped her arm, thinking about her family. "They're wonderful, and they love me, but with two older, more serious brothers, I'm kind of the odd duck."

Mick didn't say anything to that, just continued to encourage her with his silent attention.

"You can imagine how they all reacted when I told them I wanted to be a writer." She laughed, remembering. "They told me to get serious, and when they saw that I *was* serious, they worried. Especially whenever I did research. Now, though, they're really pretty proud."

"Are you close with them?"

"Oh, sure. And my brothers are great. They're both married and have kids and houses. They still worry on occasion, but meeting you would probably fix that."

Mick went still. "Did you want me to meet them?"

She'd rushed things, she realized, and said, "Not yet."

He frowned. "You said I'm different than the other guys you dated."

"Well…yeah. I never invited any of them to move in with me."

"How am I different?"

She shook her head, lost to rational explanations when it came to her response to him. "I don't know. Everything just feels different with you, sort of sharper edged. Better. I hope that doesn't alarm you. I mean, I won't start pushing for more."

Mick set his coffee aside and stripped off his jeans. "What if I push for more?"

Del felt her mouth fall open as he stepped into the tub behind her, forcing her to move up while the water sloshed inside the tub and over the sides. His hairy legs went around her, and he tugged her back into his chest. Against her ear, he whispered, "Delilah?"

"Then…" She swallowed, trying to get her thoughts collected. "Then I guess we'll just take it one step at a time."

He cupped his hand and poured water over her breasts. "Are you still sore?"

Her heart swelled and her stomach curled in anticipation. She leaned back, closed her eyes and whispered breathlessly, "No."

CHAPTER NINE

THEY SETTLED INTO a nice routine. Mick didn't want Delilah in his house, where she might see evidence of him being a cop, so he had Josh and Zack alternately bring him more clothes as he needed them. Now her closet was filled with his things.

A dozen times he thought of telling her the truth, of explaining why he'd started the deception in the first place. But he'd only known her a little over a week, and working undercover made him more cautious than not.

Their relationship grew every day. He'd have a chance to tell her everything eventually.

Meeting with his sergeant had been difficult. Mick had set it up so that Angel and Dane would be visiting when Josh came by. They drove out for pickup pizza, and Mick slipped away to meet with the sergeant. He got a new gun, which he hid away, and an update on the robbery—which wasn't promising, since they hadn't discovered anything new.

He'd eventually have to see the shrink, as policy dictated anytime a shooting occurred. But under the circumstances, the sergeant was willing to give him more time for that.

Though he could have driven himself, Mick

claimed soreness to keep Delilah with him when he went to physical therapy. She took her laptop and wrote in the waiting room while he went through a series of increasingly difficult exercises meant to bring him back to full strength. It was slow going, and frustrating, to say the least, but he knew it wouldn't be much longer before he could make love to her as he wanted to, without concern for his injury.

Often he woke at night to an empty bed, and he'd hear her in the other room, tapping away at her keyboard. Rather than go back to sleep, he usually waited for her, and they'd make love when she crawled back in beside him.

Her unusual routine suited him just fine.

There didn't seem to be any dwindling of the devastating chemistry between them, but little by little they were both less alarmed by it, and now they wallowed in the near-violent sensations. Delilah proved inventive and curious, and she had no shyness with his body, taking everything she wanted and giving back as much in return.

Ten days had passed before his sergeant called and told him Rudy Glasgow was finally awake and coherent and ready to talk. But strangely enough, he only wanted to talk to Mick. He'd actually awakened from his coma a few days earlier, but had remained stubbornly silent and still too weak to leave the hospital. There'd been no sign of the other men, but Mick wasn't giving up, and neither was the police department.

His sergeant told him to give Detective Faradon, the lead investigator for the case, a call. Mick peeked in at Delilah, saw she was totally engrossed in her story, and punched in the numbers.

He spoke briefly with Faradon before requesting that the detective use Delilah's number only for emergencies. "Anytime you need to get in touch with me, just call my place and leave a message. I'll check the calls often."

"Running a secret life?" Faradon asked.

Mick ground his teeth together. He didn't want Faradon to know that he was still keeping secrets from Delilah. "I don't want her to overhear anything," he said as an excuse. "It could taint the case if she learned of anything important."

"Just telling you is risky," Faradon agreed. "We're only keeping you informed because you were shot, which makes you damned involved, from where I sit."

"Thanks." Mick rubbed the back of his neck. "I'm glad you understand. So, you got a pen handy?" He recited his home number to Faradon, then they briefly discussed the condition of the man in the hospital before hanging up.

Now all Mick needed was an excuse to get away from Delilah. He didn't want her to know that he'd be talking with Rudy Glasgow, yet he'd made such an issue of going nowhere without her, she was bound to be suspicious if he tried to leave on his own now.

As usual, she sat at her computer working when he finished making lunch and approached her. She was nearing the end of the book, and according to her, that's when she got most involved with the story. She had to tie up loose ends and wrap up the novel with a punch. Mick considered the way her mind worked, conjuring up so many twisted mysteries, and he shook his head. "Hungry?"

Glancing up, she asked, "Who was on the phone?"

Mick stalled, then said, "Just a friend."

"Josh? Zack?"

He hated lying to her, and often he didn't even need to. She hesitated to pry, so if he just shook his head, she'd let it go at that. Sometimes it seemed to him that Delilah went out of her way to give him his privacy, to not push. That bugged him, since it took all his concentration to keep from pushing her. She came to him willingly, accepted him in all ways, but there were still pieces of her that remained hidden. It made him nuts.

Instead of answering her specific question, he asked, "What do you have planned today?"

She accepted the sandwich he handed her and took a healthy bite while shrugging. "Writing. More writing. I hope to finish this weekend. Why? Did you need me to take you somewhere?"

It amused Mick to see how she dug into her sandwich. Sometimes when she wrote she forgot everything else, including food. When her hands began to shake, then she'd remember and grab a bite to eat.

Other times she did nothing but eat while writing. She kept a variety of snacks in her desk drawer—white-chocolate pretzels, caramels, peanuts, chips. She shoveled food away like a linebacker, yet she stayed so slim, even delicate. Her metabolism astounded him.

Settling his hip on the edge of her desk, Mick

shook his head. "No, I don't want to interrupt you today. Looks like it's going well."

"It is. I've thought about this scene for ages. It's a fun one to write. Really gruesome."

He laughed at that. "Then you stay home and finish up, but I do need to go out for just a little while."

"Without me?"

"Unheard of, I know, especially with how I've depended on you." He studied her face, seeing the hurt and something more. "You don't really mind, do you?"

She hedged, saying, "Why do you need to go out?"

Going with a sudden inspiration, he touched the end of her nose and smiled. "It's a surprise."

She flopped back in her seat and gave him a mock frown. "Not fair. What kind of surprise?"

"Now if I told you that, it wouldn't be much of a surprise, would it?"

She hesitated, fiddling with the crust on her sandwich. "You don't need to buy me things, you know."

He nodded gravely, playfully matching her mood. "I know."

She didn't look appeased by his response. "You sure you're okay to be on your own?"

"I'm a big boy, Delilah."

"Ha! Don't I know it." Her lecherous grin had him laughing again.

Damn, how he loved her shifting moods, how he loved…

Oh no. He pulled up short on his wayward thoughts, frowning at himself for letting such a deep

insinuation intrude. He'd known her all of ten days—
if he disregarded the two weeks prior to their formal
meeting. He cared about her, more so every hour. No
denying that. And he was drawn to her on the most
elemental levels.

But it was far too soon to be thinking beyond that.
Far, far too soon.

She mistook his frown and sighed. "Okay, I won't
play mother hen, but please don't overdo it. It hasn't
even been two weeks since you were shot."

Glad of the misunderstanding, he nodded. "Cross
my heart."

Mick was ready to leave ten minutes later. He reminded Delilah to keep her door locked and not to
let anyone in when he wasn't there. She was still
skeptical about any personal threat, but she placated
him by agreeing. She had few visitors, other than his
friends, but she received mail from her publisher and
agent regularly. She promised Mick she would be extra careful, and he finally left.

He was anxious to get some answers, anxious to
face the man who'd put a bullet in his back.

The man who'd tried to kill Delilah.

The thought burned Mick, put a fire in his gut and
a vibrating tension in his muscles. His sergeant had
warned him not to overstep himself, to keep his cool,
and Mick had agreed, even knowing it wouldn't be
easy. The case was out of his hands, turned over to
Homicide, and they could have refused to keep him
involved. But they'd agreed to let him in to talk to
Rudy Glasgow, in hopes he'd be able to get additional
information.

Knowing Delilah would stay in her apartment alone all day made it easier to be away from her. She'd said she intended to write, and Mick believed her. Once she got involved with her stories, not much, including him, could pull her away.

He found her intensity rather endearing.

An around-the-clock watch had been placed on Rudy's room, even while he'd been unconscious. As Mick approached, the present guard came to his feet and set his magazine aside. Glancing down, Mick saw it was a periodical on martial arts. He smiled.

"Dawson, with City Vice." Mick held out his credentials for the guard to verify.

He nodded. "I was told to expect you."

"Has anyone else been in to see him? Has he talked to anyone else?"

The young officer rubbed the back of his neck. "Far as I know, he made a call to his lawyer and told the lead investigator that he'd speak with you. That's it."

"He called a lawyer?"

"Almost first thing after waking up. I heard he was real insistent about it."

Mick supposed that with an attempted-murder charge on Glasgow's head, getting a lawyer would be a huge consideration. "He's doing okay now? They expect a full recovery?"

"Yeah. He's a bit weak and shaky yet, and his leg is still healing, so they're planning to keep him another day or so, but then they'll ship him out." The guard grunted. "If you ask me, he's ready to go now, just dragging it out for the sake of a cushy bed."

Mick didn't doubt the probability of that. He pulled the door open.

The room was similar to the one he'd stayed in, only the shades were tightly drawn to keep it dim, and the TV played loudly. Mick took it all in with a single glance, then lounged against the wall. "You wanted to see me, Glasgow?"

Rudy Glasgow glanced over at him. His face was pale, his eyes shadowed, testimony to his physical state. It didn't move Mick one bit.

Rudy studied Mick for a long minute before grinning and motioning him closer. "I won't bite. Hell, even if I did, I doubt you'd feel it, I'm so damn weak."

Mick refused to respond to that prompt. He went straight to the matter most important to him. "Why'd you try to shoot her, Glasgow?"

He had to shout to be heard over the television, and it annoyed him. Rudy had soft sheets under him, plump pillows behind his head, a mostly eaten meal still on the tray beside his bed. Except for his elevated leg, wrapped in gauze where the bullet had struck, and the guard outside his door, he seemed to be pampered.

It grated that a criminal—an attempted murderer—should be treated so gently.

With a long, lethal look, Rudy said, "That bullet may have crippled me for life."

Mick bared his teeth. "No shit? That's the best news I've had all day."

"Screw you," Rudy suddenly said, lifting himself forward in a surge of anger. He kept his tone low, his voice a growl barely audible over the sound of the TV. His right hand twisted the sheet at his side.

Mick raised a brow, glad to see he'd riled the man. In his experience, information was always more forthcoming when your adversary was upset.

The information he got wasn't quite what he'd been expecting.

Slowly, by tiny degrees, Rudy's hand opened and he rested back on his pillows. He breathed deeply, as if that small fit of temper had taxed him, then a sardonic light entered his tired eyes and he actually chuckled. "But then," he said, "she's already doing that, isn't she?"

"Doing what?"

"Screwing you." He laughed again.

Feigning ignorance, Mick asked, "What the hell are you talking about?"

His laugh was bitter and mean. "That double-crossing bitch you protected. Oh, she covered her ass real good, I'll give her that."

Impatient, Mick barked, "Turn that damn television down. I can barely hear you."

"You heard me just fine, but I'll keep the set on so no one else hears. This conversation is between me and you. What you do with it after that is your own business."

"You planning on telling me something important, is that it?"

"Damn right. You," Rudy rasped, and thrust a finger at Mick, "are making cozy with an accomplice."

"Is that so?" Mick forced himself to speak casually, though a tightness invaded his chest. "And who would it be?"

"The woman you protected!"

"The woman *you* tried to kill?"

"She had it coming!"

Finally, Mick thought, finally he'd get some answers. He summoned a pose of boredom, when inside he seethed with anticipation—and something else, something damn close to dread. He blocked it; *he had to know.* "How do you figure that?"

"Because she was in on the robbery."

Mick laughed, though he didn't feel even an ounce of humor.

Rudy seemed beside himself. "Why the hell else did you think she was there?"

Mick stayed silent, not about to encourage him.

The man smirked. "My lawyer has been in contact with her, you know. He told me that she's got you moved in and under her spell. She even bragged to him that you wouldn't prosecute her, not while she's keeping you happy in bed."

"You expect me to believe this?" Mick knew Delilah hadn't talked to any lawyers. He'd been with her twenty-four-seven. Protecting her, he thought... No, he wouldn't let doubts intrude because of this scum! Delilah was an open, trusting woman. A gentle woman.

Who drove her car into rivers and learned how to hot-wire cars. A woman who kept company with criminals...

Mick shook his head. He knew every damn call she'd gotten. From her agent, her editor... But then, he'd just taken her word on that, when the strangers had called and she'd excused herself for a private conversation.

"You know she's a damn publicity hound," Rudy continued. "Don't you read at all? This is her biggest stunt yet, though we sure as hell didn't know about her twisted ending until we heard the cops coming. Then we realized she'd tipped them off. There was no other way they could have known we'd be there."

Icy dread climbed Mick's spine, chilling him on the inside, making his voice brisk. "A passerby claims to have seen you through the front window, and he called the police on his cell phone."

Rudy waved that away. "She set the whole thing up, including the guy who placed the call. Think about it—what was she doing there when she didn't buy anything? And why the hell would a real successful writer live in that dump she calls home?"

Mick had often wondered the same thing himself. But what did he know about a writer's salary, successful or otherwise? And for that matter, what did Glasgow know about how Delilah lived?

Feeling edgier by the second, Mick demanded, "Why tell me this?"

"Why?" Again Rudy leaned forward, and this time he shook a fist. "Because I'll be damned if I'll sit here and rot while she goes scot-free!"

"So you think I'll go to the police and have them arrest her? That I'll ask to have her prosecuted?"

"Cut the crap. You don't need to go to the cops because you *are* a cop. I know it, and more impor-

tantly, *she* knows it, regardless of your lame act about
being a PI.''

Mick's heart thudded to a standstill. How did this
man know what he'd said to Delilah, unless Delilah
had told him? Feeling as if a fist was tightening
around his windpipe, he managed to say, ''A cop?''

''That's right. You must really think she's stupid,
but believe me, she's a clever one. She hadn't counted
on you being in the jewelry store that day. She'd told
us she just wanted to take part in the robbery, to experience it because of her twisted way of researching
things. We'd get the goods and she'd get her insight.
She promised to pay us nicely for our trouble.

''But then I guess she decided it'd work out better
for her if she got rid of us. If anyone got wise to what
really happened, she'd be off the hook. It would have
been our word against hers, and she's fast becoming
a celebrity, while we all have records. Without any
proof to back us, she'd have walked away with a ton
of fresh publicity, and we'd all have done time.''

''You still don't have any proof—or are you stupid
enough to think I'm going to believe you?'' Mick had
bluffed with the best of them, and right now he felt
as if he'd gambled with his heart.

''Just hear me out.''

''Not if you're only going to spout bullshit.''

Again, Rudy's hands fisted in the sheets, and his
face turned an angry red. ''When she realized I knew
the truth about how she'd set us up, she saw you as
a way out. I bet she came on real strong, didn't she?
I can tell by your expression she did.'' Rudy laughed.
''She figures you'll protect her, but I want you to see

justice done. That's what cops do, right? They arrest the criminals."

Mick narrowed his eyes. "Or shoot them in the leg."

"Bastard!"

His shout was so loud, the guard stuck his head in the door. "Everything okay in here?"

Mick didn't even look at him. "Get out."

Holding up his hands, the guard said, "Just checking," and backed away, letting the door hiss shut behind him.

Mick took a step forward. His heart hammered, but he kept his expression impassive, blank. "Give me one good reason why I shouldn't take you apart."

"Why the hell would I lie? And think about it—how would I know all this otherwise?"

"Your buddies who got loose?" He stood right next to the bed now, staring down at Rudy, fighting the urge to do him more damage. "We haven't rounded them up yet—but we will."

Rudy groaned, but more out of frustration than pain. "Believe me, they're long gone. Not a speck of loyalty in their veins. No, the only one I've spoken with is my lawyer, and he gave me some gritty details that just about pushed me over the edge."

Mick didn't want to hear any details. "Give me the lawyer's name."

"Not yet." Rudy absently massaged his leg. With deep satisfaction, Mick watched the pain cloud his face. "Not until she gets what she deserves."

"Why would she tell the lawyer anything? It would only incriminate her."

The man shook his head. "He's in love with her. He would never do anything to hurt her, including sharing this information with you. He only told me because he wanted me to understand that she had no intention of getting involved in this mess, that I couldn't count on her to help me out."

"Ah." Mick made a tsking sound of false sympathy. "So you have no one to corroborate this ridiculous tale, huh? Too bad." The sarcasm didn't work as well as he'd hoped; he still felt ready to shout with rage. The *ridiculous* tale was far too close to sounding plausible to suit him.

"I don't need anyone to confirm my story. You already know it's true."

"Not so," he lied. "I don't believe anything repeated by an attempted murderer and bungling thief."

The man looked dumbstruck, then florid with rage. "She really did get to you, didn't she? I understand she wore you out that first night, drugged you, then used her mouth to put you to sleep. But you're a good sport. I mean, you paid her back in kind, right, once you'd gotten a little rest and your friends had all gone home?" Rudy jeered, his voice grating down Mick's spine. "For a wounded man, you were tireless, I'll give you that. But then with her in the saddle, what man wouldn't be?"

A red haze of pain and anger nearly blinded him. "You son of a bitch." Mick grabbed him by his hospital gown and twisted, lifting him a good six inches off the mattress. Disappointment threatened to buckle his knees. He had begun trusting her, caring about her, even lo—

No! None of that mattered now. The only way Rudy could have known the intimate details of Mick's first night with Delilah, especially the playful reference to riding, was if she'd told someone.

And why would she do that unless what Glasgow said was true? He couldn't believe he'd let his lust for her override his professional instincts.

Anguish tore through Mick, obliterating his reason, filling him with bitter regret.

On the heels of those overwhelming sensations was refreshing fury, a reaction he knew how to deal with, an emotion that gave him back his breath—and his strength. He let the rage overtake him.

He released Rudy with a wrenching motion that made the man choke and hold his throat.

Mick backed away, knowing he'd gone over the edge. He wouldn't let her hurt him like this. He wouldn't let her make him forget his duty, his responsibilities.

Goddamn it, he'd been the worst kind of fool, but no more. He didn't verify or deny Rudy's claims, he simply turned on his heel and walked out, but he heard Rudy alternately gasping and laughing behind him.

Hot purpose drove Mick, made his steps long and hard and impatient.

The guard tried to speak to him, but Mick's throat was all but closed, his thoughts, his feelings agitated, even violent. He had to collect himself, get himself under control.

And he had to see the lead investigator on the case.

He had evidence to share—and he wouldn't feel sane until he did.

DELILAH HEARD THE KNOCK and left her desk. Mindful of her promise to Mick, she asked, "Who is it?"

"Josh," a voice called back, and, leaving the chain on the door, she cracked it open.

Not only Josh stood there, but Zack, too. They made a mismatched pair, she thought, seeing them both smile at her. Josh with his dark green eyes and blond hair always reminded her of a slick cover model. He had cockiness stamped all over him, and he knew his effect on women. She shook her head. His effect was wasted on her. She had eyes only for Mick, and she liked it that way.

"Can we come in?" Zack asked.

If Josh looked like a model for *Playgirl,* then Zack, with his kind blue eyes and bone-straight, light brown hair, looked like a model for the Sunday ads, maybe for comfy house slippers. He looked warm and cozy, like a man meant for a family.

Josh was excitement. Zack was comfort.

Mick was both those things and more. He was everything. Too quickly, he'd become so important to her.

She held the door open so they could enter. "Mick's not here."

They both drew up short, and Josh, in the rear, almost ran into Zack. "What do you mean, he's not here?"

Delilah shrugged. "He said he had a surprise something or other to do and left at lunchtime, almost four hours ago. He didn't want me to go along."

They shared a look. "You promised to stay in?" Josh guessed.

She shrugged. "I had writing to do, anyway. But this overprotectiveness is getting absurd." She gave them both pointed looks to let them know they were grouped in with the overprotective absurdity. After all, they backed Mick up every time he warned her to be cautious. She wondered how they thought she'd lived this long without them all looking over her shoulder, protecting her every step of the way.

Zack put his arm around her. They were both overly familiar, treating her now as if she and Mick were a longtime couple. They'd come around almost every other day, and had learned to make themselves at home. "Grant the guy the right to worry."

"He doesn't return the favor." She didn't mean to sound complaining, but it sure came out that way.

"Meaning?" Zack asked in a gentle tone.

"Meaning he doesn't want me to ever worry and he looks annoyed if I do."

Josh dropped onto her couch. "'Course he would. He's a guy."

Del warned him with a look. "Your sexist attitude is going to get you into trouble someday." At first Josh's attitude had rubbed her the wrong way, but now she accepted him, even liked him. In small doses.

Zack nodded. "I've told him the same, but this time he's right. Mick can take care of himself."

She laughed at them. They saw everything in black-and-white, especially where men and their roles in life were concerned. Men were supposed to protect, to defend, to cherish. Even Josh, with his variety of girlfriends, treated them all as special. And Zack made his beautiful little girl the center of his life.

That thought brought another, and she asked, "Where's Dani?" She enjoyed visiting with the child. Dani wasn't the average four-year-old. She was too precocious, too aware of her surroundings.

"Gone to the movies with a neighbor and her daughter. She said to give you a hug from her." So saying, Zack pulled Del close and squeezed her, rocking back and forth.

She laughed and pushed herself away. Never in her life had she been touched so much. Her parents, once they'd realized she was different, had given her space—not necessarily space she wanted, but evidently space they needed. They hadn't known how to deal with her, so they'd dealt with her less.

Not so with these guys. The less they understood her, the more determined they were to figure her out. And in the process, they coddled and cuddled her a lot. They made her laugh, made her exasperated, made her feel important, wanted.

She enjoyed it all, the intimate, hot touching she and Mick shared, the friendly touching and camaraderie she got from Mick's friends, and the emotional touching, the acceptance, the welcome. Not a day went by that she didn't hear from one or another of Mick's family or friends.

It had never occurred to her how isolated she'd become. She wrote in a void, emerging only for research and publicity. But then Mick had saved her life, and in the process, changed it irrevocably.

"When do you expect him back?" Josh asked, even as he picked up the TV remote control and started looking for a sports channel.

Zack turned the television off. "Dolt, did you consider that she might be busy?"

Josh glanced at her. "You busy?"

Feeling rather conspicuous now, Del gestured at her desk, littered with small sticky notes and research files. "I was just writing the last chapter."

"Then we can hang out and wait for Mick?"

Zack groaned. "Writing is work to her, you idiot. How can she work if you're here disrupting her?"

Josh looked totally bemused by the idea that he might be a bother to anyone, and Del relented. "Not at all," she said. "I'll enjoy the company. I really don't know how much longer Mick will be, though." She glanced at the wall clock and saw it was nearly five. "I thought he'd be back by now."

Zack glared at Josh, which made Josh raise his brows in a *what?* expression, before asking, "You're sure you don't mind?"

"I've been writing all day. My legs are cramped." Then a thought hit her and she said, "I haven't been out running once since Mick moved in. I miss it."

Again they shared a look, and it was Josh who said, "It's not safe for you to be out traipsing around until they catch those other guys."

"Yeah, right," she scoffed. "Who's to say they'll ever catch them? Am I supposed to stay cooped up forever?" Josh opened his mouth and she rushed to say, "Don't answer that! I know what *you* think already."

He grinned shamelessly. "I was just going to say to wait until Mick is completely healed and I'm sure he'll run with you. In the park. Or someplace else that's safe."

"But not here," Zack added.

"No, not here."

Del sat down on the couch next to Josh. "Why not here?"

Josh frowned, measuring his words. "Being the intense writerly type that you are, you may not have noticed, but this area is pretty hazardous."

"Hazardous how?"

He glanced at Zack for help. Zack sat on her other side. "Unsavory types live around here."

"Really?"

"Well, yeah…you never noticed?"

She chuckled at his disbelief. "Of course I did. I also noticed the variety of people who live here, old and young, black and white and Hispanic, male and female, friendly and hostile. I love the atmosphere, the constant chaos. No matter what time of night I'm up to write, there's something going on outside. People feed my inspiration, and I write better in places like this."

Zack reached over and tweaked a tendril of her hair. "You're a nut, sweetheart."

She swatted at him, laughing.

Josh agreed. "Most women I know want to avoid the criminal element as much as possible. You're the first person I've heard who wants to embrace it."

"I write about the criminal element, remember? Most of my mysteries revolve around a villain. Besides, I go where my villains go. And that makes for some fun travel."

"Yeah?"

"Yup. I love moving."

They were just getting into that discussion when Del's doorbell rang. She glanced at both Zack and Josh, then started to get to her feet.

Josh stopped her with a hand on her arm. "Mick?"

Shaking her head, she said, "Not unless he lost his key."

Zack moved past them both. "I'll get it."

Del smiled at their determination in keeping her safe. She didn't bother telling them that she received a lot of special delivery packages from her editor. No, she just sat back and indulged them in their maleness.

When Zack opened the door, she saw two people there, a man and a woman dressed in suits. The woman gave a faint, stony smile. "Is Ms. Delilah Piper in, please?"

"Who's calling?" Zack asked suspiciously. At the same time, Del stood to better see.

The woman looked past him. "Ms. Piper?"

"That's right." Del started toward the door, but Josh kept pace at her side.

The woman flipped open her bag to display a shiny, very official badge. "I'm Detective Darney, with the city police department. This is Detective Breer. Would you mind coming with us to answer some questions?"

Josh bristled, eyeing the badges as if to verify their authenticity. "What's this about?"

At his tone, the male officer spoke up. "She's wanted downtown for questioning. That's all...for now."

Confused, Del asked, "Questioning about what?"

Both Josh and Zack flanked her, and Del appreciated their solid, comforting presence. She felt off balance and a little frightened.

Detective Breer ignored Josh and faced Del instead. "For possible involvement in the jewelry store robbery," he intoned, his voice so deep Del felt her skin prickle.

"What?" She thought she shouted the word, but it came out as only a vague, rusty whisper.

Detective Darney looked sympathetic. "You've been named as an accomplice," she gently explained. "But before any charges are filed, we'd like to talk to you."

Del had no idea what to do; she'd never faced a situation like this! She turned to Josh with a blank stare, hoping for direction. He looked furious and concerned. "Don't worry, sweetheart. We'll be right behind you."

"Mick..."

Zack gave her a squeeze. "We'll get hold of him. I promise."

She nodded, reached for her purse, and then Detective Darney had her arm, leading her out the door.

CHAPTER TEN

AT LEAST THEY HADN'T handcuffed her, Del thought with a struggling sense of humor to temper her despair. Her throat felt tight, her chest hurt and her stomach was queasy. She almost faltered as she was led through double glass doors and into a long corridor, but the police station wasn't a place to make a scene.

Detective Darney's heels tapped on the tile floor on one side of her, while Breer's heavy steps echoed as solid thuds on the other. They had her caged in—guarding against her escape? Absurd, almost as absurd as the interrogation room where they stopped.

Detective Breer pulled a chair out for her. "Would you like a cup of coffee?"

Numbness seeping in, Del shook her head. The proffered courtesies, in light of the situation, were almost laughable. She drooped down into the chair.

The plastic-covered seat squeaked beneath her. Her blouse stuck to her back from the heat and her tension, forcing her to lean forward. Sweat gathered between her breasts. The unmarked car she'd ridden in had icy-cold air-conditioning, but this room was hot, stuffy, closing in on her. Suffocating.

Once while doing research, she'd been in a room

just like this. She knew the procedure and the protocol, and tried to calm herself with the fact that she knew what to expect, though she'd certainly never thought she'd find herself in the position of being an actual suspect.

Still, she wouldn't panic. It was all a misunderstanding. And thinking that, she said, "If you get hold of Mick Dawson, he could explain to you that I was just a victim."

As if she'd summoned him, Mick strode in. He had another man behind him, and both of them wore frowns, but Mick's was darker, and very grim. Del didn't understand, and she couldn't stop herself from saying in some surprise, "Mick!" and then, as relief washed over her, "Thank God you're here."

His black-eyed glance lacked any emotion as he took a seat at the end of the table—a good distance from where she sat.

Anxiety smothered her. Mouth dry, pulse racing, Del looked down the expanse of the table to Mick. It meant something, that awful distance he'd instigated, but for the life of her, she couldn't imagine what. When he'd left her at the apartment that afternoon, everything had been fine.

He'd even told her he planned to get her a surprise gift.

Thinking this wasn't exactly the surprise she'd hoped for, Del twittered nervously. The silly sound just sort of escaped on its own, a girlish giggle, a forerunner to hysteria, making her edgier. She slapped a hand over her mouth. She didn't understand…any of it.

She swallowed hard and reached for composure. "What's going on?"

The man who'd entered with Mick held out his hand. He was large and beefy, and had salt-and-pepper hair neatly trimmed above his elongated ears. Watery, pale blue eyes were closely spaced to an overlarge nose. His suit fit his square frame loosely, and a wrinkled tie hung crooked around his neck.

He looked like a wonderful character, Del thought, someone she could put into a book. She knew she shouldn't be thinking such inane thoughts at the moment, but all other thoughts cut like tiny razors, and her mind naturally shied away from them.

She couldn't bring herself to accept the man's hand.

He eased back, putting his hand in his pocket. The other held a clipboard. "Ms. Piper, I'm Detective Faradon, lead investigator on the robbery you were involved in." He checked his clipboard, then rattled off the date and time and location.

Del concentrated on finding her breath and centering her thoughts. She had to deal with this—whatever it might be. "Could you please tell me what this is all about?"

Rather than sit, Faradon propped his hip on the edge of the table. Del expected the table to collapse under his weight, but it held.

She skipped another glance at Mick. He was staring at her with such stony concentration that it struck her like a physical blow, forcing her to flinch away.

The other two detectives watched her as well. It

was like being on display, or caught in a hangman's noose, and it hurt.

"Ms. Piper, are you acquainted with Rudy Glasgow?"

She shook her head, then stopped abruptly. "Yes, he's the man in the hospital, the man Mick shot."

"So you do know him?"

"I know of him." Her heart beat too hard, too fast. "I've read the accounts since the shooting. His name has been in the papers. He's…he's unconscious."

"Not anymore." The man surveyed her through lowered, bushy brows. His expression turned speculative, calculating. Finally, he said, "He claims to know you."

Forgetting her sweaty blouse, Del dropped back hard in her chair. Her spine offered less support than an overcooked noodle. "He's wrong," she replied flatly.

"He claims," the man continued, glancing at his clipboard, "that you set the whole thing up as a publicity stunt."

Del's gaze shot to Mick and locked with his. Neither of them blinked. Dear God, surely he didn't believe such an idiotic story.

She shook her head. "No."

"That's it?" Mick asked, his voice harsh and loud in the closed room. "No other explanations?"

Del searched his beautiful face, his once gentle face, and her heart crumbled. The flat, compressed line of his mouth, his locked jaw and dark flinty brown eyes showed his distaste.

For her.

Del winced with a very real pain. *He'd already found her guilty in his mind.* She wanted to reach out to him, to touch him, but she couldn't. She didn't think he'd let her.

"Mick?" she whispered.

His expression hardened even more and he looked away.

It hurt worse than anything she'd ever felt. She murmured to his averted face, "I can't believe you just did that. I...I really can't."

He gave her another sharp look, but this time she dismissed him.

Looking down at her hands, Del said, "I don't know Rudy Glasgow, and I didn't set up the robbery for a publicity stunt. I don't do that."

"You have been known," Detective Breer pointed out, "for your extravagant research tactics."

"Tactics that have never hurt anyone or broken any laws." She felt hollow, stiff. Wounded. "I was there that day, as I've already said, to see how a robber would set things up, but—"

"Isn't that something of a coincidence," Detective Darney asked, her voice soft in comparison to the men's, "that a robbery would take place while you were doing your research for a robbery?"

"Yes." Del's stomach churned with an awful dread. "It's an incredible coincidence."

"You've spoken with him."

Del jumped at the lash of Mick's accusation. She didn't quite look at him when she asked in a small voice, "Who?"

He rounded the table until he faced her from the

other side, giving her no choice but to meet his gaze. "Glasgow. I saw him today." He slashed a hand through the air, impatient, provoked. "He knows *things*."

"What kind of things?"

After glancing at the other people in the room, Mick narrowed his eyes on her. "Things you and I have done. Intimate details that he couldn't have guessed at."

Detective Darney turned away. The men stared at her, their attention burning hot. Embarrassment hit her first, then a wave of remorse for what Mick had clearly thrown away.

And finally her temper ignited in scalding sensation. It chased away the numbness and burned away the hurt. Her heart raced, her pulse pounded.

Very slowly, she came to her feet. "I haven't spoken to anyone about anything we've done."

"He knew it all, Delilah. He knew *details*."

She stared over his shoulder, her mind racing as the ramifications of that sank in. "Then he…he found out some other way."

"How?"

"It's not my job to figure it out." She turned pointedly to Faradon. Sweat gathered at the base of her spine. She itched from the prickling of fear, mortification, loss and anger.

"All of you," she said, addressing the whole room, "you are looking at the wrong person. I don't know Rudy Glasgow. I haven't spoken with him."

"You've told no one?"

She glanced at Mick, overcome with sadness. His

distrust would not be easy to forgive, and he would be impossible to forget. But she had no choice now. "What we've done, Mick…well, it was special to me." She got choked up and despised herself for the weakness. She wasn't used to declaring herself in front of a crowd, especially a hostile crowd. And she didn't delude herself; this crowd was hostile. They'd already condemned her.

She cleared her throat and made a last stab to reach him. "I would never have discussed our personal situation with anyone, much less the man who shot you."

For a long, sizzling moment, Mick stared at her, and she held herself still, hoping he'd smile, that he'd tell her he believed her. That he'd apologize.

He jerked away, cursing softly. His back to her, Mick ran a rough hand through his hair, and Del found herself stupidly concerned for his injury. She could feel his tension, his anger.

She ignored everyone else in the room. At the moment, the only one who mattered was Mick. What the others thought could be straightened out later. She said steadily, "If you just think about it, you'll know I couldn't have done that. That I wouldn't have done anything like that. You know me."

"Barely," he said, still not facing her.

She wavered on her feet. That he could say such a thing after everything they'd done together, after everything she'd felt for him…

She called herself a fool, even as she begged, "Don't do this."

His gaze cut toward her, accusing. "He said you

were counting on our relationship to keep you safe from the law.''

Mick's insinuation was clear. He chose to believe a man who'd shot him in the back, rather than her. Del forced herself to straighten. Later, she'd have to decide how to deal with her broken heart.

Right now, she had to figure out what to do to make the detectives believe her. That had to be her top priority.

But how? She looked around at them—and saw pity from the lead investigator, interest from Detective Breer and understanding from Detective Darney. Del hated it all, and accepted that they all considered her guilty.

''Are you arresting me?'' She was proud of her steady voice, the strength in her demand.

Faradon tapped his clipboard against the table. ''Not just yet. But I don't want you to leave town.''

''Fine.'' Del turned to walk out on wobbly legs, but he stopped her.

''Ms. Piper?''

She froze.

''I may have more questions later. I trust you'll cooperate with me?''

She turned to face him. ''The man wanted to kill me—or so everyone keeps telling me. Now that he's come up with this outrageous tale meant to incriminate me personally, I have to believe it was a deliberate act against *me*. Of course I want him convicted and his cohorts found. I'll help you any way I can.''

Looking a little bemused by that heartfelt speech, Faradon murmured dryly, ''Thank you.''

Del pushed the door open and walked out. Her neck hurt, her stomach coiled. Tears burned behind her eyes, and she fought them back.

She wanted to run, as fast as her legs could carry her. Just as she hadn't known such wonderful elation existed until she'd met Mick, she hadn't known anyone had the power to hurt her so badly.

But she held her dignity intact and walked, head held high, back down the long corridor. She was more than a little aware of Detectives Breer and Darney following behind her.

When she reached the front desk, Josh and Zack stood there, impatient and worried. Zack reached for her first, pulling her into a warm, tight embrace that was just what she needed, but not who she needed it from.

"Hey," he said, squeezing her a bit tighter, "are you okay? You're shaking."

Swallowing back a choking sob, she nodded against his chest and allowed herself the luxury of being held by him for one moment more. Then she pushed away.

Josh touched her cheek. "Mick didn't return my page yet."

It took two attempts before the words would come out. "No need to page him. He's here."

Josh and Zack frowned, their expressions mirroring each other. The irony struck her, and she almost laughed. Not only would Mick not help her, but...

"He was the one," she said, trying for a note of self-mockery in place of desperation, "who evidently brought the new evidence to the police."

Josh didn't appear convinced. "Honey, are you all right?"

"No, no I'm not." Any second now she was going to throw up. Not because of Rudy or the robbery. She was innocent, and sooner or later they'd all realize it.

No, she was sick at heart, and sick inside, because she loved a man who'd just turned his back on her, and she had no idea how she was going to recover.

A deep breath, then another, didn't really help. "Being that you're Mick's friends, not really mine, and being that he now thinks I'm a... Well, I'm not sure what he thinks." She shook her head, understanding now why he'd kept his thoughts so private—because he'd never trusted her. "All I know is that it's ugly, that everything has changed, and I have no doubt you'll both back him up as you always do. So—" she fashioned a smile out of her stiff lips and tried not to notice the concern in their eyes, the caring "—I guess this is goodbye. It's been swell, guys."

She hurried out front, with both of them rushing behind her. A taxi rounded the corner onto the adjacent street, and she jogged across the parking lot to hail it, just wanting to escape, to be alone—as she'd accustomed herself to being. She had the cab door open when Josh grabbed her arm.

"Delilah, wait."

She looked up at him—and saw Mick standing in the station doorway. "He can explain," she said, tears filling her eyes to the point where everything blurred. "Goodbye."

Josh had no choice but to release her. She didn't look back to see them talking. She knew what Mick would tell them, what he believed, and she couldn't bear to see them turn on her, too. She'd finally gotten comfortable with them, accepted them as a part of her life, a disruptive, unruly, fun part.

And now it was over.

She dropped her head forward and covered her face. *How?* she wondered, wishing she could understand what had happened, how it had all gone so wrong in the blink of an afternoon.

The man Mick had shot was no longer unconscious. And he'd told Mick something, found some way to convince him that she was involved. Mick had said he knew personal things, intimate things. That had to mean details of their lovemaking.

Judging by the way Mick had looked at her, *he* hadn't told a soul, so he'd assumed that she had done the blabbing. To a criminal. To a man who'd tried to kill her and had shot him.

And then the shock of it hit her. She felt chilled to the bone, shivering with realization, revulsion.

The cabby pulled up to her apartment, and Del handed him a twenty, not even thinking about getting change, or how much she'd tipped him. She stumbled to the steps leading to her apartment and stared up at the front door.

There was only one thing for her to do.

She had to leave.

MICK HATED TO ADMIT IT, but he was relieved to see that Josh and Zack had followed Delilah to the station. That meant she hadn't been alone when the detectives took her. He'd regretted sending for her almost immediately, but then he had a lot of regrets, and they all centered around her. He had to stop thinking with his emotions and start using his head instead.

He turned to Josh as he approached, but wasn't prepared for the solid pop in the left arm his friend delivered.

"Ow, goddamn it!" Awkwardly, he rubbed his arm and glared at Josh. "That hurt."

"Good." Josh looked ready to take another swing, this one at Mick's head. "What the hell did you do to her?"

"To Delilah?"

Zack rolled his eyes. "No, to Queen Elizabeth. Of course to Delilah. She came out of here nearly in tears."

"Not *nearly* in tears," Josh accused, his nostrils flared like a charging bull. "She was crying, damn it."

Mick hurt from his hair to his toenails, and not all of it was physical. The idea of Delilah crying only added to his pain, making it more acute when he'd thought he couldn't hurt any worse. Dully, wishing he could undo the past, or somehow change it, he said, "She's not who you think she is."

Zack went very still, then stiffened. "What did you do?"

To see his two best friends rallying to her defense added one more bruise to his already battered conscience. He'd wanted them to accept her, and vice versa. But now it hardly mattered.

In the briefest terms possible, Mick explained the

situation. He hated going through it again, hated rehashing all the ways he'd been duped, all the ways she had lied.

When he finished, Josh popped him again.

Mick squared off, unwilling to let Josh's hostility continue. "Will you quit that!"

Pushing himself between them, Zack said, "Josh has a point."

"A point?" Mick stared at him, incredulous. "All he did was hit me!"

"Because you needed to be hit," Zack explained, always the cool one, always the peacemaker. "Jesus, man, you don't know anything about women. I realize you don't date much—"

"Look who's talking."

"—but I figured you'd have picked up some things just from being around Josh, if only by osmosis."

"I know more than I care to," Mick grumbled in return. He knew that he was a lousy judge of character, that he'd allowed his gonads to overrule his good sense. That few people could be trusted, but he was too damn stupid to learn that lesson.

"Not," Josh said, pressing forward again, "by a long shot."

Mick was amazed by Josh's red-eyed, aggressive attitude, which went well beyond defensive friendship for Delilah. *He was acting territorial.* Mick closed the space between them in a heartbeat. "What the hell does she mean to *you?*"

"More than she does to you, obviously!"

Again, Zack wedged into the middle, chest to chest with Mick, forcefully moving him a few feet away from Josh. "Quit baiting him, Josh. And Mick, he's right. Why the hell didn't you talk to her privately?"

"I'm a cop," he reminded them, with an enormous dose of sarcasm and a chip on his shoulder so large his knees almost gave out. "I'm supposed to bring in the criminals." No sooner did the words leave his mouth than he winced. He sounded just like Rudy.

Josh shook his head and all but shouted, "You're also in love, you ass."

Mick stared at him, and wondered if he could reach him before Zack intervened. Probably not, judging by Zack's watchful attention. Mick settled for saying, "Go screw yourself."

"Oh yeah, that'll fix things." Josh threw up his hands. "Do you have any idea how rare a woman like Delilah is?"

Possessiveness bristled along his nerve endings, despite what had just transpired in the interrogation room. "Not more than a few days ago, you were calling her strange!"

"Strange, unique, rare." Josh shrugged. "But that was ten days ago, before I really knew her."

"You're keeping count!"

"She's damn special."

Zack nodded. "Very special."

"Did either of you hear me?" Mick demanded in a shout, so frazzled and confused he knew his hair should be standing on end. "She's dealing with Rudy. She was in on the whole thing."

Zack leveled him with a pitying look. "I don't believe it."

"Neither do I," Josh added. "If you'd talked to her privately, maybe she could have explained."

"She had a chance to explain in there," Mick roared, stabbing a finger toward the station, "and all she did was deny any connection to him."

"Maybe because she has no connection, and maybe because you threw her for one hell of a loop." Josh squeezed his eyes shut. "God, she looked so hurt, it's breaking my damn heart, and I'm not the one in love with her."

Zack raised a brow over that, but refrained from saying anything.

"She's crazy about you, Mick. She trusted you." Disgust filled Josh's tone. "And you just tossed her to the wolves."

Mick looked away from the accusation in Josh's eyes. "All I did was have her questioned."

"All you did," Josh said, grabbing him by his shirtfront and shaking him, "is show her that you don't care two cents for her feelings, that you don't trust her and that you'll gladly believe a man capable of murder rather than hear her side of things."

Put that way... Mick shook Josh off and paced across the parking lot. Heat rose from the blacktop in waves, adding to his frustration, making him sweat.

His first sight of Delilah in the interrogation room had showed her to be wilted, stunned. By the time she'd walked out she'd mustered up a bit of stiff-backed pride. But the incredible vibrancy that he'd thought an integral part of her had been gone. He shook his head, wanting to dispel the image of her beautiful blue eyes clouded with distress. "I was...sick when I got done talking to Rudy."

"Sick and stupid," Josh sneered.

Zack grabbed Josh. "Will you knock it off! This isn't helping, and to be frank, I'm beginning to be a bit suspicious of your interest myself."

Josh glared at him, then at Mick's questioning gaze. Finally, he shrugged. "If Mick wasn't interested in her, I'd have been hot on her trail. So what?"

Already on a short fuse, Mick exploded. "You miserable son of a—"

This time Zack had to leap between them, shoving at both men hard to keep them from coming to blows. "You're both causing a scene, damn it!"

Around Zack's body, Josh taunted, "What's it matter to you, buddy? You just threw her away." And then, as if that wasn't enough to curdle Mick's blood, he added, "I think I'll go *console* her."

Another struggle ensued, while Zack did his best to keep the two of them apart. Josh, muttering a sound of disgust, finally gave up and stepped away. "Fine, you still want her? Well then, go after her. But *listen* to her. And don't you dare make her cry again."

Mick, red in the neck and teeth gnashing, subsided as well. He didn't really want to take his rage out on a friend. It took him several moments, but he finally got the words out. "You honestly think there might be another explanation?"

They both nodded at him. Josh said, "I believe in her. She may be good at coming up with elaborate plots for her books, but she'd never hurt someone she cared about."

Mick wondered if, after what he'd just put her through, he could still be counted among those she cared for.

"And no way," Zack added, "would she take a chance on innocent people getting caught in the cross fire just for publicity."

Mick groaned, hearing the ring of truth in their words. Josh walked away from them both and went to stand near a telephone pole. Zack squeezed Mick's uninjured shoulder. "Yep, I'm afraid you might have blown it. Better to get there as quick as you can and start your apologies. If you give her too much time to consider what you've done, she may not be able to forgive you."

Mick stared at his feet. "I can't imagine what explanation there could be. Rudy knew things that no one should have known."

"It would be easy enough for him to guess that you were sleeping together. That doesn't take an Einstein."

"He knew…details. Specific details that went beyond—"

"I understand," Zack rushed to say, before Mick could stumble on. But Mick noticed there was a gleam of curiosity in his eyes, too.

He straightened. "I'll give her a chance to talk to me, one on one. And I hope like hell you're right, that she can clear this all up."

"Ha. I think you better do more than that. You better get down on your knees."

Mick glared at him, but as he walked away, he didn't rule out the possibility of begging. He'd never felt so miserable in his life—not when Angel had been threatened and he knew he couldn't protect her, not even when his mother had died in a stranger's shack, an empty whiskey bottle beside her. No, the thought of losing Delilah was a gnawing ache that kept expanding and sharpening until his guts felt on fire and his chest threatened to explode.

Even if she had been in on the scheme, he didn't want to lose her. He'd find a way to keep her out of jail, keep her straight, even if that meant keeping her in bed, under him, from now on.

Before he reached his car, he was running.

It occurred to him with a blinding flash of insight that if his friends were right, if Delilah was in fact innocent, he'd just left her alone and vulnerable. Anything could happen to her.

He stepped on the gas and made it to her apartment in record time.

JOSH SAW ZACK GLARING at him and he grinned, though his grin felt more sickly than not. "What?"

"Don't use that innocent tone on me. What the hell were you thinking?"

Forcing a chuckle, Josh shook his head. "I just worked him into a lather. He needed to be shook up or he'd have stood around here pondering all the possibilities, and by the time he realized we were right, it would have been too late. I saved him some time and heartache, that's all."

"So everything was an act? You're not hung up on her?"

Josh winked, and lied through his teeth. "Not at all. You know I like to play the field."

"Huh. I know you've never had a woman show complete and utter disinterest in you before."

"True." Delilah had gone from not noticing him, to grudgingly accepting him as Mick's friend, to displaying a fondness that bordered on sisterly. From the start, she'd made her preferences known, and it had been Mick all the way. Josh laughed. "I tell ya, I can live without it ever happening again."

Zack turned to look at the road. "I hope Mick doesn't kill himself getting over there."

"I just thought of something," Josh said, and reached for the cell phone clipped to his belt. "Since we both know Delilah didn't have any part of sharing that information, someone must have been spying on them."

"But how?" Zack asked. "Mick claims it was very personal in-the-bedroom stuff."

Josh grinned. "Yeah, I wish he'd elaborated on that." Zack laughed, never guessing exactly how big a lie that was. The last thing Josh wanted to hear was the personal sexual details between them. It ate him up.

Delilah, with her contrary ways and openness and brutal honesty, had stolen a piece of his heart. It was the damnedest thing he'd ever experienced, and while he was thrilled all to hell and back for Mick, he couldn't help wishing that he'd found her first.

He shook off his melancholy. Right now, all he wanted was for Mick and Delilah to be happy, and that meant Mick had to get her to forgive him. To that end, Josh wanted to figure out what had gone wrong.

"You think someone could have seen in through the bedroom window somehow?"

"I don't know," Josh admitted, "but I know who could find out."

Awareness lit Zack's eyes. "Alec?"

"You betcha." He punched in a series of numbers and waited until the call was answered. "Alec Sharpe, please. Yeah, it's an emergency."

Only a few seconds passed before Alec took the phone. "Sharpe here."

It would have taken far too long to explain, so Josh merely said, "Hey, Alec, this is Josh. Mick is kind of in trouble and you need to get over to Delilah's apartment."

To Josh's surprise, Alec didn't ask any questions, didn't ask for details of any kind. He said only, "I'm on my way," and the line went dead.

Zack looked at Josh as he closed the cell phone. "Well?"

Josh shrugged. "He, uh, he doesn't say much, does he? But he's heading over there now." He glanced at his watch. "Figuring he was at the office, I think it'll take him about forty-five minutes."

Zack frowned in thought. "With what I've heard about Alec, I wouldn't be surprised if he made it in thirty."

Then they stared at each other. Josh shifted, looked up at the broiling afternoon sun and then the glare off his car's windshield. He propped his hands on his hips and tilted his head at Zack. "You got anywhere you need to be?"

After glancing at his watch, Zack said, "Not for a few more hours. Dani was going to the pizza parlor after the movie."

They'd been friends so long, they often shared thoughts without words being spoken. "Think we should?" Josh asked.

Neither one answered, then in unison they said, "We should."

CHAPTER ELEVEN

MICK SAT OUT FRONT for several minutes, stewing in his own misgivings. He hated to admit how much he hoped, prayed, that Delilah could come up with an alternate explanation. Even now he wanted to hold her, to tuck her close and tell her everything would be all right, that he'd keep her safe and keep scum like Glasgow away from her.

He groaned. It was entirely possible that she'd set up the whole robbery, that he'd gotten shot because of her.

It was even probable, given the facts at hand.

Cowardly bastard, he accused himself, and jerked his car door open. He'd face the outcome, whatever it might be, just as he'd faced everything in his life, good and bad.

He took the concrete steps two at a time. The long flight of stairs leading to the upper level didn't slow him down, either. He bounded up them, anxious to speak to Delilah, to figure things out.

He started to knock, then decided to use the key she'd given him. She might refuse to let him in under the circumstances, so he unlocked the door and stepped quietly inside.

The apartment was silent, causing his instincts to

scream. Mick reached to the small of his back and pulled out his gun. He'd armed himself right after seeing Rudy in the hospital. He hadn't worn the gun before that because he hadn't wanted to make Delilah suspicious, and he was only a mediocre shot with his left hand. But he'd felt naked without it.

Every light in her apartment blazed, and things were scattered everywhere—boxes on the floor, cushions pulled loose from the sofa.

Fear for her clawed at him. Mick crept forward, away from the open door, then quickly ducked as the chopping block from the kitchen whooshed past him, barely missing his head. It fell to the floor with a clatter, the wood neatly splitting down the middle. He whirled and aimed.

Thrown off balance by the impetus of the attack, a small body tumbled forward and landed against his chest, warm and familiar. Mick automatically raised his gun to the ceiling while catching her.

He and Delilah stared at each other.

Slowly, Mick lowered his arm to his side, watching her warily. She stepped back and away from him, then covered her mouth, breathing hard. "Ohmigod." Her fingers over her open mouth trembled. She shook her head. "I'm sorry. I didn't know it was you."

All color had leeched from her face. Her eyes appeared huge and distressed. Everything inside Mick melted, all the suspicions and the worry and the anger temporarily replaced by the need to protect her. "Are you all right?"

Seconds ticked by while they stared at each other. She shook her head again. "No."

That was all she said before turning away and heading for her bedroom. Obviously, no one else was in the apartment, given the way she went about her business.

Mick followed her into her room, and the first thing he saw was the suitcase opened on the bed, partially packed.

His knees locked; his healing shoulder pounded with a renewed ache. "You going somewhere?"

She didn't look at him again, though her face remained pale and he could see her hands trembling. "Yes."

His throat tightened. "Where?"

"I can't tell you in here."

A frown pulled at his brows. "In here in the bedroom?" he asked, perplexed by her odd behavior.

She shifted impatiently. "No, here in my apartment."

"You heard what Faradon told you." He strode toward her, uncertain but determined. He wouldn't let her get away from him. "You're not to leave."

Her scathing glance stopped him in his tracks. "I can't very well stay here. But don't worry. I'm not skipping town. I'll still be around for you to persecute."

"Prosecute," he corrected automatically, then caught himself, realizing she'd said it on purpose. He clenched his teeth, counting to ten. Attempting a softer, more reasonable tone, he said, "I don't want to prosecute or persecute you, babe."

She went to her dresser, picked up an armload of items and dropped them haphazardly into the suitcase.

"Get out of my way," she said as she started past him to the hallway. "What are you doing here, anyway? And why are you creeping around with your gun out? Were you going to shoot me?"

She didn't wait for an answer to that outrageous insult, but marched into the hall.

"You know damn good and well I wouldn't shoot you! I wouldn't do anything to—"

"Hurt me?" She stopped abruptly. "It's a little too late to make that claim, isn't it?"

"Delilah…"

In a hurry to finish packing, she rushed off. Was she leaving her apartment rather than throw him out? Did she think he intended to stay with her still?

Actually, he hadn't thought that far ahead, but the idea of leaving her, of not having her next to him at night, her soft body his to touch, her gentle breath warming him, gave him a lost, sick feeling in the pit of his stomach.

He put his gun away, then knotted his hands to keep from reaching for her. She looked…breakable. Fragile.

She stopped in the middle of the floor, as if uncertain what to do next. Her gaze landed on her computer, and she dove toward it with a purpose, quickly pulling cords and disconnecting the monitor.

Mick used that opportunity to clasp her shoulders. Touching her made him feel better. "Delilah, listen to me."

She jerked away so violently, she almost lost her balance. "Don't touch me," she said in alarm, her eyes huge and round and filled with wariness. "Don't you ever touch me again."

They watched each other in silence. Mick was the first to finally speak. "Tell me what's going on."

For a long minute, she stared at her hands. "All right." She took a deep breath, met his gaze defiantly. "I fell in love with you. I trusted you. I knew it was too soon for that, but I couldn't seem to stop it. And you've broken my heart. I really don't think I can ever forgive you."

Her words were damn difficult to take, filling him with elation—because she loved him—and the heavy weight of sadness, because he didn't know if he could do anything about it. He chose his words carefully, watching her, gauging her reaction. "Because I turned you in?"

Her eyes closed and a tiny, very sad smile appeared. "No, because you'd think that about me at all." She looked at him again. "Here I was, letting myself go crazy for you, and you hadn't really learned anything about me at all."

The need to hold her was a live thing. He barely resisted it. "Can we back up just a bit?" When she didn't answer, he asked, "Why are you in such an all-fire hurry to leave now?"

She gave a broken sigh. "And here I thought you were so smart. Smart and brave and honorable." She reached for his hands and enfolded them in her own. Leaning so close he thought she would kiss him, she whispered near his ear, "I didn't tell anyone anything. I figure you didn't, either. That means my place has to be bugged."

Mick stood there, stupefied, watching her lean back, watching her wait for his reaction. Bugged?

A stillness settled over him, slowing his heartbeat, squeezing his lungs. *Of course her place was bugged.*

But it would have to be worse than that. Just listening wouldn't have given anyone such specific details of their first night together. No, that was something that had to be seen, too.

Almost in slow motion, Mick looked around, heart pounding with acceptance. He caught Delilah by the shoulders. "Come on."

"Where?"

"To my car. I want you out of here."

She dug in her heels, resisting his efforts. "I'm not your responsibility anymore. I can take care of myself, just like I've always done."

"We can't talk here," he insisted.

And she added with a note of sadness, "We don't need to talk anywhere. We're through."

He hadn't been willing to accept that when he'd thought her an accomplice; no way in hell would he accept it knowing she was innocent and in danger. And he didn't doubt her now, not at all. Maybe he was too anxious to find an alternate explanation, one that didn't incriminate her in any way. But this time he was going by his heart, by his guts, not by his damn pride or his conscience.

He gripped her shoulders tighter, opened his mouth—and heard someone say, "Am I interrupting?"

They both whipped around, and Mick shoved Delilah behind him. Alec lounged in the doorway, one black brow quirked in question, his equally black eyes speculative.

Mick caught Delilah's hand, dragged her resisting behind him, and stepped out into the hallway. Without a word, Alec followed. They moved to a corner and there, where no one could possibly hear, Mick asked, "What the hell are you doing here?"

"Josh called and said you needed my help." He looked at Delilah, his gaze speculative. "What's going on?"

"Damn." Mick quickly explained the possibilities to Alec. Several times Delilah tried to wiggle her hand away from him, but he held tight, and she seemed reluctant to make a scene.

Alec didn't appear the least surprised by any of it, but then he was a specialist when it came to espionage equipment. "Probably a Minicam," he said. He put his large hand on the side of Delilah's neck and bent to look her in the eyes. "You okay?"

She didn't so much as glance at Mick. "I'll survive."

Alec considered that, holding her gaze for a stretch of time, then shook his head. "I think you should go on home with Mick. Let me check things over here and... No?"

She shook her head. "I'm not going home with Mick."

"Yes, you are," Mick told her. "Alec, I just need a sec to talk to her."

Her gaze glued to Alec's, Delilah bared her teeth in what she probably thought looked like a confident smile, but instead showed her tension. "I'm *not* going home with Mick."

Alec raised his brows, waiting for Mick's response. He was saved from that fate when pounding footsteps sounded on the stairs. They all moved at once, Mick again shoving Delilah behind him while drawing his gun, and Alec stationing himself in front of them both.

Josh and Zack skittered to a halt at the sight of them blocking the hallway.

"Uh, we decided you could use some backup," Josh explained.

Mick growled, knowing Josh thought he couldn't apologize to Delilah correctly on his own.

Delilah mistook him, though. From behind Mick she muttered meanly, "Some watchdog you are if you need those two."

Mick turned to frown at her.

Alec sighed.

More footsteps sounded. Dane, gun in hand and arm extended, reached the top of the stairs in a crouch. Everyone blinked at him.

Alec said, "You got my message."

"Yeah." Dane came to his feet and tucked the gun away in a shoulder holster. "What's going on?"

Delilah stepped around Mick, glaring at all five men. "Do you all run around town armed?"

Josh and Zack shook their heads. "Of course not."

Alec, Dane and Mick said at the same time, "Yeah."

She turned away in exasperation. "I need to finish packing."

"Packing?" Josh asked, his tone filled with alarm.

"You're going somewhere?" Zack tried to step in front of her.

Alec caught her by the back of her shirt, then quickly held up both hands when she rounded on him. "Don't slug me, just listen up, okay? You can be pissed off at Mick all you want. Hell, I would be, too."

"Me, too," Josh and Zack said almost in unison, earning Mick's glare.

"But," Alec continued, "you have to think here. Don't go putting yourself in danger just to spite yourself. I don't know where you intended to go, but with everything we've just found out, even you have to realize you need someone who can protect you."

Dane crowded closer. "Just what the hell is going on?"

Mick groaned. "God, I'm getting tired of explaining this."

"Then let me." Delilah drew herself up, and she wore the meanest expression Mick had ever seen. It relieved him, because at least some of the shock, some of the hurt, had been replaced. "Mick went to the hospital to see Rudy Glasgow."

"He's awake?" Dane asked.

"Yeah," Mick said. "Unfortunately, he is."

"While there," Delilah continued, "Rudy convinced him that I was part of his little gang, a criminal to be arrested."

Her tone was so nasty, the men all held perfectly still as if frozen by her censure.

"You see, Rudy knew personal stuff—and no,

none of you need details—about what we'd done here in the apartment.''

''In the bedroom,'' Zack supplied, earning a hot glare from Delilah.

''So, of course,'' she practically sneered, ''Mick had to believe the worst about me.''

Mick swallowed hard. She'd have them all lynching him before she finished. Already Josh was seething again, and Zack kept giving him reproachful looks. Dane and Alec just seemed resigned. ''Delilah—''

''He convinced his connections in the police department to have me picked up for *questioning*.''

Everyone looked at everyone else. Dane ventured, ''Connections?''

Mick shook his head. ''Never mind.'' Delilah didn't yet know he was a cop, and he had a feeling now wasn't a good time to tell her. He had enough amends to make without confessing his own deception.

''She thinks her apartment is bugged,'' Alec finished for her, cutting to the chase, ''which would explain things.''

''Ah.'' Dane nodded. ''That'd make sense, I guess.''

''It explains it better than thinking she had a hand in that damned robbery,'' Josh pointed out unnecessarily.

Zack elbowed him hard.

Defensive, Delilah crossed her arms over her middle and repeated, ''I am not going home with Mick. I can take care of myself.''

"You know," Alec said, his lowered brows making him look more than a little fierce, "this could have all been a ploy. Why tell Mick you were involved unless someone wanted him to get angry with you, to walk away from you?"

"Which would leave you alone and unprotected," Dane finished for him. He nodded. "Someone wants to get to her, but that's impossible with Mick watching over her. So they instigated this little separation."

Still determined, Delilah said, "I have a deadline."

"Good Lord," Mick muttered, unable to believe she'd be concerned with that now.

"I don't have time to debate with you. I just want to get settled down and finish my work."

"Someone is after you, damn it!"

Even when Mick shouted at her, she didn't meet his gaze. She stared down at her feet and said, "I'll be very careful."

She turned toward the apartment door, and again she got pulled up short. Josh, standing tall and resolute beside her, held her arm. "If you don't want to go home with Mick, come to my place."

Raging jealousy shot through Mick. Growling, he took an aggressive step forward, and both Alec and Dane flattened a hand on his chest, stalling him.

Delilah smiled in regret. "I can't do that, Josh. I'd drive you crazy in an hour."

"Not so."

She shook her head stubbornly. "No, it's out of the question. I wouldn't consider imposing on you."

"Then come home with me," Zack said. "Dani would love to have you there."

"No," she answered gently, looking a little amazed by the offers. "I don't sleep regular hours, and I'd be disruptive and—"

Dane shrugged. "You know you're welcome to our place, or to Alec's."

Alec nodded. "Absolutely."

"But either way, Delilah," Dane continued, "you can't be alone. It isn't safe."

Mouth open, she shook her head. "I don't believe this. You people hardly know me. You can't really want me underfoot. And if there is some type of danger, I could be bringing it to your homes!" She shook her head again, more violently this time, as if making a point. "No, I could never do that."

Dane turned to Mick. "Why don't you go in with Alec and look around? I'd like to speak to Delilah alone a second."

"About what?" Mick asked suspiciously, afraid Dane might bury him further. He was beyond pleased that everyone had jumped to her defense, had rushed to assist her, but he'd have been happier if she'd had no alternative but to give him another chance.

"About life and love and reality."

Josh grinned. "Can I listen in?"

"No." Dane caught Delilah's arm and dragged her toward the steps. "This'll only take a minute."

DELILAH WENT GRUDGINGLY. Truth was, she didn't know what to do. Her only plan had been to get out of the apartment. She felt…dirty. Not just from Mick's impossible and hurtful accusation, but by the sickening possibility that someone had been watching her, someone had seen her making love to Mick. She shuddered with revulsion.

Dane put his arm around her shoulders and stopped at the landing at the bottom of the stairs. It was slightly cooler here, but not much. She felt hot and irritable and irrevocably wounded.

"You asked why any of us would want to take you in."

"I've never known people like you," she admitted, glad for something to think about besides the invasion of her privacy.

"We'd do it for Mick. We love him, and it's obvious you're important to him. He'd go out of his head if he screwed up this badly and something happened to you. I don't want to see him hurt that way. He's been hurt enough in his life."

The thought of Mick suffering because of her made her sadder than ever. Damn it all, she still loved him—and that was sheer stupidity on her part. Nursing her hurt, she said, "Yeah, he cares so much he thinks I'd get him shot."

"Men in love do stupid things. Our brains get all muddled. It's not what we expect, and we don't know how to deal with it."

"He's not in love."

"Wanna bet?"

"He's never said so."

"In words, maybe. But from the start he's been fascinated with you."

She scoffed, and Dane added gently, "Delilah, he took a bullet for you."

She shrugged off that irrefutable fact. When he'd

thrown himself on top of her, he hadn't even known her name, so he couldn't have had feelings for her then. And since then…well, since then everything had been too fast. She was confused, so no doubt he was, too. "Mick is a hero," she reasoned. "He'd do that for anyone."

Dane laughed. "I agree, he's pretty damn heroic. But he's still human, so you have to allow him some human faults. Like bad judgment on occasion, and jumping to conclusions. And acting before he's really thought things out—which is what I think happened today."

"Do you have any idea how badly it hurts for him to think that of me?" Her heart, once full to bursting with love for Mick, now felt cold and hard, a dull ache in her chest.

"Yeah, I do. I made the same mistake with my own wife once."

That got her attention. Delilah stared at him, fascinated.

"It's a long story," Dane said, "and I won't bore you with the details now, but I let her think I was my deceased twin, because I thought she'd had a hand in trying to murder him."

Delilah felt her mouth drop open, her eyes widen. "That sounds more outrageous than the stuff I put in my books."

Dane winced. "I know." Then he smiled. "I fell in love with Angel before I got around to telling her the truth. When it all came out in the open, she hated me. Or at least I thought she did. *She* certainly thought she did. Circumstances not a lot different from what you're dealing with now kept her with me. And it gave us a chance to work things out.''

''You think I should go home with Mick so he can make amends?''

''I think you should give your relationship every chance to work out the ugly mistakes. It's not like you two met under normal circumstances. You've been shot at, he's been wounded, someone is obviously after you for some reason—that's enough in itself to make any relationship difficult.''

''I guess.''

Dane hugged her close. ''One more thing. Mick wouldn't risk his life for just anyone. From what he said, he was already mesmerized by you before the shooting. He'd watched you, and thought about you. I understand it happens that way sometimes.''

She rubbed her face, so tired and washed-out and confused she could barely order her thoughts enough to keep talking. ''I don't know.''

''You're feeling muddled, too,'' Dane pointed out, while gently rubbing her back. ''All the more reason you should give things a chance. Go to his place, rest up, talk. I'm not saying to forgive him tonight, but at least let the opportunity exist for him to make it up to you. Give him a chance to explain. Who knows? Maybe he'll say something profound and you'll be able to forgive him.''

They heard a noise and looked up the stairs. Mick stood at the top. Had he heard their conversation? His gaze on Del, he said, ''We found something.''

''We'll be right there.'' Dane put his arm around her and started her walking. ''It's been a rough day.

Wouldn't you like to go sit down and let your mind rest for a few minutes?''

Mick waited for them, watching Del closely with his intense, probing gaze. He almost seemed to be holding his breath, he stayed so still.

"Delilah?"

The gentleness, the hope in the way he whispered her name, broke Del's resolve. She nodded. "I'll go with you."

He let out his breath in a rush.

"But this doesn't mean I forgive you."

He nodded. "I haven't forgiven myself. For now I just want to get you settled and know you're safe." Then to Dane he said, "It's an optic fiber Minicam. High-tech stuff, run from the apartment next door."

Dane halted in midstep. "Next door?"

"Led in through the vents on the connecting walls." He glanced at Del, and she could feel his suppressed rage. He held himself in check for her, but he was more furious than she'd ever seen him. "Which included all the rooms except the kitchen and the bathroom."

Thinking of the eyes that had been on her, watching her while she wrote, slept, while she made love with Mick, made her stomach lurch. In the next instant Mick was there, gathering her close despite the trouble between them. "I'll find them, babe, I swear."

Giving herself a brief respite from her pride, Del rested her head on his shoulder. God, it felt good to have him hold her again.

When Dane went ahead into her apartment, Mick led her toward Josh and Zack. He touched her chin, bringing her gaze up to his. "I think it'd be best if you waited in my car. I'll only be a minute."

Josh threw his arm around her shoulder—and Mick promptly removed it. He said under his breath, "You've pushed enough today, Josh."

Josh just grinned, and Del had no idea what they were going on about.

"Have you ever noticed the neighbors next door?" Alec asked Del as he reentered the hall.

She gathered her scattered emotions. Now was no time to fall apart. "I know most everyone else in the building, but I thought that apartment was vacant."

"Does your landlord live here?"

"Afraid not." She wrung her hands, still shaken by having her worst suspicions confirmed. "I can call him if you want to check it out."

Mick shook his head. "We'll need to notify Faradon. He'll get a search warrant."

Del looked from one male face to another. "So what do we do now?"

"We get you settled and safe." Mick's eyes narrowed. "And then I'm going to see Rudy again."

CHAPTER TWELVE

DELILAH WAITED INSIDE Mick's house while he carried in her computer equipment, which she'd insisted on bringing along. Alec had checked the hardware and software for bugs and declared everything clean, so there was no reason for her to miss her deadline.

A severe headache left her somewhat nauseous, but she wasn't sure what to do. She'd never been in Mick's home before. Whenever he'd needed something, she'd offered to bring him home, but he'd always gotten someone else to take care of it.

Now she realized why. He hadn't wanted her inside his personal domain. That would have been too close to suit him. He wanted to keep her as distant as he could while still being intimate with her. And she, like a fool, had given him the perfect opportunity by moving him into her apartment.

"Where would you like me to put it?"

She turned to see Mick standing in the doorway, his arms filled with her monitor and keyboard, watching her. Josh and Zack stood behind him, loaded down with more equipment.

Del glanced around and shrugged. "I guess the bar counter would work as well as anywhere."

Mick didn't move, even though Zack and Josh

were making impatient noises behind him. "You can use my desk."

"No, thanks." She walked away. The last thing she wanted was to further invade his privacy.

Almost an hour passed before they had her settled in. Dane had trailed them during the move, watching to make certain they weren't followed. The whole thing seemed very cloak-and-dagger to Del. Despite her profession, she'd never expected to be on the receiving end of a real mystery. Mysteries were figments of her imagination, not reality.

Mick's house, moderate in size, probably forty years old, had a quaint coziness about it. Del stood at the kitchen sink looking out the window. His backyard faced a cul-de-sac, and some distance away she could see a pool filled with playing children, another family grilling out on their patio. It all seemed so…domestic. Hard to believe she was here because someone wanted her dead.

Zack slipped his arms around her and rested his chin on top of her head. "You'll be all right."

She patted his hands where they crisscrossed her waist. One thing she'd realized through all this was that Josh and Zack were now her friends, too. She cherished that fact. "You think so?"

"I know there's no way in hell Mick's going to let anything happen to you."

She laughed at that. "Oh, I dunno. He just might decide I'm a criminal again and hand me over to them."

"Nope, ain't gonna happen. You've thrown him for a loop is all, and believe me, that's not easy to do.'' He kissed her temple, then asked, "Did I ever tell you how hard it was to make friends with him?"

She shook her head.

"He was so closed off, so damned isolated from everyone and everything. Because the fire department and the life squad are located right next door to each other, Josh and I were friends before we ever met Mick. But we all ate at Marco's and every day we'd see Mick sitting there alone. He'd just eat and leave."

It wasn't a pleasant image, his self-imposed isolation, and Del's heart softened in spite of her efforts to the contrary.

"One day some guys came in drunk and started causing problems." Del heard an odd note of enthusiasm in Zack's tone. "They were loud, disruptive, making a mess and scaring off customers. It was interesting, watching Mick go on alert, seeing how he took it all in and waited to make a move, without even appearing to notice. A waitress asked the men to leave, and one of the guys stood and took an aggressive stance. There were four of them, but Mick never hesitated to jump to her defense.

"He told the guy—nicely—to back off. A punch was thrown, and within seconds, Mick had the guy flattened. The others tried to rush him, three against one, but Mick didn't have any problem handling them." Zack chuckled. "He sure got Josh's respect that day."

"You two didn't help him?"

"He didn't give us a chance," Zack claimed defensively. "At least not with the actual fight. But afterward Josh insisted on buying him a drink—*insist* being the operative word, because Mick was hell-bent on keeping to himself—and the rest is history. It still took us half a year to get him to loosen up, to finally realize we weren't in cahoots with the bad guys. But we've been pretty close ever since.''

"You're saying Mick doesn't come by trust easily?"

"You have to get him there kicking and screaming.''

She smiled, thinking that a pretty apt picture. "Why?"

"Now that's something you'll have to ask Mick.''

"I'm glad you're not telling *all* my secrets, Zack.''

Zack gave Del a reassuring squeeze and turned to face Mick with a grin. "Just trying to help out.''

Josh stood next to Mick. "Good luck. I just got read the riot act for that very same thing.''

"You," Zack said, "had it coming.''

Mick actually smiled. "You know, Zack, sometimes it's hard as hell to tell whose side you're on.''

"I'm on the side of the right and just.'' He saluted Mick. "I suppose you're ready for us to make our exit?''

"I wouldn't be that rude.''

Josh snorted. "He told me to get the hell out.'' So saying, Josh went to Del and hugged her right off her feet. "If he gives you any problems, call me.''

Over Josh's shoulder, Del saw Mick's expression harden, and she quickly disengaged herself. "I'll be fine.''

Josh teased, "But just in case…''

Zack grabbed him by the back of his shirt and

dragged him away. "I need to get home for Dani, so we'll see you both later. Mick, if you need anything, just let us know."

Mick didn't answer; he was too busy watching Del.

She shifted uncomfortably, then heard the front door close. *Now what?* she wondered.

Mick came a step closer to her. She felt hemmed in by his imposing silence and the cold sink at her back.

She wasn't sure what she expected, but he only said, "You look exhausted. Why don't you take a warm shower while I hook up all your computer stuff? Or are you hungry? I can fix you something to eat."

She shook her head, very unsure of herself and the situation. "A shower sounds nice. But I...I don't know where it is."

Appearing pained, he closed his eyes, then opened them with a rueful sigh. "I'll show you around."

It was a two-bedroom house with hardwood floors and a small cream-and-black tiled bathroom. He showed her his bedroom, his air watchful, then the guest bedroom across the narrow hallway. Del peeked into both rooms.

His dark gaze pierced her careful reserve. "You can use whichever room you want." Unnamed emotions deepened his voice.

"Where will you sleep?"

"Wherever you want me to."

Well, heck. That put the decision back on her, and she felt too unsteady to force the issue at the moment.

She gestured toward the smaller room. "I'll use this one."

With no inflection whatsoever, Mick said, "All right. I'll put your things in there." He led her back into the bathroom. "Towels are in the linen closet right here, and shampoo and stuff is already on the tub ledge."

He started to turn away and she reached for him. The muscles in his forearm tightened when her hand closed around his wrist. "Mick?"

He looked from her hand to her face. "Yeah?"

Del wanted to groan. He was so stiff, so…formal. She had a feeling he was trying not to pressure her, but she wished he would… No, she didn't know what she wanted.

"Is there any chance they know where you live?"

"No. We weren't followed today. Dane made sure of that, and I trust him. And only my closest friends, and the people I work with, have my address."

"But…"

In the briefest of touches, his fingertips grazed her cheek. "I've got a lot of explaining to do, honey. I wanted to wait until I got you here, so you couldn't change your mind about staying with me. But now I think I have to come clean."

Del stiffened. "If you're going to hurt me again, Mick Dawson—"

"No." His fingers tunneled into her hair, stroking her warmly. "I swear, I'll do my best never to hurt you again. But what I have to say will probably make you madder than hell."

She could deal with mad, she supposed. "All right."

"Take your shower, get comfortable, then we'll sit down and lay everything out in the open."

She wasn't at all sure she liked the sound of that, but figured he was right. From here on out, she wanted, demanded, honesty. If he couldn't give her that, they had nothing.

MICK GAVE A SATISFIED NOD. He'd managed to accomplish a lot while she showered. But then, she'd stayed in there forever. Too many times to count he'd wanted to check on her, to make sure she wasn't crying or upset, but he knew getting too close to her while she was naked and wet would be his downfall.

So he clenched his teeth and worked. He had her computer, printer and fax machine all set up in a neat little organized corner. He'd given her his own padded desk chair, and taken one from the dinette set for himself. He'd hung her clothes in the closet, changed the sheets on the guest bed—a bed that had never been used. Canned chicken noodle soup simmered on the stove.

He'd called his sergeant and explained things, and spoken with both Faradon and Dane. Unfortunately, the apartment next to Del's was indeed empty, but they had been able to get some fingerprints. Running them would take some time.

Mick had just finished cutting two sandwiches into halves when Delilah walked in.

Her wet hair was combed straight back from her forehead and she'd pulled on loose shorts and a

T-shirt. Barefoot as usual, she padded toward him and pulled out a chair. "I hadn't realized I was hungry, but the soup smells good."

Mick was so tense even his knuckles hurt as he put some soup in a bowl and set it before her. They ate in silence. When she was almost finished, he said, "I'm not a private investigator."

Her head lifted, her eyes wide and cautious. "You're not?"

Because he couldn't stop himself, Mick pushed his bowl aside and took her hand. "At first I lied out of necessity. I can't tell everyone the truth, that's just a fact of my job. Why I continued to let you believe the lie, I'm not sure. I told myself that we didn't know each other well enough. Too many things didn't add up." He met her beautiful blue eyes and admitted, "Actually, I think I was just afraid."

"Of me?"

He looked down at their clasped hands. She was so small boned, so delicate despite her height. She had a willowy appearance, and he wanted nothing more than to protect and cherish her. "It isn't easy to admit, but you scare the hell out of me."

Time stretched taut while she pondered those words. She turned her hand in his and returned his hold. After taking a deep breath, she said, "Okay, so what do you really do?"

"I'm a cop. I work undercover."

She stared at him, silent.

"I'd just finished a bust when I met you, which is a good thing, since I don't have a medical release to get back to work yet, and I hate turning over a case to someone new. It screws up the work that's already been done.''

Still holding his hand, Delilah rested her free arm on the table and leaned forward, her animosity and distrust replaced by curiosity. ''That's why you were armed?''

''Dane and Alec really are PIs. But yeah, I never go anywhere without my gun. Used to be a gun would make you stick out as a cop, but these days *not* having a gun would be a bigger giveaway. The world has turned into a nasty place.''

She chewed her bottom lip. ''What you do, is it dangerous?''

''Sometimes.'' Lying to her was no longer an option. ''I mostly deal with prostitutes and drugs and gambling. Because of what I do, I live well away from where I work.''

''I noticed.''

Of course she had. Delilah was no dummy, he thought with a sense of pride. Even more encouraging was the fact that she hadn't yet pulled away from him. He took hope. ''Rudy knew I was a cop. He said you knew and had told him.''

He felt her slight emotional withdrawal when she stated, ''But now you know that isn't true.''

He rubbed his thumb over her knuckles, trying to soothe her. ''I assume he heard me on the phone, talking to my sarge while I was at your apartment.''

''Where was I?''

''The shower, the bed, involved in writing.''

''Oh.''

''Delilah...I'm sorry.''

"No, I understand."

"Do you? Because I sure as hell don't." Self-disgust rose in his throat. "That first night I spent with you, I should have told you the truth."

"As I remember it, that first night I was too busy seducing you," she said, her tone lighter, more accepting.

"And here I thought I was the seducer."

Her face suddenly paled and she swallowed. "All the while, someone watched us."

"Don't think about that." Mick wanted to pull her into his lap, to hold her close. Instead, he redirected her thoughts. "If one of Rudy's cohorts did hear me, they still wouldn't know I was undercover. The station protects my identity."

Mick could see her researcher's mind at work. She frowned thoughtfully and said, "I think I understand how all this works, although I've never interviewed an undercover officer before."

"Now's your chance," he teased, so relieved that she wasn't angry, he almost felt weak.

"You drive your personal car to the station, but then trade up for an undercover car?"

"Not exactly. No uniforms ever know who's undercover. There's a special place where we switch cars, provided by the city. Once a car gets burnt up—"

"Burnt up?"

"Recognized." She nodded and he continued. "Then we get a new car."

"Something old and disreputable?" she asked, her

nose wrinkling at the thought even as her eyes lit up with interest.

He shrugged. "Sometimes. But sometimes we get a fancy car. You never know. It depends on the case."

"You work with a partner?"

"Not exactly, but no one ever works without backup. We all carry pagers and cell phones—another common tool among criminals, thankfully. If something goes wrong, we have special codes we can dial to get help fast."

They talked for over an hour. Delilah surprised him with her understanding. But then maybe it was just her desire to learn about his profession that swayed her. He told her about how wires could be detected with special devices that ran through TVs. If the TV reception got wavy, meaning it had picked up the wire's reception, a perp might know he'd been set up, and things could get hazardous real quick.

Mick told her about his jump-out bag. It held a mask to cover his face when he made arrests, so the perps wouldn't recognize him. And about his vest, which he wore even when it was ninety degrees outside. He described the SIG Sauer guns some punks carried, and the hollow-point bullets used to make a bigger wound.

Everything he told her, no matter how gruesome, only made her curious for more. In so many ways she delighted him, excited him, alternately brought forth his lust and his protectiveness.

When she started yawning, Mick stood to put their bowls in the dishwasher. "I think it's time for you to get some rest. After everything I put you through today, you have to be exhausted.''

He turned to see her rubbing her eyes tiredly. ''I'm wiped out.'' But she didn't stand, didn't make a move to go to bed. She just stared at her hands.

Mick closed the dishwasher and stood at her side. ''You don't have to be nervous here, Delilah. My house is secure, and Faradon has someone driving by every fifteen minutes. You're safe.''

''I know.'' Still she didn't move.

Mick knelt down beside her. ''What can I do?'' he asked. He searched her face, and wished like hell he had some answers. ''I know I can't make up for not trusting you, but I'll do whatever you need me to.''

She stared at his hand on her knee. ''You don't owe me. What you did…it's understandable. I just wish you'd talked to me first. Together we might have…''

''I'm a bastard, I know.'' He worked his jaw, then pointed out, ''You haven't yelled at me at all.''

Her slender shoulder lifted in a halfhearted shrug. ''At first I was too devastated to yell. Then too hurt. Now…well, now I understand.''

''I'd feel better if you'd yell.''

Her soft mouth curled at his words, which weren't quite facetious. ''There's no point to it.''

And Mick had to wonder if that meant she considered him a lost cause, not worth the effort of a good yell.

Time, he'd have to give her time. ''Come on. I think I'm ready for bed, too.''

Looking at him through her inky lashes, she stood.

He couldn't decipher her mood, and hated the helplessness he felt.

They went down the hall together, and Mick allowed himself to hold her for just a moment. He kissed her forehead and stepped away. "If you need anything, or want anything, I'm right next door."

She nodded. "Good night."

Mick stared at that damn closed door for far too long before taking himself off to bed. He doubted he'd get any sleep, and in fact, he wasn't tired at all. His body hummed with tension, with leftover adrenaline.

He left his door ajar so he'd hear her if she called out. Lying there in the darkness, he went over all the possibilities, but couldn't come up with a good reason why Rudy would want her dead.

It had to be linked to Neddie Moran somehow. It was just too much of a coincidence for her to have known Neddie before he was killed, and for Neddie's death to have taken place so close to the attempt on her life.

Mick turned to the bedside table and picked up the phone. Hitting the lighted numbers, he called Faradon.

"It better be important," Faradon grumbled. It sounded to Mick like the man was eating, but then Faradon probably ate a lot. He was as big as a bear.

"Did you find any connection between Neddie Moran and Rudy Glasgow yet?"

"Nope, not a thing so far. But then it could be Neddie knew one of the other guys, and without their names, we're lost. The prints'll probably help. Don't worry, we'll keep digging. We're bound to turn up something soon.''

Frustrated, Mick had just replaced the receiver into the cradle and settled back when his door squeaked open.

Delilah's silhouette was outlined by the faint light coming through his windows. ''Mick?''

Mick's body thrummed to life as he propped himself up on one elbow. Unless his eyes deceived him, she wore only a T-shirt. He forced the raw hunger from his tone and asked as gently as possible, ''You okay, babe?''

She crept closer, hesitated. ''I don't want to sleep alone.''

Those softly spoken words had a startling effect on his libido, an even bigger effect on his heart. Mick lifted his sheet, inviting her into his bed.

She hurried the rest of the way to him and slipped in by his side. For a second, she kept a slight distance between them. Mick didn't move, didn't breathe, and then she turned to him and gripped him tight, and all the pent-up tension inside him exploded.

''CHRIST, I'M SORRY, so damn sorry,'' he murmured into her hair. His hold was tight and infinitely gentle.

Del cuddled closer, comforted by his scent, the warmth of his skin…. ''You're not wearing anything?''

He stilled, then said, ''I can put something on if you want.''

''No.'' She loved touching him, and she needed the feel of him right now. All of him. The hair on his chest provided a nice cushion for her cheek, and she nuzzled into him. "Just hold me, okay?"

He turned to face her, drew her closer into his body so that he surrounded her, protected her. Always. Del felt a fat tear sting the corner of her eye. God, he was always trying to protect her.

"Does it bother you?" she whispered into the darkness, into the safety of his nearness.

"Hell, yes." His large hand opened on the back of her head, his rough fingertips sinking in to cradle her scalp, massage, soothe. "When I think of those bastards looking at you, I want to kill them. I *could* kill them."

Del sniffed and laughed and continued to cry softly. She was so damned confused. "No," she chided, wanting to hear him, to borrow some of his strength. "I meant does it bother you that they saw *you*. Your privacy was invaded as much as mine."

"I hadn't thought about it," he said. "At first I was just blind with…"

"Rage? Because you thought I had lied to you?"

He shook his head, then nuzzled her shoulder and squeezed her until she squeaked. "I hate to admit it," he rumbled against her throat, "but you deserve the truth. Ugly as it might be, regardless of how damn asinine I feel about it."

"The truth?"

"It wasn't rage I felt first, but this awful drowning hurt." He pressed his mouth to the skin of her throat, her shoulder. "There aren't many people in this world who could hurt me. But thinking that you'd used me, that you were laughing at me…it knocked my legs out from under me. It was all I could do to get the hell out of Rudy's hospital room without ripping him apart.''

Del turned her face to his. ''I'm sorry,'' she said very softly, and meant it.

''Oh God, don't. Don't apologize to me!'' He sat up and switched on a light, shocking her, making her blink against the glare of it. ''You should slap my face, Delilah. Or curse me or…hell, I don't know what. But don't apologize.''

She looked up at him, her eyes welling with emotion, and his expression crumbled.

''Oh, babe, no, don't cry.''

That got her laughing again, a wobbly, pathetic laugh. ''Don't apologize, don't cry.'' She sniffed, and gratefully accepted the tissue he handed to her. She blew hard before continuing. ''I've thought about it, and I can see why you believed Rudy. We haven't really known each other that long, not long enough for unconditional trust.''

She scooted up to sit against the headboard. ''Trust doesn't really come easy to me, either.''

''Tell me what to do,'' Mick said, touching her cheek to remove one lingering tear. ''Tell me how to prove to you that I *do* trust you.''

She blinked. ''Do you?''

He settled himself beside her, and their shoulders touched. Del had the sheet to her chin, but Mick barely had it covering his lap. Even now, in a vortex of emotions, he stole her breath away. He folded his hands over his abdomen and stared at the far wall.

''Damn right I trust you,'' he said. ''I think it was

myself I didn't trust all along. But you…almost from the minute I saw you, I wanted you. You drew me like no one ever had, and that shook me because I wasn't used to anyone affecting me like that." He glanced down at her. "It's scary the way you make me feel."

Del lifted his left arm over her shoulder and curled into his side again. "Okay?"

His arm tightened. "Better than okay."

"Will you tell me about your childhood?" She felt him stiffen, felt the stillness that came over him, body and mind.

"Why do you want to know?"

"To try to understand. I've gotten the impression it wasn't great, but that kid's a part of you."

"No."

"You can't run away from your past, Mick. All you can do is deal with it."

"I've dealt with it," he muttered.

Del knew she was pushing, but it was important to her to know all of him, the good and the bad. "Then you shouldn't have any problem sharing with me." To force the issue, she added, "Since you trust me."

"That has nothing to do with trust."

"Of course it does!" Again she twisted to look at him, but he pressed her head back to his shoulder. Del grinned. "You know, even Neddie trusted me enough to confide in me. He told me about his past and things he'd done, things he regretted."

This time Mick turned her face up to him. His fingers were hard, firm on her chin. "What things did he tell you?"

"You first."

"Delilah…"

She only raised a brow, waiting.

He sighed, gave a slight shake of his head and then kissed her forehead. He settled back, and though his pose was relaxed, she felt the rigid way he held himself. "Family services took me away from my mother twice. The first time it happened, I was about five. She'd gone out partying and hadn't come back, and a neighbor reported her."

Covering her shock and her sympathy, Del asked, "How long was she gone?"

"All weekend. In those days, other than her disappearing every now and then, it wasn't so bad. The house stayed kinda picked up and she had a regular job and she still seemed to…like me."

Seemed to like me. Del's heart cried out at the hurt he must have felt. She smoothed her hand over his chest and kept quiet.

"They gave me back to her easy enough, and I was glad. Sometimes being with her was rough, but it was nothing compared to not knowing what would happen, or being stuck with strangers. My mother promised to take some classes, to get into rehab for her drinking, and voilà—I was back home."

"Were things any better then?"

He laughed. "They got worse, actually. She was embarrassed that her neighbors knew I'd been taken away, so we moved. She got a new boyfriend and started drinking even more, but she was careful to put on a good show for the folks who checked up on her.

It was another couple of years before things really went down the toilet."

Del cringed at the idea of something worse than a mother neglecting her son for an entire weekend, but again she kept silent, wanting him to talk.

"My mother had an affinity for drink first, and men second. She moved them in and out of our house, but none of them ever contributed, and most of them didn't care to see me too often. Until I was about twelve, I tried to just stay out of sight. But then her liver went bad and she got really sick, and the guy who was with her at the time took her to the hospital. She had to stay awhile, and he skipped out, so family services had me again. That was the worst. I mean, at five I probably needed looking after. But at twelve? I'd have been fine on my own, and when they finally let her out of the hospital I knew I had to take over or I'd get taken away from her for good. Not that I'd have missed her much, but..." He shrugged.

"The familiar," Del said, "is almost always easier than the unfamiliar."

"Yeah." He smoothed his fingers up and down her bare arm for a few minutes, thinking. "I was bigger than her by then, so she couldn't close me off in my room anymore or use threats against me. I could out-run her, and smacking me hurt her worse than it did me. So I told her how things were going to be."

Del shivered at the harshness of those words, at the awful reality he'd faced at such a young age. "At twelve years old, you took charge?"

"Damn right. And she listened, and did as I said, because she knew otherwise I could get her arrested."

"How?"

"She had men in the house who were thieves and cons. She'd done a lot of stupid stuff while drunk, including prostituting herself for drinks, gambling with money we didn't have, accepting stolen goods in exchange for a room—usually to someone busy dodging the law. Our television, and for a while our car, were both stolen."

Del wondered if that was why he'd chosen to work Vice, because he'd already seen the other side of it.

"A lot of the men would make big promises, some even to me. They'd talk about taking care of her, buying things, but they all lied. Family services lied, too, always telling me things would get better. And she was the worst of all—she lied every damn time she said she loved me. After that, she'd always tell me not to say anything to anyone because she'd be taken away and I'd be left all alone." He laughed, a rough, humorless sound. "I knew it was bullshit all along. Whatever maternal instincts she'd had got drowned in a bottle early on. By the time I was twelve, she'd already pretty much wiped her hands of me, but my new conditions really finished things off."

He drew a long breath. "She did as I told her, and she hated me in the bargain."

Del hugged him tight. "What, exactly, did you tell her to do, Mick?"

CHAPTER THIRTEEN

"WE SOLD OUR HOUSE, which we were about to lose anyway, since she missed more and more work from drinking and couldn't make the payments. I didn't want to end up on the street, and neither did she. I checked around and found an apartment building—the one right next door to where you rent. It was a terrible area even then, but I used the money we made off the house to buy it, and the rent from the other apartments was income. I was in charge, taking applications from renters, collecting the rent, running ads when necessary."

"You did all that at twelve?"

"There weren't a lot of choices." He smiled down at her. "But it wasn't bad. Hell, it was the best it had been for a while. She stayed drunk and ran around with every Tom in town, but she knew better than to screw with the bill money. When I got old enough, I got a job and that helped, too."

"When did you meet Angel?"

His gaze brightened with a smile of genuine warmth. "She moved in when I was sixteen. Her first son, Grayson, was just a little-bitty squirt, and she'd been in a car wreck and was barely able to get around herself. I helped her out, and she started tutoring me in the school subjects I had problems with. Angel was…she was the type of woman I hadn't seen before. She didn't lie or make things up. If something needed to be done, she found a way to do it.''

Del felt more tears gather and quickly swiped them away. ''I know she loves you.''

''Yeah. She does. She thinks of herself as a big sister, or a surrogate mother, I guess.'' Mick reached over and tweaked Del's nose. ''Now, you talk about a role model, that's Dane. Alec, too. They're both great guys.''

She caught his hand and held it to her cheek. ''They say the same about you.''

Del kissed his palm, and he asked, ''Delilah, will you forgive me?''

She hesitated to be totally honest with him. She knew that she loved Mick, and she'd rather die than hurt him. But the night was quiet, the light low, and he deserved the truth. ''I can forgive you, because I understand.'' *I love you too much not to.* ''But I don't know that I'll ever feel the same again.''

He went rigid. ''What does that mean, Delilah?''

She wished he hadn't turned the light on. She'd have preferred the concealing darkness, which made confessions so much easier. ''Since the day I met you, I've seen you as bigger than life, a knight in shining armor, fearless.''

He snorted. ''That's nonsense. Hell, I just told you, *you* scare the hell out of me.''

She shook her head; nothing really scared Mick, she knew. And she certainly didn't have that type of power over him. If she had, he wouldn't have turned on her so easily. "I write about heroes every day, but I didn't know they existed. I didn't think any man would deliberately risk his life to keep someone else safe. I didn't know a stranger would risk his life, not for me."

He frowned over that.

"I saw you as…" she shrugged helplessly "…the best of everything."

Mick shoved away the sheet and stood. Gloriously naked, he stalked to the window and looked out at the black, balmy night. A large oak blocked what little moonlight there might have been. No leaves stirred; all was silent except for the bumping of her heart.

The faint light from the bedside lamp threw a glow along one side of his body, causing shadows to dip and swell over his muscles and bones, exaggerating his strength, which she already knew to be considerable. She wanted to touch him everywhere. She wanted to eat him up. And nothing, not even her hurt, could change that.

"I come from nothing, Delilah." His voice broke the night, harsh and raw. "For most of my life, I was nothing. Despite how they feel about it, I'm like a stray that Angel dragged home and everyone accepted. I owe Angel and Dane and their whole goddamn family for showing me what family is, for letting me know how a real life could be, and for helping me to get that life. I owe them for who I am now. But if you stripped them away and left me with just myself, with just the bare bones of *me,* I'd be back at square one. And that sure as hell isn't a white knight.''

''No!'' She struggled to her knees, clutching the sheet to her throat. ''You are who you are, Mick Dawson, a strong, capable man with or without anyone else.''

He whirled around. *''I am not a damn hero.''*

He looked livid, his eyes red, his nostrils flaring. Del stared.

''Don't you dare put me on some fucking pedestal,'' he growled, ''because I'm guaranteed to fall off. I'm human, and I blunder my way through life just like everyone else.''

When she remained silent, wide-eyed and stunned, he stomped back to the bed, caught her upper arms and lifted her from the mattress, causing her sheet to fall. She worried for his injured shoulder, and his injured soul.

''You thought I was impervious to cold, too, that I had insides made of iron.''

Del sputtered. ''Don't bring up my coffee now!''

''You don't know what I go through, how I fight every day to make sure I stay deserving.''

Deserving of what? she wanted to ask, but she couldn't. ''Mick...''

''To a lot of people, right and wrong are clear-cut values. But not to me. I force those ideologies into the front of my mind all the time—that a woman strung out on drugs is wrong, not just desperate. That a young man with a gun is a criminal, not a kid trying to survive. I don't even know what a white knight is, but I know what the rules tell me, and I follow those rules to the letter.''

Del swallowed her hurt. Looking at him, seeing his pain, hurt even more. "Did those rules tell you to protect me when you knew it might get you killed?"

His jaw clenched; his entire body tightened. But his hands didn't hurt her. She knew without a doubt that Mick would never, ever physically hurt her.

"An officer has to take action when he sees a civilian threatened."

She barely heard what he said. "Did those rules insist you turn me in because you thought I was breaking the law? Or did you do that because you thought I'd used you?"

He tipped his head back and groaned. "Both."

"Mick?" She needed to touch him, to soothe him, but his hold didn't allow for that. So she gave him the only words she knew that might help. "I forgive you."

His gaze jerked to hers, hot, burning, filled with relief, with satisfaction, greed, elation.

She saw the pulse racing in his strong throat, saw the muscles in his shoulders quiver, saw the glaze of relief in his eyes.

"I want you," he groaned. "More than I've ever wanted anything. More than I wanted my mother to care, more than I wanted Angel to be safe." He shook her slightly. "More than I want my next breath. But I'm just me, and if you try to make me more than that we'll both be disappointed."

Del licked her lips. It sounded to her like he loved

her, though he hadn't quite said so. "Do you want me now?"

He lifted her a few inches more until his mouth ground down on hers, bending her head back. His tongue thrust deep. Her body came into stark contact with his, making her aware of all his hard angles and firm muscles, and the long, hard length of his throbbing erection.

Just as quickly his kiss eased and he gentled his hold. His velvet tongue licked, teased, then slowly withdrew. "I'm sorry," he murmured against her mouth, nibbling on her lips, softening them. *"I need you."*

"Your shoulder," she said in alarm, fearing he'd hurt himself.

And Mick groaned again, a sound of half humor, half awe. "Even when I act like a marauding bastard, you don't put me in my place." His expression was less strained, and a half smile curled his mouth. "You're something else, Delilah Piper, you know that?"

"Something good?" she asked.

He smoothed her hair, stroked her lips with his thumb. "Something wonderful," he whispered, and then he kissed her again, this time with such sweetness, such love, she didn't even need to hear him speak the words. She couldn't resist him. He'd tell her what she wanted to hear sooner or later, but for tonight she had him, she had his confidences, and that was more than enough.

THE SECOND MICK AWOKE, he knew the other side of the bed was empty. He sat up in a rush, panic closing in—and saw Delilah sitting in the chair by the window. He eased back, but his heart continued to stutter and his stomach still cramped. "You couldn't sleep?"

A dark shadow made up her form in the gray, predawn light, and still he sensed her smile. "Watching you is more fun than sleeping."

He realized the sheet was around his ankles, and he cocked a brow at her. It was easier to breathe now, with her so obviously teasing. "Taking advantage of me?"

"Yes."

Mick stretched and yawned. With his initial alarm gone, he realized he felt better today, less frazzled, but not completely satisfied. He didn't think he'd be content until he had Delilah committed to him one hundred percent. And that meant getting a ring on her finger and hearing her say the vows.

When she was officially his wife, then maybe he could relax.

He'd made progress last night, though he hoped like hell she'd never put him through anything like that again. He hated rehashing the past. It shamed him, reminded him of how weak he'd been, how far he'd struggled. And whether Angel admitted it or not, he always knew he'd never have made it without her. If it hadn't been for Angel, he'd be on the other side of the law right now, the one being arrested for God only knew what, rather than a cop doing the arresting.

It was an emotional struggle he dealt with every day.

He heard Delilah sigh as he stretched his left arm

high, and grinned. She was so blatant about enjoying his body, both by touch and sight. He was glad he hadn't spent his life chasing women and screwing around like so many males seemed driven to do. It made their relationship that much more special. She was the only woman who'd ever lived with him.

"I thought you'd be writing," he said as he stood and went to his dresser to get some shorts.

She turned to watch him. He knew his way in the dark, but still he flipped on the wall switch, wanting to see her better.

She looked…dreamy.

"I didn't even think about writing."

He frowned, stepped into his gray boxers and went to her. She wore his shirt, and that turned him on. Of course, if she'd been wearing nothing at all, or the sheet, or her own T-shirt, he'd have still been turned on. She couldn't breathe without making him hard.

He stood looking down at her, dreading the question he had to ask. "Did I interfere with your work?"

"How so?"

He smoothed her glossy dark hair behind her ears, touched her arched brows. "You were so upset, I thought…"

"Oh, no. When I'm upset, I usually work through it at the computer. Same when I'm excited. Or sad."

Mick shook his head. Not much got in the way of her writing.

"It's just that last night was so wonderful. *You* were so wonderful." She sighed again, a sigh of repletion and fulfillment, making him feel like that damn white knight she'd spoken of.

Then she added, "I've been thinking, too, about Neddie, about some of the stories he told me."

Slowly, Mick straightened. "Let's do this over coffee."

"Do this?"

"I have a gut feeling that whatever you're going to tell me will be the clue we've been missing. I need caffeine to digest it all, so I don't miss anything important."

Delilah stood and did her own stretching. His pulse leaped. If this wasn't so important… He eyed the bed. But no, it *was* important, and he had to see to her safety first.

"This gut feeling of yours," she asked, "is it like a cop's sixth sense?"

Mick put his arm around her and led the way to the kitchen, flipping on the lights as he went. It was only five-thirty. It'd be another hour or so before the sun lit the sky. "I just know that somehow all this stuff is related."

She nodded, took a stool at the counter—evidently more than willing to have him wait on her, which he was glad to do. "I think it has to do with the story I'm working on."

"Your newest book?" He measured coffee and turned on the machine.

She nodded. "You got anything I can snack on? I'm starved."

He remembered she'd been too upset to eat much the night before, and guilt washed over him. He scrounged around until he found her a few cookies.

"I can put some eggs and bacon on, too," he offered, and she accepted with a mouthful of cookie.

"You talk while I cook," he said.

She waved the second cookie at him. "Neddie was trying to go straight, you know? A condition of his parole was that he continue to be counseled, and part of his counseling was to own up to the things he knew he'd done wrong. So he sometimes talked to me."

"You were supposed to absolve him of guilt?"

"Not even close." She chewed on her cookie, thinking, then shuddered. "He told me some gruesome stories," she admitted. "Stuff I could never use in a book. It was too…real, and you know what they say about truth being stranger than fiction. But in a way, Neddie had this odd code of honor. He didn't hurt anyone that he didn't think needed to be hurt. I mean, he didn't just choose innocent victims."

"He hired himself out, honey. He did what he was paid to do."

"I know." She brushed the remainder of the crumbs from her hands and watched Mick lay bacon in a hot skillet. "But he only took jobs that his conscience would let him take. Like this one guy he snuffed—"

"Snuffed?" Mick eyed her, appalled at the casual way she said that.

She shrugged. "It's part of the lingo."

Didn't he know it. "Go on."

"Anyway, the guy he killed had some huge gambling debts, but Neddie said he took the job because the guy also abused his wife."

Mick made a face. "What a discerning fellow."

Delilah laughed. "That's what I said to him. And he knew it was still wrong, but he said he half enjoyed beating that guy up and then dumping him for dead, because he hated anyone who would hit a woman."

"We're in agreement on that."

In a voice as soft as butter, she said, "I know."

Mick poked at the bacon with a fork. He couldn't take her hero worship on an empty stomach, so he steered her back to the subject at hand. "What does any of this have to do with your story?"

"Well, Neddie told me that these guys tried to hire him to kill a man because the guy knew too much and wanted to come clean. They were afraid he'd turn evidence on them or something, so they wanted Neddie to kill him, then sink his car in the river."

Mick jerked around, staring at her. A limp piece of uncooked bacon dangled from the fork in his hand.

"Neddie refused. Not only because he was out of the business and trying to go straight, but because he said he sympathized with the other guy. He said they were alike, both of them wanting to be legit, and there was no proof the guy would rat. After all, Neddie said he'd never ratted anyone out before."

This is it, Mick thought with a surge of triumph. *This is the link.*

"I told Neddie about how I'd learned to escape a car that had gone into the river, and he said I couldn't have escaped if I'd been dead before it went in." Delilah tilted her head at Mick, her beautiful, light blue eyes filled with a heavy sadness. "Is that what happened to Neddie? You said he was murdered, and I know he drowned. Did someone kill him, then drive his car into the river? The paper didn't give all the details. I didn't know you were a cop, so I didn't think you'd know, either. After all, it was supposed to be confidential stuff for the ongoing investigation.''

For the first time that he could remember since becoming an officer of the law, Mick didn't even consider what was right or wrong. He set a cup of coffee in front of Delilah and pulled out the stool next to her. Their bare knees touched, his on the outside of hers. ''Neddie's wrists,'' he explained carefully, ''had bruises on them, evidence that he'd been tied up, though there were no ropes or anything on him when his body was found.''

Delilah reached for his hand, and Mick squeezed her fingers.

''He had a wound on the back of his head, too. The coroner said he'd been struck with a blunt object, knocked out just before the car went off the bridge— or possibly as the car went over. It'd be impossible to tell for sure, but as you just said, he wasn't given the chance to escape the car and swim to the surface. We're thinking whoever did it hoped the car wouldn't be found until time and the natural effects of water and cold had done enough damage to disguise a deliberate murder.''

''He had a suicide note in his pocket?''

Mick nodded. ''Yeah.''

Her lips quivered, and she drew a ragged breath. ''That's exactly what Neddie described, what he said the men wanted him to do.'' She blinked away a sheen of tears, and whispered raggedly, ''I used that whole scenario in my book.''

"The book you're working on now?"

"Yes. In the last book, the hero got away by keeping his head and doing the things I'd learned from submerging myself in a car."

Mick shuddered. He could *not* think about that now. Somehow he'd figure out a way to temper Delilah's more dangerous inclinations, without stifling her.

"But in this book," she continued, oblivious to his turmoil, "he was knocked out, a suicide note planted on him, and the heroine had to save him."

Just like Delilah to twist things around, Mick thought. But then, if any woman were capable of a rescue, it'd be Delilah Piper. He wouldn't underestimate her on anything, once she set her mind to it.

It was an enormous long shot, but Mick asked, "That whole scenario is too damn close to the truth to be comfortable. Does anyone know what's in this book?"

She nodded. "Tons of people, I'm sure. Remember I told you I was on the news, discussing my current project? We talked about that whole scene. I…I was laughing about it, bragging that it could happen, and that a woman might indeed be a hero. I never once considered that I could be putting Neddie in danger."

"Neddie didn't know about the interview?"

"I don't know." She covered her face. "He died shortly after that. He…he might have died because of *me*. Someone could have heard that radio program, someone who knew we'd become friends, that Neddie coached me on my research."

"And they might have assumed he'd told you too

much, and that you could repeat it." If Mick thought he'd felt fear before, it was nothing to what he felt now. Someone wanted to shut her up, to make certain she couldn't repeat details that might be incriminating. But he didn't know who, and until he did know, until he could get the bastards, her life was at stake.

Delilah rocked slowly back and forth in her seat as the ramifications settled around her. "I'm to blame."

With a new fury, Mick tipped up her chin. "*Wrong.* Don't even go there, babe. When you live the type of life Neddie did, then you run the risks. That's just how it is."

"He was changing."

"Maybe just a little too late." Mick pulled her into his lap. "Did Neddie give you any names, anything that might connect him with the killers?"

She thought hard, staring down at her hands. Slowly her gaze rose to his. "You know, he did say something, but I'm not sure it'll help."

"At this point, it'd have to be more than we've got."

She nodded, her brows drawn. "He said the guys who wanted to hire him should have known better, because they'd been in prison with him in '86, all of them convicted for car theft."

It took several moments for it to sink in, before Mick allowed himself to believe. "Bingo."

"You think?"

"I think it'll be easy enough to check prison records. That might do it, with your testimony. Especially if the fingerprints from the apartment next to yours match up. We should have those today."

"Is that why they tried to kill me? They knew Neddie had been talking to me? They knew he'd...told me things?"

Mick hugged her. God, she was precious to him. And she was also smart, so there was no point in hoping to protect her. Besides, he didn't want her feeling guilty for Neddie's death, not if he could help it.

"The bruises on Neddie's wrists showed that he put up a hell of a fight, that he tried to work himself free. But he didn't make it." Mick kissed her temple, her ear. "Could be they promised to let him go if he named everyone he'd talked to."

She shook her head, adamant in Neddie's defense. "No, Neddie would never have done that, not if he thought they'd hurt me."

Her innocence amazed him. "How long did you know him, sweetheart?"

"A few months. But we were friends, Mick," she said staunchly.

"That's not enough time to really judge."

She leaned back and gave him a level look. "It's longer than I've known you."

Mick scowled, not appreciating that comparison at all. "He was an admitted murderer. A car thief. Those things are not synonymous with ethics, and any man could cave when his life was on the line."

"I won't believe that."

Mick decided to let it go. She'd been hurt enough, and disillusioning her now wouldn't accomplish a thing. "Let's finish up breakfast and shower, then I'll call Faradon. He should be up by then, and if not, well, he'll get up.''

"You really think any of this will make a difference?"

"I know it will."

"I hope so," she said. "I want this behind us. I want us to take walks in the park and go to the zoo, and I want to get back to my research.''

Mick groaned. He didn't know if he could live through her special brand of daredevil study.

But he knew he didn't want to live without her, so he supposed he'd find a way to get used to it.

CHAPTER FOURTEEN

THE PHONE RANG while Mick was in the shower. He'd insisted that Del go ahead while he cleaned the kitchen, and when she'd protested, he claimed it had to be that way. If he showered with her, they'd never leave his house.

She accepted that he probably was right.

With her hair still wet and her feet bare, Del picked up the phone. "Dawson residence."

"Faradon here. Is this Ms. Piper?"

"Yes," she said shortly. Detective Faradon still wasn't one of her favorite people, not after the interrogation she'd been through.

"We got the fingerprints back and have some photos to go with them. We'd like you to come to the station and take a look, see if you can ID anyone. How soon can you be here?"

She bristled at his demanding tone. At the very least, she felt the man owed her a few apologies. "Actually, Mick and I were coming in, anyway." She didn't mention her new "evidence" because she wasn't convinced it would help. Mick could explain everything.

There was a pause, then he asked, "How soon?"

"Mick is about done showering now. I'd say we'll leave here in the next fifteen minutes."

"I'll be waiting," he said, and rudely hung up.

A few minutes later Mick came out looking nicely rugged and sexy as sin in faded, well-worn jeans and a soft gray T-shirt. He wore scuffed, lace-up black boots. As Del watched, he checked his gun.

She inched closer. "Can I see?"

He glanced up. "What? My gun?"

Nodding, she said, "A Smith & Wesson, right? Semiautomatic?"

Mick held the gun out of her reach. "No one touches my gun but me."

She rolled her eyes. "I'm not going to fire it. And I do know a little about guns."

"Research, I suppose?"

"Yes."

"Well, then you know enough to understand how dangerous they are." With a dexterity that proved how quickly he was healing, he tucked the gun into a holster at the small of his back, and smoothed his T-shirt over it. "And," he said again, "*no one* touches my gun but me."

"Fine. Whatever."

He caught her before she could turn away, and kissed her neck. It was shameful, but she immediately softened, just as he'd probably known she would.

"Who was on the phone?" he asked against her throat.

Sometimes it was annoying, loving Mick. She couldn't seem to stay angry with him, especially when he kissed her. "Your buddy, Faradon."

"He's not my buddy, he's just the lead investigator on the robbery and shooting." He kissed her again, this time nuzzling beneath her ear. It felt like her toes melted. "What did he want?"

Struggling to get her brain in gear, she succeeded in saying, "He has fingerprints and photos, and he wants us to come take a look for a positive ID."

Stepping back from her, Mick looked at the chunky black watch on his wrist. "Hell, it's barely eight o'clock. He's at it early."

Feeling hopeful for the first time, Del asked, "Do you think that means we're close to having this wrapped up?"

Mick took her arm and headed for the door. "Even with an ID, we'd still have to get hold of them, but it'd sure make it easier to track the bastards down. It's tougher to hide when everyone knows who you are. There's also the possibility that Rudy'll be more willing to talk once we have names."

The sun never did quite rise. Instead, as they stepped outside, they saw that fat purple clouds had rolled in, leaving the air heavy with the scent of rain. In the distance, lightning flickered.

Mick cursed. "Did you want to grab a jacket or umbrella?"

"I won't melt."

She saw his surprise, then his smile, as he opened the car door for her. "I'd forgotten your affinity for rain," he said.

When she raised a brow, he explained, "The day I finally met you, the day of the robbery. Everyone else had an umbrella, but you didn't even seem to notice how soaked you'd gotten.'' He slid his hand over her waist and squeezed suggestively. "I noticed."

Del smiled at that. It was nice being reminded that the awesome attraction went both ways. If Mick had indeed noticed her when she looked like a used rag mop, then his interest was as keen as hers. Maybe more so, because she hadn't paid him a bit of mind until the shooting.

Once he folded his big body behind the wheel, she told him, "I love running in the drizzling rain. It's peaceful and it stimulates my muse."

He started to make a nasty crack, no doubt about stimulating her, and Del elbowed him. They both laughed and she thought how nice it was, how right, to be with Mick this way. She wondered, once everything was settled, what would happen. When it was no longer necessary for her to stay with him for protection, would he ask her to leave? Would he ask her to stay?

Half an hour later she was still pondering that when the sky opened up. No slight drizzle this, but a raging summer storm full of power. The stuffy, humid air came alive with electricity, crackling and snapping all around them. Trees bent and dipped, leaves and debris danced across the rain-washed roadways.

Del slanted Mick a look. "Rainstorms are sexy," she whispered.

"You're sexy. Rain or no rain," he replied, keeping his gaze on the road.

She grinned, about to tell him how she'd like to spend the afternoon once they finished at the station, when they were blinded by a sudden glare. In the darkness of the morning storm, an approaching car's bright lights reflected off Mick's door. He flinched, throwing up a hand, but it didn't help. The car came from an empty side street, and rather than slowing, it accelerated to a reckless speed across the slick roadway, coming right for them.

Mick glanced out his window, gripped the wheel tightly and muttered with icy calm, "Hold on."

The car struck the back side-panel, throwing them into a spin. Del's seat belt tightened; she yelped in alarm, barely keeping her wits enough to twist around, trying to see what happened.

At the force of impact, Mick first overcompensated, and the car slewed off the road and into the mud before grasping the slick pavement again.

Del, assuming it was an accident—a result of the rainy conditions—wondered why Mick didn't just pull over. She looked over her shoulder, wide-eyed, in time to see the other car straighten and shoot toward them again.

Mick's hand flattened on the top of her head, and he shoved her down in the seat. "Stay there!"

The rear windshield exploded, glass flying everywhere. "Dear God!" Del held Mick's thigh, her face pressed into his side. This couldn't be happening! She tried to sit up, wanting only to protect Mick.

"Keep down," Mick barked, again flattening her in the seat. It suddenly hit her who was after them and why.

Del felt another impact, this time to the rear fender of the car, and there was no way to steer out of it. The car swerved off the road, slinging mud and fishtailing, and finally colliding with a scrawny tree, jarring them both hard.

Mick's head hit the wheel and he slumped.

"Mick!" She screamed his name, scrambling to get her seat belt off, to reach him. Her heart leaped into her throat, her vision clouded with fear. Before she could reach him her door was jerked open. The thunderous roar of the storm intruded, along with a spray of rain and turbulent air. Hard hands grabbed her, yanking her back. She fought them, seeing the trickle of blood on Mick's forehead, the stillness in his body.

He needed help, a hospital! But already her feet were being dragged through the mud, and no matter how she fought, she couldn't escape. The hands holding her only tightened with bruising force.

Someone grabbed her hair and wrenched her head back. "Do you want me to go back and put a bullet in him to make sure he's dead?"

That voice was rough, familiar, and Del froze, choking on her terror. "No."

"Then come along and be quiet."

A hard shove landed her facedown in the front seat of the other car, and she barely had time to right herself before two men squeezed in around her. The battered car had been left running, idling roughly. The interior smelled of smoke and stale liquor. It was dirty, cluttered.

The man on her right pressed a gun to her ribs, hard enough to make her groan, and with enough intent to scare her witless. She recognized them as the same men from the jewelry store—the men who wanted her dead.

"What do you want?" she asked around her fear, wanting, needing Mick. *Dear God, please let him be all right.*

"Shut up."

The car lurched away, tires squealing, zigzagging with a distinct lack of caution for the weather and road conditions. Wet tendrils of hair stuck to Del's face and throat. She swiped them aside and twisted to see Mick's car as they made a screeching U-turn and sped away. Right before he was out of view, she could have sworn she saw him lift his head, but it was hard to tell with the rain streaking the dirty windows and the strobing effects of the electrical storm.

Del closed her eyes on another silent prayer. Mick *had* to be okay. The gun prodded her when they made a sharp turn, keeping her own danger in acute perspective. She felt icy cold inside and out, and couldn't stop the racking shakes that made her teeth chatter and her head hurt.

Keep them talking, she thought. "How did you know where to ambush us?" she asked.

Smirking, the man lifted his hand to his head, finger and thumb extended as if it were a phone. "This is Faradon," he mimicked. "We need you to come to the station."

Her stomach roiled. "You had us bugged again?" Had these disgusting men heard Mick's heartfelt admissions about his past? She couldn't bear it.

"Nope. I didn't overhear the call, I *made* the call. Your protector was rather accommodating, sharing his home number with Faradon and asking him to leave any messages concerning the robbery on his message machine. He didn't want you to know he was a cop, you see, but he still wanted to stick his nose where it didn't belong. The son of a bitch was determined to get hold of us.'' He shrugged. ''He called his house and took his messages that way, and you went on in blissful ignorance, thinking you screwed a PI, not a cop.''

Reality sank in. One more lie Mick had told. Strangely enough, she felt more concern for his guilt, if he should find out, than she did for the lie. She understood him. She knew why he hadn't confided in her. She'd meant it when she'd said she forgave him for that. ''You got Faradon's name and Mick's number from a call he made at my place.''

''That's right. So, no, Faradon isn't expecting you. He won't send out the cavalry.''

Del looked through the mud-spattered windshield and saw they were headed toward the river. Not the Ohio—no, that would be too obvious. This was a much smaller, much dirtier river. But it was deep. And fast. Mostly isolated excepted for the occasional fisherman. But not today. Today the river was deserted.

And she knew why they were going there.

Do not get hysterical, she told herself, even as her breath hitched and her lungs constricted. She could smell the two of them in the stuffy, steamy interior of the car. She could smell her own fear and their excitement. Bile rose in her throat.

They pulled off the main road and drove through

a patch of weeds and scrub. A ramshackle outbuilding sat to their right, and a long wooden pier, probably private, stretched along the shore, then angled out into deeper water. The car bumped onto it, tires thumping along the uneven, weather-worn boards.

Though they moved slowly now, edging nearer and nearer to the end of the dock, Del felt time speeding past her. A cabin cruiser docked to their right blocked them from view of the road.

Over the river, lightning danced, temporarily illuminating the sky and emphasizing the blackness of the deep, churning water. They meant to drown her, to kill her and sink the awful, dirty car with her inside it.

The driver laughed, reaching for her upper thigh and giving her a lecherous squeeze. "It's a shame we have to end this so quickly," he sneered. "Watching you with that cop makes me want to taste you myself."

Del slugged him.

She didn't think about it, didn't weigh the wisdom with the folly. She simply snapped, then reacted on instinct. Using a technique she'd learned in self-defense classes, she brought her elbow up and back. Hard, fast. Right into his face.

"Fucking bitch." The driver grabbed for his bleeding nose and temporarily lost control of the car. The other man grabbed Del by the neck, squeezing as he shouted orders.

In that single moment of chaos, everything became clear for Del, and she knew what to do.

She ignored the fist clamped around her throat,

making it impossible for her to draw air, and instead put her efforts into a hard shove on the driver. He lost his balance, and Del wedged her foot down to the floorboards. She found the gas pedal and jammed down.

With a loud roar of the engine, the car lurched forward. The driver shouted, gripping the wheel, but Del had clamped both hands on it. They wrestled, but he sputtered blood and went blind with panic.

The hand at her throat let go to grab her shoulder. It felt like her arm had been wrenched from the socket—but it was too late. The old car went airborne off the far end of the dock, suspending time and sound and reality, then dumped hard into the icy river with an enormous splash. Hissing and sputtering, the car tipped, engine first, and began sinking.

Both men forgot about Del in their panic. They pounded at the windows, screamed as the blackness engulfed them and water began rushing in.

Del concentrated on regaining her breath. Her throat felt crushed; it hurt to swallow, even to breathe, but she did it, slow, deep. The gun had dropped onto the seat beside her, forgotten. She tucked it into her pocket. The man to her right got the window open, and a great gush of frigid river water knocked him backward into Del. His elbow caught her shoulder, his foot dug into her thigh as he scrambled frantically to get to the window again, bent only on escaping the car.

On her knees so that her head stayed in the pocket of air inside the car, Del inhaled deeply, then slithered

278 CAUGHT IN THE ACT

to the back seat. Water closed over her face just as her fingers found the window handle.

She thought of Mick, thought of everything she wanted to tell him, and did what she had to do.

MICK WIPED BLOOD from his face with one shaking hand and maneuvered the slippery, winding road with the other.

After smacking his head on the steering wheel, he'd come to in enough time to see the car leaving with Delilah—but not in enough time to stop them.

Going seventy miles an hour to diminish their lead, he'd called for backup. His actions had been by rote, because both his mind and his heart stalled the second he'd realized what had happened.

He reached the river just in time to see the car sail off the dock and hit the churning water with crunching force. Terror blinded him. He wasn't aware of slamming on his brakes. He wasn't aware of the other police cars pulling up at the same time, sirens blaring and lights flashing.

He threw open his car door and hit the ground running, his only thought to get to Delilah. The storm surrounded him, lashing his face, making his feet slip in the wet weeds and slimy mud. Just before he reached the end of the dock, he got tackled hard and then held down. He fought the restraining hands without thought, hitting someone, kicking another.

"No, goddamn it," Faradon shouted when Mick almost wrenched loose. "Hold him!"

Mick barely heard. Three men gripped him, twisting his arms, making his wounded shoulder burn like fire, but it was nothing compared to the agony in his heart.

They jerked him to his feet, and all around him men shouted orders, while sirens continued to squeal and blue lights competed with the white flashes of the storm.

Numb, Mick continued to strain against the arms holding him. Faradon stepped up close. "We have a team preparing," he said not two inches from Mick's face. "Dawson, do you hear me? They'll be in the water in ten minutes tops."

Mick shook his head. In ten minutes she would be dead.

With renewed strength he lurched forward, taking the men by surprise. They lost their footing on the slippery, weathered boards and their holds loosened. Mick broke free.

He'd taken two running steps when someone shouted, "Look!"

A spotlight searching the surface of the water reflected off Delilah's inky-black hair. She sputtered, coughed. Mick went into the water in a clean dive. With several hard fast strokes, he reached her.

When he closed his hands around her, she at first fought him.

"It's all right, baby," he said, spitting dirty water, "it's me."

"Mick?" She dog-paddled, swallowed some of the water and choked, then cried, *"Mick!"*

She clung to him. Mick felt so weak it was all he could do to drag in air. Then several men surrounded them, catching them both and pulling them to the docks.

He hoisted Delilah up first. Faradon himself leaned down. "Give me your hands, miss," he said, and Delilah reached upward.

Sloshing, shivering, she landed on the dock, and someone rushed to put several blankets around her.

"M-M-Mick?"

He heard the shivering alarm, the need, and helped to drag himself out. Officers tried to cover him, too, but he wanted only Delilah. Weaving on her feet, she reached for him, and then he had her, tight in his arms where she damn well belonged and where she'd damn well stay.

He heard her crying, and his knees went weak. He tangled his hands in her wet hair, knowing he was too rough, but unable to temper his hold. "I've got you," he said gruffly, and crushed her to him.

"Mick, c'mon, man," said a gentle voice. "Let's get her out of the rain."

As if from far away, Mick heard Faradon speaking to him. He wrapped Delilah closer and allowed them both to be led to the outbuilding. It was dry inside, that was the best to be said for it.

Faradon stood there, looking slightly embarrassed. "We're, uh, fetching some dry clothes."

Mick gulped air, swallowed choking emotions and a love so rich he couldn't bear it. Delilah clung to him, and he didn't know if he'd survive the fear of thinking he'd lost her. He lifted his head. "The bastards who took her?"

"We're looking for them. If they surface, we'll fish

them out. If not, we'll start diving until we find them.''

Delilah struggled for a moment, and Mick loosened his hold.

''Take this,'' she said, digging a gun out of her baggy jeans pocket. She held it out to Faradon, and he carefully accepted it.

''You disarmed them?'' he asked, his voice heavy with awe.

Mick pressed her face to his shoulder. ''She can explain to you later.''

Faradon didn't look like he wanted to wait until later, but then a cop wearing a slicker stepped into the doorway. He held out a bundle of clothes, wrapped in another slicker, then nodded and excused himself.

Mick said to Faradon, ''Get out. And don't let anyone else in.''

Half grinning, shaking his head, Faradon said, ''Right.''

The door shut behind the detective, and Mick forced himself to loosen his arms from around Delilah. The small building was dim, crowded with boat trailers, ski equipment, tools. Mick bent, touched his nose to hers and whispered, ''Let me get you dry, okay?''

She nodded. ''I'm all right now.''

''I know you are.'' He strangled on the words and had to stop, had to draw in a shaky breath. His hands trembled as he stripped away her sodden blankets and started to work on the fastening of her loose jeans.

''I lost my shoes in the river,'' she said.

Mick wondered if she was in shock. He needed to get her warm and dry, needed to get her to a hospital.

He needed... Swallowing hard this time didn't help. He hated it, hated himself, but tears clogged his throat. He felt unmanned, vulnerable.

Without the gentleness that he intended, he removed her clothes and turned to rummage through the bundle inside the slicker. He found a loose jacket, two more blankets.

"Lift your arms," he murmured, and she obliged. The jacket, apparently donated by one of the officers milling around outside, hung to her knees. Mick shook out another blanket, this one thankfully dry, and draped it over her.

Delilah clutched the edges together and said, "It's not really cold. I mean, it must be eighty-five outside. I'm just chilled...." Her teeth chattered, making her explanations difficult.

"Shh," Mick said, and stripped off his own shirt so he wouldn't get her wet. There was nothing he could do about his pants. He sure as hell wasn't going to run around bare-assed. He pulled one slicker over Delilah's head, then another over his own. "Let's get you to the hospital so you can be checked over," he said, deliberately concentrating on only one thing at a time.

Her fingers clutched at his arm, gripping the slicker with surprising force. "Mick, I don't...I don't want to go back out there yet."

His heart hit his stomach with her trembling words. He turned to her, opened his arms.

And she launched herself into him. "I was so—so scared," she said on a wail.

Mick wanted to absorb her into himself, to surround her always and keep her from ever being hurt again. Those damn tears got him again, and he squeezed her tighter, assuring himself that he had her, that she was okay.

Rain drummed on the metal roof of the shed and wind howled through every crack and crevice in the aged boards.

Then Delilah said something that made his knees give out. "I thought I'd lost you."

"What?"

She sniffed, shook her head while tears mingled with the wetness on her cheeks. Her words were broken, scattered and rushed. "I saw the blood on your forehead and I thought you might be dead or dying. You've already been hurt so much because of me." She leaned back to gently touch his face. "Are you all right? Truly?"

Mick dropped to his knees and stared up at Delilah, not caring that he cried, having totally forgotten about his own cut head. "*You* almost died," he groaned.

"Oh no. I knew what I was doing." She smoothed his sodden hair, her hand tender, loving. "I was afraid at first. Terrified really. But I kept thinking about you. I kept thinking what if I survived and you didn't? When I realized it was you in the river with me, I went weak. I was…well, I was doing fine until then."

Mick pressed his face into her belly. The chill had left her body and she felt warm, smelled musky and damp, and he knew he couldn't stand it, knew he was going to embarrass himself.

He held her tighter but it didn't help.

Faradon rapped at the door. "You two about done changing?"

"Go away!" Delilah yelled impatiently. "We'll be out in a minute."

Faradon grumbled something, but he didn't open the door.

Mick felt her cool hands cup his face, but he couldn't let her go, couldn't unclench his muscles. He hated feeling like this, powerless and weak and... He opened his hands on her behind and squeezed her closer, grinding his face into her, trying to absorb her.

He heard Delilah's smile as she said, "I love you, Mick Dawson. More than anyone or anything, now and forever."

He drew a shuddering breath and rubbed his face over her belly, on her borrowed blanket, drying his eyes and attempting to regain control. He had to get hold of himself. He had to...

"Tell me you love me, too," she whispered.

"I do," he said without hesitation. Only a trace of tears remained in his raw voice, not that he gave a damn. Delilah deserved to know everything about him.

"You do?" she asked.

"So much it hurts."

"I don't want you to hurt."

"Then don't ever leave me."

"Never." She slipped to her knees in front of him, still cupping his face. She kissed him, then kissed him again. She even smiled. "Will you stop calling me Delilah and call me Del?"

His shoulders shook. "No."

"Oh." She sounded surprised and disgruntled, and that went a long way toward helping him regain his discipline. Even at the worst of times, she amused him.

Finally she asked, "Well then, will you marry me?"

He actually laughed, but it turned into a groan. "I was going to ask you, you know."

"Sorry."

He touched her face, her sodden, tangled hair, her small breasts and narrow hips and long thighs. "God, I love you, every inch of you. I'll always love you, I swear it." When she gave him a brilliant smile, he added with more strength, "You've stolen forty years off my life with that last damn stunt!"

Her smile never wavered. She stood and held out her hand to him. As if *he* needed *her* assistance to stand!

He did.

He still felt wobbly, but as long as he didn't think about the moment that he'd seen that car go into the river...

He shuddered, took her slender hand and let her help haul him to his feet.

She put an arm around him and leaned her head into his shoulder. "I lost fifty years, leaving you behind in that car, bleeding. Nothing has ever scared me like that."

They headed for the door together. Just as Mick opened it, someone shouted, "I've got one of 'em!"

They followed the spotlight, and saw several cops converge on a man trying to crawl onto the muddy, thickly weeded shore. He was promptly handcuffed.

It wasn't until the next day that the police finally found the other man's body and confirmed his death. But they had two of them, Rudy Glasgow and the driver. They also had fingerprints, both from the apartment next to Delilah's and the gun she'd retrieved from the car.

It was over.

DEL FLITTED from one person to the next. She loved being in a large family, even if most of that family was male and not really family at all. They felt like family, treated her as such, and they loved Mick to distraction. That in itself made her more than a little fond of them.

At the moment, Angel and Celia were perusing Mick's new bookcases, now holding her books. Del had pretty much taken over his house. His spare bedroom served as her office, and he'd already had an extra phone line put in.

The kids were all outside playing, but they could be heard through the open windows. Every minute or so one of the adults went to check on them.

Dane and Alec were seated on the couch, Josh and Zack in adjacent chairs, all of them watching a sports channel. Now that Del was used to them, Dane no longer seemed so imposing and Alec was nowhere near as frightening. But they were still fascinating characters.

Grinning, Del dropped down on the seat between them, using each hand to pat a hard masculine thigh. The two men looked at her warily. "Now that I've finally finished my current book and got it all turned in," she said, "I've been thinking of doing a book about two PIs who—"

Mick, who'd sauntered over to stand behind the couch, covered her mouth with a large hand. Del froze.

"If either one of you wants to remain in my good graces you won't tell her anything about anything…dangerous."

Alec saluted Mick with his cola. "Sorry, but Celia knows everything dangerous involved in my job, and she's been chewing Del's ear for the past hour."

True enough, Del thought, appreciating both Celia's forthright information and the way everyone had taken to calling her "Del," once she'd explained that she only used the name "Delilah" for writing.

Everyone except Mick, that is, who swore he loved her name as much as he loved her. The charmer. He even claimed "Delilah Dawson" had a very nice ring to it. Del couldn't wait for that to become her name in fact.

Dane nodded. "Yep, I'm afraid you're preaching to the choir here, Mick. You should have gagged the women, not us."

Mick groaned with heartfelt sincerity. He'd promised to be understanding about her research, though

Del knew he wanted to keep her in a cotton-lined box so she didn't so much as stub her baby toe.

Del pulled his hand away and tipped her head back to see him upside down. "How'd you sneak in here behind me?"

Mick rolled his eyes. "Sweetheart, when your brain is plotting, a herd of buffalo could tramp through and you wouldn't notice."

Since that was true, she said instead, "But I thought you were outside playing with the kids."

"They did me in. They're vicious little brutes who keep singing about how I was saved by a woman."

Del frowned, feeling a good dose of jealousy. "What woman?"

Mick leaned down to kiss her. "You."

"Me?" He nodded, and Del said, "But I didn't save you."

The awful nightmare of the car wreck, of Mick's head injury and her dousing in the river was two weeks old now, but she still shivered whenever she thought of how close she'd come to losing him.

Angel sidled up behind the couch, too, and hugged Mick. Celia joined her, resting her hands on Alec's shoulders. Zack and Josh twisted in their seats to face Del. She felt hemmed in by them all—but now the feeling was nice, sort of comforting.

She was surrounded by friends and family.

Mick smoothed his hand over her hair, something she was now more than familiar with. "Of course you saved me," he said. "You love me, right?"

"Absolutely."

"There, you see?" Alec chimed in, nudging her

with his rock-hard shoulder. "You saved Mick from being a cynical fool who didn't believe in love."

Del looked at Mick again. With the way these people adored him, she found that hard to believe. "You didn't believe in love?" she asked skeptically, but at the same time she thought it probably explained his reticence in admitting his feelings to her. Now, of course, he told her how much he cared in a thousand different ways—including the simple words *I love you.*

Mick just smiled.

Dane nudged her next, almost knocking her into Alec's lap. "You saved him from being a control freak, too."

Del righted herself and laughed; Mick was still very much a controlling man, and she doubted that would ever change.

Zack said, "You saved him from living his life like a monk."

With a very slight blush, Del said, "Okay, you got me there." Everyone laughed.

Mick was a voracious lover, and he couldn't seem to keep his hands off her. Which she appreciated because she loved when he touched her. He'd also become a voracious reader. He'd devoured her books and claimed he couldn't wait for the next one. She'd been nearly beside herself with his praise.

Josh tossed back a drink, then asked, "So when is this wedding we're all anticipating?"

Mick frowned at his friend, but said, "I just got the church reserved for the first Saturday of next month."

"You're all invited," Del announced, "as long as you know it won't be too fancy. No tuxes, and definitely no long white lace gowns." She pulled her jeans-clad legs up onto the couch and hugged her knees. "I hate dressing up."

"I'll be lucky to get shoes on her," Mick teased, and Angel promptly corrected him. She'd been with Del when the dress *and* matching shoes were bought.

Del noticed Josh heading for the kitchen, his head down, his hands shoved into his pants pockets. She smiled at Mick, rose from the couch and went to her friend. She found him standing at the sink, watching the children play through the window. "Josh?"

He turned to her, but said nothing.

"You're happy that Mick's marrying me, aren't you?"

He looked surprised, then wary. "Why?"

"Because you're one of his best friends. I don't want to come between you."

That made him laugh. "You belong between us, honey. Mick's a lucky guy, and yeah, I'm happy for you both."

"I hesitate to point this out, but you don't exactly look happy."

"No?" He studied her face, his green eyes dark, his slight smile crooked, chagrined.

She shook her head. "*Morose* might be a better word."

Mick's arms slid around her, lacing over her stomach. "*Defeated* might work, too," he said gently.

Josh snorted.

Mick tightened his hold, surprising Del, then said, "There are plenty of women out there, Josh."

"Yeah?"

Zack stepped up. "That's right, and I intend to find one."

All eyes turned to him. Del grinned. "You're bride hunting?"

"Why is that such a surprise?"

Josh said, "Because you seldom date? Because you're the quintessential bachelor? Because no woman will ever come before Dani?"

Del slugged Josh, making him jump and rub his shoulder while grumbling.

Still frowning, she said, "No *good* woman would want to come before his daughter! Children should always be first. At least until they're self-sufficient. Besides," she added, patting Zack's chest and smiling, "Zack has enough love for a wife and several children."

"One daughter is enough! All I want now is the wife to complete the set. After all, Dani is crazy about you, Del. It made me think about what she's missing."

"Like what?" Mick asked. "You take great care of her."

"I try," Zack admitted, "but she needs a female role model. Someone quiet and intelligent and sincere."

"And sexy?" Mick asked.

Zack shrugged. "I'd rather she was domestic, if you want the truth."

"I wish you luck," Josh said with mock sincerity.

"I don't need luck, because I already have a plan. And I'm starting tomorrow."

Mick and Josh groaned, but Zack just smiled, confident in himself and his eventual success.

The rest of the family filed into the kitchen, including the children. Zack scooped up his daughter, hugged her tight.

"Time for us to go," Dane announced. "Tomorrow is a school day."

There were kisses all around, and everyone gradually left except Zack and Josh. Zack's daughter had fallen asleep on his shoulder, her blond curls disheveled, her mouth smooshed on her daddy's shoulder.

Zack pulled Del close with his free arm and gave her a smacking kiss on the mouth. "Congratulations again on the engagement," he whispered. He patted her cheek and stepped aside.

Josh set down his drink and reached for Del, catching her shoulders in his hands. He gave her the softest look she'd ever seen from him, leaned forward—and Mick's hand was suddenly between them, covering her mouth.

Mick bared his teeth at Josh and said, "Out."

Laughing, Josh pushed him aside and kissed Del on the forehead. "Your future husband is a jealous lout, did you know that?"

She waved his comment away. "Nonsense. He knows I'm crazy about him."

Josh and Mick exchanged a certain look that Del didn't understand in the least.

Shaking his head, Josh gave her a squeeze. "I'm glad you're so happy."

Holding his daughter to his shoulder, Zack grabbed Josh's collar and hauled him toward the door. "Let's go. Dani is starting to snore, and you're pressing your luck."

After they'd gone, Del asked Mick, "Okay, what was that all about?"

"What?" he asked, pretending innocence.

"That business with Josh. What's wrong with him?"

Mick looked briefly harassed. "Nothing that he won't get over," he said, and it almost sounded like a threat.

Before she could ask any more questions, he took her hand and herded her toward the bedroom.

"What do you think about Zack wanting a wife?" she asked.

Mick lightly pushed her down on the bed, then covered her with his body. He touched her cheek, her chin, the corner of her mouth. "I think he's a little jealous, too."

"Too?"

Mick kissed her. "Everyone knows I'm the luckiest man alive. When I think about the fact that you're mine, I almost can't bear it, it's so incredible. I want to tell the whole world." He smiled. "I love you, Delilah Piper."

"I'm lucky, too," she said softly. "I have you. And I did tell the whole world."

Startled, Mick leaned back. "You did?"

"Wait until you see the dedication in my next book. It's to my very own hero, the finest man alive."

She cupped his face. ''And everyone knows that's you.''

Mick frowned for just a moment, then his frown lifted and he shook his head. ''Damn, I do feel like a hero. After all, the hero always gets the girl in the end, right?''

Del laughed. ''In my books, he sure as heck does.''

YESTERDAY'S SCANDAL

GINA WILKINS

GINA WILKINS

This bestselling, award-winning author has written more than forty books for Mills & Boon Sensual Romance® and Silhouette Special Edition®. Her romances have been translated into twenty languages and are sold in more than one hundred countries worldwide.

A lifelong resident of central Arkansas, USA, Wilkins lives in a country home with her husband and three children. She has a degree in journalism from Arkansas State University, and has worked as a reporter, feature writer, advertising copy-writer and audio-visual director before beginning a full-time career in fiction writing. She is a frequent speaker at writers' conferences, but says her true passion for speaking is in schools.

Gina Wilkins has written an exciting new miniseries for Silhouette Special Edition®. *Look out for* **The Stranger in Room 205** *in July 2002,* **Bachelor Cop Finally Caught?** *in August,* *and* **Dateline Matrimony** *in September.*

Dedication:

For my friends and colleagues in Novelists, Inc., the most supportive group I have ever met.
And for Nora Roberts, my personal hero, who was there for me when I needed her during this past year.

My thanks to all of you.

CHAPTER ONE

TAILLIGHTS GLOWED red in the darkness ahead of him as Mac Cordero drove along the rural outskirts of Honoria, Georgia. He wasn't deliberately following the other vehicle. They just happened to be headed in the same direction on the narrow, hilly road bordered by thick woods on the left and a rain-swollen river on the right.

Mac had no particular destination in mind. He was merely killing time on this Friday evening, delaying his return to the no-frills motel where he would be staying until he made better arrangements for the next few months. He had things to accomplish in this oddball town, and the renovation of the 1920s-era Victorian-style house he'd recently purchased was the excuse he'd use if anyone asked why he was here. The *real* reason he was here—well, sometimes that even seemed like a mystery to him.

Because it was a warm, early-June evening, his windows were down, letting in the fresh, woodsy air and the sounds of night creatures. Neither lifted his mood, nor eased the frustration that he had accomplished so little since his initial visit to Honoria several weeks earlier. He was no closer now to solving the mystery that had brought him here than he'd been when he'd decided to pursue it.

The small car ahead of him began a steady ascent up a steep, blind hill. Mac shifted in the seat of his truck. All in all, it had been an unproductive day. He was beginning to wonder if boredom was all that awaited him here. He hated being bored.

A squeal of brakes brought him abruptly out of his thoughts. His hands tightened on the steering wheel when the taillights ahead of him swerved suddenly and erratically, then veered off to the right side of the road—straight toward the river. At the same moment, a light-colored van topped the hill in the center of the road, speeding, weaving, making no effort to slow down. Acting on instinct, Mac jerked his wheel to the right, pulling his truck to the side but stopping before it went over the edge. The van sped past, disappearing behind him.

Muttering a curse, Mac didn't waste time trying to get a license-plate number, but jumped from his truck and ran to the edge of the road. The slow-moving river looked like black ink in the darkness, shimmering with multifaceted reflections of the three-quarter moon overhead. He saw no sign of the car he knew had gone over. Kicking off his shoes, he prepared to dive in.

A head broke the water in front of him as he started to jump. He heard a loud gasp for air, followed by what might have been a broken cry of pain and fear. A moment later, he was in the cold water, reaching the woman just as she went under again.

He grabbed her arms and hauled her to the surface, noting automatically that she was lightweight, slender. His hands easily spanned her waist as he treaded water and supported her until she caught her breath. It was difficult to see her features in the shadows, but he got the impression she was somewhat younger than his own thirty-three years.

Reassured that she was stable, he asked urgently, "Is there anyone else in the car?"

"No. I was alone." Her voice was a choked whisper. "It...took me a while to get out. I had my windows down, but..."

"It wasn't as long as it must have seemed to you." He was aware that she was trembling so hard her teeth were chattering. The water was cool, but not frigid. Sensing that shock was about to set in, he tightened his grip on her. "Can you swim? Are you injured?"

"I...I don't know," she managed to say, clinging to him. "I hurt, but I don't know exactly where yet."

Because it made sense to him, considering the circumstances, he merely nodded and wrapped an arm around her to help her toward the bank. He would assess her injuries once she was safely out of the water, he decided, beginning to swim with steady, rescue-trained strokes.

The bank was steep, mud crumbling beneath his hands and feet as he helped the woman out of the river. It wasn't easy to swing her into his arms and carry her up to the side of the road. Hard shivers racked her, and he could hear her teeth chattering. Damning the darkness that kept him from seeing whether she was bleeding anywhere, Mac settled her on the gravel beside the road. "I'll be right back."

He dashed to his truck, water streaming off him, his wet socks providing little protection from the rocks on the roadbed. Ignoring his discomfort, he snatched his cellular phone and dialed 911. Grabbing the lightweight jacket he'd tossed into the passenger seat earlier, he gave the emergency dispatcher a clipped summation of his situation, requested an ambulance and then hung up.

The woman was curled into a fetal ball when he returned to her. He suspected that if there was enough light, he would see that her lips were blue. She wore a T-shirt and shorts, and her feet were bare. She'd probably lost her shoes in the river. She lay in a puddle of water, trembling.

"I've called for help," he said, wrapping his jacket snugly around her. The thin fabric seemed to make no difference at all; she seemed hardly to notice it. Shock, he thought again, and shifted her onto her back, pushing her knees upward so that her legs were higher than her head.

Only marginally aware of his own soggy, chilled condition, he smoothed wet, nape-length hair from the woman's face. His eyes had finally grown accustomed to the darkness and he could make out the woman's features. Her skin was so pale it looked like porcelain in the milky moonlight. He took another guess at her age—mid- to late twenties, perhaps. Her hair looked dark, but it was hard to tell for certain. "What's your name?"

"Sharon." Her voice was faint, but coherent, to his relief. "Sharon Henderson."

"I'm Mac Cordero."

She pulled a hand from the folds of his jacket and reached out toward him. "Thank you."

He cradled her icy fingers in his larger, somewhat warmer ones. Their gazes met and held. Her eyes glittered in the moonlight. He knew his own face was in shadow, but he offered a faint smile of encouragement. "You're welcome."

She shivered again and he tightened his hand. He felt as if something passed between them at that point of contact—warmth, emotion…something. Most likely he was overreacting to the dramatic turn the evening had suddenly taken. When he'd complained of boredom earlier, he certainly hadn't been hoping for anything like this.

A dark Jeep with a flashing light on the dash topped the hill and braked to a stop across the road. The driver stepped out of the vehicle and crossed to them swiftly, kneeling at the woman's other side. "Sharon?" he said, recognizing her immediately, "Are you hurt?"

"I don't think so," she answered, but didn't sound quite convinced.

"An ambulance is on the way. Can you tell me what happened?"

"I was leaving Tressie's house after dinner. There was a van—it came out of the driveway on the other side of the hill without stopping. I swerved, but it ran me off the road—almost as if it was intentional.''

"I saw the van," Mac added. "It never even slowed down."

The other man looked at him. "Chief Wade Davenport, Honoria Police Department," he introduced himself.

"Mac Cordero. I happened to be following behind Ms. Henderson's car, and I saw the accident."

"Judging from your appearance, I take it Sharon's car went into Snake Creek?"

Mac frowned. Snake Creek? Hardly a name to inspire confidence. He hated snakes. Yet he knew that even had the water been crawling with them, he'd have gone in after her. Years of training and practice had kicked in the moment he'd seen someone in trouble. You could take the cop out of his uniform, he thought ruefully, but it was a hell of a lot harder to break those old cop habits.

"My car." Sharon turned her head to look mournfully toward the edge of the road. "I just made the final payment."

Davenport patted her shoulder. "Let's not worry about that right now, okay?"

A siren broke the deceptively peaceful silence of the night. Davenport glanced in its direction, then turned his attention back to the soggy couple in front of him. "You said the van pulled out of the driveway just over the hill?"

Sharon nodded. "Yes. The driver didn't even

pause to see if anyone was coming from either direction.''

''That's the Porter place. The Porters left for vacation three days ago.''

''You think the van was there to rob them?'' She sounded appalled.

The police chief glanced at Mac, who had already leaped to that conclusion, then looked back at Sharon. ''I'll check that out as soon as you're taken care of. I don't suppose either of you got the number of the license plate on the van.''

''No.'' Mac shook his head, knowing he'd be able to provide little detail. ''I thought it was more important to make sure no one was trapped underwater.''

''You made the right call.'' Davenport stood as an ambulance pulled up behind the Jeep. ''I'll have more questions for you later, if you don't mind, Mr. Cordero.''

''I'll tell you everything I saw—but I'm afraid it wasn't much. It all happened too quickly.''

Two uniformed paramedics—a man and a woman—approached with swift efficiency. Only then did Mac realize that he was still holding Sharon's hand. She clung to him when he would have released her, as if he were her only lifeline in frighteningly uncharted waters. He had to gently peel her fingers away so the medics could do their jobs.

He hadn't been cold when he'd knelt beside her, holding her hand. Now, as he stepped back, he felt a chill penetrate his wet clothing. He shoved his hands into the pockets of his slacks and winced when the waterlogged fabric clung to him. Fortunately, his wallet was in the truck, so the only thing he'd ruined was a good leather belt. His shoes were still by the water's edge. He'd get them as soon as the ambulance left.

Wade Davenport returned from using the radio in his Jeep just as Sharon was being loaded onto the ambulance. "I'll come to the hospital in a few minutes to see about you," he promised her.

"All right," she answered automatically, though she was still looking at Mac. "Mr. Cordero..."

He stepped closer to the gurney. "Yes?"

"Thank you."

She had already thanked him. He answered as he had before, "You're welcome."

He watched her—and was watched in return—until the ambulance doors closed between them. Only when the ambulance had driven away did he turn back to the chief of police, prepared to answer his questions.

SORE MUSCLES CLENCHED when Sharon shifted in her seat Sunday evening, causing her to wince. She immediately regretted doing so when the man on the other side of the restaurant table frowned and asked, "Are you sure you're all right?"

Since it was at least the tenth time he'd asked in the past couple of hours, Sharon had to force herself to answer patiently. "I'm fine, Jerry. Still a little sore, but the doctor assured me that was to be expected.''

Jerry Whitaker didn't look satisfied. He seemed convinced that her injuries from Friday night's mishap were worse than the few scrapes and bruises she had told him about.

He'd been out of town for the weekend, and when he'd returned that afternoon, talk of the accident had been all over town—no surprise in Honoria, where rumors zipped from household to household with the frantic speed of a metal ball in an arcade pinball machine. Having lived here since adolescence, Sharon had learned to discount most of what she heard, but Jerry still tended to take the local gossip much too seriously.

''Tell me more about your business trip,'' she encouraged him, trying to change the subject. ''How was the weather in Charleston?''

Her attempt at diversion failed. ''Fine,'' he answered automatically, then returned to his questions about her. ''Have you talked to Chief Davenport since I called you this afternoon? Have there been any further developments in the investigation of the Porter robbery—any leads on the van that ran you off the road?''

Resigned to rehashing it all again, Sharon looked down at her plate. ''Nothing. It's as if the van disappeared off the face of the earth. If Mr. Cordero hadn't seen it, I would have wondered if I had imagined it.''

Jerry's scowl deepened. ''Ah, yes. Cordero-the-hero. That's what they're calling him around town, you know.''

Sharon wrinkled her nose. "You're kidding. That's so corny.''

"Have you *heard* some of the stories going around about what happened Friday night? Mildred Scott told me you drowned and Cordero brought you back to life with CPR. Clark Foster said you were trapped in the car and Cordero had to break a window to pull you out, nearly drowning himself. And then there's the version Gloria Capps is spreading— that you cut yourself on broken glass and almost bled to death before Cordero saved you by using his necktie as a tourniquet.''

"That's ridiculous. He wasn't even wearing a necktie." She shook her head. "It's *all* ridiculous. I was already out of the car when Mr. Cordero jumped in to help me. I'm sure I could have made it out of the river on my own.''

She didn't want to sound ungrateful for Mac's help, but she didn't like hearing she'd been cast as the hapless victim in so many improbable scenarios. She'd been taking care of herself—and the rest of her family—for a long time. It wasn't easy to let anyone else take charge, even briefly.

"Of course you would have made it out on your own.''

Sharon didn't know whether Jerry's attitude was due more to his faith in her or his jealousy that Mac Cordero had become such a romanticized figure in Honoria. Jerry had lived in this town all his life.

He'd taken over his father's insurance office a few years ago, but an insurance salesman was rarely regarded as dashing or heroic, terms that had been applied to Cordero in the numerous retellings of Sharon's accident.

She'd been dating Jerry casually for three or four months. They shared several common interests and had passed many pleasant evenings together. She'd been aware from the start that their relationship owed more to circumstance than chemistry—there weren't many singles their age in Honoria—but she wasn't looking for romance, only occasional companionship, which Jerry provided without making too many demands in return.

"I really don't understand all this fuss over the guy," he muttered, slicing irritably into his steak. "He's a contractor, for Pete's sake. Not even a particularly shrewd one, if he thinks he's going to make a profit on the Garrett place."

"I've heard he specializes in restoring old houses. He must know from experience whether or not the Garrett house is worth renovating."

Jerry shook his head stubbornly. "That eyesore is going to require a small fortune just to make it livable again. It should have been condemned years ago. The location's not bad, even if it isn't close to the golf course, like all the best new homes. Tear it down and start from scratch, that's what I would do. Maybe even subdivide—it sits on a three-acre lot. That's enough land to put in quite a few houses and more than pay for the initial investment."

Just what Honoria needed, Sharon thought. Another tacky subdivision filled with cheaply built, cookie-cutter houses on undersize lots. "Some people love the old, the historic," she murmured. "The Garrett place was practically a mansion when it was built in the early part of the twentieth century. It must have been beautiful."

"Maybe it was then, but now it's just old." Jerry shook his head in bafflement. "I've never understood what people see in beat-up antiques when they can have shiny new things, instead."

She wasn't surprised by Jerry's attitude. He had a taste for flash. He traded cars nearly every year when the new models debuted, and was always upgrading his computers and electronic equipment. The past held little appeal for him—his eyes were firmly fixed on the future. She saw no need to remind him that she had a soft spot for antiques. It was something he just couldn't understand.

Jerry's thoughts were still focused on Mac Cordero. "The guy's just a contractor. I don't know why so many people around town want to make him into something else. The rumors about him are absurd. Why can't they just accept that he's exactly what he says he is?"

The mildest speculation cast Cordero as an eccentric multimillionaire who fixed up old houses for his own hideaways. Some whispered that he was an agent for a Hollywood superstar who wanted a place to escape the press occasionally. The most incredible story she'd heard suggested he was working for an organized-crime family preparing the Garrett house for a mobster who needed to get out of New York City.

"You know how rumors get started around here," Sharon reminded Jerry. "Because Mr. Cordero chooses not to share information about his personal life, people entertain themselves by filling in the blanks with colorful details."

"So what do *you* know about him?" Jerry's question proved he wasn't as averse to gossip as he pretended—something Sharon already knew, of course.

"I don't know anything more than you do. I didn't exactly have a lot of time for personal chit-chat when I met him. All I can tell you is he seemed very…capable," she said for lack of a better description.

As much as she hated to admit it, even to herself, she had been in trouble Friday night. Yes, she'd managed to get out of her sunken car on her own, but she'd been shaken and disoriented. She probably would have gotten to the shore on her own—at least, she hoped so—only to find herself stranded on a rarely traveled country road without a car or a phone. As frightened as she had been, there had been something about Mac Cordero that had reassured her. Maybe it was the strength of the rock-hard arms that had supported her until she'd caught her breath. Or the steady way he'd held her gaze when he'd assured her that help was on the way. Or maybe it had been the way her hand had felt cradled so securely in his.

It embarrassed her now to remember the desperation with which she had clung to the stranger who'd pulled her from the water. At the time, she'd simply been grateful to have someone to hold on to.

"Would you mind if we talk about something else now?" she asked, uncomfortable with the feelings those memories evoked. "It seems that all I've talked about for the past two days is the accident."

"Of course. So, what about your car? Have they pulled it out yet? Were you able to salvage anything?"

This time she didn't bother to hold back her sigh. There appeared to be nothing she could do to distract Jerry. Pushing her unsettling thoughts of Mac Cordero to the back of her mind, she concentrated on her dinner, answering Jerry's questions with as little detail as possible.

She could only hope something would happen soon to get the town talking about something else.

"I'VE INTERVIEWED everyone I could think of who might've seen something suspicious around the Porter place, Wade. We've put the word out all over town that we're looking for the light-colored panel van that was seen leaving the scene of the crime. We're getting nothing. Apparently, the only two people who saw the vehicle were Sharon Henderson and that Cordero guy."

Chief Wade Davenport raised his gaze from the accident reports scattered in front of him to the skinny, dejected-looking deputy on the other side of the battered oak desk. "Keep asking, Gilbert. Someone had to see something."

Ever the pessimist, Gilbert Dodson gave a gloomy sigh. "I'll keep asking, Wade, but I've talked to everyone but the chickens now."

Wade leaned back in his creaky chair and steepled his fingers in front of him. "Then maybe you should start interviewing chickens."

Shoulders slumping, Gilbert nodded and turned toward the door. "I'll get right on that, Chief."

Wade muttered a curse as his office door clicked shut. He tended to take it personally when anyone broke the law in his town. There'd been a rash of break-ins about a month ago, and the culprits had never been caught. Now there'd been another—the Porter place. They'd been quietly and efficiently cleaned out by whoever had been in the same van that had almost killed Sharon Henderson.

The break-ins were connected. Wade was sure of it, even though he had no evidence to support his hunch. There wasn't that much crime in Honoria, and there hadn't been any breaking and entering going on in almost five years. Not since the O'Brien kid and his buddies had thought it would be "fun" to start their own crime ring. Kevin O'Brien was twenty-three years old now and had done his time. The first thing Wade did when the current burglaries began was to check on Kevin's whereabouts. As far as he could tell, there was no connection this time.

Which meant he had another thief operating in his

town, victimizing and endangering his friends and neighbors. And that made Wade mad.

Narrowing his eyes, he picked up the report that had been filed by Mac Cordero, the "mysterious stranger" everyone had been gossiping about. It was interesting that the previous burglaries had taken place while Cordero was in town a few weeks back buying the old Garrett place. Now there'd been another one, only days after Cordero returned to begin the renovation project. Cordero "just happened" to be driving down that back road at the same time the Porter place was being cleaned out. Maybe there was no connection there, but Wade didn't like coincidences.

Wade's wife and kids lived in this town. It was his job to keep them—and the other residents—safe. He turned his attention to Cordero's statement again, looking for anything that resembled a clue.

CHAPTER TWO

IT DIDN'T TAKE LONG for Mac to learn a few things about the woman he'd pulled from Snake Creek. Even though he didn't mingle much with the townspeople, every busybody he encountered in Honoria during the next few days—and there seemed to be many of them—was anxious to tell him all about her. He found some of the information interesting, but two comments, in particular, caught his attention.

Sharon Henderson was an interior decorator *and* a good friend of the McBride family.

The motel where he was staying was not so coincidentally located within full view of the McBride Law Firm. From the window of his room, Mac could see the firm's parking lot. He'd heard that the founder, Caleb McBride, a lifelong resident of Honoria now in his early sixties, had very recently left for a month-long Caribbean cruise with his wife, Bobbie. Their older son, Trevor, was running the law office single-handedly until Caleb's return.

Mac had watched a steady stream of clients and visitors entering and exiting the office building during the last five days he'd spent in Honoria. Some he could already identify, such as Trevor's striking, red-haired wife and two young children, and Trevor's younger brother, Trent, whom Mac had met a month ago in that same parking lot.

Late Monday afternoon, Sharon Henderson arrived at the firm.

Watching from his window, Mac recognized her immediately, though he wasn't sure how. The attractive, well-dressed woman who slid out of a nondescript sedan bore little resemblance to the wet, shivering waif he'd encountered Friday night. Her hair fell in a gleaming brown sweep to just above her shoulders and she carried herself with poised self-confidence. As she disappeared inside the law office, he told himself he could be mistaken. There was no way he could know for sure the visitor was Sharon. Even if he'd gotten a closer look at her that night, he was too far away to see her clearly now.

Drinking coffee from the coffeemaker provided in the room, he was still sitting in the uncomfortable chair watching the other building when the woman emerged again. Though he'd spent the past hour trying to convince himself he couldn't possibly have identified her, the sense of recognition hit him again the moment she walked out into the parking lot. He didn't know how he knew, but he was convinced Sharon Henderson had just dropped in on Trevor McBride.

Interesting. He'd heard she was a friend and her visit proved there was a professional relationship, as well. He wondered just how much she knew about the McBride family history...and if she shared the rest of the town's passion for idle gossip.

Maybe it was time for him to pay a call on her. He'd been thinking about doing that, anyway, for professional reasons. Now that he knew her connection to the McBrides, he had more personal motives for wanting to get better acquainted with Sharon Henderson.

"C'MON, SHARON, why can't I go? All the other guys will be there."

Sharon grimaced as her fifteen-year-old brother's voice edged perilously close to a whine. She tightened her grip on the telephone receiver, trying to get a firmer hold on her patience at the same time. "Brad, you are not going to an unchaperoned party. I know Mike Riordan's parents are out of town this week, and I don't at all approve of them allowing him to have a party at their house while they're away. As far as I'm concerned, that's just asking for trouble."

"But Mike's brother Joe is going to be there to keep an eye on things. He's a college man."

Sharon wasn't impressed. "He just finished his first year of college. That makes him barely nineteen years old. I'm sorry, but that isn't my idea of a suitable chaperon for a houseful of teenagers. The answer is no. We can go out to eat or to a movie, if you like. Or you can invite a couple of your friends over to eat pizza and play video games."

"All my friends are going to the party. No one's going to want to miss it to hang out with me."

Refusing to be swayed by his plaintive tone, Sharon responded firmly. "I doubt that everyone will be at the party. I'm sure I won't be the only adult who'll think this is a bad idea."

"Just let me go for a little while, okay? If it gets too wild, I'll call you to come get me."

"You aren't going to a party that isn't adequately supervised, and there's no use discussing it any further."

"Fine. Great. Ruin my life."

She sighed. "I'm not trying to ruin your life. I'm trying to be a responsible guardian."

"Mom would let me go if she was here."

The operative word, Sharon thought wearily, was *responsible*—something their dear, ditzy mother had never been. "Well, Mom's not here. While she's away, I'm in charge. You're just going to have to accept that."

Sullen silence was his only response.

"Be thinking about what you want for dinner tonight, okay?" she suggested, her tone conciliatory. "We can go to that new Mexican place you like so much. You'd enjoy that, wouldn't you?"

"Might as well sit at home and watch TV," he muttered.

"If that's your choice," she agreed evenly. "I have to get back to work now. I'll see you this afternoon."

He hung up without responding.

Sharon rubbed her forehead as she hung up the phone. It was Tuesday afternoon, a slow day in her home-decor shop, and for once she was grateful for the lull. Her full-time assistant was at a doctor's appointment, and Sharon was alone. Between her confrontations with her rebellious kid brother and the almost incessant calls from acquaintances still wanting to talk about the incident Friday night, she was ready for some time to herself.

With her back to the door of the shop, she slid the phone into its place beneath the counter, then turned to the paperwork she'd been looking over when Brad called. Her elbow bumped a thick wallpaper-sample book, which crashed to the floor at her feet. Muttering a mild curse, she knelt to pick it up, tucking it into the crook of one arm. What else could go wrong today?

She gasped when a man's hand suddenly appeared in front of her, offering to assist her to her feet. She hadn't heard anyone enter the shop, so it caught her completely off guard to realize she wasn't alone. She looked up and swallowed hard when her gaze was captured and held by a pair of eyes as dark and unrevealing as polished onyx.

Sharon had never considered herself a fanciful person, but the image that came immediately to mind was that of a sleek, dangerous black cat. This intriguing man was as out of place in her little shop as he was…well, in this small, sleepy town.

No wonder everyone in Honoria had been speculating about him.

Almost involuntarily, she placed her hand in his. There was an instant shock of familiarity when his fingers closed around hers, bringing back memories of how safe she had felt when he'd pulled her out of Snake Creek.

He helped her to her feet. Her voice was a bit breathless when she said, "Thank you, Mr. Cordero."

His left eyebrow rose half an inch. His voice was a deep growl that befitted the exotic animal she had envisioned when she saw him—the same voice that had echoed in the back of her mind since the accident Friday night. "I wasn't sure you would remember me."

Her smile felt wry. "I'm not likely to forget our meeting anytime soon."

His answering smile was just a slight shift at the corners of his mouth—and only added to his attractiveness, in Sharon's opinion. She hadn't gotten a really good look at him in the shadowy darkness Friday night, but now she could understand why so many women in town had been whispering about him. It wasn't often they saw a man like this.

"Six feet of sex," Leslie Anne Cantrell, the town flirt, had called him, eliciting delighted giggles from the women who'd overheard. Sharon could honestly say now that Leslie Anne hadn't been exaggerating. Any normal woman would appreciate Mac Cordero's thick black hair, gleaming dark eyes, taut brown skin and sleekly muscular build.

He wasn't a man any woman was likely to forget, she mused, no matter how they met.

Realizing abruptly that she was standing there gazing up at him, her fingers still clasped in his, she pulled her hand away and stuck it in the pocket of the navy linen blazer she wore with a muted plaid shirt and khaki slacks. Though the expression in his eyes was impossible to read, she had the unnerving sensation that he could see directly into her mind as he searched her face. "You've suffered no ill effects from your ordeal?"

"No, I'm fine. A few colorful bruises and sore muscles, but no real injuries, thank goodness."

"You were fortunate."

She nodded. "Yes, I know."

"Any word about the van that ran you off the road?"

"No. Wade—the police chief—said it seems to have disappeared. But if it's still in the area, he'll find it."

"You seem confident about that."

She couldn't help smiling. "Wade takes his job very seriously. When someone breaks the law, he doesn't rest until he catches them."

"Then I hope he catches them soon." For the first time since he'd helped her to her feet, he looked away from her face long enough to glance around her shop, Intriguing Interiors. The store was filled with rows of wallpapers and borders, shelves of order books, swatches of designer fabrics, and displays of decorator and gift items. "Nice place."

"Thank you. I bought it almost two years ago."

What might have been amusement glimmered for a moment in his eyes. "I know."

She studied him curiously. "You do?"

His mouth quirked again into that sexy semi-smile, making her pulse race in a manner that both distracted and annoyed her. She made an effort to focus on their conversation rather than the effect he had on her—something she would think about and rationalize later, she promised herself.

"Ever since I helped you out of that water, everyone in this town has wanted to talk to me about the accident—and you," he said ruefully.

She waved a hand toward the door. "That's my town. The rumor capital of the world. So what did they tell you about me?"

"That you're a very talented decorator. Which is one of the reasons I stopped by."

He had surprised her again. "You need a decorator?"

"Yes. I've purchased an old Victorian house at the end of Deer Run Lane—"

"The Garrett place," she acknowledged with a nod. "People have been talking about you, too."

The slight twist of his mouth this time might have been a smile or maybe a grimace, but either way, it was as sexy as all get-out. Feeling uncomfortably schoolgirlish, Sharon almost sighed.

"Anyway," he continued, "I'm completely renovating the place. I need a decorator. I'd like to keep the decor appropriate to the period of the architec-

ture—Victorian, but not overdone. I'll want to start
consultations soon so there will be plenty of time to
order wallpaper, light fixtures and any other decorating items I'll need. Are you interested in the
job?''

Though she loved the idea of decorating a restored historic home, Sharon felt compelled to be
honest. ''I'm not really a trained decorator, Mr. Cordero.''

''Call me Mac. I understand you've decorated
quite a few homes and offices around town. Trent
McBride, who's doing the cabinetwork for my renovation project, recommended you. He said you're
redecorating his father and brother's law offices.''

She wondered if she could ever be comfortable
using his first name. She found herself rather intimidated by this man, for some reason. It was hard to
imagine having a casual relationship with him.

''I do some interior decorating as a sideline for
my shop,'' she admitted. ''It's always been an interest of mine, and I've taken a few decorating
classes. I started out helping friends, and then other
people began to request my services. But if you want
a more experienced, better-known professional decorator, you'll have to bring someone in from Atlanta.''

He shook his head. ''I prefer to patronize local
businesses.''

She knew he had hired local carpenters, plumbers,
electricians and other subcontractors for the renovation project. She knew, as well, that he hadn't

demanded a lengthy list of credentials from everyone he'd hired. Trent McBride, for example, had only just gone into business as a cabinetmaker.

"I would certainly be interested in discussing this with you," she said, intrigued by the challenge of such a project, even as she hoped she was up to it.

He leaned a forearm against the sales counter. The casual pose brought him a bit closer to her, just enough to make her self-conscious again. His smile was slightly deeper this time, giving her a glimpse of white teeth. The job he offered was looking better and better, she thought, letting herself drift for just a moment in sheer feminine appreciation.

"Maybe we could talk about it over dinner tonight?" he suggested. "The restaurant on West Charles isn't bad."

She was on the verge of accepting—just to discuss the project, of course—when she remembered her brother. There were times when she'd left him home by himself for a couple of hours, but she didn't think it was a good idea tonight. She wouldn't put it past him to sneak out and go to the party anyway—and she wasn't going to give him that opportunity. The boy throwing the party was a notorious troublemaker, and Brad was too easily led into mischief. There had already been one occasion when he'd been escorted home by Officer Dodson; she didn't intend for it to happen again tonight.

"I'm afraid I can't tonight," she said.

If Mac was disappointed, he didn't show it. "When would be a good time for you to meet?"

"I can spare a couple of hours tomorrow afternoon, if you're free then."

He straightened away from the counter. "I'll be out at the site tomorrow meeting with subcontractors. If you want to join me there, we can do a walkthrough. It will give you a chance to look the place over, too."

Definitely intrigued—and more comfortable with the thought of discussing the job at the site rather than over dinner—she nodded. "What time?"

"Two o'clock?"

"I'll be there."

He was already moving toward the door. "Until tomorrow then."

"Mr. Cordero—"

"Mac," he reminded her over his shoulder.

"I want to thank you again for helping me Friday night."

He gave her a sudden, full smile that nearly melted the soles of her shoes. He didn't smile often, apparently, but when he did—*wow*. "Not necessary. See you tomorrow, Sharon."

She hadn't given him permission to use her first name, but it would be churlish to remind him of that now. She wasn't usually one to insist on formality— but with this man, a little distance might not be such a bad idea.

He was just reaching for the doorknob when the door opened and a plump blonde bustled in, nearly crashing into Mac. "Oh, sorry," she said, catching herself just in time.

His smile fading into a more somber expression, he nodded politely. "No problem." And then he let himself out, leaving the two women staring bemusedly after him.

"Who," Tressie Bearden demanded, "was *that?*"

Dragging her gaze away from the glass door, through which she could see him walking purposefully away, Sharon cleared her throat and turned to her employee. "That was Mac Cordero."

Tressie's eyes widened. "Cordero-the-hero? Oh, man, he's even better-looking than I've heard."

Sharon frowned. "I wish you wouldn't call him that. It's such a silly nickname."

"Hey, you were the damsel in distress he rescued," Tressie replied with an impish grin. "I would think you'd consider the nickname appropriate."

Though she was tempted to argue again that Mac had only assisted her, Sharon resisted the impulse. "How did your doctor's appointment go? Everything check out okay?"

Glancing again toward the door, Tressie answered absently. "She said I'm a healthy, red-blooded woman in my prime. So I guess it must have been Mac Cordero's gorgeous dark eyes and delectable bod that made my heart rate go crazy, hmm?"

Since Sharon had been experiencing similar symptoms during the past twenty minutes or so, she couldn't argue with Tressie's conclusion. Apparently, they were *both* healthy, red-blooded women.

Now that they'd settled that, it was time to put adolescent foolishness aside and get back to work. "About those wall sconces you ordered…"

Tressie wavéd a hand impatiently. "We can talk sconces later. What was Mac Cordero doing here? What did he say? What did *you* say? Did you find out anything interesting about him?"

Tressie was an active participant in local gossip circles and her membership in the Honoria Community League gave her an inside track to the most juicy tidbits. Her gift of gab and easy way with people made her an asset to the shop, but Sharon sometimes found her co-worker's chatter exasperating. If she told Tressie that Mac had offered her the decorating job, the news would be all over town within the hour, and Sharon hadn't even given him an answer yet. She settled for half the truth. "He said he wanted to make sure I'd recovered from the incident Friday night."

"Really? That was nice of him."

"Yes, it was."

Tressie's expression turned speculative. "Do you know if he's married or anything?"

"No, I don't know. The subject didn't come up." For some reason, Sharon would have bet he was unattached. Educated guess—or wishful thinking? she wondered with a slight wince.

Looking disgusted, Tressie shook her head. "I'd have made sure it came up. Why didn't you ask him?"

"Because it's none of my business." Sharon

could only hope the hint got through as she moved across the shop to straighten a display of clearance items. "So why don't you call and check on those sconces? They should have arrived two days ago."

Tressie hesitated a moment, reluctant to drop the subject, but then she nodded and moved toward the telephone. As much as she loved to gossip, she was efficient and hardworking, and Sharon was still grateful that Tressie had come to work for her.

Feeling a little guilty for not telling Tressie about the decorating offer, Sharon went back to work, herself, her thoughts divided between details of her business, worry about her brother and anticipation of her next meeting with Mac Cordero.

THE MAN in the gutted-out kitchen with Mac was young—no more than twenty-six—golden-blond, blue-eyed with glasses and a little on the thin side. Picturing his own solid build, black hair, dark eyes and brown skin, Mac was well aware that he and Trent McBride could not have looked more different. No one could have guessed from looking at them that they shared a blood relationship—and no one but Mac knew about that relationship. Even he didn't know exactly how close the connection was.

"So you want a state-of-the-art modern kitchen concealed behind solidly built, period-appropriate woodwork," Trent summed up with a comprehensive glance around the large, shadowy room. The electricity wasn't turned on yet, so the only light came through the filthy windows and from the two battery-powered lanterns Mac had brought with him.

The house had been empty for years, and the deterioration was pervasive—so much that there were some who openly doubted the renovation was worth the time and expense. With his experience, Mac knew better. He'd taken on more daunting projects, and the results had been both satisfying and profitable. There were plenty of people who were willing to pay for history and quality. Of course, Mac's previous jobs had been in areas with a bigger money base and more historical interest—Atlanta, Savannah, Charleston, Birmingham. It might take a bit longer to find a buyer here. But he wasn't too worried about it. He'd come to Honoria for reasons that were far more personal than professional.

Even if it cost him every dime he'd managed to accumulate in the past few years, he would consider it money well spent if he finally got some answers to the questions that had haunted him all his life.

Because Trent was still waiting for a response, Mac nodded. "I want every modern convenience, but I don't want it to look like a restaurant kitchen. We'll use appliance garages and custom cabinetry to camouflage the equipment."

Trent seemed to approve. Mac could tell the younger man was picturing the end result as he looked around the cavernous room with its big windows and massive stone fireplace at one end. "It's going to be expensive."

Mac shrugged. "Quality costs. Of course, I'll be

keeping a close eye on expenses, making sure I'm paying fair prices and spending no more than necessary.''

Trent didn't seem concerned about the prospect of close supervision. "I'll work up a detailed cost analysis for you," he offered. "If anything unexpected comes up, we'll discuss then how to handle it.''

"That's the way I prefer to do business. I'm not crazy about surprises.''

Trent smiled a little at that. "I could have guessed that from the few meetings we've had.''

Mac wondered how *Trent* felt about surprises. He could give him a whopper of one right now, if he wanted. But he would wait until the time was right—until he had his answers—before he decided how, or whether, to break his news to the McBrides.

A woman's voice came from somewhere in the front of the house. "Mr. Cordero?''

Mac swiveled toward the sound, then wondered why his pulse had suddenly quickened in response to Sharon Henderson's voice. A decorator, he reminded himself. That was all she was to him. All he intended for her to be. And this was his chance to find out just how friendly she was with the McBride family.

CHAPTER THREE

MAC FOUND SHARON waiting just inside the front door, which he had left open. In marked contrast to the dull, colorless surroundings of the run-down entryway, she looked fresh and pretty, dressed in clean, bright colors. She was studying the broken, curved staircase, her expression thoughtful. "I've never been in here before," she said when he joined her. "I didn't know what to expect."

He found it annoyingly necessary to remind himself that he was only interested in her because of her interior-decorating skills and her friendship with the McBrides—not because she was the first woman he'd been attracted to in months. Dragging his gaze away from her, he glanced around the entryway. "Most of the damage is cosmetic. This place was built to last, and it has, despite the neglect."

"It's really worth saving?"

He rested a hand on an intricately turned newel post. "I wouldn't be here if I didn't think it was."

Wearing the same contemplative look he'd just seen on Trent, she glanced slowly around the big entryway and then through an arched doorway into a room that had probably served as a front parlor. "It must have been beautiful once."

"And it will be again. Let me show you around downstairs. I'd rather save the upstairs until the staircase and upper floors have been reinforced."

She glanced up the stairs, as if she was reluctant to miss anything in the tour he'd promised. But then she turned away from the staircase to follow him along the lower floor.

He led her through the parlor, the single downstairs bedroom, what might have once been a sitting room or music room, and a long, narrow dining room. Without lights, the rooms looked even more shabby and ramshackle than they actually were. The sunlight that managed to penetrate the dirty windows turned gray and dusty inside. But Mac saw the still-intact crown moldings, the repairable plasterwork, the solid-wood paneling and hardwood flooring, and he knew the house could be spectacular again. He wondered if Sharon shared his vision.

She murmured something he didn't quite catch. "I beg your pardon?"

Looking at him with an air of distraction, she motioned to the long, fanlight-topped window at the end of the dining room. "Beveled leaded glass," she said. "And look at the detail of that crown molding. You don't see work like that anymore."

Her comments pleased him, as did the expression on her face. Oh, yeah, she was seeing what could be, rather than what was. Just as he did when he looked at this place.

She stepped closer to the window to examine the

framing. "The woodwork is in good shape all through the house? No dry rot? Termite damage?"

"Some, but minimal. There are a few places where we'll have to do some reproduction work, but not many."

She moved close to a wall to peer at the darkened wallpaper that had once been a bright sunflower design, more indicative of the 1970s than the early 1900s. "I bet there are at least a half-dozen layers of wallpaper on these walls. Homeowners often used to paper right on top of existing patterns. If that's the case, I should be able to re-create original decor by studying the earliest layers."

"I counted six layers in the master bedroom. Five in the kitchen." He'd dug through all that in his initial examination of the house's condition.

"Were the early patterns distinguishable?"

"In places, yes. You'll probably want to see it, though I'm not interested in an exact reproduction of the original decor. Just a look that's appropriate for the period."

"The townspeople have always referred to this place as a Victorian mansion, but it isn't strictly Victorian, is it? More a combination of Queen Anne, Italianate, and even a little Early American craftsman influence. Sort of a hodgepodge, but it works. It must have been spectacular."

Despite her disclaimers that she wasn't a professional decorator, he was satisfied with the observations she'd made thus far. He had seen examples of her work, having learned that she'd decorated several of the businesses he'd visited in town, and he knew she had a flair for color and proportion. Now he was even more confident that he hadn't made a mistake approaching her about this project.

Her friendship with the McBrides might be useful to him later, but it was her decorating expertise that interested him at the moment. At least, that was what he told himself, though he was all too keenly aware of how nice she looked in her pale blue spring-weight sweater and fluidly tailored gray slacks that emphasized the slender waist his hands had spanned so easily.

He reminded himself again that he didn't have time for that sort of distraction now. He might notice her blue-green eyes and sweetly curved mouth, the shallow dimple in her left cheek, the graceful line of her throat or the feminine curve of her breasts beneath the soft knit sweater she wore, but that was as far as he intended to take it. He had a job to do—and the Garrett place was only a part of it.

Though his voice was casual, he was watching Sharon closely when he led her into the next room. "This," he said, "is the kitchen."

The smile that lit her face when she saw who was waiting there was full, warm and beautiful. Mac couldn't help wondering how it would feel to be on the receiving end of a smile like that from her. "Trent," she said, and even her voice was warmer now. "What a nice surprise."

Though Mac had summed Trent up as a somber, even brooding, type, the smile he gave Sharon held a natural charm with a hint of mischief. Having heard through the local rumor mills that Trent had been involved in a near-fatal plane crash that had left him with both physical and emotional scars, Mac suspected he was seeing an echo of the cocky young ladies' man Trent was reported to have been before the crash.

"Hi, Sharon. It's good to see you again." Trent kissed her cheek with the ease of long acquaintance.

Mac found himself frowning as he watched Trent's casual touch against Sharon's smooth cheek. He cleared his expression immediately, forcing himself to study the pair objectively.

"It's good to see you, too," Sharon said. "You look great."

"So do you. I was glad to hear you weren't seriously injured Friday night."

"Only a few bruises. I was lucky. So how are the wedding plans coming along?"

A glow of satisfaction warmed Trent's usually cool blue eyes. "Everything's on schedule. Annie and I will be married the last Saturday in August."

"I know your mother is looking forward to having another wedding in the family."

Trent grimaced. "Oh, yeah. She loves a big fuss—any excuse to get the family all together."

Mac stuck his hands in his pockets.

Sharon and Trent exchanged a few more pleasantries and then the conversation turned to the project at hand. "What do you think of the house?" Trent asked.

"I have to confess, I've always wanted to come inside and look around this place." Sharon made a slow circle to study the kitchen, her attention lingering on the huge fireplace. "It's something, isn't it?"

"It definitely has potential. You're doing the decorating?"

"Mr. Cordero and I are discussing that possibility."

It was beginning to irk Mac that she continued to call him Mr. Cordero in that prim, rather prissy way. It couldn't be more opposite to the warm and informal manner in which she spoke to Trent. "Mac," he reminded her, deciding it was time for him to do a little fishing. "I take it you two know each other?"

Trent chuckled. "You might say that. Sharon and I went to the prom together."

Sharon's smile turned a few watts brighter. "Trent was a senior, I was a junior. He had already been accepted into the Air Force Academy. I was so impressed, I spent the whole evening looking at him and giggling like an idiot."

"I don't remember it quite that way," Trent said gallantly.

Mac told himself he should be pleased to hear this. After all, her connection to the McBrides was one of the reasons he was interested in her. Right? And yet he still found himself changing the subject rather more abruptly than he had intended. "Yes, well, perhaps we should talk about the renovation project now."

He stepped smoothly between them and opened the briefcase he'd left on a rough-surfaced counter. "I have some blueprints and sketches here…"

Sharon and Trent moved closer on either side of him to study the paperwork in the yellow light of the battery-powered lanterns. It annoyed Mac that he had to make such an effort to concentrate on the job instead of Sharon's spicy-floral scent.

This wasn't working out exactly as he had planned.

FORTY-FIVE MINUTES LATER, Trent left, explaining that he had an appointment with his fiancée. Sharon was touched by the eagerness that glinted in his eyes as he left. For almost a year after his accident, Trent had barricaded himself in his solitary rural home, brooding and alone. He'd held his friends at a distance, seeing no one but family—and Annie Stewart, the housekeeper his mother had hired for him against his will. Now he and Annie were planning their wedding, and Trent was learning how to smile again.

Sharon was delighted for him.

Mac cleared his throat, drawing her gaze away from the back door through which Trent had disappeared. "Prom, hmm?"

She smiled. "Yes. I wore a flame-red satin slip dress and Trent wore a black tux with a red cummerbund and bow tie. I thought we looked sophisticated and glamorous—like movie stars. My mother still keeps our prom picture on the piano with all her other family pictures.''

When Mac didn't seem particularly amused by her reminiscing, she cleared her throat and turned the conversation back to business. ''At what point would you want me to become involved with the renovation?''

''You're considering taking the job?''

She practically itched to be a part of this project. ''Yes.''

''I'm glad to hear it.''

Something about his expression and the tone of his voice made her wonder why he seemed so pleased that she would be joining the renovation team he was assembling. He didn't really know her, and he had seen only a few examples of her work. Had the recommendations he'd heard really been so persuasive?

He had said it was his practice to patronize local businesses and workers whenever possible. Granted, there weren't many professional decorators in Honoria to choose from—none, actually. ''You're sure you don't want to consult a few other decorators first?'' she asked, a sudden attack of nerves making her wonder if she was being wise to get involved with this man. With this *job,* she corrected herself quickly.

He shook his head. ''I want you.''

She really wished he hadn't worded it quite that way. Something told her those three words would echo in her mind for a disturbingly long time. ''I would certainly understand if you want to at least consider—''

''Sharon—do you want the job or not?''

Clasping her hands in front of her, she glanced around the big, old kitchen. ''Yes. I want it.''

''And you believe you can do a good job?''

She could already picture the front parlor done in tastefully restrained Victoriana, old Oriental rugs on satiny, refinished hardwood floors, strategically placed mirrors making the small rooms look bigger. ''Yes, I do.''

''Then all we have left to discuss is the money,'' he said matter-of-factly. ''I've written the decorating budget here—'' he stabbed a finger on one of the sheets of paper scattered across the counter ''—which includes your fee, itemized on the next line. Does that look like a fair estimate to you?''

She glanced at the figure, blinked a couple of times, then read it again. ''Yes, that looks fair,'' she said, her voice a bit strained.

She couldn't help remembering all those wild rumors about Mac—that he was a rich eccentric, or on consignment for a celebrity millionaire, or working for a big-money crime family. As improbable as those scenarios had sounded, money didn't seem to be a problem when it came to this project. She would be compensated very generously for the sheer pleasure of helping this sadly deteriorating building become a beautiful home again.

''I'd like you to be closely involved with the project from the start,'' he said. ''You've probably noticed I have my own way of doing things—it's not necessarily the way most contractors work, but it suits me. I assemble a team at the beginning and then involve everyone in the decision-making, utilizing their expertise in their areas. Final decisions, of course, are mine, but I'm always open to discussion and suggestions.''

"How long have you been doing this? Buying and restoring old houses, I mean.''

"Full time for almost three years now. Before that, I restored a couple of small houses as a sideline to my day job.''

"And what was your day job?''

She'd considered herself making conversation, not trying to pry, but she got the sudden feeling that Mac wasn't comfortable with her questions. "I've worked in several jobs prior to this one.''

"I see.'' She looked at her watch. "I really should get back to the shop. I have an appointment with a sales rep this afternoon.''

"I'll walk you to your car.''

She knew the layout of the house this time, so she led the way with Mac following close behind her. As she walked, she looked around again, making dozens of mental notes. She would like to return soon with a camera and sketch pad. She was so involved with her planning, she forgot to concentrate on her steps and she might have tripped over a broken board had Mac not reached out to take her arm before she reached it, guiding her around the plank.

"The floors are pretty rough,'' he said without

letting go of her. "It's even worse upstairs. Once the carpenters get started, I'm going to designate the whole house as a hard-hat zone."

"I should have been watching where I was going. I'm afraid I was too busy mentally decorating."

He chuckled. "As much as I appreciate your eagerness to get started, I wouldn't want you to injure yourself because of it."

"I'll be more careful from now on," she promised, trying to keep her tone light despite the ripples of sensation emanating from his hand on her arm.

"Good."

When he didn't immediately move away, her smile wavered. His face was only inches from hers. His dark eyes looked straight into hers. She'd never understood more clearly what it meant to be in danger of melting at someone's feet. When it came to her hormones, this man was downright dangerous.

She cleared her throat so she could speak without squeaking. "Is there something else?"

He hesitated a moment, then dropped his hand and stepped back. Without further comment, he motioned for her to continue through the house. She took care to watch her step as she walked out.

She unlocked the driver's door of the rental car her insurance company had provided until she could replace the one she'd lost in Snake Creek. Uncertain what to say, she turned hesitantly to Mac before getting in. "I'll start gathering some pictures and samples before our next meeting. I'd like to come back soon to take some measurements and photographs."

"The work crew starts tomorrow, so someone will be here pretty much all the time, Monday through Saturday. Come by anytime, but be careful around the construction."

"Thank you, I will. So, I guess I'll see you later."

"Mac," he said.

She lifted an eyebrow in confusion, wondering why he'd just said his own name. "I beg your pardon?"

"I'd like to hear you say, 'I'll see you later, Mac.'"

"Why?"

"Let's just say I like my team to be on comfortable terms with each other."

"I'm quite comfortable with you," she lied briskly.

Wearing a slightly challenging smile, he leaned against her open car door. "Then why can't you say my name, Sharon?"

He said hers easily enough. And something about the sound of it on his tongue made a funny little shiver go through her. Which was hardly a professional way to react to a business associate, she chided herself.

"I have no problem saying your name, Mac. But I am running late, so if there's nothing else, I'd better be on my way."

There was definite satisfaction in his smile when he straightened away from the door. "No, there's nothing else—for now. Drive carefully."

He didn't stay to watch her drive off, but turned

on one heel and walked back to the house. He didn't even glance over his shoulder before disappearing inside. Sharon was left staring after him. She roused herself with a slight shake of her head and reached for the key.

As she drove away, she vowed to herself that this was the last time she would allow him to turn her into a tongue-tied adolescent.

Any further exchanges between her and Mac Cordero were going to be strictly business—even though she was beginning to wonder if Mac had something else in mind.

BRAD WAS on his very best behavior Thursday evening during dinner, which pleased Sharon almost as much as it worried her. She loved her younger brother dearly, but any time he acted sweet and polite, she couldn't help wondering what he was up to.

"How are you enjoying your summer vacation, Brad?" Jerry Whitaker, who had joined them for dinner, asked encouragingly.

Looking up from the baked pork chops, rice and steamed vegetables Sharon had prepared, the boy tossed a fringe of shaggy brown bangs out of his face to look across the table. "It's okay. Better than school, anyway."

"What are you doing to keep yourself busy?"

"Baseball, mostly. Coach Cooper has practice every afternoon. And I go to the Boys and Girls Club a couple of mornings a week for tennis lessons."

Jerry smiled at Sharon. "Sounds like you've got quite an athlete in the family."

Absently returning the smile, she glanced at her brother. "Yes, Brad's very good at sports."

"What else do you have planned for summer, Brad? Hanging out at the pool with your friends? Flirting with the girls? I seem to have a vague memory of doing a lot of that back in the olden days when I was your age."

Because he knew it was expected of him, Brad chuckled in response to Jerry's exaggeration, but then his smile faded as he glanced at his sister. "Sharon doesn't let me hang out with my friends much. She's afraid I'll get into trouble."

Sharon's defenses went up when Jerry gave her a reproachful look. "That's not exactly accurate," she protested. "I certainly don't forbid Brad to see his friends. I simply ask him to let me know where he'll be and what time he'll be home."

"And I have to tell her who's going to be there, and what we'll be doing, and what we'll be eating, and—" Brad held up a finger for each point he made.

"That's enough," Sharon cut in, knowing her brother was still annoyed with her for keeping him from attending the party Monday evening.

She still felt justified in her decision, especially since she'd heard that Officer Dodson had been dispatched to send everyone home when the festivities had gotten too loud. She'd been surprised that he hadn't reported seeing signs of drinking among the underage guests. At least the kids had been smart enough not to try to get away with that—probably because they'd guessed that Chief Davenport would have someone keeping a close eye on them.

"Your brother is fifteen years old, Sharon," Jerry murmured. "You have to loosen the apron strings sometime."

Brad looked smug.

Sharon was annoyed with Jerry for undercutting her in front of Brad. Surely he knew she was doing the best she could while their flighty mother was off vacationing with a group of congenial widows she'd met over the Internet. It wasn't the first time Lucy Henderson had left Sharon in charge of the household—she'd been doing it since Sharon was a teenager, herself—but it was getting much more difficult as Brad grew older and more rebellious.

She picked up a bowl. "Have some more vegetables, Jerry."

Fully aware of the message she was really sending him, he chuckled, took the bowl and obligingly changed the subject. "What's this I hear about you working on the Garrett-house renovation?"

It had taken less than forty-eight hours for the news to get to him. Sharon wasn't sure why she hadn't already mentioned it, herself. Maybe because Jerry so rarely showed any real interest in her business, which he tended to refer to as "the little wallpaper shop." "I've been hired as the interior-design consultant. I'll help choose colors, patterns, fixtures and so on. Mac wants the house completely ready for occupancy when the renovation is completed.''

''Mac?'' Jerry murmured, lifting an eyebrow.

Funny how easily the name had slipped from her this time, proving that she'd already begun to think of him that way. ''He doesn't care much for formality.''

''I'm not sure I approve of this arrangement.'' Jerry seemed to be only half teasing. ''Apparently he's quite the romantic figure around town. Handsome, mysterious, reportedly wealthy. *And* he's the guy who saved your life last weekend. I wouldn't want you to get swept off your feet.''

Sharon forced a smile. ''I'm only working for him, Jerry, not dating him.''

''I'm glad to hear that. Why do you think he chose you as his decorator? Do you suppose his budget is more limited than rumors have implied?''

Aware of Brad listening to the conversation while he ate, Sharon tried to keep her tone humorous. ''Are you calling me a cut-rate decorator, Jerry? Hardly flattering.''

He didn't even have the grace to look sheepish. ''Now, Sharon, you know I didn't mean it like that. But you must admit, you aren't a licensed decorator. Picking out colors and wallpaper patterns has been a hobby for you.''

A hobby? She thought of the hours she'd spent reading, studying, poring over magazines, journals and sample books. She'd had several paid decorating jobs, including the recent remodeling of the First

Bank of Honoria and the upcoming McBride Law Firm project. Needlework was a hobby; decorating was a passion she'd had since adolescence. "He said I came highly recommended," she said simply, knowing it would be a waste of breath to argue semantics.

"I'm sure he won't be disappointed."

Had Jerry always had that slightly condescending tone when he talked about her work, or was she simply being oversensitive this evening? Whatever the cause, this conversation was beginning to annoy her as much as his criticism of the way she was watching out for her brother.

"I'll make sure he isn't," she said, and stood. "Who wants dessert? I baked a strawberry cake."

Brad and Jerry both eagerly accepted the offer.

As Sharon stood alone in the kitchen slicing cake, she found herself thinking that maybe she shouldn't see so much of Jerry for a while. She'd gotten into the habit of hanging out with him without really thinking about where the relationship was going. She hadn't liked the note of possession in his voice when he'd quizzed her about working for Mac. Was he under the impression that they had an exclusive relationship?

As far as she was concerned, she and Jerry were friends. They weren't lovers. Jerry had broached the possibility a time or two, but Sharon had always put him off. She wasn't ready to take that step, she'd told him. She didn't think it set a good example for Brad. Both were legitimate excuses, but the truth was, she simply hadn't wanted to become that intimately involved with Jerry. Something had always held her back.

Maybe it was because he'd never taken her breath away just by looking into her eyes, a small voice whispered inside her head. He had never caused a jolt of electricity to go through her with a simple brush of his hand. She had never actually reacted to any man's touch that way—until Mac.

The cake server slipped from her hand, clattering against the tile floor. The noise roused her from her disturbing thoughts, clearing away the image of Mac's gleaming dark eyes.

"Are you okay in there?" Jerry called out from the other room.

"I'm fine," she answered, her tone sharper than she had intended. She immediately regretted it. It wasn't Jerry she was angry with, it was herself. She was simply going to have to get herself under control when it came to Mac Cordero. And she was going to have to take charge of this situation with Jerry. It wasn't fair of her to lead him on.

Maybe it would be better if she simply concentrated on her brother and her business, at least for the next few weeks.

CHAPTER FOUR

MAC WAS in his motel room early Thursday evening when someone tapped on the door. He took another look at the photograph in his hand—a picture of a woman holding a tiny infant with Mac's dark hair and eyes—and then slipped it back into its usual place in his wallet before moving toward the door. He had to take a couple of deep breaths to release the pain and anger looking at that photo always roused in him. Only then could he answer the knock.

From long habit, he checked the peephole before releasing the lock. Curious, he opened the door and leaned against it, shoving his disturbing memories to the back of his mind. "Well, hello, Chief. Paying a social call?"

"Partially," Wade Davenport surprised him by answering. "Mind if I come in?"

Mac stepped out of the doorway and gestured toward the two chairs beside the window. "I would offer you a drink, but all I have is half a can of soda—and it's probably flat."

Glancing around the rather spartan motel room, Wade asked, "Are you going to be staying here long?"

Was the police chief just making friendly conversation, or keeping tabs on the stranger in town? Mac shrugged. "I've been looking for an apartment to rent for the duration of the renovation job. I talked to the manager of the complex on West Elm this afternoon. I'll probably move there next week."

Wade wandered to the window and glanced out. "Not much of a view. The McBride Law Firm's parking lot. The McBrides are related to my wife, you know. Caleb's her uncle, Trevor's her cousin."

"There usually are a lot of family connections in a small town like this one," Mac observed, following Wade's glance. He wondered if the police chief would be so cool if Mac told him about his own family connection to the chief's wife.

Turning away from the window, Wade sat in one of the chairs. Mac settled in the other. "What can I do for you, Chief?"

"Call me Wade. Seems more appropriate between colleagues, don't you think?"

"Colleagues?" Mac repeated carefully.

"One cop to another."

Long experienced at concealing his emotions, Mac kept his posture relaxed. "Cop to *ex*-cop is more accurate."

Wade nodded acknowledgment of the distinction.

"Any particular reason you've been checking up on me?"

"You've come to my town at the same time as what passes for a crime wave in these parts. Seemed appropriate."

''You always keep this close an eye on things around here?''

''That's why they pay me the big bucks.''

Because Mac knew how little small-town police chiefs typically earned, he chuckled dryly. ''Careful. Start talking about big bucks and I'll suspect you're on the take.''

''Marvella Tucker slips me a dozen home-baked cookies about once a month. She's ninety years old, likes to drive her big old car right down the middle of Main Street. She thinks I won't ticket her if she keeps baking cookies for me.''

''Is she right?''

Wade grinned and patted his stomach. ''What do you think?''

''I think I need to figure out a way to get on Mrs. Tucker's cookie list.''

''So what's a former vice cop doing remodeling an old house in this burg? How'd you choose the Garrett place?''

''Still checking up on me?''

''Making conversation,'' Wade corrected him. ''I used to be with Atlanta P.D. Burned out, came to Honoria for the slower pace and better working hours. What brought you here?''

Mac lifted a shoulder. ''Mine's a similar story. Got tired of working vice and decided I needed a change. Old houses have always interested me, so that's the direction I took. It's satisfying work.''

''My wife and I live in a house her father built more than forty years ago. There's always something needing repairs, but I still prefer it to one of those new cut-and-paste houses. Emily says it has character.''

"Most old houses do," Mac agreed.

"You never told me how you found the Garrett place.''

"I saw a photo in a real estate listing. It looked as if it had potential, so I came here to check it out. You know the rest.'' The answer was only partially true, but close enough not to bother Mac's conscience overly much.

"You've got the town all abuzz, you know. Nothing the folks around here like better than having someone new to talk about.''

"So I gather.''

"They're good people, for the most part. The gossip only occasionally turns vicious.''

Mac thought Wade was being generous, considering how often the gossip had turned against his wife's family. It hadn't taken him long to figure out that the McBride name had been synonymous with scandal for several generations.

No one but Mac was aware that there was one scandal yet to be revealed. One in which he was intimately involved. One for which he deserved some sort of revenge—once he found out who to direct it toward.

"So what's the buzz on me?" Mac asked casually. "What made you think you needed to run a check?"

Wade shrugged. "What would you have done in

my position? The only stranger in town just happened in the vicinity of the very isolated Porter place when it was being robbed. No real reason for you to be out there. Last time you were in town, when you were buying the Garrett house, someone broke into Joe Baker's storage shed and took an RV and some other expensive sporting goods. I make it a practice to be skeptical of coincidences.''

Through narrowed eyes, Mac studied the other man warily, having trouble reading Wade's affable expression. He wasn't sure why the chief was telling him all this. If the guy really suspected he was involved, would he be quite so open about it? Was Wade saying Mac's law enforcement background cleared him of suspicion, or that circumstantial evidence still pointed his way? ''I guess I'd have done the same in your position. But I'm not your thief.''

''That's what my hunch tells me.''

''How accurate do your hunches generally turn out to be?''

Wade grinned lazily. ''Oh, about ninety percent.''

''Ten percent margin of error. Not bad. So, who's your hunch telling you to go after?''

His smile fading, Wade sighed. ''Unfortunately, it isn't leading me anywhere. I literally haven't got a clue yet. Just a feeling that I've got four break-ins that are all related, and that there's something going on in my town I don't know about. And that pisses me off.''

''I'll keep my eyes open. Sometimes an outsider sees or hears something the locals miss.''

"Especially an outsider who worked vice for a number of years, I'd imagine. I'd appreciate your insight if something catches your attention."

Though he didn't really expect to be in a position to identify a local crime ring, Mac nodded.

Wade planted his hands on the arms of his chair and pushed himself to his feet. "We'll have to swap shop talk soon. Over lunch at Cora's Café, maybe. Tasted her pies yet?"

"No, not yet."

"Then you're in for a treat. She makes the best I've ever had—and I'm something of a connoisseur when it comes to desserts." With a last glance out the window toward the McBride Law Firm, he moved toward the door. "I'll see you around, Mac."

Still clueless as to the real purpose behind the chief's visit, Mac saw him out, then watched from the window as Wade drove away.

He had an itchy feeling that Wade Davenport wasn't an easy man to mislead.

"YOU SHOULD HAVE INVITED him to dinner," Emily McBride Davenport chided her husband later that evening when he mentioned his call on Mac Cordero.

Looking up from the block tower he was building with their almost-two-year-old daughter, Claire, Wade lifted his eyebrows in surprise. "Now, why would I do that? We don't even know the guy."

Watching from the couch where she'd been reading a book, Emily pushed her mop of golden curls out of her face to frown at him. "He's new to town, Wade. He's probably lonely."

"I'm not so sure about that. He seems like the self-contained sort. Probably prefers his solitude. You know he's turned down most of the invitations he's received from well-intentioned townsfolk."

"Most likely because he could tell most of them just want to pump him for personal information," Emily retorted.

He smiled as he guided the red block gripped in Claire's chubby hand to the top of the tower. "And isn't that what *you'd* like to do?"

Emily looked offended. "Of course not. I'm not interested in his personal business. I just think it would be neighborly to have him to dinner."

"I don't make a habit of bringing strangers home unless I know my family is safe with them."

Emily rolled her eyes, as she so often did when she felt Wade was being overprotective. "You like him, Wade. I could tell from the way you spoke of him."

He did sort of like him, actually—even if he wasn't quite sure he trusted him. Just because Mac Cordero had bravely jumped into a river to save Sharon Henderson's life, and just because Wade had learned that Mac was a former police officer from Savannah didn't mean the guy had no ulterior motive for being in Honoria.

He knew Mac had lied to him at least once that afternoon—when he'd said he'd come here after seeing a photograph of the Garrett house in a real estate ad. The Realtor had told Wade that Mac had approached her, asking what old homes were available in this area. He hadn't seen the house and then come here, as he'd claimed—it had actually been the other way around. So why the lie?

There was a reason Mac had come to Honoria— and Wade had a hunch he hadn't yet heard the whole story.

MAC DECIDED to have dinner at Cora's Café Friday evening. He'd been thinking about her pies ever since Wade had mentioned them the day before. Because it was a nice spring afternoon, still sunny and warm at six o'clock, he decided to walk the half mile from his motel to the café.

Honoria's downtown section had fallen victim to urban sprawl, leaving abandoned buildings and boarded-up storefronts behind. There had been some effort to revitalize the area, but the new development on the west side of town had taken a heavy toll in this neighborhood. Mac studied the shabby old stone storefronts and thought of the history and traditions that had been abandoned here and in so many other small towns.

A group of teenage boys wearing baggy clothes and fashionably surly expressions loitered on the sidewalk in front of a seedy-looking store-turned-arcade. Mac counted seven boys, none of them over seventeen, four holding cigarettes. Tough guys, he summed up swiftly—at least in front of their buddies. Wanna-be rednecks. Trouble waiting to happen. He'd seen boys this age and younger packing guns and pushing drugs on street corners in Savannah.

The boys completely filled the sidewalk, blocking Mac's path. He could step into the street to go around them, but there were a couple of cars coming and he wasn't in the mood to play dodge-the-Ford. "Excuse me," he said, focusing on the boy who looked least likely to be a jerk.

The boy started to move, but two of his pals closed around him, their expressions challenging. They were bored, Mac thought, and hungry for excitement—even the negative kind. If it were up to him, they'd all be put to work, flipping burgers, pushing brooms, picking up trash, if necessary.

Without speaking, the boys watched for his reaction to their defiance. One of them—the tallest and probably the oldest—took a drag from a cigarette and blew the smoke directly into Mac's face. Mac didn't react, his narrowed eyes still locked with those of the first boy he had approached. He kept his voice very soft. "Perhaps you didn't hear me. I said excuse me."

The boy swallowed visibly and shifted his weight backward.

"C'mon, Brad, you chicken," someone muttered. "We were here first. Make him go around."

Again, Mac kept his voice very quiet, an intimidating trick he had perfected during his years on the force. "Just step aside, and I'll be on my way."

"Don't let him push you around, Brad," one boy ordered.

"Shut up, Jimbo," Brad muttered, glancing up at Mac, who stared steadily back at him.

"Better not start anything you don't want to finish, boy," Mac advised, never taking his eyes off the teenager's tense face. The boy looked familiar, he couldn't help thinking. Something about his wide, blue-green eyes reminded Mac of Sharon Henderson.

His cheeks burning in resentment and embarrassment, Brad moved out of the way. Mac walked on at the same leisurely pace as before, not bothering to glance over his shoulder at the boys. He heard some of the other kids giving Brad a hard time for backing down, and another make an unflattering comment about Mac's Latino heritage, but he didn't react and they made no effort to purse further trouble with him.

They weren't quite as tough as they pretended to be. Which didn't mean they couldn't turn dangerous if someone didn't get them under control soon, he mused as he pushed open the door of Cora's Café. He was glad he wouldn't have to deal with them again.

AN OVERSIZE HARD HAT slipping to one side of her head, Sharon peered through the viewfinder of her camera Saturday afternoon. Ignoring the sound of hammering coming from the second floor above her, she framed a shot of the leaded-glass window in the dining room of the old Garrett house. She snapped the picture, then lowered the camera, wondering if she should try another angle.

From behind her, someone straightened her hat. A ripple of electricity ran through her, and she didn't have to hear his voice to know it was Mac. "This should fit tighter," he said.

She wasn't sure what he would see in her expression, so she fussed with her camera as an excuse to avoid turning around for a moment. "I found it sitting in a box in the entryway. It was the only hard hat I could find."

"Then I'll have to get you one of your own. This won't protect you much if something heavy were to fall."

Almost as if to illustrate his words, a crash came from upstairs, followed by what might have been a muffled curse. Sharon glanced up at the stained ceiling and smiled. "Point taken."

"How long have you been here?"

"About an hour. I've already taken photos of the kitchen and the parlor. I was just finishing up in here."

"What else do you need?"

"I was going to take a few pictures in the downstairs bedroom. I don't suppose I can go upstairs yet?"

He shook his head. "Not today. The crew's up there testing the floors and patching holes. I'm reasonably sure the structure is safe, but I don't want you wandering around up there until I'm sure."

"And when will that be?"

He shrugged. "They'll be finished later this afternoon. They haven't found any problems so far."

Although she understood his caution—after all, he was the owner of the house now and therefore liable in the case of accidents—she was still impatient to get upstairs and explore. "I'd be very careful."

His smile was pleasant but unyielding. "Next time."

"Has anyone ever mentioned that you can be awfully bossy?" she asked him a little too sweetly.

He chuckled. "Around here, I *am* the boss."

"I'll just finish up downstairs, then—boss." She turned to snap one more shot of the window, then moved toward the bedroom.

He fell into step beside her. "Getting any great ideas?"

"A few." Unfortunately, the only ideas that struck her as she entered the bedroom with Mac had nothing to do with decorating. Never mind that the room closely resembled a shadowy cave filled with dust and cobwebs. Or that one windowpane was broken, letting a warm breeze whistle through it. Or that there wasn't a stick of furniture. It was still obviously a bedroom, and she and Mac were alone in it.

What was it about this man that he could affect her just by looking at her in that smoldering manner? She hadn't blushed since high school, but she was dangerously close to it when he put a hand at the small of her back to guide her around a nail sticking up from a floorboard. The heat of his skin penetrated the thin, scoop-neck T-shirt she'd worn with jeans and sneakers for her exploratory visit here.

"The architect recommended taking out this fireplace and replacing it with doors leading out to a garden," Mac said. But even that strictly-business comment sounded oddly intimate because he had murmured it into her ear.

Grateful for an excuse to move away from him, she crossed over to the stone fireplace in question and made a pretense of studying it. "It would bring more light into the room, of course, and easier access to the outside. But I wouldn't do it."

"You'd keep the fireplace?"

She turned to look at the center of the room, picturing a big white-painted iron bed there, covered in eyelet and mounded with pillows. A rocking chair in one corner. Fresh flowers on an old chest. A fire burning in this wonderful stone fireplace. Two people cuddled in the bed—she refused to picture faces. "I would definitely keep the fireplace."

He nodded. "I had already decided to do that. I'll convert the small window in the west corner to a glass-paned door leading outside. That should provide enough natural light to brighten the room a little during the day, but I didn't want to sacrifice the fireplace."

"I'm glad. It's really lovely." She rested a hand on the heavy oak mantelpiece. "I've always wanted a fireplace in my bedroom," she mused almost to herself.

"The romantic type, are you?"

She dropped her hand and squared her shoulders. "Not particularly. I've always considered myself the practical type. A fire is a nice way to take away a chill on cold winter evenings."

"Mmm." He made it clear he didn't quite accept her self-description. "Will you have dinner with me this evening?"

She swallowed before asking, "Do you want to talk about my ideas for the decorating? I'm afraid I don't have much to discuss with you yet, since I just—"

"No," he cut in quietly. "This has nothing to do with business."

He was asking her for a date. She hadn't dated anyone but Jerry in months—primarily from lack of interest in going out with anyone else who had asked during that time.

She couldn't claim a lack of interest in Mac; the opposite was actually her problem. She was, perhaps, *too* interested in him. She supposed some people—her assistant, for example—would consider that an odd reason to hesitate about accepting his invitation. But Sharon had always considered herself a shrewd judge of people, and something told her Mac wasn't exactly what he seemed to be.

It wasn't that she was afraid of him, or even that she didn't trust him—but she was definitely wary of him. Should she follow through on her undeniable attraction to him, or listen to her instincts and avoid further complicating her life?

His left eyebrow lifted. "I didn't think it was that difficult a question."

"You aren't a member of a crime family, are you?"

"I beg your pardon?"

"According to local rumor, you're either an eccentric millionaire, a flunky for an eccentric movie star, or you're a member of an organized-crime family. The first two possibilities don't worry me overmuch, but I would definitely be concerned about the latter."

His chuckle was disarming. He didn't laugh often, and it was a pleasant sound. "I am not a crook," he assured her, the cliché making her smile. "I don't work for anyone except myself. As for the millionaire part—I'm afraid not."

Remembering Tressie's question, Sharon asked, "Are you married?"

"No. I'm single, straight and unattached. Are there any other juicy tidbits you want to quiz me about?"

"I probably haven't even heard all the talk," she confessed. "Those were just the stories that made it to my shop."

"Do you always take gossip so seriously?"

She had to smile at that. "Hardly."

"Is there anyone who would object to you having dinner with me?"

She thought of Jerry, but shook her head. "I'm not seeing anyone special, if that's what you're asking."

"So…?"

It was as good an evening as any to go out. Brad was going on an overnight campout with his base-ball team, sponsored by the coach and several team dads. Having made an excuse to Jerry after her re-cent decision to spend less time with him, Sharon was free for the evening. She had planned to spend a little time to herself for a change perusing deco-rating journals and making preliminary notes for the renovation project. Instead, she heard herself saying, "All right. What time?"

His only reaction was a brisk nod—as if there had been no real doubt that she would accept, she couldn't help thinking. "Seven? I'll pick you up."

Sharon thought of the inevitable ramifications if she and Mac were seen sharing a cozy dinner-for-two in town. There would certainly be talk. Specu-lation. Questions. She wasn't accustomed to being the center of gossip. She'd always been the quiet and responsible type. Everyone knew her mother was a lovable flake, that her father had died of a heart attack thirteen years ago, and that her little brother tended to hang with the wrong crowd, but they had never attracted the sort of interest that the McBrides or some of the other longtime Honoria residents garnered.

"I could cook," she suggested, wondering whether her alternative was actually more or less reckless than dining in public. "You're probably tired of restaurant food by now," she added quickly, not wanting him to take it the wrong way. "Maybe you'd enjoy a home-cooked meal?"

"I would very much enjoy a home-cooked meal. Restaurant food gets a little tiring after a while." He seemed to take the question at face value. She hoped he wasn't reading more into the offer than she intended.

She nodded, hoping she wouldn't regret the impulsive invitation. She couldn't quite believe she had invited Mac Cordero into her home.

One thing she was certain of—this was the only bedroom in which they would be alone together that day.

CHAPTER FIVE

MAC FELT smug as he parked his car in Sharon's driveway Saturday evening. He would have been satisfied to buy her a meal in a crowded restaurant. Dining in her home, where they could talk privately and without interruption, was even better than he had hoped for.

He planned to make good use of the evening. He would just have to be careful not to raise her suspicion with the questions he intended to ask.

He wondered if she was a good cook. It had been months since he'd eaten a meal that hadn't been prepared in a restaurant kitchen. Although he had to admit the blue plate special at Cora's Café had been pretty darned close to home cooking—and Wade hadn't exaggerated the quality of her pies.

Sharon's house was a frame-and-brick ranch-style in a middle-class neighborhood. One of the cookie-cutter houses Mac usually disdained, but he assumed it had been chosen more for affordability than taste. Sharon opened the door almost the moment his finger touched the doorbell. Apparently, she had been waiting for him.

"I wasn't sure what you're serving," he said, holding out a bottle of wine. "I brought white."

She took it without meeting his eyes or touching his fingers. "Thank you. This is perfect. We're having Cornish hen. I hope you're hungry," she added brightly as she closed the door behind him. "I'm just putting finishing touches on dinner. It looks like it might rain later this evening, doesn't it? The weather guy said there's something like a seventy percent chance. Of course, we need the rain, but I hope it doesn't ruin my brother's camp-out with his friends. If you'd like to wash up before dinner, there's a—"

"Sharon." Mac couldn't help smiling. "Breathe."

She went still, then grimaced. "I was babbling, wasn't I? Sorry."

Her nervous chatter hadn't prevented him from noticing how nice she looked. She'd changed out of the clothes she'd worn earlier, and was now wearing a pastel yellow blouse and light khaki slacks. The pale colors accented her glossy brown hair and creamy-peach complexion. He considered telling her how pretty she looked, but he was afraid that would set her off again. Instead, he glanced around her living room, admiring the bold use of color and texture in her decorating. "Nice place."

"Thank you. Please, sit down. Can I get you anything to drink before dinner?"

He settled on the boxy, red-print sofa. "No, thank you."

"I'll just put the wine away and check on dinner. I'll be right back."

True to her word, she wasn't gone long. Mac was still sitting where she'd left him, studying the comfortable living room. "You decorated this room?" he asked to start the conversation.

Sharon perched on the very edge of a straight-backed armchair upholstered in red, gold and green stripes. "It's my mother's house, actually, but she had me do all the decorating. Mother's on vacation in Europe for the summer, and I'm staying here with my younger brother until she returns. After that, I plan to move into a place of my own—probably an apartment for a while."

"You said your brother's on a camping trip?"

"Yes. His baseball team is having a father-son camp-out. Our father died when my brother was just a baby, but they encouraged him to go, anyway. I always feel so sorry for poor Brad when things like this come up—it makes him so much more aware of not having a father, himself. It isn't easy on him."

No, it wasn't easy. Mac clearly remembered father-son camp-outs from his own youth. He'd never had a father to take him, either. He wondered if it had made Sharon's brother as angry and resentful as it had made him. And he wondered if Brad's mother and sister had overcompensated for that loss. Mac's own mother hadn't allowed him to wallow in self-pity—and he still appreciated her for that. "How old is your brother?"

"Fifteen." Seeing that he looked surprised by her answer, she added, "He's almost eleven years younger than I am. My parents had given up on having a second child, and were completely surprised when Brad came along.''

Brad. Remembering the teenager with that name on the street corner last night, Mac wondered if it could possibly be the same boy. If so, Sharon certainly had her hands full. The crowd that boy had been hanging out with looked like trouble with a capital T in Mac's opinion. ''Your brother doesn't mind having his older sister as a baby-sitter?''

Her grimace was expressive. ''We've had our differences, but we're getting along fairly well for the most part. It would be easier, of course, if he was in school, so I wouldn't have to worry about keeping him entertained during the day.''

''He doesn't have a summer job?''

''No. He's involved in several sports and he isn't old enough to drive yet, so it isn't really feasible for him to have a job now. I offered to let him work at my shop for the summer, stocking shelves, sweeping up and dusting, that sort of thing, but he was afraid he'd be bored. I don't want to ruin his summer.''

It was Mac's opinion that school should be held year-round, with break time built in throughout the year. Since few schools had adopted that schedule, he believed kids who'd reached the teen years should have jobs to keep them out of mischief and teach them a work ethic. After all, school terms had been built originally around farm life, when most of the students had worked in the fields during the summer months. They certainly hadn't sat around on their butts watching the tube, playing video games or hanging around on street corners looking for trouble with strangers. Mac, himself, had taken his first job when he was twelve.

It wasn't honest work that caused boredom, as Sharon and her brother seemed to believe, but lack of anything productive to do. Yet Mac had learned long ago that it was best to keep his opinions to himself when it came to other people's kids—or, in this case, kid brothers.

After a moment of silence, Sharon sprang to her feet. "Dinner will be ready in just a few minutes. Make yourself comfortable—are you sure I can't get you anything?"

"No, I'm fine. I'll just wash up—down this hallway?"

"Yes. Second door on the right."

Mac wandered back into the living room after washing his hands. His attention was drawn to a cluster of framed photographs arranged on an old upright piano in one corner of the room. A quick study confirmed that her brother was the boy Mac had encountered outside the arcade. *Great,* he thought with a shake of his head. Sharon's brother already hated him. Not that it mattered, he supposed. It wasn't as if anything serious was developing.

The photograph he was looking for sat at the back of the grouping. In it a young, blushing Sharon stood beside a teenager Mac might have mistaken for Trent McBride's mischievous younger brother, had he not known it was Trent, himself. His handsome face was creased with a big sloppy grin and his arm was around Sharon's waist. They had been a very attractive young couple.

He returned to the couch so Sharon wouldn't walk in and catch him snooping through her photographs, but the image of Sharon and Trent was still very clear in his mind. He knew Trent was happily engaged to someone else now, but there was clearly some sort of history between him and Sharon, even if nothing more than an innocent friendship.

She appeared in the doorway, looking little older than the girl in the photograph as she gave him a slightly shy smile. "Dinner is ready."

He followed her into the dining room, unable to resist admiring the graceful sway of her hips as she led the way. Just because he hoped to pump her for information didn't mean he couldn't appreciate spending an evening with an attractive woman.

"THIS LOOKS GREAT," Mac said, sitting at Sharon's beautifully set table a few minutes later.

"I hope you like Cornish hen. I forgot to ask what you prefer when I offered to cook."

"When it comes to food, there's very little I *don't* like," he admitted, reaching for his napkin. "Except sushi. Never developed a taste for that."

"I've never tried it. Sushi bars aren't exactly common in this area. I love most seafood, though."

"It tastes pretty much like you'd expect raw fish wrapped in seaweed to taste. I'm more of a meat-and-potatoes guy, myself."

"Then it's a good thing I prepared meat and potatoes tonight, I guess."

Swallowing a bite of creamy scalloped potatoes, he murmured, "Oh, yeah."

She seemed to relax a little in response to his enjoyment of the meal. "It's nice to cook for someone who appreciates my efforts. Brad would rather order pizza or pick up burgers than eat home-cooked vegetables."

"He'll get over that."

"I hope so. It's a constant battle to get him to eat well."

"Is your mother a good cook?"

"When she pays attention to what she's doing, she's an excellent cook. My mother's a bit of a daydreamer. An artist. She's been known to get distracted and put pepper in pudding or sugar on scrambled eggs. She even poured coffee on Brad's cereal once."

"She sounds…interesting."

"Brad teases her. He asks her how we'll be able to tell if she ever gets senile?"

Mac chuckled and took another bite of fresh asparagus. "You said she's an artist?"

"Yes. She teaches art at the junior high school."

It seemed like as good an opportunity as any to slip the McBrides into the conversation. "Trent mentioned that both his mother and sister-in-law are teachers. I suppose your mother knows them?"

"Everyone knows everyone in Honoria. Trent's mother, Bobbie, has taught at Honoria Elementary for more than thirty years. She seems to have no intention of ever retiring. Trevor's wife, Jamie, teaches speech and drama at the high school. She graduated from Honoria High, then spent almost ten years acting in New York before coming back to teach.''

"You never had an urge to teach, yourself?"

She shook her head. "I've always loved decorating. After I finished high school, I took a two-year interior-design course and some business classes at the local college. I worked in a wallpaper store for a couple of years, and when the owner decided to sell, my mother encouraged me to buy it. It was a little scary, making that investment, but Caleb McBride helped me with the paperwork and details, and so far, I'm holding my own.''

The McBrides again. As interested as he was in Sharon's own story, Mac knew he should probably start directing the conversation the way he wanted it to go. "Caleb's the attorney?" he asked, though he already knew the answer.

"Yes. He's Trent and Trevor's father. They have a sister, too. Tara lives in Atlanta.''

"Trent mentioned that his parents are away on vacation.''

She nodded as she reached for her wineglass. "A cruise. It's their first vacation in longer than anyone can remember. Caleb's a dear, but a real workaholic—they practically had to carry him onto that ship. He had a minor heart attack a while back, and his family has been making him take better care of himself since."

Mac took a sip of his own wine, then set his glass back on the table, keeping his tone offhand. "I get a little confused about the relationships around here. What exactly is the family connection between the McBrides and the people who built the old house I bought?"

"Didn't Trent tell you?"

"We haven't talked much about the history of the place, just the plans I have for it."

"Well, the Garrett house was built by Trent's great-great grandfather, I think. His grandmother—Caleb's mother—was a Garrett and I believe the house was built by her grandfather."

"So the McBrides and Garretts are longtime residents of Honoria."

"Oh, yes. But there aren't many Garretts left—a couple of distant cousins in Carrollton. And Caleb's the only McBride left of his generation, as far as I know."

"He was an only son?" Again, it was a question Mac already knew the answer to, but he wanted the conversation to unfold naturally. Casually.

Sharon seemed comfortable enough with the topic. "No, Caleb had two brothers, Josiah Jr. and Jonah. They're both dead now."

It had infuriated Mac when he'd first arrived in Honoria and learned that two of the older McBride brothers were dead. It had reduced his chances of getting revenge by two-thirds. His original plan had been to make someone suffer the humiliation and disgrace his mother had endured. To make it publicly known that a McBride had fathered and then abandoned a child, leaving a vulnerable woman alone to deal with her shame.

But it was hard to humiliate a dead man. And unless Caleb McBride was the culprit—which even at this early stage of Mac's investigation seemed unlikely—it didn't appear that Mac would find the retribution he'd craved for so long. But at least maybe he could finally find some answers.

"The McBrides don't seem to have a particularly long life span."

She frowned thoughtfully. "I don't know about that. I think Jonah died in an accident when he was only in his early forties, but Josiah Jr., was older. He died of emphysema and lung cancer after years of heavy smoking. Poor Emily had to put her own life on hold for years to take care of him—which wasn't an easy task. Her father was a...difficult man. I remember being very intimidated by his perpetual scowl back when I was a teenager."

Filing that tidbit away, Mac went along with the conversation, looking for other tidbits of information. "Emily is the police chief's wife?"

"Yes. Emily Davenport now."

"No siblings to help her out with her difficult father?"

"She has an older half brother, Lucas, but he had a falling-out with his father—and with most of Honoria, for that matter—and he left town after high school. Fifteen years later, he came back to visit his sister. Their father was already dead then.''

No mention so far of congenital ailments in the McBride family, something Mac needed to know, especially after… ''I didn't realize Mrs. Davenport has an older brother. I don't think I've met him.''

''No. I've only met him a couple of times myself. He's nine years older than Emily. Lucas and his wife live in California and only come back to visit a couple of times a year. But they'll be here in August for Trent's wedding, I'm sure.''

It was increasingly obvious that she didn't share her town's penchant for idle gossip. So far, all Sharon had done was answer his innocuous questions without much embellishment. While Mac admired her discretion, it wasn't getting him very far. He took a calculated risk with a bolder question. ''You weren't kidding when you said the folks around here like to gossip. Am I mistaken, or do the McBrides seem to attract more than their share of talk?''

Sharon wrinkled her nose. ''You aren't mistaken. It seems as if there's always one scandal or another involving the McBrides. It's unfair for the most part, I might add. They're really a very nice family.''

''If you say so.''

That noncommittal comment brought her chin up in defense of her friends. ''I do say so. I've known them for ages and they've all been very nice to me and my family. I certainly hope you aren't letting a few spiteful locals make you question your decision to hire Trent for your renovation team.''

"I don't base my hiring decisions on idle chatter.''

"Good," she said with a brisk nod. "Any large family in a small town is going to attract its share of gossip, of course. Every big family has its share of scandals—divorces, unwed pregnancies, that sort of thing—and the McBrides are no different. But most of the accusations leveled at the McBrides have later proven to be completely unfounded. Like when Sam Jennings accused Emily of embezzling from his accounts at the bank—he was just trying to stir things up. Sam's also the one who led everyone to believe Lucas killed Roger Jennings, when all along it was Sam himself—and Roger wasn't the first person Sam killed, either.''

Mac set down his fork. "I don't think I followed all that.''

Sharon made a sound of exasperation, and shook her head. "Sorry. It just makes me so mad that people are telling you these stories about the McBrides. They really don't deserve the treatment they get around here.''

"No one mentioned anything about murder to me.''

She pushed a strand of hair out of her face, still looking annoyed. "No, of course not. Everyone knows the truth now. I suppose I should tell you the story so you won't go away with a misconception about Lucas.''

"I wouldn't want you to betray your friends' trust just to satisfy my curiosity," Mac murmured, feeling vaguely guilty about the lie.

"It's common knowledge around here now," she said with a shrug. "Even though it all happened more than four years ago, it was a huge scandal and people still like to talk about it. It started when Emily was a toddler and her mother—Josiah Jr.'s second wife, Nadine—apparently ran off with a married man, Al Jennings. Josiah was always very bitter after that, and mixed very little with the townspeople. He and Lucas, his son by his first wife, who died of pneumonia, didn't get along well. Actually, Lucas didn't get along well with many people, because he had such a temper as a boy. Probably because his own mother died so young and his father was such an unpleasant man. Especially after Nadine disappeared with Al."

"It sounds like enough to make anyone surly."

Smiling a little in response to Mac's wry comment, Sharon continued, "Anyway, Lucas had a sort of hate/hate relationship with Roger Jennings—the son of the man Nadine supposedly ran away with. Roger blamed all the McBrides for his father's defection, and Lucas took the brunt of it because he and Roger were close in age. One night very soon after Lucas finished high school, they had a particularly bitter public quarrel. Roger died that night."

"How?"

"He fell off a cliff on McBride land, close to Lucas's house. It was all very tragic and very mysterious and, needless to say, the local gossips had a field day. They all decided Lucas killed Roger. They had him tried and convicted even before the funeral. There wasn't enough evidence to arrest Lucas, but the people who never liked him, anyway, didn't care about that. They made life here so unpleasant for him that he felt he had to leave. He took off in the middle of the night, and no one heard from him for years.''

''Which, of course, only made him look more guilty in the eyes of his accusers.''

''Exactly. Fifteen years later, Lucas came home to visit his sister, Emily, and the truth came out. Nadine McBride and Al Jennings were murdered by Al's own brother, Sam. It turned out Sam had been a jilted lover of Nadine's, and he killed her and Al in a jealous rage. When Sam's nephew, Roger, came too close to finding out the truth several years later, Sam pushed him over the cliff, making it look as if Lucas was the real murderer.''

''You had a triple murderer living right here in Honoria?''

''He was my dentist when I was a teenager. I always thought he was sort of weird, but I never dreamed… Anyway, he even tried to do away with Rachel, Roger's younger sister, when she stumbled onto the truth four years ago. Had it not been for Lucas and Wade rushing to her rescue, he might have killed her. Now Sam is in prison where he belongs and Lucas is married to Rachel and living quite happily in California.''

Mac had followed the tale with only a slight effort. "So Lucas married the sister of the man he was accused of murdering?"

"Yes. He owns a successful software company now. He's made loads of money, which might have something to do with why the whole town practically salutes him every time he comes back to visit."

"Success can be the best revenge."

She scowled. "I despise hypocrisy. The same people who were whispering about him now pretend they believed he was innocent all along."

Shifting a bit uncomfortably in his chair, Mac prompted, "So that's when all the gossip about the McBrides began?"

She shrugged. "There were a few other incidents, but that was the most dramatic. The other stuff has been generally exaggerated."

"And I thought nothing exciting ever happened around here."

"We've had our share of scandal. But personally, I prefer a quieter, more peaceful existence. If I'd wanted excitement, I'd have moved to a big city instead of settling down here to be close to my family."

Thinking of some of the "excitement" he'd seen as a vice cop, Mac decided she'd made the right choice.

Sharon nodded toward his glass. "Would you like some more wine?"

"No, I'm fine, thanks."

"I had a couple of thoughts about the renovation project this afternoon—specifically, the little front parlor. Would it be possible to change the doorway to an arch to match the shape of the fanlights in the entryway and dining room?"

He would have liked to ask a few more questions about the McBrides, but there was really no way to pursue it now without arousing Sharon's suspicions. "Actually, that's something I've already discussed with the builder," he said, going along with her for now.

He hadn't forgotten his main purpose in being here this evening. He would find a way to learn more about the McBrides later.

BY CONVINCING HERSELF this was a business dinner, Sharon was able to relax considerably during the remainder of the meal. It was easier to talk about decorating with Mac than to make social small talk. She was still annoyed with herself for babbling on about the McBrides the way she had. She'd let her irritation with the local gossips and her natural inclination to defend her friends carry her away.

Mac had probably been bored by the whole conversation about people he hardly even knew. In all likelihood he considered her as big a gossip as the others he'd encountered around here.

Better, she thought, to stick to business.

Her awkwardness with Mac could be attributed to the fact that it had been a long time since she'd spent an evening with any man other than Jerry, who tended to dominate conversations with talk about himself. An evening with Jerry was usually entertaining—and never made her as nervous and self-conscious as this supposedly simple dinner with Mac. Maybe because Jerry didn't have Mac's habit of studying her across the table as if everything she said or did was inherently interesting.

Seeing that Mac's plate was empty, she asked, "Would you like coffee and dessert? I made a strawberry cake. It's sort of my specialty."

A decidedly odd look crossed his face. "Um…thanks, but strawberries make me break out in hives."

Of course they did. There seemed to be some force at work to cause as many awkward moments as possible between the two of them. "Something else, then? I have ice cream or…"

"Just coffee, thanks. Dinner was so good I've eaten too much already."

"Why don't we have our coffee in the living room. I have a few sketches I'd like to show you in there."

His grin was a brief flash of white, both wicked and disturbing. "Are you offering to show me your etchings?"

"Behave yourself," she said sternly, not sure whether she was talking to him or to her own suddenly activated hormones.

"Yes, ma'am." He stood when she did and reached to move her chair out of the way for her. "Can I help you clear away the dishes first?"

She couldn't help smiling. Mac had the kind of old-fashioned manners that she'd been trying to teach Brad—with only partially satisfying results. "Are your parents still living?" she asked impulsively.

He seemed to go still for a moment. And then he replaced her chair without looking at her. "I was raised by my mother. She died three years ago."

Something in his voice told Sharon he hadn't quite recovered from the loss. Her tone was gentle when she asked, "Was she the one who taught you to be such a gentleman?"

Though the question appeared to disconcert him a bit, he nodded. "My mother was a real stickler for manners. 'Stand up when a lady stands, Miguel.' 'Take your hat off indoors, Miguel.' 'Say please and thank you, Miguel.'"

Intrigued by this fleeting glimpse into his past, she cocked her head. "Miguel? That's your first name?"

He gave her a funny little bow. "Miguel Luis Cordero."

"When did you start answering to Mac?"

He shrugged. "That came from my mother, too. She grew up in San Juan, but she wanted me to have a more mainstream American upbringing. She gave me her father's name, but she thought it would be easier for me to answer to a more common nickname."

He was reaching for his dishes as he spoke. Sharon rested a hand on his arm to stop him. "I'll take care of these later. Why don't you just go on into the living room and I'll bring the coffee.''

He glanced at her hand on his arm, then raised his eyes to hers. And once again she understood what it meant to be held captive by someone's gaze. She wasn't sure she could look away if she tried. She was relieved when Mac broke the contact.

''I take my coffee black,'' he said.

She deliberately stiffened her knees. ''I'll be right in.''

She lingered in the kitchen a few minutes longer than was absolutely necessary, giving herself a chance to recover from that moment of connection between them. She was fine with him as long as they stuck to business, but every time she became aware of him as a sexy, single male, she froze. It wasn't that she had anything against sexy, single males, but with Mac she had the feeling things could get complicated—and not only because she would be involved with him professionally for the next few months.

CHAPTER SIX

SHARON ASSEMBLED a tray with two cups of coffee and a plate of chocolate cookies, just in case Mac changed his mind about dessert. When she carried the tray carefully into the living room, she noticed Mac sitting on the couch, examining an antique-reproduction lighting catalog she'd left on the coffee table. "These wall lights you've marked with adhesive strips—are you considering them for the Garrett house?" he asked.

Setting the tray on the coffee table, she settled on the couch next to him to study the photographs. "No, I've ordered those for one of my customers who's redoing her bedroom. She has a house full of Mission and Shaker antiques, and I thought those fixtures would go well with her decor. But there are several others in the catalog you might want to look at for your project."

"I like this one," he said, and pointed to a corner of the page farther from her, so that she had to scoot a little closer to examine the photo he'd indicated.

"That *is* nice," she agreed. "I can envision it in the downstairs hallway, can't you? It would nicely illuminate that dark corner outside the dining room."

He turned a page. "What about something like this in the parlor?"

She leaned a little closer, studying the ad with a thoughtful frown. "Well, it's pretty, of course, but do you really want to go with that look? This fixture is more representative of the 1950s than the 1920s era, but we can certainly mix styles, if that's what you'd like. Some decorators recommend mixing styles and periods for a more complex and eclectic—"

"*You're* the designer on this project," he reminded her. "What I want you to do is decorate the house as if you were going to live in it yourself."

She glanced at him with a smile. "What makes you think I'd want to live in a restored Victorian? How do you know I wouldn't prefer stylized chrome and glass from the 1980s? Or the Danish Modern look of the 1960s?"

"Because I saw your face when you got your first look at the Garrett place. I watched you run your hand over the moldings in the master bedroom. I saw the way you practically melted over the beveled-glass fanlight in the dining room. It was lust, Sharon. Pure, heart-pounding, skin-dampening lust."

It took her a moment to respond coherently to his wholly unexpected side trip into rather erotic fancy. "I, um, love the house, of course—or at least the house I know it can become—but I'm not sure I would describe my feelings as, er—"

"Lust?" He smiled a little. "You don't think the word is appropriate?"

"Well, no, not really. I'll admit I have a certain passion for decorating. I'm excited to be a part of your team. And I certainly might fantasize about owning a place like the Garrett house, myself. But *lust* is perhaps too strong a word to describe my feelings."

He gave a low chuckle. "You've just used the words *passion, excited,* and *fantasize* pretty much in one breath—and you accuse *me* of using too strong a word?"

They were supposed to be talking business, not swapping innuendoes. Somehow this conversation had gotten completely out of hand. She made a weak effort to get it back on track. She looked at the catalog again. "Do you see anything you like?"

"I definitely see something I like," he murmured, bringing her gaze back up to his. He wasn't looking at photographs. His intense dark eyes were focused on her face.

"I, um…" What had she meant to say? The words were gone, having slipped from her suddenly overheated mind like wisps of steam.

She didn't realize he had lifted his hand until she felt his fingertips against the side of her face. What was it about his touch that electrified her, even as it gave her an incredible sense of security? Was it the memory of the way he'd held her the night they'd met? Had that dramatic introduction made her react differently to him—or was it something about the man, himself?

"What did you ask me?" she murmured, trying to clear her thoughts.

"Nothing." His gaze was on her mouth now.

She cleared her throat. "Do you want…?"

His eyes rose to hers again. "Do I want…?"

What was it she'd started to offer? "Coffee."

His smile twisted wryly. "Coffee," he repeated. Neither of them moved.

"This," she said after a moment, still feeling the weight of his fingers against her face, "is what some people might call an awkward moment."

"It doesn't have to be." His thumb moved, tracing across her cheek to her lower lip. "We can go back to talking about fixtures."

Her lip quivered beneath his touch. Talk? She wasn't even sure she could speak coherently.

She could insist on keeping the evening strictly business, and Mac would go along with it. She could move to another chair, away from the feel and heat of him, and he wouldn't try to hold her back. It would be the sensible, practical, *Sharon* thing to do.

Funny, she mused, studying the strong shape of his mouth. She hadn't been quite herself since her car sank beneath the surface of Snake Creek. She hadn't seen things in quite the same light—her job, this town, Jerry. Her life. Maybe because she'd come so close to losing it all. The accident had made her very aware of everything she had—and everything she'd only dreamed of.

She realized abruptly that it would have been a shame if she had died without ever meeting Mac Cordero. Without really knowing what it meant to melt at a touch.

His mouth was very close to hers now. If she reacted so strongly to the feel of his hand, what would it be like to kiss him? Did she really want to miss this chance to find out?

Taking her silence as permission, he covered her mouth with his.

Okay, she thought, somewhat relieved that no fireworks exploded around her, no cymbals crashed in her ears. It was just a kiss, like the kisses she had received before. Just a pleasant, gentle press of lips. Nice, but it certainly wouldn't change her life.

Lulled into relaxing, she closed her eyes and tilted her head for him. Her lips softened, parting just a little. She raised a hand to his shoulder, letting it rest lightly there. Just a simple kiss between two unattached adults, she assured herself. If nothing else, it would satisfy their curiosity, and then they could get on with business.

The tip of his tongue touched her lower lip, eliciting a slight shiver of reaction. Okay, so it was a pretty good kiss. There was no reason to hurry through it. She slipped her other arm around his neck and parted her lips a bit more.

A moment later, her head was spinning, her pulse racing, her toes curling—and she would have sworn there were fireworks going off and cymbals crashing somewhere around her. Every cliché she'd ever heard had just become real for her—and this tricky, unprincipled male had deliberately waited until her guard was down before springing them on her.

Just a kiss? Right—like a tornado was just a stiff breeze.

Somehow his arms had gone around her, and his hands were sneaking into places they shouldn't be, but she didn't want him to move them. Which only proved how good he was at being bad.

His tongue swept her mouth, taunting and teasing until she couldn't resist responding with a few tentative thrusts of her own. Which only seemed to encourage him to take the kiss deeper.

This was why, she thought somewhere in the back of her mind, she had been so jumpy around Mac from the start. Somehow she had known almost from the first time she'd seen him that this would happen—and that it wasn't going to be uncomplicated.

She'd known all along that Mac wasn't like the forgettable men she had dated in the past.

She couldn't think clearly with his arms around her, his mouth on hers, his tongue sparring with hers. It was wonderful. Heady. Exciting. She couldn't seem to care that she had known him only a week. That she still knew very little about him.

All that mattered at the moment was that she'd felt a connection to him from that first dramatic meeting. That she'd been drawn to him every time she had seen him since. That his eyes, his touch, his voice affected her in a way she'd only fantasized about before.

His right hand slid slowly up from her hip, leaving a shivery path behind him. He pressed lightly against the small of her back, urging her closer. She tightened her arm around his neck, letting her fingers burrow into his thick ebony hair.

She didn't know how this had happened, exactly—but she couldn't be sorry it had. It really was a spectacular kiss.

His hand moved again, sliding around her waist to pause perilously close to her breast. Even as she ached to feel him there, she felt herself pulling back.

"Too much?" he murmured against her mouth, moving his hand to a more innocuous position.

"Too soon," she amended candidly.

Very slowly, he drew back. He wasn't smiling, she noted. He didn't look particularly pleased with himself for slipping so neatly behind her defenses. In fact, he looked almost as startled as she felt—and almost as dismayed.

Because he was so very good at masking his emotions, his expression cleared almost immediately. He pulled his hands away from her. "Our coffee's getting cold," he said, his voice only marginally huskier than usual.

Actually, a cold drink sounded pretty good to her just then, considering that she'd been on the verge of overheating. She scooted several inches away from him and reached for her coffee. It annoyed her that her hand wasn't quite steady when she picked up her cup. Just a kiss? Had she really thought it could be that easy with him?

Mac cleared his throat. "I should probably go."

She glanced instinctively at her watch, not certain whether she was relieved or reluctant that he was ready to leave. "It's still early."

"Mmm. More time to get into trouble if I stay," he murmured.

The glint of humor in his eyes made her smile, even as she felt her cheeks warm. He made it clear enough that he would have liked the embrace to go further. And she had to admit that deep down inside, she shared the sentiment. But as she had said, it was entirely too soon to be flirting with that sort of temptation.

She'd known Jerry for ages and hadn't kissed him the way she had just kissed Mac. She hadn't wanted to, for that matter.

"Besides," Mac added, setting his half-emptied coffee cup on the tray, "it's starting to rain."

She hadn't heard the rain until he said that. She hadn't been aware of anything outside this room, actually. For the first time in a while, she remembered her brother. The thought was accompanied by a ripple of guilt that he'd been so far from her mind only moments earlier.

"I hope the fathers on the camp-out made plans for rain," she murmured, looking toward the window in time to see a brief flash of lightning.

"They're idiots if they didn't. The forecasters have been predicting rain for days."

His blunt tone made her smile again as they stood. "Do you always plan for every contingency, Mac?"

"I try." He paused in front of her, reaching out to brush a strand of hair away from her still-tender mouth. His expression was somber. "I didn't plan on you."

Her smile faded. She certainly understood that sentiment. Mac—and her unexpected reaction to him—had certainly thrown *her* for a loop. But some surprises were rather nice ones, she thought as he stroked her cheek lightly again.

Not quite knowing what to say, she walked him to the door. She started to say something about working up design boards for the Garrett house, but it seemed rather foolish to talk business now, to pretend there was nothing else developing between them.

"Thanks for the dinner," he said as they paused at the door. "You were right, it was nice to eat a home-cooked meal for a change."

"I'm glad you enjoyed it. Next time I'll remember about the strawberries." She spoke without thinking, only then realizing that she had just implied there would be more evenings like this.

His mouth quirked into a slight smile. "For another dinner with you, I would even eat strawberries."

Smiling back at him, she quipped, "And risk breaking out in hives? I'm flattered."

"You should be. I hate to itch."

Twisting her hands in front of her, she looked up

at him, suddenly awkward again. "It sounds as if it's starting to rain harder."

A rumble of thunder underscored her words. "You aren't afraid to be alone during thunderstorms, are you?"

"Just the opposite, actually. Would it surprise you to hear that I like thunderstorms?"

"It might have, earlier today. Now—no, it doesn't surprise me at all."

Since they'd kissed, he meant. Since they had created their own storm—and it had been very obvious that she'd liked it.

Another roll of thunder made her glance at the door. "You'll get wet. Let me find you an umbrella."

"I won't melt." He reached for the doorknob. "Good night, Sharon."

"Good night, Mac." It was becoming easier to say his name—perhaps because it would be ridiculous to call him Mr. Cordero now.

He hesitated with one hand still on the doorknob. He placed his free hand behind her head and tugged lightly, bringing her mouth to his for a brief, but still effective kiss. "I'll see you soon," he murmured, the words a promise. And then he was gone, disappearing into the night.

Sharon closed the door behind him, then sagged for a moment against it, her cheek pressed to the cool wood. So much for pretending there was nothing but business between them. Or that she even wanted it that way.

SOME COP HABITS were hard for Mac to break. Keeping detailed notes was one of them. Sitting at the shaky table in his motel room, he studied the yellow legal-pad pages spread in front of him. On one sheet, he had started a rudimentary family tree. At the top, he'd written the names Josiah McBride and Anna Mae Garrett. On the next line were the names of their three sons, Josiah Jr., Jonah and Caleb.

Beneath Josiah Jr., he had written "Lucas, 40," and "Emily McBride Davenport, 31."

He studied those names for a moment, remembering what he'd learned about the eldest McBride brother. Josiah Jr. had apparently been humorless, withdrawn, moody—distant even to his own children. Could Mac's mother have fallen in love with a man like that?

Apparently there had been something about Josiah that some women had been drawn to. He'd married twice, though the second wife had taken a lover soon after. The lover with whom she had been murdered.

According to Sharon's timeline, Josiah had been between wives when Mac was conceived. Which might explain why he would start an affair with a Puerto Rican maid in a Savannah hotel, but it didn't fit with the story Mac's mother had told him. His father had been a married man, she had explained with an old sadness in her musical voice. Although he had talked about leaving his wife for her, his sense of family loyalty had finally drawn him away.

The guy had never known that he left Anita Cordero carrying his child. Anita had refused to use her baby as a marriage trap.

Was it possible that Josiah's marriage had been nothing more than a convenient lie? A coward's way of ending an affair that had lost its novelty for him?

Had Josiah McBride Jr. been Mac's father? If so, it didn't seem as if the man had any reputation left to ruin. Apparently, he'd left little respect or admiration behind when he'd died.

He shoved the unfinished family tree aside in frustration. He had no answers yet, and wouldn't come up with any tonight. Perhaps he would learn more the next time he found an opportunity to discuss the McBride family with Sharon.

Sharon. His mind was suddenly filled with the image of her face. The way she had looked after he kissed her—her skin flushed, her eyes heavy-lidded, her lips damp and reddened. She would never know how hard it had been for him to pull away. It had been too long since he'd held a woman in his arms. Since he had lost himself in a kiss that cleared his mind of questions, plans, memories—leaving nothing there but hunger.

He'd told the truth when he said he hadn't expected to meet her. Even when he'd made the calculated decision to use her knowledge of the McBrides, he hadn't intended to seduce any information out of her. The kiss had been unexpected, unplanned, and had nothing to do with the McBrides or anyone else except Sharon, herself. He had kissed her for no other reason except that he had wanted to. Needed to.

He hadn't planned on that at all.

BRAD WAS HOME early Sunday morning, in a more passive than usual mood after his camp-out. The organizers had planned for rain; the festivities had been moved inside a one-room building at the campground that was usually rented out for parties and family reunions. Though he'd probably had only a couple of hours' sleep, Brad was in a mellow enough mood that he didn't even complain—much—when Sharon insisted he accompany her to church.

Not that it had done much good, she thought ruefully as the service ended. He'd slept through the entire sermon. She poked him discreetly, and he woke with a muffled snort. "Time to go," she said.

He gave her a sheepish smile. "Good. I'm hungry."

She laughed and patted his arm. "Of course you are. You're breathing, aren't you?"

As usual, it took her a while to leave, because so many people detained her. Among the usual casual greetings, there were still a few who wanted to talk about the incident in Snake Creek. Sharon found it hard to believe only eight days had passed since that night. Maybe it seemed longer because she had chosen not to dwell on the experience.

She'd made a special effort not to think about it at all, though she hadn't been able to block the images from her dreams. The only thing that had kept those dreams from becoming nightmares had been the mental echo of Mac's voice, soothing and reassuring her. She'd chosen not to give too much thought to that, either.

Pushing the memories and Mac to the back of her mind, she made her way steadily to the parking lot, where still more members of the congregation waylaid her. Brad waited nearby, shifting from one foot to another, letting out an occasional gusty sigh.

"It's good to see you looking so well, Sharon," Emily Davenport said, smiling over the head of the baby girl in her arms. "I've thought of you often during the past week."

Sharon responded appropriately, then tickled little Claire's dimpled chin. "Hello, sweetie. You get more beautiful every time I see you."

"Say thank you to Miss Sharon, Claire," Emily instructed, though the child was only interested in the activities going on around her.

"Where's Clay?" Sharon looked around for Emily's thirteen-year-old stepson, then spotted him talking to her brother. "Oh, there he is, with Brad. Goodness, that boy seems to have grown six inches since I saw him last, and it's only been a couple of weeks."

"Same with Brad. They're becoming young men, aren't they?"

"I'm afraid so," Sharon agreed pensively. "Is Wade working this morning?"

Emily's smile faded. "Yes. Someone broke into

Discount Motors during the storm last night. They stole a car from the lot and some computer equipment from the office.''

Sharon frowned. It was bad enough that these kinds of crimes were happening in their town, but it especially bothered her that it had occurred so close to where her brother and his friends had been enjoying a wholesome evening of fun. Discount Motors was only half a mile from the campground. That seemed to make the crime even worse, for some reason. ''Does Wade think this break-in is related to the one at the Porter place last weekend?''

''He's certainly pursuing that possibility.'' Emily shifted her daughter into a more comfortable position on her hip. ''We're having a cookout at our place next Saturday. Would you and Brad like to come? Clay would love it. There are never any teenagers for him to talk to at our family gatherings.''

''It sounds like fun. We'd love to come.'' Though Clay was a couple of years younger than Brad, it was a friendship Sharon wanted to encourage. Clay was a good kid—smart, funny, outgoing. Popular with the good crowd, even if being the police chief's son earned him no points in other circles. Sharon worried about Brad getting involved with the wrong crowd. Clay Davenport was exactly the sort of friend she wanted for her brother.

''Great. Then we'll see you around noon on Saturday. Oh, and feel free to bring a friend if you like.''

Sharon suspected Emily was hinting about Jerry.

Matchmaking was the second favorite pastime in this town, right behind gossiping. "Is there anything else I can bring?"

"How about one of your famous strawberry cakes? Wade always goes on about how good they are."

Sharon couldn't help laughing a little. "Not everyone likes strawberries. But I'll make a cake, anyway, just for Wade."

"He'll be your slave."

Sharon laughed again. "I'll keep that in mind."

"Sharon, I'm hungry," Brad complained.

Emily smiled in understanding. "We'll see you Saturday."

"I'm looking forward to it." Sharon turned to her brother. "Okay, Brad. Let's go find something to eat before you collapse."

MAC WAS ON THE ROOF of the Garrett house Sunday morning when someone hailed him from below. He looked curiously over the edge, then masked his surprise. "Well, hello, Chief. Another friendly social visit?"

Wade Davenport grinned lazily up at him. "What you doing up there, Mac?"

"Communing with nature. Hang on, I'll be right down." Abandoning his inspection of the roof, Mac descended the ladder he'd propped against the back of the house. Wade waited for him at the bottom. "I'm beginning to wonder if you're following me around, Chief."

Wade put a hand on the ladder, as if to test its sturdiness. "Just thought I would stop by while I was in the neighborhood."

Mac suspected the chief had a specific reason for being in the neighborhood. And he would bet Wade had stopped by the motel first. "What can I do for you?"

"I wondered if I could talk you into giving me a tour."

"Sure," Mac agreed easily, wondering what, exactly, was behind the request. "Be happy to."

"I'd appreciate it. I've always been curious about this place, but I've never had an excuse to look around. My wife's great-grandfather built this house, you know."

"So I hear. We can go in through this door, which will take us into the kitchen."

Wade didn't move toward the door. His attention was focused on a large, padlocked storage building at the back of the yard. "Actually, I'd like to have a look inside that outbuilding first. If you have no objections, of course."

Mac pushed his hands into the pockets of his jeans, keeping his stance casual. "Any particular reason?"

"Oh, just curiosity."

Yeah, right. "This is just a wild guess, but has there been another break-in recently?"

"Mmm. Last night, out near the campground. Why do you ask?"

Shaking his head, Mac moved toward the outbuilding. "Never mind. Let me show you my storage shed."

Wade followed close at his heels. "You understand, of course, that this is just a request. I don't have a search warrant or anything official like that."

Mac leveled a look at the other man over his shoulder. "Now why would I be concerned about search warrants? This is just a friendly social visit, right?"

"You got it," Wade drawled cheerfully.

Pulling a key from his pocket, Mac opened the heavy padlock and swung the door open. Power lines ran from the outbuilding to a temporary construction utility pole set up nearby, so he was able to reach inside and snap on the bare lightbulb that hung from the rafters. He then stepped back, allowing Wade full access to the building filled with tools and materials. "There you go. Check it out."

A cursory glance seemed to satisfy the police chief. "Yeah, that's pretty much what I expected to see. You've got some expensive tools in there. You might want to step up your security, considering the problems with theft we've had around here lately."

"I'll keep your advice in mind. Thanks." Mac snapped the padlock into place again, tugging at it a couple of times to make sure it was secured. "C'mon, I'll show you around inside. I imagine you'll want to peer into all the nooks and crannies."

"Will I find anything interesting in those nooks and crannies?"

"Only if you're interested in dust and cobwebs."

Wade shrugged. "I'm easily entertained."

Half an hour later, they'd explored the entire house—every nook and cranny. The only questions Wade asked during the tour involved the renovation, itself. He seemed genuinely interested in the project, but Mac was discovering it wasn't always easy to tell what observations were being made behind the chief's expression.

They finished back outside at the ladder. "Thanks," Wade said. "That was very interesting."

"I hope it answered your questions."

"Most of them."

"If you have any others, you know where to find me. I'll be moving into a furnished apartment on West Elm tomorrow afternoon. If I'm not here, I'll most likely be there."

"I'll remember that. Er—I guess I really shouldn't leave without asking one more question. What, exactly, did you do last night?"

"I had a business dinner with Sharon Henderson, my decorator," Mac answered evenly, stressing the professional relationship for Sharon's sake. "I was back in my motel room at just after nine o'clock. I watched a *Star Trek* rerun on cable, caught the late news, then read for an hour or so before going to sleep. Want to know what I dreamed?"

Wade laughed. "Hey, I'm a cop, not a psychiatrist."

"Just checking."

The chief left, saying only that he would be seeing Mac around. One hand squeezing the back of his neck, Mac watched him leave.

Damned if he could figure that guy out. He had the distinct feeling that Wade didn't seriously consider him a suspect in the break-ins, but was generally leery about him, anyway. He would have to be careful not to do anything to further pique the chief's suspicions, especially when it came to the McBrides. He had a feeling Davenport was extremely protective of his wife, and wouldn't allow anyone to bother her. No matter what the family connection turned out to be.

CHAPTER SEVEN

SHARON WAS STILL in her shop ten minutes after closing time on Monday. Tressie had already gone home and Sharon would have followed suit had she not been waiting for her brother. He'd spent the afternoon at a movie with friends who were supposed to have dropped him off twenty minutes ago.

She was beginning to worry. Against her better judgment, she'd given him permission to ride with a sixteen-year-old friend with a driver's license and a car, a decision she'd been second-guessing all day. She'd probably been swayed by Jerry's accusations that she was being overprotective of her brother, that she needed to start treating him like a young man rather than a child. And Brad had been on his best behavior for the past few days, which naturally made her more inclined to indulge him occasionally.

She hoped she hadn't made a mistake.

When the telephone rang, she snatched it up. "Intriguing Interiors."

"I thought I might find you still there."

It hadn't been necessary for Jerry to identify himself, of course. She recognized his voice immediately. "Yes, still here," she said. "I was just about to lock up."

"How was your day?"

"Busy. And yours?"

"The same. You heard about the break-in at Discount Motors, I guess."

"Yes, Emily mentioned it at church yesterday."

"I carry their insurance, and I've spent all morning with Bob Hickey, trying to get a list of everything that was stolen or damaged. Bob's a nice guy, but not the most organized business owner. He…"

Distracted by the sound of the door opening, Sharon looked up paying only marginal attention to what Jerry was saying. She'd expected to see her brother enter the shop. She was surprised when Mac Cordero strolled in, instead. It was even more difficult after that to pay attention to Jerry's play-by-play recitation of his workday. She smiled at Mac and motioned to indicate that she would be right with him.

Jerry was still talking. "And then Martha Godwin called. Boy, was she wound up today. She's decided that she…"

Realizing that Jerry wouldn't be taking a breath anytime soon, Sharon covered the mouthpiece with her hand and spoke softly to Mac, who leaned against the counter nearby. "Hi."

"Want me to wait somewhere else while you finish that?"

Jerry was still going on about Martha's eccentricities. "No, you're fine," she murmured to Mac. "This won't take long."

"Anyway," Jerry said suddenly in her ear,

"we're both too tired to cook this evening. Why don't we go out? We'll take Brad, of course. He'll want pizza, I suppose."

Looking away from Mac, who was thumbing through a wallpaper-sample book to occupy himself while she finished her call, Sharon said, "Thanks, Jerry, but we can't tonight."

There was only a hint of disappointment in his voice. "I guess you already have plans for the evening. I knew it was short notice, but I thought it was worth a try. So...I'll talk to you later, okay?"

She wondered if he was beginning to catch her hints that they should spend less time together. Now that she had forced herself to look objectively at their relationship and had come to the conclusion that it wasn't going anywhere—more importantly, that she didn't really even want it to—she saw no reason to continue. They should both feel free to pursue other...interests, she thought, glancing sideways at Mac. She hoped she wouldn't have to spell it out to Jerry—that would be so awkward and uncomfortable—but she was prepared to do so if necessary. "Sure. We'll talk later."

It had been a brief, unremarkable conversation, on the surface no different from dozens of chats they'd had before. Yet Sharon had the odd feeling that she had just made a significant change in her life as she disconnected Jerry's call and turned to Mac.

He looked up from the wallpaper book, his grave dark eyes searching her face. "Everything okay?"

"I hope so." After putting the telephone away,

Sharon tucked a strand of hair behind her ear, suddenly feeling shy with this man who had kissed her senseless less than forty-eight hours before. "Is there something I can do for you, Mac?"

He hesitated just long enough to make her aware of how many answers there could be to that particular question. And then he smiled. "Actually, I stopped by to give you my new address."

"You aren't staying at the motel now?"

"No. I've moved into an apartment on West Elm."

"Are you pleased with it?"

He shrugged. "It's clean, anyway. Better than a motel room."

"It's furnished?"

"The basics are provided. Enough to satisfy my needs for now."

"What about linens? Cookware? Dishes?"

"I have all that. I carry a couple of boxes of necessities with me from job to job."

She frowned. "It sounds rather bleak when you put it that way. Don't you have a permanent home somewhere?"

"I own a house in Savannah. It's rented out now."

"So you've just been moving from job to job?"

"For the past few years."

"You don't have a family?"

"I'm divorced."

"Oh." She hadn't really considered that he might have once been married. She wondered what had happened to his marriage. Why he lived such a lonely existence now. Had his heart been broken? "No children?"

"No."

She studied his face. There'd been something in that stark single syllable. Something in his voice. A flash of emotion in his eyes. Pain? Regret? A touch of anger? Or was she letting her imagination get completely away from her?

He changed the subject before she could ask any more questions. "Are you finished here for the day?"

"Yes. I'm waiting for my brother. He was supposed to have been here half an hour ago."

"He hasn't called?"

"No. He went to a movie with some friends. They probably stopped by the arcade afterward and let time get away from them."

"That's typical of teenagers, I understand."

"Yes—but Brad knows I expect him to be on time."

"It must be difficult being responsible for a teenage brother. Does he usually follow your rules?"

"He hasn't given me much trouble so far. An incident or two. Some backtalk. No open rebellion yet."

"Still, I bet you'll be glad when your mother comes home."

Mac didn't know her mother, of course. Having Lucy home wouldn't make much difference. She let others take over—usually Sharon. As for Brad—

well, Sharon worried about what would happen when school started again. It had been at school that Brad had hooked up with the wrong crowd in the first place. She wasn't at all sure Lucy could do much if he got into any more trouble. Lucy indulged, she didn't discipline.

"So what's the penalty for being half an hour late?"

"I haven't decided yet. I'll probably take his video game away for the evening. Maybe TV, as well."

"Mmm. That'll show him," Mac murmured.

Sharon shot him a suspicious look. Was that an implied criticism? He was the one who'd said all teenagers did this sort of thing. Did he expect her to ground Brad for life?

The door opened and Brad rushed in, red-faced and panting. "I'm sorry I'm late, sis. Jimbo ran out of gas and we had to—"

The jumbled words came to an abrupt halt when he spotted Mac. He froze practically in midstep. Sharon knew he was startled to find someone else in the shop after closing time, but she couldn't imagine why his cheeks suddenly turned beet red and his face drew into a sullen scowl.

"Brad, this is Mr. Cordero," she said, rushing to fill in the strained silence. "Mac, my brother, Brad Henderson."

"Nice to meet you, Brad."

His gaze on his shoes, Brad muttered something incoherent.

Sharon lifted an eyebrow. Her brother was sometimes awkward, but rarely outright rude. "I'm not sure Mr. Cordero heard that, Brad."

Mac shook his head. "No, it's fine. I'll clear out now. I just wanted to give you my new address."

"Thank you. I'll probably come out to the site tomorrow to take pictures upstairs. It's safe to do that, I presume?"

"As long as you stay clear of the workers. I expect to be there most of the day tomorrow. I'll see you then."

She smiled at him. "See you then."

He looked for a moment at her smile and then raised his eyes to hers again. She had the strangest sensation that she had just been virtually kissed. Her lips actually tingled.

The man really was making her crazy.

Mac turned toward the door then. "See you around, Brad," he said as he passed the teen.

Brad didn't reply.

"You were rude to Mr. Cordero, Brad," Sharon chided when the door closed behind Mac. "I doubt he heard a word you said."

"I don't like him."

She was surprised by the growled response. "What do you mean? You only just met him."

"I don't care. He seems like a jerk to me."

"Honestly, Brad. You shouldn't form judgments about people without even getting to know them. Mr. Cordero is a very nice man." Even as she said it, she was aware of how insipid the word *nice* seemed when applied to Mac.

Brad didn't buy it. "He's a jerk. And I don't like the way he looked at you."

Sharon reached for her purse. "Don't be silly. Let's go home now and get some dinner. And we're going to talk about why you were more than half an hour late."

"I told you, it wasn't my fault."

"We'll talk about it later," she repeated, keys in hand as she moved toward the door.

"Jerry said last Friday night that he was going to try to take us out for pizza or something tonight. Didn't he call?"

"He called, but I turned him down."

"Aw, man! Just because I was a few minutes late?"

"I had several reasons." She let him exit the shop ahead of her.

Brad muttered under his breath as she locked the door. Sharon sighed. It was going to be a long, stressful evening. The only bright spot in the past hour had been Mac's unexpected visit.

CAMERA IN HAND, Sharon stepped through the front door of the Garrett house at just after five Tuesday afternoon. She had passed several vehicles leaving as she arrived, so she assumed work had ended for the day. Mac's truck was still in the parking lot, alongside one other car she recognized as Trevor McBride's.

Wondering why a lawyer was visiting a construction site, she paused just inside the front door at the rack Mac had set up to hold spare hard hats. She couldn't help smiling when she spotted a brand-new, bright yellow hat at the end of the row. Neatly lettered across the front was the word *decorator*.

The hat fit almost perfectly when she settled it on her head. It made her feel very much like a member of the team—a feeling she was starting to enjoy. Somewhat proprietarily, she glanced around the entryway and into the front parlor, imagining how beautiful and welcoming this view would be once she finished her part.

Heavy footsteps on the temporarily reinforced stairs made her look up. Mac and Trevor were on their way down. Neither was wearing a hard hat—probably because the construction work had ended for the day. She studied them as they descended. Two very strong, attractive men, she mused. One dark and sleek, the other golden and slender.

She imagined there would be quite a heated debate among her friends as to which man was the most attractive of the two. As for her—well, she thought as she focused on Mac, there was really no question.

Trevor smiled when he saw Sharon. Mac didn't smile, but there was a sudden gleam in his dark eyes that made her knees quiver for a moment. Because it seemed safer, she concentrated first on his companion. "Hello, Trevor."

"Hi, Sharon. Nice hat."

"Thank you." She glanced at Mac with a quick smile. "It's new."

"Very fetching. Interesting place, hmm?"

"Very. I haven't been upstairs yet, but I'm itching to reveal the potential of the downstairs."

"It's a bit of a maze upstairs, but there's definite potential there, too. Mac just gave me a quick tour. I haven't been in here since I was a kid and I was curious if the place looked anything like I remembered."

"And did it?"

"Not much," Trevor admitted. "But that was a long time ago."

She laughed. "You make it sound as if you're an old man."

He chuckled. "There are days when thirty-two feels pretty old. Especially when I'm trying to keep up with my six-year-old son and three-year-old daughter."

"How is your family?"

"Fine, thank you. I'll give them your regards."

"Do that."

Trevor turned to Mac, who'd been waiting patiently while they exchanged pleasantries. Thanking him again for the tour, Trevor shook Mac's hand, then explained that he had to hurry home to his family. Sharon and Mac were left alone in the house when Trevor closed the front door behind him.

"I was surprised to see Trevor here," Sharon commented, just to fill the sudden silence.

"Trent said something the other day about Trevor

wanting to look around the place before we changed everything. I sent a message for him to stop by anytime.''

"It was nice of you to take the time to walk him through.''

"I had no other plans. And I understood his curiosity.''

"And now I'm the curious one. I can't wait to get upstairs and look around.''

"Then what's keeping you?'' he asked, motioning toward the stairway.

Very aware of Mac following close behind her, she climbed the stairs, wondering what she would find at the top.

As Trevor had commented, the upstairs resembled a maze, with lots of little rooms opening off meandering hallways. To add to the chaos, the workers had started tearing out walls already, leaving gaping holes behind.

Mac guided her through the mess, pointing out features that would remain, describing the changes, even asking her opinion on a couple of options. She took several snapshots, though she knew it would look very different once Mac was finished.

Studying a particularly interesting wall line, she turned and found Mac standing directly in front of her. "Um…there's not a lot of natural light up here, is there?''

The way he was looking at her, she could tell he wasn't really thinking about the renovation. "There will be more when we're finished," he said, his eyes never leaving her face.

She moistened her lips, trying to keep her mind on the job. "You're making a lot of changes."

"Yes. But the basic style and structure of the house won't change."

"I know. That's what I find so intriguing about this project."

He lifted a hand to straighten her hard hat, though it already felt straight. He left his hand there when he'd finished, maintaining the contact between them. "Doesn't anything else about this project intrigue you?"

She swallowed. Now, how was she to answer that? "Um…"

"Coward," he murmured just beneath his breath.

Her left eyebrow rose in response to the challenge. "I beg your pardon?"

"Nothing." His attempt at looking innocent was almost laughably ineffective. She didn't think Mac would be trying out for the Honoria Community Theater anytime soon. Innocent was just not an expression he could pull off.

Feeling more at ease with him now, she walked the fingers of her right hand up the front of his denim shirt, holding the camera in her left hand. "If I were a coward," she asked, "would I be here now? Alone in this old house with a guy some people say is involved in organized crime?"

Even though she had spoken lightly, he frowned. "I told you, I am not … "

She covered his mouth with her fingertips. "I know. I was only teasing."

Moving swiftly, he caught her hand and held it against his lips, planting a kiss in her palm. Funny. She'd never realized there were quite so many nerve endings in her palm. And every one of them sparked to life when Mac's lips brushed her skin.

His head still slightly bent over her hand, he looked at her through his dark lashes. No man had ever looked at her the way Mac did. Others had looked *at* her—Mac seemed to look right into her. And, oh, how it made her feel.

Without releasing her, he slid his other hand behind her neck and gave a gentle tug. She never even considered resisting.

This kiss was as startlingly powerful as the ones they had shared before. She might have thought she would be better prepared this time for the effect his kisses had on her. She'd have been wrong.

She wasn't sure how her arms ended up around his neck. She didn't remember putting them there. She only knew they felt right there. She didn't know what had happened to her camera, though she supposed the slight thud she'd heard at her feet a moment earlier might be a clue. Fortunately, it was an inexpensive and durable model. Not that she cared at the moment.

He twisted so that she rested over his arm, giving him better access to her mouth. His movements were bold. Decisive. There was a hint of wildness in this kiss. A whisper of danger. She wouldn't have expected to be drawn to either. But she was.

From the beginning, Mac had appealed to a part of her she hardly recognized, herself.

He lifted his head, searched her face for a moment, then covered her mouth with his again. The kiss went on for an eternity, and when it ended, there was no doubt left in her mind that he was as affected by the connection between them as she was. His left arm surrounded her, supporting her. His right hand was at the small of her back, pressing lightly, holding her against him. There was no question that he wanted her—and what an experience it was to be wanted by a man like this!

"Did you plan this?" she asked.

"I planned to have you in my arms again since I left your house the other night," he admitted.

"I'm not sure if I should respond by being flattered or insulted."

"Just as long as you respond," he murmured, then kissed her again.

She most definitely responded.

"This is crazy," she murmured between kisses. "We hardly know each other."

He caught her lower lip gently, briefly, between his teeth, causing a current of electricity to race through her. Then he lifted his head. "I'm all for getting to know each other better."

She trailed a fingertip along the strong line of his jaw, realizing that her initial shyness around him was almost gone. "I'd like that."

"Have dinner with me tonight?"

"I have to pick up my brother from baseball practice in half an hour. I was planning to make spaghetti for dinner tonight. Why don't you join us?"

His mouth twisted. "I don't think your brother likes me very much."

She was surprised he'd picked up on that. She still didn't understand Brad's antagonism toward Mac. "He just doesn't know you. Brad's going through an awkwardness stage. I'm sure he'll like you if he spends time with you."

Twisting a strand of her hair around his finger, he gave a slight shrug. "Maybe. Maybe not. Does it matter a great deal to you?"

She felt as if it should. It had always seemed important that Brad liked Jerry. It made things easier when they spent time together. But she wasn't going to let Brad's attitude prevent her from spending more time with the most fascinating man she had met in…well, in her entire life.

"Come for dinner," she said. "Brad will behave."

"What time?"

"Seven."

"I'll be there." He slid his hand into the hair at the back of her head. "You said you have another half hour?"

"Almost."

He smiled as he tossed her hard hat aside and lowered his mouth to hers again. "Sounds like enough time to get to know each other a little better."

CHAPTER EIGHT

"HE'S COMING to our house for dinner? I'm leaving."

Sharon sighed. "I really don't understand your antagonism, Brad. You only met Mac for a couple of minutes."

"I've seen him around town. He's a jerk. Strutting around like he's some hotshot who's better than the hicks around here."

Appalled, Sharon stared at her brother. They stood in their living room—she'd waited until they arrived home before springing the news on him about who was joining them for dinner—and he faced her from the center of the floor, his shaggy hair tumbling into his anger-flushed face. He needed a haircut, she thought inconsequentially. He was beginning to look like someone she didn't know. He certainly sounded like a stranger. "Who's been saying these things to you? I can't believe those are your words."

"Everybody's been talking about him."

"I thought I'd taught you not to listen to the malicious gossip that goes on around this town. You have the intelligence to form your own opinions,

Brad. You have to get to know someone before you decide whether you like him or not."

"I know all I want to know. He just wants to make some fast money off the old Garrett place and then he'll move on. I don't see why we have to entertain him while he's here."

"How about simple hospitality? He doesn't know many people in town."

"He doesn't belong here. He isn't even our kind."

Sharon felt her eyes narrow. "Would you like to explain that comment?"

Apparently deciding he'd come too close to crossing her personal line, Brad backed down, but not by much. "Nothing," he muttered.

"If I thought you were making a slur against Mr. Cordero's ethnic background, I would send you to your room and make sure you didn't come out again until the school bell rings in the fall. I will not tolerate any form of bigotry in my household, is that clear? But I'm sure that's not what you meant, because our mother did not raise us that way."

His hands shoved in his pockets, Brad stared at the floor, refusing to answer.

"Mr. Cordero will be joining us in about an hour. You will wash up and prepare yourself to be polite, understand?"

"I bet Jerry won't like it that you're spending so much time with this guy."

"I don't consult with Jerry before I invite someone to dinner. Jerry and I are friends, Brad. That's it.''

Brad looked suddenly stricken. "You're not going out with this Cordero guy, are you?''

Choosing her words carefully, Sharon answered, "I like Mac. He's an interesting man. He and I are working together on the renovation project, so I will be spending quite a bit of time with him during the next few months. If you would just give him a chance, I'm sure you would like him, too.''

"Why can't I just go to Jimbo's for dinner?''

She was tempted to let him, just to avoid any unpleasantness in front of Mac. But it seemed too important to teach her brother about proper behavior—and especially about tolerance. She didn't know which of his friends had been filling his mind with such garbage, but she had no intention of letting it go on. "Because we're having company for dinner and I want you to be here. Now go get cleaned up.''

Muttering beneath his breath, Brad stamped upstairs. Sharon watched him worriedly, wondering what was happening to her little brother. Was this typical teenage behavior, or something more? She wished Caleb and Bobbie McBride were in town. Their practical, sometimes blunt advice, along with their experience at raising teenagers, had been valuable to her on many occasions.

Shaking her head, she went into the kitchen to start dinner, hoping she hadn't made a big mistake in inviting Mac to join them.

The telephone rang fifteen minutes before Mac was due to arrive. Sharon answered on the kitchen extension. "Hello?"

"Hi, sweetie."

"Mom." Casting a quick look around the kitchen to make sure nothing needed her attention at the moment, Sharon leaned against the counter for a chat. "How's the Riviera?"

"Oh, darling, it's wonderful. I wish you and Brad were here to enjoy it with me."

Sharon was sure that was true. Lucy had always believed in the more the merrier. Unfortunately, she'd never quite gripped the concept that "more" also involved more money. "I'm glad you're having a nice time."

"I miss my babies, of course. How are you and Brad?"

"We're fine, Mom." She decided against telling her mother about Brad's growing rebelliousness. There was nothing Lucy could do about it long-distance. And little she would do, even if she were here, Sharon admitted to herself.

"I wasn't sure you'd be home. I thought maybe you'd have a date with Jerry."

"No. Not tonight." That was something else she had no intention of discussing just now. The list of safe topics was shrinking rapidly, she thought. "Tell me what you've seen and done since the last time you called," she prompted.

Lucy immediately launched into an eager and colorful monologue that Sharon could only half follow.

Keeping an eye on the clock, she made appropriately interested noises. At five minutes until seven, she broke in to say, "Do you want to talk to Brad before you have to go?"

"Of course I want to talk to my little boy."

Sharon almost sighed. Lucy's "little boy" was five-eight and a hundred forty pounds. Three inches taller than Sharon and twenty pounds heavier. Sharon could only catch glimpses of the sweet-natured child he'd been. And she wished she could better understand the moody young man he'd become. At least if her mother was here, there would be someone to share the worry. "I miss you, Mom. I'll be glad when you're home."

"I know, darling. Just a few more weeks."

"I'll get Brad for you."

Brad took the call on the phone in his room. Sharon had just replaced the receiver in the kitchen when the doorbell rang. She'd asked Brad not to upset his mother with his complaints. She hoped he was complying with her request.

"What's wrong?" Mac asked when she opened the door.

She immediately smoothed her expression. "Nothing. Come in."

Being Mac, he didn't let it go at that. "Something's bothering you," he said as he closed the door behind him. "What is it? Is there anything I can do?"

"Really, Mac. It's okay. I'm just a little concerned about my brother."

"Why?"

She shrugged. "He's a teenager."

His mouth twisted a little as he nodded. "I don't envy you."

She could understand that. Few men would willingly take on the responsibilities Sharon had shouldered. Even though she hoped to have her own place soon, she was realistic enough to know that she wouldn't be able to completely distance herself from her family's problems. Lucy was just too scatterbrained and disorganized to manage well on her own and *definitely* not firm enough to deal with Brad's stubborn moods.

Lucy had indulged Brad too much, and for that matter, so had Sharon. They'd both felt that they had to make it up to him somehow because he'd lost his father so young. Perhaps they'd gone overboard. It was difficult now to suddenly become a disciplinarian.

Mac looked around. "Where is your brother?"

"On the phone with Mom. Probably telling her what an ogre I am," she muttered.

"Every teenager needs an ogre for a guardian."

"You're probably right."

Taking a step closer to her, he reached out to trace her lower lip with a fingertip. "Since I'm *not* a teenager, perhaps you could save this stern frown for your brother?"

Realizing she'd been scowling since he'd arrived, she smiled slightly against his finger. "Sorry."

"That's better."

Brad appeared at the top of the stairs just then. He was obviously displeased to catch them standing so close together, Mac's hand still resting lightly against the side of Sharon's face. The glare he gave them was almost cold enough to cause frostbite.

Mac dropped his hand and moved away, taking his time about it. "Hello, Brad. Nice to see you again," he said casually.

"Hey."

Sharon wasn't exactly pleased with Brad's curt response, but at least it had been audible. He knew better than to be blatantly rude to a guest in their home. At least, she hoped he did.

MAC DIDN'T TRY to push the boy into further conversation during dinner. He and Sharon discussed the anticipated progress of the renovation for the upcoming week, then turned the discussion to national politics, a subject that interested them both. Keeping his head down, Brad concentrated on his food, apparently content to be ignored.

Eventually Sharon seemed to decide it was time for her brother to join in. "How's your food, Brad?" she asked pleasantly. "Do you need anything else?"

"It's fine," the boy replied without looking up from his plate. "Can I have some more bread?"

She passed him the basket of wheat rolls, which he accepted with a muttered, "Thanks."

Because he could tell that Brad's sullenness was disturbing her, Mac said, "This is really good, Sharon. I've always liked spaghetti."

He was rewarded with a smile. "It's my mother's special recipe. She's a very good cook when she pays attention to what she's doing. Remember the time she accidentally used cayenne pepper instead of paprika, Brad? We nearly burned the linings out of our mouths."

The boy didn't share her amusement. "My mom's a great cook," he said, sounding defensive.

Mac shrugged. "Everyone makes mistakes. My mother used to get distracted and burn the plantains. I started thinking of the smoke alarm as a dinner bell."

"Plantains?" Sharon repeated. "I've never had them."

"They look a little like bananas. In Puerto Rico, they're often fried and served as a side dish."

"What other Puerto Rican dishes did your mother make for you?"

He could tell she was relieved that the conversation was moving again, so he decided to expand a bit. "We had arroz con pollo quite often—that's yellow rice with chicken, one of my favorite meals. And asopao, a heavy rice soup, with either chicken or shrimp. Paella. And for dessert, flan. No one made it the way my mother did. I still dream about her flan sometimes," he joked, though it was the truth.

"I like *American* food," Brad muttered.

"Like spaghetti?" his sister asked sarcastically, nodding toward Brad's empty plate.

He flushed and ducked his head again.

A hint of apology in her expression, Sharon turned to Mac again. "Did you ever live in Puerto Rico?"

"No. I visited there once, but I was born and raised in Savannah."

"Which explains the Southern accent," she teased lightly.

"Yes, ma'am."

"Do you speak Spanish?"

"Well enough to make myself understood. I had to learn it pretty much on my own. My mother wanted English to be my primary language."

Sharon tried again to pull her brother into the conversation. "Brad's taking Spanish in school."

"Only because I've got no choice," Brad said immediately. "They won't let us graduate without two years of a foreign language. Don't see the purpose in it, myself. English is the only language I need to know."

Sharon's little brother was in danger of becoming a bigot, Mac mused, remembering some of the slurs he'd heard muttered behind him the evening he'd encountered Brad and his friends outside the arcade. Typical gang mentality. Band together against suspected outsiders. Create an image of superiority by perceiving and treating others as inferiors. Someone needed to get this kid away from that crowd before he got into trouble.

Not that it was any of *his* business, of course.

"I made brownies for dessert," Sharon said,

smoothly changing the subject. "I hope you aren't allergic to chocolate, Mac."

"I have no problems at all with chocolate."

"Can I take mine up to my room? I want to read my new sports magazine."

Sharon gave Brad's request a moment of consideration. "We do have company."

"Don't let me keep you from your magazine," Mac said with a slight shrug.

"Okay, Sharon?"

She gave in. "I suppose it's all right."

The boy practically bolted upstairs.

Sharon looked contritely at Mac. "I'm sorry. I don't know what gets into him when he's around you. I guess you intimidate him, for some reason."

Mac, of course, knew exactly why Brad still resented him. The kid hadn't gotten over being embarrassed in front of his friends. But he was just going to have to get over it. Mac wasn't going to disappear—not until he was good and ready, anyway.

"Let me help you with the dishes," he said, reaching for his empty plate.

"Oh, that's not—"

"Sharon," he cut in firmly. "This is the second time you've fed me. Let me help."

She smiled and caved. "If you insist."

Since Sharon admitted to being the clean-as-she-cooked type, it didn't take long to load the dishwasher and straighten the kitchen. By the time they'd finished, a fresh pot of coffee had brewed.

They carried their cups and plates of pecan brownies into the living room. They'd talked while they worked. Mac was surprised about how easily he conversed with Sharon. He usually found it harder to make small talk. But now he knew it was time to get down to the real reason he was here—or at least that's what he told himself—to find out more about the McBrides.

"Trevor McBride seems like an interesting guy," he said, keeping his tone light as he held his coffee cup and reached for a brownie. "He looks a lot like Trent, but I got the impression when he visited the site this afternoon that they're not much alike on the whole."

"Not a lot," Sharon agreed from the chair she'd chosen near the couch where Mac had settled. "I always thought of Trevor as the more grounded brother. Like their older sister, Tara, he excelled in school—valedictorian, class president, that sort of thing. No one was surprised when he followed in his father's footsteps and went East to law school. He made quite a name for himself in Washington, D.C., before moving back here to raise his children after his wife died so tragically young."

"Had to be tough on him. Being left with two small children to raise, I mean."

"Yes, it was very hard on him. He was lucky to have had his parents here to help him out. They're a very close family. They rally around each other without hesitation when one of them is in need. Then he and Jamie got married, and they seem very happy now. He and the kids are all crazy about Jamie, and she obviously feels the same way about them.''

Mac found it hard to identify with a family that unhesitatingly supported each other through every difficulty. It was a luxury he and his mother had been denied. "The McBrides have had their share of troubles, haven't they?''

"Like all big families, I suppose,'' she said with a shrug.

Not much help there. "I was thinking about Trent's plane crash. I understand he'd been on his way to a career in the air force until the crash grounded him.''

She nodded, looking distracted, her eyes on the staircase. Thinking about her brother again? Mac wondered. But at least she was answering his questions.

"Yes, Trent always dreamed of being a pilot. He was as smart as his sister and brother, but grades weren't quite as important to him. He made A's only because he needed them to get him into the Air Force Academy. Tara and Trevor were always rather serious, very focused. Trent was the clown. The daredevil. I suppose that's hard for you to believe now. The crash changed him so much. He's just now learning to enjoy life again. Thanks in no small part to his fiancée, Annie, he's learned that he can be happy doing something other than flying.''

"It couldn't have been easy for him to give up the one thing he'd always wanted.''

Sharon shook her head. "I'm sure it was the hardest thing he's ever done. His family was so worried about him. Bobbie told me once that she wasn't sure he would make it through—but I always knew he was stronger than that."

"You wouldn't still be carrying a torch for the guy, would you?"

That got her attention. She let out a peal of laughter that was obviously genuine, to his satisfaction. "Good heavens, no. I've always considered Trent a friend. In fact, I probably think of him more like a brother—a cousin, maybe—than anything else."

"Just checking out my competition," he murmured, pleased when she blushed prettily.

"It isn't Trent," she assured him.

"Oh?" He lifted an eyebrow. "Someone else?"

"I've told you, I'm not romantically involved with anyone. I have male friends I see sometimes, but that's all."

He gave her a wicked smile that made her blush deepen. "Good."

She made a pretense of concentrating on her coffee, looking so flustered and vulnerable that it was all Mac could do not to pull her into his arms and make her flush with desire rather than embarrassment. He cleared his throat and forced himself back on topic. "Trevor's several years older than Trent, isn't he?"

She seemed grateful that he'd veered into less personal waters. "Almost six years, I think. Trent's twenty-six, and Trevor is thirty-two."

"And their sister is older?"

"A year older than Trevor," she agreed. "Tara's thirty-three. Um—about your age?" she hazarded, obviously hinting.

"The same," he agreed. "I'm thirty-three." He wondered if the fact that he and Tara McBride had been born only months apart made it more or less likely that they had the same father. He couldn't help wondering how Sharon would react if he made that speculation aloud. She'd proven to be even more helpful than he'd hoped in providing information about the McBrides—but something told him that would stop abruptly if she suspected he had an ax to grind against the family she obviously admired so greatly.

"I'm looking forward to meeting Caleb and Bobbie McBride," he commented, hoping he wasn't pushing his luck. Mac had a pretty strong suspicion that Caleb wasn't the man he was searching for but he might as well find out everything he could. "The way everyone in town talks about them, they sound intriguing."

Sharon smiled. "They are. You'll like them, I'm sure. Caleb's a true Southern gentleman. Jamie says he plays the part of the small-town Southern lawyer to the hilt. She's crazy about him, of course—as I am."

"He's the founder of the McBride Law Firm, right?"

"Right. He opened the practice long before I was born."

"I, um, suppose he has to travel quite a bit in his line of work."

Laughing a little, Sharon shook her head. "Caleb never leaves Honoria. You wouldn't believe what his family went through just to get him to take this vacation. He calls himself the original homebody, someone who is perfectly happy to live his entire life in the town where he was born. I don't remember him ever being gone for more than a day or two at a time, and never without his wife and family to accompany him."

So Caleb never left Honoria. Mac nodded somberly. "He and his wife sound very close. They must be a lot alike."

"I'm sure they are in some ways. But Bobbie— well." She seemed to grope for the most suitable adjectives.

He chuckled. "I've heard she can be…intimidating."

"The people who told you that were probably in her class at one time. She's the terror of Honoria Elementary—and the best teacher in town. Fiercely loyal to her family and friends, a bit gruff but very good-hearted, bossy but well-intentioned. There are some people who are put off by her bluntness, but I'm very fond of her. She and Caleb are a wonderful couple—the perfect foils for each other. They both have something very special to offer. They've been married for almost forty years."

"Are there any McBrides you don't like?" Mac asked, shaking his head.

She laughed. "No, not really. My own family is so small—just Mom and Brad and me, and a few distant relatives we don't see very often. I must admit, I've always been a little fascinated by the McBride clan."

"It shows."

Her mouth twisted. "I suppose that's why you and I always end up discussing them. You must wonder if I ever talk about anything else."

Had she actually convinced herself that she was the one who kept bringing the McBrides into their conversation? If so, Mac had been more subtle than he'd believed—or she was more worried about her brother than she was letting on, which was more likely. Deciding to be content with the progress he'd made for the evening, as well as feeling guilty for manipulating Sharon this way, Mac changed the subject. "Did you get all the photographs you needed today? Will you be out at the site again tomorrow?"

She shook her head. "I'm going car shopping tomorrow afternoon. I can't keep renting."

"Did your insurance come through for you?"

She shrugged ruefully. "To a point. I took a loss, of course, and I'll have to finance a new car."

"It's damn unfair, isn't it? Whoever was driving that van should be the one paying. It wasn't your fault the idiot decided to run you off the road."

"I know. And you're right. It is unfair, and it makes me furious, but I suppose I'll have to live with it until Wade catches the guy. Even then the chances are slim I'll ever be reimbursed, I suppose.''

''I'm afraid so.''

''I try not to think about that night very often,'' she said, looking into her coffee cup. ''It's too disturbing for the most part. But I can't help wondering sometimes…''

''Wondering what?'' he asked gently, sensing she needed to talk.

She looked up at him. ''The van seemed to come at me so deliberately. You don't think—you don't think it was deliberate, do you? To keep me from testifying about what I saw, or somehow identifying him, I mean? Am I letting my imagination run away with me when I think along those lines?''

She was asking for reassurance that someone hadn't deliberately tried to kill her. Knowing how horrifying that possibility must be to her, Mac wished he could give her the reassurance she wanted. But in this, at least, he had to be honest with her. ''I don't know, Sharon. Maybe it was an accident, but under the circumstances, maybe it wasn't. You can bet it's a question your friend Wade will ask if he ever gets his hands on the guy.''

''When, not if,'' Sharon corrected him automatically. ''Wade will catch him.''

From what he was learning about the very thorough police chief, Mac understood why she spoke so confidently. If the driver of that van was still in the area, there was a good chance Wade would catch him. But it was more likely that he was long gone.

Too many crimes like that were never solved, an endless source of frustration to those who worked in law enforcement, and one of the reasons Mac had wanted out.

"Try not to dwell on it," he advised her, knowing that wasn't as easy as it sounded. "You're safe now. It isn't as if you could identify anyone."

"I know. I just can't help remembering every once in a while…" Her voice trailed off as she shivered, and he pictured her reliving the terror during sleepless nights. His fist tightened around his coffee cup. He wished *he* could get his hands on the guy who had almost cost Sharon her life.

She shook her head. "I'm fine, really. And I'll never forget the way you helped me that night."

"I'm just glad I was there. So, is anyone going car shopping with you tomorrow? Or do you prefer to handle that sort of thing on your own?"

"Brad wants to go, but fortunately he has baseball practice. I'm afraid he would try to talk me into buying something completely impractical—like a Corvette or a Viper or something equally out of my price range. I'm quite sure he won't approve of the sensible sedan I intend to buy. My friend Jerry— he's an insurance salesman here in Honoria—offered to go with me, but Jerry's the take-charge type. He'd never let me get a word in edgewise with the car salesperson. He means well, but I'd prefer to handle the purchase myself."

"If you'd like some company, I'd be happy to go

with you. I'd only give my opinion when you ask for it.''

She looked intrigued. "Are you sure you have the time?''

"I'll make the time—if you want me to go along.''

"Actually, I would appreciate having a second opinion. I thought about asking Trevor or Trent, but I wasn't sure either of them would be available.''

"I'm available.''

Her smile made him glad he'd taken the risk of offering his company. She was obviously pleased— which pleased him in return. "I'd like that.''

"So would I.'' And he was well aware that it had very little to do with finding out more about the McBrides.

Because it was getting harder with each passing moment to sit so close to her without touching her, he set his coffee cup on the table and stood. "I'll see you tomorrow.''

She rose with him. "You're leaving?''

He glanced at the staircase. "It seems like the wisest choice.''

Following his glance, she nodded. "Maybe you're right.''

"Where do you want to meet tomorrow?''

"My shop—noon?''

"I'll be there.''

She followed him to the door. Casting one more quick look at the empty staircase, he reached out and pulled her toward him for one long, thorough kiss. It was all he allowed himself—but he simply couldn't leave without it. She returned the embrace with an eagerness that suggested she had needed it as badly as he did—or was that only wishful thinking on his part?

As he drove back to his apartment, Mac tried to analyze exactly what was going on between him and Sharon Henderson. He wanted her—he'd be an idiot to deny that. But he also wanted any background she could give him about the McBrides, especially Caleb and his brothers.

And yet somehow, he had the uncomfortable feeling there was even more between them than that. And he wasn't at all sure what to do about it. His one attempt at commitment had ended in pain and bitterness—he had no intention of going through anything like that again. Especially with a woman who might very well hate him when she found out why he was really here.

CHAPTER NINE

MAC STUDIED the McBride family tree taking shape on the yellow legal pad. Two hours after leaving Sharon's house, he sat at the small round table in the eat-in kitchen of his temporary apartment, his notes spread in front of him. He'd been trying to concentrate on the few new tidbits he'd learned, rather than the way Sharon's mouth had felt beneath his. He'd made an attempt to remember the reason he'd come to Honoria in the first place, rather than the look of reciprocal desire he had seen in Sharon's eyes.

Thinking of Sharon tonight could prove to be far more uncomfortable than brooding on bad memories.

"Caleb and Bobbie McBride," he had written at the top of a fresh sheet of paper. Beneath the names, he'd noted that they'd been married for nearly seven years before Mac's conception—which meant Caleb could have been the married man who'd had an affair with Mac's mother. Although it was possible, Mac was having trouble believing it. There were certain other things that didn't fit at all. Caleb had long been established as an attorney in town, a job that seemed to require no travel. From what everyone said, he and Bobbie were very happily married, almost perfectly suited. So why would he risk everything to have an affair? Especially since Caleb's oldest child, Tara, was Mac's own age, which indicated Caleb and Bobbie had certainly been getting along at least reasonably well thirty-three years ago.

Everything Mac had heard about that branch of the McBride family indicated that they were almost TV-sitcom perfect—a small-town lawyer and a schoolteacher with three attractive, intelligent, popular and successful kids. If scandal really was a McBride legacy, it seemed to have affected that group less dramatically than the others.

Caleb's children seemed to have grown up in the kind of home Mac had secretly fantasized about when he'd been a lonely boy whose single mother worked too long and too hard, leaving him alone too much to daydream about what his life might have been like if things had been different.

He'd watched other boys with their dads and he had wondered what it would be like to have a father of his own. He'd gone through stages of resentment, anger, even rebellion that his father hadn't wanted to be a part of his life. Much like Brad Henderson, he realized. Brad definitely needed a strong male influence in his life, rather than two women who seemed to have gotten into the habit of overindulging him.

Mac had been fortunate to have a mother who had been determined to help him make something of himself, and a few good male role models—a couple of favorite teachers, a coach and a police officer neighbor who'd taken Mac under his wing. He knew Brad was involved in sports, so maybe the boy had a few guys who cared enough to keep him in line, show him what being a real man was all about.

He wondered if Sharon's friend Jerry was one of Brad's role models.

He'd heard about Jerry, even before Sharon had casually mentioned him. Rumor was that Sharon and Jerry had been dating for a while, though no one seemed to think it had gotten serious yet. There'd been a few who felt the need to mention the guy to Mac—as if obliquely warning him that he could be intruding on posted property. Mac had decided to take his cues from Sharon, herself—and she'd certainly given no indication that any other man had a claim on her.

He didn't think she'd appreciate the terms in which he was thinking about her, he thought with a frown. She wasn't property to be claimed by any man, including himself. And yet he was aware that he still didn't like thinking about Jerry. He was sure he wouldn't like him—and he'd never even met the guy. Which meant that what he *really* disliked was the thought of Sharon spending time with any other man.

Slamming his pencil onto the table, he shoved his chair backward and stood. He didn't want to sit here identifying with Sharon's fatherless kid brother, or brooding about her other male friends. And there didn't seem to be any more conclusions he could reach about the McBrides tonight. He still knew almost nothing about Jonah, Josiah Jr. and Caleb's younger brother. He was the remaining piece of the genetic puzzle Mac was trying to assemble.

Mac needed to figure out a way to somehow include Jonah McBride in his next conversation with Sharon. At the moment, that seemed much easier than trying to figure out a way to entice Sharon into his bed.

SHARON HAD KNOWN when she accepted Mac's offer to look for a car with her that the friendship growing between them would no longer be private. She might as well have posted a notice in the *Honoria Gazette* that she was dating him. She knew people would talk. But she didn't really care. She and Mac were single, unattached adults. There was no reason at all why they shouldn't spend time together.

She had such a good time that Wednesday afternoon. She enjoyed being with Mac, valued his advice, appreciated the way he stood back and let her do her own talking and make her own decisions. And she savored the way he looked at her, making her feel feminine and desirable and special in a way no other man had ever made her feel. She was aware that she was becoming majorly infatuated with this man, but she told herself she could handle it.

At least, she hoped she could.

She had hardly parked her new car in the garage that evening when the telephone rang. Tossing her purse aside, she grabbed the kitchen extension. "Hello?"

"Hello, Sharon. It's a pleasant surprise to hear your voice rather than your answering machine."

She grimaced. It was obvious from Jerry's tone that he wasn't happy—and she could guess the reason. "Hi, Jerry."

"I hear you got a new car this afternoon."

"Yes. I was planning to call you first thing in the morning to update my insurance. How did you hear about it?"

"Charlie Hayes came by my office just before closing time to give me the information on his new pickup. He mentioned that he'd seen you at the dealership."

Sharon remembered chatting with the retired school principal who'd once been her mother's boss. She had introduced him to Mac. "Mr. Hayes looks good, doesn't he?" she said. "He seems to have fully recovered from his bout with cancer."

She'd had a faint hope Jerry would allow her to direct the conversation, but she wasn't surprised when he said, instead, "Charlie told me you'd brought a friend with you."

"Yes," she answered evenly. "Mac Cordero volunteered to go with me when I mentioned my plans for the afternoon."

"Perhaps you've forgotten that I also volunteered."

"No, I didn't forget. But I didn't want to take

you away from your office. Mac had some free time this afternoon.''

''Rumor has it you've been spending quite a bit of time with this guy.''

So people *had* been talking. ''I am on his renovation team,'' she said rather lamely.

''And the project isn't anywhere close to where your services are needed. From what I hear, they've just started tearing out walls and old fixtures and wiring. It'll be weeks before they start rebuilding.''

''Mac has asked me to be involved at all stages. He likes my ideas.''

''I'm sure he does,'' Jerry muttered.

Because that comment seemed juvenile, Sharon chose not to respond. ''Would you like to hear about my new car? It isn't fancy, but it's—''

''What I would like to hear,'' he cut in curtly, ''is just what is going on between you and Mac Cordero.''

She wondered why Jerry suddenly sounded so priggish. She'd never really thought of him in those terms before. Of course, she had never really done anything to annoy him this much before. ''I don't owe you any explanations, Jerry. Nor do I have to ask your permission to see other people.''

''Is this why you've been avoiding me lately? You're seeing this Cordero guy?''

''I don't think it's a good time to discuss this.''

''And when *is* a good time, Sharon? Every time I've suggested getting together lately, you've had an excuse.''

That was true, she realized with a grimace. She'd been trying to send gentle hints to Jerry, when it would have been better to tell him outright that she wasn't interested in him romantically. That she valued his friendship and hated to lose it, but she couldn't commit to a relationship that realistically was going nowhere. "Perhaps we could have dinner one night next week?"

There was a taut, lengthy pause. "Don't do me any favors."

"Come on, Jerry. There's no need to..." But Sharon's words were met by a dial tone. He'd hung up on her. She sighed in exasperation.

"He dumped you, didn't he?"

The voice from behind her made her start, the phone still clutched in her hand. "Brad, you startled me," she said, shaking her head as she replaced the receiver. "I nearly jumped out of my shoes. Do you want to see my new—"

"Did you let Jerry break up with you?" her brother interrupted.

She realized only then that Brad looked furious.

She spoke calmly. "Jerry and I didn't 'break up.' We weren't involved in that way. You make us sound like your high-school friends who go steady."

"He's mad at you because you've been hanging out with Cordero, isn't he?"

Sharon was beginning to resent this line of interrogation from her brother, especially so soon after Jerry's cross-examination. "This really isn't any of your business."

"I heard you took him with you when you went looking at cars today."

"How in the world—"

"Why did you do that? Didn't you know everyone would talk about it?"

"I don't see anything wrong with taking a friend shopping with me."

"It makes you look like you're chasing the guy."

"Brad!"

"Jimbo says you can't trust a guy like that. Traveling from place to place, never sticking around. Hitting on women wherever he goes, looking for an easy—"

"Jimbo doesn't know what he's talking about," she snapped. "And, frankly, neither do you."

"I know the guys are all making fun of you. They think you're stupid to fall for a jerk like that. They told me if I don't talk some sense into you, he's going to make a fool of you. You'll end up like Connie Moser if somebody doesn't stop you."

Sharon had to roll her eyes at that. Connie Moser was a sixteen-year-old single mother who'd become pregnant after a summer fling with a boy her own age who'd come to Honoria from Saint Louis to visit his grandparents. She hardly saw a correlation. "Give me credit for a little more sense than that, will you, Brad? You're being ridiculous. Mac and I are both adults. Why shouldn't we go out if we want?"

"You already have a boyfriend. Jerry."

"Jerry is *not* my boyfriend." She found herself

raising her voice in frustration, and realized she was coming close to getting into an undignified shouting match with her maddening younger brother. She took a deep breath to steady herself. "I'm not asking your permission to date Mac."

"So how come I have to ask *your* permission to do anything?"

"Because, whether you like it or not, I'm the adult in charge in this household, at least until Mom comes home. I've tried to be fair and I've tried to cut you a great deal of slack, but when it comes down to it, the final decisions—and the responsibility—are mine. Frankly, I don't consider it an ideal situation, either, but Mom asked us this favor and we both agreed to it, so we're going to uphold our end of the deal."

"But—"

"You have neither the right nor the responsibility to 'talk sense into me' about anything I do. I don't have to seek your approval, and I have no interest whatever in Jimbo's opinion. Have I made myself very clear?"

Sullenly refusing to answer, Brad only nodded, looking down at his feet.

"Go upstairs and wash up. Dinner will be ready in half an hour, and then we'll need to leave for church. I'm sure you remember that you have youth group tonight."

He looked as though he wanted to argue, but he didn't. For one thing, he probably knew he'd pushed her too far. And for another, she knew he enjoyed his youth group meetings, though he wasn't in the mood to admit that—or anything else—to her now. He swiveled and left the room, his steps much heavier than they needed to be.

She waited until he was out of sight and then sagged against the counter, her anger dissipating and leaving her shaky. How on earth had she ended up in this situation? What had made her think she could handle this? Her mother had made it sound so simple—just keep an eye out for Brad for a few weeks, make sure he didn't get into trouble and take care of the house until Lucy returned. No problem, right?

Wrong. Sharon could feel the whole arrangement beginning to crumble around her and she wasn't at all sure what to do about it. Brad was changing. Openly challenging her in a way he'd never done before. Maybe it was only natural for a boy his age, or maybe it was something more serious than that— how was she to know?

She wished again that Bobbie and Caleb McBride were in town.

Maybe she could talk to Wade Davenport. His son was a teenager and seemed so well adjusted. Maybe the police chief could offer some suggestion. Or what about one of the other men in Brad's life? His baseball coach. His tennis instructor. Officer Dodson, who seemed to have the boys' respect even though he kept a close eye on them. Would any of them know what to do?

For some reason, she found herself wanting to talk to Mac, though he didn't have a teenager and didn't even know Brad, really. She thought just hearing his voice would make her feel better—and that realization worried her almost as much as Brad's tantrum had.

MAC WAS GETTING into the habit of eating dinner at Cora's Café. He wasn't the only regular, and it wasn't hard to understand why the place was so popular. The food was good. There was a different blue plate special every day, so he didn't get bored with the menu. And then there were Cora's pies...

Loneliness wasn't a problem during his meals, either. Cora's longtime employee, Mindy Hooper, was jovial, dry-witted and naturally talkative. She made a point to stop by his table and visit whenever she had a few moments. Her manner toward him wasn't flirtatious. Though she couldn't have been more than forty, she treated him in an almost maternal fashion—the same way she behaved toward most of the other customers.

Although Mac had only been in town for a couple of weeks, she already seemed to consider him a local, having learned his choice of dinner beverage, his favorite salad dressing, the way he drank his coffee, and that he liked every flavor of pie except strawberry. It was nice to be so easily accepted by someone who took what she knew about him at face value without being overwhelmed by curiosity to learn more.

Other diners occasionally stopped by Mac's table to greet him—people he'd met through the renovation project, some he'd encountered in other places such as the post office and hardware store, and a few friendly folks who just wanted to stop and introduce themselves. Although he wasn't particularly interested in making friends in Honoria—he had no plan to return once he'd accomplished his personal and professional goals—he made a point to respond to the greetings pleasantly enough. There was no reason to be impolite, he figured.

Pleasantly full and in a pretty good mood Thursday evening, he left the café and headed for his truck, which he had parked nearby. He would rather have spent the evening with Sharon, of course, but he figured they both needed some time apart. The hours they'd spent car shopping the day before had been very pleasant—almost *too* nice, as far as he was concerned. He hadn't learned anything new about the McBrides—in fact, he'd hardly given them a passing thought. And it bothered him that his growing desire for Sharon was beginning to interfere with his purpose for being in this town.

He'd come too far in this quest to let it go now. He couldn't allow Sharon—or anyone else—to get in his way of finding the truth. Once he had his answers, it would be entirely up to him to decide what to do with them. He had told himself he didn't really care who got hurt when the truth came out. As badly as he'd been hurt during his lifetime, he deserved to have his payback.

But being around Sharon made him question his

actions and his motives. Made him begin to wonder if some things were more important than revenge.

He definitely needed some time away from her.

Lost in his thoughts of Sharon, it took him a moment to notice the deep gouge that ran down the driver's side of his truck. It was a long, ugly scratch that ran from fender to fender, cutting through the black paint to reveal the gray metal beneath. Deliberately inflicted—most likely with a nail, a knife or some equally sharp object. It had not been there when he'd parked the truck barely forty-five minutes earlier.

Whoever had done this had known exactly what sort of damage he was doing. And who he was doing it to. Mac had no doubt that nearly everyone in this nosy little town recognized his truck by now.

Last time he'd been in Honoria, he'd rented two different dark, nondescript cars, hoping he could learn something about the McBrides without calling attention to himself. Of course, he hadn't realized then just how little actually went by without notice in this town, how the slightest change from the ordinary was cause for suspicion. He'd almost been accused of stalking Annie Stewart, when it had actually been Trent McBride he'd been observing. It had taken some glib talking on his part to get him out of that one, having to convince Trent that he had been looking to hire him for the renovation team, not keeping an eye on him or his girlfriend.

On this trip, he'd driven his own functional black pickup with its distinctive markings and chrome accessories. And now it had been deliberately targeted…

Hearing running footsteps, he whirled just in time to see someone disappear around a corner down the street. Someone who'd probably been hiding in an alley or behind another vehicle when Mac went past.

Someone who very strongly resembled Brad Henderson.

"Dammit," he muttered and whipped his cell phone out of his pocket. He punched in Sharon's number. She answered on the second ring.

"Where's your brother?" he asked without bothering to identify himself.

She sounded puzzled. "He has a ball game this evening, but he's having dinner first with the rest of his team. Why?"

"Where are they having dinner?"

"Probably at the new soda shop on Maple Street. They all like the burgers and shakes there. What's this all about, Mac?"

The soda shop was only a few blocks away from Cora's Café. There was no doubt that Brad could easily have walked the distance. He might even have had someone with him; just because Mac had seen only one boy didn't mean there hadn't been more who'd slipped away unnoticed. "My mistake," he said to Sharon. "I thought I saw Brad, but I must have been wrong."

She didn't buy his glib explanation. "Mac?"

"Don't worry about it, okay? Sorry I disturbed you."

"But—"

"I'll talk to you tomorrow. G'night, Sharon." He closed the phone and slipped it back into his pocket, trying to determine his next move.

"What happened here?"

Mac turned, and recognized the man who had spoken as one of the police officers he'd met the night Sharon had been run off the road. Dolan? Dobbins? Dodson, he remembered. "Evening, Officer."

The other man, who looked to be about Mac's age, closed the door of the aging SUV he'd just climbed out of. "I'm on my way to dinner at Cora's, but I see you've got a problem here. Anything I can do?"

Mac glanced at the gouge and shook his head, irritated all over again. "No, thanks."

"You'll be wanting to make a police report, I imagine. That scratch looks like it was put there on purpose. Have you already made yourself some enemies in town, Mr. Cordero?"

"Not as far as I know. There's no need for you to make a report, Officer. I can handle this."

"Now, don't you go trying to handle trouble like this on your own. I know you were once a big-city detective, but me and Wade are the law around here."

It was all Mac could do not to grimace. Was the guy *trying* to sound like a bad movie stereotype of a Southern-hick cop? If so, he was doing a hell of a good job. "I said I'll take care of it, Officer. But thanks for the advice."

Dodson shrugged. "Suit yourself. Guess I'll go have my dinner, then."

"The coconut pie is especially good this evening," Mac said genially.

"I'll keep that in mind. See you around."

Mac nodded and opened the driver's door of his truck. Whoever had inflicted the damage was long gone now, of course, probably safely among the rest of the ball team and ready to swear he—or they—had never left the group. But Mac had no intention of letting it go that easily. He wanted to have a few words with Sharon Henderson's kid brother. And the boy had better listen, if he knew what was good for him.

"I'M TELLING YOU, Chief, I don't like that guy. He gives me the creeps."

Wade studied Gilbert Dodson over steepled fingers. "What is it, exactly, that you find so creepy about him?"

"That attitude of his. All cool and superior. Like he knows something everyone else doesn't. I'm telling you, Chief, I'd keep looking at him in regard to those break-ins. I'd bet he has something to do with them."

"You've been trying to convince me of that for more than a week now, Gil, but you haven't brought me any proof." Wade leaned farther back in his chair, making the springs squeak. "Bring me something I can work with, and I'll do something about it. But until then…"

He left the rest of the sentence hanging.

Dodson sighed with his usual pessimism. "I'm doing my best, Chief."

"I'm sure you are, Gil. So go out and do some more of it."

Nodding heavily, Dodson shuffled out of Wade's office.

Gilbert seemed convinced Mac Cordero was up to something nefarious, Wade mused, still staring at the empty doorway. His officer's dislike of the other man was curious—Gilbert usually got along just fine with everyone.

Wade was starting to have more questions than answers—about many things. And it was really getting on his nerves.

Looked as if it was time to pay Mac Cordero another call.

CHAPTER TEN

SHARON LEFT her shop as soon as Tressie returned from her lunch break Friday afternoon. "I'll be back later," she said on her way out.

"Enjoy your lunch," Tressie called after her. "I hope you'll be sharing it with someone...interesting."

Since Tressie had been teasing her mercilessly all week about Mac, Sharon let the barb sail by unchallenged. For one thing, she *did* plan to see Mac while she was gone. She wanted to ask him exactly what he'd meant by that strange phone call last night.

Knowing it would only set Brad off again, she hadn't mentioned the call to him, but she'd questioned him closely about what he'd done before she'd arrived at the ballpark to watch his game. He'd shrugged carelessly and told her he and the rest of the guys had eaten dinner at the soda shop and then headed for the park to change into their uniforms and warm up. Nothing special, he assured her. Just ask any of his friends.

It bothered her that he hadn't quite been able to meet her eyes during the conversation.

Mac's truck was parked outside the Garrett house,

along with a few others. She was glad she'd caught him before he left. Now if she could catch him in private for a few minutes to ask him…

She saw the scrape on his truck almost as soon as she got out of her car. Walking slowly toward it, she winced as she studied the long slash of metal, bared where the black paint had been scraped away. While she knew it was possible the damage had been caused by accident, deep inside she knew what had happened. Someone had done this on purpose. A malicious act of vandalism—or an ugly message.

"If you're here to see me, you almost missed out," she heard Mac say from behind her. "I was just about to leave for lunch."

She turned to look at him, motioning toward the truck behind her. "When did this happen?"

"Yesterday evening—while I was having dinner at Cora's Café."

"You discovered it just before you called me?"

"Not long before."

"You thought Brad did this."

"The possibility crossed my mind," he said, and there was something in his expression she couldn't quite interpret.

"Mac, you can't possibly believe—"

Talking and laughing loudly, two workers Sharon knew emerged from the front door of the house and headed toward the outbuilding where the supplies were kept. On their way past, they called out greetings to her, which she returned with forced patience before looking at Mac again. "You really don't think…"

"Have you eaten?" he asked.

She frowned. "No."

"I haven't, either, and I'm starved. Let's talk about this over lunch, okay?"

"Well, I…"

He opened the driver's-side door to his pickup. "Let me help you in."

Since the vehicle was rather high off the ground, she silently accepted his hand for assistance, climbing into the truck and sliding across the bench seat to the passenger's side. She was glad she'd worn a functional gray pantsuit today rather than the long, straight black skirt she'd almost put on that morning.

She waited only until Mac was behind the wheel with the engine running. "I hope you don't really think Brad would do something like that to your truck. Or to anyone else's, for that matter."

"Do you like barbecue?"

It was obvious he wasn't going to discuss his truck or his suspicions. Since she couldn't actually force him to talk about it, she fastened her seat belt and sat back. "Yes, I like barbecue."

"Someone told me Bud's Place makes a great pulled-pork sandwich. Sound good to you?"

"The food is fine, but Bud's Place is strictly a drive-through. There are no dining facilities."

"So we'll take the food to my apartment. It isn't far, and we can talk in private there."

His apartment. Sharon moistened her lips and

twined her fingers together in her lap. It *would* be best to discuss this in private, she thought. She certainly wouldn't want anyone to overhear Mac say he suspected her brother of vandalizing his truck. There was no telling how fast *that* rumor would get around—or how it might be embellished along the way. "All right. We'll talk at your place."

If he was particularly pleased or surprised by her agreement, she certainly couldn't tell.

BUD'S PLACE WAS popular for take-out lunches, so the line of vehicles at the order window was long, even though the lunch rush had passed. Mac ordered two pulled-pork sandwiches with coleslaw, a large order of seasoned fries, two fried peach pies and two large iced teas. The only choice Sharon was given was whether she wanted mild or spicy sauce on her sandwich. She chose mild. Mac ordered spicy.

His apartment complex was aging but relatively well maintained. It catered to contractors and work crews and others who were in town only temporarily. People who were only passing through—like Mac, she thought with an odd, hollow feeling.

He escorted her into a ground-floor apartment on one end of the main building. The furnishings, she noted, made the place seem more like a motel suite than an apartment, but at least it wasn't cramped. The decent-size living room held a couch, two armchairs, a coffee table, an end table and a TV on a rolling stand. An efficiently compact eat-in kitchen opened off to one side of the main room, and a bed-

and-bath combination off to the other. Set into the back wall of the living room was a door that led out to a tiny brick patio that held two plastic lawn chairs and looked over a neatly groomed grassy compound.

''Not bad,'' she said.

Mac shrugged. ''It suits my needs for now.''

For now. Again, a reminder that he wasn't here to stay. Could Sharon see him off with a smile, grateful to have known him even for that brief time, or would she be left brokenhearted when he moved on to the next project?

She decided she wouldn't think about that right now. One problem at a time, she told herself as she and Mac spread their lunches on his table. She'd noticed that Mac had cleared away a stack of legal papers to give them room; she assumed they were notes about the renovation project.

''About the damage to your truck,'' she said as soon as they'd taken their seats.

''Did *you* do it?'' he asked with one of his disconcertingly inscrutable half smiles.

She blinked. ''No. Of course not.''

''Then don't worry about it. I'll take care of it.''

''So you *don't* think Brad had anything to do with it?''

He took a bite of his sandwich, neatly avoiding an answer.

''I know Brad has been unfriendly to you, but that's only because he doesn't adjust to strangers very quickly. He really isn't a bad boy. He's gotten into mischief a time or two, but he's never vandalized anything before. He wouldn't do anything that destructive or malicious.''

''Mmm.'' Mac bit into a French fry without elaborating.

''You do believe me, don't you? You have to admit, I know my brother better than you do.''

''Of course.'' He finished his sandwich and eyed the peach pies while she seethed in frustration on the other side of the table. ''Everyone was right,'' he commented after a moment. ''This really is good food. Want a fried pie?''

''You aren't going to talk about this with me, are you?''

''I'm perfectly willing to discuss this good food with you.''

''That isn't what I meant and you know it. I'm trying to talk to you about Brad.''

''I see no purpose in discussing your brother just now. I have no proof that he damaged my truck, and you're convinced he didn't. That's really all there is to say about it at the moment.''

''It bothers me that you still seem to believe Brad is capable of doing something like this.''

''You pointed out, yourself, that I don't know the boy as well as you do. It will probably take a little more time for me to form my own opinions about what he is or is not capable of doing. All I know for certain at this point is that he dislikes me, for reasons of his own. That doesn't bother me, particularly, unless it comes between you and me. And then I suppose I would have to do something about it.''

He'd spoken so dispassionately. Did it really not bother him that Brad disliked him so intensely? It would trouble her if a member of Mac's family took an immediate and unwarranted objection to her. Maybe that only further illustrated how different she and Mac were. Or maybe her family and friends didn't matter all that much to him because he didn't expect to be a part of her life for very long.

''Here,'' he said, pushing a paper-wrapped pastry toward her. ''Have some pie. Guaranteed to put you in a better mood.''

She sighed and accepted the dessert. ''You are an infuriating man, Mac Cordero.''

He chuckled softly. ''Now there's something I've never heard before,'' he murmured, obviously lying.

Shaking her head, she unwrapped the pie and bit into it. It was good—packed with sweetened dried peaches in a cinnamony filling, the flaky, half moon–shaped pastry crust deep-fried to just the right crispness. He was right; it was hard to be in a bad mood while eating a fried peach pie, but her worry about the conflict between Brad and Mac had only been suppressed, not eradicated.

''WOULD YOU LIKE me to make some coffee or anything?'' Mac asked when they'd washed down the last of the pie with their iced tea.

''No, thank you.''

He stood and gathered up the leftover garbage,

tossing it into a wastebasket. "When do you have to be back at work?"

"No specific time. Tressie's quite capable of running the store while I'm out. If she needs me, she knows I always have my cell phone nearby."

He reached out with the swiftness of the jungle cat she'd often mentally compared him to and pulled her toward him. "Well?" he challenged. "Are you going to let your kid brother's tantrums come between us?"

It sounded so foolish the way he said it. Letting a teenager set the rules for her. It was long past time for her to make her own rules. Her own choices. Her own decisions.

It seemed easier to show Mac her answer than to tell him. Pushing all her worries to the back of her mind, she focused solely on the moment. What she wanted now.

She wanted Mac.

Resting her hands on his shoulders, she rose on tiptoe to offer her mouth to him. She didn't have to offer twice.

He didn't even try to lull her into a sense of security this time. He went straight for the explosions and the fireworks, stunning her senses, shattering her defenses, clearing her mind of anything but him. All she could do was to hold on—and try to set off a few fireworks of her own. Apparently, she succeeded. She heard Mac's breath catch in the back of his throat, and felt his whole body grow taut.

He locked his arms around her and deepened the

kiss, invading and staking every inch of her mouth. She thought it only fair that she should have the same privilege. He seemed to agree, since he put up no resistance when she claimed her right to explore.

His skillful hands were as bold as his clever mouth. He traced her curves with his fingers, as meticulously as a blind art lover studying a famous statue, seemingly intent on exploring and memorizing by feel alone. Yet Sharon wasn't made of marble. Every nerve ending reacted to his touch, leaving her feeling as though tiny electric charges were sparking all over her body. She had the fanciful sensation that she would almost glow if someone turned out the lights.

She hadn't been fanciful before she'd met Mac.

Dragging his mouth across her cheek, he nibbled his way to the soft hollow behind her ear, where her pulse pounded wildly against his lips. Even if she had wanted to, she couldn't have hidden her reaction to him. She had been vulnerable to Mac from the beginning, and she suspected he knew it. She had to trust that he would not use that knowledge against her.

It wasn't easy for her to put that much faith in a man who was still very much a stranger. There was so much about Mac she still didn't know—deeply hidden aspects of him she sensed but didn't quite understand. She could only hope that her trust in him would prove justified.

He lifted his right hand to the back of her head, buried his fingers in her hair, and tightened them until she was held gently, but securely, in place, gazing up at him. The move was an almost aggressive one on his part, but she had no fear as she stood in his grasp. Oddly enough, she felt safe there—the way she always felt when Mac held her.

His voice was rough when he said, "This is between you and me, Sharon. No one else."

She could hardly think of anyone *but* him at the moment. "I know."

"You aren't what I expected to find here," he muttered, his lips hovering only a breath above hers.

Her fingers flexed against the firm muscles of his upper arms. "What did you expect to find, Mac?"

"Myself," he answered after the slightest hesitation. And then covered her mouth with his before she could ask him to elaborate.

This kiss was different, somehow. There was a new hint of masculine arrogance in his attitude—as if he'd won some sort of victory. She really should call him on it, remind him that nothing had been decided, no irreversible steps had been taken. She might even have convinced him of it—had she completely believed it, herself.

She slid both arms around his neck, allowing herself to sink against him. His right hand fell to the small of her back, pressing her more snugly against him, giving her unmistakable evidence of where he wanted the next step to take them. It had been building toward this from the start, the urgency intensifying with every kiss, every touch, almost every glance that passed between them.

As cautious as she had been during the past few years, every action deliberate and carefully considered, every potential consequence studied and weighed, she found it hard to believe that she was even considering a reckless fling with this man. She wouldn't be acting on impulse, exactly. She knew precisely what she would be putting at stake—her heart, her reputation, her relationship with her brother. Even her professional status, since she would be getting involved with a client, which was never a prudent choice.

Yet when Mac held her this way, when he kissed her with a hunger that seemed at times to border on desperation, she found herself believing that no risk was too great. Being with Mac could well be reward enough for whatever price she might have to pay.

He slid his hand beneath her fitted top. His fingertips brushed against the frivolous scrap of black lace she wore underneath. A slight shudder went through her at the thought of having his hand against her sensitive bare skin.

Attuned to her reactions, he murmured against her mouth, "Am I frightening you?"

"No," she managed to say candidly, though her mouth was dry and her heart seemed to be tap-dancing in her throat. "You're seducing me."

He gave a low groan and crushed her mouth beneath his again, pulling her so tightly against him that she was quite graphically convinced that she wasn't the only one being seduced.

Long, heated moments later, he broke off the kiss

with a gasp. "This wasn't why I brought you here," he groaned.

Distracted by the firm line of his jaw, she traced it with a fingertip. "Why *did* you bring me here?"

"To, uh…" He caught her wandering hand and pressed a kiss against it. "To talk."

It occurred to her that she hadn't seen him without a shirt. She didn't know if his chest was smooth or furry. She would bet on smooth. Curious to discover if the bet would have paid off, she unfastened a button of his shirt. "What did you want to talk about?"

He seemed to hold a silent debate between several options, then apparently rejected them all. "Never mind," he growled as she undid two more buttons.

She slid one hand slowly into the opening she'd made. *Smooth,* she thought. *I win.*

She rewarded herself by lifting her mouth to his again. As eagerly as he responded, he seemed to be under the impression that *he* had won something.

"Mac," she murmured into his mouth, sensing a slight hesitation.

He caught her lower lip gently between his teeth. "Mmm?"

"I need to be back at work in another hour or so."

His lips moved against her flushed cheek. "That doesn't give us much time."

"No," she whispered, surprisingly bold. "So let's not waste any of it."

Moving with a speed that made her a bit dizzy, he swung her into his arms and began to move to-

ward the bedroom. She laughed breathlessly, clinging to him as excitement and anticipation mingled
with shivery trepidation. She knew this wasn't a safe
or sensible choice, but the woman Mac had dragged
out of Snake Creek was much more adventurous
than the old Sharon had been. She didn't believe in
wasting opportunities.

Mac had left his bed neatly made that morning.
He tumbled with her onto the top of the covers,
pushing pillows to the floor with a sweep of one
arm. Sharon's heart was beating so hard in her chest
she was surprised it wasn't shaking the bed. This
was *not* what she'd expected when she'd dressed for
work that morning. This wasn't at all the sort of
thing that ever happened in the middle of her workday.

Not that she was complaining, she decided as
Mac's mouth closed over hers again.

She felt a tremor in his hand when he fumbled
with the buttons of her jacket. Muttering a curse
beneath his breath, he tried again, having more success this time. She felt cool air on bare skin when
he gave her an endearingly sheepish smile. "Sorry.
I really wasn't prepared for this."

She had expected him to be smoother, more polished. It delighted her that he wasn't. This glimpse
of vulnerability made her even more certain that
Mac Cordero was as special as she had come to
believe.

"Changing your mind?" she asked, sliding her
hands inside his open shirt.

His response was half laugh, half groan, making his chest vibrate against her fingertips. "Hardly."

"Good." She pushed his shirt off his shoulders, baring him from the waist up. She felt her insides turn to jelly as she looked at him. *Beautiful* was all she could think as she gazed at his taut brown skin, sleekly defined musculature and flat, firm stomach. There were scars, as well, evidence of a hard life. But, overall—perfection.

She couldn't wait to see the rest of him.

He'd gotten his momentary, uncharacteristic lack of composure under control. His fingers were skillful when he returned to the task of removing her clothes. And when the trim gray pantsuit lay on the floor, along with the lacy garments she'd worn beneath, he revealed a talent that left her dazed.

Demonstrating the attention to detail she'd observed in his work, he concentrated on exploring every inch of her, his hands and mouth moving over her slowly and painstakingly. Leaving her breasts damp and heaving with her gasping breaths, he moved lower, tracing her ribs, nibbling her belly, making her squirm with a pleasure so intense it almost hurt. She wanted to reciprocate, to do some exploring of her own, but he had somehow drained all her energy. She wasn't even sure she could lift her head from the pillow. The only movements she seemed capable of making were completely involuntary.

She tried to focus on the physical, rather than the emotional, elements of their lovemaking. The heat of Mac's skin against hers. The roughness of his work-callused fingers. The sound of his uneven breathing in her ear. The feel of his heart pounding against his chest. The hardness of the erection straining against the zipper of his jeans. Her own reactions—racing pulse, tightened throat, oversensitized skin. A deep, wet ache in her lower abdomen.

It was safer concentrating on those sensations than on the feelings bubbling inside her. The heart-swelling emotions threatened to overcome her, bringing a hint of tears to her eyes and a certainty that nothing would ever be the same for her after this.

She couldn't think about that now. She had other things to concentrate on—like what Mac was doing with his right hand at that moment. And, oh, was he doing it well!

He laughed softly when she tugged at him with impatient hands. "In a hurry to get back to work?" he asked in her ear.

She was in no mood to be teased. "Mac—"

"What do you want, Sharon?"

"You," she whispered, moving against him in a way that made it very clear what she wanted.

"Happy to oblige, ma'am," he murmured, reaching for the snap of his jeans.

He kept condoms in the nightstand. Sharon didn't want to think just then about whether he stored them there as a general precaution or because he found himself in frequent need of them. She decided, instead, to be grateful he had them available now.

It didn't take him very long to return to her, but it felt like forever. She wanted him so badly, she ached. Desperately needed him to appease the hunger he'd created in her. "Now," she demanded, reaching for him.

Amusement mixed with desire in his voice. "You really are the take-charge type, aren't you?"

She cupped his gorgeous face in her hands. "I've had to be," she answered simply. "Does that worry you?"

"*You* worry me," he said, and the amusement was gone now. "But that doesn't seem to make any difference."

She didn't always understand this man, but that didn't seem to make any difference, either. She brought his mouth to hers. "*Now,* Mac," she said against his lips.

He settled between her raised knees. The muscles of his back bunched beneath her hands as he prepared to thrust forward—like a sleek cat getting ready to spring, she thought, still enamored with the imagery.

Holding himself very still, he looked at her, his dark eyes burning with roiling emotions she couldn't begin to interpret. She only knew that she trusted him. "Sharon," he growled, "whatever happens—don't regret this."

"No," she whispered, utterly certain that she was telling the truth. "No regrets."

His muscles rippled, and he moved again—and the mental image of a wild, dangerous animal dissolved into shards of pure sensation. She was no longer able to maintain coherent thought.

Her fingers curled into his shoulders, as if clinging to sanity. A choked cry lodged in the back of her throat, trapped there by the press of his lips against hers. She could do nothing more than whimper as he pushed her higher and farther, toward a conclusion they both desperately craved.

He tore his mouth from hers with a harsh groan, and the cry he had imprisoned escaped her. Thin and quivery, it seemed to echo in the small room as shudders of release coursed through her, again and again.

Even as the echoes died away and the shudders subsided, Sharon realized that she'd been right to be wary of this. She'd been afraid her life would never be the same. Now she knew for certain she'd been right. Everything had changed.

Now that she had been with Mac Cordero, she would never again be content with ordinary.

CHAPTER ELEVEN

MAC FELT as though dozens of people were watching when he climbed out of his truck at the Garrett house. As if there was someone standing in every window, gaping and speculating. He hadn't felt that way when they'd left the site together, but he did now. Things had changed.

His concern was for Sharon, not himself. Knowing the way rumors circulated in this town, and the pleasure the locals took in embellishment, he hated to think of Sharon being the subject of those tales. He hadn't given much thought to it before, never having cared particularly what people said about him, but it was different now. He found himself suddenly feeling protective and possessive, two emotions he hadn't intended to feel.

He'd told himself all he wanted from Sharon was some information, not sex. Now he didn't know what the hell he wanted. He only knew he couldn't let Sharon be hurt by his personal vendetta. For the first time since his world had fallen apart two years ago, he cared about someone else's feelings besides his own.

He helped her out of his truck. She smiled up at him, her eyes glowing, her cheeks flushed, her hand resting so trustingly in his, and it made his stomach tighten.

He wouldn't hurt her, he promised himself.

"I have to go back to the shop," she said, making little effort to hide her reluctance.

He didn't want to let go of her hand, but he did. "I know. I have to get back to work."

"Mac?"

She'd learned to say his name so beautifully. The single syllable sounded almost musical from her lips. And he was starting to feel like a foolish sap standing here mooning over her. "Yeah?" he asked, more gruffly than he had intended.

"I had a great lunch."

Damn, he wanted to kiss her. It was only the thought of those watching eyes that held him back. "So did I," he said, instead.

Proving she wasn't oblivious to possible onlookers, either, she glanced quickly at the house before reaching out to touch his hand. "No regrets," she reminded him.

Damning to hell anybody watching, he lifted her hand to his mouth, pressing a quick, hard kiss against it. "I'll call you later," he promised as he released her and stepped back.

She smiled, and turned toward her car. Something stopped her just as she reached for the door handle. "Emily Davenport invited me to a party at her house tomorrow afternoon," she said, looking at him over the top of her car. "She encouraged me to bring a friend. Would you like to go as my guest?"

A party at the Davenport house. He was sure every McBride in Honoria would be in attendance, maybe a few from out of town. A great chance to get a good look at them, maybe pick up a bit more information, he realized. This was the reason he'd cultivated Sharon's friendship from the beginning, wasn't it? Because she gave him better access to the McBrides. So why was he suddenly feeling like a snake?

"I'd really like you to come," she added when he hesitated.

"Is your brother going to be there?"

She bit her lip, and he could tell that she'd forgotten her brother temporarily—and that she was flooded with sudden guilt because of it. "Yes," she said after a moment. "He'll be there. But he'll behave himself, I guarantee that. And maybe after you spend a little more time with him, you'll realize that he couldn't possibly have…well, you know."

Mac glanced at the scrape on his truck, and remembered that fleeting glimpse of Brad Henderson disappearing around the corner of a building. Because he'd made a vow to himself that Sharon wouldn't be hurt, he chose to keep that memory to himself. He could handle a punk kid with an attitude problem. "If you're sure I wouldn't be out of place, I'd like to come with you tomorrow."

She smiled. "Great. Do you want to ride with us or meet us there?"

"I'll meet you," he decided, choosing to forgo the car ride with her brother.

"Okay. See you there. One o'clock. Do you know where they live?"

Wade and Emily Davenport lived in a house that had been built by Josiah McBride Jr., who had a one-in-three chance of being Mac's father. "Yeah. I know where they live."

"Great. Um—call me tonight?"

"I will." He watched her get into her car and drive away, giving him a little wave as she disappeared down the driveway. It took him back for a moment—his wife used to wave to him like that when she drove away.

She hadn't waved when she'd left the last time. Her shoulders had been slumped with grief and defeat as she had driven away. And, knowing when it was time to let go, Mac hadn't tried to stop her.

He'd decided his course that day—that he would find the answers to the questions that had haunted him all his life. That he would make someone pay for the pain he and his mother had suffered. Pain that had carried over to destroy his marriage. And now another woman was in a position to be hurt by him.

If there was a curse involved with being born a bastard McBride, then the most generous thing for him to do would be to stay far away from Sharon Henderson. Unfortunately, he was afraid it was already too late to protect her.

"Hey, boss," a jovial carpenter called out on his way to the supply building. "Didya' have a nice lunch?"

Mac's first instinct was to belt the guy. And then he realized the question had been asked without any ulterior meaning, that he was the one who was making too much of it. "Yeah, it was fine," he said, trying to keep his tone pleasant. "How's it going in there?"

"Moving along at a good pace. This house is going to be spiffed up and ready to sell in no time."

As far as Mac was concerned, it couldn't be too soon.

He was beginning to think he'd made a terrible mistake by coming to Honoria.

SHARON MADE SURE her hair was neat, her lipstick was fresh, her clothes were straight and her expression was unrevealing before she entered her shop. Finally confident that there were no clues to be found in her expression about how she'd spent her lunch hour, she walked in with her head high and a cheery smile on her face.

"Oh, my," Tressie said after taking one look at her. "You must have had an interesting lunch."

Sharon's jaw nearly dropped. "Why did you say that?"

"You were with Mac Cordero, weren't you?"

"How do you know?"

"I can tell by the glow in your eyes."

Sharon scowled.

Tressie laughed again. "I'm only teasing you, Sharon. Kyle McAllister stopped by for his wife's wallpaper borders, and he said he saw you and Mac picking up barbecue at Bud's.''

''Dammit, can't someone even eat a sandwich in this town without everyone talking about it?'' Sharon felt like stamping her feet in frustration. It was hard enough trying to figure out for herself what was developing between her and Mac. It made it even more stressful when she knew everything they did was being watched and whispered about.

Tressie merely shrugged. ''You know this town, Sharon. It's infuriating at times, but that's just the way things are. How do you think I found out my weasel of an ex-husband was running around with that health-club bimbo, hmm? I always suspected he had some emotional problems, but I never knew he was completely stupid. He seemed shocked that I heard about his affair—he thought he'd been so very clever. He should have remembered that secrets have a way of coming out in this town.''

For some reason, Tressie's words made a funny prickle of apprehension course down Sharon's spine. She didn't know why. While she was trying to keep her relationship with Mac private for now, it wasn't as though they were trying to conceal any great secret. They weren't doing anything wrong. They were falling in love, and they didn't want to do that in the public eye.

She felt the blood drain suddenly out of her face. Falling in love? Was *that* what they were doing? She didn't know about Mac, but the words felt all too right to her.

Tressie was looking at her in concern now. "Sharon? You okay?"

Forcing a smile, Sharon pressed a hand to her stomach. "Barbecue in the middle of a workday. I'll spend the rest of the afternoon popping antacids."

"You're sure you don't want to talk about anything? I'm a pretty good listener, you know. And, believe it or not, I can keep my mouth shut when I'm asked to."

Knowing the offer was sincere, and that Tressie really would respect her privacy, Sharon was tempted. It might make her feel better to share what she was going through with another woman—her excitement, her worries, her hopes, her fears, the roller-coaster of emotions that went along with falling in love.

While Sharon had a lot of women friends, there was no one she felt comfortable confiding her most private emotions to, especially since her closest friend from high school had married and moved away a year or so ago. Her mother and Bobbie McBride, two confidantes she'd always counted on, wouldn't be back for a while yet. She'd been keeping so much to herself lately—her dissatisfaction with the rut she and Jerry had fallen into, her developing attraction to Mac, her growing concerns about Brad. She would certainly value any advice she could get.

Still, she heard herself saying, "Thanks, Tressie, but everything's fine. Just busy, as usual. Did you hear anything yet about that order we placed for Mabel Watson?''

Tressie was obviously reluctant to change the subject, but a long look at Sharon's expression must have convinced her that she really had no choice. She sighed and shook her head. ''I'll go call about it right now.''

''Thank you. I have some paperwork to do, so I'll be at the computer if you need me.''

''And you know where to find me if you need me,'' Tressie countered.

''Yes, I do. Thank you.''

Sharon spent the rest of the afternoon trying to concentrate on work and failing abysmally. The heady euphoria of lovemaking had faded, leaving only a deep, warm glow inside her. An occasional flash of memory made her catch her breath and close her eyes, instantly transported back to the bed in Mac's apartment. But for the most part she found herself spending more time worrying than savoring.

She kept picturing that ugly scrape on the side of Mac's truck. Whoever had inflicted it had wanted to cause damage. It had been malicious and calculated. A random act of vandalism or a personal attack against Mac? Who in town disliked him that much?

Other than Brad, of course.

She didn't want to believe her brother capable of something like that, even though it was obvious Mac didn't share her faith. Brad was her little brother. He went to church with her. His raggedy old teddy bear still sat on a shelf in his closet. He wouldn't have deliberately caused hundreds of dollars' worth of damage just because he'd taken an irrational dislike to Mac, would he? Of course not.

But what if…?

The telephone rang. Knowing Tressie was busy with a customer, she reached for it, grateful for the distraction. "Intriguing Interiors. May I help you?"

"Hey, sis. Tommy's having a pool party next Friday and he wants to know if me and Jimbo can spend the night. His mom will be there and everything. Is it okay?"

Thinking of Mac's truck again, she wondered if she should ask Brad about it. If there was any chance he'd been involved…

"Tommy's mom said you can call her if you want to ask her anything, but she'd like to know as soon as possible so they can make plans. Is it okay?"

She gave his request another moment's thought. She was beginning to have doubts about Brad spending so much time with Jimbo, but Tommy seemed like a decent kid. She'd met his mother, a PTA officer and soccer mom who, while spreading herself a bit thin with all her volunteer activities, seemed involved in her two sons' lives. "I suppose there's no harm in it."

"Cool. Thanks, Sharon."

He sounded so genuinely pleased and grateful that she couldn't help softening. "You're welcome, Brad. Promise me you'll be good."

"Sure. No problem."

The guarantee was given so glibly that she

couldn't take much reassurance from it. "Brad," she began impulsively, suddenly needing an answer about Mac's truck.

"Mmm? I've got to go. Jimbo's waiting for me. We've got baseball practice."

She swallowed the words she'd almost blurted. This wasn't the time to question him, not about something so important. Not over the phone. And not while Jimbo was waiting for him.

Besides, she reminded herself, she didn't really believe Brad had done it. More likely Joe Wimble had gotten drunk again and felt like causing trouble. Until someone had decided to try his hand at larceny recently, Joe's drunken shenanigans had been the worst crimes Honoria had seen since Sam Jennings had been hauled off for murder more than four years ago.

Her little brother wasn't a criminal. She was sure Mac would see that for himself soon.

They only needed time.

WORK FINISHED for the day, Mac locked the Garrett house and headed for his truck. He found Wade Davenport leaning casually against the driver's side.

His first instinct was to curse. He was tired and confused, and he needed some time alone. He was in no mood to be interrogated by the police chief. His nod was curt. "'Afternoon, Chief."

"Hey, Mac, how's it going?"

"Can't complain."

"Nasty scratch on your truck here. Get too close to something?"

"Apparently."

"Do you know who did this, Mac?"

"Not for certain, no."

"But you have suspicions?"

Mac only shrugged.

"Officer Dodson's concerned that you've got a feud going with someone. He said he got the feeling you were planning to handle this yourself."

"Now comes the part where you tell me you don't want any trouble around here, right? I know the speech, Chief. Your officer already gave it to me."

"Yeah, but did you listen?"

Mac let silence be his answer.

Wade shook his head, glanced at the scarred truck again, then changed the subject. "We found the van that was used in the Porter robbery."

That brought Mac's head up. He was most definitely interested in any progress that had been made in apprehending the bastard who'd almost killed Sharon. "Just the van? Or did you find out who was driving it?"

"No, it was abandoned. And wiped clean. It doesn't appear we're going to learn much from it."

"Registration?"

"It was stolen from a used-car lot in Carollton a couple of days before the Porter break-in. No witnesses to that theft."

Hardly encouraging news. "Where did you find the van?"

"Officer Dodson found it in the garage of a vacant house a couple of streets back from the motel where you were staying."

Mac sighed. "You don't suppose I was driving the van *and* following Sharon in my truck, do you?"

Wade chuckled. "I doubt you're that talented. You asked where the van was found. I told you. That's all."

"Still have your suspicions about me, Chief?"

Wade's lazy grin never wavered. "Let's just say you aren't a man I would make the mistake of underestimating."

"I've been invited to a party at your house tomorrow. Do you feel safe having me around your family, or would you rather I decline?"

If Wade was surprised, he didn't let it show. "We'd be delighted to have you. Did Trent ask you?"

"Actually, it was Sharon."

"I see. Well, any friend of Sharon's—" He didn't bother finishing the cliché, but straightened away from the truck and stuck his hands in his pockets. "I guess I'll be seeing you tomorrow, then. My wife will be delighted to meet you. She's heard about you, of course, and she's been curious."

Mac had decidedly mixed feelings about meeting Emily McBride Davenport, the woman who was either his cousin or his sister. "I'll look forward to meeting her."

"I guess I'd better get home for dinner. If you change your mind about making a report on your truck, let me know."

Without responding, Mac watched the chief climb into his Jeep and drive away.

Being among the McBrides tomorrow could be very interesting—or prove to be a huge mistake, he thought. One of many he'd made since coming to Honoria.

He hoped that making love to Sharon Henderson didn't turn out to be the biggest mistake he'd made yet.

MAC DECIDED to eat at Cora's again that evening. Because it was a Friday and many locals tended to eat out on weekends, there was more of a crowd than usual. He had to park down the street, close to the arcade. There was no group of boys on the sidewalk outside the place this time, he noted in satisfaction. He wasn't really in the mood for another confrontation.

He had just reached the arcade when Brad stepped out the door, accompanied by the tall boy who'd egged him on the last time. Brad's first reaction at seeing Mac was surprise. The surprise changed quickly to what Mac interpreted as half-guilty defiance. "Hello, Brad," he said, meeting the boy's eyes.

Brad looked down at his shoes and nodded stiffly.

Another couple of steps brought Mac closer. "How have you been? Keeping yourself busy?"

Brad shrugged.

"Oddly enough, I spotted a boy who looked very much like you in this same area just yesterday evening. He was running down the street. Like he'd done something wrong and was trying to get away before anyone saw him."

"I don't know what you're talking about," Brad muttered, his eyes shifting away.

"Hey, man, leave my friend alone," the bigger boy said, stepping closer. "He ain't done nothing."

Mac answered without looking away from Brad. "If that's true, he has no reason to be concerned."

"Are you concerned about this guy, Brad?" the bigger boy asked mockingly.

"Be quiet, Jimbo," Brad muttered. "I can handle this."

Mac glanced dismissively at Jimbo before speaking again to Brad. "Looks to me like your buddy here is just itching to get you in trouble, Brad. Maybe you need to ask yourself if he's really a pal."

Brad straightened his shoulders. "I pick my own friends."

"Yeah—so do yourself a favor and choose wisely."

"You going to take advice from the player who's been doing your sister, Brad?" Jimbo jeered.

"Shut *up,* Jimbo!"

Even as Brad rounded on his companion, Mac was moving. A moment later, Jimbo was pinned against the brick wall behind him, Mac's hands fisted in the boy's designer-label shirt. Caught completely by surprise, Jimbo had gone pale, his eyes wide, his mouth hanging open. He was perhaps an inch taller than Mac, but there was no doubt who was the dominant male in this confrontation.

"One more word out of your mouth about Brad's sister, and you'll be sorry you were ever born," Mac said very quietly, his nose only inches from the kid's. "Is that very clear?"

"Let him go." Brad sounded both furious and terrified. "He didn't mean anything."

Keeping his eyes on Jimbo, Mac asked, "You let your friends talk about your sister that way, Brad? Does she really deserve that?"

"He was just trying to make you mad."

"It worked." Mac tightened his hands on Jimbo's shirt. He wouldn't really hurt the kid, of course— but he'd make him think he would.

"Hey! Let him go, Cordero." The order came from just behind them.

Maintaining his grip, Mac glanced over his shoulder. Officer Dodson was approaching at a half run, his gloomy face creased with a frown. "What's going on here?"

"Just having a chat with the boys, Officer," Mac replied affably.

"He's—he's crazy, Dodson. Arrest him or something," Jimbo stuttered.

"I think we've heard enough of your opinions, Jimbo," Mac suggested.

"Okay, Cordero, let him go. You can't go around

town assaulting our kids—not unless you want to end up in jail.''

"Okay, Jimbo, I'm letting you go," Mac said. "I'm assuming you've gotten my message. Watch your mouth from now on."

The boy stumbled when Mac abruptly released him. "Well?" he demanded, turning to the hovering officer. "Aren't you going to cuff him?"

Mac smiled faintly. "I think Officer Dodson understands that I wasn't assaulting you. Just giving you a little demonstration. If you're going to act like a tough guy, you better be tough enough to deal with the trouble you stir up."

Dodson didn't look as if he knew what to do. His first choice would probably be to lock Mac up just for causing trouble. Another part of him seemed to want to just walk on and have his dinner, forgetting he'd seen anything at all.

Taking pity on the guy, Mac stuck his hands in his pockets and stepped away from the boys. "Trouble's over, Officer. I'll behave."

Looking relieved, Dodson nodded curtly. "Good. Don't you boys have somewhere to go? Brad, ain't your sister waiting for you at her shop?"

Shaken, and keeping his gaze averted from Mac, Brad nodded and took a few steps away.

Jimbo was still staring at Dodson in disbelief. "You're not going to do *anything?* You're just going to let him strut away like he's some kind of big shot or something?''

"Give it a rest, Jimbo," Dodson said wearily. "Quit while you're ahead."

The boy gritted out a curse that was even uglier because of his age, and spun on one heel. "C'mon, Brad."

"Brad," Mac said as the boy scuttled past him.

Brad gave him a nervous, angry look. "What?"

"For your sister's sake, I'm letting you off the hook about my truck. I won't be so generous a second time."

The boy's eyes were so hot with emotion it was a wonder Mac's skin didn't blister. But then he turned and stamped off in the wake of his obnoxious pal.

Dodson gave a heavy sigh. "Do you go looking for trouble, Cordero, or does it just follow you around?"

"Let's just say I deal with it when I find it."

"You're starting to worry me, Cordero. I don't think you fit in around here."

Mac chose not to comment.

The officer shook his head, his expression morose again. "I'm hungry. I'm going to eat. Stay away from the kids, okay? I can't let you get away with something like that a second time."

"There shouldn't be a second time. Enjoy your dinner, Officer." Mac turned and headed back toward his truck. He was no longer hungry.

CHAPTER TWELVE

"YOU HAVEN'T TOUCHED your dinner, Brad. Aren't you hungry?"

Brad looked up from playing with his food. Something in his eyes made Sharon's throat tighten. He looked so troubled. "Brad? Honey, is something wrong? You've been so quiet all evening. Aren't you feeling well?"

He shrugged. "I feel okay."

"Didn't you and Jimbo have a good time at the arcade?"

"Jimbo can be a real jerk sometimes," he muttered.

So that was the problem. Brad had quarreled with his friend. She relaxed a little. That wasn't so bad. Teenagers squabbled all the time. And she'd been wanting him to spend less time with Jimbo, anyway. "Do you want to talk about it?"

"No."

"Are you sure? I can be a good listener."

"I don't want to talk about it, okay?"

"Fine. There's no need to snap."

Brad muttered something incomprehensible and went back to toying with his dinner.

"I talked to Emily Davenport this afternoon," she

said, trying again to make conversation. "She said Clay is really glad you're coming to his house tomorrow. He likes you, you know."

"He's a kid."

"He's a nice kid."

"He's okay."

Sharon considered telling Brad that Mac would be attending the cookout too. She rejected the idea because he was already in such a bad mood. He was likely to refuse to go altogether if he knew Mac would be there. She had to trust that he wouldn't be terribly rude in front of their friends. And that spending more time with Mac would help her brother accept him better.

Brad shoved his plate away. "I'm really not very hungry. I think I'll go read or something."

She started to remind him about the dishes, but decided she would just as soon do them herself tonight. It seemed easier in the long run than dealing with Brad in this disposition. "All right. Let me know if you need anything."

Rubbing her aching temples, she started cleaning up when he left. She was so tired. She looked forward to being alone in her bedroom where she could think about the events of the day and prepare herself for tomorrow.

The telephone rang just as she finished cleaning the kitchen. She sensed who was calling even before she answered. Her hunch was confirmed when Mac spoke. "How's it going?" he asked.

"It's a little strained around here this evening,"

she answered candidly. "Brad's in one of his moods."

"Did he mention his encounter with me earlier this evening?"

She frowned. "You talked to Brad today?"

"I ran into him and his friend when they were coming out of the arcade. I don't blame him for not wanting to tell you about it, but I imagine you'll hear soon enough. I'm sure there were witnesses."

She closed her eyes and leaned against the counter, her head starting to pound harder. She just knew she wasn't going to like this. "What happened?"

"Not a lot. Brad's buddy Jimbo shot off his mouth and I politely informed him that his attitude could use some adjustment."

"Brad seems angry at Jimbo tonight."

"He should be. The guy's a certifiable jerk. Why do you let your brother hang out with him?"

"They've been friends for years. Jimbo has some family problems. His parents are divorced and his father's out of the picture, which gives the boys something in common. He's living with his grandparents now while his mother tries to get her life back together. He's not a bad boy, really—just angry and hurt."

"Excuses only go so far, Sharon. He's old enough to make his own choices now. Someone needs to make it clear to him that his choices have consequences."

Sharon wondered if they were talking about Jimbo now—or Brad. "What did you say to them?"

"Not much. I just made it clear that I won't tolerate much from either of them. And I told them to stay away from my truck."

"You still think Brad did that?"

"If he did, I'm sure he had help and encouragement from his buddy. Your brother seems to be more of a follower than a leader. He's going to have to watch that he doesn't follow someone straight to jail."

Growing defensive now, Sharon lifted her chin and tightened her grip on the telephone. "Thank you for the advice, Mac, but I know my brother. He isn't quite as weak-minded as you believe."

"I never said he was weak-minded. I just pointed out that he's walking a thin line."

"Then I'll help guide him. It's support he needs, not threats."

"When it comes to teenagers, it sometimes takes both."

"I'm sure you mean well, Mac, but—as people often say—it's easy to tell other people how to raise their kids when you don't have any, yourself."

The silence that followed her words was so heavy and so fraught with tension that she realized she must have unwittingly hit a nerve. Always overprotective of her family, she'd allowed his criticism of Brad to make her angry, and she'd struck back. She drew a deep breath. "Mac, I—"

"Don't apologize," he cut in. "You say anything

you feel like saying to me, okay? I'm not interested in tiptoeing around in carefully polite conversations with you. That's not what I want from you.''

''What *do* you want from me, Mac?'' she risked asking.

After another momentary hesitation, he replied, ''That's not a question I can answer right now.''

''Fair enough,'' she murmured, telling herself it was foolish to be disappointed.

His short, dry chuckle was barely audible through the phone lines. ''You're going to be satisfied with that? You don't want me to start spouting poetry or promising you the moon and stars?''

''I don't want poetry or promises. I just need you to be honest with me.''

There was another pause. And then Mac cleared his throat. ''I'm trying.''

Something in his voice made her sense deeper meaning to his words. She knew there were things about Mac he hadn't told her. Parts of himself he hadn't yet allowed her to see. But they'd only known each other a matter of weeks. The explosive connection between them had developed so rapidly. The rest would come with time, she hoped. For now, they had to rely on trust.

She was painfully aware that she had already taken a huge risk of trusting Mac with her heart.

''Maybe it would be better if I skip the cookout tomorrow,'' he suggested after a moment. ''You know everyone's going to be watching us. And your brother would certainly enjoy the party more if I'm not there.''

Her first reaction was to adamantly shake her head, even though he couldn't see her. ''No. I really want you to be there. You'll meet my friends—the ones you haven't already met, of course. As for Brad, he needs to spend more time with you to get over his initial antagonism. And frankly, I think you need to be around him for the same reason.''

''You think we've got a testosterone tussle going on, do you?'' he asked, sounding amused now.

She smiled. ''I hadn't thought of it quite that way, but it's possible, isn't it?''

''Actually, that's exactly what it is,'' he surprised her by admitting. ''A new male has moved into the area and the young studs are peeing all over the place to mark their territory.''

She was startled into a quick laugh. ''I definitely wouldn't have phrased it in those terms.''

''That's because you're not a guy.'' He sounded almost cheerful all of a sudden.

Bemused by his rapidly changing moods, Sharon decided to encourage this one. ''I'm glad you've noticed.''

''I noticed that right off.''

''So you'll be there tomorrow?''

''If you're sure you know what you're doing.''

''I'm very sure. I want you there.''

''And I want you—anywhere I can get you.''

The murmured comment made her blush. ''Mac—''

"Weren't you the one who said you want me to be honest?" Without giving her a chance to respond, he added, "See you tomorrow, Sharon."

He hung up without further comment.

Sharon replaced her own receiver slowly. She thought about going straight up to Brad's room to talk to him about this irksome feud he had going with Mac, and to confront him once and for all about whether he'd damaged Mac's truck. But something held her back, just as it had during dinner. She found herself oddly afraid to challenge him—maybe because she wasn't sure she wanted to hear his answer.

Just the possibility that Brad had been involved was overwhelming to her. She felt totally unqualified to deal with anything of this magnitude. Property damage that extensive was a matter for the police to handle, not an older sister. It should more likely result in someone being sent to jail, not sent to his room. Maybe she didn't want to admit the culprit could be Brad because she just didn't know what she would do if it had been.

Mac had assured her he'd taken care of the problem. Was she being totally cowardly and irresponsible to leave it at that?

She just couldn't handle this tonight. Too much had happened today. She couldn't process any more. Her whole life had changed that afternoon and she needed some quiet time alone to deal with that. There would be time tomorrow to figure out what to do with Brad.

She had fallen in love. Surely she deserved at

least a few hours to savor the feeling before dealing with the inevitable ramifications.

EVEN AS HE PARKED his truck in the Davenports' crowded driveway, Mac was half convinced he was making a mistake. His relationship with Sharon was complex enough in private; taking it public this way could only complicate everything. Add to that his secret connection to the McBride family and this afternoon was likely to prove very awkward for him. He wasn't crazy about parties, anyway—and he definitely had no experience with family gatherings. So what the hell was he doing here?

Okay, so he already knew the answer to that question. He was here partly to discover more about the McBrides—but mostly because Sharon was here.

An aging pickup Mac recognized as Trent McBride's pulled into the long driveway and parked behind Mac's truck. Trent climbed out of the driver's-side door, then turned to assist his fiancée out. "Hey, Mac," Trent said, showing no surprise at seeing him there.

"Hello, Trent."

"You remember my fiancée, Annie Stewart?"

"Of course. It's nice to see you again, Ms. Stewart."

Petite and deceptively delicate-looking, she smiled up at him. "Please call me Annie."

"Only if you'll call me Mac."

"Of course. Trent's been keeping me informed about the progress of your renovation project. He said the house is going to be spectacular when it's finished. I know the cabinetwork will be beautiful,'' she added with a proud look at Trent. ''Have you seen any of the furniture Trent makes, Mac? He's very talented. He's made some of the most beautiful rocking chairs I've ever seen.''

''Annie,'' Trent murmured, looking abashed by her bragging.

Mac looked from one to the other. ''I'd like to see the rockers. I've always got an eye out for quality furniture.''

''I'll show you sometime. Right now, I'm more interested in lunch.'' Trent reached into his truck and pulled out a small cooler. ''C'mon, Mac, we'll show you around.''

''Can I help you carry that?'' The cooler looked heavy, and Mac knew that Trent had sustained a back injury in the plane crash.

Trent scowled. ''Thanks, but I've got it.''

Annie rolled her eyes in response to her fiancé's curt tone. ''He *never* admits that he needs help, whether he does or not,'' she murmured.

''I said I've got it. Now, do you two want to eat or stand here running your mouths?''

Mac chuckled and held out his arm to Annie. ''Shall we?''

She slipped her hand beneath his elbow and dimpled up at him. ''Why, thank you, sir.''

Trent glanced over his shoulder. ''Careful, Mac. I'm the jealous type.''

Aware of the dry humor in Trent's voice, Mac

responded in kind. "Don't worry. I think of her almost like family."

It was a sick joke, of course, and at the McBrides' expense. But Mac had to entertain himself somehow.

Following Trent around the side of the big old white-frame, black-shuttered house with its wraparound porch, Mac steeled himself for what was to come.

The backyard was large and nicely landscaped, shaded by big, spreading trees and decorated with masses of colorful flowers. It was a warm, cloudless day, and the adults and children mingling around a large, smoking barbecue grill and several picnic tables were dressed in lightweight, brightly colored clothing. Quite a welcoming and domestic sight, Mac thought wryly. Like a scene from a Disney movie.

Probably because he was looking for her, he spotted Sharon immediately. She was standing beside one of the picnic tables talking with three other women. He identified the striking redhead as Trevor's wife, Jamie. Though he hadn't been introduced to her, he'd seen her entering the law firm enough times to know who she was. The fresh-faced blonde was Emily Davenport. He had seen her from a distance, though he'd made no effort to meet her before now. He didn't recognize the cool-looking woman with dark auburn hair standing next to Sharon. He'd never seen her around town.

They were all very attractive, but the only one

who made Mac's pulse rate increase was Sharon. She wore her hair down in a smooth, glossy curtain to her collar. The bright sunlight brought out rich, warm highlights, and he could almost feel the silken strands in his hands again, almost smell the clean, fresh scent of her shampoo. She wore a sleeveless, scoop-neck white blouse that closed down the front with tiny buttons, and khaki shorts that revealed a modest, but delectable stretch of legs.

He found himself fantasizing about releasing the buttons of her blouse, stripping away her shorts to expose the parts of her he had so painstakingly explored in his bedroom only twenty-four hours earlier. He forced himself to clear his mind of those thoughts before he embarrassed himself.

She smiled when she saw him. He remembered the first time she'd visited the Garrett house, when she'd been surprised to find Trent McBride waiting in the kitchen. Mac had wondered then how it would feel to be on the receiving end of one of her bright, warm, generous smiles. Now he knew. It felt great.

Wade, Trevor and another man were gathered around the barbecue grill, holding beers and frowning intently at the sizzling meat. Trent glanced at Mac and chuckled. "They look like they're performing brain surgery, don't they?"

Spotting them, Wade handed his beer to Trevor and ambled their way. "Hey, guys. Annie, you look lovely as always."

She smiled. "And you are as charming as always."

"How's that dumb mutt of yours?"

"Bozo is just fine, thank you. And he isn't dumb," she added firmly. "Just—unconventional."

Trent snorted. "The mutt's got the IQ of a bowl of oatmeal," he muttered.

Annie pretended to be offended, but she was smiling. "Admit it, Trent, you like my dog."

Trent shrugged ironically. "He and I have come to an arrangement. We'll each share Annie—to a point."

Wade turned to greet Mac. "Good to see you, Mac. Trent, give me that cooler and show Mac where we keep the beer."

Having made his point by carrying the cooler this far, Trent relinquished it without argument. He led Mac to a large, ice-filled metal tub that held a variety of canned beverages. Sharon and her companions joined them there.

"Hi, Mac."

He accepted a dripping can of cold beer from Trent, then turned to acknowledge Sharon's greeting. "Hi, yourself."

"It's a beautiful day for a cookout, isn't it?"

The words were merely polite trivialities, but her eyes said so much more. She was glad to see him. And it shook him to realize how much that meant to him. "Yes, it's very nice."

He pulled his gaze from her and glanced around the lawn, noting that the only children in evidence were three blond little girls, not much more than toddlers, playing with some plastic toys on the grass near the picnic table where the women had just been sitting. "Did your brother decide not to join you today?" he asked Sharon, wondering if Brad had chosen to stay away rather than chance another meeting with him.

"Brad's inside playing video games with Wade's son, Clay, and Trevor's son, Sam."

"A day like this and they're playing inside?"

Having overheard Mac's question, Wade grimaced. "I told them they could stay in there until lunch is ready, but then they're joining us out here in the fresh air. The problem is that Lucas just sent Clay a new game and of course they couldn't wait to try it out."

"Remember I told you about Lucas, Wade's brother-in-law who owns a software-design company in California," Sharon said. "Brad thinks it's just about the coolest thing in the world that Clay's uncle has a company that creates video games and that Clay gets to try them out before they even hit the market."

"Let me introduce you to our other guests, Mac," Wade offered, playing the gracious host. "You know Trent and Trevor, of course, but you haven't met their brother-in-law, Blake Fox. He and Tara live in Atlanta with their daughter, Alison—the littlest one over there. Blake, this is Mac Cordero, the contractor we told you about."

Shaking Blake's hand, Mac noted that the other man was golden-haired, blue-eyed and built in a way that some might have described as elegantly slender.

He had the look of a 1940s film star—probably deliberately enhanced by his choice of loose, perfectly tailored clothing. But there was a sharp gleam of streetwise intelligence in his bright blue eyes that was entirely modern.

The guy fit in well with the fair-skinned, light-haired McBrides, Mac thought, aware again of the dramatic contrast between them and himself.

"Good to meet you, Mac," Blake said, and though his manner was quite casual, Mac had the sensation he'd just been studied, memorized and categorized. Blake had the look of a hustler, or a particularly slick con man. Mac had encountered several of them over the years. He knew Tara was a lawyer—maybe she'd married one, as well, he thought as he returned the greeting.

Blake turned to the auburn-haired woman who'd approached as the introductions were made. "Mac, this is my wife, Tara."

Extending her hand, Tara smiled warmly, dispelling his initial impression of coolness. "It's very nice to meet you, Mr. Cordero. My brothers have told me you're remodeling the Garrett house. I've always thought it was a fascinating old place. I'm glad someone else recognized its potential."

"Okay, I've waited long enough." The woman Mac had identified as Jamie McBride pushed good-naturedly forward, multiple earrings dangling, numerous bracelets jingling. Her flame-red hair was chopped in a stylishly haphazard fashion and her willowy figure was boldly displayed in a brightly colored, spaghetti-strap top and brief denim shorts. Her lips, fingernails and toenails were all painted a bright fuchsia. "I want to meet this fascinating man who has the whole town talking."

Trevor sighed. "Mac, allow me to introduce my wife, Jamie. If your first impression is that she's basically a fruitcake—well, you'd be right."

Jamie laughed and punched her husband's arm. "I just want to meet him, Trev. It isn't often we get a dashing stranger in this town."

It was obvious to Mac that this stage-actress-turned-high-school-drama teacher loved attracting attention with her unconventional behavior. Happy to oblige, he took her outstretched hand and bent to press his lips to it. "It's a great honor to make your acquaintance, Mrs. McBride."

She giggled. "I know a rogue when I see one—and I adore them. You can stay."

"Very considerate of you. Especially since this is my house." After making the dry comment to her cousin's wife, Emily Davenport stepped forward to be included in the introductions. "I'm Emily, Mr. Cordero. I'm so glad you could join us today."

"I appreciate your hospitality. And I answer to Mac."

Jamie nodded firmly. "That's good. This is a cookout, not a business meeting."

"Mommy. Claire's eating grass again," the eldest of the three little girls playing by the picnic table announced, causing all the adults to spin around.

Mac watched as Jamie immediately abandoned

her outrageous behavior and responded maternally to her stepdaughter, Abbie, who had loudly tattled on her little cousin. Emily diverted little Claire's attention from snacking on the grass, and the men went back to their cooking.

For a moment, Mac couldn't look away from the children. His son would have been about their age now, he thought. He could easily picture dark-haired, dark-eyed Emilio toddling on the grass with these pretty little girls. The image made him almost flinch with an old, long-suppressed pain.

Sharon placed a hand on his arm. "Mac? Is everything okay?"

He forced a faint smile. "Everything's fine. I was just watching the kids."

"Cute, aren't they? I wish Caleb and Bobbie were here, so you could meet them, too. They're such a wonderful couple."

"Yeah, I'd like to meet them." Caleb McBride might prove to be the only man still living who could provide the answers Mac was looking for. He sure as hell didn't seem to be making much headway on his own.

During the next few hours, Mac couldn't quite understand why his mood grew steadily darker and heavier. The company was entertaining, the food delicious, the weather perfect. With the exception of Brad Henderson, who had almost turned purple when he saw Mac, everyone had been very friendly. But it seemed the more pleasantly the afternoon progressed, the grimmer Mac felt.

The McBride relatives chattered spiritedly all through the meal, catching up on recent events in each other's lives, sharing tidbits of innocuous gossip from around town, bragging about their children. And then they lapsed into reminiscing, sharing embarrassing tales about each other, teasing mercilessly, finishing each other's sentences as they tried to explain to the spouses and guests who didn't already know the stories. The anecdotes were amusing. Mac chuckled at the appropriate times and made the right comments, but he couldn't say he was actually enjoying them.

"Remember the time Trent got locked in Grandma McBride's root cellar?" Tara shook her head with a smile as she addressed her brothers and cousin. "He was just a toddler, not much older than our Alison is now. Savannah got hysterical. She'd just read a book about the Lindbergh baby and she was convinced Trent had been kidnapped. She didn't calm down until half an hour or so after Trent was found."

"I can't say I remember that," Trent murmured, looking uncomfortable when his fiancée smiled quizzically at him.

"Savannah?" Mac asked, playing his part.

"Our cousin," Trevor explained. "She's a year older than Tara. Her father, Jonah, was our dad's youngest brother. Uncle Jonah died when Savannah was only ten. Trent and I don't even remember him."

"Neither do I," Emily said, "but I wish I did. Everyone who knew him loved him."

"I remember him a little," Tara said. "He was a lot like our dad—very good-natured, always cutting up. He had a deep laugh and carried butterscotch candies in his pocket. He was a salesman and he often brought gifts for everyone when he came back from a trip. And he absolutely adored Savannah."

"He spoiled her rotten," Trent commented. "She grew up thinking she was a princess because her daddy always told her she was."

"Yes, well, she had to get over that when she became the mother of twins," Tara said matter-of-factly.

So everyone had loved Jonah McBride, the salesman who'd often been away on trips. Had Anita Cordero loved him, as well? Wouldn't it be ironic if the man she'd spent her life missing and hoping to someday see again had died less than ten years after he'd deserted her?

How would Jonah's little princess react to finding out she had a younger brother she'd never known? A brother who had been denied the camaraderie and memories she shared with her cousins. A brother who had never known what it was like to be spoiled by a doting father.

"Is everyone ready for dessert?" Emily asked, standing. "We have several types. Wade and Clay, Sharon brought her strawberry cake that you both love so much."

Wade and his teenage son immediately wore identical looks of greed. "Sharon makes the best strawberry cake I've ever tasted," Wade told Mac. "Wait'll you try it—pure heaven."

Sharon laughed softly. "Mac's allergic to strawberries. He'd be better off having some of Emily's famous German-chocolate cake."

"I like German chocolate," he assured her, aware that some of the others were looking at them speculatively now—probably because Sharon had spoken about him in such an indulgently familiar tone. If they hadn't already suspected something was going on between him and Sharon, they probably did now.

Somehow during dessert the conversation turned to the rash of break-ins lately, and the near-tragic accident through which Mac and Sharon had met. It was during that discussion that Mac learned Blake Fox was a private investigator in Atlanta; Wade seemed to value his advice about tracking down the culprits. Aware that Mac was listening closely, Wade turned to him at one point and said, "Do you have anything you'd like to add, Mac?"

"Sounds to me as if you've got it covered," Mac answered with a slight shrug.

"What would *he* know about police work?" Brad muttered across the table, his tone jeering. "He just fixes up houses."

"Tell that to some of the crooks he put behind bars in Savannah," Wade answered, implicitly rebuking Brad for his rudeness.

Mac swallowed a groan. He hadn't meant for this to come up today. He should have known better. Even among this relatively discreet group, secrets seemed to have a way of coming out.

CHAPTER THIRTEEN

"YOU WERE A COP, Mac?" Blake asked, apparently the first to understand the reference.

He nodded, almost feeling Sharon's startled gaze on his face. "For ten years. I retired a few years ago to become a restoration contractor, something I'd always been interested in trying."

"I don't suppose you want me to mention your citations? Or the fact that you retired after being shot in the line of duty, saving a group of innocent bystanders from a lunatic with an assault rifle?"

Wade's expression was so bland Mac was half tempted to punch him, just to see if it ruffled him. The chief really had investigated him thoroughly. Hell, he'd probably even talked to Mac's superior officers in Savannah. He'd been right when he'd assumed that there wasn't much that slipped past Wade Davenport.

"You were *shot?*" Sharon whispered, looking pale.

He shook his head reassuringly. "Just grazed. Hardly a scratch."

It was a lie, of course. He'd been hospitalized for ten days. But he saw no need to go into that now.

Jamie McBride was the one who broke the startled silence, and of course she did it with an outrageous comment. "Cordero-the-hero," she murmured, tongue in cheek. "That's what they call you around town, you know, because you saved Sharon's life that night. Just imagine the name you'd pick up if they heard about *this*."

Mac felt his cheeks darken, the closest he'd come to a blush in years. Wade laughed. Trevor rolled his eyes in resignation at his wife's impudence. Brad Henderson made a sound of disgust and pushed away from the table. "C'mon, Clay, let's go check out your new game. I'm starting to get nauseous."

"That boy really doesn't like you, Mac," Wade said when the teens had left, with Trevor's almost-seven-year-old son tagging eagerly along.

"It's just taking him longer than most people to respond to my natural charm," Mac drawled in return, making Wade chuckle.

"Mac thinks Brad is a bit threatened because Mac and I have become friends," Sharon said, looking concerned about her brother's behavior.

Trent shrugged. "Makes sense. Teenagers don't like change."

"That's what I told Mac," Sharon agreed quickly. "All Brad needs is some time and understanding—"

"And a good swift kick to the butt," Trent murmured.

Mac chuckled at Sharon's expression. "That's what I told *her*."

"Sympathy and understanding only go so far with

teenagers,'' Wade advised Sharon. ''Sometimes it takes a tougher approach.''

Sharon sighed and lifted a hand to her temple. ''Okay, I'll try.''

''Brad's a good boy,'' Emily said firmly. ''Don't let them upset you, Sharon.''

Sharon looked only marginally reassured.

One of the younger children—either Emily's Claire or Tara's Alison, Mac tended to mix them up—toddled up to him and set a stuffed toy on his knee. She looked up at him with enormous blue eyes, apparently waiting for him to make a comment. ''That's, uh, real nice, Claire,'' he added, figuring the odds were pretty good that he was right.

''That's Alison,'' Abbie informed him with a haughtiness that was rather pronounced considering she wasn't even four yet. ''Claire's over there.''

He really wasn't faring very well with the younger set here today, Mac thought resignedly as the little girl he'd misidentified bustled happily away.

The child looked healthy, he mused, watching her chubby little legs pumping along. All the McBride descendants looked downright robust. He fervently hoped the same would prove true of any future offspring. No parent deserved the kind of heartbreak he had been through.

He glanced at his watch. The afternoon was well advanced. Shadows were lengthening in the yard. The kids were starting to look tired. And so was he, he imagined. He needed to get away.

Sitting next to him, Sharon leaned closer, masking her voice beneath the lively chatter of the others. "You look as though you're getting ready to bolt."

"I need to run by the house," he said. "The electricians were there this morning and I like to make sure everything's locked up after the crews leave."

Sharon stood as he did. "I'll walk you to your truck."

Looking only at her, he smiled a little. It calmed him to focus on her at the moment. Helped him concentrate on the present rather than the past.

Mac took his leave of the others, all of whom assured him they'd been delighted to have him there.

"I'm so glad you could come, Mac," Emily said, her hand in his. "Please visit us again."

He looked into her friendly blue eyes, seeing nothing but warm sincerity in her expression. A very nice woman, he thought. Would he ruin her comfortable life if he pursued his private investigation, if he made it publicly known that her father could be his, as well? He hadn't really cared when he came here who might be hurt or embarrassed if the truth was revealed, but that was before he'd met the McBrides. Before he'd been welcomed so graciously among them.

Whether they knew it or not, they were his family—and he didn't know how much, if anything, he owed them because of that coincidence of genetics.

Sharon was still thinking of her brother as she accompanied Mac around the side of the house.

"Brad really will come around, Mac. He just needs time."

Time. He considered that a moment. It would be several months before the renovation was finished. While it wasn't absolutely necessary for him to oversee every day of the work, it was his practice to be very actively involved in his projects from beginning to end. He enjoyed the work, and took great satisfaction in watching the daily progress.

It was *not* his practice to get involved with a woman in town during his jobs. There had been the occasional encounter since his divorce; he hadn't quite lived a monk's life since his divorce. But not far from it. And none of the few other women had made him question what he wanted or where he was headed the way Sharon did.

They paused together beside his truck. Sharon reached out to touch the deep scratch across the door. "You're going to have this repaired, aren't you?"

"Eventually."

She drew a deep breath, the action pushing her breasts against the thin fabric of her summery blouse. Again, his fingers itched to have a go at that row of tiny, flirty buttons. Her next comment brought his attention abruptly away from her cleavage.

"I want you to bill the repairs to me," she said firmly.

He studied her determined expression. "Forget it."

"I'm serious, Mac."

"So am I. You aren't paying for my repairs."

"Look, I know you still think Brad had something to do with this. And even though I really hope you're wrong, I believe in taking care of my responsibilities. If there's even a possibility that he's the guilty party, then I should pay for—"

"I said forget it." He wasn't about to let her take this any further. "Regardless of what I believe about the person who did this, I know for certain that it wasn't you. You aren't going to pay for it."

"But if Brad really did—"

"If Brad's guilty, then it should be up to him to make restitution, not you. I won't take your money, Sharon."

"But—"

"Have you even asked Brad if he had anything to do with it?" he asked gently.

Her stricken expression was answer enough.

"You haven't," he interpreted. "You're afraid of what he might say."

She sighed and rubbed her temples. "I'm such a coward."

Catching her wrists, he pulled her hands away from her head. "You," he said, "are the least cowardly person I've ever met. I can't imagine many other women your age who would have accepted the amount of responsibility you've taken on this summer. You're the one who deserves a vacation, but it seems like everyone's taking one except you. No one could expect more of you than what you've already given.''

Her hands cradled in his, she shook her head. ''I don't mind watching out for my brother while my mother takes a trip that was the chance of a lifetime for her. It's just—well, not quite as easy as I'd expected.''

''So don't take on more stress than you've already got. I'll take care of my problems, even if they involve your brother. Neither Brad nor I need you to handle this for us.''

She bit her lip, seeming to contemplate his words for a moment. And then she gazed up at him again. ''Mac? Why didn't you tell me you were a police officer?''

He winced. ''It didn't come up?'' he offered lamely.

She only looked at him.

He sighed. ''I don't know. It just never seemed like the right time to mention it.''

''Or maybe you thought it was something I had no need to know about you?''

He wasn't sure how to answer that.

She let him off the hook with a slight smile and a shake of her head. ''It's okay. I'm not trying to learn all your secrets. I just wondered.''

All his secrets. He glanced toward the house where so many of the McBrides were still gathered. ''Sharon—''

''I guess I'm just a little stressed today.''

''I don't want to cause you any more.''

She squeezed his hands. "Don't worry about it. I can handle it."

He remembered the vow he'd made to himself that he wouldn't hurt her. He devoutly hoped it was a promise he would be able to keep. Taking a chance that they wouldn't be seen—and not really caring at that moment if they were—he leaned over to brush his lips across hers. Her mouth was warm and soft and clung to his for a moment before he straightened away from her. It wasn't easy for him to release her hands and step back. What he really wanted to do was toss her into his truck, take her to his apartment and spend the next twenty-four hours making love to her.

At least twenty-four hours.

"I want to see you again," he said, his voice gruff. "When can you get away?"

He didn't think he needed to clarify that he wanted to see her alone. She smiled at him in a way that let him know she understood. "Soon," she said. "I want to be with you, too."

He almost kissed her again. Instead, he reached for the door handle of the truck. "I'll call you later."

"You do that," she said, then turned to rejoin her friends.

So what, exactly, had he accomplished? he asked himself as he turned out of the Davenports' driveway and onto the road that would take him to the Garrett house. He'd learned that there was a good chance Jonah McBride had been his father—something he'd already figured. He'd caused Sharon to be embarrassed by her brother's behavior—and they'd both known it was a possibility. And, even though he knew the McBrides weren't prone to gossip, he'd made the relationship between Sharon and himself the focus of attention at least briefly that afternoon.

What *had* he accomplished? Damned if he knew.

But it was becoming harder and harder for him to think of the McBrides as just a group of people who owed him answers and apologies.

JAMIE WAS POISED to pounce almost the moment Sharon returned. "Well?" she said while the others were busy taking care of the little ones and putting away cookout supplies. "Anything you want to share with me?"

"What do you mean?" Sharon asked, though she knew very well what had piqued Jamie's curiosity.

"You're seeing Mac Cordero, aren't you? I'd heard around town that you are, and now that I've seen you together, I think the rumors might have some merit for a change."

Sharon still wasn't sure who'd started that rumor. She and Mac had been very discreet. They'd hardly been seen in public together. She could only assume that some of the construction workers had reached certain conclusions from watching them together— which only proved that men were just as bad as women to spread gossip, she thought with a shake of her head.

"Mac and I have been spending some time together. But it's still very early, Jamie. Much too soon to make any predictions."

Jamie laughed and patted Sharon's arm. "Don't worry, I'm not starting a betting pool. I just thought it was sweet the way he looked at you. It feels great to have a guy walking into walls when you're around, doesn't it?"

Flustered, Sharon laughed. "He doesn't actually—"

Jamie waved her hand dismissively. "I was speaking metaphorically, of course. Mac could hardly take his eyes off you all afternoon, even though he was very discreet about it. He's like Trevor, I think. It isn't easy for him to express his emotions, but he feels them very deeply."

Sharon remembered the afternoon when she had watched Mac and Trevor descending the stairs of the Garrett house side by side. Even though they were very different physically, she'd had the feeling that they were quite a bit alike in other ways.

"I guess you've heard Jerry's been telling everyone in town that you dumped him for Mac."

Sharon frowned. "No, I hadn't heard that. Has he really been saying those things?"

"I'm afraid so. He's really quite bitter about it."

Sharon put a hand to her head. "I wish he wouldn't do that. It isn't as if Jerry and I were ever really a couple. There was never any talk of a future between us."

"Men." Jamie heaved a dramatic sigh. "There's no understanding them."

Sharon heartily agreed.

Abruptly turning serious, Jamie touched Sharon's arm again. "I know your mom's away and you have a lot on your plate now, with your brother and everything. I remember how terrifying it was starting a new relationship. I know how it feels to fall for a complex, exasperating man with emotional baggage—which I would bet big money describes your Mac as well as my Trevor. If you ever need to talk, you know where to find me."

"Is it that obvious?" Sharon heard the touch of wistfulness in her own voice. "That I'm falling for him, I mean."

Her eyes ruefully sympathetic, Jamie smiled. "Sweetie, you might as well be wearing a sign."

Sharon groaned.

"Maybe I'm just particularly sensitive to it because it hasn't been that long since it happened to me," Jamie encouraged her. "Maybe no one else noticed."

Glancing automatically at the others, Sharon decided that every other woman there seemed to be surreptitiously watching her and Jamie. Oh, yes, she thought. They had noticed.

She might as well have been wearing a sign.

MAC WAS SITTING at his kitchen table again, brooding. His notes were spread in front of him, but it was the photograph in his hand that held his attention. A bottle of bourbon sat on the table, a half-empty glass near his elbow. He didn't drink often, but tonight there had seemed to be no reason to stay completely sober. He had nothing better to do and no one to do it with.

From the snapshot, his ex-wife and infant son gazed up at him. The picture had been taken in a hospital. Karla sat in a wooden rocker with four-week-old Emilio in her arms. Several tubes were attached to the baby, leading to equipment outside the boundaries of the shot. Emilio had never known a day without tubes or needles. Two weeks after this photo had been taken, the child had died, as quietly and unassumingly as he had lived.

Mac was in the photograph, too, kneeling beside Karla's chair. He hadn't wanted to have this picture taken, but Karla had insisted, and it had seemed like little enough to do for her during that nightmarish ordeal. It was ironic that she hadn't wanted to take the photograph with her when she left him.

The doctors had told them that Emilio's birth defect was genetic, something passed down through generations. Having been adopted as a baby, Karla knew nothing of her own genetic histo_y. Mac, of course, knew only that there had been no history of the disease on his mother's side. There had been tests available to find out which of them carried the gene that had caused Emilio's death, but Mac hadn't bothered to take them. It had been too easy for him to shoulder the blame, himself.

Perhaps Karla had been tested during the past two

years. Mac wouldn't know. He hadn't talked to her since they'd drifted apart in the weeks after they'd lost their child.

It had been Karla who had filed for divorce, even though Mac had tried to talk her into giving their marriage another try. He'd even offered to go to counseling with her—and he hated that sort of thing. But she hadn't been interested. Whatever love she'd had for him in the beginning had been lost in grief and anger and bitterness. And his own distance.

Mac accepted his share of the blame for the end of the marriage. He'd lost his mother only six months before Emilio's birth, and he'd still been reeling from that devastating loss. He and his mother had been very close. They'd had to be. They were all the family each of them had.

Still grieving for his mother and trying to deal with the facts he'd learned after her death about his own parentage, he hadn't been adequately prepared for the second blow of losing his son. Maybe he hadn't been supportive enough of Karla during the difficult six weeks that Emilio had lived. Or maybe what they'd had simply wasn't strong enough to survive that kind of hardship.

He'd thought attraction, passion and affection were enough. Apparently, he'd been wrong.

What he was starting to feel for Sharon was entirely different than what he'd shared with Karla. But how was he to know whether this was any more real? Any more lasting?

The doorbell rang, drawing him out of his painful

reverie. He wasn't expecting anyone, which meant there was a good chance this wasn't something he wanted to hear. He sighed heavily, took another sip of his bourbon and rose.

A few moments later, he opened the front door to find Sharon Henderson standing on the other side.

"I probably should have called," she said, eyeing him uncertainly.

Aware that his hair was tousled, his shirt half unbuttoned and his feet bare, he cleared his throat. "No. I was just relaxing. Come in."

He moved aside to hold the door open for her. After only a momentary hesitation, she entered his apartment.

He closed the door behind her.

SHARON COULDN'T TAKE her eyes off Mac's face as she stepped inside his living room. As usual, his expression gave away little of his thoughts, but she had become strangely attuned to his emotions. She sensed that he had been feeling sad this evening. "What's wrong?" she asked.

"Nothing. You just caught me by surprise."

She really should have called. She had never been the type to act on impulse, but she'd done a lot of things that were out of character for her since Mac had come into her life. "I found myself on my own for the evening and I wondered if you would be interested in keeping me company for a few hours. But if you have other plans..."

"On your own, huh?"

"Yes. Clay and Brad talked me into letting Brad spend the night there. They'll probably play video games until dawn."

"And you thought maybe you and I could play a few games of our own?"

She loved the way his mouth quirked when he sort of smiled. "Only if you're interested, of course."

He reached out to tug her into his arms. "I am most definitely interested," he assured her, his mouth close enough to hers that she could feel the warmth of his breath on her face.

"You've been drinking," she murmured, noting the faint scent of alcohol and the slight flush on his cheeks.

"Yeah. Are you worried that I'm a closet drunk?"

She thought about it only a moment before shaking her head. "No. I think you've had a drink tonight because you were upset about something."

"Something like that."

"Did it help?"

His mouth twisted. "No."

She raised a hand to his jaw. "Is there something I can do?"

Catching her hand, he planted a kiss in the palm. "Oh, yeah."

The fervency of his reply made her smile. "Why don't you tell me what you need?"

He slid his hands down her sides, gripped her hips

and pulled her closer. "Why don't I show you, instead?"

Wrapping her arms around his neck, she murmured into his mouth, "That would work."

He didn't carry her to bed this time. They walked side by side, their bodies close together, their steps slow. They both knew there was no reason to hurry.

They left the overhead light off, turning on the small, dim lamp beside the bed for illumination. Sharon pushed Mac's shirt off his shoulders and then reached for the snap of his jeans. She intended to take a much more active role this time.

Because she was looking, she found the white scar low on his back, just above his left hip. Her fingertips brushed the puckered flesh. "This is where you were shot?"

"It wasn't that bad. My injuries were never life-threatening."

Kneeling beside him, she pressed her lips to the scar. "It must have been very painful."

The way he flinched when her lips touched him, she'd have thought he was in pain now. And perhaps he was, she mused with a secret smile. But it was a good pain this time—an ache only she could soothe.

Standing unselfconsciously nude in front of her, he lifted her up and reached for the first tiny pearlized button on her white summer top. "I wanted to do this all afternoon."

"I know." She smiled wickedly at him, remembering Jamie's comment about how good it felt to have a man "walking into walls." "I could tell by the way you looked at me."

Brushing his lips across her forehead, he murmured, "Sometimes I worry that you see too much when you look at me."

She didn't know how to answer that, so she didn't try. Instead, she placed a hand on either side of his face and brought his mouth to hers.

By the time the kiss ended, her blouse and bra were on the floor and her shorts were puddled around her feet. Mac lifted her out of them and fell to the bed with her. "You are so perfect," he half groaned, running his hands over her.

"Not perfect. I have a scar, too."

"Where?"

Feeling deliciously mischievous, she smiled and ran a finger across his lower lip. "Why don't you try to find it?"

It was a challenge he accepted with enthusiasm. There wasn't an inch of her he missed in his search—not an inch he didn't touch or kiss. Even after he found the small scar from her childhood appendectomy, he kept looking—just in case, he informed her gravely, there was a flaw he had missed. Not until he'd kissed his way to her toes did he pronounce her as perfect as he had believed her to be.

By then, she could hardly think clearly enough to remember what he'd been looking for.

He was doing it again, she thought weakly. Clouding her mind with passion and pleasure, keeping her so dazed and befuddled she could only lie against the pillows and gasp. Calling on all her strength, she pushed herself off the pillows and pressed him onto his back. "My turn," she said firmly.

He spread his arms. "Knock yourself out."

Her breath catching on a giggle, she bent over him. It wasn't the most romantic invitation she'd ever had, but it was sincerely offered, and that was what mattered. By the time this night ended, she promised herself, she would know his body as well as he knew hers.

It wasn't easy keeping him still while she explored him. He kept wanting to roll her beneath him. Sharon had to hold him in place with a firm hand. He could easily have overpowered her, of course. He wouldn't even have had to put much effort into flipping her onto her back and pinning her there with his own body. But he let her set the pace, even though he almost quivered with impatience.

He jerked violently when she took him into her hand. Groaned deep in his chest when she placed her mouth on him. And a few long, emotion-filled moments later, he did something she hadn't expected from this strong, hard man. He begged. "Sharon—please…"

The request affected her in a way no amount of machismo could have. She melted. "Mac—"

They moved together, a fluid, silent duet of desire. It took only a heartbeat for him to don protection, and then another for him to bury himself so deeply inside her she felt as if he had become a part of her.

She couldn't have begun to guess how much time passed—minutes…hours…days. There were no words, no coherent thoughts. Only ragged breathing and broken cries. And so much raw, honest emotion that her heart seemed to swell almost to bursting with it.

She was so desperately in love with this man. It didn't seem to matter that they'd known each other such a short time, or that there were still secrets between them, at least on his part. She loved him. Whether that love would lead to a happy ending— well, that remained to be seen.

CHAPTER FOURTEEN

HIS CHEEK on her breast, his arm across her, Mac lay on his stomach next to her as they very slowly recovered their breath. Their sanity.

"Tell me this isn't a fantastic dream," he muttered after a while, without lifting his head.

She laughed. "I don't think you had *that* much to drink before I arrived."

"Half a glass."

"So which was more effective at making you feel better? The booze? Or me?"

He lifted his head to give her a faintly reproachful look. "Fishing?"

Unabashed, she touched his face. "Yes."

"You are infinitely better than bourbon."

She grinned. "I'll take any compliment I can get."

Propping himself on one elbow, Mac smoothed her tangled hair away from her face. "You're in a feisty mood tonight."

"I guess being bold and bad does that to me."

"'Bold and bad'? Is that what you're feeling?"

"Of course. I don't do things like this. Ever. I'm always sensible and responsible. I don't take chances, I don't have flings and I don't act on impulse. Not usually. Not until you came along."

He considered her words, and he didn't look entirely pleased by them. "A fling," he repeated in a murmur.

"For want of a better term."

"I don't care for that one."

"Do you have a better word to offer?" she challenged, still in that oddly daring mood.

"No," he said after a brief pause. "But it isn't a fling."

It wasn't much—but it was something. She decided to be satisfied with that for now.

Her hand rested on his side, just inches from the scar on his back. "Why did you quit the police force? Was it because you were shot?"

"Not entirely. I was just tired of giving everything I had to a job and not seeing any real results for my efforts. I'd put one drug dealer behind bars and three more would take his place. For every at-risk teenager we set straight, we lost a dozen more. I started dreading going in to work in the mornings. I felt more and more like I was trying to put out a forest fire with a squirt gun."

It pleased her that he'd answered her so candidly, giving her another glimpse into his character. She didn't think less of Mac for walking away from a job that had grown frustrating for him; she knew it was because he had cared so deeply that he couldn't stay. "So you went into the restoration business, where you could see definite results. You take something old and neglected and you make it useful and beautiful again.''

''Something like that,'' he said with a slight shrug. Despite his offhand tone, she could tell her assessment had been on track.

Because he seemed in a mood to talk, she risked another personal question. ''How did your wife feel about your change of profession? Was she relieved?''

''Actually, she rather liked being married to a cop. A contractor wasn't nearly as exciting to her.''

That couldn't have been the only reason the marriage ended, she mused. ''How long were you married after you quit police work?''

''About a year.''

It must have been a difficult year, she decided, studying his expression. But maybe she didn't want to talk about his marriage right now, after all. ''Tell me about your mother,'' she said, instead.

His eyebrows lifted. ''You really *are* feeling chatty, aren't you?''

''I'm sorry. Would you rather I be quiet?''

''No. Ask anything you like. What do you want to know about my mother?''

''From what little you've told me about her, I can tell you were close to her. She must have been very special.''

''She was.'' His voice held a mixture of pride and wistfulness, making it clear he still missed her very much.

''She was born in Puerto Rico?''

"Yes. She was married in San Juan when she was seventeen. She followed her husband to Savannah, where he went to work on the docks and she found work as a hotel maid. A year later, he was killed in a job accident, leaving her a widow before her nineteenth birthday."

"And pregnant with you—how terrible for her."

"No. Her husband wasn't my father." There was no emotion in his voice. "My mother fell in love with another man almost ten years later. He was married to someone else. I was conceived from that relationship. Her very Catholic family turned against her because she had a child out of wedlock. She raised me on her own, without any help from anyone."

"Your father?" she murmured, studying his impassive face.

He shrugged. "I never met him. He had no interest in staying behind to deal with the devastation he had caused in my mother's life."

"She must have been a very strong woman."

"She was. She never accepted any assistance from anyone. She raised me on what she earned as a hotel maid. By the time I was five, she was the head housekeeper. She never made a lot of money, but what she had went to my health care and education. I started working to help her out when I was just a kid, but it was always a struggle to convince her to take money from me."

"She named you Miguel, but she called you Mac. And she made sure you could speak English."

"As I said, she wanted me to fit in. She hoped I would become a doctor or a lawyer. But when I chose to enter the police academy, instead—following in the footsteps of a neighbor I admired and who had always taken an interest in mentoring me—she couldn't have acted more proud of me."

"You loved her very much, didn't you?"

"I adored her."

His simply and sincerely worded reply made her throat tighten. She would like to think that if she ever had a son, he would speak of her with the same respect and devotion with which Mac remembered his mother.

"After my mother died," he said, looking into the distance over Sharon's head as if gazing into his past, "I found out that she had put every extra dollar she made into life insurance policies naming me as the beneficiary. Even after I was grown and supporting myself, she felt she needed to provide for me."

"It sounds as though she adored you in return."

"She did. I used the insurance money to establish my new business. I think she would have approved."

"She gave you the ability to pursue a dream, even if it might have been different from her dreams for you. Yes, I'm sure she would have approved."

"You'd have liked her, I think."

"I'm sure I would have loved her." How could she not have loved the woman who had raised this very special man?

Mac gave a little shake of his head, as if shaking off the memories, and moved a hand over her bare body. "Have we talked enough now?"

She reached up to brush back a lock of silky black hair that had fallen onto his forehead. "Do you have something else in mind?"

Lowering his head to her breast, he murmured, "Something's bound to come up."

She giggled, and then gasped when his tongue swept over her nipple. "Okay," she said breathlessly, her fingers tightening in his hair. "That's enough talk for now."

He gathered her closer. "Good."

SHARON WOKE at 2:00 a.m., thirsty and disoriented. After taking a moment to gather her bearings, she turned her head on the pillow to look at Mac. He was soundly asleep, his limbs sprawled, his mouth just slightly parted. Sleep didn't soften his features much, she mused. Even now he looked powerful and strong. Still slightly dangerous.

She knew now that there was a soft side hidden behind that stern exterior. A side he would allow few people to see. She felt fortunate to be one of them.

She lay there for a moment, just watching him. Fantasizing and hoping...

Her thirst finally pulled her from the bed. She snatched Mac's denim shirt from the floor where she'd thrown it earlier and slipped her arms into the sleeves. It was long enough on her to serve as a short robe, covering her enough for modesty's sake. Wrapping it around her, she headed for the kitchen.

Mac had left the light on. The kitchen table was cluttered with papers. An open bottle of bourbon sat next to a half-empty tumbler. The cap lay beside the bottle.

Automatically reaching to replace the cap, she paused when her gaze fell on a photograph lying on top of the scattered papers. In it, a dark-haired woman held a tiny, black-haired, black-eyed baby. The setting was obviously a hospital. In the picture, Mac knelt beside the chair, his right hand resting protectively on the baby's head, as if to protect the child.

He looked very much like a worried father.

Her fingers shook a little as she reached out to touch the photo. She could picture Mac sitting here alone, sipping his drink and staring at this photograph. Only one explanation occurred to her. Had this child been Mac's? He had told her he and his wife had no children. Could their baby have died?

No wonder she had sensed such sadness in him when she'd first arrived. Did it still hurt him to talk about it? Was that why he hadn't told her?

He deserved his privacy. Prepared to step away from the table, she moved her hand from the photograph. It was then that the name McBride caught her attention. It was written in block letters at the top of one of the legal-pad pages. *All* of the pages, she corrected herself, looking slowly from one sheet to another.

Why was Mac compiling a comprehensive file about the McBride family?

They were all there—parents noted at the tops of the pages and offspring listed beneath. He'd even recorded the ages of each of the cousins.

She had given him much of this information herself, she realized, remembering several conversations in which the McBrides had been discussed fairly extensively. She'd actually been embarrassed by her babbling, worried that Mac had been bored. But now she wondered if she had been manipulated by an expert.

But why?

A pen lay on the pad, as if recently abandoned. Only a few lines had been written on the top page. "Jonah McBride. Wife, Ernestine. Daughter, Savannah, 34. Traveling salesman. Unhappy marriage."

He'd learned this information only a few hours earlier, she thought, pressing a hand to her stomach.

"Would you like to go through my wallet, too?"

She jumped when he spoke from the doorway behind him. Whirling on him, she scowled. "Don't you dare go on the offensive with me! Why are you spying on my friends?"

Leaning against the doorjamb, wearing only a pair of unsnapped jeans, he didn't change his expression. "Is that what you think I'm doing?"

That stoic, inscrutable look on his face only made her madder. "And don't play word games. It's obvious what you're doing. You have everything but their shoe sizes written here."

He only continued to look at her.

"Mac, I want answers."

"So do I. But we don't always get what we want."

Clenching the back of a chair so tightly her knuckles whitened, she glared at him. "Were the McBrides the reason you came to Honoria?"

He didn't respond.

"Were they the reason you were so friendly to me? Because of my friendship with them? Were you using me to get to them?"

Mac sighed and shoved a hand through his hair. "Sharon, calm down. We need to talk."

"I'm perfectly calm. And the only words I want to hear from you are an explanation of what these pages mean."

"Can't you just believe me when I tell you I don't mean the McBrides any harm?"

"You're asking me to trust you?"

"Yes." His eyes bored into hers. "That's exactly what I'm asking you to do."

Releasing the chair, she twirled her fingers in the front of his oversize shirt, abruptly aware of how little it covered. Strangely enough, she felt more naked now than she had in his bed wearing nothing at all. "Before I make that decision, will you answer just one question for me? Honestly?"

"That depends on what you ask," he said guardedly.

"*Did* you first ask me out because of my friendship with the McBrides?"

"Yes."

His starkly honest answer made her heart sink. "Damn," she whispered.

Mac had used her. He'd just admitted it. It seemed that Brad had been right. She would try to remember to apologize to him—after she'd had a good cry.

"I want to get dressed now," she said, moving toward the doorway in which he stood.

He didn't move, but continued to block her passage. "Maybe it started out that way, but that isn't why I'm here with you now."

"I'd like to believe that," she murmured, unable to meet his eyes. "But I saw what you've written on these pages. I don't know what you're doing, or why, but I know you got part of that information from me. You used me."

"In some ways, that's true. And I'm sorry. But—"

"Please let me get dressed, Mac," she begged miserably. "I can't think clearly like this."

He hesitated for one tense moment, then moved aside.

She almost dashed to the bedroom.

She couldn't look at the rumpled bed while she gathered her clothes and took them into the bathroom to dress. Her thoughts were whirling, her stomach clenching. She had plunged so swiftly from euphoria to despair that she could hardly process what had happened to her. She still didn't have a clue what Mac was up to, but it didn't really matter just then. She knew she wasn't going to like it. If there was a simple, innocuous explanation, he would have told her already. And he had already admitted that he'd first been interested in her because of her connection to the McBrides.

Foolishly enough, she'd thought it was her personality he'd been drawn to. Her talent, perhaps. Hell, she wouldn't have been this upset if he'd confessed that he'd only wanted her for her body. But to use her against her friends, to pump her for information about the people she liked so much, and who had been so good to her...well, that really hurt.

Whatever he was up to, there was no excuse.

Dressed again in her blouse and shorts, she wished she had worn something more formal that evening. It wasn't easy to be cool, clipped and intimidating in shorts. But she intended to try. She took several deep breaths before she stepped out of the bathroom. She wasn't eager to face Mac again.

He was still in the kitchen. The photograph had been put away, she noted. So had his notes. The bourbon bottle still sat on the table, capped now. The tumbler was empty.

Mac leaned against the counter, his arms crossed over his bare chest. "Do you feel better now?"

"No." She wasn't sure she would ever feel better again, not as badly as he had hurt her tonight. "Will you tell me now why you're gathering information about my friends?"

"I can't, Sharon. Not yet."

"Do you ever plan to tell me?"

He hesitated for a long time before answering. "I don't know. I haven't decided."

"Does it have something to do with your police work? Are you undercover for some reason? Do you think any of the McBrides are involved in something illegal?"

He was shaking his head even before she paused for a breath. "I'm not a cop, Sharon. Not anymore. My reasons for being here are strictly personal."

"And you won't tell me what they are."

"There are people who might be hurt. I don't know yet if I want to be responsible for that."

"You must have known when you came here that someone could be hurt. Didn't it bother you then?"

"I didn't know them then."

That made her pause to study him. He sounded as if he had begun to like the McBrides. As if he was having second thoughts about whatever had brought him here.

She thought of what she had seen on those pages. The names of Caleb and his brothers, their wives and children. Notes about their jobs and their marriages.

My mother fell in love with another man. He was married to someone else. I was conceived from that relationship.

And his mother had called him Mac.

The insight came to her in a stunning flash. "You're looking for your father."

A muscle in his jaw was the only part of him that moved.

"Is that it, Mac? Do you think Caleb or one of his brothers was the married man who had an affair with your mother?"

He ground out a curse through clenched teeth, and then sighed. "I know one of them was. I just don't know which one."

"*How* do you know?"

"I found the name in my mother's papers after she died. Just the last name. She probably never expected me to find it, or to make anything of it. I contacted her sister in Puerto Rico, who confirmed that she knew the man's name was McBride and that he was from a place called Honoria, Georgia. She knew that because my mother told her. Mother expected to live in Honoria someday, when her lover divorced his wife and married her."

Aware of the bitterness in his voice, she asked gently, "Your aunt didn't know his first name?"

"Only the last name—and only because my mother told her that she called me Mac because my father's name was McBride. A tribute to the man who abandoned her."

"So you came here to find out for yourself."

"I figured he owed me some answers. I didn't know when I started this that most of the suspects were dead."

Imitating him, she folded her arms and tried to speak unemotionally. "Have you decided which one it was?"

He shrugged. "I figure Jonah is the most likely suspect."

She remembered what he'd written about Jonah. "Traveling salesman. Unhappy marriage." He was probably right. "Jonah's been dead for years."

"I know."

"His widow and his daughter are still living, of course. Ernestine is a very proud and snobbish woman. It would humiliate her to learn that her husband had an affair and fathered a child while they were married."

"I didn't come here to humiliate an innocent bystander. His wife wasn't to blame for what he did. Mother knew he was married when they started their affair. She foolishly fell in love anyway. And she believed his lies that he loved her enough to marry her."

"What about Savannah? If Jonah was your father, that makes her your sister. Don't you want to get to know her?"

His face hardened. "I came here to find answers, not a new family. If Jonah had been alive, I might have tried to hurt him as much as he hurt my mother. I wouldn't have cared much about who got hurt along with him. But he's dead. It's too late for me to do anything to him. His widow and his daughter have nothing to do with me. I have no reason to have anything to do with either of them."

The hardness in his voice shocked her. This wasn't the man she had fallen in love with. This was a stranger. Angry, bitter, cold.

This was the man who had callously used her for

his own purposes. She wasn't even sure this man was capable of love.

Was this only another side of the Mac she'd thought she knew? Or had she completely deluded herself while falling in love with a stranger?

"There is still one McBride brother living. Caleb," she said quietly. "Is there any chance…?"

Mac shrugged again. "He's been happily married for nearly forty years. He rarely leaves Honoria. I'd say it's far more likely that Jonah was the sperm donor in my case. From what I've heard about him, I can understand why he fell in love with my mother. I just can't understand why he left her."

"Caleb will be home in a week. Are you going to ask him if he knows anything about this?"

"Don't you think I have that right?"

"The right to cause an uproar in a very happy family?" She shook her head. "I don't know."

Mac's voice turned even colder than it had been before. "My mother died still loving the man who'd broken her heart. She never got over him, never stopped hoping he would come back to her. She named me after him, dammit. I have a right to know who did that to her. The duty to seek retribution on my mother's behalf."

"Retribution?"

His eyes glittered like black stones. "Whichever McBride seduced my mother, he would not have wanted his gutless actions widely known by his children, his grandchildren, his neighbors and friends. And the way gossip travels around this town, it wouldn't take long for everyone to know if I choose to drop a few well-placed words.''

The thought of Mac deliberately causing that kind of pain to so many people made her sick. She could understand his anger. She could even understand his desire for revenge. But to know that so many innocents would be hurt in the process—and that in the long run, nothing would really be accomplished... She just couldn't approve of that.

She didn't know what to say. She only knew that the entire situation broke her heart. But what hurt her the most was the fact that Mac had used her for his own purposes.

Though he didn't move, he seemed to physically withdraw from her. ''It's obvious whose side you're on.''

That brought her chin up again. ''I'm not on anyone's side. I won't be put in the middle of your private war, Mac. You've used me to this point, but I won't let you use me any longer.''

''It was more than that,'' he muttered.

''Was it?'' She kept her voice steady with an effort. ''Earlier tonight, I asked if you had a word to describe our relationship. You didn't. Do you have one now?''

Placing a hand on the back of his neck, he started to speak, then fell silent.

''I didn't think so.'' She turned on one heel toward the doorway.

''You're leaving?''

''Yes.'' She didn't look back. She didn't want

him to see the tears forming in her eyes. "Don't worry, Mac, I won't say anything about what I've learned here tonight. I won't interfere with your vendetta, but I won't help you, either. Whatever information you dig up now, you won't be getting it from me. And whatever you do with that information is entirely your decision. I only hope you make the right choice."

"What about the job?"

She couldn't believe he'd brought that up now. It was wounded pride that made her square her shoulders, turn, and face him without expression. "I'd recommend that you bring in a professional decorator from Atlanta. This time you'll probably want to hire someone on the basis of their training and experience, rather than their friendship with a family you want to destroy."

"That wasn't the reason I hired you," he said flatly. "When it comes to my jobs, I choose the best people—and you're the best. I'm holding you to your professional obligation."

"Fine," she snapped. "This assignment will look good on my résumé. I suppose it's only fair if I use you in this."

He inclined his head in an almost royal gesture. "Just do a good job."

"I always do." She turned and left, before she ruined her cool performance by bursting into tears.

BRAD FOUND Sharon crying Sunday evening. She had been proud of herself for not giving in to tears since she'd left Mac's house in the wee hours of the morning. But something made her think of him Sunday evening, after she thought Brad was in bed, and the floodgates opened despite her efforts.

She was sitting in the kitchen, an untouched cup of herbal tea in front of her. Her elbows resting on the table, she buried her face in her hands and sobbed quietly. It hurt so badly to think that she had risked so much and had been given so little in return. She hadn't been naive enough to think that he'd fallen in love with her at first sight, but she'd thought there was something real between them. Something that had a chance of lasting forever.

She'd obviously been more naive than she'd thought.

She'd been nothing more to him than a pawn in a calculated quest for revenge. Because of his manipulation, she had unwittingly aided his assault on her friends. It hurt so much she wasn't sure she could bear it.

"Sharon? What's wrong? What's happened?" There was a note of panic in Brad's voice as he spoke from the doorway behind her. He had seen her cry so rarely that he must have assumed something terrible had happened.

She caught her breath and mopped at her face with her hands. "It's okay, Brad," she said, trying to speak reassuringly. "Nothing's wrong."

"You're crying."

"I'm just feeling sad this evening. Women do that sometimes."

He didn't buy it. "Something's happened. Someone's hurt you. It's Cordero, isn't it? What did he do?"

She sighed. "Brad, please. Let it go."

"Did he say something about me?"

"It wasn't about you. It had nothing to do with you."

"But he said *something*."

"We had a disagreement. My feelings were hurt, but I'll recover, okay? Things like this just happen sometimes."

"So you won't be seeing him anymore?" Brad asked hopefully.

"I'm still working for him on the Garrett house renovation. But our relationship is strictly professional from now on."

"Why don't you just tell him to stuff his renovation job?"

"Because I have a business to run. And a professional reputation to uphold. I can't just walk away from a business commitment in a huff because the client hurt my feelings."

"I told you about that guy. I told you he wasn't as cool as you and everyone else thought he was."

Funny that her first instinct was still to defend Mac. He and his mother had suffered a great deal because of his father's callous abandonment. His mother certainly wasn't blameless in the affair, but Mac had admittedly adored her. He had owed her everything. It was only natural that he would want to defend her. And if he'd also lost a child not long after his mother passed away, then it made sense, knowing him, that he would turn that grief to anger.

She couldn't blame him for wanting to lash out at his absentee father. But she wouldn't excuse him for being willing to hurt so many other people in the process. She hadn't deserved to be one of his casualties.

"There are some things about Mac you don't understand," she told her brother quietly. "He isn't as bad as you think."

Brad snorted in disgust. "You've still got a thing for him, don't you? Even after he made you cry."

Wearily, she rubbed her aching temples. "Brad, please. I don't want to talk about this tonight. You're supposed to be in bed."

"I was thirsty."

It was a late-night foray for water that had caused Sharon such pain in the first place, she couldn't help remembering. "Get a drink and then go back to bed. We'll talk again tomorrow," she said.

"But—"

"Brad. Please."

He grumbled, but poured himself a glass of water. Downing it quickly, he set the glass aside, then paused by her chair to awkwardly pat her shoulder. "The guy ain't worth crying over, sis. He'll get his, don't you worry."

"Just stay away from him, Brad. Please. For my sake."

He muttered something she didn't quite catch and moved on toward the doorway.

Sharon watched him leave with a worried frown. She really hadn't handled that well, she thought. He had caught her off guard, at a time when she wasn't thinking clearly enough to deal with him. She had messed everything up today, she thought with a dispirited sigh.

She didn't know what it was going to take to get her life back on the comfortable track she had established before Mac Cordero came to town.

CHAPTER FIFTEEN

THERE WAS ALWAYS a lot of time to think during a stakeout. Mac had gotten some of his best ideas while sitting in a car or at a window, waiting for something that might or might not happen.

On this particular Friday night, he was sitting in a deeply shadowed hollow beneath a huge oak tree on the outskirts of the property surrounding the Garrett house. It was almost midnight and he'd been sitting there an hour, so he'd had plenty of time to think. Not that he hadn't already done far too much thinking in the six days that had passed since Sharon stormed out of his kitchen.

It was a clear, fragrant evening, the light breeze just slightly cool against his face. Only a slice of moon floated in the inky sky, so the shadows were deep, hiding their secrets in darkness. Mac knew he was just as well concealed in his black shirt and jeans. A part of the summer night, with secrets of his own to hide. Somewhere above him, an owl hooted, sounding as if it was mocking him as the fool he knew himself to be.

He hadn't seen Sharon since she'd walked out of his apartment. He knew she'd been avoiding him—and, to be honest, he'd been doing the same. He still couldn't remember the hurt in her eyes without flinching. He hadn't been able to tell her that he hadn't used her—because, truth was, he had. And, worse, he had done it intentionally.

He hadn't meant to fall in love with her in the process.

She'd wanted him to put a name to what he felt for her, to convince her that it was more than sex, more than convenience. He hadn't spoken because he hadn't known what to say. His track record with commitment was lousy. He'd already hurt her once, he didn't want to risk doing so again. Her brother hated him, and so would her friends if they found out why he was here. It was a hopeless relationship—and Sharon deserved better.

In a way, it had been very unselfish on his part to let her go before he hurt her again, he told himself. So why did he still feel like such a slug? Like someone who belonged in the shadows, hidden away from the sunlight?

Why did it still hurt so badly to think of her walking away from him?

A sound behind him made him tense. Sitting absolutely still, he listened as the voices grew closer. He recognized one as Brad Henderson's.

"I'm not sure about this, Jimbo. I think maybe we'd better—"

"Come on, Brad, you're not chickening out, are you? Not now."

"It's just—well, what if we get caught? What if Tommy's mom finds out we snuck out?"

"We won't get caught. Trust me. Me and Tommy know what we're doing. His mom sleeps like the dead when she takes one of her pills, and Tommy watched her take one tonight. And we've got Gil on our side."

"I don't know—"

Another boy spoke this time, his voice gruff with impatience. "C'mon, Brad, you hate this guy. You said he deserved this."

"It's going to be a piece of cake, Brad." Jimbo, again. "We use these bolt cutters to cut the locks on the storage building, help ourselves to the best tools, and then we'll have a little fun in the house. Gil said that fancy glass is leaded. Original. *Real* hard to replace. That'll show Cordero what happens when he pushes us around."

"I don't have a problem with breaking his windows," Brad muttered. "He deserves that for being such a jerk. But the stealing...I didn't know you guys were involved with that."

"Don't get preachy on us, Brad," Jimbo warned. "We haven't taken anything from anybody who didn't have insurance to cover it. And you sure have liked it that we've had extra money to spend on food and arcade games and movies and stuff. You didn't worry about where the money came from when we were spending it, did you?"

"Well, maybe—but the Porter place, guys. I didn't know it was you driving that van. My sister could've been killed."

"I told you—I didn't mean for that to happen. I

panicked, okay? I'd never driven a van like that before. But she's okay now. And you're making up for it tonight. You said this bastard made her cry. Here's your chance to make *him* pay.''

Mac felt like the bastard they had called him— the bastard he was—when he thought of Sharon crying over him. She hadn't deserved that. She didn't deserve this, either. His anger with her brother grew.

''I don't know,'' Brad said again, and there was temptation as well as fear in his voice.

''I'm tired of this,'' the third boy announced flatly. ''Let's do it, guys. Brad, are you with us or not?''

''He's with us. Ain't you, Brad?''

''Yeah. I—I guess so. Just give me a minute, okay? You guys go on and I'll meet up with you.''

''He's backing out,'' the other boy announced scornfully.

''No, I'm not. Really. I just—I just need to pee, okay? I'll be there in a minute.''

''You better. Come on, Jimbo. Let's do it.''

''Right with you, man. Don't let us down, Brad.''

Mac listened while the other boys moved toward the house. Brad stayed where he was, cursing frantically beneath his breath, obviously torn between joining his friends and making a run for it. Feeling as if fate had stepped in to give him a break, Mac decided it was time for him to assist the boy in his decision making.

Brad never had a warning. Mac had an arm around him and a hand over his mouth before the kid knew he wasn't alone. It wasn't hard for Mac to overpower the skinny, panic-stricken teenager. "Be still before you get hurt," he said quietly into Brad's ear. "You know who I am, don't you?"

Brad nodded stiffly.

"Your friends are walking straight into Chief Davenport's arms. He's waiting for them behind my storage building. He'll probably let them cut the lock before he moves in, just to make sure of what they're up to. And then he'll put them behind locks they won't be able to cut."

Brad groaned.

"I'm giving you a break, kid. Not because I think you deserve it. To be honest, I think it would do you a world of good to spend some time in juvenile detention. But you see, I know that would devastate your sister. And unlike you, that matters very much to me."

Brad moved sharply, forcing Mac to tighten his grip. "Don't argue with me, boy. If you really cared about your sister, you wouldn't be here doing something that you know would break her heart. You wouldn't be hanging out with a guy who trashes her reputation. The same guy who almost killed her less than a month ago. What kind of man chooses a jerk like that over his own family? You're damn lucky to have a sister like Sharon. You should be her defender, not one of the people who hurts her."

Brad jerked his mouth free of Mac's hand. "*You* hurt her. You made her cry."

"You're right," Mac said evenly. "And I deserve

every name you want to call me. But you're her brother.''

Brad couldn't answer that.

''We're too far out of town for you to walk safely back at this hour. My truck is parked a hundred yards up the road from here. Go wait in it for me. The keys are in my pocket, but I left the doors unlocked. You should recognize the truck. It's the one with the big, ugly scratch down one side.''

Brad muttered something Mac didn't even try to catch.

''Unless you want to join your friends with Chief Davenport, of course. But I wouldn't recommend it. From what I heard, they deserve what they're going to get. You just squeaked by. Now, I can take you home to your sister or I can turn you over to the cops. Your call.''

''I'll wait in your truck,'' Brad conceded grudgingly.

''That's the first smart choice I've seen you make yet, boy.'' Cautiously, Mac released him, half prepared for him to run. But Brad only stood there, his head down, his shoulders slumped, looking suddenly younger than his fifteen years.

''Get in the truck,'' Mac urged. ''I'm going to make sure everything's taken care of at the house. I'll drive you home when I'm finished.''

''Are Jimbo and Tommy really going to jail?''

Mac hardened his voice. ''If you're tempted to feel sorry for them, spend the time while you're waiting for me thinking about how easily your sister could have drowned in Snake Creek.''

Without comment, Brad shuffled off toward Mac's truck.

Mac found Wade and two of his officers beside the storage building, Jimbo and Tommy handcuffed between them. Jimbo was sniveling, Tommy looked sullen and defiant.

Mac spoke to Wade. "Looks like you got your perps."

"Yeah. Got 'em just as they were about to help themselves to your tools."

Clicking his tongue, Mac shook his head at the boys. "Now, is that any way to treat a guest in your hometown?"

They both glared at him.

Turning his back to them, Mac looked at Wade again. "Thanks for tipping me off, Chief. I am, most definitely, pressing charges."

"No kidding. Uh—we rather expected to catch more than two of them."

Keeping his expression impassive, Mac shrugged. "I guess their friends had enough sense not to get involved in this."

"I'm glad to hear it."

Mac was aware that Officer Gilbert Dodson was notably absent from the crime scene. "I'm sorry about your man, Wade. It always gets you when a cop goes bad, doesn't it?"

His face strained, Wade nodded. "Yeah. It does."

"If you don't need me for anything else right

now, I've got an errand to run. I'll see you sometime tomorrow."

"Yeah. See ya', Mac."

Brad was waiting in the truck, slumped down on the seat, the most miserable kid Mac had seen in a long time. He climbed behind the wheel and slammed his door. "Your buddies are in cuffs. Be glad you aren't."

"I am." The admission was made grudgingly. "I guess I should thank you for what you did for me."

Mac started the engine. "I didn't do it for you, remember?"

"I know. You did it for Sharon."

"Fasten your seat belt." He drove the truck onto the road and headed for town.

"Are you going to tell her?" Brad asked after a tense pause.

"Don't you think I should?"

The boy looked down at his tightly entwined hands.

Mac gave him another minute to worry, then said, "I'm not going to tell her. The whole point of this is to keep her from finding out what a moron you almost were."

Though he obviously resented Mac's blunt words, Brad was hardly in a position to protest. "What about when she hears about Jimbo and Tommy? If they're going to jail, everyone will be talking about it."

"And she knows you started the evening in their company. You're just going to have to tell her you found out what they were planning and chose to go home rather than get involved with something you knew was wrong. Don't lie to her, just stick to that story.''

Brad looked out the passenger window as Mac turned onto the street where he lived. He waited until Mac parked in the driveway before saying, ''If you hadn't stopped me, I'd have been in jail right now.''

''Are you just figuring that out?''

''No. I just—well, thanks, okay? I really didn't want to go to jail. I didn't have anything to do with those other break-ins, I swear. I didn't even know Jimbo was involved until he told me tonight. He didn't think I'd go along with them before, but he thought I might tonight.''

''Because it was my place they were hitting this time.''

''Yeah.''

''They thought you hated me enough to help them. Then once they had you involved, it would have been easy enough for them to continue to control you by threatening to turn you in for this one.''

''I guess.''

''Trust me, that's how it works. I've seen it a hundred times. That's how Gilbert Dodson was able to get the kids to steal for him. He got them involved, strung them along with money and gifts, then coerced them into staying with him. Not that your buddies tonight seemed to need much coercion.''

"I didn't know Officer Dodson was crooked. I thought he was a straight-up cop. I knew a lot of the guys liked to hang out with him, but I thought he was just…you know, mentoring them or something."

Sensing that the boy was still badly shaken from his near brush with the law, Mac kept his voice calm and steady. "He 'mentored' them straight into jail. Even cops can go bad when they let greed and stupidity take over. They start feeling superior to everyone else, for one reason or another, and they begin to think the rules that apply to ordinary folks don't apply to them."

"Jimbo told me tonight that they only stole from people who were jerks. And everyone had insurance, so nobody really lost anything."

"Do you agree with that line of reasoning?"

After only a moment, Brad shook his head.

"The insurance companies lose—and so do the people who have to pay higher rates. The crime victims who have to pay deductibles and then scramble to replace their belongings lose. You saw what your sister had to go through to replace her car and the things in it. It cost her quite a bit—and it wasn't her fault."

"I don't need the lecture. I didn't steal anything. I wouldn't have gone through with it tonight. Even against you. I've been raised better than that. But I probably would have gotten into trouble, anyway, because I'd have run after them and tried to stop them. Nobody would've believed me."

"Probably not."

Brad sighed wearily. "Jimbo said you wanted me out of the way so I wouldn't interfere with you chasing after my sister. He said you would do anything you could to come between us. He said if I hassled you enough, you'd decide she wasn't worth it and you would leave us alone."

"If I wanted you out of the way, I'd have let Chief Davenport haul you off tonight, now, wouldn't I?"

"Yeah. I guess."

"Yeah. Go on in now. It's late. And don't scare your sister. Ring the bell and let her know who you are."

"I will." Brad didn't seem to know quite what to say at that point. Mac knew the kid still had major issues with him. He was obviously torn between his previous dislike and his gratitude that he'd been spared a traumatic ordeal.

"Go on in, Brad," Mac repeated quietly.

Brad apparently decided they'd said enough. He opened the door and slid out of the truck.

"Brad?" Mac spoke before the boy closed the door.

"Yeah?"

"This is two strikes against you now. Three strikes and you're out. Is that clear?"

"There won't be another one."

"Make sure of that."

Showing he wasn't entirely cowed by the events

of the evening, Brad shut the door with somewhat more force than necessary.

Mac backed out of the driveway, then stopped a few yards down the deserted street until he saw Sharon open the front door to her brother. Then he drove off quickly, hoping she hadn't spotted him. It would be difficult for Brad to explain how he'd ended up riding home in Mac's truck without telling her exactly where they'd met up.

Maybe he'd done something good tonight, he mused as he headed for his apartment. Maybe he'd put a confused kid on the right path. Or maybe by letting Brad off the hook tonight, he'd only contributed to the development of a juvenile delinquent.

All he knew for certain was that, whatever the results of his actions, he had done it all for Sharon.

He owed her that much, at least.

BY SATURDAY AFTERNOON, Mac had decided to leave town.

Though it wasn't the way he preferred to do business, he could oversee the renovation project from a distance, leaving a foreman in charge of the day-to-day supervision. Maybe the job wouldn't be handled with his usual, almost obsessive attention to detail, but it would be adequately completed. He could then put the place up for sale and forget he'd ever started this futile quest.

That would probably be the best move for everyone, he thought with the memory of Sharon's smile haunting the shadowy back corners of his mind.

He stood in the master bedroom of the Garrett house. The workers had all left for the afternoon and the house was still, the silence as heavy as Mac's mood. Since most of the work to this point had been upstairs and in the kitchen, this room had hardly been touched. It still looked almost exactly the same as it had the first time he'd seen it.

Sharon loved this room. The big fireplace. The high ceiling. The wide, detailed moldings. The wooden floor that would soon gleam with a satiny sheen again. She'd confided to him that she saw this room decorated in lace and antiques. A decorative white-iron bed. Old stained-glass shades on bedside lamps. A thick, handmade rug on the floor.

She wouldn't actually be choosing the furniture for the house, of course—that would be up to the future owner. But she'd already talked about the wallpaper and lights she would select, as well as the fixtures for the attached bath. She'd made him see it all so clearly.

He could picture it now as he stood there alone in the dust and the shadows. The soft lights. The fire. The big bed, rumpled from lovemaking. The mental image made him yearn for things he couldn't quite identify—or perhaps he just didn't have the nerve to try.

A sound from behind him brought him out of his lonely thoughts. Someone was in the house with him. Though he wasn't expecting anyone in particular, Trent McBride had said he might stop by with a sample cabinet door for his approval.

Yet somehow he knew it wasn't Trent. He turned very slowly to face the door and wait for her.

Sharon looked a bit uncertain as she stepped into the room, her gaze locking immediately with his. She wore a sleeveless, scoop-neck, pale yellow knit dress. That particular shade of yellow was her favorite color. He knew that small detail about her—along with so many other tidbits he'd filed into his memory. Like the faintly floral scent of her shampoo. The way her pulse fluttered in her throat when he kissed her there. The way her fingers twined in his hair when he made love to her, and twined together in front of her when she was nervous.

They were entwined that way now, her knuckles almost white with the pressure she exerted on them.

"How did you know where to find me?" he asked, realizing she had walked directly to this room.

The question seemed to confuse her a little. "I don't know."

It wasn't important, of course. "Why are you here?"

"I need to talk to you."

"What about?"

He watched her take a deep breath, the movement stretching her thin knit dress across the breasts he had kissed until she sighed with pleasure. He raised his gaze from them with an effort.

"Brad told me what you did for him. I don't quite know how to thank you."

"Er—what did he tell you?" he asked cautiously, uncertain of what he should say.

"Everything," she answered simply. "Starting with keying the side of your truck and ending with you stopping him before he broke into your place last night."

He was frankly surprised. "Did he now?"

"Yes. If it wasn't for you, Brad would be in jail today. Maybe he deserved to be—but I'm so very glad he didn't have to go through that. We owe you so much—"

"You owe me nothing," he said flatly. "I heard the boys talking. I knew Brad had not been involved in any of the previous break-ins. I could tell he was being led into something that deep down he wanted no part of. I just helped him make the right choice. I'm surprised he told you, though."

"He said he needed to. He was so shaken by what almost happened that I don't think he slept a wink last night. He cried when he told me about it. He was so disappointed in Jimbo and Tommy and Mike—another boy who'd been involved in the previous break-ins. So disillusioned by Officer Dodson's involvement. And so stunned and grateful for what you did for him, even after the way he had treated you."

"I told him I didn't do it for him."

"I know." She took a couple of steps toward him, her eyes holding his. "He told me that, too. He said you did it for me. But I think you did it for both of us."

Even though she stood close enough for him to catch a faint scent of her floral shampoo, he didn't reach out to touch her. He had to fist his hands in his pockets to stop himself from trying. Gratitude and indebtedness were not what he wanted from Sharon—even though he still didn't know what, exactly, he did want.

She seemed perplexed by his silence. She cleared her throat. "Brad didn't know how you and Wade learned of the boys' plans last night."

"Wade got a tip. One of the kids spouted off to a friend, who got a conscience and told his father the whole story. Wade had already been following his own hunch on Dodson and he found a storage-warehouse in Carollton with a unit full of stuff taken in area break-ins. The unit had been rented under an assumed name, but the storage warehouse owner identified Dodson from a photograph. As for last night—the kid with the big mouth had been bragging about what they were going to do to the 'cocky Latino' who'd come to town and stirred up so much trouble. So Wade was ready for them last night."

"And Wade told you?"

"He heard they might try to pull Brad in because of his antagonism toward me. Because of my friendship with you—and his own—he gave me a chance to intercede. Had Brad gotten all the way to the storage building with the other kids, there would have been nothing Wade could do. He was already skirting the ethical line to bring me in."

"I'll have to thank him—"

"No. As far as Wade knows officially, Brad was never there. I've never confirmed that he was, nor will I. The other boys won't say anything, and even if they do, they have nothing on him. Brad was never involved. Let's leave it at that."

Her eyes were so sad and troubled, it made his chest ache to look at her. He wanted very badly to reach out to her. He contented himself with smoothing a strand of hair away from her face. His fingertips brushed her warm, flushed skin, and the temptation was strong to press his lips to hers, but he restrained himself.

If he kissed her now, and she responded, he couldn't know if it was only gratitude motivating her actions. He couldn't accept that.

He dropped his hand, shoving it back into his pocket.

Sharon moistened her lips, as if she sensed how close he had come to kissing them. And then she spoke again, her voice firmer this time. "Brad *was* involved in damaging your truck. He said he let Jimbo goad him into it because of a confrontation they had with you. One they felt they lost."

"I've always known it was Brad. I saw him."

"But you didn't pursue it. Again, for my sake."

He merely shrugged.

Her chin lifted in a show of pride. "I'm sorry I didn't listen to you. And I *am* going to pay for your repairs."

"You are not paying for anything and that's the end of it. If Brad makes the offer, I'll let him work it off doing cleanup around the site. I won't take money from him that he would probably get from you, anyway.''

She didn't look entirely satisfied, but she let it drop. Wrapping her arms at her waist, she chewed her lower lip, looking as though she couldn't decide what to say next. The distance between them seemed suddenly more pronounced than the three feet or so that separated them physically.

He hated it.

"Caleb and Bobbie McBride got back in town this morning. I don't know if you heard."

"No. But I knew they were due soon." He wished she hadn't brought up the McBrides, reminding him of the biggest area of contention between them. It still stung that she'd so quickly taken their side, that she had seemed so judgmental of him for pursuing a goal she didn't approve of. It appeared that the McBrides had everything—including Sharon's loyalty and affection.

And if he kept thinking along those lines, he would digress into maudlin self-pity, he thought with a touch of disgust.

Her head lowered now, she looked up at him through her lashes. "Have you decided what you're going to do? Are you going to ask Caleb if he's your father?"

"I'm leaving town," he said abruptly. "I'll probably be gone by the middle of next week."

Sharon looked to be in shock. "You're leaving?" she repeated, staring at him.

He nodded. "I'll pick a foreman to be in charge of the project. I thought I'd ask Trent if he's interested in the job. Then I'll check in with him every day or two for reports, and make a personal visit every few weeks. Any decorating problems you encounter or questions that come up, you'd talk to him, and he'll relay them to me. The same with the other subcontractors."

"But, Mac, why? Why do you have to leave?"

"Because of the nature of this town," he answered bluntly. "If I stay here, renovating my grandparents' house, working side by side with my cousins or siblings or whatever the hell they are to me, something's liable to get out. You figured out why I came here, there's a chance others might do the same. Maybe I wanted to hurt someone when I came here, but that doesn't matter now. There are too many innocents in the line of fire. Too little to be gained by continuing. You win. The McBrides win. It's time for me to retreat."

Looking distressed, she reached out to him, laying a hand on his arm, her fingers curling into the thin fabric of his shirt. "I can't agree with you," she said. "There's no reason anyone should ever find out the truth, unless you want them to. All you have to do is put away your notes and be discreet. You have so much invested in this project. You know you want to see it through."

He looked at her hand on his arm, thinking how easy it would be to pull her against him and crush her mouth beneath his. His voice was just a bit hoarse when he said, "I'm not leaving entirely because of the McBrides. It's also because of you."

Her fingers clenched spasmodically. "Why because of me?" she whispered.

"I've caused you enough trouble. I don't want to make you feel awkward around your friends. Or around me."

Her eyes suddenly swam beneath a sheen of moisture. His heart twisted as she leaned toward him, her lips slightly parted, her gaze beseeching. "Mac, I—"

From the front of the house came a sudden heavy pounding on the door. Drawn so abruptly out of their tense exchange, both of them jumped and turned instinctively in that direction.

"That's probably Trent," Mac said, raising a hand to the back of his neck, which had tightened almost painfully. "He said he might stop by."

Her head down, Sharon took a step back from him. "I guess I'd better go. I just…I just wanted to thank you."

"It wasn't necessary. But it's good to see you," he added, thinking again how pretty she looked. She brightened the dark, gloomy room just by standing in it in her pale yellow dress. The only drawback was knowing she would soon be gone again.

Without speaking, she walked with him to the front door. Mac couldn't think of anything to say. He assumed the same was true for Sharon.

They were both struck truly speechless when he opened the door to find Caleb McBride standing on the other side.

CHAPTER SIXTEEN

SHARON FELT her heart stop when she recognized the man on Mac's doorstep. What was Caleb doing here? Had he somehow found out why Mac was in Honoria?

"Sharon," he said, spotting her with a bright smile. "This is a nice surprise."

"It's good to see you, too, Caleb," she said, presenting her cheek for his kiss of greeting. "How was your vacation?"

"Bobbie enjoyed it," he said, his expression wry. "I found it very pleasant, but I was ready to come home about a week ago."

"I'm sure you couldn't wait to get back to work," Sharon teased lightly, though from the corner of her eye she watched Mac watching them.

Mac had to be asking himself the same question that kept repeating in her mind. Why was Caleb here? She had no doubt that Mac recognized the older man; he'd done his homework quite thoroughly. How did it feel, she couldn't help wondering, for Mac to meet his uncle for the first time this way?

Caleb turned to Mac and extended his hand. "I'm

sorry. I was distracted by your lovely guest. I'm Caleb McBride.''

Sharon thought Mac hesitated for a fraction of a moment before taking Caleb's hand. "Mac Cordero," he said. "It's nice to meet you."

"I hope you'll forgive the surprise visit. My curiosity made me impatient. My mother grew up in this house, which is why I was very intrigued when I heard you planned to restore it. And especially since my son is a member of your renovation team."

"A valued member," Mac said graciously. "Your son does beautiful woodwork. It's hard to find anyone these days who puts so much time and effort into his work."

"Yes, he's very talented. We're quite proud of him."

Standing to one side of them, Sharon thought Caleb appeared to be watching Mac very closely, studying his face as if something there intrigued him. Or was she letting her imagination run away with her?

"Is your contracting business based here in Georgia, Mac?" Caleb asked.

Mac nodded. "I was born and raised in Savannah. I still maintain a home there."

For some reason, Sharon found herself holding her breath as she watched Caleb's expression change. The genial, country-lawyer smile he always wore so easily seemed to slide off one side of his face. Her breath left her in one long, shaky sigh.

"I once knew a woman in Savannah whose name

was Cordero,'' Caleb murmured, his voice not quite steady. ''Anita Cordero.''

As still as he was, Mac could have been carved from wood. There was no expression on his face. And Sharon thought she might be the only person in Honoria who could read the emotion in his eyes. ''Anita Cordero was my mother.''

Caleb swallowed audibly. ''Was?''

''She died three years ago.''

''I'm very sorry to hear that.'' Caleb lifted a hand to wipe his mouth. His fingers shook. ''Your—er— father. Is he still living?''

''I don't know. I never met him.''

''Do you mind if I ask how old you are?''

''I'm thirty-three.''

''My God.'' Caleb put out a hand to press it against the nearest wall.

Sharon reached out to him quickly. ''Caleb?'' She glanced worriedly at Mac. ''He had a heart attack two years ago.''

''No.'' Caleb held up his free hand. ''I'm all right. Just…shaken.''

Mac took a small step forward, looking worried. ''Do we need to call for medical help?''

Still holding the wall, Caleb ignored the question. ''Why did you come to Honoria, Mac?'' he asked, his voice husky.

Mac looked at Sharon. She shrugged helplessly. He drew a deep breath. ''I came to find some an- swers. I had no real plan about what to do with them once I found them.''

Caleb couldn't seem to take his gaze off Mac's face. "You have your mother's features. Her eyes."

"I know." As if he was becoming overwhelmed by all the emotion in the room, Mac stuffed his hands in his pockets. "I don't imagine I look at all like my father's family."

Seeming to gather his strength, Caleb straightened, his voice steadier now. "Sharon, dear, I wonder if you would excuse us for a little—"

"No." Mac's tone was sharp as he took a step closer to her. "Sharon knows my story. She stays."

Sharon looked uncertainly from one man to the other. "I don't mind," she said. "We can talk later, Mac."

"No." He reached out to take her hand, and despite his almost arrogant tone, something about the gesture was oddly pleading. As if he needed her with him. There was no way, of course, that she could leave now. She nodded and curled her fingers around his.

Caleb glanced at those locked hands, and at Sharon's face for a moment. Then he turned to Mac. "I met Anita Cordero almost thirty-five years ago. I was consulting on a very lengthy, complicated legal case in Savannah, and it was necessary for me to stay in a hotel room for weeks at a time. My marriage was going through a difficult period and Anita became very special to me. I wanted to spend the rest of my life with her—and then my wife told me she was pregnant."

With Tara, Sharon thought, her heart in her throat. Dear God, Caleb McBride was Mac's father.

Caleb continued firmly. ''My wife and I had tried for several years to have a baby, but we'd begun to believe it would never happen. Her announcement staggered me. She was carrying my first child—and I was in love with another woman. I told Anita everything. She told me I had to go home to my wife. She wouldn't break up a family, she said. She told me that we were never meant to be together. That the time we'd shared was never really ours. And then she asked me never to call her again. She made me promise I would never look back. And she became furious when I stupidly offered to send her money. She was a very strong-willed woman. And I was a very weak-willed man.''

He must have been attracted to strong women, Sharon thought. Bobbie was one of the most domineering women she'd ever met. Everyone had always thought Caleb and Bobbie's marriage worked so well because he very contentedly allowed her to have her own way. Sharon had never dreamed that Caleb had concealed so much behind that fatherly-lawyer image he had perfected.

''She never told me about you,'' Caleb finished, looking straight into Mac's eyes. ''I never knew.''

So Mac's father hadn't deliberately abandoned him. He had never known he left a son behind when his love affair ended. Did knowing that ease any of the hurt and anger Mac had carried around for so long?

Mac sighed very faintly. "You never looked back." It wasn't a question.

"I tried very hard not to," Caleb corrected him. "It was all Anita asked of me. I've made a good life for myself here with my practice and my family, I'll admit that. But I can't say that I never looked back."

Mac's fingers tightened almost imperceptibly around Sharon's, as though seeking strength for what he needed to say next. "Just over two years ago, I lost my six-week-old son to a very rare genetic birth defect. A problem with his blood. The doctors told me the condition was hereditary, that it would have shown up somewhere in my family history. Does that sound familiar to you?"

Looking understandably distressed by Mac's loss, Caleb shook his head adamantly. "There's absolutely no history of genetic birth defects on either side of my family. I would know if there was."

Sharon hoped Mac had found some comfort in that reassurance. She couldn't imagine the pain he must have gone through when he'd lost his child. The anguish of not knowing whether it had been his absent father who had passed on that gene.

Still without expression, Mac nodded. "Then you've answered all the questions I had when I came here. There's no need for you to worry. I no longer need the revenge I once thought I wanted."

Caleb wiped his face with his hand again. "Mac—she named you Mac?"

"Miguel Luis. She called me Mac—after you, I

know now, though she never told me your name. When she died, I learned that my father was a McBride from Honoria. I didn't know until you told me that it was you, and not one of your brothers.''

"So you literally came here on a private quest for answers. That must have taken a great deal of courage.''

Mac shrugged. "I just needed to know.''

"Your mother was a very special woman, Mac. I'm sorry I caused her, and you, so much pain with my weaknesses.''

"My mother bore part of the blame—but you're right. She was very special. She gave me a good life.''

"I'm happy to hear that. And now that we all know the truth—''

Mac broke in with a shake of his head. "My mother didn't want to break up your family, and neither do I. I've met all your children and your grandchildren. They're nice people. From what I've heard, your wife is a fine woman. There's no need to hurt any of them by stirring up the past. I plan to leave town soon. You needn't worry that I'll cause you any trouble.''

Still holding Mac's hand, Sharon rested her free hand on his forearm, bringing them closer together. It had been a very gracious concession. She was as proud of him as she was saddened for him.

This time it was Caleb who shook his head. "I intend to tell Bobbie the whole story. Our children, too. Your siblings have a right to know that they have another brother, and you deserve to get to know them. I've lost thirty-three years of my eldest son's life. I don't want to waste any more time.''

Sharon felt her eyes well with fresh tears. The emotion in Caleb's voice was so strong, so touching that it went straight to her heart. Was Mac equally affected?

The gruffness of his voice told her that he was. ''I doubt that either your wife or Trevor would appreciate hearing you refer to me as your 'eldest son.'''

''Bobbie will have the most difficult time with it, of course,'' Caleb admitted honestly. ''But she's a strong woman with a few old secrets of her own. We've made a comfortable life together here. She won't throw it away easily. As for Trevor—all of my children have big, generous hearts. And there is nothing they value more than family. You are their brother, Mac. Once you get to know them, you'll understand how important that is to them.''

''And what about you?'' Mac challenged.

Caleb blinked rapidly. ''You're my son. Once you get to know *me,* you'll understand how important that is to me.''

Sharon could almost feel Mac begin to panic. ''I didn't come here to join your family,'' he said bluntly. ''I've gotten by just fine without a father, without siblings. It's too late for me to learn how to deal with them now. I think it would be best if we all just agree to keep this to ourselves.''

Caleb squared his shoulders, and Sharon realized

that Mac hadn't inherited all his stubbornness from his mother. "I let Anita talk me into leaving without looking back," he said. "I know now what a tragic mistake that was. I won't make it a second time. I'm telling my wife the truth. You do what you have to do, Mac—but I hope you'll choose to stay for a while. God knows you don't owe me a thing, but I'd like to find out if there's a chance you can ever forgive me."

Mac released Sharon's hand and stepped away from her, causing her arm to fall to her side. "I've hurt too many people in my life. I won't cause any more pain. You were all getting along just fine before I came here," he said, glancing at Sharon to include her. "You'll do the same again after I leave."

Sharon decided it was time for her to join the conversation. She faced Mac with her hands on her hips. "Don't you think it's up to us to decide how we were getting along before you came here? Maybe we think our lives will be better for having you in them."

"And if I think you're wrong?"

"Then maybe we'd like the right to try to change your mind." She stepped toward him and placed her hand on his rigid arm again. "You're a good man, Mac Cordero. You care about other people, even though you sometimes try to hide your feelings. But that stiff-necked pride of yours is only going to hurt you in the long run if you aren't very careful. It sounds as if you got it from your mother. But perhaps it would have been better for everyone if she hadn't let her own pride rule her actions.''

She knew she had taken a risk with even that slight criticism of his mother. To her relief, Mac didn't seem to take offense—maybe because he was simply too distracted by his own confused emotions.

''No one here is asking for any lasting commitments from you, Mac,'' she added gently. ''We only want the chance to get to know you better. To see what the future has to hold for us all.''

She hadn't forgotten that Caleb was there, that he heard every word she was saying. But reaching Mac now seemed much more important than protecting her own pride. Something told her that if she missed this chance, there might not be another one. And she wasn't willing to risk that.

''Maybe it's too late for me to be your father, Mac,'' Caleb added quietly. ''But I hope it's not too late for me to be your friend.''

Mac drew a deep breath, his shoulders seeming to relax a little. ''I need some time to think.''

''Of course.'' Caleb cleared his throat, then glanced at Sharon before looking back at Mac. ''It would take a very special man to win this fine young woman's heart. And a very foolish man to reject that gift. Since I have no right to offer you fatherly advice, I'll leave it at that.''

Mac only scowled, reminding Sharon very much at that moment of her notoriously stubborn younger brother.

''I'll see you both around,'' Caleb said after a

momentary pause, moving backward toward the door, his eyes still locked on Mac's face as if he was reluctant to look away. "I have some long-overdue things to take care of at home."

"Caleb—good luck." Sharon didn't know what else to say.

"Thank you, dear. Good luck to you, too."

Sharon suspected she was going to need it.

THE OLD HOUSE was almost eerily silent after Caleb left it. Filled with soundless echoes of raw, painful emotions. Sharon stood as still and quiet as one of the ghosts that probably haunted the place, watching Mac as though afraid he would disappear if she took her eyes off him.

He was filled with a sudden, bone-tired weariness. "I need a drink," he said. "I have some sodas in a cooler in the kitchen. Do you want one?"

She seemed only momentarily taken aback by the offer. "Yes, I'd like that."

He motioned for her to proceed him. He noted that she glanced over her shoulder a time or two on the way. Was she concerned that he would take the opportunity to escape while her back was turned? As tempting as that was in some ways, he had no intention of doing something like that. Not just yet.

The cooler was a small, electric unit he'd set in the kitchen to hold cold drinks for himself and the work crews. He didn't allow beer on his sites, but cold drinks, juices and water were always available. He noted automatically as he opened the door of the unit that the supply had been almost depleted. He would have to restock before the crew returned Monday morning.

"What do you want?" he asked Sharon.

She reached past him and took out a diet soda. He selected a beverage for himself, then closed the door. He popped the top on the can, then just stared at it, his thirst gone. Suddenly, he wasn't sure he could swallow.

"Mac?" Sharon set her own can on the plywood-covered countertop. "Are you okay?"

He avoided looking at her, uncertain what his expression might reveal. "I'm fine."

Very gently, she removed the untouched can from his lax fingers and set it beside her own. And then she went up on tiptoe and wrapped her arms tightly around him. He stiffened for a moment in surprise, but then gathered her closer and buried his face in her soft hair.

He was tired of fighting, tired of trying to resist her.

Without a word, she pressed a kiss to his throat. How could she know what he needed most right then? Could she actually read his mind, or had she learned him so well in such a short time?

She lifted her head to look at him, and pressed a cool hand against his warm cheek. Her smile was tremulous. Completely understanding. As if she knew what he was feeling even better than he did.

He lowered his mouth to hers, hesitating just before he made contact. She slid her hand to the back of his neck and brought their lips together. And he almost groaned with sheer pleasure. It had been days since he'd last kissed her. It felt like weeks.

Tenderness flared almost instantly into passion. Mac was almost consumed with the need to make love to her, to lose himself in her. To make the rest of the world disappear, leaving only the two of them in it.

Had he really thought he could walk away from her so easily? He knew now that he'd only been fooling himself.

He reached beneath the short hem of her dress, sliding his hands up her bare legs to her hips. His fingers curled in the fabric of her sheer panties, kneading her tight bottom. She really was perfect, he thought. Even her pale little appendectomy scar was perfect to him.

She moved in response to his touch, pressing against him, inflaming him further. The setting couldn't be more wrong for this. They were in a half-gutted old house, surrounded by the scent of sawdust. For Sharon, there should be flowers, candles, silk and lace. Someone better than a battered ex-cop with so much emotional baggage he practically needed a bellhop.

She didn't seem to care about any of that. Her mouth was as avid as his, her hands as greedy. And when he ripped off his shirt, draped it over the counter and lifted her onto it, she spread her knees eagerly so that he could step between them.

He took her there, on the counter, using protection

he carried in his pocket more from habit than anticipation. They didn't even undress, removing no more than necessary. It was rough and fast and awkward—and Mac had never needed anything more in his entire life.

His knees were weak when they finished. He had to brace himself against the counter on either side of her, his forehead resting against hers. His breathing was loud in his own ears, seeming to echo in the cavernous, empty kitchen.

When he was sure he could speak coherently, he said, "I didn't mean for that to happen."

Her arms were still around his neck, her face against his. "I know. But I'm glad it did."

He pulled back a few inches to look at her. "I didn't want gratitude from you before, Sharon. I don't want sympathy from you now."

She smiled and laid her hand against his face. "You always underestimate yourself."

He gave her a faint smile in return. "That isn't a mistake I'll ever make with you."

"See that you don't," she answered, her tone a little saucy.

He kissed her lingeringly, knowing he had just implicitly committed to staying in Honoria for a while. He didn't know what was going to happen, exactly—with the McBrides or with Sharon. But Sharon had asked him to give them all a chance to find out what the future held for them.

It seemed he still had at least one more question left to answer.

EPILOGUE

MAC STOOD in the master bedroom of the Garrett house, surveying the room with deep satisfaction. Above his head an old-fashioned ceiling fan turned lazily, stirring the humid, late-August air. Early-evening sunlight streamed through the windows and the paned glass door beside the big fireplace, casting a soft glow and extending his shadow across the gleaming wooden floor.

It was a beautiful room, he thought, almost begging for furniture and occupancy. His team had done a great job in here, as they had with the other parts of the house that had been completed thus far. The renovation was more than half finished. The place would be ready for habitation by Christmas.

"I thought I would find you in here. This seems to be your favorite place to think."

He turned with a smile to greet Sharon as she walked into the room. She had changed out of the fancy dress she'd worn to Trent's wedding earlier that day, and now wore jeans and a T-shirt, as he did. They had been invited to a casual dinner later at Caleb and Bobbie McBride's house with Tara and Trevor and their families. Trent and Annie had already left for their honeymoon. Sharon and Mac had decided to meet here, since Mac had wanted to check on some things that had been done that morning.

"There's a peaceful feeling in here. It does help me think," he admitted. "I believe it's my favorite room in the house."

"It's definitely mine." She wandered over to the fireplace, as she often did, and rested her hand on the mantelpiece, looking inside as if she could visualize a fire burning there, even on a very warm day like this one.

She belonged in this room, he mused, watching her. It suited her perfectly. Just as he had discovered how well his bed suited her in their past few weeks together.

He would soon find out if she agreed with him.

She spoke before he could. "The wedding was lovely, wasn't it?"

He felt his mouth twist. "Flowers and music and cute little kids in ruffled dresses. They'd have been just as married if they'd stood in front of a justice of the peace wearing shorts. From the expression on Trent's face most of the morning, I think that's exactly what he would have preferred."

Sharon laughed softly. "You men just don't appreciate romance."

He shrugged.

Her amusement faded into sincerity. "Thank you for going with me, Mac. I know you were reluctant, but I thought it was important for you to be there.

And I think Trent was glad you came, even though he can't admit it just yet.''

Mac's newly discovered half brothers were still having trouble getting over their anger that Mac had deceived them so thoroughly when he'd first arrived in town. Jamie had told Mac that Trevor was having trouble learning to trust people again after the painful scandal with his first wife and their fickle Washington, D.C. cronies. What he had seen as betrayal on Mac's part—and Caleb's—had hit him hard.

Trent, too, was still reeling from so many changes in his life. The end of his air force career, the occasionally inconvenient physical limitations resulting from his accident, his new career as a carpenter, falling so deeply in love for the first time in his footloose life—the acceptance of a half brother, one who just happened to be his employer, hadn't been easy for him. He hadn't understood why Mac had felt it necessary to approach them with such subterfuge, rather than simply making his agenda known from the start. It had been Caleb who had asked his sons to forgive Mac—and to try to understand what Mac had been through. How much he had suffered while they had grown up so loved and protected by the father Mac had never known.

Mac didn't want their sympathy—but he was beginning to want their acceptance. He was tired of being alone. He needed family. And he thought they would get there, eventually. It would just take time and patience, on all their parts. Today had been a giant step in the right direction.

"No matter how he grumbled about all the fuss, I've never seen Trent look happier," Sharon said, fully convinced that everything would work out for the best now that the truth was out.

Trent had looked more than happy, Mac mused. He'd looked deeply, thoroughly satisfied—as if he'd just been given everything he'd ever wanted.

It had been an interesting day, all in all. Mac had been aware that he had drawn almost as much attention as the bride and groom, at least from the unrelated guests in attendance. He'd been aware of them watching him, looking in vain for resemblances between him and the McBrides. Watching him with Sharon, wondering what was going on between them. Eavesdropping on his conversations with Caleb and Bobbie, curious about *that* relationship, as well.

Mac knew they hadn't heard anything to start the rumor mills running again. He and the McBrides had been congenial, friendly, polite. As for Bobbie— well, he'd never met a woman exactly like her. Quite frankly, she rather terrified him. Once she'd gotten over the shock of finding out who he was, she had brusquely decided to accept him. And for Bobbie McBride, acceptance included full entitlement to giving advice and directions—all for his own good, of course.

Despite his healthy wariness of the woman, Mac actually liked her, oddly enough.

As for Caleb—he was trying very hard to figure out how to be a new father to a fully grown man.

Their relationship was still awkward, to say the least—but a bond had formed. Though he was still cautious, and still dealing with a lot of old anger, Mac was beginning to have a tenuous hope that the bond would only grow stronger during the years ahead. He would never have the relationship with Caleb that Trevor and Trent had, of course—but maybe they could form their own connection. And maybe it would be a bonus for both of them in the long run.

Tara had had the hardest time dealing with Caleb's actions thirty-three years ago. She had to know that it was only because of her arrival that Caleb and Bobbie had stayed together back then. Mac suspected that she had idolized her father, placed him on a pedestal that no mere human was worthy of, and it hadn't been easy for her to learn that Caleb had flaws just like everyone else. But Mac believed the wounds would heal, again with time. Already Tara was making friendly overtures toward him, letting him know she held no grudges against him for what had been done to all of them so long ago. She was a strong and gracious woman, and she had a heart big enough to accept another brother once the bruises faded.

It was a strong family with very close ties. They would survive this scandal, just as they had weathered so many other trials in the past.

"Did you notice how happy Annie looked that her mother came to her wedding?" Sharon asked, running a fingertip along the mantel as if looking for dust. "She wasn't sure her mother would have the courage to defy her father, who disapproves so strongly of Annie's marriage, but I could tell she was thrilled to see her there. Maybe that family is healing, as well. It's important for families to learn to forgive and move on. To be together. I know I was glad to have my mother and Brad with me today, our family all together again to celebrate our friends' good fortune."

She wasn't just talking about Annie Stewart's family, of course, or her own. She was referring to the McBrides, as well—letting Mac know, as she had so many times before, that she believed it would all work out for the best. Her unflagging optimism was one of the things he admired most about her.

Changing the subject, she glanced up at the slowly turning ceiling fan. "They've done a wonderful job in here, haven't they? And the rest of the house is really shaping up fast. It will be ready to put on the market in no time."

"Do you think I would have any trouble selling it?" he asked, watching her closely.

"No." She sighed wistfully. "I'm sure it will sell very quickly. It's such a beautiful home."

"Still lusting after it for yourself?"

She wrinkled her nose as he reminded her of that early conversation between them. "Don't I wish."

"Do you wish that, Sharon? Would you be happy living in this house?"

Her smile faded as she turned to him. "I'm not quite sure what you're asking."

He cleared his throat, oddly nervous now. "I'm asking if you'd like to live here. With me. In this house. As my wife."

It wasn't the most coherent proposal in history. Definitely not the most poetic. He'd probably just confirmed her earlier declaration that he had no appreciation for romance. But if sincerity carried any weight with her, it had come directly from his heart.

Apparently, earnestness was as touching to her as frills and flowers. Her eyes filled with tears.

"*Don't* cry," he ordered with quick male panic. And then added uncertainly, "Unless that's a good thing, of course."

She dashed at her cheek with one hand, smiling shakily. "That depends."

"What do you mean? I just proposed to you."

She stayed where she was, watching him with a puzzling air of expectancy.

"Well? Are you accepting or not?"

"I don't know."

He frowned at her. "What do you mean, you don't know? Why don't you know?"

"You haven't told me yet why you're asking."

He sighed. Apparently, she was going to insist on the frills, after all. Once again, he spoke from his soul. "I'm asking you to marry me because I love you. I fell in love with you when I pulled you out of that river and I've fallen more in love with you every day since. I expect I'll continue to fall harder every day I'm fortunate enough to spend with you in the future. I want you to be my friend, my partner, my lover, and the mother of my children. I will give you my absolute loyalty and undying affection in return. I will be a good son-in-law to your nice, ditzy mother, and a big brother and role model for Brad. I believe I have a lot to offer you, Sharon—but so much more to gain if you say yes.''

He'd started her tears flowing again, but he didn't try to stop them this time. He'd figured out that they were, indeed, a good thing.

''You had me when you told me you love me,'' she whispered. And then she threw herself into his arms.

''Is *this* a yes?'' he asked, just to make sure.

''Yes. Definitely yes.''

He covered her mouth with his before she could change her mind.

COMPROMISING POSITIONS

VICKI LEWIS THOMPSON

VICKI LEWIS THOMPSON

With more than fifteen million books in print
worldwide, Vicki Lewis Thompson may well have
contributed to global warming. Her distinctive blend of
sizzle and humour has earned her awards with *Romantic
Times* and *Affaire de Coeur* magazines. She's also a seven-
time finalist for the Romance Writers of America's
coveted RITA® award. Living in Arizona, USA with
her husband and a very spoiled tuxedo cat, she spends
much of her time in the pool and is waiting for
someone to invent a waterproof laptop.

Look out for Vicki Lewis Thompson's super-sexy
Sensual Romance™ **The Nights Before Christmas**,
available November 2002!

Dedication:

To the members of the
Phoenix Desert Rose Chapter of RWA.
A more dedicated, hardworking bunch couldn't be
found. I'm honoured to be one of you.

CHAPTER ONE

IF ONLY somebody needed him.

Mick Farrell spun around in his secondhand office chair to keep from dying of boredom. The creak of the chair was the only sound in the office. The secondhand telephone sitting on his secondhand desk, a telephone with two lines to handle the overload, was silent. There was no overload.

As Mick stared into space, he pictured an imaginary meter running for rent and utilities on this nine-by-nine cubby, which he'd leased for a year. Air-conditioning alone cost a fortune, especially in the middle of a Phoenix summer.

A week ago he'd moved in the desk, the chair, an empty file cabinet and the telephone. He'd hung his karate certificates and awards on the wall, and when that hadn't seemed like enough firepower, he'd added his diploma from Arizona State to illustrate that he had brains as well as brawn.

His buddy Craig had suggested a cool poster or two, but Mick wasn't sure about that. Artwork on the walls might soften his image, and he wanted his clients to think of him as a tough guy. Craig had lent him two folding chairs that sat across from his desk in preparation for cradling the fannies of his clients.

But there were no clients, despite all the flyers he'd put on car windows in downtown Phoenix, the ads he'd run in the *Arizona Republic* and the notices he'd mailed to everyone he knew.

In all his preparation for starting his own bodyguard service, he'd never pictured sitting for a week with no calls. Okay, no business calls. He couldn't count calls from Craig or his sister Holly. Even his mother had called once to ask how it was going. He wished they wouldn't bother, because every time the phone rang, he got all excited, thinking he had a client on the line.

When fielding calls from friends and relatives, he had to admit nobody had hired him yet. Then they'd try to cheer him up by pointing out that a week wasn't very long, but their perkiness only made everything worse somehow.

They were right—a week wasn't very long. At least he hadn't thought so until he'd had to spend the seven days in this silent office waiting for the phone to ring. Whenever he left, like to get some take-out for lunch, he came back hoping the answering machine light on the phone would be blinking. Sometimes it was, and then it would turn out to be Craig or Holly or a wrong number.

He'd caught up on all the back issues of his karate magazines and each day he read the paper—all of the paper. That still left a lot of time on his hands. His slacks and dress shirt weren't the right outfit for serious karate practice, so instead he'd practiced drawing his .38 from the small holster strapped to his ankle.

He could only do that for so long before becoming cross-eyed with boredom. Guns weren't his thing and he'd only use it as a last resort, but he couldn't offer complete protection without it.

As a kid he would have loved the idea of spending a whole week teaching himself to be a quick-draw artist. But the thrill had definitely worn off that activity. He couldn't consider bringing in a TV or a sound system, either. He'd put his office address on those flyers, and he couldn't risk having somebody come in and discover him watching

Oprah or listening to his old Genesis albums. You never knew what could turn people off.

He really wanted this business to work. All his friends had found their niche in life, and even his little sister was happy as a clam with her bookstore job. He was the only one who hadn't figured out what he wanted to be when he grew up. This could be it. But first he needed clients.

After glancing at his watch and confirming that it was only 10:46 in the morning, he sighed and leaned back, his gaze fixed on the frosted glass window in the office door. His name wasn't on it. That would have taken yet another chunk of his savings, and he'd decided to wait until after his first assignment. Then he'd hire someone to paint his name on the window as a celebration of his first piece of business.

A shadow fell over the frosted glass.

His heart began to pound and he leaned forward, almost afraid to hope. The shadow wasn't very big, which ruled out Craig. It could still be Holly, although she was supposed to be working at the bookstore today.

The doorknob turned, and he grabbed the telephone receiver, a blank pad of paper and a pen. "I could probably work that in," he said while the dial tone droned in his ear.

The door opened and he pretended to be engrossed in his phone call as he scribbled his birth date on the paper and the first lines of the Gettysburg Address. The scent of perfume drifted toward him—not Holly's brand. Good.

He resisted the urge to glance up. "Let me double-check with my assistant and I'll get right back to you," he said with what he hoped was crisp efficiency. "Thanks for calling Farrell's Personal Bodyguard Service. Goodbye."

Keeping his eyes on the pad of paper, he wrote "The quick sly fox jumped over the lazy brown dog," tore the page from the pad and folded it in half before giving his attention to his visitor, his first potential client.

Then he blinked in surprise. Stacy Radcliffe—returned from the Big Apple. He hadn't seen Stacy since…since she'd flown back to Phoenix for Holly's college graduation four years ago.

She grinned at him, showing off those perfect pearly whites. "Hey, Mick."

"Hey, Stacy." For many reasons, Stacy Radcliffe made him uncomfortable. For one thing she was a babe, but off-limits because she was Holly's best friend. Holly had once said that she and Stacy knew everything there was to know about each other. That had clinched it for Mick. He wasn't about to get involved with somebody who would divulge all their activities to his little sister.

For another thing, Stacy was the only child of wealthy parents, and she'd never wanted for anything. While Mick and Holly had struggled financially to put themselves through college, Stacy had been treated to an all-expenses-paid education at a prestigious Manhattan school for the performing arts. Then Mommy and Daddy had subsidized her for the past several years while she tried to make it as a dancer on Broadway. Mick thought a woman of twenty-six should be earning her own way by now.

But the chief reason Stacy made him uneasy had to do with a secret. Twelve years ago she'd caught him in the high school parking lot one balmy spring night having a serious make-out session. That alone wouldn't have been so bad, considering he'd been eighteen and only doing what most guys his age did best. Unfortunately, he'd been doing it with the wife of the school board president in the back seat of the school board president's Lincoln Town Car.

The episode hadn't been his idea. He'd attracted Mrs. Robinson types ever since he'd turned sixteen, and in those early days he'd been tempted more than once. If Stacy hadn't shown up, he'd probably have done the deed with Cassandra Oglethorpe.

Stacy had been fourteen that year, a freshman like his sister. He'd figured she'd blab to everyone, including Holly, that he'd been making out with Cassandra Oglethorpe while Cassandra's husband presided over the April school board meeting. Cassandra had escaped the meeting for a cigarette break and had come over to watch Mick doing laps on the lighted track. Apparently those little gym shorts had given her ideas.

After Stacy had caught them, Mick had braced himself for the fallout, figuring Oglethorpe would pull his diploma at best, press charges at worst. Disappointing his parents had bothered Mick, but more than that he'd hated the idea of his baby sister becoming disillusioned about the brother she idolized.

The fallout had never arrived. Miracle of miracles, Stacy must have kept her mouth shut. Mick always wondered if she'd been saving it to use later. But poor Oglethorpe, fifteen years his wife's senior, had died of a heart attack not long ago, so Mick didn't think the scandal would have the same punch now.

All the same, he'd still rather not have anyone know, especially Holly. He didn't like Stacy carrying this secret about him when he didn't know when she might decide to reveal it.

He wondered if by any chance she was here to hire him as a bodyguard. As much as he needed the business, he hoped not. Guarding Stacy would be way too complicated.

"So where's your assistant?" she asked.

He didn't know what she was talking about. "What assistant?"

"The one you were going to check with before you accepted the assignment just now."

"Oh." He felt heat climbing up his neck. "I don't have one." He wished she didn't look so sexy standing there in her snug capris and a red top held up by two very skinny straps. She wore her brown hair shorter now. It used to fall around her shoulders and partially conceal her slender neck. Now there was plenty of golden skin to admire, and he was having a tough time ignoring the view.

She lifted her eyebrows. "So you made that up about an assistant?"

He'd forgotten how expressive she could be with those eyebrows. "Yeah." No need to tell her he'd made up the phone call, too. "I'd like people to think that I—"

"Say no more." She slipped onto one of the folding chairs and settled her small designer purse in her lap. "I understand completely. And I'm here to help."

"Help?"

"Yes. When Holly told me what you were up to, I decided to come right down and offer my services."

As was often the case with Stacy, he was at a loss for words.

She leaned toward the desk. "Mick, you just told someone on the phone that you have an assistant. I agree that it makes you seem more professional. So here I am."

He tilted back in his chair, trying to act casual as hell, as if women like Stacy came strolling in to offer their services on a regular basis. "I don't understand how you could do that. You're a dancer. You have a career in New York."

"I may be a dancer, but I don't have a career in New York." Her mouth curved in a sad smile. "There, I actually said it. Finally admitted the ugly truth. I'm washed up."

He didn't know how to respond. Although he'd always disapproved of what he saw as her parasitic lifestyle, he hated seeing anybody give up on a dream. Besides, her brown eyes had gone all soft and vulnerable, and he was a sucker for that look.

Finally he took a stab at being helpful. "Listen, I'm sure it takes a long time to make it on Broadway. Years, I'll bet. You probably just need to—"

"I need to quit, is what I need to do. Yes, it takes years, and I've devoted almost six to this quest. I'm no closer now than when I started. More than that, I've taken a good look at the competition. I'm good, but they're great. I'm ambitious, but they're driven. The healthy thing is to face the facts and move on."

This sure wasn't the Stacy Radcliffe he knew. She was beginning to sound like an adult instead of a spoiled brat. But the spoiled brat had been easier to resist. Now he found himself feeling sad for her because she'd poured so much time, energy and her parents' money into a failed venture. That had to hurt.

"I'm sorry it didn't work out," he said, and discovered that he meant it. She'd made the pep squad as a freshman, so he'd watched her going through her routines on the sidelines when he wasn't otherwise engaged on the football field. He'd also seen her perform in the school musical that year, and despite himself, he'd been impressed that a fourteen-year-old had such outstanding moves.

Actually, he'd been more than impressed. He'd been turned on, and thoroughly ashamed of himself for lusting after a child. But she was no child now.

"Maybe it's fate," she said. "Here I am back in town at the exact time that you're opening this business. You need an assistant and I need a job. Kismet."

Now this was more like the old Stacy—full of unrealistic expectations and positive the world was ready to do her bidding. She probably couldn't imagine that his budget was too tight to hire a janitorial service, let alone a full-time assistant.

He cleared his throat. "Uh, I don't think you have the right qualifications."

"Of course I do! I've had voice lessons, so I would be perfect to answer your phone. And that's for starters. Here's my plan—I'll answer your phone and handle public relations for you. During lulls in business, you can start teaching me karate, and before you know it, I'll be ready to assist you in the field, too."

His chair let out a loud squeak as he sat forward. "You've got to be kidding."

"Nope." She smiled at him. "I think it would be a blast."

"Oh, I'll just bet you do. I'm sure you picture yourself acting out scenes from *Remington Steele* or *Moonlighting*."

"Hey! You used to love those shows as much as Holly and I did, so don't make fun of them like you're so above it all."

"Yeah, I liked those shows, but this isn't TV." He settled into his stern lecture mode, one he'd perfected after years of dealing with a little sister. "It's real life and it's hard and it's dangerous. The world is full of kooks and weirdos, and you never know what they're gonna do."

She rolled her eyes. "Like I don't know that after living in New York for six years."

"But you weren't exactly looking for tense situations. That's what the bodyguard business is about. I've been training for years in order to be qualified for this. For the past six months I've been practicing at the shooting range, too, so I can handle a .38 with speed and accuracy. I take this seriously. Very seriously."

Instead of acting cowed by his lecture, she laughed. "Just

like I thought. You're doing this because it sounded too fun for words.''

Which he was. But he couldn't let her know it. ''I'm doing it because I want to help make the world a safer place.''

''Good!'' She continued to grin at him. ''That's very good. How great that you've found a job that includes noble motives along with the excitement factor.''

''I'm not in this for excitement.'' Or he'd better not be, because so far the excitement quotient was nonexistent.

''Of course you are. Don't forget that I have the dirt on you.''

Oh, God, here it came. Blackmail City. ''Uh, about that night in the parking lot, I—''

''I'm not talking about your sex life—but there's another example. It's all part of your personality. You're a thrill seeker, Mick.''

''I am not!'' But he had been, back when she'd known him. That's why his parents had dragged him to karate class, to settle him down.

''Come on. When we were kids you practically made a religion out of riding the Colossus at Magic Mountain. And then there was that bungee-jumping period, which almost drove your parents into an early grave. Don't tell me you're not in this for the thrills.''

''I'm not,'' he said. ''I've grown up.'' Most days he thoroughly believed that, but seeing Stacy again, he wondered if a little wildness still lingered. ''Let's cut to the chase here. Are you planning to use that parking lot thing to get your way?''

Her expression brightened. ''Wow. What a concept. I hadn't thought of it.''

He squeezed his eyes shut and cursed under his breath.

''My goodness, you're still worried about that coming to

light, aren't you? I had no idea. I thought it was old news, especially now that poor Mr. Oglethorpe is no longer with us.''

Gazing at her, he weighed the option of telling Holly about the incident himself and disarming Stacy. After all, it *was* old news. Holly would probably laugh about it. And yet...he couldn't imagine himself confessing such a thing to his little sister, even after all these years. It was an embarrassing story, and he felt a certain obligation to protect Cassandra, too. Maybe that was misplaced chivalry, but it was the way he felt.

She stared back at him. She'd always been a cheeky little thing. ''I suppose it isn't the sort of thing you'd want people to know right when you're starting a business,'' she said.

''No, it isn't. But it's not only about me. If word got out it might hurt Cassandra's reputation. She moves in pretty elevated circles these days, from what I hear. But if hiring you is the only way I'll keep your mouth shut, I still can't do it. In the first place, I have no money for that. In the second place, you don't just learn karate in a few lessons.''

''I'll bet I could pick it up faster than you think. As a dancer I've had to learn balance, and my legs are really strong. I'm in good shape.''

He could see that. She was in excellent shape, too good, as far as he was concerned. ''Even assuming I had the money to hire you, which I don't, what about your parents? They would never go for this.''

''I'm twenty-six years old. I don't need a permission slip from my parents to take a job. We can negotiate the salary. I don't need—''

The phone interrupted her, and before he could grab it, she did.

''Farrell's Personal Bodyguard Service.'' She sounded exactly right when she said it, too, like a professional receptionist. "How can we help you?" she added, as if she'd been practicing.

He figured Craig was on the line. Either Craig or Holly. He hoped it was Holly, because Craig would give him a hard time over it. Craig had tried to date Stacy once upon a time, but she'd ignored his attempts. Understandably, Craig wasn't a Stacy Radcliffe fan. He wouldn't appreciate hearing her voice on the phone, especially if he suspected she was sitting on a folding chair belonging to him.

Mick motioned for her to give him the phone, but she shook her head.

"I see," she said. "Let me put you on hold for a moment, Mrs. Oglethorpe, while I check with Mr. Farrell on that."

Mick was sure he'd heard wrong. His luck couldn't be this bad.

Stacy leaned over and pressed the hold button on his secondhand phone, thereby displaying some awesome cleavage. "It's Cassandra Oglethorpe." She studied him for a reaction.

From the warmth of his cheeks, he knew he was giving her one. "I don't believe it." His voice was a tad on the hoarse side. "It's Holly on the phone, and this is some sort of shakedown you two cooked up."

"Trust me, it's Mrs. Oglethorpe. She wants to hire you." Stacy maintained a deadpan expression.

He began to believe she was telling the truth. "Hire me for what?"

"I find myself wondering the same thing. Maybe you're touchy about that parking lot incident because you're still carrying on with Mrs. Oglethorpe."

"I'm not! That night was the end of it, I swear!"

"Then maybe she wants to renew the acquaintance."

Mick's stomach churned. "This is a bodyguard service, not an escort service."

"Oh, she says she needs a bodyguard. She wants to spend the Fourth of July and a couple of days after that up at her cabin in the White Mountains, but her ex-fiancé is making threats, so she's afraid to go alone." Stacy batted her eyelashes at him. "Even though it's short notice, she wonders if you can come up and protect her."

Mick groaned. "Wonderful."

"So do you want me to tell her you aren't available? I mean, it is next week, after all. Maybe I should tell her you're booked."

"Maybe...or maybe not. No...I don't know! What if this is legit? She has tons of money, thanks to Oglethorpe's investments, and she's very influential. If she's really in need of a bodyguard, it's a great opportunity."

"Then you want me to tell her you *are* available?"

Mick stared at her in misery. "If it's a hoax, I don't want to spend three days fighting her off."

Stacy's eyes filled with a devilish light. "Is that what you were doing in the parking lot, fighting her off?"

He ground his teeth together. "No. I was younger then."

"So was she." She held the receiver out and looked it over, as if evaluating Cassandra Oglethorpe. "Poor lady. She's past her prime and you're no longer interested."

"Stacy, damn it! When I was an eighteen-year-old stud I had no discrimination! Now I do. So sue me for being young, horny and stupid."

"I have a solution for your problem."

He didn't think he wanted to hear what it was. But he was desperate. "What?"

"Hire me as your assistant and take me with you to Mrs. Oglethorpe's cabin. But don't tell her that's what you're planning to do. It can be a surprise. That way, if she's on the up-and-up, she should be glad for an extra person. But if she's not, at least you'll have a chaperon. And she can't very well say anything, considering that she is requesting a bodyguard.'' Stacy sat back and looked pleased with herself.

Somehow from the moment she'd first suggested working as his assistant, he'd known that it would turn out this way. Stacy Radcliffe usually got what she wanted. Apparently she'd abandoned her Broadway career and, for some reason he had yet to figure out, she'd decided it would be fun to play at being a bodyguard.

He probably had Holly to thank for Stacy appearing on his doorstep. No doubt Stacy had headed over to see Holly as soon as she'd hit town, and Holly had naturally filled her in on Mick's latest endeavor.

''I don't think we can keep Mrs. Oglethorpe waiting much longer,'' Stacy said, glancing at the blinking light on the phone. ''And, as you said, she has tons of money. By the way, what are we charging for this assignment?''   .

Mick had determined his rates a long time ago, but that was when he'd expected to get all of the fee. At the moment that didn't seem likely. So when he gave Stacy the amount, he raised it by twenty percent.

She lifted her eyebrows. ''Not bad. Not bad at all. How much do I get out of that?''

''I haven't said I was hiring you.''

''You will.''

Mick sighed. He didn't have much choice in the matter. Fortunately, the situation, assuming it was genuine, didn't sound too dangerous. He ought to be able to handle an angry middle-aged fiancé and keep Stacy out of harm's way at the same time. If Cassandra had made the whole thing up to get him alone, then he really needed someone around to help keep Cassandra in line.

But, damn, what a way to start his new career. He felt the same way he had when Stacy had opened the back door of the Lincoln Town Car twelve years ago—screwed, blued and tattooed. "You get twenty percent," he said.

Her smile was triumphant.

"But this is only temporary," he added. "A trial run. Nothing cast in stone."

She didn't look as if she believed a word of it. She had him by the privates and she knew it. "Thanks, Mick. You won't be sorry."

"I'm already sorry." With another sigh he gestured toward the phone. "Better seal the deal with *our* client."

CHAPTER TWO

AFTER FINALIZING the arrangements with Cassandra Oglethorpe, Stacy decided to leave Mick's office before she wore out her welcome. Besides, she still had to move a few of her belongings from her parents' house to her apartment. She promised Mick she'd report to work promptly at nine the next morning, flashed him a smile that communicated far more confidence than she felt and took off.

This job with Mick was a shaky proposition, no doubt about it. But she didn't have much in the way of marketable skills, and her mother had begged her not to get a minimum-wage job flipping burgers at McDonald's or stocking the shelves at Kmart. Working for Mick would seem like something she'd taken on for the hell of it because she craved adventure. Nobody would suspect she desperately needed the money.

As she drove her red BMW convertible up the 101 toward her parents' Scottsdale home, she wondered if she should sell the car, despite her mother's request that she keep it for the sake of appearances. Her mother had claimed that people would talk if Stacy Radcliffe started driving a beater.

Stacy thought her mother was fighting a losing battle. The family fortune was gone—lost through a series of bad investments—and the debt load was mounting as her mother struggled to maintain the status quo.

Her father seemed perfectly willing to liquidate and start over, but not her mother, and her mother was calling the shots at the moment. She'd begun looking for ways that her husband could make money at home, so he wouldn't appear to be working.

For now, Stacy had decided to go along with her mother's subterfuge, since her father was willing to. After all, she owed both of them a lot. They'd provided her with everything a young girl could have wanted, and the least she could do was be cooperative now that the tide had turned against them.

Personally she didn't mind gearing down. The concept brought its own kind of freedom, and she was beginning to realize that her parents' expectations had kept her in a straitjacket. Although she hated seeing her mom and dad in financial trouble, she felt guilty relief that they couldn't support her dancing career any longer. She'd been staying on in New York so as not to disappoint them, but she'd had it with auditions and rejection, productions that folded after one night and cranky stage managers.

And when that creepy guy Gerald had become fixated on her, that had really freaked her out. She'd been about to call her parents and suggest coming back to regroup when her mother had beat her to it. Her mother had wanted her to live at home, of course, but Stacy knew that would never work. Even if she moved from her old room to the guest house, she'd still feel like a kid again under Mommy and Daddy's thumb. They loved her, but they had yet to accept that she'd grown up.

But in order to afford an apartment, she needed a job. With all her mother's restrictions, she'd been at a loss as to what kind of job until she'd talked with Holly and found out about Mick's new business.

Despite her uncertainty about working with him, she had to smile when she thought of their interaction this morning. He was so cute. He'd always been terminally cute, with those bluer-than-blue eyes and that shock of untamed, ma-hogany-colored hair. When she'd still lived in Scottsdale, she definitely would have gone out with him if he'd asked.

But he hadn't asked. According to Holly, he'd been wor-ried about dating his little sister's best friend, afraid that she'd repeat the details of their dates to his sis. If that was the reason, it irritated the hell out of Stacy. Hadn't she proved herself trustworthy by not telling anyone about that night in the parking lot?

That night had marked the end of her childhood and the beginning of her erotic fantasies about Mick. She'd had re-hearsal for the school musical and had been standing outside waiting for her mother to pick her up when she'd heard noises coming from the white Lincoln Town Car not far away.

The school board president couldn't have been making those noises. She'd passed the meeting in progress on her way out. Curiosity had always been a failing of hers, so she'd crept over to peek in. For at least thirty seconds she'd stood with her nose plastered to the window and her four-teen-year-old body experiencing all sorts of delicious feel-ings.

Mick and Mrs. Oglethorpe had been so absorbed in each other that they'd had no idea she was there. She could have crept away unnoticed, but the temptation to get the best of Mick, who'd teased her and Holly unmercifully for years, had been too strong. Opening the back door, she'd asked conversationally, "How's it going, Mick?"

Mrs. Oglethorpe had screeched, and Mick had cursed. Then he'd turned his head to look over his shoulder at her. She'd never seen such a fierce expression on his face.

"*Go away,*" he'd said in a tight voice.

She'd had enough performance experience to pull off nonchalance, even though her heart had been beating like crazy. She'd shrugged. "Okay. Good to see you again, Mrs. Oglethorpe. Bye, Mick." Then she'd closed the door and walked calmly back to the front entrance to wait for her mother.

From that day forward, whenever she'd imagined making out with anyone, it had been Mick in her fantasies. She'd heard that men who'd been initiated into sex by older women were supposed to know more about pleasing a lover. She couldn't prove the theory, but the guys she'd been involved with later on had evidently not been taught by someone older and more worldly. As she'd endured their clumsiness, she'd continued to think of Mick and what he might have learned from Cassandra Oglethorpe.

And now Stacy would be working for him.

As she pulled into the circular drive of her parents' hacienda-style home, she waved to the gardener who was trimming the pyracantha bushes near the arched entry. Her father had offered to take over the landscape work, but her mother wouldn't hear of it. They'd had a gardener for years and they would continue to have a gardener, she'd said.

Stacy parked the car and decided to go in through the front patio gate. If her mother kept her usual schedule, she'd be taking a swim in the pool before lunch while her husband was out at the club with his golf buddies. Stacy guessed her mother and father were keeping the same schedule.

Her mother's desperate attempt to maintain things as they'd always been was perfectly understandable. Evie Radcliffe had been protected from harsh realities all her life, so she wasn't equipped to deal with them. She'd been born into money and had married money. The wealth must have seemed endless.

But now that Stacy looked back on her father's business dealings, she realized that he'd never been particularly astute. He was a dreamer, not much more talented at practical business matters than his wife. But he'd inherited so much that it had taken him years to lose it all.

She unlatched the wrought-iron gate and walked through it into the cool patio. Fifty-year-old mesquite trees had been trimmed and nurtured to grow large and protect the area from the blistering summer heat. On the far side of the patio another gate led to a tidy little guest house, also shaded by large mesquites.

Only the pool, centered in the yard like the turquoise stone in a Navajo necklace, caught the sun. And sure enough, Stacy's mother was churning away through the water, getting in her usual twenty laps. She might be broke, but she refused to be fat.

Stacy sat in a cushioned lounge chair and waited for her mother to finish. Evie was a good swimmer. She could also ride a horse, sail a boat and water-ski. Unfortunately none of those skills would help her in her current crisis.

It was even more unfortunate that she hadn't encouraged her daughter to go into a sensible profession, either. Although Stacy would love to help her parents, she couldn't imagine how, other than to take care of herself for a change.

Evie didn't catch sight of Stacy until she'd climbed out of the pool. "Goodness!" she said with a reproving smile. "You should have announced yourself."

"Didn't want to interrupt your laps." Rising from the chair, she handed her mother the thick beach towel that had been lying on a table nearby.

Evie pulled off her bathing cap and shook out her chin-length hair, cut and colored ash-blond by one of Scottsdale's best salons. "I certainly could have made up for it tomorrow." She took the towel. "Thanks, sweetheart. Can you stay for lunch?"

"Sure. Then I'm packing up a few last things and heading over to the apartment."

Evie grimaced. "That apartment seems so unnecessary."

"It's all part of Mother Nature's grand plan, Mom. If I were an orangutan, I'd be staking out my own tree by now. If I were a woodpecker I'd be building my own nest. If I were a coyote, I'd be—"

"Oh, for heaven's sake. You're not a wild animal, you're my daughter. And I do wish your father and I could have seen the place before you signed the lease. It might be completely unsuitable."

"It's fine, Mom." No way Stacy would have ever let her mother influence her choice of an apartment. Her mother would have insisted she rent something far too extravagant. "A palace compared to what I had in New York."

"Don't remind me of that dingy little hole-in-the-wall! Come on in. I'll shower off and then we can eat a little of the crab salad Yolanda made this morning."

Not long afterward they were seated at the Mexican-tiled breakfast bar sharing lunch the way they had so many summer days in the past during Stacy's idyllic childhood. She'd never truly appreciated the luxury of having her mom around so much back then, when so many of her friends' mothers had pursued careers that had taken them out of the home most days.

But a career would sure help her mother right now. Stacy looked with new eyes at the spacious kitchen and thought of all the parties over the years. The hub of the celebration usually turned out to be right here at the breakfast bar. Her parents were fantastic hosts with a flair for casual elegance. Stacy couldn't imagine them living anywhere else, but they couldn't keep the house much longer at the rate things were going.

Nevertheless, her mother discussed a new decorating scheme for the dining room as if she had the money to implement it. Stacy went along with the discussion as if she believed the new wall coverings and window treatments would actually be ordered.

"By the way, I got a job today," she said during a break in the conversation.

Her mother paused with her fork in midair. "Doing what?"

"I'm going to be Mick Farrell's assistant."

Evie frowned and put down her fork. "Didn't he just start some sort of personal protection business?"

"Right. He's a bodyguard."

"So what would you be doing as his assistant?"

Stacy knew better than to lay out her plans for advancement. If all went as planned and she became proficient in karate, she'd make herself so valuable to Mick that he'd eventually consider her a full partner in the business. But Evie wouldn't like the idea of her daughter becoming a bodyguard.

So Stacy provided only part of the truth. "I'll be doing office stuff, mostly. I convinced him that it will look more professional if he has someone answering the phone and handling the office details."

"Well, you're right about that." Evie gazed at her. "Didn't you used to have a crush on him?"

Stacy didn't think her mother had noticed that. "No, of course not. I mean, he's Holly's brother. That would be too weird."

"I don't think so. And I think you did have a crush on him. Whenever you knew he'd be around, you'd primp for hours."

"Girls at that age do that all the time anyway. Mick's just a good friend, that's all."

Her mother's gray eyes sparkled. "Or so you say."

Aha. Her mother had figured out a way to tell her friends about this job. She would explain that Stacy had thought it would be fun to work for Mick Farrell, a guy she'd always been attracted to. Stacy wasn't happy about her mother's too-accurate-for-comfort conclusion, but if she kept denying it, she'd arouse even more suspicion.

"Well, I can't imagine that he's paying you much," her mother continued, "so why don't you let me cover your rent for the time being?"

Stacy put her hand over her mother's to soften the refusal. "Thank you, but I think it's time I supported myself." And she would, somehow. Before she'd left New York she'd sold her few items of furniture. Because she'd bought them when she'd thought money was no object, they'd brought a good price. Assuming she could continue to work for twenty percent of Mick's income, she'd be fine.

"Look," her mother said, "I know you don't want to take money because you think we can't afford to give it. That may be true for the time being, but I'm sure things will get better soon."

"I'm sure they will, too, Mom." Then she switched topics, bringing up a local political scandal to distance them from any more personal discussion. Until and unless she wanted to confront her mother about their slide into bankruptcy, she might as well steer clear of the subject.

Later her mother helped her carry out the last few boxes of her belongings and stash them in the convertible. "There's that big Fourth of July thing coming up at the club," Evie said. "Fireworks and a buffet dinner. More people are in town than usual this year, so it should be fun. Why don't you bring Mick?"

Stacy was caught by surprise. "Um, Mick's been hired by a client for the Fourth." She'd forgotten about the annual club event. Even if Mick couldn't go, she'd be expected to be there. She'd hoped to slip out of town on the Fourth without telling her mother, but that didn't look likely now.

"That's too bad," her mother said. "I guess it's good that work's coming in, though. As for you, I don't know if there's anyone else in town you'd like to invite, but if not, there's no need to bring a date." Evie hoisted a box of Stacy's old CDs into the back seat of the car.

"Um, I may be going along on that assignment with Mick," she said.

Her mother turned, her eyes wide. "Going with him? But why?"

"I can't talk about it, Mom. When people hire body-guards, they don't want everybody spreading the word."

"I wouldn't spread the word." Evie looked wounded by the comment.

"I'm not saying you would, but I'm not supposed to tell anybody the details."

"I understand that, but I'm your mother and I'm con-cerned for your safety. Office work is one thing, but I as-sume the actual job involves some degree of danger."

Stacy took pity on her. "It's okay, Mom," she said more gently. "This assignment is a piece of cake. You don't have to worry."

"That's easy for you to say, isn't it? Maybe I should talk to Mick. I really don't like—"

"Mom, I'm not your little kid anymore." Stacy struggled to remain patient. Her mother's reaction was normal, espe-cially considering she was an only child. "You gave me strict instructions about the type of job I could get, so now that I have one that won't embarrass you, you're going to have to leave the subject alone, okay?"

Evie gave her a long look. "You promise me you will be careful?"

"I promise. Anyway, Holly's the one who suggested I ask Mick about a job, and Holly wouldn't want me to get into anything dangerous.'' Of course Holly didn't know Stacy's plans for advancement, either.

"Speaking of Holly, I'll bet she wouldn't mind knowing you're interested in her brother.''

Stacy told herself to stay calm. "I'm working for the guy. For all I know he already has a girlfriend.'' Now that was an unsettling thought. Surely Holly would have said so if he did.

Evie lifted her hair from the nape of her neck. "I doubt it. When I ran into his mother recently she was buying a wedding gift for yet another relative and complaining that she didn't think Mick would ever settle down. So if he's seeing anyone, it's not very serious.''

"Maybe so, but like I said, I'm only his employee.''

"At this point, anyway. I always liked Mick. I realize he wasn't raised with your advantages, but I think he could amount to something one day.''

Stacy decided to ignore the matchmaking implications of the statement. "I hope he does. I could use a raise.''

Her mother sighed. "I hate that you have to worry about money. I really, really hate it.''

"It's good for me, Mom.'' She gave her mother a quick hug and went around to the driver's side of the car. "See you soon.''

"And you will be very careful on this secret assignment?''

"Very careful.'' She got into the car.

"If you get into a problem, you can call me, anytime, day or night. I'll come right over.''

"Thanks, I appreciate that.'' Stacy recognized the love that prompted her mother's offer. She didn't doubt for a minute that her parents would drop everything and come running if she needed them. That was nice to know, but on the other hand, she wished they'd start seeing her as a competent adult capable of handling her own crises. She started the car.

"When are you going to invite us to see your apartment?" her mother called, shading her eyes from the sun.

"Soon. Just let me get it fixed up first."

"All right. We'll see you soon then."

Stacy drove off with a wave of her hand. She didn't know how long she could stall her mother on coming over to see the apartment, but she'd hold her off as long as possible. One look at the tiny, somewhat shabby one-bedroom and Evie would go into orbit, claiming that no daughter of hers would live in such substandard housing.

Maybe if business really picked up for Mick, she'd be able to move into something nicer. In the meantime, she had to keep her mother far away from her living quarters. Evie wasn't equipped to handle the shock.

MICK ARRIVED at work ten minutes early the next morning. With his newspaper tucked under his arm and his Starbucks iced coffee in his left hand, he put the key in the lock and opened the door. When he cashed his check from Cassandra, he'd hire someone to paint his name on the frosted glass. It hadn't taken so long, after all.

Once inside the office he checked the message light on the phone. As usual, it was steady and green.

Walking around his desk, he put down the coffee and the newspaper before he rolled out his office chair and sat down. He'd spent a little extra time getting dressed this morning, and he'd worn the blue silk shirt and paisley tie Holly had given him for Christmas. He probably shouldn't be excited about this new development of having Stacy here today, but he was. Adrenaline pumped through him at the prospect of her coming in the door any minute.

He should be more suspicious, considering that the call

from Cassandra Oglethorpe had coincided perfectly with Stacy's arrival. There was still a good chance Holly and Stacy had staged the whole thing. After all, he'd never actually talked to Cassandra, so it could have been Holly on the other end of the line.

If those two had cooked this up as an elaborate hoax, then Stacy had become an excellent actress during her years in New York, because he'd been totally convinced by her eager expression when she'd proposed herself as his assistant. He had to believe she'd been sincere. Surely all those psychology courses he'd taken had given him some insight into human nature.

Of course, sincere or not, this was only a lark for her, something to tide her over until she decided what she wanted to do now that New York was no longer an option. Actually, Stacy might work out great. When he'd heard her answer the phone he'd realized how much classier she made his business appear. Not only that, taking her up to the White Mountains would keep Cassandra at arm's length.

Despite the dicey personal angle, he was thrilled that Cassandra had hired him. The money from that job could keep him afloat for a while, and if he managed to avoid insulting Cassandra, she might let him use her as a reference. Even better, she might recommend him to others.

So about the time Stacy decided the bodyguard business wasn't her cup of tea, which was inevitable, he might very well have his business up and running. Then he could hire a real assistant, someone who had qualifications and needed the job.

In the meantime it could be fun having Stacy around, although he'd have to make sure he didn't let himself get carried away. She was still Holly's best friend. He could hire her, make use of her good telephone skills, and then cheerfully let her go on to something else when she was ready to call it quits.

He took the lid off his coffee and snapped open his newspaper, bringing it up to hide his face. When Stacy walked in, assuming she did, he didn't want to be sitting there staring at the door waiting for her.

No sooner had he taken his first drink of coffee than the door opened.

"I'm here!" Stacy announced.

"Hey." He took his time lowering the newspaper, as if he'd found something fascinating in it and had to read the final paragraph. But he was so glad she'd shown up. Her offer to be his assistant hadn't been a joke, after all. That meant Cassandra was a genuine client, and he had a business going.

Finally he took a sip of his coffee before gazing up at her. Oh, she was here, all right. She was *so* here. Her short, white dress hugged her hips and bared her lovely knees. The matching jacket was cropped high and cut so as not to disguise a bit of that tempting figure.

He almost choked on his coffee.

She sat down across from him, unhooked a large purse from her shoulder and pulled out a monogrammed leather notebook. "I think every employee should bring something special to the job, something only they can offer," she said.

She brought something special all right. This formerly dull little cubby fairly hummed with sexual excitement. "So you brought a notebook with your initials on it?" he asked.

She flashed him a saucy smile. "Very funny." She flipped open the notebook. "I made some notes last night. As you know, my one area of expertise involves the world of show business."

"Right." He had no idea where she was going with this.

"No offense, Mick, but yours is the dullest office I've ever been in."

He *was* offended. "Maybe if I had your kind of money I could jazz it up, but secondhand was all I could afford."

"There's nothing wrong with secondhand."

"How would you know?"

"Oh, come on. Don't get all defensive. Let me be of some help to you."

"Like how?" Damn it all, he felt defensive. It made his blood boil to have her waltz in here in that outfit that probably cost more than his entire set of office furniture and announce that his surroundings were dull.

"Now, listen, Mick. You're starting a business. You need to create an image that will draw people in. Maybe you're not in entertainment like I was, but you still have to attract customers." She held up one of his flyers. "Holly gave me this."

"It has everything on there." He still sounded defensive. "But I assume you think there's something wrong with it?"

"Well, for one thing, it's white. For another, there are no graphics."

"I'm on a budget—"

"Budget, smudget. Holly knows something about doing stuff on the computer and she offered to help you for free, but she said you didn't want anything fancy."

"I wanted it to look professional," he muttered.

"Professional does not mean boring." She pulled another flyer out of the pocket of her notebook. "Look at this."

He took the fluorescent orange paper with a frown. "Too flashy. It— Hey, that's me!" He stared at a picture of himself competing in a karate tournament. The side of his foot had just connected with his opponent's jaw. Below the picture bold letters proclaimed that Mick Farrell Gets the Job

Done. Then the company name, address and phone number were listed, along with his credentials.

"Holly and I fooled around with some ideas last night," she said. "This is the one we both like the best."

Mick shook his head. "I couldn't pass something like that out. It's too…too…"

"Exciting?"

"I think the word I want is *boastful*."

"Oh, for heaven's sake!" She gestured toward his phone. "Do you see that thing ringing off the hook?"

"No, but—"

"Starting your own business is one of the riskiest financial ventures in the world. In a sense, that's what I was trying to do in New York, and I didn't make it. After six years there, I can tell you that what they say is true. Sex sells."

"*Sex?*"

"Absolutely. Your first client called you because she thinks you're a sexy guy."

"You don't know that."

"Yes, I do." Her gaze was level. "But you can't depend on your past reputation to keep you in business. You have to promote a sexy image in the here and now."

He couldn't believe how he'd totally lost control of the situation. One minute they were talking about flyers and the next minute they were back to his sex life. "I'm not selling sex, damn it!"

"Of course you're not. You're selling protective services. But there's something sexy about that, and if you don't exploit it, just a little, you may not succeed. I understand the value of promotion and, believe me, underlying a huge percentage of it is good, old-fashioned sex appeal."

"I still don't want—"

"It's your choice, Mick. You have two options, as I see

it. You can either sit here and wait for the phone to ring until you run out of money—''

"You don't know that will happen."

She cruised right past that comment. "*Or* you can let me show you how to use your natural sex appeal to your advantage. Which will it be?"

CHAPTER THREE

STACY REALIZED that hitting Mick with a new business approach could backfire on her. But over a Chinese take-out dinner in her apartment, she and Holly had concluded that Mick needed a major publicity boost if he expected to get this business off the ground. Because Mick was Stacy's only viable employment opportunity, she had a big stake in his success.

She and Holly had picked up supplies on the way to Holly's apartment and used Holly's computer to create the new flyer. When Stacy had noticed the framed picture of Mick sitting on Holly's bookcase, she'd suggested scanning it in. The results, from Stacy's point of view, were outstanding.

Mick was obviously not as impressed as she was, but he continued to study the flyer in his hand. At least he hadn't completely rejected the idea.

Finally he looked up. "Does Holly know about the Oglethorpe job?"

"Of course not. I had to tell my mom I was going on an assignment with you because she was expecting me to be at the Fourth of July bash their country club always has. But she doesn't know what the assignment is about."

His expression was guarded. "Or who it's for?"

Stacy's irritation surfaced. "No, she does not know who it's for! And I resent your implication that I'd talk about the office's confidential business."

Mick sighed. "I'm sorry. Obviously I'm paranoid about having Cassandra Oglethorpe as my first client. I don't know why I couldn't have a normal assignment for my first job, like protecting some rich dude's kid on the way to school. Then I wouldn't be in this mess." He tossed the flyer on the desk.

"That's the whole point." Stacy grabbed it and rattled it for emphasis. "You need to market yourself better. Let's print up some of these. I'll bet you'll be amazed at what will happen."

"What will happen is that my friends will never let me live it down."

"So, which is worse, being teased by your friends or watching your career go down the tubes for lack of business?"

He eyed her silently.

"It shouldn't be a tough question, Mick."

"Okay. I'll try the flyer."

"Good." She consulted her list. "Next item. You should probably change how you dress."

He blinked in surprise. Then he glanced down at his shirt and tie. "This is a *very* good shirt." He brushed a speck of lint from his tie. "In fact, I'll have you know Holly bought me this shirt and tie for Christmas. And my mom helped her pick them out."

Stacy didn't want to mess with sentimental family interactions, so she decided to tread lightly. "And they're beautiful. The shirt brings out the blue in your eyes. But you weren't a bodyguard when they bought you that shirt. It's not form-fitting enough."

He stared at her.

"Don't look at me as if I'm crazy. I know what I'm talking about. I've been through a million auditions, and I know how much clothing affects the way people react to you. I don't care how competent you are, you have to look the part. If you're going to guard people by using your martial arts skills, then you have to show off your muscles. And lose the tie.''

"I've seen plenty of bodyguards wearing ties!" He crossed his arms protectively over his chest. "What about Kevin Costner in that movie with Whitney Houston? He wore a tie all the time.''

"That was years ago. Besides, that movie wasn't about trying to expand his business. He'd just been hired by *Whitney Houston,* for God's sake. As far as I know, you have Mrs. Oglethorpe, and whoever that was on the phone when I came in yesterday. Is that a client I should know about, by the way, now that I'm working for you?''

His face turned a dull red. "That wasn't a client.''

"Oh.'' So he had a girlfriend. She hadn't expected to be so disappointed. "Sorry. Didn't mean to pry into your personal life.''

"It wasn't anybody.''

"Mick, it's okay. I'm guessing it's a woman Holly and your family don't know about, right? Your secret's safe with me.'' Her imagination ran wild. Maybe his girlfriend was an exotic dancer, or maybe she'd barely turned eighteen, or maybe she was another older woman like Mrs. Oglethorpe. Or maybe—

"No, I mean it was literally *nobody.* When I saw someone was about to come in the office, I picked up the phone and pretended to be taking a business call, so I'd look busy.''

"Oh." She was so pleased with that information that she grinned at him like an idiot. "Now that was a smart move. And it shows that you understand how important it is to give the right impression.''

"I thought this shirt and tie was the right impression.''

She shook her head. "Not exciting enough. I'm thinking you might wear a form-fitting, collarless shirt. In black."

"Black? But it's a hundred and fifteen out there!"

"You could keep it at the office, and change into it when you get here. I'm only talking about wearing it when you meet with clients. For that, you should dress all in black. You might even consider letting your hair grow so that you could tie it in a ponytai—"

"Hell, no! The black outfit, maybe. To be honest I can sort of picture what you mean, although I think it's kind of ridiculous. But I'm not growing my hair so I can wear a ponytail. Forget that."

He acted so upset at the idea of long hair that she almost giggled. "Okay. No ponytail. Unless we got you a fake one that you could clip on whenever you—"

"No."

Because he looked somewhat unreceptive, she decided it was time to back off. She'd written several more things on her list, but she decided to save them for later. Right now might not be the time to suggest that they should choreograph some karate demonstrations. She'd also wait before pulling out the prop she'd brought to add zing to those demonstrations.

"Tell you what," she said. "Why not leave me here to cover the phone, do a little filing, whatever, and you go down to the copy shop and order those flyers, so we can start the ball rolling?"

He laughed. "Filing. Right. There's nothing to file. And the phone never rings, either."

"That's okay. If I have time on my hands, I'll make some calls to see if I can drum up business for you."

"Yeah?" For the first time he looked genuinely interested in one of her ideas. "Who would you call?"

"Flyers are good, but they're passive. Last night I made

a list of places where people with money gather in this town—you know, the sort of clubs where my parents and their friends hang out. Wealthy people are the most likely to need your services, so I plan to call each place on my list and get the word out.''

''That sounds like a good idea, but…wouldn't you hate doing that?''

''Why would I?''

He shrugged. ''I sure would. Mailing stuff and putting flyers on cars is one thing. Calling people up and asking them to hire me would feel really weird. Like begging for their business, or something.''

She'd suspected he felt that way, but she was delighted to hear him admit it. Now she knew he really needed her. ''It's always hard at first, but I had to work through that in New York. If I hadn't been willing to promote myself I wouldn't have landed any jobs. As it was, I'm sure I wasn't aggressive enough. The difference here is that I'm not promoting myself, I'm promoting you. That's ten times easier.''

He gazed at her and slowly nodded. ''Good point. You know, I'll be honest, Stacy. When you came in yesterday I thought hiring you was a big mistake. But I'm beginning to see how you could really help me.''

Her reaction caught her by surprise. For the first time in ages, someone thought she'd be of real use, and the idea brought a lump to her throat. She cleared it away, embarrassed that she could be moved by such a little crumb of validation. ''Good,'' she said. ''I'm glad. Now why don't you go take care of the flyers while I get busy?''

''All right.'' He stood. Then he glanced down at his Starbucks. ''I should have brought you something. I'm so used to my routine that I didn't even think about it.''

She stood, too, and picked up her purse in preparation for

moving around to his side of the desk. "Never mind. I'll be fine."

"Maybe I should get a coffeepot for the office."

Stacy laughed. "Then we'd just fight about who was supposed to make the coffee. I don't drink that much of it, anyway. No problem."

"If you say so, but I feel as if I'm leaving you here without any amenities. I didn't notice it so much when I was by myself, but—"

"I don't need amenities." She was touched by his sudden concern.

"In any case, I'll leave the newspaper for you, in case you get sick of making those calls. And I won't be gone long." He circled the desk.

"Take as long as you need." She started around the other end of the desk, so she could take his chair. "In fact, I was wondering if you'd make me a set of keys while you're out."

"Uh, yeah. Sure."

She sat in the upholstered chair that was still warm from his body heat. Something about taking the chair he'd just vacated made him seem very close, even though he now stood on the other side of the desk. She wondered what it would be like to be in his arms. Settling back in his chair felt a little like that, especially since the scent of his shampoo and aftershave lingered.

He shifted his weight from one foot to the other, but made no move to leave. "If anyone should come in, which I doubt, you can tell them I'll be right back," he said.

"I'll tell them." She tried to clear any seductive thoughts from her mind as she gave him what she hoped was a businesslike glance. But the seductive thoughts wouldn't go away. Even with the generous cut of his shirt, she could tell how well developed he was. In New York she'd known lots of men with muscles like his, dancers who could lift her six feet in the air without breathing hard. But for the most part, those men had been gay.

Mick took the flyer and folded it before tucking it in his shirt pocket. "Guess I'll head off to the copy place." Still he hesitated. "Should I take off the tie now?"

How about the tie, the shirt and the slacks? "If I were you, I'd take it off," she said. "As you said, it's a hundred and fifteen out there."

"Okay." He unknotted the tie and pulled it off. Then he unfastened the top button of his shirt. "Better?"

Oh, yeah. "Much better." Those simple acts had made her salivate. She had no trouble understanding why Cassandra Oglethorpe had hired him to keep her company for a few days. Her nerve endings hummed and her nipples tightened. She would have to start controlling her reactions better, because a man with his experience might be able to pick up on her interest.

"Are you sure you'll be okay?" he asked. "It's pretty boring in this office."

There was nothing boring about it at the moment. She looked away to keep from laughing. "I'll manage."

"If you're sure." He headed toward the door. "I'll be back before you know it." Then he finally walked out, closing the door behind him.

God, he was a hottie. She flapped the lapels of her jacket to cool herself down. But she stopped in embarrassment when he opened the door and poked his head back in.

"Why are you fanning yourself?" he asked. "Is it too hot in here?"

She tried to look nonchalant. "Not really. I should have worn a dress with more natural fiber content. This one doesn't breathe very well."

"Well, if you get too warm, the AC control's on the wall here by the door."

"I'll remember that."

"I forgot to say that we'll close the office for lunch, if you have any errands to run or anything."

"No errands."

"Then maybe we'll go out together and grab something."

It wasn't a very romantic invitation, but it still made her heart pound. "Sure."

"Good." He smiled his boyish grin. "See you soon."

Oh, Lord. When she was convinced he'd really left, she collapsed back against the chair and took several deep breaths. She was pitiful. He told her she might be useful and nearly made her cry. Then he suggested they eat lunch together and she was reacting as if he'd asked her out on a big date. Apparently the girlhood crush she'd had on Mick was still in full bloom. Not only that, she was far needier than she'd thought.

When she'd set out to fix her financial situation, she'd never imagined that her personal life needed fixing, too. Now it appeared that her years of battling Broadway had taken a toll on her self-esteem. She'd have to be very careful not to let Mick know how vulnerable she was right now.

A balance of power was the only way this joint venture would work. Therefore she didn't want him to suspect her money problems, but even more, she didn't want him to suspect that she had absolutely no idea where she fit in this crazy world.

THE FLYER was a big hit at the copy shop, much to Mick's surprise. While he walked a block down the street to have extra keys made, the flyers were printed. By the time he came back to pick them up, several of the employees had gathered around to ask about his karate experiences.

Even customers in the shop wanted a flyer to take home. Considering that the same information had appeared on his first version, he had to conclude the fluorescent color and the picture made all the difference in grabbing everyone's attention.

Stacy had been right.

She'd also been sexy, saucy and tempting as hell sitting across the desk from him in her crisp little white dress. Natural fiber content aside, it was quite a dress. He'd had to work hard to keep his gaze from following the rise and fall of her breasts. And there were other charms to ignore. At least twice he'd become mesmerized by the fullness of her lower lip and had barely managed to catch enough of her conversation to make an appropriate response.

If she was anybody else, he'd have asked her out by now. But this was Stacy, and the most he dared was a quick lunch during working hours. This job was a passing fancy for her, and he needed to keep reminding himself of that so he wouldn't do something stupid.

Yet she continued to show him that she was exactly the person he needed in the office right now. Even if he'd thought of calling around to the exclusive clubs in town, he wouldn't have done it in a million years. But she was cool with the concept, both because of her auditioning in New York and because she'd moved in those wealthy circles all her life.

If she'd been right about the changes in the flyer, she could be right about his style of dress. He hadn't thought of himself as auditioning to be somebody's bodyguard, but in a sense he was. He'd never had reason to worry about his image before. After college he'd worked as a karate instructor because he couldn't decide what else to do.

The job lacked thrills and didn't pay much, although he'd

enjoyed the kids. Teaching would have been a decent sideline, but he couldn't imagine devoting his life to it.

Then his best friend Craig, who was earning far more as an accountant than Mick ever would as a *sensei,* had suggested Mick use his martial arts skills to make some real money. Together they'd researched the need for personal protection services in Phoenix and had decided that Mick should take out a small-business loan, invest in some extra training and hang out his shingle. Craig had offered to handle the books for free the first year.

Mick only hoped he'd have some entries in those books. With Stacy on the job, he just might.

On the way back to the office he passed a men's clothing store and, on an impulse, went in. Sure enough, they had the type of shirt Stacy had been talking about. At least he thought that's what she meant. Rather than buy it without her, he decided to bring her back here during their lunch hour and make sure.

The whole idea of a costume felt funny to him, but he'd do what it took to create some traffic through that office. He thought of Stacy sitting there now and picked up his pace, despite the sweltering morning. His picture on the flyer might attract some attention, but if he put her picture on it, that would attract even more attention. If only she meant what she'd said about getting into the business, he could imagine how much of a draw she'd be.

But he couldn't take her seriously. That would be a huge mistake. In the meantime, though, he ought to bring her something to drink, so she wouldn't think he was a terrible employer.

He stopped at the Starbucks where he always bought his iced coffee and ordered one of their frozen coffee drinks. Most women he knew liked those. Then he added a brownie for good measure.

As he approached the door of his office he could hear her on the phone, her voice animated. He couldn't resist listening to her pitch without her knowing he was there. He stepped back a little so that his shadow wouldn't fall against the frosted glass window in the door.

"Oh, he's *very* good," she said. "You should see all the awards he's won for martial arts. I would have no trouble trusting him with *my* life, I'll tell you that." Then she laughed. "That doesn't hurt, either. Nothing like having a guy who's both competent *and* cute."

He shouldn't be eavesdropping, he decided. Her compliments were having a very dangerous effect on him. His blood warmed, and he had the urge to go in there, pull her out of that chair and kiss her, just to see what would happen if he did. Not a good idea. He could just picture the conversation between Stacy and Holly after a stunt like that:

So how was your first day working with my brother?

Uneventful until he stormed into the office and kissed me.

Thinking of his sister hearing all the gory details cooled him off considerably. But once he walked into the office he was in trouble again. She'd taken off the jacket to her dress. The sleeveless effect and the scooped neck provided way too much temptation under the circumstances.

But he couldn't very well ask her to put the jacket back on. He glanced at the thermostat and concluded she'd left it at the original setting, probably to try to save him money on air-conditioning. To hell with that. He needed her to cover up. His hands were full but he used his elbow to nudge the setting lower before walking over to the desk to put down the box of flyers, her frozen drink and the brownie.

"I'm sure he'd be happy to give a demonstration," Stacy said, smiling at him. "Maybe even this week."

A demonstration? His stomach churned. He wasn't a performer like she was. Tournaments were one thing, but the idea of putting on a show for the people from the country club, people who wouldn't normally have anything to do with him, scared him to death. He started waving his hands to signal that he didn't want to do anything like that.

"Oh, you'll be impressed, all right." Stacy frowned at him. "Listen, another call's coming in, so if I could put you on hold for a quick sec, I'll be right back." She punched the hold button and looked at Mick. "What?"

"What do you mean, a demonstration?"

"It's an excellent way to showcase your abilities." She pushed the button on the telephone again. "Samantha? Sorry about that. The word's getting out about Mick Farrell, obviously. So as I was saying, it's good to see someone like Mick in action." She swiveled her chair so her back was to him.

He walked around the desk and tried again. *I don't want to do that,* he mouthed silently.

"Oh, darn it, Samantha. There goes that other line again. I'll be right back." Jabbing at the button, she gave Mick an exasperated look. "You're not making this pitch any easier, you know."

"What pitch? What the hell are you getting me into? I don't want to put on some sort of performance, for crying out loud."

"Don't be silly. There'll be nothing to it. I—"

"Nothing to it?" His panic increased. "How can you say that?"

She sighed. "All right, I won't make Samantha any promises. Let me finish the call and then we'll talk about it."

"We sure as hell will talk about it. And who's Samantha, anyway?"

"The activities coordinator at my parents' club." Stacy went back to her call. "Wow, this phone is going crazy. I'll have to juggle a few things to work in that demonstration, so let me call you back in a little while, okay? Right. Good talking to you, too. Bye.'' She finally hung up the phone and glanced at him. ''Mick, don't be stubborn. It's a good idea to show people what you can do.''

''I don't agree. And, besides, how am I supposed to show them? I can't just go out there and do some fancy kicks. I need an opponent, and I don't want to—''

''I've already thought of that. You can use me.''

''You?'' He laughed. ''Nobody is going to believe that you're a real threat to me.''

''I thought of that, too.'' She leaned over and fumbled through her large shoulder purse.

Oh, God. By leaning that way, she'd allowed the top of her dress to gape open, and he could see...way too much for his own good. He shouldn't look. He shouldn't be standing here staring down her dress and thinking about what it would be like to touch those lovely breasts of hers, when what he really needed to do was nip this demonstration idea in the bud. But speaking of nipping...

She moved so fast, and he was in such a sexual daze, that before he knew what was happening she'd left the chair and grabbed him around the waist. Then she poked something hard into his ribs.

He looked into her eyes, and they were no longer soft and appealing. Instead, they glittered with purpose. He felt totally disoriented. ''Stacy?''

''Do as I say,'' she said, ''or I'll put a bullet right through you.''

CHAPTER FOUR

STACY TOOK great satisfaction in Mick's amazement. Keeping her expression as murderous as possible even though she wanted to laugh, she waited for a flicker of fear in those blue eyes. Or apprehension. Apprehension would do. After all, he didn't know the gun was a toy or that she hadn't developed a dangerous attitude while she was living in big, bad New York City.

Instead, once his obvious shock passed, he gazed at her with studied calm. "So shoot me."

"Shoot you?"

"Yeah. Put a bullet right through me, like you said you would if I didn't cooperate." All his attention was focused on her, but he gave no indication that he was nervous.

She frowned. "Are you crazy? You're not supposed to tell someone to go ahead and shoot if they have a gun pressed against your rib cage." She had to concentrate on the gun-against-the-rib-cage part, because mostly she was aware that she was hugging him.

This might be the first time as an adult that she'd ever put her arm around him and, wow, it was cozy standing here like this. He was warm and solid. In fact, unless she was mistaken, a certain part of him below his leather dress belt was getting more solid by the minute. Interesting.

But that was the only real reaction she was getting out of him with this stunt. It was a nice reaction. The longer she stayed here looking up into his eyes, the nicer the reaction seemed. She was getting all warm and juicy herself, now that she took time to notice. If he would put *his* arms around *her,* then they'd have a really good thing going.

Well, except for the toy gun, of course. She was willing to drop the gun. Too willing, especially considering that she was trying to make a point, and mutual sexual attraction wasn't it. "Shouldn't you be trying one of your fancy karate moves to neutralize the situation?" she asked.

"Too late."

"What do you mean, *too late?* Aren't you some advanced level of black belt?"

"Yes. But as long as you have a potentially loaded gun shoved up against my ribs, I can't risk using karate to disarm you. I might not move fast enough to avoid the bullet."

"Oh." So obviously she'd have to dream up a different scenario for the demonstrations they'd put on. She wondered what had caused him to lose his concentration. Maybe what was going on down below his belt was giving her a clue. "But now that I'm here, couldn't you do something?" she asked.

"I am doing something."

No joke. But surely he wasn't referring to his erection. "You are?"

"Yes. I'm watching you very carefully. If you give me an opening, I'll take it. Otherwise I'll try to defuse the situation."

From what she could tell, his defusing tactics weren't working. "I thought you'd be able to disarm me somehow."

"Only if you lose focus. But I'm warning you, Stacy, this is a dangerous game you're playing. Is the gun loaded?"

Which one? she thought, and had to bite the inside of her cheek to keep from laughing. "Why? Are you an eensy, weensy bit afraid?"

"It's kind of hard to be afraid of an attacker who uses

words like *eensy* and *weensy*. But I'm plenty concerned. Loaded guns aren't anything to mess with, even in fun. If this is a joke, and I'm assuming it is, then I hope you're not playing around with a loaded weapon.''

The words coming out of his mouth sounded so older brother, but the reaction going on behind his fly sure wasn't. Maybe this trick of hers had turned out okay, after all. His head might be telling him she was young and kind of stupid, but his body didn't care. His body wanted to rumble.

Amazing how a guy could be in danger of having a hole blown right through him and yet there was that determined soldier down below his belt, standing at attention and ready for action. Or, and this was a fascinating concept, maybe a little danger stoked Mick's fire. That would explain his tendency toward thrill seeking. And she'd bet he still had that tendency, even if he'd tamed it some.

She decided not to tell him the gun was a fake…yet. Instead she planned to have a little more fun. She gazed up at him and tried something a drama coach had told her was a sexy move if you had the right kind of mouth, full and pouty looking. The coach had mentioned that Stacy had the right kind.

Parting her lips slightly, she edged her tongue out and ran the tip along her bottom lip.

Mick's eyes grew a shade darker, and he seemed to be struggling to maintain that calmness he was so proud of, the calmness that would help defuse the situation.

Stacy wasn't into defusing. She stroked her tongue slowly along the underside of her top lip.

Mick's eyes grew darker yet, and his breathing changed. ''Stacy, I don't know what you're trying to prove, but—''

''Have you ever made love at gunpoint?''

Desire flared in his eyes. ''No.'' His voice rasped in the

stillness of the office. "Besides, I know this is all a big joke."

"Is it?" She nudged the incriminating bulge in his pants.

He swallowed. "A guy can't be blamed for having a normal reaction."

"But I could be ready to shoot you." She lowered her voice to a seductive purr. "Does the thrill of danger get you hot?"

"No." His breathing grew labored. "I don't think you're ready to shoot me."

"But you don't know for sure, do you? You don't know if this gun is loaded or not. I think that's turning you on." She brushed against his fly again.

"Why are you doing this?" He was beginning to sound desperate.

"Oh, maybe because of all those years you treated me like a dumb little kid not worthy of your notice."

"Believe me, I noticed you."

"You did?" She discovered her own voice wasn't all that steady as she tucked herself in closer.

He groaned softly. "Give me a break, Stacy. You've been strutting your stuff around me for years. You think I didn't notice?"

"Why would I think that? You never did anything about it."

His laugh was ragged. "As if I would, and have you give my little sister a detailed accounting. No, thanks."

"I wouldn't have told Holly anything."

"Yeah, right." His gaze burned into hers.

"I wouldn't! I didn't tell about you and Cassandra, did I?"

"That was different. You knew I'd get into trouble if you told. But there would be nothing stopping you from spilling everything you and I did."

Now she was getting angry. "Nothing except common decency. Consideration. For want of a better word, *class*."

"Ah, yes, class. Thank you for bringing that up. I knew there was another reason I didn't make a move on you in the old days but, as we've already seen, my brain isn't working at its best right now."

She stared at him in confusion. "What are you talking about?"

"I'm talking about you as a debutante and me working my way through school waiting tables. I'm talking about you driving a Beemer and me barely able to afford wheels."

"What? Are you telling me you didn't ask me out because I had more *money* than you?" She was so outraged that she jabbed the toy gun deeper into his side. "I wish this *was* loaded!"

"Aha." He reached between them, grabbed the barrel and twisted the toy gun out of her hand.

"You are such a jerk." She backed away from him, breathing hard. "It's a good thing your sister doesn't have your prejudices or I would have been minus a best friend."

"It's not so important with girls." He examined the gun in his hand.

"Why the hell not? Holly couldn't afford a Halston original for the prom, but that didn't stop her from suggesting that she and her boyfriend double-date with me and Alex."

His head came up. "Alex who?"

"Alex Connelly, another person who wasn't worried about me being too rich for his blood."

"You went to the prom with Alex *Connelly*? Oh, Stacy, you shouldn't have done that."

"I don't know why not." She wasn't about to tell him that she'd spent the whole night fighting Alex off. She'd found out later that he'd nailed three-quarters of the girls on the pep squad and she'd been next on his list. "We had a great time."

"You did not. You're not that kind of girl."

"How do you know what kind of girl I am? You never even bothered to find out."

He held up the gun. "You're the kind of girl who teases a black belt with a toy, which doesn't make you the sharpest tool in the shed. Lucky for you I noticed that twitch at the corner of your mouth and knew you were trying to keep from laughing."

She fought the urge to find something and throw it at him. He'd probably think that was immature, so she controlled herself. "You did *not* notice a twitch. You thought it was a real gun, and you even wondered if it was loaded. Besides, you said you couldn't do anything about it once I had you in that position."

"Actually, I was pretty sure the gun wasn't loaded, so I could have taken the risk of disarming you earlier. But I wanted to make sure I didn't hurt you in the process."

"Oh, *right*." She stomped around to the other side of the desk. "You didn't want to do anything about it," she said, pointing a finger at him, "because you were having a pretty good time. Because I turned you on, Mr. I-Don't-Date-Rich-Girls."

A red flush crept up his neck. "That was a mere reflex."

"An inconvenient reflex, too, wasn't it? Because you don't want to admit that when you snuggle up to Ms. Debutante, you get a massive erec—"

"Hidey-ho, friends and neighbors!" Mick's friend Craig breezed through the door. "Whoa, Nellie! What's with the heater?"

"Stacy—"

"Stacy wanted to see your gun," Craig finished. "Of

course she did. Hello, Miss Stacy Radcliffe, Broadway star.'' He swept a bow in Stacy's direction.

''Hey, Craig.'' She could sense his wariness under the bluster. They'd never made it past the uncomfortable fact that he'd wanted a date and she hadn't. Although he was a nice guy and many women thought his red hair and freckles were adorable, he didn't excite her. It took Mick to do that. Unfortunately.

''So how come you're visiting the offices of Farrell's Personal Bodyguard Service?'' Craig asked. ''Need a bodyguard?''

''No, actually I'm—''

''Stacy's going to help me out with the phone for a little while,'' Mick said.

She wished to God she didn't need this job so much, or she'd let him know what he could do with his phone. All this time she'd thought he'd avoided her because of Holly, when the real reason was that he had too big an ego to deal with a woman more well off than he was. She was *so* not telling him about her reduced financial situation.

''But you don't get any calls except from me, your sister and your mom. Oh, and didn't your dad call once, too?''

Mick rubbed the back of his neck. ''I got a legitimate call yesterday.''

''Really? Who from?''

''Cassandra Oglethorpe.''

Craig whistled. ''Now there's big bucks for you, m'boy. A guy in our firm handles her taxes, and considering the case of pricey wine she sends him every Christmas, I'm guessing she's loaded. Can you tell me what she needs, or is that privileged information?''

''Sorry, can't tell you,'' Mick said. ''I only told you her name because as the accountant you'll see it on the check anyway.''

Stacy noticed the tinge of color in his cheeks, but she doubted Craig picked up on it because obviously he didn't know anything about the overtones of this assignment. That fascinated her. She would have thought Mick had confided in his best friend about the escapade with Cassandra. After all, Craig wouldn't turn him in.

But it looked as if he didn't kiss and tell, and she and Cassandra were the only other people who knew about that parking lot rendezvous. Apparently Mick really did have a streak of gallantry and didn't want Cassandra's reputation tarnished, even in the eyes of his best friend. That spoke well of him.

It also emphasized how private he was about personal matters. Under the circumstances she could forgive him for being skittish about taking up with his little sister's best friend. But she might never forgive him for resenting her privileged upbringing. It wasn't her fault that she'd been born a Radcliffe. And how ironic that he probably had a better-looking bottom line at the moment than she did.

"So you have a wealthy client," Craig said. "That's good. Congratulations. If she passes the word, you could start building this business into something outstanding."

Mick looked over at Stacy. "Um, Stacy has some ideas about that, too." He put down the toy gun and reached for a flyer.

"You know, that .45 is making me a little nervous," Craig said. "I could have sworn you had a .38, because you thought that would be enough. If you've moved up to a .45 within the first week, you'll be toting an AK-47 by the end of the year."

Mick glanced back at the gun. "Oh, it's not real."

"Okay. That's good. That slows my heart rate considerably. But why are you playing with it?"

Stacy decided that if Mick was willing to mention her

contribution to the flyer project, she might as well advance her cause for the rest of the publicity. "I brought the gun today," she said. "I thought Mick and I might use it when we put on demonstrations around town."

"So *that's* it," Mick said. "Well, I don't think—"

"Demonstrations?" Craig's eyes widened. "I can't believe you've talked the Mickster into doing demonstrations."

"She hasn't," Mick said. "I'm barely able to live with this new flyer, but I have to say it sparked some interest in the copy shop, so maybe it will help."

"Let's see that thing." Craig took the flyer Mick held out and glanced at the picture. "Hey, I remember this. It's from that tournament in L.A. where you won everything in sight."

"It's a dramatic way to highlight his abilities," Stacy said.

"If the color doesn't blind you first." Craig glanced at Stacy. "I take it this was your idea?"

She lifted her chin. "Yes, it was." And if Craig was going to be stupid enough to shoot down her plans because he was still holding a grudge against her for those rejections back in high school, then Mick could easily go along with Craig and her efforts would come to nothing.

"I hate to admit it," Mick said, "but I think she was right. My other flyer was boring."

Stacy was surprised that he'd come to her defense.

"*I* helped you with that boring flyer, my man," Craig said. "You said you wanted something understated and professional."

"Maybe I was wrong. We'll find out after I distribute these flyers."

"If it works, I'm all for it." Craig laid the flyer on the

desk. "But don't forget that you got Cassandra Oglethorpe with that boring flyer you and I designed."

"True." Mick looked over at Stacy, as if expecting her to contradict him.

She wasn't about to. "It can't hurt anything to have two kinds of flyers out there," she said.

"No, I suppose not." Craig eyed her as if trying to decide whether she was his buddy's friend or foe.

In truth she was neither. She would have liked to be Mick's friend, but if he thought of her as a spoiled brat that didn't seem likely. And she could hardly be his enemy because helping him build a thriving business was in her best interests.

As for Craig, she hoped he wasn't allowing their previous history to color his judgment. She'd like to think they were on the same side, both of them trying to help Mick. She couldn't tell from Craig's expression what conclusions he was drawing about her.

"So what brings you to this neck of the woods?" Mick asked.

"Hunger pangs. I thought you'd like to join me at the deli down on the corner for a Reuben sandwich. Stacy's welcome, too, of course."

She sincerely doubted that.

"I'm up for a Reuben," Mick said. He glanced at her. "Would you like to come along?"

She would, but only if she could be a mouse in the corner hearing what the two guys had to say about her. They *would* discuss her presence in the office—guaranteed. She'd also hoped that she and Mick would spend part of the lunch hour shopping for a sexier shirt for him to wear, but she knew better than to bring that up in front of Craig.

Maybe it was time to retreat a little. "Thanks, but I'm not really that hungry," she said. Then she glanced at the iced coffee drink and brownie on the desk. "Was that for me?"

"Um, yeah." Mick looked a little uncomfortable, as if he weren't sure he wanted Craig to catch him in the act of bringing her treats. "The place was on my way back from the copy shop, and I thought you might need a snack."

"Great. I'll just munch on that while I mind the phone. You guys go ahead."

Still Mick hesitated. "Want us to bring you something from the deli?"

"No, thanks." She remembered the French catering service her mother had used in the good old days. Stacy couldn't afford their food now, but she wasn't above tweaking Mick with her supposed wealth. "If I get hungry, I'll just order up something from Antoine's."

"Oh." Immediately Mick's hesitation vanished. "Right. See you later then."

"Bye, Stacy," Craig said. "If you talk to Antoine, give him my best. I handle his taxes now."

"I'll tell him you said hi." As she watched Craig and Mick go out the door, she wondered if Craig thought she'd rejected him all those years ago because he didn't come from a wealthy family. That hadn't been the reason at all, but if Mick thought that way then Craig might, too. Besides, it wasn't true that she'd dated only high-society types.

Or was it? Come to think of it, the guys all had come from families with money. But those had been the ones who'd asked her out, with the exception of Craig. She'd met them through the country club, or at the endless parties her parents gave.

She'd never stopped to think that less privileged boys might not have wanted to risk taking her out in a beat-up old car to a fast-food place and a round of miniature golf. Not that she hadn't done those things, but she'd been escorted to the hamburger stand and goofy golf in a new sports car, not an old junk heap.

Well, except for the times she'd ridden around in Holly's car. She had fond memories of that '65 Ford Galaxie, with room enough for her, Holly and four of their best friends. Her girlfriends had come from various economic backgrounds, and it had never seemed to matter.

Or maybe *she* hadn't thought it mattered. Now that she was more sensitive to the issue, she wondered if any of those girls had resented her designer clothes and family vacations to Europe. When she'd landed a part in the school musical as a freshman, had anyone thought that her private dance lessons with an ex-Broadway star were the reason she'd won the role?

She picked up the phone and called Holly at the bookstore. Holly was the only person who knew that she was no longer in the chips, and Holly was sworn to secrecy, so they could discuss this issue.

She waited while the person who answered the phone went to find Holly, who was working back in the storeroom.

"This is Holly Farrell. How can I help you?"

"Did you resent me for having so much money back in high school?" Stacy asked, skipping an introduction.

"Why? Did my idiot brother tell you that?"

"No. He said that *he* resented me. Well, not in so many words, but that was the gist of it. So I was furious and sort of wished I had a real gun instead of a fake one, although not really. But then I got to thinking that maybe—"

"Back up. What fake gun? What are you up to over there?"

"I pulled a fake gun on him to show him that he and I could put on karate demonstrations at places like my parents' country club."

Holly gasped. "You didn't."

"Yeah, I did. And he thought the gun was real, too, no matter what he says."

"Wow. That was a dangerous stunt, kiddo. What did he do?"

"Well, he—" Stacy caught herself. No matter how much she'd love to describe Mick's reaction, every incriminating bit of it, she couldn't. That was exactly what he'd meant about getting involved with his little sister's best friend. "He acted very calm and controlled, even though I had what he thought was a loaded gun shoved against his rib cage," she said. "And then when he told me about the rich girl thing, I got mad and told him I wished the gun was loaded, and that's when he took it away from me."

"The karate training really has made him cool under fire," Holly said. "Which is good, considering what he's gone into. My poor parents are still kicking themselves. Here they wanted him to learn karate as a kid so he'd stop taking stupid risks, and then he uses his training to become a bodyguard."

"So they're not happy about it?" Stacy knew all about overprotective parents.

"Not happy. Now they're praying he gets married soon, because married guys are usually more careful. Anyway, lucky for you that he didn't break your arm when he thought you might have a real gun. You shouldn't mess around with him, Stace. Seriously."

"You're probably right." *In more ways than one.* "Anyway, we're off the subject. Did you resent me for the clothes and the shoes and the spa treatments?"

Holly paused.

In that brief hesitation, Stacy had her answer. "You did. God, Holly, I had no idea. Was I insufferable? Did I parade my wealth around for everybody to see?"

"No, no, you didn't. You were pretty good about it. Very

good. It was my issue, and it taught me a lot about envy. But I love you, girlfriend. I loved you before, when you were rolling in it, and I don't love you any more or less now because you're broke.''

A lump of emotion stuck in Stacy's throat.

"Stacy, are you okay? Look, you were wonderful about having that money. You shared so many experiences with me that I would never have had otherwise. You know what? I didn't resent you. Never you. I just sometimes wished that I could waltz down to the most exclusive dress shop in Scottsdale and buy whatever outfit I wanted. Or that I could ask my dad to buy me a brand-new red sports car and he'd just do it. I used to wish that kind of thing.''

Stacy cleared the lump from her throat. "Thanks for sticking by me, Holly, even if it was tough sometimes.''

"It wasn't so tough. Believe me. I loved those Aspen skiing vacations when your folks took me along. Listen, I have to go back to work. Want to do something later?''

"Yes. Yes, I do. I want you to help me pick out a shirt for your brother.''

"You're buying him a shirt? Does this have something to do with the gun thing?''

"Sort of. I'll explain when I see you.''

"I can hardly wait. Bye.''

"Bye, and thanks for being my friend.''

"My pleasure.''

After Stacy hung up the phone she made another call to make sure she had some room left on her credit card. She had to be very careful about purchases these days, and she tried not to use her credit card at all. But some things could not be put off. A sexy shirt for Mick was one of them.

CHAPTER FIVE

BY THE TIME Craig hit the elevator, he was giving it to Mick with both barrels. "What in God's name are you doing hiring Stacy Radcliffe to answer your phone? If you really needed a woman to do that, which I doubt, I could have found you at least ten people more qualified and in greater need of a job!"

"I know." Mick wondered if he should finally tell Craig about Cassandra Oglethorpe. He'd always wondered if that teenage mistake would come back to haunt him, and now it seemed to be doing exactly that.

But, damn it, he didn't want to tell Craig about Cassandra. Besides being a woman whose breasts he'd fondled, she was now a client, his first client. For all he knew she'd hired him legitimately, maybe even as a way of apologizing for trying to seduce him so long ago. Dredging up that embarrassing incident and telling Craig all about it wasn't a very good way to thank her for giving him her business.

"Did you hear what Stacy said just now?" Craig continued, gathering steam. "She plans to *order up something from Antoine's.* I don't know what you're paying her, but I doubt she'll make in one day what she could spend on a lunch order from Antoine's. It's nuts, Mick."

"I know," he said again. "But she has some good ideas."

"The flyer has yet to be tested, and I can't picture you putting on demonstrations for the country club set. I realize business has been a little slow at first, but that's to be expected. And see, you just got Cassandra Oglethorpe. That's only the beginning. You don't need to run around putting on demonstrations. Besides, how can Stacy help you do that? Is she trained in karate?''

"No."

"And there's paperwork involved with taking on an employee. Are you aware of that? I was thinking of setting you up with a Simplified Employee Pension Plan, but if I do that, you have to include her. Now there's a joke, you contributing to Stacy Radcliffe's retirement account."

Mick's head began to ache. He hated complications, and they seemed to be multiplying. "I don't know anything about what you have to do when you hire an employee. I've never had one before."

"You shouldn't have one now. There's this wonderful new invention, the answering machine. There's another one—call forwarding. You could get a pager and a cell phone, and not one of those communication aids requires filing a W-2 form! What were you thinking?"

"I don't know." Unless he revealed his history with Cassandra, he couldn't explain his behavior in any way that Craig would understand...except maybe one. "Look, Holly sent her over, and...well, I've always thought she was kinda cute."

"Ahhh." Craig leaned against the back wall of the elevator. "Well, I can't fault you there. As you know, so have I. But she doesn't date guys like us, buddy. And to make matters worse, now that she's working for you, you're in danger of being sued for sexual harassment if she misinterprets something you say or do."

"Oh, God." Mick groaned. Still, he didn't really think Stacy would slap a lawsuit on him if he tried something. He didn't want to hurt Craig's feelings, but after the gun episode with Stacy, he thought she might be interested in a little one-on-one with him, even with his piddly bank balance. "The thing is, she wants me to teach her karate."

"I see." Craig nodded, and there was a touch of envy in his expression. "You, *sensei,* her, grasshopper."

"Something like that." The elevator slid open and they headed out of the building. Mick's appetite had vanished. Somehow he'd become caught in a no-win situation. He could either bad-mouth a client or pretend he was planning to take advantage of an employee.

"So, in the course of the course, so to speak, you thought you might get a little hands-on opportunity with the gorgeous Ms. Radcliffe."

Mick's frustration made him walk faster, despite the heat. "You know what? Probably not. Because you're absolutely right, I could be walking right into a sexual harassment suit. Chances are she won't have anything to do with guys like us, so I'd be setting myself up for rejection or worse. Who needs that? Besides, making a move on her while teaching karate would be unprofessional. I'd be discrediting my *dojo.*"

"And goodness knows we wouldn't want that." Craig was puffing. "Never mind the prospect of financial ruin. Maintaining the honor of the *dojo* is way more important. Hey, could you slow down a little? I think it's about a hundred and thirty out here today."

"Oh. Right. Sorry." Mick slowed his pace.

"So now that we've established that hiring Stacy was a colossal blunder, are you going to fire her when you get back to the office?"

"I really can't do that." He searched for a reason he could tell Craig. "Holly would be on my case if I fired her so quickly."

"But you will fire her eventually."

"Yeah. As soon as I can. In the meantime, maybe I'll go along with a couple of her ideas." He decided to try out another one on Craig. "She, um, she wants me to dress differently."

"Like how?"

Mick pushed open the swinging door into the deli and was greeted with a blast of chilled air. "She thinks I should buy one of those collarless shirts in black, and make sure it fits sort of tight, in order to show off...well, so people can see..."

"Your muscles!" Craig started to chuckle.

"Could you keep it down?" Mick glanced around and hoped he wouldn't see anybody he knew as he headed for a line of people waiting to place their orders.

"I hate to say this, but she's probably right on that score." Craig got in line behind him. "With that shirt, you look more like an accountant than a bodyguard."

"What about Kevin Costner in that movie with Whitney Houston?"

"You're not that type of bodyguard. He was into the celebrity thing, and he had all kinds of gizmos and gadgets. Surveillance toys. He was more like a Secret Service guy, which is what he dressed like, come to think of it. But with you, people should be imagining they've hired Bruce Lee or Chuck Norris. I think Stacy's right. You need a different look."

Mick was happy Stacy had scored at least one point in Craig's mind. "See, she knows that kind of stuff because of her experience on Broadway. She knows how somebody should promote himself."

"Yeah, well, I still don't see that as a reason to keep her on once you're up and running. Anyway, order your sandwich. You're next."

Mick let the subject drop until after he and Craig were

seated. They had a favorite table by the window where they could look out on the busy downtown street and watch for women. At the moment Mick wasn't much interested in ogling females. He had all he could handle sitting up in his office right now.

Once they'd both started on their sandwiches, he returned to the topic of Stacy. "I promise she won't be a permanent fixture or anything," he said. He needed Craig to be okay with her working in the office for a little while. After all, Craig was providing the bookkeeping temporarily, and if it hadn't been for him, Mick might never have thought of going into this business. He wanted to keep Craig happy.

Craig put down his sandwich. "I'm just sorry she's a fixture in the first place. But I suppose she'll get tired of the whole thing soon, anyway. You know she's only doing it for cheap thrills." He picked up his dill pickle and bit into it with a loud crunch.

"I'm sure you're right, but she's willing to work for twenty percent of my first fee from Cassandra Oglethorpe. I've already tacked on twenty percent to the amount I quoted Cassandra, so I'm not out anything, except for all that pension junk you mentioned. Damn, do I have to worry about medical insurance and stuff?"

"Could be." Craig regarded him impassively.

"Damn."

Craig finished off the pickle while he gazed at Mick. By the time he'd swallowed the last of it, his expression was more sympathetic. "Are you sure you're not expecting this relationship to go beyond the office? I wouldn't blame you for wanting it to, but it's risky from a business standpoint, and from a personal standpoint it's a dead end. Just ask me."

"I'm sure." He hadn't been so sure when she was teasing him with that tongue-around-the-lips routine, though. At that moment he'd been deep into a fantasy of kissing that soft, plump mouth. He'd also imagined peeling off her little sundress and kissing the rest of her. Worse yet, he'd discovered something unsettling about himself. He hadn't stamped out his thirst for thrills, after all. Apparently the threat of danger *did* turn him on.

He'd known all along that was the attraction with Cassandra. She was at least fifteen years older than he was, and although she was reasonably attractive, she wasn't beautiful. They had nothing in common, and she wasn't the kind of woman he was drawn to. He would never have been excited about her rendezvous suggestion back in high school if the plan hadn't been dangerous.

Of course he hadn't expected to get caught back then, just like he hadn't expected to be shot today. Back in his bungee-jumping days, he hadn't expected the line to snap, either, but he'd never been absolutely sure it wouldn't, and therein lay the thrill of it all. Apparently he was still susceptible to the promise of that kind of thrill.

Craig swallowed another bite of sandwich. "I'm picking up vibrations from you, old buddy. You may think you've given up on getting jiggy with Ms. Radcliffe, but I say the possibility is still lurking in the back of your mind. And I know you—when you get involved with somebody, you really get involved. Even if she doesn't claim harassment, she could put your heart through the shredder before she decides to traipse on back to the Big Apple."

"That's just it. She seems to have given up on her dancing career. I guess the competition was harder than she thought." Every time Mick remembered that sad look in her big brown eyes, he got a pang in his chest. "I feel kind of sorry for her."

"Omigod. This is not good. As we've discussed too many times to count, you are way too softhearted."

"I'm just saying that when you have to give up a dream, then—"

"Okay," Craig interrupted. "Let's do a reality check here. There are lots of people in this world you could legitimately feel sorry for. The counter person at the dry cleaners who's a single mom struggling to make ends meet. And then there's the guy at the cigar shop who lost a leg in 'Nam. And the cleaning lady in my office complex whose son is in jail—we can feel really sorry for her. But Stacy Radcliffe? The girl who drove a BMW convertible to school the day she turned sixteen? I don't *think* so."

"Hey, rich people have feelings, too."

"I'm sure they do." Craig wiped his mouth with his napkin and tossed it beside his plate. "And they can hire expensive therapists to help them deal with those feelings. They don't need the likes of you and me to feel sorry for them."

"Okay." Mick wasn't sure how much of Craig's attitude was connected to Stacy's rejection years ago, but he decided enlisting Craig's sympathies for Stacy wouldn't work. "Then forget about feeling sorry for her. She's willing to answer my phone for the next few weeks, and because of the extra I tacked onto Cassandra's fee, it's not costing me anything yet. Maybe, since I'm not paying her until then, that loophole can keep me from having to file all those government forms right away."

"Maybe. I'll look into it."

"I like the idea of somebody answering my phone. It does seem classier. And anybody else I hired would need to be paid on a regular schedule, but Stacy doesn't need the money, so she can afford to wait until I get a check from my first job."

Craig nodded. "Okay. I can see you're set on this. Just as long as you don't entertain any ideas about after-hours activity, then maybe it's a good thing. All I'm saying is that she's the kind of woman who inspires those kinds of ideas, so you'll have to watch out.''

"I'll watch out, Craig. You've succeeded in making me very, very cautious.''

Craig laughed. "I sincerely doubt that. You're a lot of things, but cautious isn't one of them.''

"Well, in this case, I intend to be.''

Craig gazed at him. "Good.''

STACY WASN'T SURPRISED when Mick came back from lunch alone. Craig wouldn't be eager to spend more time in her company.

She'd been about to call the English riding club her mother belonged to and find out if they'd like a demonstration by Farrell's Personal Bodyguard Service, but instead she replaced the receiver so she could talk to Mick.

He sat in a folding chair across from her and glanced at the remains of her brownie and iced coffee. "I thought you were going to order some lunch.''

"I'm not that hungry.'' Actually she was getting very hungry. The brownie and coffee were wearing off, but she'd hold out until five. She wasn't sure where the nearest fast-food place was, and she didn't plan to ask, either. Tomorrow she'd bring her lunch in order to save money, and she'd disguise her thriftiness by pretending she was dieting.

"I shouldn't have bought you the brownie and spoiled your lunch. It's not good to fill up on sugar and then skip the nutritious stuff.''

She rolled her eyes at the comment. It was sort of cute the way he kept trying to act like a big brother. She'd never had one before, so she didn't exactly hate his behavior. Still, she wanted him to see her as a capable adult, not a wayward child. She was getting mighty tired of everyone, from her parents to Mick, treating her that way.

Crossing her arms on the desk, she leaned forward. "Mick, I'm all grown-up now. Just because you bought me a brownie doesn't mean I had to eat it. I realize that you're used to watching out for a little sister and you toss me in the same category as Holly. But I am not your little sister."

"I'm well aware of that." For a moment, sexual tension flickered in his eyes. Then he seemed to mentally douse it. "But for the time being you are an employee, and you'll do a better job if you eat right and don't load up on the sugary stuff. I didn't help the situation any by bringing you a brownie."

At that moment she realized something very liberating. She'd never been an office employee before, but he'd never been a boss, either. The nearest he'd ever come to being in charge of someone was Holly, so he lapsed into that behavior because he didn't know proper protocol, either.

"How about this approach?" she said. "I'll handle my own food and drink while I'm on the job if you'll promise not to comment on my choices."

He nodded. "Sounds fair."

"Craig doesn't like the fact that you hired me, does he?"

Mick looked uncomfortable. "He was just confused because he didn't think I could afford to hire anybody right now."

"And he doesn't know anything about you and Cassandra Oglethorpe, does he?"

"No." He gazed across the desk at her. "What? Why are you smiling at me like that?"

"I guess because I'm so impressed that you've protected Cassandra all these years, even to the point that you didn't tell your best friend about that episode. Most guys wouldn't have been able to resist bragging a little."

"Maybe it's only because I'm too embarrassed."

"In front of another guy? Come on. She's a sexy woman. You'd get all kinds of points as a stud if you told your friends that she came on to you, not to mention the points for daring to try something in her car in the school parking lot."

Red crept up his neck to his face, and he shifted in his seat. "Could we talk about something else? Like…like the demonstrations, for example. I don't want to do that."

"So I gathered." While he'd been at lunch she'd worked out her bargaining strategy, because she figured the demonstrations would solve two problems. They would get Mick out of this office and into the public eye, and they would force him to teach her some karate. "How about this? We do one for my parents' country club, and if you don't get any clients from that, then we won't do any more."

He let out a gusty sigh. "You keep saying *we,* like you're going to do it with me. You have no idea how much training you'd need to be ready for that. So the whole idea is no good."

"The idea is *great.* You keep forgetting that I'm a highly skilled dancer. I will learn faster than you ever imagined. If I weren't wearing a dress today, I'd be able to show you right now what an easy time you'll have with me."

He coughed. "You might want to rephrase that."

"Oh, loosen up, Mick." She couldn't help teasing him. "In fact, why don't you lock the door and I'll strip to my underwear and show you what I can do? No one will ever know."

He nearly knocked over the chair as he scrambled to his feet. "Absolutely not!"

"Why?" This was fun. "Think you couldn't resist me while I'm wearing nothing but Victoria's Secret?"

He'd begun to quiver. "That's not it."

"Sure it is." She loved being able to get this kind of reaction out of him. She wasn't entirely sure what she wanted to do with that reaction, but knowing she sexually excited him was terrific news.

"We have to get something straight." His voice was strained. "You talked your way into this job, but now you're definitely my employee. You're getting a W-2 form, and maybe something called a Simplified Employee Pension."

"Pension? I don't need a—"

"I might have to give you one. Regulations."

Talk of pensions and regulations had a way of ruining the mood she'd been having such a good time creating. "I'll bet you don't have to give me a silly old pension."

"Not only that, but I'll probably have to look into medical and dental insurance, and deal with red tape that won't quit. The bottom line is that we're gonna be totally and completely official." He swiped the air with one hand. "Which means that questionable behavior can become sexual harassment, and we're not going there."

"Sexual harassment? Or for pity's sake. All I was going to do was show you some of my dance moves."

"I don't want to see any of your dance moves."

"How are you going to understand that I'll be an excellent karate student if you won't even let me show you my dance moves?"

Heaving a sigh, he folded his arms and gazed at the ceiling. "Okay, we'll work on the karate."

She punched both fists in the air. "Yippee! When?"

"Tomorrow."

"Terrific." She could hardly wait. Once he realized how much promise she had, he would begin to see her as a true partner in this business. Maybe, for that reason, she shouldn't tease him sexually anymore. "What should I wear?"

"I'll bring you a *gi*, but you'll probably want to wear a white T-shirt under it. Most women do." He cleared his throat. "In fact, make sure you do."

She was so tempted to take that line and run with it, but she controlled herself. "Is it one of those white pajama thingies?" If a *gi* was what she was picturing, it had a wrap front and nothing to keep it closed but a tie belt. She'd bet Mick would be plenty nervous if she didn't wear that T-shirt.

He looked pained. "It's white, but if we're going to do this we might as well start out right. Call it a *gi*, not a white pajama thingy."

She clasped her hands together and bowed. "As you say, master."

"*Sensei.*"

She glanced up. "Say what?"

His mouth twitched as if he might be trying not to laugh. "Call me *sensei*. It means *teacher*."

"Oh. Cool. I am going to be so awesome at this. Wait and see, Mr. *Sensei*, sir. I am going to knock your socks off."

His grin broke through. "Maybe so, but between now and tomorrow you might want to try working on something that may seem totally foreign to you, but it's very important for a karate student."

"Sure, anything. You'll be amazed at what a quick study I am. What is it?"

He laughed. "Humility."

CHAPTER SIX

"SO HOW'S IT GOING with my brother?" Holly asked the minute Stacy joined her at a table in the Fiesta Mall's food court.

"I'll tell you in a minute. First I have to eat." Wedging her purse between her feet, Stacy grabbed the fat bean burro nestled against a pile of rice and two tacos on her plastic plate. As she took a huge and unladylike bite, warm refried beans oozed between her fingers. She chewed, swallowed and licked her fingers clean before taking another generous mouthful.

Her mother would have been horrified at the way she was inhaling this food in public. A lady would use a knife and fork on the burro, but she didn't have time for that. God, she was hungry. She'd never been this hungry in her life.

But then she'd never spent an entire day in a food-free environment, either. During dance rehearsals somebody had always shown up with sandwiches or pizza or pretzels. Food had been easy to come by on the streets of New York.

New York was also where she'd learned to love eating with her hands. Come to think of it, New York had undone much of the society training she'd received at her mother's knee. She'd wanted to fit in with the other troupe members, and that wouldn't have happened if she'd demanded a seafood fork with her order of shrimp or turned up her nose at drinking beer from a bottle.

That was another good reason for not living at home. Her

manners weren't as refined as they used to be, and her mother would surely have tried to fix that.

Stacy had arranged to meet Holly at the mall and, in the process, had announced her plans to scarf down some food immediately. Holly hadn't been interested in eating this early and had wandered over to a coffee bar to buy an iced latte. Stacy had headed straight for the Mexican concession because the food was filling, cheap and quick. It also tasted fabulous, but anything might have tasted fabulous to her right now.

Glancing up, she found Holly staring at her. "'Scuse my manners," she said. "But I'm faint with hunger." Then she polished off the burro and took a drink of her cola before picking up a taco.

"No doubt." Holly grinned at her. She'd recently had her hair cut in a short, elfin style that made her look as if she should be painting toys in Santa's workshop. "'Scuse my staring, but I've never seen you chow down like that. I had no idea anyone could work up such an appetite answering the phone."

"Mm-hm." Stacy finished off the taco. Gradually the urge to consume large amounts of food was fading. She dabbed at her mouth with the napkin she'd forgotten to put on her lap. "The thing is, I was running late, so I didn't eat breakfast. Then I thought Mick and I were going to grab some lunch, but Craig showed up so they went to lunch instead."

"You mean Mick went off to eat with Craig and didn't give you a lunch break? That's inexcusable. I'm calling him tonight and giving him some instructions about how to treat an employee, especially when that employee happens to be my best friend. I can't believe he didn't—"

"It was my own fault," Stacy said. "When I found out that Mick had always thought of me as a spoiled little rich girl, I told him I would have Antoine's deliver something. It was childish of me, but I couldn't resist. Of course I couldn't afford that, so when he came back from lunch I told him I wasn't hungry, after all.''

Holly put down her latte so fast the ice sloshed against the rim of the cup. ''You mean you haven't told him about your financial problems?''

''Nope, and I don't want you to, either.''

''He wouldn't spread it around, if that's what you're worried about.''

''No, I'm not worried about that.'' Mick might doubt her ability to keep a secret, but she didn't doubt his, not after the way he'd protected Cassandra all these years. ''I just don't want him to know I'm desperate for this job. I plan to be so valuable that he'll keep me on because I'm an asset to the business, not because he feels sorry for me.'' She lifted her second taco and prepared to take a bite.

''Oh.''

Stacy put down her taco again. ''What do you mean, *oh?*''

''Nothing! I just figured you'd tell him, that's all. If you don't want to, that's okay by me. I can see your point, and I'm sure you're doing the right thing.'' Holly's smile was intended to sweep away all questions.

It didn't work on Stacy. She concentrated her attention on her best friend, who'd never been able to tell a decent lie. ''Holl, why do you want me to tell Mick about my parents losing all their money?''

''I don't! I just thought you would.'' Holly jabbed the straw into her slushy drink several times while watching the results, as if mixing the contents of her cup had become the most important job in the world.

''Yes, you do. When I said I didn't plan to tell him, you sounded *very* disappointed—about as disappointed as you were the time you found out that my father had been teasing you about knowing Shaun Cassidy personally."

Holly looked up, her gray eyes troubled. "You're right about my brother having a prejudice about your money. I thought if he knew you weren't rich anymore, he'd… um…well, the two of you might—"

"I knew it!" Stacy slapped her palm on the table. "You sent me over there because you're trying to start something between Mick and me."

Holly's chin lifted. "That wasn't my only reason. He needs somebody to help him get this business going, and he won't take any advice from me or my parents."

"But it was a reason?" Stacy was pretending to be more upset than she really was. Secretly she was flattered that Holly would try to engineer such a move.

"Okay, I have *always* thought you two would be good together. And not just because you're my best friend and it would be cool to have you for a sister-in-law."

"*Sister-in-law?* You are trying to get us *married?* Holly, I am so not ready to get married." The concept gave her cold chills.

"Why not?"

"Well, because…" Stacy paused. Her first reaction had been absolute panic, and she hadn't stopped to think why. "Because I'm only twenty-six?" she said finally.

"Lots of girls we graduated with are married. Some of them even have kids. JoAnn Detmar has three."

"That's scary." Stacy picked up her plastic fork and took a bite of rice. This was not a comfortable topic, and she still wasn't sure why that was.

"Wasn't there anybody in New York that made you consider marriage, even a little bit?"

"Not really. I think of marriage as something you get into when you know where your life is going, and in New

York I had no idea whether I'd make it as a dancer or not. Now I know that's not my future, but I don't know what is." She gazed at Stacy. "And I certainly don't want to get married and have kids because I can't think of anything better to do."

Holly sighed. "I wouldn't want you to do that, either. But I've had this fantasy of you and Mick together, and *he's* not getting any younger. Plus my parents are right. If he got married, he'd think more carefully about the risks he takes than he does now. So here you are, both in the same town, working in the same office.... What are the chances that you'll match up like that again?"

Stacy couldn't help laughing at the earnest way Holly was pleading her case. Besides, laughter relieved the tension she felt every time she thought of herself getting married. "I had no idea you were so stuck on this."

"I know. I never said anything because you seemed set on the dancing career and I knew Mick didn't want to move to New York, so it seemed impossible. But now you're back! I wanted you to make it big, Stacy. I really did. But since you didn't, I think maybe it was meant to be, you coming back here and my brother still being single."

Stacy hated to spoil Holly's fantasy. Holly had always had a terrific imagination, which was why working with books fit her perfectly. But real life didn't usually turn out like the stories Holly loved so much.

"I can see you aren't buying this," Holly said. "But I'm telling you, it would work. First there's Mick, shy on the outside, while on the inside lurks a wild streak that not everybody can handle. Then there's you, the exact opposite—bold on the outside and shy on the inside."

The shock of being suddenly revealed jolted Stacy. "You've never said that you see me that way."

"I'm not sure I did see you that way until you came home

this time and admitted you didn't have what it took to succeed on Broadway. That's when I looked past the hype and realized a shy person was hiding inside the superconfident performer.''

Stacy took a deep breath. ''You know, it's a wonder you've put up with me all these years. Between my money and my ego, I must have been a real pain in the ass.''

''You were not!'' Holly grabbed Stacy's clasped hands and squeezed. ''You were fun and exciting and generous. Maybe I was a little overwhelmed, a little intimidated, a little jealous. But I was proud to have you as my friend.'' She grinned. ''You were my status symbol.''

''Ouch.''

''Everybody needs them when they're teenagers. You had money and fame and I had you. Mick had his sports, and girlfriends galore. All of us were walking around trying to be such big shots, or, in my case, the best friend of a big shot. You and Mick would never have worked out seven or eight years ago, but now…'' She gave Stacy's clasped hands one more squeeze and released them. ''Now I think you might.''

''How could we? You just got finished telling me we're opposites.''

''I used the wrong word. What I meant to say was you would complement each other.'' She wove her fingers together. ''You know, dovetail. Where he's weak, you'd be strong, and vice versa.''

The conversation was getting too intense for Stacy. ''I think you've been spending an unhealthy amount of time in the self-help aisle of your bookstore. And besides, Mick has made it very clear that as long as I work for him, there will be no hanky-panky. He thinks I'd sue him for sexual harassment.''

Holly laughed. "Oh, right. I'll bet he said that after he had lunch with Craig."

"True."

"The guy invented paranoia. Did you tell my brother how ridiculous that idea is?"

"I guess. Sort of. Maybe. But that doesn't matter, because I don't think he trusts me."

Holly studied her for several seconds. "So tell him about your new circumstances. I'm sure that would go a long way toward establishing trust."

Stacy shook her head. "I won't have him feeling sorry for me. It's bad enough that I told him I failed as a professional dancer. He got that sympathetic look on his face, and I wanted to bite my tongue. I'd rather have him be suspicious than sympathetic."

Holly threw up both hands. "Okay. But I warn you, Stacy Radcliffe, if my brother ends up shoving some fifth-rate sister-in-law down my throat because you wouldn't cooperate at the critical moment, I'll—"

"Now who's paranoid?" Stacy said. "You and Craig make a good pair."

Holly turned bright red.

Stacy stared at the unexpected reaction and gradually began to smile. "Hey, did I accidentally guess something?"

"We've been out a couple of times." Holly's nonchalant shrug was unconvincing, especially in combination with her pink cheeks. "No big deal. We didn't tell Mick about it, though, because, as you know, my brother is impossible when it comes to the guys I date. I want to see if this is going anywhere before I spring it on Mick. And Craig, being the King of Paranoia, agrees with me."

"My lips are sealed. But I think this is kinda cool." Then a new thought came to her. "Is that why you're so intent on matching me up and marrying me off? Because you're feeling the urge?''

"No!" Holly looked even more embarrassed. "Marriage is the farthest thing from my mind."

Stacy wasn't sure she believed her, but she accepted the answer because the whole concept of her and Holly being marriage-bound was freaking her out. "Good," she said, "because we are way too young to be thinking like that. I don't care what JoAnn Detmar has been up to. We're different."

"Absolutely."

Not very convincing, Stacy thought. Maybe for Holly the time was ripe for finding a mate, but not for Stacy. "You've been on your own for a while," she said. "But I really haven't. All these years I've been supported by my parents, I've felt that they should be able to call the shots. Now, because the money's gone, I'm finally free." She put her hand on Holly's arm. "I'd love to be your sister-in-law, Holl, and I love that you want me to be. But the thought of marriage…" She shuddered. "I can't deal with it. Not when I'm just starting to spread my wings."

"Oh." Holly looked disappointed. "I guess I see what you mean."

"That's not to say it isn't the perfect thing for you, though."

"Me? I'm not so sure about that. I treasure my freedom, too."

"Maybe not as much as me," Stacy said.

Holly gazed at her for a long time. "No, maybe not," she said.

It was a sobering moment for Stacy. For six years she'd been immersed in show business and had somehow imagined that time was standing still back here in Phoenix, that everything had stayed pretty much the way she'd remembered it from high school. Instead, people she knew, even her best friend, had been moving toward the next stage in their lives.

When she'd assumed that she'd become a Broadway star, she'd pictured herself having a series of torrid affairs and never doing anything so traditional and boring as getting married and having kids. Now that she wasn't destined to be a Broadway star, maybe she would get married some day.

But not yet. For the first time in her life she was out from under her parent's thumb, and she wanted to take time to enjoy it. This gig with Mick was the perfect way to start.

She picked up her tray. "Come on," she said to Holly. "Let's go find a sexy shirt for your brother."

MICK ARRIVED at the office early enough to change into his *gi* and figure out how he'd turn the small office into a temporary *dojo*. Luckily a maintenance man rode up in the elevator with him, so he asked the guy to help him move the desk against the wall. That created a usable open area, although Mick would have preferred more space.

Locking the door, he changed into his *gi*. The industrial-grade carpet didn't feel nearly as nice under his bare feet as the hardwood floor he was used to, and he'd have to watch out for rug burn, but he'd make do.

By the time Stacy walked in a little before nine, bringing her trail of expensive cologne with her, he'd run through some warm-ups. They'd released some of his tension, but not enough. One glance at Stacy and the tension returned. Unless he could get rid of it somehow, his muscles would fight him the whole time he tried to teach her some basic skills.

"Wow, you look official," she said.

"That's the idea." And she looked gorgeous, as always.

Today her short skirt and jacket were the color of a ripe peach, and her strappy high heels matched. He was glad he'd bought her the more expensive *gi*. The lady obviously was used to wearing the best.

She glanced around the office, her eyes wide. "Did you move that desk by yourself?"

"Sure." When he realized she actually believed him, he smiled and shook his head. "Not really. The maintenance guy helped me."

"I would have helped you."

It hadn't occurred to him. "I don't know. That's a pretty heavy desk."

She set her large purse against the wall. "You still think of me as some weakling, but dancing is a very physical activity." Then she pulled back the lapels of her jacket. "See? I wore a white T-shirt, like you said."

When he'd suggested a T-shirt, he'd imagined a shapeless cotton one, the standard-issue type that was only sexy when wet. Instead she'd worn a scoop-necked spandex job. He supposed she hadn't meant to thrust out her breasts when she opened her jacket, but she had, and he found himself staring. And salivating.

"Is the shirt okay?" she asked.

"Uh, sure." He cleared his throat and glanced away, hoping to hell his face wasn't the color of a fire hydrant as he headed over to the gym bag he'd dropped in a corner. "Fine. Let me get your *gi*." *And get my erection under control.* He unzipped the bag and pulled out the folded cotton uniform.

"I have something for you, too."

He turned to discover her holding a black collarless shirt. The material looked like silk and he didn't dare imagine what the shirt had cost. If it fit, he'd have to pay her for it, and his budget probably wouldn't stretch that far. The financial differences between them always had a cooling effect on his libido, which in this case was a good thing.

"Do you like it?" she asked.

"Um, it looks expensive."

"Good. I wanted it to." She held it out. "You need to look both sexy *and* prosperous. But don't worry about the cost. It's my gift to you."

Pride jabbed him hard. He'd pay for the damn shirt if he had to take out an advance against his credit card. "I can't have you doing that. Tell me how much it was."

"More than you would have paid, but it's the perfect shirt. Holly helped me pick it out, so it should fit like a glove." She glanced at the bundle in his hand. "Is that my uniform?"

"Yes. But about the shirt, just tell me—"

"How much do I owe you for the uniform?"

"Nothing, for now. I think you'd better decide if you like karate before you decide if you want to keep it." Because he'd splurged on a really nice one, he hated the thought of it being shoved to the back of her closet. When she ultimately decided to give up on this crazy idea, he'd take it back and find someone else who could use it. Therefore he didn't intend for her to pay.

"So is it mine or not?"

"It's yours for as long as you want to study karate."

Her eyebrows arched. "Then I should have it for a long, long time. You'd better let me pay you for it."

"No."

"Then it's a gift?"

He could see where this was going. "Look, this is a specialized uniform, and if you give up on karate there's no reason to have it, so you can return it to me. The shirt, on the other hand, isn't the sort of thing I can imagine giving back."

"I can't imagine giving back the *gi*, either. So let's make an even trade."

"Stacy, you're being unreasonable."

"*I'm* being unreasonable? What about you?" She shook the shirt at him like a matador teasing a bull. "You know what your problem is? You're still hung up on how much money I have. Because I'm rich, I'm not allowed to buy you something, because that would damage your precious pride. But you are allowed to buy me something, thus proving to me that you have money you can throw around, just like I do. The whole situation is dumb, Mick."

He considered the bundle in his hand. If he traded with her, then he'd never be able to ask her to return it. It probably would end up crumpled in the back of a cedar-lined closet behind her rack of imported Italian shoes. He really hated knowing a perfectly good *gi* would go to waste, but they seemed to be at a standoff.

Closing the distance between them, he held out the uniform. "All right. It's a deal."

"Great." She took the *gi* and handed him the shirt. "I'd love for you to try it on. If Holly's advice was wrong and it doesn't fit, I'll take it back tonight and get you a different size."

"You mean try it on now?" Sure enough, the material felt as expensive as it looked. The only time he'd ever felt silk against his skin was when a woman had worn it to bed. Therefore the fabric reminded him instantly of making love. Not good.

"I think you should put it on before you get all hot and sweaty. I assume we'll both work up a sweat doing this?"

"Uh, yeah. Probably." Oh, God. Between the silk shirt and her perky breasts under the white spandex, he'd abandoned thoughts of karate in favor of another activity that would make them all hot and sweaty. And now she was suggesting that he get partially undressed.

Yet she had a good point. If she'd paid as much as he thought for this shirt, then he'd better try it on right now.

"I thought we'd get pretty vigorous," she said. "I brought along some supplies so I can freshen up in the bathroom after we're finished. Now go ahead and put on the shirt while I take off my suit."

"*What?* Hey, wait a minute!" He nearly dropped the shirt as she laid the *gi* on the edge of the desk and shrugged out of her peach-colored jacket. "Don't do that!"

"Oh, relax." She slung her jacket over the back of his desk chair and reached for the button at the back of her skirt.

"Stacy, don't you dare undress in this office."

"It's hardly undressing. This isn't exactly a T-shirt. It's more like a leotard. You can't even see my underwear." She stepped out of the skirt.

He nearly had a heart attack. He'd forgotten that her nickname in high school had been "Legs" Radcliffe. She looked like Miss America standing there in her snug white leotard and high-heeled sandals.

Seemingly oblivious to the havoc she was causing, she leaned down to pull off a shoe, a move that accentuated the toned curve of her backside. Then she shifted her weight to take off the other shoe. Her toenails were painted. Peach.

He'd never sucked a woman's toes in his life, but he wanted to suck hers. In a spontaneous, totally unintended expression of desire, he groaned.

Stopping in midmotion, her hand cradling the bottom of her shoe, she glanced up. "Is something wrong?"

His voice was a harsh croak. "Yes."

CHAPTER SEVEN

STACY COULD HARDLY mistake the expression of lust in his eyes, which had turned navy-blue with desire. He clutched the silk shirt so tightly in his fist that his knuckles showed white beneath his tan.

She'd obviously turned him on, big time. Yet he'd probably never believe she hadn't meant to. She really wanted to succeed as his working partner, and mad passion at this critical stage would definitely screw that up.

Unfortunately the look in his eyes had prompted her insides to do the happy dance. One move on his part and she'd be ready to rumba. But so far he'd managed a reasonable distance between them.

"Sorry about that," she said. "Guess I've spent too much time in musical theater. Backstage everybody runs around half-naked."

He swallowed.

She probably shouldn't have mentioned the half-naked part. "What I mean is, nobody thinks anything of stripping— Oh, never mind." She jerked off her remaining shoe, tossed it to the floor and grabbed the white bundle he'd given her. "I'll put this on and solve the problem." But the pieces weren't familiar to her, so she fumbled a bit. And her hands were shaking for some silly reason. "Which of these thingies is the pants?"

"The one in your left hand." He sounded desperate.

"Okay. I see now. Okay. Here I am, stepping into the

pants. Except I'm not sure how the drawstring is supposed to work." While she fiddled with it, the pants fell down again. "Whoops."

"Put the string through those loops in front."

"Oh." She gave him a quick glance. He still looked as if somebody had bopped him in the head with a rubber mallet. "You could turn around, you know."

"Oh. I could." He sounded like a robot. He even moved like one when he turned his back on her. Gone was the fluid movement, the easy grace.

"I really wasn't trying to cause a problem, Mick." She managed to get the drawstring tied and in the process decided these pants would definitely cure whatever ailed him. She'd never seen a more unflattering fit in her life. "I came here thinking of the lesson as similar to a dance rehearsal. In New York we'd come in, peel off our street clothes and get to it."

"It might be better—" He paused and cleared his throat. "It might be better if you didn't explain anymore."

"I guess you're right." Boy, was she conflicted. Her body was telling her to proceed with the program and initiate some contact with the muscled guy standing not far away. But her mind warned her that if she started down that unprofessional path, she could kiss a career in the personal protection business goodbye. And she needed a new career.

Putting her arms in the sleeves of the uniform's coat, she tried to make sense of the little ties on either side. Finally she gave up, wrapped herself in the thing and secured it with the white belt that had fallen out of the bundle when she'd unrolled it.

"You can turn around, now," she said. "I'm all covered up."

He turned, and he looked slightly more composed. "You must think I'm an idiot."

"No." Inside her loose cotton outfit she was still quivering in reaction to the tension between them. "I'll bet you've been concentrating so hard on setting up this business that it's been a long time since you've had any—" She stopped the explanation immediately when she realized what she'd been about to say.

"Sex," he finished for her. "Yeah, it's been a while, but that's no excuse. You'd think I was still eighteen." He gestured toward her coat. "You'll need to wrap that the other way, and then I'll show you how to tie the belt."

"What difference does it make how I wrap the coat?"

"Custom. Left over right is how it's done. The way you've done it, right over left, is how they prepare bodies for cremation."

"Yikes!" She quickly untied the knot of the belt, tossed it on the desk and folded the flaps of her coat the other way. Then she reached for the belt.

"Wait. The belt alone won't hold it closed. You need to tie those little strings on each side. Plus the jacket should hang evenly."

She looked at the strings. "I had no idea this was so complicated. What do I tie first?"

He took a deep breath. "I'll show you." He laid the silk shirt on the desk and came toward her.

"Are you sure that's wise?"

"Look, we have to be able to work together. Next Wednesday we'll head on up to Cassandra's cabin for three days. Maybe it's good that I'm confronting my problem now."

Our problem. Three days with Mick would be filled with temptation. She'd proposed to act as his chaperon, but maybe Cassandra would become hers. Stacy cleared her throat. "There's a lot more to karate than I thought. I can't even get the outfit on right."

"There is a lot, so don't think you'll be trained and ready by the time we head for the White Mountains." He knelt in front of her and took hold of the lapels of her jacket. "With this thing, first you make sure these are hanging evenly." He adjusted the lapels with brisk efficiency.

In the process, the cotton material rubbed over her breasts, and her nipples tightened. "Okay."

"Then you tie the strings on the right side into a bow." He sounded perfectly in control of himself. "And then the strings on the left side."

But the more he worked with the material, the more aroused she became. If he was this good at dressing her, he'd probably be excellent at undressing her. She closed her eyes and wondered if he could hear her heart beating.

"You're not watching what I'm doing. You won't know how to do it if you don't watch me."

She opened her eyes and looked down, meeting his gaze as he tilted his face upward to look at her. And there was that heated connection again, the one that sent sparks flying and made her tremble with yearning.

"Damn," he said softly.

"Double damn," she murmured, and sank to her knees, facing him. "Mick, there's powerful chemistry going on between us."

He cleared his throat. "Tell me about it."

"Do you think it's because you're feeling deprived?"

He reddened. "Maybe. How about you?"

"Uh…it's been a while for me, too." She was embarrassed to admit how long. David had been her only lover while she'd lived in New York, and he'd gone home to Nebraska more than a year ago. "What can I say? There are a lot of gay guys in the dance world."

"So this could be about both of us needing a good—"

"But we won't do that," she said quickly. "That would mess up our working relationship."

"No, we won't do that," he said, his expression stormy. "But what *are* we going to do? Every time I look at you I want to kiss you…for starters."

Her pulse kicked up another notch, but she tried to stay semirational. "Then maybe you *should* kiss me and get it over with. A kiss is no big deal. We can still work together after a kiss. It's possible we'd both hate it."

"But we might love it. It's too risky."

"But if we don't do it, then this tension will never go away. Come on. Kiss me. We'll probably find out our mouths don't fit right, or we don't like what the other one does, tongue-wise."

He smiled, but tension still lurked in his gaze. "Tongue-wise?"

"You know. Everybody has a favorite technique—the slide, the thrust, the tickle, the tease. And techniques don't always mesh." Just thinking about sharing a kiss involving tongues heated her blood to boiling, but then again she'd been fantasizing about Mick for so many years that reality was bound to be a letdown. That would be a good thing for both of them.

"Which technique do you like?" Huskiness betrayed the emotion underneath his lighthearted question.

"Doesn't matter. You can't change yours to fit, not after all the years you've been kissing. It either works for me or it doesn't. A first kiss can be more disillusioning than a first time in bed."

"I see." The light of challenge flared in his eyes. "And you think one or both of us will end up disillusioned if we kiss each other."

"It could happen." She wondered if maybe she'd taken

a wrong turn. Now he might be determined to disprove her theory, and then they'd both be sunk.

"In karate we're taught to stay out of volatile situations." He reached up as if to cup her head in his hands. Instead he combed his fingers through her hair, drawing it back from her face.

She quivered at the gentleness of his touch. "I guess this qualifies as volatile."

"Definitely." He combed his fingers through her hair again. "You need to tie this back, out of the way."

She closed her eyes, enjoying the sensation of having her hair stroked. "Before you kiss me?"

His breathing roughened. "I'm not going to kiss you."

"It feels like you are." Keeping her eyes closed, she parted her lips slightly.

His breath caught and his hands stilled. "I shouldn't take the risk."

As disappointment washed over her, she realized how much she wanted this kiss, needed this kiss, no matter what the outcome. Her lashes fluttered upward and she gazed into his smoldering eyes. "But you always were a daredevil."

"Never more than now. This is suicide." He combed his fingers through her hair again, pulling it back and closing his fist around it, almost as if he intended to tie it back for her. "Your hair's even softer than it looks."

Her womanly instincts overrode every bit of good sense. "So's the rest of me."

The heat intensified in his eyes. "I'll just bet it is."

"And you want to find out for sure, don't you?"

He didn't answer, but the look in his eyes did.

"Come on, Mick. You weren't built for risk-free living."

He tightened his grip on her hair. "And you? What were you built for?"

His hold on her hair had an electrifying, caveman feel to

it that thrilled her to her toes. "I'm still trying to find that out." Heart pounding, she moistened her lips. "Wanna help me?"

Leaning over her, he exerted steady pressure on her hair, drawing her head slowly back until her mouth was angled perfectly to meet his. "Yes," he said, his voice thick with desire. He stroked the exposed column of her neck and cupped his hand around her throat. "Yes, God help me, I do." Then his mouth came down, hot and demanding.

Instantly she knew she was in big trouble. Mick didn't have technique. He had talent. With one hand fisted in her hair and the other encircling her throat as he kissed her, the message was primitive, possessive, wildly exciting. She lost her power of reason and could no more analyze what he did with his tongue than list the sensations coursing through her.

All she knew as she clutched his shoulders and moaned in delight was that he could have anything he wanted. Anything.

His mouth lifted a fraction. "This was a mistake," he muttered.

"Yes," she said, panting. "Let's keep making it."

And, bless the man, he seemed to agree. As his mouth reconnected with hers, he slid his hand inside her jacket. She loved the caress, hated the material separating her nipple from his fingers. But she hadn't learned quick costume changes for nothing. In no time she'd slipped her arms free of the coat.

Mick caught her fever and released his hold on her hair. While he continued to make fabulous love to her mouth, he helped her pull her arms out of the leotard and shove it to her waist. All that remained was her white satin bra, and soon that lay on the floor beside them.

Then he cupped her breasts with a groan of satisfaction. Knowing how well he kissed, she could imagine the wonders he'd visit on her aching breasts. Cupping his face in both hands, she guided him to her throat, her collarbone and at last her tingling nipple. Sure enough, his mouth seemed created to give her pleasure in that way, too.

Staying limber through dance had its advantages. As the fires raged in her, she abandoned all modesty, placed her hands flat on the floor and arched her back, thrusting her chest toward him.

A fierce, eager sound rumbled in his throat as he leaned over her and took what she offered. She hung her head back and cried out in sensual delight. She'd never surrendered to such pure animal lust in her life, and it felt glorious.

When the phone rang, she was too far gone to care, too immersed in her jungle of passion to be interrupted by the demands of civilization. "Let it go," she pleaded.

His voice rasped with frustration. "I can't." He eased her back to a kneeling position. "I have to answer it." Getting to his feet, he lurched toward the desk and fumbled with the receiver. "Hello? I mean, Farrell's P-Personal Body-guard Service." He coughed, as if to disguise his heavy breathing. "Hey, Craig." He paused. "No, I'm fine. We were…moving furniture, and I was closest to the phone."

Gradually Stacy's erotic haze dissipated. What had she been thinking? Obviously she hadn't been thinking at all, and now Mick would fire her. She grabbed her bra from the floor and scooted around so her back was to him while she put it on.

Moving quickly, she pulled up her leotard top and shoved her arms back into the sleeves. She stood in order to try to arrange the coat of her *gi* correctly. She would be so fired and she wouldn't learn karate and she'd be back at square one, with no job prospects. What a mess.

"Yeah, that sounds good," Mick said into the phone. "Okay, buddy. Thanks. Bye."

Bracing herself for his dismissal, Stacy turned around. "Mick, I—"

"I am so sorry," he said. "So very sorry but—"

"Don't say it!" She crossed her arms over her stomach to hold the coat closed. "Please don't. I'll dress in ugly clothes. Baggy, ugly clothes. I'll stop wearing makeup and perfume and even deodorant if you think that would help."

He shook his head, his gaze troubled. "It wouldn't. The thing is, I don't see how I can—"

"Give me another chance. Let me show you how sexless I can be. I really want this job, Mick. And if you fire me, how are you going to handle the situation with Cassandra?"

"Fire you? Who said anything about firing you?"

"You did! You said *I'm so very sorry but....* That's what people say when they're about to let you go. That's what the casting director would say after I'd auditioned and didn't get the job. *I'm so very sorry but you don't have the right look. I'm so sorry but you aren't what we had in mind.*" Her emotions were all stirred up from their wild make-out session, and now, damn it, she was battling tears.

"Stacy, how could I fire you? I was as much to blame as you. You really could sue me for sexual harassment if I fired you now."

"Oh, for pity's sake! You know I wouldn't do that. Not even if you fired me. But please don't. I need—" She caught herself before she admitted that she needed the job. "I need to find a new direction for my life, and I really think this might be it." She took a shaky breath. "I promise I'll never let you touch me again."

"I'm the one who needs to make some promises. And I promise not to ever lay a hand on you again, Stacy, if you can forgive me for what just happened."

As she gazed at him, honesty prompted her to let him off

the hook. "There's nothing to forgive," she said quietly. "I loved every minute of it."

He groaned. "I'll have to ask you not to say things like that."

"Right. You're perfectly right. I won't say things like that. I won't say anything that's not directly related to our working relationship. I will be as efficient and sexless as a stapler."

"Good luck."

She stood a little straighter. "I'll have you know I can be *very* efficient."

"I'm sure you can. It's the sexless angle that I don't think you'll be able to cover, and that's okay, because I'm going to ignore that portion of your...personality. But in order to do that, I have to forget about teaching you karate. That's what I've been trying to say."

Her hopes for this new career plummeted again. "But I have to learn! Otherwise, how can I help you in the field?"

"I never really expected you to do that."

"I know, but *I* expected me to do that."

He sighed. "It's too much to learn in a short time. By the time you were proficient enough to be of some help...we're talking a couple of years, at least, probably more."

"Less. Much less. Let me prove it to you. Give me some lessons."

"I can't. It would involve too much close contact, and I'm obviously very susceptible to you. I thought I could count on my sense of honor, but that didn't stop me from...from..." His eyes grew smoky again.

She knew that look. If she didn't call a halt they'd be back on the floor in no time, and then he really would fire her. "Okay, you won't teach me karate. I'll learn it on my own." She had no idea how, considering her finances.

"That's what I should have suggested in the first place. I can recommend a very good teacher. I don't know if he's available, but if you take private lessons, you will learn faster."

"Thank you. I'll look into it." She would do nothing of the kind, but she would go to the library and see what she could find on the subject. "You're going to be surprised at how much I pick up in a short time. I want us to be able to do those demonstrations, and I hope to start setting them up when we come back from the White Mountains."

"We'll see."

From his expression she was pretty sure he had no intention of doing those demonstrations. He'd tolerated the new flyers, and he'd be pleased if they brought in more business, but he probably didn't intend to keep her on once they'd completed the assignment at Cassandra's. After that, so long as he didn't indulge in any more craziness like this, he'd probably feel free to let her go.

"What did Craig want?" she asked.

"He told me that if I didn't pay you anything except a portion of the fee for Cassandra, you would be considered an independent contractor and I wouldn't have to get into the pension and insurance stuff."

"You mean if that's *all* you ever paid me." Sure enough, she'd been absolutely right about his plan.

"Right. If I put you on some kind of salary, then I have to think about your benefits." He blew out a breath. "Look, for some reason Craig seems to have mellowed a little on this deal, but he still thinks you're doing this for the hell of it and you'll get bored soon and leave."

"Craig's wrong."

He gazed at her without responding.

"He's wrong, and I'm going to prove that to you." Stacy scooped up her jacket, skirt and shoes. "Now, if you'll excuse me, I'll head down to the bathroom and change back into my work clothes."

CHAPTER EIGHT

MICK WAS EXTREMELY unhappy with himself. He'd handled this whole business poorly. Worse than poorly. Stacy had come in this morning expecting a karate lesson, and instead she'd been mauled. Maybe she'd enjoyed the mauling, but that didn't excuse his behavior.

The fact that she'd brought him a present made him feel even worse. He glanced at the black silk shirt on the desk. He might as well use this time when Stacy was gone to try it on. It was the least he could do.

As he was taking off the coat to his *gi*, he thought of what a disaster the whole uniform episode had turned out to be. Thank God the phone had interrupted them, but someone might just as easily have opened the office door. It was the Cassandra Oglethorpe syndrome all over again.

He thought he'd outgrown that kind of stunt. Apparently not, and he'd put Stacy at risk this time, not to mention his professional reputation and his brand-new career. What an idiot.

No doubt Stacy was telling the truth about the informality backstage at a Broadway theater and how she'd approached this morning's karate lesson. Much as he'd like to believe she'd intentionally been provocative, he didn't think so. Not this time. No, the blame all belonged to him.

He laid the coat on the desk and picked up the black shirt. The tactile association with the expensive silk was the same as always for him—something that felt this good belonged on a beautiful woman, at least until he'd stripped it off of her. But Stacy had bought it for him with the intention of sprucing up his image, and he needed to find out if it fit or not.

The buttons slipped from the buttonholes easily, as if the manufacturers didn't want to cause the shirt's owner any inconvenience by making him struggle with the task. The pearl-gray buttons were as smooth as polished marble. Everything about this shirt was sexy.

After unfastening the smaller buttons at each cuff, he slipped his arms into the sleeves. The silk tickled the hair on his arms and he remembered when Vivian, a woman he'd dated for nearly a year, had taken off her black silk panties and trailed the soft undies all over his naked body.

He'd loved it, and that Christmas she'd bought him silk boxers. He'd ruined them in the washing machine and had decided he wasn't classy enough to own such things. If he kept this shirt, he'd take it to the cleaners, which was one more expense he couldn't afford.

But damn, it felt good when he put it on. He buttoned it up, and the silk rustling over his chest affected him so much that he was afraid he'd get another erection. He'd just finally recovered from the one he'd had during those moments of madness with Stacy.

If he thought too much about that experience—the fullness of her mouth and the ripeness of her breasts—he'd be right back where he'd vowed not to go again. But something about this shirt made him think of surrender.

He tucked it into the waist of his *gi*, and that was another mistake. His briefs rode low on his hips, which left lots of territory for the silk to tease. It whispered over his navel and the sensitive small of his back. For a man used to cotton, the effect was sinfully sweet. It made him think of sin, too, and that wasn't good.

"I like it," Stacy said from the doorway.

He turned, afraid she still might be rumpled from their encounter. To his relief she looked totally together—her makeup repaired and her hair combed. The white leotard under her jacket showed no signs of having been pulled down and bunched at her waist so that he could... He'd better not think about that.

Clearing his throat, he glanced away. He had to control his thoughts better.

"What do you think?" she asked.

He wasn't sure how to answer that. The shirt reminded him of pleasures he'd rather not think of while Stacy was in the vicinity. "It feels...very expensive."

She smiled. "That can be a very good thing. As I said before, you want to project prosperity. If that shirt can make you look and feel successful, then it's well worth it."

"I don't think I can accept—"

"Mick, please don't reject my gift. You're doing me a big favor by hiring me as your assistant and giving me a sense of purpose, now that I've left Broadway. I want to show my appreciation."

He felt like sixty kinds of a heel. "Don't make me out to be some sort of nice guy, because I'm not." Even now he was having trouble ignoring the sheen of lipstick on her mouth and the gentle rise and fall of her breasts. "A nice guy wouldn't have taken advantage of—"

"Stop right there. You didn't take advantage of me. We enjoyed some mutual pleasure. Neither one of us is to blame. But I agree that if we continue down that road, our working relationship will be compromised. I don't want that." Her brown eyes gleamed with determination.

No matter how much he tried to tell himself that she couldn't be serious about this job, he had a gut instinct that she was very serious about it. That didn't make sense, considering that she was Stacy Radcliffe, debutante, but he couldn't shake the feeling that she would hang in there and try to learn the personal protection business.

Unfortunately she had no idea how difficult and time-consuming her training would be. In the meantime he couldn't afford to keep her on if all she could do was answer the phone and do the filing. He figured she was doomed to fail at the task she'd set for herself.

That bothered him more than he wanted to admit. The only way to lessen her sense of failure was to cut her loose now, before she invested any more time in the project. She'd already promised she wouldn't sue for sexual harassment if he fired her.

"Stacy, I've changed my mind about taking you on the Oglethorpe assignment," he said. "I'm a big boy. I can keep her from getting too friendly, if that's even what she's planning. It might not be."

"You're not taking me?" Her eyes grew wide. "Then does that mean—"

"It means that there never was a job here in the first place. You're trying to create one, and you're even willing to study karate in order to do that. I can't in good conscience encourage you when I know how long you'll have to train and how hopeless the whole idea is."

She regarded him with dismay. "Mick, I—"

"Listen, I was wrong to hire you on the basis of some supposed awkward situation with Cassandra." He hated seeing the intense disappointment in her expression, but he steeled himself against it. "I'll handle Cassandra. You should cut your losses and look for some other job."

"But I don't know what else I could do."

God, but this was difficult. And Holly would be furious with him for not giving Stacy more of a chance. But he'd only be setting her up for a fall. He—

The phone rang again. She started for it, but he waved her off. If he wasn't planning to keep her on, then he needed to answer his own damned phone.

He picked up the receiver. "Farrell's Personal Bodyguard Service. How may I help you?"

"Mick Farrell?"

"Yes."

"I saw your flyer," the male caller said. "The one with you kicking the guy in the head. That was a great flyer. It really got my attention."

"I'm glad." Score one for Stacy.

"With all the kidnapping going on these days, I'm getting nervous about my family's safety. I'm considering putting somebody on retainer to keep an eye on things. When could we sit down and talk about it?"

His first legitimate client. And it was all due to Stacy, the woman he was trying to fire, the one who had no options for other employment. He knew how it felt to be groping for your purpose in life. He'd been there quite recently, and he didn't think having a rich mom and dad would help much.

"Let me check my schedule and get back to you," Mick said to the guy on the phone. Then he quickly took the man's name and number and promised to call him before noon.

After he hung up, he gazed across the room at Stacy. If he'd expected her to ask who the caller was, she didn't seem inclined to.

Instead she looked resigned to her fate. "You're right," she said. "I'm not qualified to be your assistant, and I have no idea how long it will take me to learn enough karate to be useful to you. You really don't need me. I'm sure you could use the twenty percent of Cassandra's fee for something better than having me around."

"Maybe not." He gestured toward the phone. "That was someone who saw the new flyer. He wants to get together and talk about putting me on retainer so I can cut the risk of having a member of his family kidnapped."

"Really?" Her expression brightened. "That's *wonderful*, Mick."

He wanted to see her smile. He really, really wanted that. "I figure he wouldn't have called without that new flyer. So I'd like you to stay, after all."

"Absolutely not."

"What?" He'd thought she'd jump at the chance. "Why not?"

"Because I can tell by the look in your eyes that you're offering me this out of pity. We don't know if the new flyer was the reason he called. He might have called if he'd seen the old flyer, too."

"It's not pity, damn it! It's fairness. You're responsible for this piece of business, assuming I get the job, and I'll bet he won't be the only one calling. And even if I don't do those demonstrations you've talked about, you still made the contact and got some people interested in the concept of a personal bodyguard. That alone could generate some activity."

Hope began to glimmer in her eyes. "I don't want to be a rock around your neck."

"You won't be, Stacy." She might be a temptation and a trial, but she wasn't capable of being a rock around his neck. He'd already been impressed by her dedication and creativity.

"Let me think about this." She stood quietly and studied him for several seconds. "That shirt really does look outstanding on you."

"If you won't stay, I'm not keeping it, and that's final."

She gazed at him for a little longer. Then she took a deep

breath. "Okay, I'll stay, on one condition. You won't put me on salary, because then you have to worry about all those pesky benefits. You can continue to pay me the way you're doing for Cassandra's job, twenty percent of the fee."

Now he was beginning to feel cheap. "Maybe you *should* get benefits. That's what any other employer would offer you."

"But I don't want any other employer. I want this job, and I don't care about benefits."

"Let me talk to Craig about it. I don't even know what it might cost. Maybe the whole thing isn't very expensive, and considering what you've already done for the business, you deserve benefits." He knew she was probably covered seven ways to Sunday under plans carried by her parents, but that didn't matter. He was her employer, so it was his responsibility to see that she had medical insurance, maybe even dental insurance. Weaseling out of that wasn't right, no matter what Craig said.

"Tell you what," she said. "Let's put the benefits thing on hold until after this weekend. By then you'll know if this guy who just called is serious, and we'll know how we work together on an assignment. Then we'll talk about whether I should get benefits or not."

Mick nodded, because her reasoning made sense, but now that he was committed to having her as an employee, he wanted everything set up right. No employee of his would walk around without benefits, not if he had anything to say about it.

She crossed to the desk. "I guess we'd better get to work. What time do you want to meet with this guy? I'll call him and set something up."

"I could meet him right now."

"Nope." She smiled at him. "That would let him know

you have nothing else to do but run over and see him. I could tell him that you could work him in this afternoon around three, if that sounds okay."

"Of course I could go at three. Or two, or four, or any-time he's available. Don't you think I should be more flex-ible? He must be important if he's worried about somebody kidnapping his family."

Stacy picked up the notepad where Mick had scribbled a name and number. "Whoa-ho! Vincent Chalmers! He owns half the office buildings in downtown Phoenix, probably even this one."

Mick couldn't even begin to think what a client like that could mean to his fledgling business, and he sure didn't want to take a chance on losing him. "Like I said, shouldn't I give him a choice of times?"

"Nope." Stacy glanced over at him. "Trust me on this, Mick. When you deal with a person like Chalmers, you need to be as busy and in demand as he is. He'll respect that and be even more eager to hire you."

Mick felt uncomfortable with that, but if anybody knew how to handle the rich and famous, Stacy did. "Okay. But if he waffles at all, give him another option."

"Fine." Stacy picked up the phone and punched in the number. In less than two minutes she'd completed the call, and Mick had an appointment with Vincent Chalmers for three o'clock that afternoon. "See?" She gave him a tri-umphant smile. "No waffling. He needs what you have to offer."

"I guess so." Mick was amazed. Apparently he needed what Stacy had to offer, too, and he'd nearly thrown it away. Still, he had to be careful not to take *all* she had to offer, or they'd both be in trouble.

"And I assume when you go to see him this afternoon, you'll wear that shirt."

He hesitated. Accepting such a sensuous gift as this shirt seemed like a step in the wrong direction. The material alone turned him on, and now each time he wore it he'd remember the morning he'd allowed himself to be carried away by lust.

"It's perfect for a meeting with someone like Chalmers."

Mick glanced at her. "You've met him?"

"He's come to parties my parents have given. He's a Bruce Lee fan, so I can see how he'd be attracted to that flyer. Wear the shirt, Mick. It won't kill you."

No, but it might mess with his mind. "Okay. And thanks."

Her shoulders relaxed. "I'm *so* glad you decided to keep it." Crossing to where she'd left her large purse, she rummaged around and pulled out a department store bag. Then she came over and handed it to him. "Here's two more, one in navy and one in maroon."

He backed up and spread his hands in protest. "No way. One is bad enough, but three? No way."

She shoved the bag toward him. "You can pay me a Christmas bonus if you want, but take the shirts."

"Nope." He folded his arms. "Not taking the shirts." Folding his arms against his chest was a whole new experience in this shirt. The material slid against his skin like cool water. He loved it.

She placed the bag on the desk. "If you get the job with Chalmers, you'll be seeing his family a lot. You can't very well show up in the same shirt all the time, and once you appear in one of your boring business shirts you'll lose points."

"It's my abilities that are important here." The subject really made him cranky. "Clothes shouldn't make such a big difference."

"Maybe not, but in the world you're hoping to work in, they do."

"I'd never thought of that angle, and I can't say that I like it much."

Stacy perched on the edge of the desk, which made her short skirt ride up a couple of inches. "Aren't you being a wee bit hypocritical on this issue?"

"Me? I've never cared about clothes." Not true. He cared a great deal about the hemline of that skirt she was wearing. She had the smoothest, most golden thighs he'd ever seen.

"I beg to differ," she said. "According to you, I can't practice karate unless I have the exact right uniform, and then I have to make sure the hem of the jacket is even, and all the ties are tied correctly, and if I don't fold the lapels the right way, somebody's liable to shove me into a crematorium. Then the belt is a whole other matter, and I understand that color is super important."

"That's different." And he didn't want to talk about that, either, because talking about it reminded him of how her breasts had risen to meet his mouth, and how she'd moaned when he'd kissed her there.

"It's not different," she said. "Clothes send a message, and you'd better adapt that message to the activity you're pursuing, or you start out with a handicap. You advised me on how to wear a *gi* this morning, and now I'm advising you how to dress for your meeting with Chalmers."

Her short skirt was sending a message, all right, and it had bypassed his brain and gone south. If he stood here discussing clothes much longer, neither of them would be wearing any. "I'm going out for coffee," he said. "Want me to bring you any?"

"Sure." She grinned. "Are you going like that?"

He glanced down in horror, certain his erection was jutting out in obvious eagerness. He discovered nothing of the kind, fortunately, but he was still wearing the pants to his karate uniform. If he walked onto the streets of Phoenix wearing those and this black shirt, he'd be taken for a rapper dude, and that definitely wasn't his intention.

"No. I'll go change first."

"See? You made my point beautifully. You are what you wear."

Then what are you when you're wearing nothing at all? He didn't ask the question. In her case, the answer was obvious. She would only improve with every piece of clothing removed from that gorgeous body.

He cleared his throat. "If I get the job with Chalmers, then I'll buy those two extra shirts from you."

"With your first check from him," she added, shifting her weight again. "Not until then."

"With my first check." She had the most beautiful legs he'd ever been privileged to ogle. He'd bet her inner thighs were as soft as her breasts. Desperate to escape before he made another big mistake, he grabbed his gym bag and headed for the door. "See you soon with coffee."

"I'll be waiting."

"Shouldn't be long." He sounded so casual as he left the office, but inside he was trembling. *I'll be waiting.* Try as he might, he couldn't erase the image of Stacy waiting for him in a totally different venue—lying against a mound of snowy white pillows in a bed big enough for playing. And he knew what she'd be wearing. It would be the only thing she was wearing, and he would delight in taking it off as he slipped each pearl-gray button free....

CHAPTER NINE

HOLLY CALLED STACY that night from work. She usually pulled the Friday evening shift at the bookstore and when things were slow she sometimes called to chat. This time she caught Stacy in the middle of watching the instructional videotape she'd rented from Blockbuster. She'd planned to spend the weekend seeing how much she could learn from it.

"What's going on?" Holly asked. "You sound out of breath."

"I'm following the exercises on this karate video, and it's not as easy as it looks."

"No kidding. What are you trying to do, impress Mick at your next session?"

"Not exactly." Stacy fought the urge to tell Holly everything. Confiding in her best friend would be terrific therapy right now. But she'd promised Mick that she wouldn't blab intimate details, and she couldn't tell Holly the whole story without hinting at what had transpired. "The thing is, I've decided not to take lessons from Mick."

"Really? Why not?"

"Um, because I think it undermines our employer-employee relationship."

"Oh, for heaven's sake! It's already undermined by the fact that you've known him since you were a kid. What's the matter, was he mean to you?"

"No." Stacy decided this had become way too complicated. Holly actually wanted her to get involved with Mick, so she'd be happy about the recent developments, but Stacy couldn't tell her and violate Mick's privacy. She couldn't be too secretive, either, or Holly would suspect there had been some unusual office procedures going on today.

"I'll bet he was too tough on you," Holly said. "I've seen him when he gets into *sensei* mode, and it's damned intimidating, even for a sister who knows perfectly well he's a softie at heart."

Stacy struggled to come up with something to say that would be true, yet wouldn't reveal too much. "A big part of the problem is that he doesn't think I'm serious about learning it and becoming his assistant in the field."

"Well, that's because he still thinks you have all the money in the world. I wish you'd tell him the truth about that."

"Nope. He would never have accepted those shirts, for one thing."

"So he liked them?"

"I think so." Stacy sure liked them. She'd never forget walking into the office and getting her first glimpse of him in the black shirt. Resisting the urge to go over and wrap her arms around him just to experience that silk-over-muscle feel had taken extreme willpower.

"You're probably right that he wouldn't have accepted the shirts if he'd known you're broke. Listen, Stace, promise you'll tell me if you get to the point where you can't pay the rent. I have some savings."

"Oh, Holly, that's so sweet of you." Stacy's eyes misted. She'd live in a cardboard box down by the Salt River before she'd take her friend's savings to pay her rent, but the offer touched her. "I'll let you know if things get that bad. I don't think they will."

"Let's hope not."

"If fact, Mick had a very promising appointment today. From the sound of things, I think he'll get another assignment soon—a very good assignment." She couldn't resist. "And the call came because of the flyer you and I made."

"Yeah? That's awesome! See, I knew you'd give him a boost. I'm going to tell Craig. Eventually he'll have to admit this was a great plan."

Stacy grabbed the chance to switch topics. "Are you going to be seeing him, then?"

"Uh, yeah, we're going out tomorrow night. That's one reason I called, to see if you and Mick would like to come along. Believe it or not, Craig said it was okay with him."

"Holly! Mick and I are not a couple! You can't invite us on a double date with you and Craig. He's my boss and I'm his assistant."

"And he's Craig's best friend and you're mine. What's wrong with both of us wanting to go out with our best friends?"

"Forget it," Stacy said. "Putting aside Mick's preferences for the moment, I can't believe Craig really wants me around."

"You might be surprised."

"Well, of course he's not going to bad-mouth me, knowing we're best friends, but he doesn't like me, Holly."

"And I say his attitude's changing, and the four of us would have fun."

It would be Mick's worst nightmare. "It would be inappropriate. And, anyway, I need to spend the weekend watching this video and trying to get the hang of karate. I have to take the video back on Sunday night, so I hope to have it memorized by then."

"Knowing the way you pick up dance routines, you will. Whoops, there goes my other line. If you change your mind, give me a call, girlfriend."

Stacy hung up the phone and pushed Play on her remote. As she worked to get into the stance they were showing on the video, she thought about Holly's matchmaking dreams and hoped Holly hadn't confided them to Mick. That could ruin everything.

STACY WAS DELIGHTED when more responses to the flyer kept Mick out of the office Monday and Tuesday. Many of the appointments she made for him were dead ends, but a few looked as if they might develop into assignments.

Mostly Stacy was glad he'd been scarce for two whole days. It cut down on the temptation factor at a critical time. Wednesday morning they'd leave for the White Mountains, and she didn't want to jeopardize that trip in any way.

Besides, she needed to work on her karate. Although she'd returned the video, she'd found several books at the library, and she wore loose clothing to work so that she could practice what she was reading. Kicks were her favorite thing because she could groove those in while she talked on the phone.

She kicked to the front, to the back, to the side. To test herself after she'd finished a call, she'd open the file cabinet drawers and close each one with a well-placed kick. A couple of times she was afraid she might split the seam in her slacks, but fortunately they were good slacks with excellent tailoring, so the seam held.

One book had mentioned that not everybody could kick high enough to reach an opponent's head, so Stacy had decided to make that her specialty. In every chorus line, she'd been the highest kicker. Now maybe that skill would count for something.

On Tuesday she brought an uninflated beach ball to work and, once Mick left, she blew it up and set it on top of the file cabinet. By squinting her eyes, she could imagine the beach ball was the head of Gerald, the crazy guy who'd scared her so much back in New York.

She'd never forget the helpless feeling of being subtly stalked by Gerald. He'd never done anything illegal, so she hadn't felt justified in notifying the police, but she'd felt threatened, all the same. He'd sent her countless love notes and had attended every performance of the last musical she was in. Afterward he was always at the stage door with flowers. She'd made certain that she left with a group so that she'd never had to confront him alone, but still, his constant presence had creeped her out.

She never wanted to be that vulnerable again.

In karate, she'd found a way to counteract that feeling. Her vulnerability diminished a little more every time her foot made contact. After many tries she was finally able to smack that ball with the edge of her foot and send it flying across the room.

Punching with her fists didn't interest her as much. She couldn't imagine how a girl could do that regularly and maintain a decent manicure. Not that she didn't work on the recommended hand and arm movements—she did. But in her heart she knew her talent lay in her kick.

Actually, she had a second strong point—her lung power. After years of voice lessons, she knew how to project. She could yell *eee-ya!* with such force and authority that she thought even Mick would be impressed.

But she wasn't ready to unveil her skills yet. She suspected her form was still pretty sloppy and she definitely didn't know what to do with her hands and arms. She was miles away from being able to break a board with the back of her hand, and she wasn't all that eager to try it.

Her kick and yell, though, were awesome. She had a gut-level conviction that she was perfectly suited to the personal protection business. All she needed was a little more time to prove it.

Tuesday afternoon she glanced at her watch to gauge how soon Mick might return. She wanted to have her shoes back on and the beach ball deflated before he walked through the door. By her calculations she had at least a half hour left before he was likely to walk into the office again.

Setting the beach ball on the file cabinet, she turned her back on it and imagined her stalker poised behind her. Come to think of it, Gerald had been a sort of squarish person, like the cabinet, although he'd had more hair than this beach ball. Greasy hair. And the most sinister smile…

"Eee-ya!" She whirled and kicked the beach ball so hard it ricocheted off three of the four walls before it finally bounced on the floor. Then she heard the knob turn on the office door.

Grabbing the beach ball, she lunged for the desk chair and shoved the ball under the desk as Mick walked in.

"Is everything okay?" He glanced around the office. "I heard someone yelling in here."

"It was me," she said. Beneath the desk she turned the beach ball with her toes until she found the release valve. She couldn't imagine how she'd explain the ball, so her best bet was to quietly deflate it while it was still under the desk. "I rented some Bruce Lee movies over the weekend, and I thought, if nothing else, I could practice my karate yell."

He gazed at her. "I hope you're not trying to teach yourself karate by watching movies."

"Now that would be silly, wouldn't it? I'll hire a private teacher, just as you suggested. How did your appointment go?" She nearly had the valve stem open.

"Okay. But she had a long-distance call come in from her sister, so she asked me to come back another time." He sat in one of the folding chairs across from the desk. "She's an older woman who loves to shop, and she carries lots of cash. She worries about purse snatchers and muggers, so she's thinking of hiring me to tag along on her shopping trips, but she hasn't quite made up her mind to spend the money.''

"Doesn't sound like a very exciting assignment." She nudged the plug from the valve stem and air hissed out. It made more noise than she'd anticipated, so she stretched and sighed to cover the noise. "Ahhh, the holiday is almost here," she said, a little louder than necessary. "I'm looking forward to a trip to the mountains, yesss, I am. Yesss, I really am. Oh, yesss." The stupid ball had more air in it than she'd thought.

Mick stared at her. "Stacy, what's that noise?"

"What noise?" She tried to plug the valve with her little toe, but that made a squeaking sound, as if she had a mouse loose under the desk.

"Something's going on, and you know it." He got up and came around to investigate.

"Okay, it's a beach ball. I was in here playing with a beach ball. You said yourself that it could get terminally boring working in the office by yourself, and you were right." She held up the sagging piece of plastic.

"You're playing with a beach ball? How weird is that?"

"I *like* beach balls. They bounce."

He stared at her as if considering whether she was in need of medication. "And you're in your bare feet." His confused expression suddenly cleared. "You were practicing more than your karate yell, weren't you?"

"Would you believe indoor soccer?"

"No, I'd believe you're trying to impersonate Bruce Lee, although what the beach ball has to do with anything I haven't a clue." Crossing his arms, he gave her a stern look. "Karate is nothing to mess around with. You can't watch a couple of movies and think that you know what you're doing. You could get seriously hurt.''

"Don't be ridiculous.'' She stood, still holding the deflated beach ball. "I'm a trained dancer, and I know my limits. Besides, I've been reading up on it.''

"There is no way you should try to teach yourself. You could strain something or pull something, and no telling what sort of bad habits you'd get into.''

His attitude really bugged her. "I'll have you know I am *very* good at kicking, already. In fact, if you'll stand back, I'll show you.''

"Stacy, I don't want you to keep this up. I'll find you a teacher, if you don't want to take the time. Just—''

"What's the matter? Are you afraid to discover I'm a natural at this, which would threaten your precious ego?''

He threw up both hands. "Okay! Go ahead and demonstrate your supposed skill. I hope you are a natural. Otherwise you're taking a big chance on hurting yourself.''

"First I have to blow up this beach ball.''

"Fine. Blow up the beach ball.''

She took the valve stem between her teeth to hold it open while she inflated the ball. While she was doing it she happened to glance over at Mick. His expression had changed. From the way his eyes were darkening, she had to assume that watching her blow up a beach ball was giving him naughty thoughts.

His jaw tightened, as if he might be trying to control those thoughts. She didn't have much sympathy for him. Instead of scolding her for taking chances, he should be praising her for her ingenuity.

She finished inflating the ball and placed it on top of the file cabinet. Then she opened each of the four drawers. "This would be more impressive if the drawers were full of files, but at least this gives you an idea.''

He stood, arms folded. "If you hurt your foot or strain a muscle, I'm not taking you to the White Mountains tomorrow. I can't have you limping around when I have to concentrate on whatever situation Cassandra has up there."

"Don't worry your pretty big head about it." She got into position with her back to the file cabinet. "Move back some more. I wouldn't want *you* to get hurt."

"Good point." He stepped back. "You might miss the file cabinet and kick me."

"Don't think I haven't considered it." She was mightily irritated with him, but she took several deep breaths to calm herself. She'd learned that from dance, but the karate books had emphasized deep breathing, too.

So much transferred from one discipline to another, but she had to admit that there were huge differences. She'd learned respect for those differences in the past few days, but she still thought Mick should give her more credit for being able to accomplish something on her own.

She was ready now. "Eee-ya!" She spun and kicked the bottom drawer shut. Like a whirling dervish, she continued to yell and spin, kicking each drawer shut right up to the top. For her grand finale, she kicked the beach ball. Her aim was excellent. The beach ball thumped Mick soundly on the head before bouncing off the walls.

Breathing hard, she propped her hands on her hips and gave him a triumphant grin. "How was that?"

He had the oddest look on his face. "Good." His voice sounded strained. "Good. Listen, I gotta go take care of some things." He started for the door. "I'll see you tomorrow."

"Wait." She couldn't figure out why he was acting so strange. Maybe she really had threatened his ego with her demonstration. "Are we meeting here?"

He turned, his hand on the knob. "Oh. I could pick you up, I guess."

"That's okay." She didn't want him to see her apartment and realize how modest it was. "It's easier if I come to your place. What's the address?"

He rattled off an apartment complex that wasn't very far from hers and gave her the number.

"I'll be there at nine," she said.

"Right. Bring plenty of clothes." With that he left.

Plenty of clothes? That was an odd parting remark. But then his whole reaction to her karate demonstration had been weird. Apparently he really hadn't been prepared for her to show such expertise so early on.

Oh, well. That was his problem. She shrugged and went to retrieve the beach ball.

SHE WAS AMAZING. His blood pounding through his veins, Mick hurried out of the building, desperate to put some distance between him and that unbelievably sexy woman. He'd expected to get a good laugh out of watching her kick the file cabinet drawers shut. He hadn't expected to be turned on beyond belief as he watched her spin and kick with more grace than some of his top students.

In the process her blouse had come partially untucked from her slacks, and her hair had become deliciously mussed. As she'd stood there panting, a huge smile on that gorgeous mouth of hers, he'd barely managed to keep from grabbing her and kissing her senseless.

He headed for the parking lot and hopped into his little Jeep. Although it had air-conditioning, he preferred to leave the canvas top off and let the breeze cool him down, even in the summer. Right now he needed that breeze, big time.

A drive in the desert for some serious four-wheeling would get rid of his tension, but he discarded the idea. The

night before he'd given the Jeep a good wash, and he'd
rather not arrive at Cassandra's with his vehicle covered in
dust. Besides, he'd have Stacy riding with him tomorrow.

Stacy. How in hell was he going to spend three days
living under the same roof with her and control himself?
What a stupid situation. Cassandra might be lusting after
him on the one hand, and he'd be lusting after Stacy on the
other. As for Stacy, he wasn't really sure what she wanted.
But more and more, he had to conclude she really wanted
to be his assistant.

While watching her perform for him, he'd been incredibly
turned on and barely able to think, but now that his brain
had begun to function again, he realized two things. She
relished the prospect of becoming a bodyguard, relished it
for the excitement and risk involved. And although she'd
displayed some natural talent for karate, she really didn't
have the slightest idea what she was doing.

That combination put her at risk, and if he didn't get her
involved in some serious training, her thirst for adventure
would make her dangerous to herself. His stomach twisted
in fear, and he understood how his parents must have felt
when he'd first demonstrated his love of risks. Karate had
worked to knock some sense and caution into him, so maybe
it would do the same for Stacy.

Without fully realizing where he was going, he ended up
parked in front of the storefront building that housed the
dojo where he'd trained ever since he was nine. Glass covered the entire front wall of the rented space, and he could
see the class in progress, kids about the same age he'd been
when he'd started. The class was sparsely attended today,
probably because tomorrow was the Fourth and many families had already left town.

Despite the heavy afternoon heat, Mick leaned on the
steering wheel and watched from outside. Going in would

disturb the dynamics of the session, and he didn't want to do that. But he did want to speak to Joe, the *sensei,* once the hour was over.

He loved this place that had become for him a second home, an anchor. His parents hadn't understood the wild impulses simmering underneath his shy-guy exterior, impulses that had tempted him to agree to meet Cassandra in the parking lot. But here, they had understood. They'd taught him self-discipline and the ability to channel those impulses he couldn't control into *karate-do,* a way to a better life.

This afternoon his self-discipline had held. But last week—he wasn't very proud of last week. He'd probably always known that Stacy could tap into his wild side, and he'd rightly kept away from her. But somehow she'd slipped in under his radar. The next three days would be a real test of his resolve.

A sparring session with Joe would center him again and prepare him for that test. He hoped Joe had the time after this session was finished. His gym bag sat behind his seat, packed as always with his *gi.*

Several minivans pulled up in front of the *dojo* as the class finally came to an end. The handful of students bowed to their *sensei* before putting on their shoes and trooping outside to meet their waiting parents.

Getting out of the Jeep, Mick grabbed his gym bag and walked toward the door. He could tell from Joe's alert attention that he'd seen Mick coming.

Once inside the door, Mick set down his gym bag, took off his shoes and socks and bowed to the *sensei* while murmuring *osu,* the traditional greeting.

"*Osu,* Mr. Farrell." Joe bowed in Mick's direction.

Despite the years they'd worked together, they maintained the formality of the *dojo,* and Mick had always found that comforting. His life outside this place could tilt and spin like a carnival ride, yet life in the *dojo* remained calm.

"Would you have time to spar now, *sensei?*" Mick asked.

Joe bowed again. "I would be delighted, Mr. Farrell."

Mick walked quickly to the back room and changed into his *gi*. By the time he'd returned, he already felt more in control.

Joe gave him a vigorous workout. Even though he was twenty years Mick's senior, he'd also had twenty extra years to perfect his skills. No matter what Mick threw at him, Joe was ready with a response. Exhaustion claimed Mick before Joe looked winded.

"Enough, *sensei.*" Breathing heavily, Mick stepped back and bowed. "You are still too much for me."

Joe smiled and bowed, too. "One day you will surpass me, Mr. Farrell. You have great talent."

Mick took several deep breaths. "Thank you, *sensei.*" Now that he'd worked the sexual tension out of his system he was more sure of what he wanted to do. "I have found another who is very talented," he said. "I'm hoping you might have room for private lessons."

"Private lessons?" Joe looked surprised. "That would be very expensive."

"She can pay," Mick said. "And she vould be well worth your effort."

He hoped he wasn't taking too much of a chance. If Craig was right, Stacy would grow bored with karate and abandon it. Then Mick would feel he'd wasted his *sensei*'s time. He'd never brought a student to this *dojo* who hadn't turned out to be a dedicated disciple.

Instinct told him to take the risk with Stacy. She'd been awesome today, considering that she'd picked up all that she'd shown him totally on her own. With good instruction, she would go far in the art.

"Bring her to me," Joe said. "And we'll see."

"I'll do that. Next week." He liked the idea of setting up that meeting. If he kept his attention focused on introducing Stacy to karate, then he might be able to ignore the incredible temptation she offered every time he looked at her.

Bowing to Joe, he returned to the back room so that he could change clothes again. He felt a hundred percent better now. If he could maintain the sense of peace he felt right now, he would be able to survive the next three days without making a total fool of himself.

CHAPTER TEN

MICK WAS STASHING a small suitcase in his Jeep when Stacy pulled into the parking lot of his apartment complex. He'd worn the navy silk shirt, she noticed with a smile of satisfaction. He really did seem to like those shirts, and they looked fabulous on him.

The shirt was tucked into bun-hugging jeans. Add to that his cowboy boots and a pair of wraparound shades, and Stacy was drooling. The combination of ruggedness, mystery and sophistication created one fascinating package—a package she would definitely not unwrap. This job was too important.

As she drove toward him, he glanced up. "Let me move the Jeep," he said, "and you can park in my spot under the canopy."

"Okay." She put her car in reverse and backed up to give him room. As she sat with the motor idling, she pressed the controls that raised the convertible top and the windows. She noticed that his Jeep was all buttoned into its canvas top, which disappointed her. She'd hoped to drive up to the mountains with nothing but the roll bar between them and the sky.

Maybe he didn't want to fool with covering the Jeep later in case the thunderclouds sitting on the horizon built into a storm this afternoon. The monsoon rains hadn't officially started, but today could be the day. Then she had an inspiration.

Instead of swinging into the parking spot he'd vacated, she turned off the engine and climbed out.

Apparently she'd confused him, because he hopped out, too. "What's the matter? Didn't I give you enough room?"

"Plenty. I just had a thought. I noticed you put the top on your Jeep, which makes sense this time of year. But if we took my car we could ride up there with the top down, and if it starts to rain we can easily put it up again."

He looked even more confused. "I thought you'd want air-conditioning on the way up."

"That's not necessary. We'll be in cool country before you know it."

"Okay, but what about your hair?"

"I'll wear my Diamondbacks cap. So, wanna take my car?"

He shook his head. "If you really want the Jeep open, I'll take the top off. Those clouds won't turn into anything until later anyway, and I'm sure Cassandra has a garage. But I thought you—"

"I would love to ride up there in an open Jeep," she said. "It would be tons of fun."

He still seemed doubtful. "But it'll be kinda hot until we gain some altitude."

"That's why I wore shorts." Then she realized he wasn't dressed for the heat. "Oh, but you didn't."

"No, but that's okay."

Now she was afraid he'd swelter. "Listen, Mick, I know that I'm the one who advised you on the proper dress for your image, but for this trip I think you could wear something cooler, like shorts."

"No, I couldn't. The jeans hide the gun strapped to my ankle. Now let's go."

"The gun." Despite the hundred-degree heat, a chill went through her. Of course he'd already told her that he carried a gun, but somehow she'd spaced the information. And it wasn't a toy gun like the one she'd used on him last week; this one shot real bullets.

He studied her for a long moment. "You know, taking you up there is a bad idea."

"No, it's not! I just—"

"You're freaked about the gun, and don't pretend you're not. Until I mentioned it, you were thinking of this as a vacation in the mountains. You even said yesterday that you could hardly wait to get away."

"I was only making conversation to hide the hissing of air from the beach ball. I know this is a serious trip, and that it's doubly important because it's your first assignment. For a second there I forgot about the gun, but now I'm cool with it." She wasn't, exactly, but she'd get there.

"I don't believe you." He sighed. "Look, just go back home. See the fireworks at the country club with your parents tonight. That's where you belong, not driving up to Cassandra Oglethorpe's with me. We both know that."

"Oh, no, we don't! I'm going with you, Mick!" She sounded too desperate, like a little kid begging to tag along with the big kids, and she hated that.

"I don't think it's a good idea."

"Well, I do." Taking a deep breath, she forced herself to stay calm. "My reaction is perfectly normal. I've never been around guns before, but that doesn't mean I can't get used to them."

"I can handle this assignment alone, Stacy."

"You think so? Who made the first move in that parking lot situation twelve years ago?"

He shifted his weight and cleared his throat. "She did."

"What if she creeps into your bed in the middle of the night?"

"Uh, well, I'll just…tell her I'm not interested."

"And risk insulting her? You can avoid the whole thing if you take me. I'm a light sleeper. If she leaves her room, so will I. Then she'll be forced to pretend she's out of bed checking on strange noises. Everyone keeps their dignity."

Mick started to say something, then hesitated and gazed off into the distance. "Damn," he said softly.

"You know this could be a bogus assignment, Mick."

"I know. But what if it isn't?" He glanced back at her. "If it's legit, I shouldn't be taking you."

"Why not? You can guard me, too. Vincent Chalmers plans to hire you to guard his entire family, which means you'll be responsible for more than one person at a time, so you should certainly be able to watch over Cassandra and me. Besides, if there is an irate ex-fiancé, he won't be interested in going after some unknown female. He'll be keyed in on Cassandra."

"Maybe."

She sensed him weakening. "No maybes about it. When a guy gets a fixation, it's specific to that woman, not some random thing. That's what's scary about it." *Like Gerald.* "They become obsessed and start thinking that if they can't have you, nobody can."

"You say that as if you have some experience with the problem," he said quietly.

She hadn't realized that the agitation in her voice had given her away. "Okay, I have had some experience, unfortunately."

"When?" His casual stance changed subtly, as if he'd put himself on alert.

She sensed more than saw the difference, but it made her feel incredibly safe. Had Mick been with her in New York, she wouldn't have worried about some silly old stalker. "During my last gig, right before I came home," she said. "Somebody started sending me love letters and signed them

Gerald. Then this scruffy guy started showing up at the theater, and I just knew it was him.''

''You can usually trust your instincts on things like that.''

''I did, although he was never aggressive, but I had this feeling that eventually, if I continued to reject him, that he was capable of…I wasn't sure what, but there was a look in his eyes that scared the stuffing out of me.''

Mick's expression remained sober. ''When you left, do you think he had any idea you were coming to Phoenix?''

She stared at him, and her stomach began to knot up. ''You don't think he would *follow* me here?''

''I hope not, but it's possible.''

The knots in her stomach tightened. ''He was this really ratty-looking guy, Mick. I figured he might even be homeless. Somebody like that wouldn't have the money to get to Phoenix, would they? And, besides, it's a big city. I can't believe he'd be able to locate me.''

''Depends on whether you made any effort to cover your tracks when you rented an apartment and got a phone.''

Which she hadn't. Phoenix seemed like such a long way from New York. ''Now, stop it,'' she said. ''You're scaring me. I'm sure he wouldn't have the money to follow me here. He's probably obsessing about some other dancer by now.''

''Probably. But when we get back I'm going to check out the security at your apartment. Did you happen to get a second-floor place, by any chance?''

''Garden apartment,'' she admitted. The term sounded so glamorous, and yet they were the cheapest in the complex because they barely peeked up above ground level. She had to climb down six steps to reach her front door, and she couldn't have Mick check out the place or he'd know how meager her resources were at the moment.

''A garden apartment. You mean the kind that's like a semibasement job?''

"That's the kind. It's very nice," she said with a lift of her chin.

"I suppose it has window wells?"

"Well, yeah."

"Good God. What were you thinking?"

"Without them I'd have almost no light—that's what I was thinking. Do you expect me to live in a cave?"

He scowled. "That's not such a bad idea, under the circumstances. Do your parents know about this Gerald character?"

"I didn't want to worry them." She was getting really, really scared. The thought of Gerald following her to Phoenix had never entered her mind.

"And what do your parents think of this garden apartment deal?"

She hesitated long enough for him to guess the truth.

"They haven't seen it," he said.

"Not yet. The apartment's fine, though. Perfectly fine." But as soon as possible she was moving. The second floor would be nice, and the third floor even better.

Mick shook his head. "It might be fine for someone else. Someone like me. But it's dicey for single women to rent that kind of place. It's too easy for someone to hide in the window well while they work their way in."

Because he was making her feel like a careless idiot, she became even more defensive. "You're exaggerating. I just came from New York City, remember? Living in Phoenix is a piece of cake compared to that."

He took a step closer. "If I'm exaggerating, you're underestimating. Just because you're back on familiar territory and it doesn't have the same reputation as New York doesn't mean you don't have to be careful. Gerald or no Gerald, you need to think of these things."

She had the feeling that if he'd dared, he'd have shaken his finger at her.

"I *am* careful," she retorted, standing her ground, even inching closer to show that he didn't intimidate her. "I have a regular lock and a dead bolt." A dead bolt she didn't always remember to use.

Sometimes when she was home she forgot to lock up at all. After all, she was in Phoenix. She'd grown up here. It just felt safer than New York. Or it had, until Mick had started scaring her to death.

"I'll take a look at the situation when we get back," Mick said. "And an alarm system might be a good investment, too."

Finally she realized that he'd used the phrase *when we get back*, not once, but twice. "So you're taking me with you to Cassandra's?"

"It beats leaving you here when you have a potential weirdo on your trail and you're living in a garden apartment."

She bristled. "So you're taking me for my own good?"

"Something like that. You'd better move your car. It's blocking my neighbor's spot."

"I don't want you to take me for my own good! I want you to take me because I'm an asset to the team."

Mick sighed. "Okay, then. I'm taking you because of that, too."

"Now you're patronizing me."

He stared down at her, his eyes hidden by the dark glasses. He was a lot closer to her than she'd realized, so close that she could see a muscle twitch in his jaw, and a little spot of dried blood where he'd nicked himself shaving. She wondered if he'd nicked himself because he'd been excited about taking this trip with her.

She could smell his aftershave, too, and that stirred her

up, because the last time she'd been this close to him he'd kissed the living daylights out of her.

"Better to patronize you," he said in a low voice, "than to rip off your clothes and make love to you."

Her heart began to pound. "That's not a good idea." It sounded like a wonderful idea.

"No, it's not. Now go move your car. We need to get on the road."

Her heart was racing so fast she didn't trust herself to speak. The words would come out wobbly, for sure. She nodded and walked back to her convertible.

SHORTS. She'd had to wear a pair of snug denim shorts, after he'd made a point of telling her to bring lots of clothes. As Mick whipped through freeway traffic on his way out of town, he hoped that those smooth, golden legs tucked under his dash wouldn't cause him to wreck.

The rest of her outfit was reasonable—a white Polo shirt, Ralph Lauren, of course, and pricey running shoes. But, on Stacy, even casual clothes managed to look seductive. It was a hell of a thing to deal with. She dominated his peripheral vision. He was aware of each time she moved her arm and absently brushed the side of her breast, causing a faint, tempting jiggle under the knit.

The Polo shirt softly draped her upper body, defining yet disguising the gentle swell beneath it, the swell that lifted sweetly with each breath she took. The material covering her reminded him of the cloth draped over a just-completed work of art. He wanted to unveil Stacy. Maybe the fact that he'd kissed and fondled her breasts had something to do with his preoccupation.

He grimaced. Yeah, just maybe.

Then, too, he'd gone way too long without some sort of sexual outlet. Unfortunately he'd reached a stage in his life when he wanted more than sex from a woman, so that made dating a whole lot more complicated. Although he hadn't let his parents know because they'd be on his case even more than they already were, he was ready to settle down. Lately he'd started thinking about kids, and a little house in the suburbs.

Just his luck that someone like Stacy had showed up, someone who pushed all his buttons and was totally wrong for what he needed. He needed wife material, a woman who'd be deliriously happy living in a tract house with a big mortgage and getting pregnant with his babies. That wasn't Stacy Radcliffe. No doubt her parents had some Yale or Harvard lawyer type all picked out for her.

But, damn, he wanted Stacy anyway. Even knowing she didn't fit into his future plans, he wanted her more than he could remember wanting anyone in a very long time.

"You're hot in that shirt, aren't you?" she asked, raising her voice above the rush of air streaming past the Jeep.

He was hot, all right, but not because of the July sun. "I'm fine."

"Unbutton it."

"Don't need to."

"Oh, don't be silly. Nobody will even notice."

Before he realized what she was doing, she'd reached over and unfastened three buttons, bing, bing, bing. "Stacy, cut it out!" He would have grabbed her hand, but traffic was too heavy to be arm wrestling with Stacy.

"Doesn't that feel better?"

"No." But it did. The breeze ruffling the lapels of the partly open shirt helped cool him down after the jolt of having her supple fingers unhooking his buttons. That was way too close to a fantasy he'd had in the wee hours of the morning as he'd tossed and turned.

"Want me to button them up again?"

"No!"

"See, I knew you'd be cooler that way." She grinned at him. "I like the look. It's sort of seventies, John Travolta-ish. You'll need to button it up before we see Cassandra, though. No point in teasing her with something she can't have."

That was exactly what Stacy was doing—teasing him with something he couldn't have. A week ago he would have said it was something he didn't even want. But a week ago he'd never have thought Stacy Radcliffe would put her salon-styled hair in a ponytail and pull it through the back of a Diamondbacks baseball cap so that she could ride in his open Jeep.

A week ago he wouldn't have said that she was dedicated to learning karate and becoming his assistant, either, but here she was, endearingly earnest about it. Now that he knew about Gerald, he understood her interest in karate. People approached martial arts from different directions. He'd wanted more self-discipline in his life, but Stacy obviously wanted more control over her safety.

But once she got that, would she move on? Probably.

If he kept that in mind, he might be okay. Keeping Stacy as an assistant meant that he could make sure she learned enough basic karate to protect herself and get through the first heady excitement of the sport without mishap.

Maybe she'd even convince Holly to take some lessons. He'd tried to teach his little sister a few things, because he wanted the women he cared about to have some self-defense skills. She'd told him he was too bossy, and he hadn't been able to convince her to take lessons from someone else instead.

Holly had never had a scare like Stacy's recent experience, so she didn't see the need for training, but Stacy could talk her into it if anyone could. But as he thought about the friendship between the two women, his stomach rolled with dread.

He was afraid to ask what Stacy had or hadn't shared with Holly about recent developments. For all he knew the passionate moment in the office had been fodder for many long conversations between them.

God, he hoped not. If anything could keep him from giving in to temptation, the image of Stacy and Holly dishing about it later should do the trick. He hoped it was enough of a deterrent, but every time he glanced over at Stacy, her bare legs soaking up the sun and that baseball cap pulled down over her eyes, his whole body ached.

As they left the desert floor and began climbing, the sun lost some of its bite and the traffic eased. Mick loved driving through Arizona's open country, where every bend in the road brought a new vista of brush-covered plains and a horizon dominated by mountains. Deep greens and browns colored the ranges in the foreground, while the more distant mountains faded into smoky mystery.

This was the land of red-tailed hawks and glossy ravens, of scrub oak and juniper pine. Eventually the sky, so blue you could hardly believe it, would be pierced by stately ponderosas, and at that elevation they might be lucky enough to spot an eagle. Mick wasn't much into poetry, but whenever he left the city and rediscovered this scenery, he thought poetry would be in order.

"This is great, Mick!" Stacy shouted over the roar of the wind. "It's been ages since I've driven up here. I'd forgotten how beautiful it is."

"I like it, too," he said. Some understatement. But some things couldn't be described in words, like the way Stacy was affecting him each time he glanced at her. Her cheeks had been whipped pink by the wind and her smile was filled with obvious pleasure. Beautiful didn't begin to embrace the way Stacy looked.

Try as he might, he couldn't remember a time he'd enjoyed a trip more. He hated for the drive to end because, once it did, he'd have to deal with whatever screwy situation Cassandra had going on. And he'd also have to deal with his increasingly potent urges concerning Stacy. As long as he was driving he had to keep his hands on the wheel and his attention on the road, so those urges could be controlled. But soon that wouldn't be the case.

Very soon, in fact. The forest had begun to close in and the air was much cooler and fragrant with the scent of evergreens. As they drove through little mountain towns that weren't much more than a café, a post office and a gas station, they passed dirt roads that led off into the trees, and occasionally a roof line or a chimney edged upward through the pines.

He'd given Stacy the directions and she was studying them.

"We need to look for an old gas station with deer antlers mounted over the door," she said.

"I'm looking. Haven't seen it yet."

"Oh, there it is!" She pointed off to the right. "Now, a mile past that is the road leading to her place." She leaned toward Mick and peered at the Jeep's instrument panel. "Are you watching the odometer?"

"Yep." And he'd be able to concentrate so much better if she'd stop leaning in close and bombarding him with her perfume.

"How are you going to introduce me to Cassandra?"

"As my assistant," he said.

"She knows some of the same people my parents know. I wonder if she'll ask what happened to my dancing career."

He heard the note of vulnerability. Stacy might be resigned to the loss of that dream, but it still had the power to make her voice hitch. "Just tell her you find the bodyguard business to be more interesting," he said. "And that you're in training with Joe Santori."

"Who's that?"

"My *sensei*. He's the best karate master in the valley, probably in the whole state. Anybody who knows anything about martial arts has heard of Joe."

"But I'm not in training with him."

"You will be. I asked him to take you on."

When she didn't say anything, when she didn't even thank him or ask any more questions, his chest tightened with anxiety. He didn't want to go back to his *sensei* and tell him that a promising student had rejected his kind offer of private lessons.

He looked over at her. "Did I make a mistake in asking him?"

She shook her head, and her eyes looked sparkly, like they were filled with tears or something, which seemed like a strange reaction.

He had to concentrate on the road, so he couldn't check it out for sure. "Then you'd like to take lessons from him?"

"I would love to," she said, sounding sort of choked up.

"Stacy, is something wrong? You don't have to take lessons from him, but if you really want to learn, he's the best."

"Nothing's wrong." She cleared her throat. "I just didn't know you had that much confidence in me."

Oh, God, she *was* choked up, all because he'd respected her efforts enough to put in the good word with Joe. And that was causing something potentially dangerous to happen in the vicinity of his heart.

Bad news. He couldn't fall for this woman. Falling for

Stacy Radcliffe would be insane, and he didn't need Craig to tell him that.

But she was so appealing, with her self-taught kicks, and her pleasure in the ride up here, and her Diamondbacks cap, and her smooth skin, and her full breasts, and her wonderful mouth and her—

"That might have been the road back there," she said. "The one we just passed."

He pulled onto the gravel shoulder and looked at the odometer. Of course that was the road, and he'd been so involved in thoughts of Stacy that he'd missed it completely. "I'll turn around."

She put a hand on his arm. "Thank you for talking to your *sensei* on my behalf."

He didn't dare look at her or he was liable to throw off his seat belt and come across the gearbox to take her in his arms. "You're welcome." He checked for traffic and started to pull out.

"Wait!"

He slammed on the brakes, causing both of them to jerk against the seat belts. "What? It's clear."

"You might want to button up your shirt before we drive down that road."

"Oh." In spite of the ease of buttoning the shirt, he had trouble, but finally he managed it. "Okay, let's go." He waited for traffic to clear again and made a quick U-turn.

Moments later they were bumping down a dirt road toward a large clearing up ahead. Through the trees Mick glimpsed a huge, three-story house covered in weathered cedar shingles. The glass set into giant windows flashed in the sunlight and the smell of wood smoke hung in the air.

As they drew closer he could see that a wide deck wrapped around the entire second floor. If the native rock fireplace climbing one side of the house was as imposing inside as it was outside, they'd be able to roast a whole pig in it. An American flag large enough to drape a Cadillac hung from a bracket attached to the deck. Apparently that was Cassandra's nod to the holiday.

"If this is a cabin, then Buckingham Palace is a bungalow," he said as he parked the Jeep in front of the house.

"It's big, all right," Stacy agreed.

A movement on the deck caught his eye, and he figured their hostess was coming to meet them. "I think Cassandra— Oh...my...God."

Cassandra Oglethorpe, a frosted glass in one hand, stood at the top of the stairs leading up to the deck. She was wearing a bikini.

CHAPTER ELEVEN

THE WIDOW OGLETHORPE had been taking care of herself, Stacy thought as she gazed up at the blonde posing artfully on the top step. Even though Cassandra had been a trophy wife and years younger than her husband, she was at least forty-five by now.

But she sure as heck didn't look it standing there in an ivory bikini that did wonders for her voluptuous body and golden tan. Stacy supposed she'd been working on that tan while lying on one of the redwood lounge chairs spaced around the open deck.

Designer sunglasses were pushed to the top of her head, casually holding her tastefully highlighted tresses back from a smooth forehead. Her hair was shoulder-length, with a soft curl reminiscent of Surfer Barbie. She wore beaded mules, and a gold ankle bracelet winked in the sun.

Stacy discovered that the scene in the back seat of the Lincoln Town Car took on a different meaning now that she could see that Cassandra hadn't become an old hag. She had definitely been picturing someone less…less everything. Mick had held this woman in his arms—they had a history, and Cassandra looked miles from being old news. Stacy discovered an unpleasant fact: she was jealous.

But she'd die before she'd admit it. "You may be sorry I came," she murmured to Mick in an easygoing, we're-just-chums tone.

"Nope. I'm eternally grateful," he replied under his breath. "I think we know the answer to our question."

"Oh, I think we do."

"Stick close," he muttered before he climbed out of the Jeep. "Hello, Mrs. Oglethorpe."

"Hello, yourself. And please call me Cassandra. Who's your friend?" She spoke with determined courtesy, as if Mick had dragged along some mangy, untrained and boisterous puppy.

"I'd like you to meet my assistant, Stacy Radcliffe."

Stacy stepped down, crunching dry pine needles under the soles of her running shoes. She felt like a windblown female jock in comparison to the glamorous woman at the top of the stairs. "Hello, Mrs. Oglethorpe."

"Stacy Radcliffe? Evie's daughter? I thought you were busy performing on Broadway." Her expression said clearly that she'd like Stacy to return to her stage career ASAP.

Stacy was glad she'd prepared herself for this question. Her failure still stung, but with luck Cassandra wouldn't know that. "I was, but helping Mick in the bodyguard business interests me more right now."

"I see."

"I'm, uh, training with Joe Santini."

Mick chuckled as he pulled both of their suitcases out of the Jeep. "Good one, Stace. She means Joe Santori, of course, but sometimes she teases him and calls him The Great Santini."

Damn. Stacy grinned to cover her flub. "Right. A big tease, that's me. Listen, I know it's rude to simply show up like this without notice, but I didn't find out until the last minute that I'd be able to help Mick on this assignment, and we just hopped in the old Jeep and drove up here. And wouldn't you know that both of our cell phones are on the blink." Stacy pulled off her Diamondbacks hat and combed her fingers through her tangled hair, but she doubted it helped much.

"Of course you're welcome here, Stacy," Cassandra said. "But Mick, I didn't realize when I hired you that you had an assistant who accompanied you on your assignments." She sounded like an indulgent parent scolding a naughty child. "I hardly think this is a big enough job for two people."

She's already plotting to get me out of the way so she can have Mick to herself, Stacy thought, and wondered how Cassandra planned to go about it. Whatever she had in mind, it wasn't going to work. Mick was here to guard Cassandra and Stacy was here to guard Mick.

"Whether the job is big enough or not," Mick said, "the beauty of this is that you get two for the price of one."

"What a good idea." Cassandra said with no enthusiasm whatsoever. "Come in and we'll get you both settled."

Had she not been toughened against rejection by her years in show business, Stacy might have wanted to slink away in embarrassment for having the gall to present herself where she wasn't wanted. But Cassandra wasn't half as nasty as some of the casting directors she'd encountered.

Mick started toward the stairs with both bags. "I take it everything's been quiet so far?" he asked Cassandra.

"No sign of Leonard, if that's what you mean." Carrying her drink, Cassandra strolled toward the large double doors leading into the house. "However, I'm taking no chances. I've put you in the bedroom adjoining mine."

Stacy almost laughed at the obvious move. "Perhaps there's a room right across the hall for me." She skipped up the stairs after Mick. She might not have glamor on her side, but she had youth and agility. "I'm a light sleeper, so I'm sure I'd hear an intruder."

"Unfortunately, that room has recently been fumigated,"

Cassandra said. "But I have a cozy little spot on the garage level. When I bring my housekeeper up here to clean, that's where she stays."

"Sounds great." Yeah, just terrific. Banished to the dungeon. But Stacy decided she'd take the maid's quarters for the time being. Before nightfall she'd figure out a way to move.

Cassandra opened the door and the three of them walked inside. Stacy came close to echoing Mick's quick intake of breath. The place was impressive. Stacy's parents had never owned a cabin in the mountains, but several of their friends had. This ranked right up there with the most plush she'd seen.

Top-of-the-line leather furniture, hand-woven Indian rugs, original Western art and beamed ceilings made it look like a retreat that might be featured in *Architectural Digest*. Enormous windows looking out on the forest gave the impression they'd climbed into a luxurious tree house.

"I was about to have lunch." Cassandra gestured toward a rustic table beside a window. The table was set for two.

Stacy wondered if she'd planned to dine in her bikini. "It's a lot cooler in here than out on the deck," she said. "I think I'll change into my jeans before lunch."

"By all means." Cassandra took another sip of her drink before leading the way toward a closed door to the right of the kitchen. She unlocked it and stood back. "Right down these stairs you'll find a bedroom and a bath. Make yourself at home." She took another swallow from her glass. "I'll show Mick to his room and set an extra place for lunch."

There was a little too much emphasis on the word *extra,* in Stacy's opinion. And now that they were in a more enclosed space, she caught the scent of gin, which confirmed that Cassandra wasn't swigging lemonade from that tall, frosted glass she held.

Stacy glanced at Mick, and he looked worried. "I'll be right back," she said. "Sing out if you need me."

"Will do," he said.

Feeling a lot like Cinderella, Stacy started down the stairs. But the manners her mother had drummed into her at an early age wouldn't allow her to openly protest her room assignment. She'd simply work around it.

At the bottom of the stairs were two doors. The one on the right was ajar so that she could see into the maid's quarters she'd been assigned. The one on the left apparently led into the garage. When she discovered the door was locked and required a key to open it, she concluded that Cassandra must be super-protective of whatever pricey vehicle was parked in that garage.

Then she turned her attention to the maid's quarters, and reluctantly admitted the bedroom and attached bath were small but cute. An antique iron bedstead sported a cushy mattress, fluffy pillows and a handmade quilt. In the bathroom, a pedestal sink and claw-foot tub continued the motif. The Oglethorpe housekeeper lived well.

Stacy changed quickly into a pair of jeans. It was even chillier down here in the semibasement. After unpacking a sweatshirt and pulling it on over her head, she stood on tiptoe to look out the high, narrow window. She had a mole's-eye view of a carpet of pine needles and a couple of pine cones that had dropped from the tree nearby. She glanced up through the branches of the tree and noticed clouds moving in, which explained the drop in temperature. Mick would have to put his Jeep in the garage before lunch if he wanted to keep the seats from getting wet.

Turning away from the window, she walked over to a small oval mirror that hung above an antique dresser. Combing her hair and reapplying her lipstick made her feel a little more presentable. She still looked very all-American girlish compared to Cassandra, but if the weather cooperated, their hostess wouldn't be able to keep that bikini on much longer without risking frostbite.

When Stacy left the room, she noticed that the door at the top of the stairs was closed again. Cassandra had probably done that out of habit, she thought as she climbed the steps. Then she turned the knob and decided that habit had nothing to do with it.

The door was locked.

THE MINUTE Stacy started down to the basement, Mick headed toward the stairway leading to the second floor. The sooner he deposited his suitcase up there, the sooner he could come back down, out of dangerous territory.

"Whoa, Mick!" Cassandra hurried after him. "Where's the fire?"

"I need to get rid of this suitcase so I can check out your security measurements." He winced. "I mean measures."

Cassandra laughed. "You're adorable. Is my bikini distracting you?"

"Not at all." Mick lied.

"Because I can change clothes. In fact, why don't I do that? While you're unpacking I'll take this off and slip into something else."

"That's okay." He didn't know which alternative was worse, to have her stay in the bikini or come upstairs with him and start changing clothes in the room next to his. "The bikini's fine. Barely noticed it. And you certainly don't need to come upstairs with me. Just point me in the right direction and I'm sure I can find it."

"Now what sort of hostess would I be if I sent you upstairs to find your own room?"

The same kind who sent Stacy downstairs to find hers. But he didn't say that. This was his first job, and he had to salvage what he could out of a tricky situation. "I'm sure you have things to do to get ready for lunch," he said.

"It's ready."

"Even so, I can settle myself in." Maybe if he stalled long enough Stacy would come back and he'd have some added protection.

"Nonsense. I'll show you the room." Cassandra plopped her glass down on an intricately carved credenza as she whipped past, her mules clicking on the hardwood floor. "Come right this way."

The winding staircase made of wrought iron and distressed wood looked like a piece of sculpture. Mick tried desperately to concentrate on the beauty of the staircase and ignore the deliberately provocative walk and the tight buns of his hostess as she mounted the steps ahead of him.

"I have an alarm system," Cassandra said over her shoulder, "but the darned thing hasn't worked right from the day they installed it."

"Want me to take a look at it?"

"Don't bother. It's very touchy, and the squirrels set it off if they happen to be scampering along a windowsill, so I disengaged it because it was driving me crazy. I thought having you spend a few days would be a nice alternative."

"I appreciate the business," Mick said.

Her laugh was low and seductive. "I thought you might."

Mick gulped. This scenario was way too familiar. Twelve years ago Cassandra had lured him into the back seat of the Lincoln with that soft laughter.

It wouldn't work on him now, of course, but the eighteen-year-old kid inside him still remembered the forbidden thrill of being seduced by Cassandra. He didn't want her, but a guy would have to be embalmed to be totally indifferent, especially given their past history. Thank God Stacy was here. He hoped she'd reappear soon.

"This is your room." Cassandra sashayed through the doorway and paused just inside the room. "I hope you like it."

He was forced to walk past her to take his suitcase inside. Moving quickly, he ducked in. He should have had plenty of room, but she must have shifted her position, because her breasts rubbed against his arm as he passed.

The room had a bed and dresser, but he barely noticed anything more than that. "It's great." He dropped his suitcase to the floor and turned toward the door. "I'm glad lunch is all ready, because I'm starving."

"That's a shame." Cassandra closed the door and leaned against it. "I was hoping you might want to talk about old times first."

His heart hammered. "I'm—I'm not sure what you mean."

"Aren't you?"

"Mrs. Oglethorpe—"

"Cassandra."

"Cassandra, then. I hope you didn't misunderstand when I took this job. I'm a professional bodyguard, and that's why I'm here."

"Of course you are. I think it's the perfect job for a big, strong man like you." Her gaze swept over him. "If I'm not mistaken you've bulked up quite a bit since high school. Not that you weren't an eyeful back then. Oh, how I loved watching you run in those tiny little gym shorts."

Mick's face heated. "It would be best if we didn't discuss that episode." Surely Stacy had finished changing clothes by now. If she came into the living room and didn't find them there, he hoped she'd have the initiative to come upstairs and look for them.

"I don't want to discuss that episode." Cassandra walked toward him. "I'd like to finish it."

Oh, dear God. "I'm afraid that's not possible."

"I think it's totally possible. And, by the way, isn't Stacy the little girl who interrupted us that night?"

"Yes." Mick's vocal cords felt stiff. "But that was for the best, Mrs. Oglethorpe—Cassandra. I'm here as a professional, and it would be best if we—"

Cassandra stepped closer. "Did you see that movie with Kevin Costner and Whitney Houston?"

This felt a lot more like *The Graduate* than *The Bodyguard.* "I, uh—"

"He's guarding her, and yet he sleeps with her." She ran a finger down Mick's chest.

He leaped backward. "I'm not sleeping with you, Mrs. Oglethorpe!"

"Why not? No one has to know." She moved forward.

As he backed up, he came flat up against the bedroom wall. "Stacy would know. She's probably downstairs right this minute, wondering what happened to us. She might even come up here looking for us."

"I wasn't about to risk having history repeat itself." Cassandra smiled. "Don't worry about your little friend Stacy. We have plenty of time to be alone."

A chill swept over him. "Why is that?"

"I locked her in."

"You *what?*" Mick grabbed Cassandra by the shoulders and shoved her aside. "You locked her in down there? How did I miss that?" He hurried toward the door and flung it open.

"You were hell-bent on getting upstairs, that's how," she called after him. "I was hoping that reflected your eagerness to renew an old acquaintance."

As Mick charged down the stairs, cursing himself as he went, he wondered why he didn't hear Stacy banging on the door wanting to be let out. She knew he needed her to stick close, so she must have changed clothes pretty fast, which meant she'd have tried to open the door by now.

"Stacy!" He ran across the living room and unlocked the door to the basement. He couldn't believe that Cassandra had locked that door without him realizing it. He'd better get his head in the game or he wasn't going to be of any use to anybody. "Stacy!" he yelled again as he pounded down the stairs.

"I'm here!"

Her voice came from behind him, and he nearly stumbled as he spun around.

Sure enough, she was standing at the top of the stairs, peering down at him. Her DKNY sweatshirt was ripped, and her jeans were covered with smudges. Her face and hands were pretty grubby, too.

He took the steps two at a time and pulled her into his arms. "God, Stacy, you look like you tunneled out of the basement."

"I damn near did!" Apparently, she wasn't ready to be cuddled, because she pushed away from him and her voice was tight with fury. "I crawled out a window. A very tiny window. And I broke two nails and ripped my best sweatshirt." She lifted her chin and glared at him in defiance. "And now I'm off to give Cassandra Oglethorpe a piece of my mind, whether you approve or not, Mick."

Wow. She was something. He felt emotion click on inside, warm and intense. "I approve," he said. "Let's go."

"I'm going to offend her, Mick." Stacy stomped across the living room. "Just so you know."

"I don't care." And he didn't. First client or not, Cassandra had stepped way over the line, and he had several things to say to her, himself. If she caused problems for him, he'd deal with that. Stacy could have been hurt crawling out that window. Nobody locked his assistant in the basement and got away with it. Nobody.

But the fact that Stacy had taken action instead of helplessly yelling and beating on the door impressed him. It really, really impressed him.

"Cassandra!" Stacy called. "We're coming to talk to you!"

"No need to shout the house down." Cassandra appeared at the top of the spiral staircase wrapped in a floor-length black robe. She glanced at Stacy and her eyes widened. "Good Lord, what happened to you?"

"*You* happened to me. You locked me in, so I crawled out the window."

"Dear child, you were *not* supposed to crawl out the window. You were supposed to stay down there and fret until someone came to let you out."

"Stacy's not the fretting kind," Mick said. "Cassandra, what you did is inexcusable."

Cassandra sighed. "I suppose it is, given how it turned out. I had hoped that you'd be more cooperative, Mick. I thought locking the door might be doing us both a favor."

Stacy put both dirt-smeared hands on her hips. "So you admit that you hired Mick so that you could get him up here and seduce him?"

"Well, that was a consideration."

"Then we're leaving." Stacy turned to Mick. "Right?"

"Right," he said. "You can keep your fee, Cassandra. Obviously you don't need a bodyguard."

"I might," Cassandra said. "I didn't make that up about Leonard. He probably won't show up, but he's fairly upset that I broke off our engagement, and he put some nasty threats on my answering machine."

"You could be making that up," Stacy said. "Like you

made up the story about the other room upstairs being fumigated so you could lock me in the basement.''

''I could, except that I saved the tape to play for Mick.'' She glanced at him. ''Do you want to hear it?''

Oh, how he hated complications. A minute ago he'd been charged up and ready to take Stacy out of this place. But if there really was a threat to Cassandra and he left her alone on this mountain, and something happened to her, he'd never forgive himself.

''You could have faked the tape, too,'' Stacy said.

''She's right,'' Mick said. ''How are we supposed to know if the tape is legit or not?''

''I guess you can't, for sure.'' Cassandra descended the stairs. ''So if you want to leave, then leave.'' She gave him a weary smile. ''Damn, but it's a blow to my ego to realize I don't have it anymore. I was so sure I could seduce you.'' Her gaze flicked over to Stacy. ''You brought her on purpose as a chaperon, didn't you?''

''I—''

''I'm Mick's assistant.'' Stacy wiped her grimy hands on her jeans. ''We work together on his cases. That's why I'm here.''

Cassandra looked at Mick, then back at Stacy. ''Pretty dedicated assistant to crawl out of that window and ruin your manicure. Usually when a woman goes to that extreme she's protecting her territory. I don't blame you, Stacy. He's gorgeous.''

''Now wait a minute,'' Mick said as heat climbed up his neck. ''Stacy and I aren't—''

''All right, all right,'' Cassandra said. ''Have it your way. The fact is, I really am nervous about staying here tonight by myself. Leonard once told me that Fourth of July would be the perfect opportunity to shoot someone, because with all the fireworks, nobody would think anything about the noise.''

Mick glanced over at Stacy to see how she was taking this information.

Some of the indignation had faded from her expression. She met Mick's gaze. ''Maybe we should stay.'' She turned to Cassandra. ''That is, if you'll promise to leave Mick alone.''

''I'll do better than that. After dinner tonight I'll go up to my room with my trusty bottle of Tanqueray and I promise not to come down again. If Mick moves the sofa so it blocks the staircase and sleeps there, that should guarantee my safety and his honor. I won't be climbing over the sofa to get to him. I have my standards.''

''And where will I sleep?'' Stacy asked.

Cassandra's smile was calculating. ''If you're so worried about whether I'll bother Mick, then maybe you should share the sofa with him.''

''You know I won't do that.''

''We'll find another alternative,'' Mick said, although, try as he might, he couldn't seem to think of a better solution. The potent image of sharing the big, comfy sofa with Stacy all night had taken up every available brain cell. He'd give five years of his life to do exactly that.

CHAPTER TWELVE

IN THE SILENCE that followed Cassandra's outrageous suggestion, Stacy's mind whirled with visions of making love to Mick on the sofa all night. Of course she would never do that, but she had to figure out her options. She could borrow Mick's Jeep and leave, but a trusty assistant shouldn't bail at the first sign of trouble.

And despite what Cassandra said now, no telling what would happen if Stacy abandoned the field. Mick wouldn't want to go along with any attempted seduction—at least Stacy hoped he wouldn't. But there was a chance, considering how glamorous Cassandra was, that she might finally wear him down. She might not be willing to climb over the sofa, but she might lure Mick into doing it.

Stacy shouldn't care if that took place. That was Mick's problem. But her insides twisted with jealousy every time she thought of Mick with Cassandra. No, she couldn't leave him here alone with such a babe.

And now that she believed this Leonard person might actually show up, she didn't relish sleeping down in the basement apartment alone, either. She'd had to jimmy the window with her curling iron in order to squeeze out. At the time she hadn't been worried about the damage because she'd been convinced there was no threat. Unfortunately the window might not lock securely anymore.

"You don't have to work it all out now," Cassandra said. "Nobody can make a decent decision on an empty stomach.

Stacy, why don't you wash off some of that grime in the kitchen? Then we'll have lunch and, after that, you can both confer and let me know if I'll have a bodyguard tonight or not.''

When it finally came to her, the solution was so simple that Stacy couldn't believe she hadn't thought of it. Apparently she'd been blinded by lust. She glanced at Mick. ''I'd rather make the decision now. I vote that we stay, and we'll put the sofa across the stairs with Mick on it. That makes perfect sense to me. And because I don't care to be alone in the basement, all things considered, I'll sleep up in your room, Mick.''

The tension eased from his face. ''Oh. Yeah, I guess you could. I hadn't thought of that.''

Cassandra nodded. ''All right then. It looks as if the three of us are here for the duration. Now let's eat.''

DURING WHAT turned out to be a delicious lunch of pasta-and-chicken salad, Stacy congratulated herself on coming up with the solution. But she couldn't help wondering why Mick hadn't thought of it first. There was the slight possibility that he'd been as captivated by the picture of sharing the sofa as she had. The idea that he might have wanted to spend the night with her made her toes curl.

But it would be such a mistake. Office romances usually caused problems. In this case, when she and Mick were the only two people in the office, it could spell disaster. Once started, an affair either turned into something serious or it fizzled out.

Because she wasn't interested in something serious at this point in her life, that left her with the fizzling-out situation. She couldn't imagine in general how anyone could work together after having a love affair fizzle out, and specifically she couldn't imagine how she and Mick would manage it.

So the best course would be never to get started, which was what she'd decided days ago.

Unfortunately she found herself having to decide all over again whenever she looked at Mick. Cassandra was right about at least one thing—he was gorgeous. And tonight they'd be sleeping under the same roof. If she hadn't come up with an alternative, they might have been sleeping on the same sofa.

But she, brilliant woman that she was, had come up with an alternative. And it was the wise course of action. Yes, it was certainly wise. But every time she glanced up and caught Mick gazing at her across the lunch table with that special glow in his eyes, she longed to be foolish, if only for this one night.

After lunch Stacy moved her belongings upstairs and used the guest bathroom to get cleaned up. Mick took that time to put his Jeep in the garage, fix the lock on the window in the maid's quarters and check all the other locks on the outside of the house.

Following a shower, Stacy wrapped her freshly washed hair in a towel, put on her terry bathrobe, and walked into Mick's former bedroom to change clothes. While she dried her hair and dressed, she reviewed the current state of affairs.

After the incident today, she was even more certain that she'd be good at this bodyguard business. Sometime between confronting the locked door and crawling out the window she'd come to the conclusion that she'd found exactly what she was destined to do with her life. Instead of becoming frustrated by the locked door, she'd accepted the challenge with a rush of eagerness.

Sure, she'd been ticked off, but she'd been exhilarated, too. She couldn't think of a single moment in her dance career, not even opening night of her first Broadway musical, that had given her that same visceral charge. Cassandra had done her a huge favor by locking her in.

Besides that, Mick had already promised to set her up with the best karate master in the state. How she'd afford those lessons was anybody's guess, but she'd find a way, because the training was vital to her new career. If Mick had been impressed with her initiative in climbing out the window, then she had an excellent chance of staying on as his assistant.

Giving in to the physical attraction between them could only mess that up. So she wouldn't do it. With renewed determination, she headed downstairs.

MICK COULDN'T ever remember a day quite this strange. By midafternoon a serious thunderstorm was in progress, which forced all of them to stay inside. Mick tended the fire while Stacy and Cassandra talked about people he didn't know, society people. He noticed with interest that Cassandra seemed to be gradually warming to Stacy.

Their discussion seemed like idle chitchat to him and he'd about decided to find something to read when Stacy suggested that she and Cassandra come up with a list of potential clients for Mick's business. Cassandra, who had continued to sip from a frosted tumbler that she refilled whenever it got low, thought it was a terrific idea.

She went in search of her address book, then found a pad of paper and a pen and handed it to Stacy. "You can mention me as a reference," she said. "Have anyone who's interested contact me."

"Thank you, Cassandra," Mick said, stunned that she'd make the offer after what had happened that morning.

From her position in a large wing-backed armchair, Cassandra glanced over at him. "Just because you won't sleep with me doesn't mean I don't want to help you launch your new business, Mick.''

He knew from the heat in his cheeks that he was blushing, and he didn't have the foggiest notion how to reply to such a statement.

"Isn't he adorable?'' Cassandra said to Stacy. "I can't imagine how you can resist him.''

Now it was Stacy's turn to blush. "I, um, work for Mick. It would be unprofessional if we—''

"Absolutely,'' Mick said, coming to her aid. "Stacy and I respect each other's boundaries, Cassandra.''

"Boundaries, schmoundaries. What a lot of politically correct BS. But that's your business, isn't it?'' Cassandra took a long swallow of her drink. "Okay, let's make up that list.''

Mick wondered if Cassandra had a point. Maybe it was ridiculous for him to give up the possibility of making love to Stacy. Most guys would say it was.

As she worked on the list, she was curled up on the big leather couch, the one they'd decided to move in front of the staircase after Cassandra went to bed, the one where he'd envisioned, for one brief moment, making love to her. Mick wondered if Stacy would go to bed at the same time Cassandra did, or if she'd stay downstairs a little longer.

He wasn't sure which to hope for. Too much time spent alone with Stacy and that sofa in the same room might be more temptation than he could handle. She'd always turned him on, and now he'd discovered that she had more grit than he'd ever imagined. He still couldn't get over that stunt of climbing out the window.

He would have loved to see that. What a little tiger. Yet now she looked so refined in clean designer jeans and a soft gray sweater that was probably cashmere. If he could pillow his head on that cashmere, he'd never ask for anything again in his life.

Now that was a lie. Once he'd pillowed his head on her breasts he'd want to get rid of the cashmere altogether. After that he'd be inspired to unfasten the hip-hugging waistband on those designer jeans.

And regardless of what Cassandra thought was best, getting physical with Stacy would lead to chaos. He couldn't make love to her for a multitude of reasons, not the least of which was his lack of condoms. He was beginning to understand why some guys always carried them.

But he didn't, and that was actually a good thing, because without that obstacle, he'd be plotting all kinds of moves on Stacy Radcliffe.

God, she was beautiful sitting there in front of the fire. She'd nudged her shoes off and tucked her feet under her while she wrote down Cassandra's suggestions for potential clients. She looked so tidy and contained, like a package neatly wrapped and waiting for some lucky guy to come by and discover the treasures inside.

He wanted her so much that watching her was giving him an erection, so he looked into the fire instead. That was no help, because the dancing flames reminded him of heat, and he'd never been hotter than the moment he'd peeled away Stacy's leotard.... Damn. It was a good thing she'd chosen to sleep upstairs.

Somehow he made it through the afternoon, but he was beginning to realize that keeping Stacy on as his assistant was impossible. He couldn't have her tagging along on his assignments, which was exactly what she wanted and probably what she was suited for. But he could hardly be expected to function in a constant state of arousal.

Breaking the news to her would be horrible, and unfair, because she was doing an outstanding job. He would never have thought of spending the afternoon pumping Cassandra for referrals, and yet by dinner Stacy had three pages of names, addresses and phone numbers.

What kind of heel accepted that sort of help and then fired the person who'd made it happen? But he could think of no other way. As business associates they were doomed.

STACY HAD SUGGESTED coming up with a list of clients without expecting Cassandra to go along with it. To her amazement, Cassandra embraced the idea with enthusiasm. But when Cassandra also spent a fair amount of time casting speculative looks at Mick while they worked, Stacy began to wonder if the client list was another weapon Cassandra planned to use to get what she wanted.

As dinnertime neared, Cassandra refilled her glass from the wet bar and announced that she had another address book upstairs. She asked Stacy to come and help her find it because the search involved moving a few cardboard boxes.

"I'll be glad to help with that," Mick said.

"No, I'd rather you stayed down here and tended the fire," Cassandra said.

Stacy was doubly surprised. Here was a golden opportunity for Cassandra to get Mick alone in her bedroom, and instead she wanted Stacy. Filled with curiosity, she followed Cassandra up the stairs.

When they reached Cassandra's opulent bedroom, Cassandra waved her over to one of two chintz-covered armchairs in a corner of the room. "There's no second address book," she said, taking the other chair. "I wanted to tell you privately that I'm officially relinquishing the field to you."

Stacy gulped. "I...don't understand."

"I'm giving up. Mick has no interest in me, judging from the way he barely glanced at me all afternoon. Yet he couldn't take his eyes off of you. Obviously I don't have a chance with him and, just as obviously, you do.''

"But—"

"Hear me out. After what I did to you this morning, I think you deserve an explanation."

Stacy couldn't agree more. "All right."

Cassandra took a long sip of her drink. "I was acting on old information this morning. Twelve-year-old information, to be exact. I don't know if he ever told you what took place after you discovered us in the back seat of the Lincoln that night."

Stacy shook her head. She wasn't sure she wanted to know.

"Well, nothing happened. Our Mick had an attack of conscience, and he insisted that I fasten all my clothes back together. He blamed himself for allowing things to progress so far, but he said that I was a beautiful woman he'd want to make love to under any other circumstances. It was quite a speech for an eighteen-year-old."

"Yes." Stacy was incredibly relieved they hadn't made love. She also had no trouble picturing Mick saying those things. He would want to take care of Cassandra's feelings and assume the responsibility for what had happened, even if she'd been the one who'd come on to him in the first place.

"I thought he was too sweet for words, and I never approached him again, because I knew he wouldn't want to get involved with a married woman. But then my husband died and I began to think about Mick again. He's only fifteen years younger than I am, Stacy. That shouldn't be a shocking difference. Men take up with women fifteen years younger and nobody says anything."

"True."

"I'm not making excuses—well, maybe I am—but I

didn't think inviting Mick up here for a few days and hoping that we could pick up where we left off was such a crazy idea.''

Stacy gave Cassandra a level glance. ''But locking Mick's female assistant in her room so you could seduce him was a very crazy idea, in my opinion.''

To Stacy's surprise, Cassandra grinned. ''Oh, but if it had *worked,* then what a triumph! Middle-aged woman snatches sexy stud from beautiful young thing. I would have been canonized by my girlfriends.'' She shrugged. ''But I give up. Or let me say I give up on Mick Farrell.''

''If you say so.'' Stacy wasn't sure whether to believe the woman or not. She'd proved that she could be very crafty.

''Now that doesn't mean I won't look around for some other delicious guy in his age range, but I wanted to start with Mick, for old time's sake. Anyway, allow me to congratulate you on your victory and also tell you that I certainly didn't mean to make you go through that window. It was a good move, though. I could tell Mick was impressed.''

Stacy's pulse quickened. She thought he'd been impressed, too, and remembering how he'd looked as he'd run up the steps toward her, she felt an urgent twist of desire deep inside.

She covered her reaction by leaning back in the chair with feigned nonchalance, exactly as she'd learned to do in acting class. ''Whether he was impressed or not, I have no intention of getting romantically involved with him.''

''Whyever not?''

''Because he's my boss, and I want to keep my job.''

Cassandra let out a hoot of laughter. ''You are going to let something practical and boring like a job stand between you and making love to that man?''

Making love to that man. It had a certain ring to it. "The job's not boring, and I really need this…" She caught herself just in time. "I really need a sense of accomplishment."

Cassandra gazed at her, and slowly the laughter faded from her eyes. "Okay, I understand that. Don't let me make fun of you for having ambition. I've never allowed myself to have any, because it seemed easier to marry a man who had ambition." She turned her glass around in her hands.

"You're talking about Mr. Oglethorpe?"

"Yes. Marrying Harvey Oglethorpe was a very practical decision on my part. I turned down a chance to have a really exciting relationship with a guy very much like Mick, a guy who didn't have much money." She surveyed the contents of her drink. "And I regret it to this day."

In spite of getting locked in the basement by this woman, Stacy felt her sympathies stirred.

"You come from money," Cassandra said, glancing up, "so maybe you don't think Mick is suitable for the long-term."

"That's not the—"

"All right, all right." Cassandra held up her hand. "It's the job you're worried about, or so you say. But, honey, if I were you, I'd sacrifice the job in a minute for the chance to create something special with Mick Farrell."

Wild talk. Dangerous talk. The leather sofa appeared in her mind, looking wide, soft and inviting…. She fought to keep a grip on her resolve. "You're assuming he's interested in me."

"That's a safe assumption. You should have seen the way he bolted to your rescue when he realized I'd locked you in. And that's not counting the way he's been looking at you all afternoon when he thinks nobody will notice."

Excitement licked through Stacy.

"I'd give anything to be twenty years younger and in

your shoes," Cassandra continued. "Mick is sweet, he's principled and he has the body of a god. He's a forever kind of guy, and they don't come along very often."

Somewhere in the course of the conversation Stacy had allowed her guard to slip, and now she felt as if she were talking to an older sister who had only her best interests at heart. "But what if I'm not ready for a forever kind of guy?" she asked. "What if I'm miles away from wanting a forever guy?"

"You are?"

"I don't want to be tied down right now. I want to get fully launched in this new career first."

Cassandra waved aside the comment. "If Mick's right for you, he won't tie you down."

"Maybe not, but marriage seems so restrictive to me. I'm so afraid I'll end up like my mother, who has no skills or—" She stopped in embarrassment as she realized she'd described Cassandra. "I'm sorry. That sounded—"

"True. It sounded true. That's me, in a nutshell, too. But you won't ever be financially helpless. You have what used to be called gumption. The only time I have gumption is when I'm going after a man, but otherwise I'm a real wuss." She chuckled. "Your mother and I wouldn't dream of crawling out of that window, not in a million years."

"Maybe not."

"I'm sure not." Cassandra stood. "Take it from a woman who drinks far too much and who screwed up her chance for happiness. You and Mick have reached that critical turning point where the two of you can either light a bonfire or throw water on the blaze. Once that moment's gone, you might be out of luck." She walked toward the door. "Oh, and in case neither of you are prepared, there are condoms in the guest bathroom medicine chest."

Stacy gulped. "Oh."

"Makes it seem a little more real, doesn't it? And now I need a refill for my drinky-poo. Let's go back and tell Mick we couldn't find the address book, after all."

Stacy recovered her voice as Cassandra stood. "Uh, I was wondering something." She stood, too.

"I sleep like a rock, if that was your question. That's why I need a bodyguard."

"No, that wasn't it. I… What about that guy you rejected all those years ago? Is there any chance that he's—"

"I checked on that, too." Cassandra's smile was sad. "Married with three kids and a grandbaby on the way. He found a wonderful woman who doesn't care how much money he makes, and he's happy as a clam. I wouldn't shake up his world for anything. Now let's go downstairs."

FOR DINNER Cassandra warmed a pot of stew, and Mick was ready to compliment her cooking skills when she announced that her housekeeper had prepared and packed enough food to last three days.

"The booze, of course, was already here," Cassandra added, leaving the table to pour herself another drink.

She'd refused to let Mick bartend for her. He suspected that she didn't want him to keep track of how much she'd had, and over the course of the day she'd had quite a bit. But she'd paced herself and hadn't stumbled or slurred her words. He didn't think she was drunk.

"Are you sure neither of you would like a small libation?" she asked. "Surely one wouldn't hurt."

"Thanks," Mick said, "but it might. I have to be alert."

"I have to be alert, too," Stacy said.

Cassandra waved a finger at her. "No, no. If he's a Lert, then you must be a Lertess."

When Stacy and Mick both laughed, Cassandra looked pleased with herself. "A Lert and a Lertess. I like that."

Mick began to revise his opinion; Cassandra might be drunker than he thought.

"I'm beginning to feel silly about this Leonard business, Lert and Lertess," Cassandra said as she returned to the table. "It's pouring buckets outside, so I can't imagine even the most murderous ex-fiancé would venture up here on a night like this."

Stacy looked across the candlelit table at her. "That's logic talking. What does your gut tell you?"

"That Leonard is crackers and capable of anything," Cassandra said.

"Then I'm glad we're here," Stacy said.

"So am I. It's been a most entertaining Fourth of July." She lifted her frosted glass. "To fireworks."

Mick smiled and touched his water glass to Cassandra's tumbler. "Not much chance of that in this weather."

"That depends." Cassandra took another sip of her drink before pushing back her chair. "You know, all this activity has worn me out. I think I'll retire and leave you two to clean up the dishes."

She'd caught Mick completely by surprise. He stood. "Of course we'll clean up, but—"

"It's only seven!" Stacy said. "Sit by the fire while we do the dishes. Surely you aren't ready for bed yet."

"Ah, but I am." Holding her glass, Cassandra stood, walked over to the liquor cabinet and picked up the bottle of Tanqueray. "The dishwasher's on its last legs, so don't be alarmed if it sounds like a really bad heavy metal band. See you two in the morning. Don't forget to scoot the sofa in front of the stairs."

Mick watched helplessly while Cassandra made her unsteady way up the spiral staircase, leaving him alone with a woman who made him tremble with barely controlled desire. The clatter of dishes brought his attention back to the table.

Stacy was busily clearing. "I'm feeling tired, too," she said. "So let's get these out of the way and then I'll turn in, myself."

"Right. Good plan. We've all had a big day." Heart racing, he picked up his dishes and followed her into the kitchen.

CHAPTER THIRTEEN

IF IT HADN'T BEEN for her years in New York, Stacy wouldn't know much about doing dishes. In Scottsdale, her mother's housekeeper, Yolanda, had handled the operation of the dishwasher and the hand washing of fine china, crystal and silver. Before Stacy had left for Manhattan, she'd asked Yolanda to teach her how to load a dishwasher.

Per Yolanda's instructions, she always rinsed the dishes first. Setting her pile on the kitchen counter, she turned on the hot water and picked up an earthenware bowl. The trick was to concentrate on the task at hand and forget that she was alone with Mick. All through dinner she'd tried to get a handle on her situation, and she was no closer than she had been when Cassandra had announced where she could find condoms.

She had a decision to make, and she'd expected to have a little more time in which to make it. The sudden move by Cassandra had caught her by surprise. Now she needed to finish up the kitchen chores and escape to her room for some more thinking. In the meantime, she'd keep her gaze firmly on the sink and dishwasher in front of her.

A slight movement of air and the scent of aftershave told her Mick had walked around her to put his dishes on the counter next to hers. He set them down with a solid thunk, and she knew with absolute certainty he was watching her. Her hand shook slightly as she held the bowl under running water.

"You don't need to rinse them."

She didn't glance in his direction. Looking at Mick was too dangerous right now. Her heart was going wild merely at the sound of his voice close by. "That's how I do it."

"You're wasting water."

If he could succeed in being irritating, that would help. "If you don't rinse them, food will cake onto the dishes," she said. Yolanda's words, exactly. If there was a slight quaver in her voice, the running water in the kitchen and the storm still raging outside would cover it up.

"Cassandra uses well water, and you need to be careful with that. It's a precious resource up here."

He'd definitely succeeded in irritating her. "It's pouring outside," she said. "Maybe we should take the dishes out there." But irritation might not be strong enough to stave off the powerful emotions rolling through her.

"Stacy, I'm only saying—"

"That I'm screwing it up!"

She twisted the handle and shut off the water before whirling to face him. Oh, God, he looked so damned good. Her chest heaved as she struggled to draw a normal breath. "All right, if you know so much about this, then you do it."

His eyes were dark, his jaw tense. "All right, I will."

She didn't dare hold his gaze for any length of time. If she did, she'd be lost. She lowered her glance. "Let me get out of your way."

"Good idea."

But they couldn't seem to manage it. What should have been a simple maneuver turned into a clumsy attempt to change places that caused them to jostle against each other.

At the unintended body contact, Stacy thought she might faint. "Sorry," she said. "I'm usually—"

Strong fingers gripped her upper arm.

She looked up into Mick's intense expression and swallowed. "I'm usually more grace—"

She gasped as he pulled her roughly into his arms. And with a muttered curse he brought his mouth down hard on hers.

She'd thought she still had a decision to make, but from that first fusion, mouth to mouth, the decision was out of her hands. Mick was in charge now, pressing her against the curved edge of the granite counter, gripping the back of her head and tilting her mouth so that he could take the kiss deeper, and deeper still.

His tongue made demands. Her body surrendered with a rush of moisture. Before she realized what she was doing, she'd unbuttoned his shirt clear down to his belt. She'd wanted to do that from the first moment he'd modeled one of the shirts for her. She'd wanted to tunnel her fingers through his chest hair while feeling the silk of his shirt brush the back of her hands.

He groaned against her mouth, and his kiss became more fevered. She stroked his powerful muscles, loving how they flexed in response, thrilled to feel his nipples grow hard when she swept her palms across them.

The slide of cashmere up her back became yet another caress, and she abandoned her exploration of his chest to lift her arms. Taking his mouth from hers, he drew away long enough to guide the soft sweater over her head. She slipped her arms free.

She thought he'd toss the sweater aside. It could land on the floor for all she cared. Instead he used the sleeves to tie it gently around her waist. Even when he was ruled by fierce desire, he didn't want to ruin her sweater.

And that was the moment she fell helplessly in love with Mick. Passion blended with the warm lava flow of complete trust. Whatever happened between them now, it would be okay. She was okay with Mick.

When he unfastened her bra and eased it away from her breasts, she watched his face. The dazed appreciation she saw in his expression fulfilled every fantasy she'd ever had of how a man might look at her. He made her feel like a goddess with one glance.

She'd thought from his wild first kiss that he'd be tearing her clothes off by now, but instead he'd slowed the pace. She was ready to urge him back to full throttle.

"You can throw that on the floor," she said softly.

"No." He laid her bra on the counter, fumbling a little to put it there while he kept his gaze on her breasts. "Last time it was too fast. I didn't—" He paused to clear his throat. "I didn't even stop long enough to look at you. That's a crime."

She glanced down at the breasts that seemed fairly ordinary to her, yet made this man tremble and sigh when he looked at them. She didn't have much of a tan this summer. She hadn't been back in Arizona long enough, and no golden line crossed the top of her breasts as it had when she was a teenager. Her skin was the same creamy shade all over. Sort of boring, from her standpoint.

Yet Mick continued to be fascinated by the view. He traced the rim of her collarbone, then trailed a finger down her cleavage. She watched the path of his finger as it climbed the curve of her breast, circled a darkened areola and nudged one taut nipple.

She was more sensitive there than she realized. More needy. A tiny whimper escaped from her lips.

His gaze flew to her face. "What?" he asked softly.

She looked into his eyes, sure that he could see naked desire in hers. "I want…I want your mouth there."

"I know."

He didn't seem to get it. "Now," she said.

He shook his head. "Too fast." Then he glanced down at her breasts again and traced a second path. This time when he flicked her aching nipple, she moaned.

"That's better," he murmured.

"Better?"

"If we're going to do this, we're going to do it right." He plucked at her nipple with his thumb and forefinger. Once.

She could barely breathe as she waited for him to repeat the motion with her other nipple. "And what…are we going to do?"

"I'm going to love you, and you're going to enjoy the hell out of it." His voice was husky. "And you can be as loud as you want." He leaned down and took her other nipple tenderly between his teeth. With a long, slow tug, he worked his way to the tip and released his hold.

She moaned again. She was beginning to understand his plan, and understanding was making her shake with anticipation. She should tell him about the condoms upstairs. And she would, but…she was a very bad girl. She wanted to find out what he had in mind first. And, besides, coherent speech was becoming more and more difficult. "But you. What about you?"

"Don't worry about me right now."

"I can't be loud," she said. "Cassandra .light—"

"No, she won't." He shoved the dishwasher closed and pushed a button, turning it on. Sure enough, it made plenty of noise. Then he picked up a dangling sleeve from her sweater and began stroking it over her breasts.

"The dishwasher—" she gasped as he leaned forward and licked right where he'd been stroking her with the cashmere "—isn't ready."

He smiled. "No, but you are." Holding the sleeve taut

between both hands, he flicked it back and forth across her nipples, driving her into such a frenzy with the soft friction that the blood roared in her ears.

"I thought…you didn't want to waste water."

"Some things are worth wasting water for." Then he dropped the sleeve, leaned down and closed his mouth over her breast.

And God help her, she did cry out. It was as though a mooring line reached from the tip of her breast to the tip of her womb. As he drew on her nipple, that line vibrated. With each quiver, it tightened another notch.

Beside her, the dishwasher whooshed and churned; outside, the wind rushed through the pines and threw rain against the window. But those sounds faded, and she heard only the moist lap of Mick's tongue and the sweet suction of his mouth. His ragged breathing matched her soft moans as he tugged her closer and closer to paradise.

Cupping her breasts in both hands, he molded and lifted them toward his eager mouth. His caress was so fluid, so mesmerizing, that she missed the transition. While continuing to stroke her breasts, he'd kissed his way downward and dropped to his knees before she even realized what he intended.

But she loved his intention. Instinctively she cupped her aching breasts, still needing to be touched there. But he was busy elsewhere, unfastening her jeans, circling her navel with his tongue. As she watched him ease her jeans down and then her panties, she began to tremble.

He gazed up at her, his eyes hot, his lips parted. Self-conscious, she took her hands from her breasts.

"Don't be shy with me," he murmured. "Take risks." Capturing her hand, he slid it between her thighs. Her palm rested against her damp curls, and her fingers curved naturally, wanting, yet not quite daring. He pressed against her middle finger and it slipped smoothly inside.

Her heart pounded frantically. She was so hot and wet. He pushed her finger in deeper, and she felt a quick throb, a promise of what lay ahead.

He drew her hand away and licked her finger clean while she gasped and quivered in reaction. Then he pressed her hand there again. "Once more," he urged. This time he gazed up at her as he held her hand in place and rocked his own over it. "You are so beautiful. Your eyes are sparkling and your cheeks are pink and your mouth is so sexy. I love your mouth."

With each gentle motion of his hand moving hers, her climax hovered nearer. She gulped for air. "Mick, I—"

"Not yet." He eased her hand away again and guided it up toward her mouth. "Your turn."

A shiver of sensual adventure went through her. "You want me to…"

"Yes." He cupped her bottom and kneaded gently. "Find out how delicious you are."

She touched her tongue to her finger and tasted freedom. Wicked, wild freedom. Seeing the intensity in his eyes, she understood her own power, and it made her bolder than ever before. Watching his reaction, she took her time, running her damp finger over her lips, licking it slowly, then finally taking it fully into her mouth and sucking.

Mick gripped her tight and looked as if he might catch on fire just looking at her.

"How was that?" she whispered.

He nodded, obviously speechless.

And she was ready to explode. "What now?" she asked.

"My turn again," he said, his voice hoarse. "Lean back."

Gratefully, she did. She was trembling so much that without the counter to support her, she might have crumpled to the floor. She discovered that the cashmere sweater around her waist cushioned and protected her from the cold granite of the countertop. She wondered if Mick had thought of that, too.

His warm breath tickled as he moved in close, and she wondered if her heart could stand the pace. Gently he kissed her curls and gazed up at her. ''Spread your legs for me, Stacy. I want all of you.''

Shameless wench that she was, she followed his instructions. And, oh, sweet heaven, did he take all of her. And wild woman that she'd suddenly become, she watched him do it, which made the experience twice as explosive. To see his mouth *there,* his tongue right *there,* to know that the gusto of his movements tousled his hair and roughened his breathing—she'd never known anything so arousing in her life. The tension built to unbelievable proportions as she shivered and shook.

She didn't last long. In no time he'd released all that mounting tension and she was crying, laughing and gasping with pleasure. Such pleasure. A thought rocketed across her lust-crazed mind—she would do anything for pleasure like this. Anything.

UNBELIEVABLE. Mick stayed with his mouth pressed against Stacy's quivering femininity until her cries died away and he felt her body go slack. Then he eased back and drew her to her knees before he gathered her into his arms. Her response had been beyond his wildest dreams, and he'd had some wild dreams about Stacy.

She'd let him love her right here in the middle of the kitchen. Never mind turning out the lights or finding a bedroom with a closed door. At last he'd found a woman whose sense of adventure matched his.

She turned him on as no woman ever had. He'd love to make her come again the same way, except that he wasn't sure he could take it. His penis was so rock hard that he wondered if it was painful pushed against her belly.

It was damned painful to him. But he hadn't thought beyond this point, beyond what he'd planned to do for Stacy. And in his view, he couldn't rightly plan beyond that. What happened next was up to her, after all.

Some women felt grateful enough to reciprocate and others didn't. Without condoms, he was pretty much at Stacy's mercy, unless she left him alone to take care of himself. That wasn't what he'd call neighborly, but then he didn't know how Stacy thought about such things.

She snuggled close, propping her head on his shoulder and kissing his neck. The pillowy softness of her breasts tucked against his chest only increased his agitation. Her nipples were still tight with arousal, and they rubbed erotically against his skin each time she moved. His jeans pinched something fierce, but he'd tough it out and see what happened.

And then, wonder of wonders, she slid a hand between them, making a space so she could work on his belt buckle. But as slow as she was being about it, and trying to do it one-handed at that, he thought he might come while she was still fiddling around.

He swallowed, unsure he had his vocal cords under control. "Do you…have something in mind?" Sure enough, he sounded stoned.

Her lips moved to the hollow of his throat. "I do," she murmured.

"Then you need to be quicker about it."

She leaned away from him. "Is that so?" Her slow smile taunted him. "And you, were you quick with me?"

"Women are different," he said in a voice gritty with desperation.

"So glad you noticed."

"I noticed. Please, Stacy," he groaned. "Use two hands."

With a low chuckle, she leaned farther back and had his buckle unfastened in no time. Then she gazed at him and deliberately ran her tongue around her mouth, the way she had in that crazy scene with the gun. "I need your help."

A red haze of lust settled over him. "Tell me what to do," he said, barely recognizing his own voice.

"Stand up," she murmured.

He wasn't sure how he managed to stand, as wobbly as he felt, but he did.

"Now lean against the counter."

He sagged against the cool granite and pressed his lips together to keep from begging for what he needed.

Mercifully she didn't tease him with the undressing part. In very little time she'd opened his jeans and shoved down his briefs. "Oh, yes," she whispered, and wrapped both hands around his shaft.

He clenched his fists and squeezed his eyes shut to keep from ending the proceedings immediately. That would be a relief, but he wanted more than relief. He wanted to remember this forever. Something this incredible might never happen again.

But how he'd keep from coming, he had no idea, considering how close he was when she was doing nothing more than holding him. When she— Oh, jeez, now she was using her tongue, lapping him gently. He clenched his jaw and swallowed a groan. That was good, so good.

Praying that the visual stimulation wouldn't finish him off, he opened his eyes. And there was that pink tongue of hers doing all sorts of wonderful things to his penis. Then she cradled his straining balls and fondled them while she continued to treat him like a melting ice cream cone.

When he thought it couldn't get much better, she looked up at him and held his gaze while she worked her magic. He'd never imagined anything so wild as looking into her eyes while she licked him.

At last, her gaze still locked with his, she slid her lips down over his shaft. That full, sexy mouth was wrapped all around him, and he was going crazy inside, never wanting the sensation to end, knowing he couldn't last even another second.

Her cheeks hollowed, and he began to shake. Reaching behind him, he gripped the edge of the counter. Slowly she drew back as far as the tip, still watching him. By the time she'd started on the downward stroke again, he'd surrendered to the inevitable. With a deep, guttural cry he buried his fingers in her silken hair, held her still, and erupted with a force that left him gasping.

A violent earthquake couldn't have rocked him any more than this. He gulped for air as the climax rolled through him in constant waves that seemed to have no end. He'd never experienced anything like it. He wanted to keep this feeling forever, and yet…he might never know such pleasure again.

CHAPTER FOURTEEN

STACY DIDN'T HAVE time to consider the implications of her behavior until later—after Mick had sunk to his knees on the floor beside her and showered her with kisses, after he'd sat down, leaned against the dishwasher and scooted her onto his lap.

She remained blissed out until the dishwasher clicked over to the dry cycle and the rain stopped. The silence that followed seemed to invite misgivings. She'd really stepped over the line this time. What's more, she'd done it during a wild, impulsive moment instead of giving the matter the serious thought it deserved.

An hour ago she'd had options. An hour ago she hadn't engaged in fantastic oral sex with her employer. She didn't regret the experience, but if she wanted to continue working for Farrell's Personal Bodyguard Service, her options had narrowed to only one.

She had to marry the boss.

The decision was a sudden one, but the only solution that made sense for both of them. If they got married, they could continue to work together, because this fantastic sexual tension would be channeled into their marriage.

As she considered the marriage thing, she waited for panic to set in. After all, she'd vowed to keep herself free to explore her options. Yet Mick was the only option she wanted to explore, and she'd never felt so free in her life as now, after they'd made love.

So instead of panic, she began feeling all warm and happy inside. Marrying Mick would mean years of loving each other, years of feeling his strong arms around her, years of working together in an exciting profession.

And, eventually, once she'd established herself in the bodyguard business, they could have children, at least two. Growing up as an only child, she'd always wanted a sister or a brother. Mick would understand that, because he'd had Holly. Holly! She would be overjoyed. Stacy could hardly wait to see her face when she heard the news.

Of course, if Mick didn't like the idea of getting married, there would be no news and she would be unemployed. To her amazement, the loss of the job carried far less impact than the potential loss of Mick. But by marrying him, she could have both.

The bald truth was that, without really meaning to, she'd fallen in love with the guy. Committed, forever after, 'til-death-do-us-part kind of love. Now that she was getting used to the idea of marrying him, she realized he was the only person in the world she'd ever thought about marrying. But she'd always deep-sixed the idea, because he was Holly's brother and because he'd never shown any interest in her.

Now he was definitely showing interest.

Mick leaned forward and nibbled her earlobe. "Okay, what's going on in that fertile brain of yours?"

Stacy hadn't thought much about how a proposal should go, but the obvious fantasy was having the love of her life drop to one knee and hold out a sparkling engagement ring. But she needed to know where Mick stood on this question, so she couldn't wait around for that. "I realize this is sudden, but I think we should seriously consider getting married."

He stopped in midnibble. After a long silence, during

which she grew quite nervous, he spoke. "You do." It wasn't a question.

"You hate the idea." Her happy feelings shriveled.

"I didn't say that."

"You didn't have to. I can tell by your unenthusiastic response." She started to get up, but he held her fast.

"Don't go running away," he said. "You caught me by surprise. Will you tell me why you think we should seriously consider getting married?"

Because I love you. I'm beginning to realize I've loved you for years. But she was too intimidated to say that now. "Because we work well together and we...play well together."

"We've been working together less than a week, and we've had one round of oral sex. I'll admit it was fantastic, but—"

"Let me go." She struggled to get away from him. Her job was doomed, but it was his reaction to the idea of marrying her that brought tears to her eyes. What had been a life-altering moment for her had been mere fun and games for him. "Forget I said anything."

"Stacy, I can't possibly forget it." He finally let her go. "But I'm afraid you're overreacting to what happened."

"Oh, I see." Hurt more than she would ever admit, she untied her sweater from around her waist and pulled it over her head. The cashmere whisked away the first dribble of tears, and she blinked back the next onslaught. "You think this is just a lark for me, and that I'll change my mind pretty soon, just like you think the job is a lark and I'll get bored with it before long."

"No, I don't think the job is a lark for you. I think you're serious, which is why we have to talk about the future."

She zipped up her jeans and grabbed her bra. "We have no future—in any sense of the word."

"Stacy, we never had a future. Your parents would no more want you to marry a man like me than—"

"My *parents?* Do you honestly think I'm going to allow my husband to be chosen by my *parents?* What sort of social caste system do you think I belong to, anyway?"

"I'm not saying they'd choose him, but they'd take one look at me, a relatively poor guy who's trying to start a business, and they'd think I was marrying you for your money and contacts."

"They would not!" Because she had no money and soon the contacts would disappear, too. But she was furious that he'd use her background as an excuse to reject her suggestion of marriage. "And if that's the way you see it, why did you make love to me?"

"I—I shouldn't have."

"You're damned right, you shouldn't have." Snatching her bra from the counter she stomped out of the kitchen. "Move that sofa across the end of the stairs after I go up. I won't be coming back down," she called over her shoulder.

As she stormed through the living room and up the spiral staircase it was a wonder she didn't bump into anything or stumble on the steps. Tears streamed down her cheeks and dripped on her cashmere sweater.

Damn Mick. Damn him for being so gorgeous. Damn him for finally showing her what she was meant to do and then snatching it away. Damn him for making love to her and letting her discover that she was crazy about him.

And, most of all, damn him for not being in love with her.

MICK FELT a hundred years old as he got up off the floor. When he had his shirt and jeans done up again he walked into the living room and stared at the dying fire. He loved her. He'd probably loved her for years and not been willing to admit it because she was so out of reach.

But that episode in the kitchen had forced him to realize that she'd been hovering in his mind all along, the perfect woman for him. That's why he'd resented her money, because it was a barrier, just as her friendship with Holly had been a barrier.

He shuddered to think of Stacy going back to Phoenix and spilling everything to his sister. But she probably wouldn't. In fact, he was virtually certain of it. If he hadn't trusted her not to tell all to his sister, he wouldn't have allowed himself to be so vulnerable.

She'd allowed herself to be vulnerable, too, and she seemed to temporarily imagine herself in love with him. After giving up her career, she was at loose ends, and marrying him might seem like the logical thing to do, especially when her hormones were raging. He couldn't let her make that mistake, no matter how much he was tempted to take her up on her offer.

Marriage to Stacy. Now that she'd introduced that concept, he might never be satisfied with anyone else. No doubt, wouldn't be satisfied with anyone else. If there was any good to come out of this, it was the self-knowledge that he'd been hoping for Stacy all along. Now he could try to get over it. What a dumb cluck he'd been to yearn for someone like her all these years.

Unfortunately, the yearning wasn't likely to go away anytime soon. He wanted her to be his wife and the mother of his children. But Stacy wouldn't be happy in a mortgaged house in the suburbs. He didn't even know if she wanted kids. But, oh, God, could he picture her growing round and beautiful as she carried his child.

With a sigh, he tackled the job of moving the sofa. It was a heavy sucker, and he enjoyed the challenge of getting it across the room without scratching the hardwood floors. He did it, a little at a time.

When that task was finished, he banked the fire, checked the locks on all the doors, especially the one leading to the basement, and turned out the lights. It was early yet, but he was dog-tired, so he picked up a cotton throw and headed for the sofa.

Tomorrow he'd let Stacy take the Jeep back to town. As he sat down and pulled off his boots, he was glad she was upstairs tonight, so that he could watch over her. Maybe he'd talk her into spending her nights with Holly until he could check out that garden apartment of hers, because he needed to stay here with Cassandra and make sure her vacation wasn't disturbed. It would be boring, but he deserved to be bored for losing his control with Stacy.

Cassandra might try to console him in unacceptable ways, but he wasn't worried about that anymore. He could handle any misplaced sympathies now that he knew that she wouldn't be insulted by rejection. Cassandra was a more together woman than he'd given her credit for. She drank *way* too much, but that wasn't his responsibility. Keeping her safe from an attacker was.

Removing the .38 from the strap around his ankle, he tucked it under the pillow at the end of the sofa. He didn't expect Leonard to show up here, but Cassandra needed to take some precautions while she was in town and more accessible to her ex-fiancé. He'd help her do that.

Although he didn't think Leonard was prowling around, he took off his jeans and socks so that he'd have more freedom of movement if necessary. The leather sofa was cool as he stretched out on it and pulled the throw over him. Cool was good. A bed of nails would have been better.

He heard the steady creak of someone walking the floor above him and felt even worse. Stacy was pacing around up there on his account, and there wasn't a damn thing he could do about it.

STACY ROAMED the confines of her room and listened to Cassandra snoring away next door. She needed to work through the mess she'd created before morning came and Mick sent her back to town. Instinctively she knew that would be his next move.

The main problem was that she was in love with him, but he wasn't in love with her. That hurt, but what did she expect? He'd never noticed her until this past week, while she'd noticed him beginning at age five. She'd met Holly in kindergarten first and then later had a glimpse of Holly's older brother, a worldly fourth-grader.

After an hour of pacing, thinking and staring out the window, Stacy concluded that maybe she shouldn't give up quite so easily. Maybe, if she gave Mick a chance, lust would transform itself into love. It was the only way she could make this come out okay. Otherwise, if she ended the relationship, she'd put an end to her new career and the possibility of marrying her true love.

Stakes that high were worth fighting for. She wandered into the guest bathroom, took two condoms out of the cupboard and tucked them in her pajama top pocket. Still, she couldn't make herself go down those stairs yet. Deciding to march into battle again was different from actually doing it. He might turn her away.

For one thing, she had no sexy nightwear. She'd brought an old pair of Winnie the Pooh flannels because she'd thought the nights would be chilly and she hadn't expected to be seducing her boss. Worse yet, the heavy socks on her feet were even more sexless than the kiddie pajamas.

Sitting on the bed, she took the socks off. So her feet would be cold. If her maneuver worked out, they wouldn't

stay cold. Then she unbuttoned her pajama top and tied it
beneath her breasts. At least she had nothing on under the
pajamas, and they were soft. In the dark he might not notice
Pooh, Tigger and Eeyore parading around on the material.

She brushed her hair, spritzed on some cologne and
turned out her bedroom light. Nothing ventured, nothing
gained. Taking a deep breath, she walked into the hall.

At the head of the staircase she paused to let her eyes
adjust to the darkness. She'd have to climb over the back
of the sofa, and that would be sort of uncool, but she
couldn't figure out another way. Fortunately now that the
rain had stopped, the clouds had drifted away and moonlight
shone through the large windows of the living room.

Because of the curve of the staircase she could see Mick
on the sofa, although he was nothing more than a lumpy
shadow. Her heart raced as she imagined making love to
him on that sofa. Real love this time, the kind that he
wouldn't be able to dismiss. She took another deep breath.

Okay, she could do this.

She started down the winding stairs, creeping quietly. Her
plan was to wake Mick with a kiss, although she wasn't
sure how she'd do that, considering that climbing over the
sofa probably would alert him to her being there. Maybe
she'd lean over the sofa and whisper his name. Yeah, that
was better. She could climb over later, once she was assured
of her welcome. Maybe he would lift her over. That would
be romantic.

As she descended, a movement by the window caught her
attention. She stopped to look more closely, trying to make
sense of it. She concentrated very hard on the shadows in
the room and finally figured out that a person was walking
slowly toward the sofa. But she'd seen Mick lying there
asleep.

The blood roared in her ears as she realized who the figure had to be. As she stood in frozen horror, the person raised his arm. *He had a gun.*

In the instant that she realized what was about to happen, adrenaline shot through her. Pelting down the stairs, she let out her best karate yell and leaped, feet first, across the back of the sofa. The man screamed as she crashed down on top of him. There was so much noise she couldn't tell if he'd shot the gun or not, but she'd damned well ruined his aim.

Gasping for breath, she started pummeling the man beneath her, trying to find his eyes so she could gouge them out. If he'd shot Mick, she would kill him with her bare hands. The guy kept screaming.

Finally, over the din, she heard Mick shouting her name. Thank God he wasn't shot, or at least not enough to be rendered unconscious. She kept scratching and clawing at the man under her, giving Mick time to get off the couch and grab his gun.

"It's okay!" Mick shouted. Then he pulled her off the guy, urging her to her feet. "I've got him covered!"

The man lay in a crumpled heap, moaning and swearing.

"Don't move," Mick said. "I have a .38 pointed at your head, and my aim is excellent."

"Cassandra tried to kill me," the man whined.

"That wasn't Cassandra." Mick turned on a light.

Her chest heaving, Stacy looked down at the guy, who was dressed in a black sweat suit. His gun, a menacing instrument with an attachment on the barrel that was probably a silencer, lay several feet away. Apparently she'd knocked it out of his hand when she'd jumped on him.

Cassandra appeared at the top of the stairs, looking shaken and scared. "I've called the police," she said. "They're on their way."

"Good," Mick said. "Is this Leonard?"

Cassandra shuddered as she stared at the man huddled on

the floor. "Yes, that's the slimeball I almost made the mistake of marrying."

Leonard stayed curled in the fetal position, his eyes squeezed shut. "I loved you!" he cried. "And you tried to kill me!"

"No, that was my assistant, Stacy, who tried to kill you." Mick kept his attention on Leonard. "And what in hell did you think you were doing, Stacy?"

"Saving you! He had a gun trained right on you, and you were sleeping!"

"Wrong. Take a look at the sofa."

She did. And there was the lumpy silhouette she'd seen, undisturbed. She glanced over at Mick and noticed that he was wearing his silk shirt and little else. He looked very sexy and absolutely furious. "Where—where were you?"

"Over in the corner," he said in a tight voice. "I heard him working at the basement door lock, so I stuffed a few pillows under the blanket and hid in the shadows. I figured if he thought I was on the sofa, I could catch him by surprise from behind and knock him unconscious without having to use my gun. At least that was my plan, until you came screeching down the stairs. You realize you almost got yourself killed?"

She began to shiver. "I didn't think about that. I only—"

"You have to think, damn it!"

So she hadn't saved his life, after all. She'd screwed up again.

"Don't yell at her," Cassandra said. "She was ready to sacrifice herself on your behalf. She—"

"I don't *want* her to sacrifice herself on my behalf!" Mick roared. "And what the hell is that on the floor, anyway?"

Stacy glanced down and noticed a couple of little white packets lying next to Leonard. They must have fallen out of her pocket during the scuffle. Her face hot, she started to retrieve the condoms.

"Stacy, don't you dare go near that bastard," Mick said. "I'll get them."

"But I—"

"Don't move, woman. You've already done enough crazy stunts for one night." Keeping the gun steady, Mick stooped down and picked up the packets. Then he lifted the hem of his shirt and tucked them inside the waistband of his skimpy briefs.

Stacy was reminded of the time she'd gone to a male strip joint with Holly and the patrons had tucked money in the dancers' even skimpier briefs. She didn't think Mick would want her to make that comparison right now.

Sirens sounded in the distance.

"The police will be here any minute," Mick said. "Go on upstairs and get some clothes on, Stacy."

"Okay." With a heavy heart, she climbed over the sofa and started back up the stairs. Instead of completing a successful seduction, she'd managed to put even more distance between her and Mick. Now he probably didn't even want her for an assistant, let alone a life partner.

At the top of the stairs, Cassandra came over and put her arms around her. "I didn't see exactly what happened, but I'm sure you were very brave. Don't let Mick take that away from you."

"She was very stupid," Mick muttered.

"No," Cassandra said. "She was brave. You're the one being very stupid right now. Come on, honey. Let's get you some proper attire and me some breath mints before the cops arrive."

WHEN THE POLICE had finally hauled Leonard away and the two women had gone back upstairs, Mick sank down on the sofa and rested his head in his hands. As he thought about Stacy running downstairs to face an armed man, the shakes he'd managed to control while the cops were there began to take over.

Leonard could have killed her. He could so easily have aimed that gun right at her and shot her dead. The shock of a wailing banshee coming at him must have scared him so bad he didn't have the presence of mind to open fire.

But it could have been different. Mick hugged himself and tried to stop quivering. He'd brought Stacy up here. If she'd died trying to protect him, he would have been the one who'd caused her death. He would have snuffed out the life of the woman he loved.

He groaned and doubled over, unable to deal with it. Then a ray of light pierced the fog of his suffering. *She'd nearly died trying to protect him.* Was it possible that he'd misjudged the depth of her feelings? They'd known each other a long time. Was it even possible that she'd cared about him all these years, just as he'd cared about her?

Nothing else would explain what she'd done. When she saw Leonard, she could have shouted a warning. But as she'd admitted, she hadn't stopped to think. She'd reacted as he would have if he'd had to protect her. She'd thrown herself in harm's way. For him.

As the thought burned itself into his brain, he knew he had to talk to her, hold her, apologize for shouting and blaming. She wasn't trained yet. And even a trained person could lose perspective when faced with danger to the one they loved. And maybe, just maybe, she loved him.

As he stood, he glanced down at his bare legs. He hadn't bothered to put on his jeans, even after the police had slapped the cuffs on Leonard. They'd already seen him standing there in his shirt and undies, so he hadn't thought there was much point in pretending modesty after that.

He didn't need his jeans for what he planned to do next, either. All he needed were the two condoms he'd tucked in the elastic of his briefs. He thought about those as he climbed the stairs. He wondered if she'd found them here or brought them along. If she'd brought them, that put a whole different spin on things.

Apparently she'd been coming downstairs to seduce him when she'd stumbled into his trap for Leonard. He remembered now what she'd been wearing—Pooh pajamas. But she'd tied the top in a sexy way. No, he couldn't believe she'd brought the condoms. If she'd bothered to do that, she'd have thrown in a sexy nightie to go along with them. The condoms probably belonged to Cassandra.

At the top of the stairs he noticed both Stacy's and Cassandra's doors were closed. Even with Cassandra's door closed, he could hear her snoring. Good. He didn't relish an audience, and he had a feeling that he and Stacy might be making some noise. Heart pounding with anticipation, he approached Stacy's door and turned the knob.

The door was locked.

CHAPTER FIFTEEN

STACY THOUGHT she'd heard footsteps, and when the door knob rattled she knew that Mick, the man whose life she *hadn't* saved—no way, José—was outside her door. She wondered why. Maybe he had some more lectures to deliver that couldn't wait until morning.

Throwing back the covers, she got out of bed and walked over to the door.

He rapped quietly. "Stacy," he murmured. "Let me in."

"Why should I?"

A pause. "Because I want to talk to you."

"*Beep*. Wrong answer."

She heard a soft thump, as if he might have let his head fall against the door. She felt a little bit sorry for him, but not much. After a great deal of reflection, she'd decided that he'd acted like a jerk by getting so angry with her downstairs. She still loved him, but that didn't mean she couldn't see that he'd acted like a jerk.

"Stacy?"

"That's my name. Don't wear it out."

His chuckle sounded weary. "Oh, Stacy. I've been such an idiot."

Aha. Now they were getting somewhere. "A total idiot."

"Yeah, total. But I was scared out of my mind at the risk you took. When I'm scared I sometimes…get mad."

The warm tone of his voice drew her nearer. "You were scared?"

"Scared shitless."

"Why?" She laid her cheek against the door.

"Because I—I think I'm falling in love with you."

She closed her eyes. Her throat felt tight, and she had to clear it to get the words out. "You only *think* you are?" She reached for the lock and turned it slowly, noiselessly, but she kept her hand on it, so she could snap it shut again. Only thinking he loved her wasn't enough.

"No. I know I am. I'm in love with you, Stacy."

"What a coincidence. I'm in love with you, too." When she stepped back and opened the door he nearly fell into the room. He must have been leaning against it as she had.

They stood there staring at each other.

"That wasn't a trick, was it?" she said at last. "A trick to get me to open the door?"

"No trick." His voice trembled. Slowly he reached behind him, closed the door and turned the lock. "Marry me," he said.

"Yes, oh, *yes!*" She threw herself into his arms.

"Oh, God, Stacy." He picked her up and tumbled them both onto the bed. "If anything had happened to you, I—"

"Kiss me." She kicked the covers aside and pulled him close. "Explain later."

But as his lips met hers, she realized no explanation would be necessary.

He held her face in both hands and kissed her with such unbelievable tenderness. No man had ever kissed her that way, as if she were the most precious creature in all the world.

"Thank you for risking your life for me," he murmured. "I'll need at least fifty years to prove that I'm even slightly worthy of what you did." Then he kissed her again, so sweetly that it brought tears to her eyes.

"That's good," she said in a choked whisper when he lifted his mouth from hers. "Now let's get it on."

His laugh was shaky, as if he didn't have total control of his emotions, either. "Okay, let's," he said, easing her to her back and nuzzling her throat as he began unbuttoning her pajama top. "I want you, Stacy. You know how much I want you. But I...it's a different kind of wanting this time."

Tears pricked her eyes again. A dream coming true could sure make a girl weepy. "I know. Me, too." She reached for the buttons of his shirt. "But I still want you naked."

"I want you naked, too. The sooner the better." He pulled off her pajama bottoms and flung them across the bed. Then he paused. "Or maybe not completely naked."

"You want to make love to me while I'm wearing a Pooh pajama top?"

"Maybe, but we'll save that idea. Now I want to make love to you while you're wearing my silk shirt."

She was thrilled that her gift had been such a hit. "You like it that much?"

"I like it that much." He wiggled around and finally got his shirt off. Then he helped her with her pajama top and tossed it aside. "There. Now put your arms through the sleeves."

As she became enveloped in the silk, the combination of the slippery material and Mick's aroma touched off explosions of heat within her. "Mm." She took a quivering breath. "This shirt is making me lose focus on the sweetness and love thing. I'm leaning toward the lust thing."

"That's okay." His breathing had become a little uneven, too. "We can stand a little lust with our sweetness and love. Now close your eyes. We need light." He leaned over and switched on the bedside lamp. "Oh, *yeah.*"

She opened her eyes slowly to find him looking at her

with such single-mindedness that she shivered in anticipation. Then she allowed herself to enjoy her first view of a nearly naked Mick.

Cassandra was right. This was a forever kind of guy. He even looked like one, with shoulders broad enough to support her deepest troubles, and a powerful chest where a loving heart beat.

She laid her palm over it and felt the rapid thrumming. She looked into his eyes.

"That's how you affect me," he said.

She glanced lower, to where his briefs barely contained him. "That's not the only way I affect you," she said, looking into his eyes again.

His smile was strained, his gaze dark and stormy. "No, that's not all."

"Are you still carrying…"

"Yes, ma'am. Thanks to you."

She checked it out, and sure enough, the edges of two little packages peeked out of the elastic waistband. Sweet tension curled inside her, and she reached for the waistband.

He caught her hand. "In a minute. First…let me play." He drew one lapel of the shirt over her breast. Her nipple dented the soft material, and he brushed his palm across it, back and forth, creating such tantalizing friction that she moaned.

"This is what I've thought about every time I put on one of these shirts." His voice was hoarse with desire. "You naked under the shirt, and me touching you this way." He massaged her breast through the thin covering of silk.

She loved seeing the hunger in his eyes, loved knowing she put it there. His touch was stealing her breath. "That feels…good," she whispered.

"Very good. But I need this, too." Drawing the material away, he sucked slowly on her nipple until she writhed with pleasure. With his mouth at her breast and the slide of silk over her back, she felt surrounded with sensuality.

Tension built within her, taunting her, making her beg for him to fill her.

Yet still he did not. The shirt was large on her, so large it reached to midthigh. As he continued to suck at her breast, he used the bottom hem of the shirt to stroke her inner thigh. Then he moved higher, feathering the damp petals of her femininity with the luxurious silk.

When his teasing made her gasp in frustration, he drew the silk away and plunged his fingers deep. Two quick strokes and she came, arching off the bed with a breathless cry.

Dazed by the fury of her climax, she lay panting while she watched him peel off his briefs. She'd thought that he'd given her more than enough satisfaction, but apparently not. The sight of his erect penis started the throbbing ache all over again. "Hurry," she murmured.

"Damn things." He fumbled with the condom, and had to start again. "Someday soon—"

"Yes. Soon."

He glanced up, his gaze intent. "Babies?"

"Yes. Babies."

He swallowed. "I love you."

"I love you, too." Wow, she was ready to cry again. By the time he'd rolled the condom on and moved between her thighs, her tears were flowing. "I'm sorry." Her voice was choked with emotion. "I don't mean to cry. It's just that I'm so…so…happy."

"Don't be sorry." He leaned down and kissed her damp cheeks. "I love that you're crying with happiness."

"I can't—" she paused to sniff "—can't seem to help it."

"Cry all you want." He probed her gently as he gazed

into her eyes. "But don't close your eyes. Keep looking at me."

Her heart hammered with eagerness and she blinked back her tears.

"I love you." He slipped in a little more.

Her breath caught.

"Your eyes are like stars right now." He pushed in deeper.

She clutched his hips and smiled dreamily. "I feel like a supernova."

"Almost there," he murmured. "In a moment you won't be able to tell where I leave off and you begin."

"That's what I want."

"Now." With a groan he buried himself completely within her. "Oh, my wonderful Stacy." His whole face seemed lit from within as he gazed down at her. "My life could end right now and I'd die a happy man."

"Me, too." She held on tight, unable to believe how perfectly they fit. "Except I'd die a happy woman."

He grinned. "But we're not going to die, at least not for a very long time." He eased back and slid forward again.

Oh, that felt absolutely fabulous. "Not while we're having so much fun."

"Exactly." He began a slow rhythm that kept time with his promises. "We're going to live…and make babies…and have wonderful sex…for at least fifty…or sixty years." He gasped and squeezed his eyes shut. Then he opened them again. "Lust is taking over, Stacy."

Her body was quickening in time with his, and she could hardly find the breath to speak. "Go for it," she cried softly as she matched his rhythm.

He increased the pace. "In case I forget to say it, I love you."

"In case I forget, I love you, too!"

As he pumped faster, his words became a soft chant of passion. "Oh, Stacy...my sweet Stacy...there...right there...now come...come for me, my love."

Then with one powerful thrust, he catapulted them both into a rainbow world, where glory showered down amid their cries of pleasure. And she knew as she wrapped her arms around him and rocked him in that ancient ritual of completion, that their lives would never be the same again.

NEVER IN HIS wildest dreams had Mick imagined such happiness as he cuddled with Stacy. The night was young, and he'd already made a quick trip across the hall to retrieve the rest of the condoms, in case one more wasn't enough to see them through.

The way he felt right now, with Stacy tucked into the curve of his body, he didn't think one more would be enough. As he cupped her breast in one hand, he could practically guarantee that one more wouldn't be enough.

She'd taken off the silk shirt, because now that he'd experienced that thrill he wanted a totally naked Stacy in his arms. She sighed, and it was the musical sound of a satisfied woman. Mick figured he'd like to hear a few more of those sighs before the night was over. He felt like an eighteen-year-old stud.

"I can't believe how perfect we are for each other," Stacy said.

"I know what you mean. In one way, making love to you is new and exciting, but in another, it seems as if we've been lovers forever."

"I feel that way, too." She snuggled against him. "And we're interested in the same things."

As he began getting hard again, he pushed back her hair to kiss the nape of her neck. "You mean like silk shirts?"

"Well, yes, but I meant like karate."

"Oh. Right." More than ever he intended to introduce her to Joe, because she'd just proved how reckless she could be without training. But now that he'd experienced having her in the line of fire, he knew he could never bring her on another assignment. He wasn't sure how she'd take that. He hoped their new understanding would help smooth things over.

"I wonder if we should call the business Farrell and Farrell Personal Bodyguard Service," she said.

"That's an idea." He wasn't crazy about the direction of the conversation. He decided to try a slightly dishonest tactic. He slipped his hand over her hip and between her legs.

She laughed. "I think your mind's on other things."

"I think yours is, too." What a thrill to find her so hot and wet already.

"Mm." She shifted to give him even better access. "We have a little problem here."

He stroked her slowly, wanting to build up to the finale. "I'm not finding any problems."

"I mean, when we go on assignments together. We can't let sex…distract us…oh, that's nice, Mick." Her breath came quicker now and her body moved restlessly against his.

"Glad you like it." He was so hungry for her. Throwing back the covers, he grabbed a pillow, slid down to the foot of the bed and rolled between her thighs.

"Mick! What are you—"

"I can't help it. You're delicious." He shoved the pillow under her bottom and blew softly against her curls. "Unless you mind."

Her laugh was breathless. "As if."

Oh, this was good. A soft bed, the perfect angle, and a woman so aroused that the scent and taste of her made him delirious. He feasted, indulging himself shamelessly as he drew out the pleasure. And then, at long last, he took her over, exulting in her wild cries.

Then he eased back up beside her and held her while she continued to quiver. He felt like a god.

At last she quit trembling and smiled up at him. "That's what I mean," she said. Then she took a deep breath. "We can't let those kinds of things happen when we're on assignments together. It would be totally unprofessional."

"We won't let it happen." He combed her hair back from her face and placed little kisses on her cheeks, her nose, her chin. "The thing is, it's too dangerous for you to be there anyway. I'm sure you agree. I mean, soon you'll be pregnant, and then—"

"Wait a minute." She captured his face in both hands and looked into his eyes. "What do you mean, too dangerous?"

He worried about that stubborn expression of hers and tried to keep his voice calm. "Stacy, we're going to have a family. I can't let the mother of my children take chances with her life."

"That's what I thought you were saying! Well, why should I let the father of my children take chances with his life?"

"That's not the same thing." This wasn't going well at all. But surely she could see that—

"It's *exactly* the same thing." She squirmed out from under him. "And if you think by marrying me you'll have the right to dictate to me on this matter, then you've sadly misjudged the situation." She sat up and pulled the covers up to her chin.

When a woman covered herself, it didn't bode well for the outcome of the discussion. He'd learned that much.

With a sigh, he sat up and faced her across the bed that suddenly seemed much too wide. "Stacy, listen. I went into this career because I have years of karate experience. On top of that I added months of extra training so I could handle a gun. I can take care of myself in dangerous situations. You can't.''

"Maybe not yet." Her lower lip quivered. "But I'm a hard worker, and you said yourself I have real promise."

"As a karate student, yes. But I went through hell when I realized how close you came to being shot tonight. For God's sake, woman, I love you! If anything should happen to you…I can't even imagine such a horrible possibility. How can you expect me to take you along on assignments, knowing the risk?''

She lifted her chin. "*Because* you love me."

"That's nuts!''

"Then you're not planning to use me as your assistant anymore?''

"In the office, I'd love to have you as my assistant.''

"Oh." Her tone was ominously calm. "So I'm to be your secretary, and that's it?''

"No, that's not it." He blew out a breath in exasperation. "I want you to be my wife, my lover, the mother of my children, my best friend, my companion, my soul mate. I don't care about the secretary thing. The rest I care very much about.''

"But you don't want me to be your assistant bodyguard.''

"No, damn it! And I don't think that's unreasonable.''

"Well, unfortunately, I do.''

He gazed at her in frustration. "Do you understand at all how I felt when I saw you leaping into the path of that guy's gun?''

"Yes."

"Then you must know why I can't—''

"I felt the same way when I thought he was about to shoot you as you slept on the sofa.''

"Exactly! You just made my point for me. I wasn't *on* the sofa, because I'd placed myself in a less vulnerable position. You, on the other hand, placed yourself in a *more* vulnerable position. Now do you see what I'm talking about?"

Her jaw tightened. "I see that I need more instruction. I was hoping to get that from both Joe and you. Apparently I'll have to rely entirely on Joe. And then I'll have to look for some other bodyguard who will hire me, since you won't."

"Stacy, for God's sake! You can't be serious about this."

She studied him for several long seconds. "You know very well that I am. I guess you thought that wedding bells and baby carriages would be enough of a substitute, but that's outdated thinking, Mick. I'm afraid I'll have to reject your marriage proposal, after all. It comes with too many strings attached, and I value my personal freedom."

He shook his head in disbelief. "Don't do this. You love me. I know you do."

"I do love you. I probably always will." Her voice quivered. "But if you're going to be such a chauvinist, I'll have to forgo the pleasure of m-marrying you." She pressed her lips together and swiped at her eyes.

A knife seemed to twist in his gut. "Stacy, please." He reached for her.

·She shrank back from his touch. "No, Mick. I need for you to leave now. Otherwise you'll only make this more difficult."

"It couldn't be more difficult! You're killing me, here. One minute I think I've found the love of my life, and now you say it's over. How can that be?"

"I'm not the love of your life. The real love of your life would be thrilled to stay put and keep the home fires burning while you're out slaying dragons. I want to be out on the dragon trail with you, so that lets me out of the running for the love-of-your-life position. Now go.''

He stared at her, still hoping for a miracle.

''Go, damn it!'' She picked up a pillow and threw it at him.

He could have dodged it, but he let it hit him. If she'd had anything more substantial to throw, he would have welcomed that, too. Pain on the outside might help him forget the incredible pain on the inside.

Putting on his briefs, he picked up his shirt and started for the door. ''Give this more thought, please,'' he said. ''I think karate's a great idea. There are tournaments you could enter. We'll put on those demonstrations you were so excited about. We—''

''If you're not going to take me out in the field, there's nothing to talk about.''

Well, he wasn't going to take her out in the field. He wouldn't have that on his conscience. And he was reasonably sure that if he didn't, she'd have trouble finding a job elsewhere. If he had to give her up in order to save her, then that's what he'd do. Even if it killed him, which it very well might.

Without another word, he left the room, closing the door behind him.

CHAPTER SIXTEEN

STACY TRIED to keep up a good front the next morning as she and Mick said goodbye to Cassandra and drove away from the cabin. But she didn't think Cassandra was fooled. She repeatedly asked them to stay on for the next two days, as if she thought by keeping them around she'd be able to fix whatever was wrong between them.

But Mick was the only one who could fix that, and Stacy saw no signs of him changing his mind. He looked like hell, as if he hadn't slept at all, but there seemed to be no give in his expression.

Once they'd pulled onto the highway, he glanced over at her. "I still want to marry you," he said. "I'm not taking that back."

"But you won't help me become a bodyguard, right?"

His jaw flexed. "Right."

"Then we have nothing more to say to each other." She'd decided a few things during the long night. Number one, she'd get whatever job was available, and if that embarrassed her mother, too bad. Number two, she'd suggest to her parents that they open a bed-and-breakfast to keep the wolf from the door. She wasn't sure where that idea had come from, but she'd spent a lot of time staring into the dark, and the thought had popped into her head.

Number three, she wouldn't tell Holly anything about what had transpired between her and Mick. That would leave her with no one to confide in about her heartbreak, but keeping this secret would be her final gift to Mick. He was a chauvinistic jerk, but she loved him and she didn't want to cause him any discomfort with his little sis.

The drive back to Mick's apartment in Phoenix was the longest ride she'd ever endured in her life. Beside her sat Mick, the yummiest guy she'd ever known, and he wanted to marry her. All she had to do was abandon her vision of this exciting new career, and she could have Mick.

There had been a moment there in the kitchen after he'd given her the most amazing climax of her life when she'd thought she'd be willing to do anything to keep him. Apparently she wasn't willing to give up her personal freedom. Cassandra's prediction that Mick wouldn't stand in the way of her goals had been wrong.

Although she'd turned the question over in her mind a million times, she couldn't come up with a compromise. One of the reasons she'd stuck with dancing for so long was that nothing else had appealed to her, and she'd been determined to have a career. Being a bodyguard was exactly right for her, but she might never have realized it if she hadn't decided to work for Mick.

As his apprentice she could have worked into the job while getting paid, but now that he'd denied her that opportunity she'd have to spend years preparing herself before she could reasonably expect to get on with someone else. In the meantime, she'd find some source of income that would pay the bills.

She could become an exotic dancer, she thought with a grim smile. And what a great revenge that would be, because Mick would hear about it through Holly. But her mother would have a fit. A fast-food job was one thing, but prancing around on a stage half-naked was beyond what she could expect her mother to endure.

Finally Mick pulled into the parking lot of his apartment

complex. The rains had come to Phoenix the night before, too, and the asphalt was steaming under the midmorning sun. In her present frame of mind, Stacy thought the parking lot looked like her image of hell.

Mick pulled in beside her car and shut off the motor.

"I guess that's it," she said, preparing to get out.

"Come up to my apartment," he said. "We need to talk this thing out."

She didn't think he had talking in mind. He wanted to get her alone and let the chemistry between them work its magic. He thought in the midst of more spectacular sex, he could bring her around to his way of thinking.

And he might be able to do exactly that. After the episode in the kitchen she'd proposed, abandoning her fears of marriage. A few rounds up in Mick's bedroom and she might abandon her career hopes, too.

She wasn't up to testing it. "Unless you've changed your mind about my role in Farrell's Personal Bodyguard Service, we're finished with our negotiations." She got out of the Jeep.

He didn't say that he'd changed his mind, but he got out, too, and insisted on helping her transfer her suitcase from the Jeep to the trunk of her car.

"Do you need a formal letter of resignation?" She was glad she was wearing her sunglasses today, and doubly glad he was wearing his. Somehow she managed to keep her voice steady. "Or can I verbally quit right now?"

"Don't quit." His voice was far from steady. "I'm sure there's an answer, if we just look at a few more options."

She closed the trunk. "Mick, I don't think you have the slightest intention of helping me train to become a full-fledged bodyguard. I think you want to use sex to convince me to give up my plan."

"Okay, forget going up to my apartment." He sounded

truly desperate. "We can go get coffee. Come on, Stacy. You'd expected to spend three days in the White Mountains, so you can't tell me you have other things to do."

"But I have other things to do. I need to look for a job."

He sighed. "No, you don't."

"Yes, I do. I need to support myself while I learn what's necessary to become a bodyguard."

"Come on, Stacy. We both know this isn't about the money."

Now that she'd lost him, she decided her secret didn't matter anymore. "Actually, money is a concern of mine," she said. "This isn't something I want you to broadcast, but my parents are having serious financial problems."

His jaw dropped.

"That's one of the reasons I came home," she said.

When he found his voice, the volume had gone up considerably. "Why the *hell* didn't you tell me that?"

"Because I know you. I wanted to be hired on my own merit, not because you felt sorry for me."

"Stacy, I can't believe you didn't tell me this. I just can't believe it. Does Holly know?"

"Yes. She's the only person who does."

He blew out a breath. "God, I haven't given you any money yet! Can you pay your rent? Do you need—"

"I'm fine for now." This was exactly what she'd been afraid of. The last thing she wanted was his sympathy. "I'll be even better when I have another job."

"You can have *this* job, damn it!"

"No. I don't want this one. I'll find something else."

"Like what, for example?"

He sounded as if she were unemployable, and that really stuck in her craw. She was being bad to suggest something she'd never do, but she couldn't help herself. A girl had to have a good exit line. "I hear they need dancers down at The Body Boutique."

"Good Lord. Tell me you wouldn't do that."

"See you, Mick." Using all the dramatic training she possessed, she came up with a smile before turning to walk toward the driver's side of her car.

"Stacy, you can't get a job there!"

She shrugged and unlocked the door. "Gotta make money. Bye." Getting in the car, she started the engine and rolled down the windows. Despite being parked in the shade, the car was like an oven.

"Stacy!"

She ignored him and dropped the gearshift into reverse. She would have preferred putting down the canvas top, because driving away in a convertible was always more dramatic if the top was down, but in this case a speedy exit was better than a dramatic one. She backed out of the parking space, gave Mick and his thunderous expression a little wave, and took off.

God, it was hot in Phoenix in the summer. She really needed to look for a job, but she might take a dip in the apartment's swimming pool before she started going through the want ads. The main thing she had to avoid was calling Holly. If she allowed a couple of days to pass she might not be so inclined to spill her guts.

But she wondered how she'd survive those days, considering that her heart was so well and truly broken. She dreaded going back to her apartment. Coming home from a trip early was always a bummer, and this time...this time was the worst of the worst. If only Mick didn't think the way he did—but she couldn't get caught up in the world of "if only."

The drive to her apartment didn't take long. She was mere blocks from Mick, and that didn't help her state of mind, either. She put down the top before she turned off the engine. Maybe tonight she'd take the convertible out for a spin under the stars, provided it didn't rain again.

Rolling her suitcase behind her, she trudged down the steps to her apartment, letting the suitcase bump along after her. Damn, she was depressed, and she wasn't sure what to do about it, either. Normally she'd call Holly, but that wasn't an option.

The minute she opened the door, she sensed something different about the place. A coffee mug was on the counter, and she didn't remember leaving it there. A magazine lay open on her little bargain love seat. She usually picked up after herself better than that, especially before going away for a few days.

She wondered if her parents had somehow found out where she lived and talked the manager into letting them in. But that didn't seem likely, and they wouldn't have left stuff lying around in any case.

Maybe being distracted about Mick had made her absentminded. She pushed aside her uneasiness and rolled the suitcase down the short hall that led to her bedroom. But the closer she came, the more the hairs on the back of her neck rose. She was used to the way her apartment smelled—a combination of her cologne, brewed coffee and the citrus-scented cleaner she used. Something smelled different in here. Very different.

And there was something else, something that had been bothering her ever since she'd walked in. She'd turned the air-conditioning down before she left to save money. The apartment should have been warm, but it wasn't. If anything, it was on the cold side. Maybe the thermostat had malfunctioned.

Then she walked into her bedroom and screamed. A raggedy-looking man was lying on her bed. And not just any man. Gerald.

He stood and smiled at her. "I was wondering when you'd come home, Stacy. I've missed you."

MICK WASN'T ABOUT to let that be the end of things. If he had anything to say about it, Stacy was not getting a job dancing at The Body Boutique. Definitely not. He didn't care how broke she was—and the thought of Stacy without money was only beginning to register—she was not strutting around on some smoky barroom stage half-naked. He'd drive over to her apartment, that *garden* apartment of hers, and talk her out of it.

But, unfortunately, he didn't know where it was. He didn't even have her phone number. Somehow in the crazy rush of all they'd been through, he'd never taken down that basic information. Then again, Stacy might have avoided giving it to him on purpose as part of her plan to hide her financial situation from him. Holly would have her address, though.

Grabbing his suitcase, he headed inside. After turning up his air-conditioning, he picked up the phone and pushed the speed-dial for Holly's number. He hoped to hell she was home.

Miraculously, she was, but she was obviously surprised to hear from him, considering that he'd told her he'd be gone for three days. Then he heard a male voice in the background ask who was on the phone.

He knew that voice. "Is Craig over there?" he asked.

"Uh, yes, as a matter of fact." Holly sounded reluctant to admit it. "Do you want to speak to him?"

"No, I'm just curious as to what he's doing at your apartment in the middle of the day. Or at any time of the day, come to think of it. Or night."

"I *knew* it," Holly said. "I just knew you'd be this way about it."

This must be the day for shockers, he thought. "You're *seeing* Craig?"

"Sort of."

"What do you mean *sort of?* You either are or you aren't! Which is it?"

"I am! So there! And if you give either of us a hard time about it, I will personally—"

"It's fine with me." Any other day, Mick might have asked more questions. He might even have asked to talk to Craig so he could find out what Craig's intentions were toward his little sister. But right now he didn't have the time.

"Fine with you? Are you sure?"

"I'm sure. Listen, Holly, I need Stacy's address and phone number."

"You don't have it already? And weren't you supposed to be with her for three days? What's up with that?"

Mick massaged the bridge of his nose. He was getting a headache. "We had a...disagreement. She'll probably tell you about it."

"Don't count on it."

"Why not? I understand she told you all about her parents being on the skids."

"She *told* you?" Holly sounded delighted. "That's great!"

"She should have told me a hell of a lot earlier than this."

"She had some issues," Holly said.

"I'm sure you know all about them, too." He couldn't keep the irritation out of his voice. "You probably know most of what's been going on between Stacy and me."

"I do not. She's been extremely closemouthed about her dealings with you."

His heart twisted. So she hadn't been confiding in Holly about their relationship, and that left her with no one to talk to—except him. To hell with the phone, he was going over there. "Okay, just give me the address," he said.

"All right. You should have it anyway, for W-2 forms and stuff."

"She quit." He hadn't meant to blurt that out.

"She did? Why?"

"I, um, told her I wouldn't help her become a bodyguard."

"Why not?" There was a sharp edge to the question.

"Because it's too dangerous."

"Oh, boy. You really did it this time, big brother. She's going to become a bodyguard anyway, you know. She told me how excited she is about the idea, and once she latches on to something she's not likely to let go."

Mick felt panic nibbling at his nerves. "She said she'd get a job dancing at The Body Boutique to finance her karate lessons. Do you think she might actually do something that stupid?"

"Doesn't sound stupid to me," Holly said. "If you won't help her, then she'll have to do whatever is necessary to pursue her goal. Those dancers make good money."

Mick groaned. "That's not the point. The point is—"

"The point is that you're standing in the way of her dream. You can either help, or she'll have to go around you in any way she can. As her best friend, I'm asking you to help her."

"But aren't you worried about her safety?"

"Sure! And I'm worried about yours, too! But if you love someone, you encourage them in what they want, if it's at all reasonable."

Mick's patience snapped. "This isn't reasonable, damn it!"

Silence greeted his outburst.

"Well, it isn't," he said more quietly.

"You really care about her, don't you?" Holly asked.

Mick swallowed hard. "Yeah."

"Then help her, Mick. You're the best person for the job. Don't let her go to strangers for this. You be the guy."

"I'll think about it. Now give me the address."

She did, and shortly afterward he said goodbye. Once he'd worked things out with Stacy he'd deal with the Craig situation. Actually, the more he thought about it, the better he liked the idea of Holly and Craig together. But he had some instructions for Craig about how Holly was to be treated. And Craig better never, ever break her heart.

Outside in the sweltering heat again, he hopped in the Jeep and set out for Stacy's apartment. She lived close, and that was good. On the way over he thought about what Holly had said, and in his heart he believed her. Although he'd like to think Stacy would never make it in the bodyguard business without his help, she might. She'd developed a taste for risk, and he knew firsthand what that was like.

But if her training wasn't thorough she'd be in more danger than ever. If he supervised everything he could be sure that her training was thorough. And yet the thought of deliberately preparing her for this profession scared the bejeezus out of him.

The irony of it all didn't escape him. Here he was, the original risk taker, ready to settle down and become more cautious, and the woman he loved was only beginning to discover the thrill of adventure. He could spend years chasing after her to make sure she didn't kill herself.

Still, if they went on assignments together he'd always know what she was getting into. That was a damned sight better than if she worked for somebody else, somebody who didn't consider her the most beautiful, awesome, spunky woman in the world.

He found the apartment with no problem and walked down the steps to her front door. Somebody nearby was having a whale of an argument, he thought. Domestic violence always made him queasy.

As he rang her doorbell, he decided the argument was going on in the adjacent apartment, and it sounded bad enough that he and Stacy probably should call the police. In fact, maybe he should even interfere himself. When she didn't answer the door, he pounded on it, determined to be heard over the noise.

He'd about decided that she wasn't home, after all, when a crazy yell splashed over him like ice water. Stacy's karate yell.

Grabbing the knob, he twisted it and put his shoulder into the door, expecting to have to break the thing down. Instead the knob turned easily and he hurtled inside. The action was happening down the hall, probably in her bedroom. He thought about the guy from New York and felt sick to his stomach.

Drawing his .38, he fought down the urge to charge in there, but that wouldn't help Stacy. Instead he forced himself to move quietly down the hall.

Stacy yelled again, and somebody landed a blow. He winced, praying the blow hadn't landed on Stacy.

"Stop!" a male voice screeched. "Stop and I'll go away!"

Mick hurried forward and stood in the doorway of the trashed bedroom. A scruffy man crouched on the floor, clutching his groin. A lamp lay smashed nearby, and he was bleeding from a cut on his head. But it was the kick in the balls that had obviously brought about his surrender.

Stacy stood, the second bedroom lamp raised over her head. She was panting, her right cheek was scraped and her blouse was untucked, but otherwise she looked okay.

Mick wanted to pulverize the guy anyway. It took all his control not to walk into the room and pistol-whip him within an inch of his life. "I'm here," he said.

She glanced up and cried out in surprise. "Where did you—"

"I was in the neighborhood. Want me to take over with this piece of garbage?"

Slowly she lowered the lamp as the guy continued to moan. "I have it handled."

His chest tightened. She was so damned beautiful. And too damned fearless. He'd have his work cut out for him in the years ahead. "I see that you have it handled. But maybe you'd like to go wash up while I escort your friend out of your apartment. He's fouling the air."

She took a shaky breath. "I guess...I guess that would be okay."

Mick walked over and shoved the .38 against the guy's neck. "On your feet."

"I don't think I can walk!" the man wailed.

"Then crawl out of here. I don't give a damn how you leave." Mick glanced at Stacy. "I'd appreciate it if you'd call the police."

"Sure."

"Oh, and about that bodyguard job." His heart squeezed, but he made himself say it. "If you still want the position, it's yours."

She gasped.

"But it comes with a wedding ring attached."

She began to tremble. "Oh, Mick, I—"

He gave her a quick smile. "Let's get rid of this bozo, and then we'll talk."

AN HOUR LATER they were back at Mick's apartment, but they weren't talking. Instead they were involved in a different sort of communication.

"Oh, yes," Stacy said with a moan. "Yes, just like that."

Mick leaned down to kiss her as he slid back and forth inside her moist heat. "I could do this all day."

"Maybe not." Stacy added a rotation of her hips to the rhythm.

"Mm. Or maybe not. That was sexy."

She treated him to the movement again. "I learned it in dance."

His breathing grew uneven, his strokes deeper. "I sure like it."

"A movement like that would come in handy at The Body Boutique."

"But you're not working there." He picked up the tempo. "You have a job."

"With you." She matched his rhythm, digging her fingers into his buttocks. "As a bodyguard."

"At least I'll know where you are."

"Right here." She felt the contractions begin.

"Right here with me." He looked into her eyes. "Forever."

"Forever." Then she rode the whirlwind, safe in the arms of the man she loved.

EPILOGUE

Two years later

MICK DROVE HOME from the *dojo,* although it was actually Stacy's turn to drive. She'd given up her turn because she was so busy admiring the black belt she'd been awarded that night. She couldn't stop looking at it, and Mick couldn't stop looking at her. With the trouble he was having keeping his eyes on the road, they'd have been wise to take a cab.

Trading off the driving chores was one of the little ways Stacy liked to maintain balance and control what she called Mick's chauvinistic tendencies to smother her. No matter what she thought, he wasn't into smothering, but he damned sure wanted to protect this feisty wife of his. Two years ago he'd finally realized that the only way to protect an independent woman like Stacy was to make sure she could protect herself.

Joe had said he'd never seen such a gifted student, which would have hurt Mick's feelings if Joe hadn't been talking about the woman Mick loved more than life itself. With his help, on top of Joe's teaching, and intensive practice at home and in class, she'd managed to become a black belt in two years, Joe's first student to manage such a feat.

Her parents had come to the ceremony. Mick found that incredibly sweet of them, considering how nervous they'd been ever since Stacy had announced her intention of learning karate and working alongside Mick.

He liked Stacy's parents. He wasn't sure if he'd have liked them rich, but now that they were middle-class and running a B-and-B, he liked them just fine. Once he'd decided he had to have Stacy, her money or lack of it had ceased to be an issue. Yet he was relieved not to have to deal with wealthy in-laws.

Holly and Craig had come to the ceremony, too. Because of Stacy's interest in karate, Holly had taken classes. Although she'd never be as dedicated as Stacy, she'd learned enough so that she could defend herself reasonably well. That pleased Mick.

He still wasn't used to seeing his sister married to his best friend, but the concept was growing on him. And he'd darn well better get used to it, because any day now he'd become Uncle Mick to Holly and Craig's baby. He could hardly wait, and he'd worked hard to conceal his jealousy. He'd always assumed he'd present his parents with the first grandchild.

He glanced over at Stacy for the hundredth time and wondered if she remembered the promise she'd made two years ago, soon after their marriage. After how hard she'd worked to become a black belt, he didn't feel right reminding her of it. At least not tonight.

"I keep wondering if I'll wake up," Stacy said. "I'll wake up and discover it's the day of the test, and I haven't passed yet."

"You were a shoo-in." As they skimmed under the streetlights, he tried to catch glimpses of her face. He swore that she was becoming more beautiful each day. Holly insisted that Stacy looked the same and that it was Mick who was becoming ridiculously besotted with his wife. That could be. Right now he sure did ache for her.

"I could have flunked," she said. "This is the hardest thing I've ever had to learn."

"And I've told you several times what Joe thinks of you. He says you were born for karate."

"That's not all he thinks I was born for." There was a smile in her voice. "He told me tonight that I should give some thought to passing on my talents."

"You mean teaching?" Mick wasn't surprised. Joe was always on the lookout for gifted students who could help with the beginning classes.

"No, not teaching."

"Then I don't get it."

She reached over and laid her hand on his thigh. "He thinks you and I should get pregnant."

Mick nearly drove up on the curb.

Laughing, Stacy withdrew her hand. "Maybe we should table the discussion until we get home."

Mick's throat tightened. "Is there...something to discuss?"

"Well, sure. You may not feel the way you did two years ago. I mean, we have the business running beautifully, and maybe you don't want to interrupt—"

"Stacy, are you saying that you want to get pregnant?" His pulse kicked into high gear at the thought.

"I promised you we could try once I became a black belt."

"I know, but—"

She laughed again. "Why do you think I've been working so hard to get there?"

Mick began to tremble. "I've never made love to you without a condom."

"Well, tonight's the night, big boy."

It was a wonder he got the car into the garage of their little starter house. As it was, he knocked over the trash cans. By the time they were inside the door that led into the kitchen, clothes were already flying.

He took her on the kitchen floor, and it seemed fitting, considering that they'd begun their lovemaking history in Cassandra's kitchen. The undressing was pretty wild, and he ripped her silk panties away in his eagerness. But once the way was clear, she was so wet that he slipped effortlessly inside.

She moaned. "Oh, Mick. This is unbelievable. Think of what we've been missing."

"I can't think. I can only feel." They always left the light over the stove burning when they went out for the night, and it was that glow that he used to see her face as he stroked in and out.

She'd never looked more radiant.

Her breath came in quick little gasps. "Do you want a boy...or a...girl?"

"I just want a baby." He felt his climax building, and for the first time he would pour himself into her. Moisture filled his eyes and he blinked it away. Surely he wasn't crying. "Our baby."

She touched his face. "You're crying."

"No."

"Yes." She was as choked up as he was. "Oh, Mick, I love you so. Thank you for waiting."

"The waiting's over." He shifted his angle slightly, knowing after two years of loving her exactly how to make her come.

"The waiting's over," she repeated breathlessly. "Give me...a baby."

"Yes, my love. Yes." He pumped faster and she began making the joyous sounds of a woman on the brink of orgasm. One more deep thrust sent her over. She cried out his name and arched against him.

"I love you," he said in a voice hoarse with tears. Then he gasped and buried his seed deep within her.

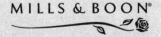

Coming next month…

BETTY NEELS

THE ULTIMATE COLLECTION

A stunning 12 book collection beautifully
packaged for you to collect each month
from bestselling author Betty Neels.

On sale 5th July

*Available at most branches of WH Smith,
Tesco, Martins, Borders, Eason, Sainsbury's
and most good paperback bookshops.*